Teriayne

Gold Hall

the Cliffs

aldia

the Egg

N

Herelia

Arro

Iliyat

the Tarn

Merrivale

Liya Pass

River's Bend

the Wild

Haya Gap

ssumara

pper Hall

Haya

the North Shore

Zosteria

Storm
Cape

Iron Hall

Istria
Bay

South Shore

the Beacons

Mar

Salya

the
hundred

0	20	40	80 MEY
0		100	200 MI.

ash

Bronze Hall

SHADOW GATE

SHADOW GATE

BOOK TWO OF CROSSROADS

Kate Elliott

TOR®

A Tom Doherty Associates Book
New York

SHADOW GATE: BOOK TWO OF CROSSROADS

Copyright © 2008 by Katrina Elliott

Edited by James Frenkel

Endpaper map by Elizabeth Danforth

A Tor Book
Published by Tom Doherty Associates, LLC
175 Fifth Avenue
New York, NY 10010

www.tor.com

Tor® is a registered trademark of Tom Doherty Associates, LLC.

Library of Congress Cataloging-in-Publication Data

Elliott, Kate.
        Shadow gate / Kate Elliott.—1st ed.
            p.   cm.—(Crossroads, bk.2)
        "A Tom Doherty Associates Book."
        ISBN-13: 978-0-7653-1056-9
        ISBN-10: 0-7653-1056-2
        I. Title.
        PS3555.L5917S53   2008
        813'.54—dc22
                                2007047697

First Edition: April 2008

Printed in the United States of America

0 9 8 7 6 5 4 3 2 1

For Constance and Kit,
who aren't afraid to wrangle with the difficult issues troubling the universe,
and who keep me honest and always show support

AUTHOR'S NOTE

IN THE HUNDRED, any and every set and sequence of patterns is seen as having cosmological significance. Every number has multiple associations. For instance, the number 3 is associated with the Three Noble Towers present in every major town or city (Watch Tower, Assizes Tower, and Sorrowing [or Silence] Tower); with the Three States of Mind (Resting, Wakened, and Transcendent); with the Three Languages; and with the Three-Part Anatomy of every person's soul (Mind, Hands, and Heart). The number 7 is associated with the Seven Gods, the Seven Gems, the Seven Directions, and the Seven Treasures.

Folk in the Hundred measure the passing of time not via year dates set from a year zero, but rather through the cyclical passage of time. The standard repeating twelve-year cycle is named after animals, in the following order: Eagle, Deer, Crane, Ox, Snake, Lion, Ibex, Fox, Goat, Horse, Wolf, Rat. However, this year cycle is meshed with the properties of the Nine Colors to create a larger cycle of one hundred and eight years. A clerk of Sapanasu, or anyone else who can do this kind of accounting, could thereby identify how long ago an event happened, or how old a person is, depending on what color of animal year in which he or she was born.

Each animal and color, having its own particular and peculiar associations, lends to all events in that year and to people birthed therein specific characteristics. Therefore, Keshad, born in the Year of the Gold Goat, combines Goat characteristics of cleverness, vanity, strong will, jealousy, pride, a deep sense of purpose contrasted with instability of shallow purpose, and a talent for seeking wealth, with Gold qualities like energy, intellect, intensity, dishonesty, envy, and aloofness.

SHADOW GATE

PART ONE: AWAKENINGS

1

MARIT WAS PRETTY sure she had been murdered. She recalled vividly the assassin's dagger that had punctured her skin, thrust up under her ribs, and pierced her heart. Any reeve—and Marit was a reeve—could tell you that was a killing blow, a certain path to a swift death. In the moment when life must pass over into death and the spirit depart the body, the misty outlines of the Spirit Gate unfold. The passage between this world and the other world had opened within her dying vision. But her spirit had not made the journey.

She woke alone, sprawled naked on a Guardian altar with only a cloak for a covering. Her eagle was dead. She knew it in the same way you know an arm is missing without looking to see: Your balance is different. Her eagle was dead, so she must be dead, because no reeve survived the death of her eagle.

Yet that being so, how could she stand up, much less stagger to the edge of a drop-off so sheer she hadn't noticed it because she was disoriented? She stepped into thin air before she knew she'd mistaken her ground, and she was falling, falling, the wind whistling in her ears. The earth plunged up to meet her.

Then she woke, sprawled naked on a Guardian altar with only a cloak for covering, and realized she had been dreaming.

Sitting, she rubbed her eyes. The place in her dream had been a narrow ledge without even a wall to warn of the drop-off. This place was high and exposed, an expanse of glittering stone untouched by vegetation. She rose cautiously and ventured to the highest point on the bluff. She stood at the prow of a ridgeline. The vista was astonishing: In front lay a lowland sink dropping away to a wide cultivated plain that extended toward a distant suggestion of water; to her right spread a pulsing green riot of forest so broad she could not see the end of it; behind, ragged hills covered with trees formed a barrier formidable not because of their height but because they were wild. The wind streamed over the ridge, rumbling in her ears.

She knew right where she was: on the southernmost spur of the Liya Hills, an excellent spot for thermals that an eagle and her reeve could spiral on for hours with a view of the Haya Gap. The vast tangled forest known as the Wild lay to the south, and the lowland plain that bordered the arm of the ocean known as the Bay of Istria ran east.

She knew right where she was.

Aui! She was standing on a Guardian altar.

So far nothing had happened to her. But that didn't change the unalterable fact that she had broken the boundaries that forbade all people, even reeves, from entering the sacred refuges known as Guardian altars. She had broken the boundaries, and now she would be punished according to the law.

That being so, what had happened to her lover, Joss, who had after all been the one who had persuaded her to follow him up to an altar?

There was only one way to find out: walk to the main compound of Copper Hall, which lay about midway between the cities of Haya and Nessumara, and find out what was going on.

The altar wasn't so difficult to get down from after all. A stair carved into rock switchbacked down the stone face and into a sinkhole that twisted to become an ordinary musty cave with a narrow mouth hidden by vegetation. She ducked under the trailing vines of hangdog and pushed through a thicket of clawed beauty whose thorns slipped right off the tempting fabric of the cloak. Clusters of orange flowers bobbed around her, which struck her as odd because clawed beauty only bloomed in the early part of the year, during the season of the Flower Rains, and that was months away.

Except for the rest of the afternoon and the following days it rained in erratic bursts as she trudged through the woodland cover. The trails she followed became slick with puddles and damp leaves. She slopped alongside cultivated lands. Farmers, bent double in ankle-deep water, transplanted young rice plants. Women dragged hoes through flooded fields, skimming off the weeds and setting them aside for animal fodder. The sun set and rose in its familiar cycle. As she moved toward the coast and low-lying land, the dykes and edges had their own distinctive flora: pulses, soya, hemp, with ranks of mulberries on the margins. She kept her cloak wrapped tightly around her, but anyway people were too busy to notice her.

Soon enough paths joined cart tracks that joined wagon roads that met up with the broad North Shore Road. Although the original Copper Hall had been built on the delta, the main compound was now sited about forty mey south of Haya on one of a series of bluffs overlooking the Bay of Istria with a lovely vantage and good air currents swirling where land met sea.

It had been years since she had walked to the turning for Copper Hall. Once Flirt had chosen her, she had always flown. The paved roadbed was raised on a foundation and surfaced with cut stones fitted together as cunningly as a mosaic, flanked by margins of crushed stone. From an eagle, you didn't notice the remarkable skill and craftsman's work, or the stone benches set at intervals as a kindly afterthought. From an eagle, one's view of the roads turned from textured ramps of earth, gravel, and paving stone into the all-important solid lines linking cities and towns and temples.

She trudged past the triple-gated entrance to a temple dedicated to Ilu, the Herald. The gatekeeper slouched on a wooden bench under a thatched lean-to, staring disinterestedly at the road. His dog whined, ears flat, and slunk under the bench. She wrapped her cloak more tightly, but no one—not the gatekeeper and none of the folk walking along the road—paid the slightest attention to her. Salt spray nipped the air. Fish ponds lined the rocky shore. The bay gleamed gray-blue in late-afternoon light, waves kicking against the seawall.

On the seaward edge the land rose into a series of high bluffs while the road curved inland past rice fields lined with reeds and salt grass. As the sun set, she found an empty byre to shelter in against the night rains, its straw mildewed. She didn't really sleep; she lay with eyes closed and thoughts in a tangle, never quite coming into focus.

She woke at dawn and rose and walked, and at last saw the stout stone pillar carved with a hood and feather in relief and the huge wooden perch, freshly white-washed, that marked the turning to Copper Hall. She was home.

Wiping tears from her eyes, she plodded up the long slope toward the high ground, feeling more and more winded, as if all the life and spirit were being drained out of her. As if she was afraid. How would she be greeted by her comrades at the reeve hall? She had broken the boundaries. She would have to accept punishment.

Aui! She had to find out what had happened to Joss, protect him if she could or back him up on his reckless decision to investigate the Guardian's altar in Liya Pass. Hadn't he been right? Wasn't it true that something was terribly wrong?

No person in the Hundred had stood before a Guardian at an assizes since her long-dead grandfather was a boy. Anyway, an old man's memory might be suspect. The meticulous records stored in Sapanasu's temples recording the proceedings of assizes courts where Guardians had presided might, in fact, be explained as a conventional form used by the clerks and hierophants of the Lantern to account the decisions made by wandering judges who were otherwise perfectly human.

Many said the Guardians had abandoned the Hundred. Others said the Guardians had never existed, that they were only characters sung in the Tales. Yet on the Guardian's altar up on the Liya Pass, she and Joss had discovered bones—the bones of a murdered Guardian, maybe, because a pelvis could have been splintered in that way only by a tremendous fall or a massive blow.

But all the tales agreed that Guardians couldn't die.

The reeve hall was a huge compound surrounded by fields and orchards and open ground where a pair of reeves—relatively new ones, by the look of their tentative maneuvers—were learning to harness up under the supervision of a patient fawkner. She didn't recognize the young reeves, but she was pretty sure the fawkner was her good friend Gadit, although she was holding her body at a canted angle, as if her right shoulder was stiff from injury.

High watchtowers stretched up as little more than scaffolding. She did not recognize the pair of very young men lounging on gate duty, but their bored faces and listless chatter irritated her. They did not bother to challenge her, and they ought to have; she was an unlikely sight, with her naked feet and calves and a cloak clutched tightly around her body, yet she walked through the gate unremarked. She would have words with Marshal Alard about their lackadaisical attitude.

It was difficult to remain annoyed in the familiar environs she loved: the wide-open land-side parade ground with its chalk-laced dusty earth; the low storehouses side by side in marching order; the barracks and eating hall sited where the high ground dipped, making a bit of a windbreak; the high lofts set back to either side, and beyond them the seaward parade ground that overlooked the cliff and the choppy bay.

Most reeves must be out on patrol, since she did not recognize the few faces she saw. Two very young fawkner's assistants scurried toward the lofts with harness draped awkwardly over their backs. A youth shuffled past holding a cook's ladle while sneezing and wiping his nose. A young woman seated on a bench was sniveling while Marit's dear friend and fellow reeve Kedi spoke in the tone of a man who has said the same cursed words a hundred times:

"It's done, Barda. When an eagle chooses you, you've got no choice in the matter."

"But I don't want this. I never wanted it." She wasn't a whiner. She was genuinely overwhelmed, her eyes rimmed red but hollow-dark beneath; her hands were trembling. "I was supposed to get married tomorrow. All the temples agreed it was an auspicious day for a wedding, Transcendent Ox, in the Month of the Deer, in the Year of the Blue Ox. Especially for a long and steady and calm alliance. That's all I ever wanted, and I like Rigard, only now his clan has called off the wedding. They've broken the contract, because now I'm a reeve. I was just walking to market and the bird dropped down out of the sky and I screamed I was so scared. Don't you see? My life is ruined!"

Kedi sighed in that weary way he had. His hair had been trimmed back tightly against the skull, almost shaven bare like a clerk of Sapanasu, and when he shifted to slap away a fly Marit realized he was leaning on a crutch. He wasn't putting any weight on his left leg.

"Heya! Kedi!" she called.

But he was too intent on the young woman. "I know it's not what you wanted. But let me tell you that every reeve in this hall envies you for the eagle who chose you."

"Trouble? It's a stupid name. She scares me."

"She's the most beautiful and best-tempered raptor in the Hundred."

Trouble! Marit wanted to ask what had happened to Trouble's reeve Sisha, a particularly good friend who besides could hold more ale than anyone, but Kedi had launched into an energetic description of Trouble that would make the hardest heart melt, so she walked down the alleyway between storehouse and fawkner's barracks that led to the marshal's garden.

Alard had loved flowers, the more resplendent, the better. So Marit was startled to see that his carefully nurtured beds of azaleas and peonies and heaven-full-of-stars had been replanted into ranks of practical herbs, as though the cook and the infirmarian had snuck in when the old man wasn't looking.

She climbed the steps to the roofed porch, where she paused, listening to the shush of a broom around the corner in a steady accompaniment to voices murmuring beyond the closed doors. Ladiya appeared butt-first, attention focused on lines of dirt forming ranks along the boards.

"Can I go in?" Marit asked.

The old woman still had her back to Marit and did not answer. She tilted her head to one side until it rested against the thin wall. Eavesdropping.

As the voices from inside were raised, it was impossible not to overhear.

"You've been marshal for one month. I'm surprised you waited so long to get rid of me!"

To hear his voice, healthy and strong and angry, hurt like a dagger to the heart, but it was the pain of unlooked-for joy that brought tears to her eyes. He was still alive.

"Joss, you have the makings of a good reeve—of an excellent reeve, perhaps—but you are *out of control.*" The words were emphasized in a firm voice, entirely calm and utterly sincere. She knew that voice very well. It went on speaking, each word crisp as if with frustration hooded. "Still, with things the way they are, and the problems in Herelia, I can do nothing but send you to Clan Hall to get you out of my jesses. I will let the commander deal with you, thank the gods, so that I do not have to. I have enough to deal with here. If I could keep you belled I would, but I cannot. In the old days, so they say, a rogue and errant reeve was subject to execution for the kind of insubordination we have seen from you, the repeated breaking of the law, going time and again to Guardian altars despite knowing that it is absolutely out of bounds, despite knowing what happened the first time you did it. But we do not have the luxury now of punishing you in that way. The gods know we need you, and especially we need Scar. So I am sending you to Clan Hall and that is final. You leave *today.*"

The last word rang. Afterward, there came a pause. Marit braced herself for the storm.

Instead of an answer, one of the doors was slammed open and Joss—as handsome as ever!—charged with all his loose-limbed passionate grace out of the chamber and past Marit without giving her a glance.

"Joss," she said. "Sweetheart."

He was already gone.

Ladiya turned around as a reeve whose short hair was laced with silver walked onto the porch in Joss's wake.

"Did you overhear all that?" he asked without a sliver of amusement, but he wasn't angry either. Masar was the most upright, bland, and humorless person Marit had ever known, and she had known him pretty well, having taken him as a lover for half a year when she was a lot younger. He'd been as humorless in bed as out of it, and he'd accepted her departure from the affair with a straight face and never in the years after showed the slightest sign that he resented her or, for that matter, pined after her. He was absolutely rock solid, a person who would back you up and risk his life to save yours and never ever cross the line past which proper behavior became improper.

Except that he was holding the marshal's staff with its jessed and hooded cap, the mark of authority in Copper Hall.

Ladiya said, "It's hard to resist a lad with good looks and the charm to back them up, but even I can see how he's gone wild since her death. Three years now, it's been. You would think he'd have devoured or drunk it off by now. You're going easy on him, Marshal."

Marshal?

Masar said, "I keep hoping he will settle down. I do not know what else to do. Nor do I need to. He is Clan Hall's problem now."

"Masar," Marit said. "Ladiya. What happened to Joss? Where is Marshal Alard?"

She extended a hand, touched Masar's elbow. "How long have I been gone—?" Faltering, she gingerly patted Ladiya on the upper arm to get her attention.

They neither of them looked at her or appeared to hear her voice or feel her hand. She might as well not have been standing there, for all the notice they took.

At last it all made sense. As the thoughts lined up in their neat ranks, a weight—more of terror than pain—settled in her chest. All that long way she had walked from the Guardian's altar across the plain, for days and days she had walked and only now did it occur to her that she had not eaten or drunk or even truly slept. No one had spoken to her or acknowledged her.

No one had seen her.

And for that matter, her feet weren't dirty.

"Great Lady," she whispered, as Masar beckoned to Ladiya and they walked past her back into the marshal's cote and slid the door shut in her face. "Great Lady . . ."
Prayers failed.

That girl named Barda had stated that she had intended to marry tomorrow, an auspicious day made especially so because it was also the Year of the Blue Ox.

Marit was pretty sure she had been stabbed by an assassin's dagger in the Year of the Black Eagle. Three years before the Year of the Blue Ox.

The cloak fell open as she extended both arms and stared at the paler skin of her palms, like a ghost's hands against her brown complexion.

Joss had "gone wild since her death."

Three years it had been, according to Ladiya.

Three years.

Now she understood the punishment laid on her.

MARIT WALKED OUT of Copper Hall, one clean foot set in front of the other clean foot and the first again and the second again, out to the turning, and there she stared one way along the North Shore Road and after that the other way. People were out and about, going on their business and their lives. They couldn't see her, because she was dead.

Is this what it means to be a wandering ghost, one whose spirit has failed to cross through the Spirit Gate?

She wept without sound because no one could hear her. At length she got bored of standing there and crying to no purpose. She turned north and walked toward Haya. The mey passed smoothly; no wonder she didn't tire. Questions dove like stooping eagles.

Do I even exist?

If no one can see me or hear me, then why can I see and hear myself?

What do I do now?

Late in the afternoon with the waters of the bay settling into their twilight calm and the light fading in the east, she saw the triple-gated entrance to the temple of Ilu beside the road and wondered if she could overnight in the lean-to. The bored young apprentice sitting as gatekeeper would not care. He would not even see her.

He was playing ticks-and-tacks in the dirt with a stick and pebbles. His dog whined and cowered, and the youth looked up and down the road and, seeing nothing, scratched its head absently. The temple compound was set back from the road, separated by gardens where the envoys and apprentices grew vegetables. The last workers were shouldering their hoes and rakes and laughing together as they headed up the track toward the compound walls. One shuffling figure wandered through the rows, bending to finger the strong green shoots.

A woman broke away from the laborers. "Here, now, Mokass. Come along. It's time for our gruel."

The lone figure skipped away from her, gabbling in a singsong voice. With a most unholy oath, the woman chased after him. He bolted, giggling, for the gate, a white-haired old man with bent shoulders and bowed back but nimble legs. The dog lifted an ear and barked once. The young gatekeeper heaved up, muttering.

"Oh, the hells. Not again." But he wasn't really angry.

The old man skittered to a halt beneath the gate, staring at Marit. He leaped back a single hop, and raised both hands palms-out.

"Death, death!" he chanted. Tears flowed suddenly. "Go away, fearsome one!"

"Can you see me?" Marit demanded.

"I never did it! I never stole that coin. Anyway, you don't want anyone here. Just walk on."

The woman caught up with him and took hold of his right arm. "Here, now. Don't go running off. It's time for our gruel." She nodded at the gatekeeper. "Good work, Lagi."

"I did nothing. He just stopped of his own accord and started babbling."

"He's gods-touched," said the woman with as much fondness as exasperation. "Poor old soul."

"I beg you," said Marit. "Mokass. Is that your name? I need your help."

"You've got no call to be knowing my name! Go away! We don't want you here."

The dog took courage from the old man's defiance and began to bark at Marit. In sympathy, more dogs within the compound started up a yammer.

"Aui! Mokass, just come along, now you've got them all going. My ears will swell up and drop off from the noise!" The woman dragged on him, and he wasn't strong enough to do more than stumble along unwillingly behind.

"Have to send death off!" he cried. "Go away! Go away!"

"In the name of the Lady, I beg you, Mokass," Marit called after him. "Go to the reeve hall and tell that the ghost of Marit sends warning: Beware Lord Radas of Iliyat. Let someone warn Copper Hall: Beware Lord Radas. He's the one who had me and my eagle killed."

"Hush, now! Sit!" Lagi towered over the dog, scolding. "You cursed beast! What's gotten into you?"

Mokass hopped, waving his hands as though batting away a swarm of wasps. "Aui! Aui! Her eagle is copper. I was born in Iliyat, did you know that? But I won't tell any tales. They're all lies." He did not look back over his shoulder, and his companion crooned soothingly as they walked away.

Marit sank into a crouch and covered her head with her arms, just sat on her heels and rocked. But it did no good. Nothing changed. The cursed dog kept barking, and finally the youth whapped him a single hard blow to shut him up, and that was too much for Marit. She jumped to her feet and ran off, not wanting the poor dog to be punished for doing its duty just because the only person who could see her was an old man not right in the head.

She walked through the night with its scraps of clouds and a Sickle Moon fattening toward the half, and at last she fumbled with the clasp and tore off the cloak and flung it aside with a scream of frustration and grief and fury and fear. She ran, as if by sprinting she might churn Spirit Gate into being and race through it to the other side, where she could find peace.

The running caught up with her. She began to cough, and could not take in air. A wind rose off the bay, howling up the road and over the fields. She staggered to a halt and fell to her knees, bracing herself on her hands as she gulped and hacked and gagged, her vision fading in and out. The world tilted and spun. She pitched forward, hit the gravel with her shoulder, and tumbled onto her back. A white mist rose off the road, rippling and billowing. Blown by the raging wind, the cloak slithered along the ground. Rising to envelop her, it molded itself to her face until she could not breathe. She fought and clawed, but it devoured her.

There was no pain.

SHE WOKE ALONE, sprawled naked on a Guardian altar with only a cloak for a covering. Her eagle was dead, so she must be dead, because no reeve survived the death of her eagle. Since it was too much trouble to try to make sense of the world, she slept.

In her dreams she trudged up hills or slogged through swampy coastlands, searching for the man she loved or for her eagle or for an answer. She wandered, lost and alone, and kept falling, falling, until she woke again with the cloak wrapped around her. She found herself in a new place, one she did not recognize except it was high and exposed and the stone ledge on which she lay glittered with a twisting pattern grown into the rock.

It was a Guardian altar, just like the ones before.

She had a headache as bad as if she'd been sucking sweet-smoke, drugged and dazzled for days, as good an explanation as any although how she had gotten up to a Guardian's altar she could not figure. It seemed she was only now truly waking up. Probably she had dreamed the entire journey to Copper Hall.

She felt thirsty and hungry, and she wanted clothing because the winds on the height chilled her. With the cloak clasped at her throat, she climbed a treacherous path down to the base of the altar, bloodying her feet and hands. She stumbled through sparse highlands forest and happened upon a shepherd's high pasture cottage, uninhabited in the cold season. Here she found a storeroom with old but serviceable tools and hunting equipment. She also found humble clothing, needing a wash that, she discovered later, hadn't gotten out all the clinging lice, and a stash of nuts and moldering nai to be pounded into a paste for a stale porridge.

The thing is, when you're not sure if you have become a ghost or perhaps something more frightening, you are wise to choose prudence. When a winged horse lands in the highlands meadow where you are sheltering, where you are trying to make sense of what has happened to you, you don't chase it away. You investigate, because you are still a reeve in your heart. In a small bag hooked to the back of the saddle, you discover a modest offering bowl like those beggars carry, and a polished black stone. The offering bowl presents no surprises; it is just a bowl. But when you place the stone in your left hand to get a better look at it, a sharp pain strikes up your arm and a flash like lightning sears you.

When you wake again, to find yourself on the ground with dirt and debris covering you as though a storm has blown over you or days have passed, and that cursed horse slobbering across your face as it nuzzles you, then you discover that the stone has vanished.

But at night, you can call light from your palm.

Marit was weak, too exhausted to travel. She lived in the shelter through the cold season, gathering and hunting. Once she had gained enough strength, she cut herself an exercise staff to work through the conditioning forms taught to reeves.

The winged horse vanished for intervals that never lasted longer than a day. She never saw it graze in the meadow or drink from the cold stream, which made her suspect that it, too, was a ghost: the ghost of a Guardian's winged horse. The Guardians were dead and gone. She had herself seen the bones of a dead Guardian, the day she was murdered on the Liya Pass. Most likely this state of being betwixt and between was indeed the punishment she had received for walking onto a Guardian altar when everyone knew it was forbidden.

But at least Joss still lived. He had survived. That was her consolation.

2

A new year arrived with the heat and the Flower Rains. She prepared travel food. When she left, she traveled along animal tracks and footpaths through high, dry country unfamiliar to her. Walking was such a slow way of traveling, especially since the worn leather straps of the sandals she had taken from the hut kept breaking. Yet if she walked in bare feet, her soles got cut and bruised.

The winged mare tagged after like a love-struck youth. When the path was reasonably smooth, she practiced riding. Except for that morning of its arrival, she did not see it fly.

Not until the day the bandits attacked her.

She heard them long before she saw them.

"We've been tramping up here for months and found nothing. I say we go back to Walshow. I'm wanting hot spiced soup from Shardit's kettle."

"That's not all you're wanting from Shardit's kettle. Not that she don't dole it out to anyone with enough coin to pay the tithing." Cruel laughter floated over the trees.

Marit paused on a mostly washed-out track where she was picking her way among stones and steep water-cut trenches. Reluctantly, she had taken the knife and the bow from the shelter, not liking to steal but knowing she couldn't survive without them. She shut her eyes, listening. The wind chased up the ridge through pine and tollyrake. She smelled a sweet-sour scent, like a festering corruption in flesh.

"Shut your ugly muzzle, arsehole. She's my wife."

"We all know what she was before, heh heh. Didn't she get thrown out of the temple for asking for coin—?"

A scuffle broke out: the distinctive smack of fist against flesh; men egging the combatants on; feet scraping and sliding on earth; breath coming in bursts and gasps.

"Stop that!" A stouter weapon thumped heads. "Cursed fools. Keep your minds on our task."

"Yes, Captain. Yes, yes," they said, but she heard resentment and fear in their voices.

"Move on out, then. Move out."

"Captain! See there! Is that the one we're looking out for?"

Their tiny figures were perfectly visible where the path bent through a clearing a very long distance below, beyond earshot. Hearing them had distracted her from looking so far. But she could see them.

And they had seen her.

She swore under her breath, losing track of their voices as they burst into activity, some racing up the path while others spread out to make a net of men along the hillside to capture her in case she tried to sneak past them. She had only seven arrows, and the knife was just a knife, the blade not longer than her hand.

"The hells!"

She began climbing back the way she had come. The horse blocked the track, lowered its head, and shoved her.

"Great Lady! You useless beast! Get out of my way."

It raised its head and stared at her, affronted.

"I beg you, please," she added impatiently. "I can't fight them. I have to run."

It unfolded its wings. They were astonishing, as pale as its silvery-gray coat and too fragile to lift such weight.

"Curse it." She tugged her stolen pack more tightly on her shoulders and ducked under one wing to come up at the saddle from behind. The wings rose over the mare's shoulders, sprouting out of a deep barrel chest thick with muscle. She made awkward work of mounting but fixed her legs into the straps—

The horse leaped.

She shrieked as she lurched sideways, grasping the post to stop from falling as the mare beat with heavy wing-strokes into the sky. Then she started laughing with relief and nerves as they rose higher, and the men came into view. One loosed a single arrow, which fell harmlessly back to earth, although she wished it might loop back and stick him in the chest.

The mare's flight seemed snail-like compared with the effortless sail of her eagle. It passed through the edges of several promising thermals, but unlike an eagle, it did not catch them and rise. It flew no faster than a horse could gallop, its thin legs imitating the gait as if it were running along an invisible road. Slow, slow, slow. Below, the company continued its dogged pursuit, scrambling up the trail.

"We're in for it now," she said to the horse, who flicked an ear. "Cursed if I don't think they're out looking for me in particular, although why I should think so, I don't know. I must have escaped that woodsmen's camp after all. Maybe these are friends of theirs, or the very men from that camp in pursuit of me. Lord Radas might have put them on my trail. But the one man said Walshow. That town lies beyond High Haldia, up in Heaven's Ridge. That's well to the north of the Liya Pass and far away from Iliyat."

Above the trees, where they flew, she had a better grasp of the land around her. She knew she was no longer on the Liya Pass, and nowhere near the vale of Iliyat, where Lord Radas ruled. And she certainly wasn't anywhere near Copper Hall. She had seen country like this during the year she had flown her apprentice's circuit as a newly trained reeve: in the high mountain escarpments of Heaven's Ridge. Steep ridges and peaks dominated the northern and northwestern horizons, a wall to separate the Hundred from the dangerous lands beyond. She and the mare flew above the foothills, a wilderness known to reeves as a haunt of bandits and other folk tossed out of their home for criminal behavior; it was also the remote nesting territories where eagles mated and raised their young out of sight of human eyes.

How had she gotten here, hundreds of mey away from the place she had died?

If she had died. Yet she could not shake that horrible dream of walking to Copper Hall. It had seemed so real. Yet if she had died and become a ghost, why did she get cold? Why did her hands and feet get scratched? How could these men see her? That twenty gods-touched men would have flocked together in the barren backcountry defied belief, because the temples prized any man or woman gifted with the spirit sight, even the ones who were cracked in the head like the old man Mokass. It was almost as if she had been a ghost then, and no longer was. How could that happen?

They lost sight of their pursuers. The mare shifted balance for a ponderous turn. Marit's legs ached as she clung to saddle and post. To be harnessed under an eagle was a very different sensation from sitting astride a horse; the view was worse from the horse, for one, with those wings getting in the way of her sight. The rise and fall of the wings distracted her until a light glinted ahead, halfway up a black cliff face rising out of a wooded hill. As the horse flew straight for the rock wall, Marit realized that she had no reins and could not control its flight. They galloped through the air straight at the escarpment, and the shadows opened to reveal a cleft and a wide ledge. The mare sailed in. Its hooves struck stone. Marit hissed between gritted teeth as the horse stamped to a halt.

She dismounted, staggered, and dropped to her knees. The mare folded its wings and ambled to the back of the cleft where a fountain burbled from a deep fissure in the cliff. It lowered its head to drink. Across the broad ledge a pattern glittered, whether in sunlight or the growing edge of shadow. It was like a crystalline labyrinth grown into the stone, a twisting pattern whose like she had seen before.

Gods preserve her. The mare had brought her to a Guardian's altar.

Aui! What did it matter now?

She rose. No one and nothing stirred. She set a foot on the entrance to the labyrinth, then the other. The pavement pulsed as if she were feeling the heartbeat of the Earth Mother. She paced its measure. With each change of angle in the path's direction, the world shifted. She saw far beyond the isolated ledge into distant landscapes: surging ocean; a fallen stone tower above a tumble of rocks lapped by soft waves; rain pattering in tangled oak forest; a vast gleam of water—not the sea—bordered by dunes; a high peak slipping in and out of streaming cloud; a homely village of six cottages beside a gushing river; a pinnacle overlooking a wide basin of land surrounded by rugged hills; a dusty hilltop rimmed by boulders where a presence tugged at her . . . and she faltered.

"Here you are," said a man's voice. "I've been waiting for you."

She did not move, sure that to take one step back or one forward would break this inexplicable link. She saw no face, only a suggestion of gold light, but she felt him as strongly as if he were standing behind her. She hid her own face by pulling up the hood of her cloak.

"You must be confused," he said. "I can help you. What is your name?"

Cursed if she was going to say that out loud to a stranger! She recognized the voice, but couldn't place it. A sour-sweet smell drifted within the lines, making her want to sneeze.

"I'm hesitant to say so," she said, measuring her words. "Who are you? How can I know I can trust you? Where are you, and how is it you can speak to me? I have many questions."

"All shall be answered as you gain your strength. You're just awakening. Here, now, let me introduce myself. I am Radas."

The name pierced her like a dagger to the heart. She was cold, then hot, breaking into a sweat.

But another man might be named Radas. It wasn't an uncommon name. "Where are you from, Radas?"

"I am lord of Iliyat. I have the resources to help you. Only stay where you are, and I will come to fetch you."

The hells he would!

Lord Radas of Iliyat had ordered her death. He was responsible for the murder of her eagle. He was a killer, and she smelled his corruption even here, not knowing how far away he was or, indeed, how they could be talking at all.

She had flown ten years as a reeve. A lie to buy herself time to edge out of a bad situation was nothing she couldn't handle easily. "I will wait for you here. How long will it take for you to reach me?"

She felt him nod, but she understood that he could not physically reach her from where he was now despite the magic that allowed them speech. "I have men in the area, searching for you. If you see them, you'll be safe with them. But they won't be able to reach you at the altar. That's where you must meet me. Stay where you are. It will take me two days to get there. You haven't told me your name?"

How persuasive he sounded! If it weren't for knowing he was responsible for the murder of her eagle, if it weren't for remembering how crisply he had ordered the men under his command to rape, mutilate, and then kill her, she would never have suspected what manner of man he was just by the pleasant tone of his words.

"I'm Ramit," she said. "I'm so very confused. Can you tell me what has happened to me?"

"All in good time. You mustn't rush these things. Some explanations are best accomplished face-to-face."

I'll just wager they are, she thought, and found herself shaking as she took another step, as the dusty hilltop vanished and a damp vista of marshland overhung by low clouds came into view. Cursing furiously, she strode to the center of the labyrinth, ignoring the landscapes flashing dizzily past. She stumbled down to the crevice, where water trickled into a basin from which the mare had been drinking. She unhooked the bowl from her belt and held it under the spring. Still trembling, she lifted the bowl to her mouth and drank her fill. The cold water burned her lips and throat. She started to cry, gulping sobs that doubled her over. Dead, slaughtered, and that poor chained Devouring girl dead by her own hand after being abused in ways that Marit was sure were worse than what little the girl had voiced aloud. Dead, lost, wandering.

Alone.

Panic swelled like a black cloud, ready to swallow her. She clawed for the steady heart that had taken her through so many years of reeve's work; she fought past the tears, and found her strength.

Enough!

She had no time for this. Two days she had, if he had been telling the truth. Knowing what manner of man he was, she knew he might as well have been lying.

She wiped her face with the back of a hand as she rose and looked around. What magic sustained the Guardian's altar she did not know. How the maze wove its sorcery into the angles of its path she could not guess, because there was actually only one route to walk once you started on the path. The many landscapes visible from within remained invisible now that she stood at the center, but by an odd trick of the view she could see from here at the center a complete vista of the ordinary land around her, all the approaches to this pinnacle, even those that ought to be blocked from her view by spurs and heights.

A pair of hawks floated on a thermal far above. To the west, on an impossibly narrow path, a mountain goat picked its way along the slope. A thread of smoke rose beyond the nearest hill, but it smelled of sheep and a drowsy shepherd strumming a simple tune on a two-stringed lute. A family of rock mice skittered below thickets of sprawling heath-pink. Stunted pine trees grew low to the ground, and spiny broom poked its first flowers from their hairy sheaths. The wind moaned along the height. Otherwise, the land was empty. She was utterly alone.

The mare waited beside the burbling crevice, watching her with interest or, perhaps, disdain. Beside the horse, a bridle hung from an iron post hammered into the rock.

With some difficulty, she slid the harness over the mare's head and, after a few problems with the ears, got it correctly settled and buckled. She had grown up in a village, and while her own family hadn't been wealthy enough to own horses or even a donkey or mule, as a girl she had hired out on occasion to the stable master at the local inn and learned the rudiments of harness care and use. Those skills had aided her when she had first come to the reeve hall, after Flirt had chosen her.

Flirt was dead.

The wind stung her eyes. A weight crushed her chest, a haze of grief rising to fill her vision and weaken her body. But she could not succumb now. She could let Flirt's death overwhelm her, or she could use it to make her strong enough to do what must be done. First, evade Lord Radas. Second, observe, and decide what to do next. This simple plan must sustain her as she walked into an unknown landscape: her life after the death of her eagle, or her death after her own death.

She led the mare to the edge of the cliff. The sheer drop did not dizzy her. Reeves learned quickly not to fear heights. Or maybe the great eagles never chose as reeves any person likely to fall prey to that particular fear.

The mare balked, wanting to stay.

"We're getting as far from here as possible, do you understand me? That man killed me, or tried to kill me, even if he wasn't the one who wielded the knife. I'll never trust him, and neither should you."

After a pause, as if considering her words or deciding whether it was worth a confrontation, the mare opened her wings. Marit mounted. They flew.

THE MARE DID not want to take her in the direction Marit wanted to go, but Marit held the reins, and forced the issue. Beyond the eastern hill in the direction of the thread of smoke lay a box canyon utterly without life or interest beyond dusty green thickets of spiny hedge-heath and bitter-thorn. The smoke came from a pile of brush smoldering at the very end where the walls fenced you in, an excellent spot for an ambush. They came to earth, the mare tossing her head and snorting. Whispers hissed from thickets along the slopes, but no one appeared. The sound might only have been the way the wind clawed through the buds and leaves, but she had a cursed strong feeling that whoever was there had *seen* her.

It might have been the passage of a drizzling rain, quickly laid down and quickly vanished as soon its hooves touched earth. It might have been the way the mare turned, once on the ground, and headed straight out of the trap with a determined gait despite branches of bitter-thorn raking her flanks and tearing a pale gray feather from her wings. Those wings, folded tight, protected Marit's legs.

"That's the second warning you've given me, or maybe the third," said Marit, bending low in case some cursed fool decided to loose an arrow or fling a spear.

As they cleared the canyon and found themselves in a rugged intersection of hills and ridges with the suggestion of a valley opening away to the southeast and the sharp spine of the high mountains to the west, Marit wondered if she had imagined the ambush.

"You choose," she said to the mare. "Anywhere but north."

The mare took flight, bearing due south according to the sun. Steep hills were easily cleared. Almost before Marit realized they had come upon human life, they sailed over a high meadow where a flock of sheep grazed. The youth watching over the flock plucked strings, head bent over a two-stringed lute.

The mare trotted to earth out of sight of the meadow, and Marit left her with reins loose, hoping the horse wouldn't stray. She cut through a stand of pine, thick with scent, and brushed through knee-high grass at the meadow's edge. The lad played intently, biting a lip. His concentration gave him charm. A handsome dog emerged from behind him and ran toward her with ears raised, interested but not particularly suspicious. The dog raced around her as she advanced, and a startled blat from one of the grazing sheep caught the boy's attention. He looked up as Marit paused a stone's toss from him.

His eyes opened wide. Equally startled, she took a step back.

He grinned and set down the lute. "The hells!" He whistled, and the dog pattered over to him. "Usually he barks," the boy added. He was old enough to be sent to the high pastures with the sheep but not quite old enough to be called a man. "Where did you come from?"

"Just over the ridge." The box canyon wasn't all that far from here, truly, although she wasn't entirely sure how to reach it traveling on the ground. Reeves sometimes lost that skill, seeing everything from on high.

"You're not from around here. Are you hungry, or thirsty? I've got plenty."

"I would appreciate a bit." Reeve habit died hard: you ate and drank whenever opportunity offered, as you didn't always know in the course of a patrol when you might have leisure to eat and drink again.

He shared a cursed sharp cider and a ball of rice neatly wrapped in nai leaves, poor man's food but filling nonetheless.

"I'm surprised to see anyone up here," he said with nice manners which, together with his pleasant features, would make him a favorite among women when he got a bit older. He was water-born, judging by the pattern of tattoos ringing his wrists. An attractive youth, but forbidden to her because she was also water-born. "We're about as far west as folk live. You can see how the mountains rise." He indicated a barrier of grim peaks to the west. "Nothing beyond that but the flat salt desert."

"You've seen it?"

He laughed. "Not myself. My uncle claims to have climbed the Wall, to see onto the deadlands. He said they stretched for a thousand mey, farther than he could see even from the mountains' edge, nothing but pale gold to the flat horizon. Maybe it's true, or maybe he just said so to impress the woman he wanted to marry. He did bring back a shard of an eagle's egg. From a nest, so he said. Said he climbed to it, and fetched it out. But he did talk blather. I bet he just found it on the trail, fallen from a high place."

He carefully asked no questions, plying her with highlands hospitality, offering a second flask of cider. He was an open lad, sure she wasn't a bad person because the dog—whose name was Nip—tolerated her. She was just utterly stunned to be having a commonplace conversation.

"I see you've a lute there. Have you always played?"

"Surely I have, since I could pick one up. Would you like me to play for you?" He was sure she would like to hear him; everyone always enjoyed his playing.

She nodded, settling more comfortably cross-legged beside him. He plucked a pair of tunes and hummed a melancholy melody that made her eyes water. Thin clouds chased across the high landscape. As the sun passed into shadow, she shivered at the unexpected draft of cool air seeping down from above and pulled her cloak more tightly around her torso.

"Listen, ver. I'm called Marit. I'm lost, truth to tell, and I got lost by running from a nasty pack of bandits who aren't too far from here by my reckoning. I'm not sure it's safe for you. You might be safer walking back to your village, wherever you came from, and warning them that dangerous men are wandering out here looking to make trouble."

He shrugged with a peculiar lack of concern. "We've had trouble for years with that crew, most of them out of Walshow and other places north of here. But we've made our own defenses." With a sly grin, he indicated Nip. "You'd be surprised what that dog can do when he's roused. We've learned to defend ourselves. It wasn't so bad before, when I was a nipster—a toddler, like. The elders say it was peaceful then. Still, the troubles are all I've ever known. But your bandits won't be finding this pasture. I'm surprised you did."

"How long have bandits been wandering up here? How can they feed themselves? How do you know they're come from Walshow? How far is it to Walshow from here?"

He snapped his fingers. Two more dogs appeared out of the grass. They were bigger than Nip and had massive muzzles and powerful chests. They loped over to sniff at her, then slipped away to resume their patrol. "You're a reeve, aren't you?" he asked. "We see them now and again, hunting around here."

"Do you? Where do they hail from?"

He shrugged. It was obvious he was telling the truth and never thought once of lying to her. He didn't even feel he needed to lie, he was that confident. "I don't know. They keep to themselves, although it's true that a time or two we've had a bit of help from them when packs of men came drifting down out of Walshow."

"They're not patrolling out of Gold Hall? Clan Hall hasn't the resources. I suppose Argent Hall or Horn Hall might fly these parts. Don't they oversee your assizes?"

He looked at the ground, dense with the green growing breath of plants feeding on the early rains and the promise of a fresh year. It almost seemed that he darkened in aspect, pulled shadows over himself as he changed his mind about trusting her. He was hiding from her, flashes that pricked at her vision

what if she knows?

a snake winds through underbrush, tongue flicking

keep a vessel as of clay about your thoughts, it is the only protection against the third eye

She blinked back tears and realized he was not speaking.

Fear makes you cold. Shivering, she clambered to her feet. Nip barked as the other dogs circled in. There were five dogs that she could now see, but three wagged their tails tentatively. None threatened her; they simply remained vigilant.

"You're one of them, seeing into me," he said in a hoarse voice. "You're death. Have you come to kill me?"

The speed of his transformation from pleasant companion to frightened lad shocked her. She took a step away from the ugly emotion she had roused in him. "What do you mean?"

He scrambled to his feet and backed away, holding the lute as if it might shield him from attack. "She hides us, it's all she can do against the others, for they have all become corrupt and soon their shadow will darken every heart. It's just that the dogs didn't bark at you. Why is that? What power do you have that can charm the dogs? Is it all for nothing, all that she has done for us to spare us?" Tears ran down his cheeks. He wept for what his folk had lost. And he continued backing away, angling so she had to turn to keep facing him.

Desperately, she said, "I don't know what you're talking about. I'm seeking answers. I'm lost."

"That's what they all say. That's what she warns us they will say, trying to get inside us, to get past the defenses she taught us to build. Nothing is safe. Nothing."

For so many years the protection had held. Now, in an instant, all had fallen, fallen. The shadow will grow, and in the end it will consume even those trying to hide from it.

Marit swayed, struck by the hammer blow of his fear and grief. The sun cleared a cloud; its light forced her to raise a hand to spare her eyes. He had turned her, so the sun's glamour blinded her.

He whistled. The dogs bolted into action, rounding up the bleating sheep. He grabbed a pack that had lain concealed in the grass. Silver ribbons to mark the new year fluttered from the buckle of the pack where he had tied them. The Year of the Silver Deer followed the Year of the Black Eagle, only in that case why weren't there only two ribbons tied to his pack, appropriate to the Deer? Why were there eight ribbons, the number of the Fox? He loped away from her with his lute in one hand and the pack bumping up and down on his back.

The Year of the Silver Fox would fall nineteen years after the Year of the Black Eagle. So why was he celebrating it now?

She didn't call after him. She recognized futility when she saw it. Anyway, she was still trembling with a fear that penetrated her entire body. She hadn't "seen" into him. It was a trick, him speaking and her too tired or anxious to notice, or maybe a kind of magic she'd never heard of except in the tales: the magic of misdirection common to clever thieves and cunning jaryas. But he had recognized the change. He'd known she was doing it. That's when he had run.

The lad and his dogs drove the sheep out of the meadow while she watched. The dogs yipped excitedly, eager to be on the move. Behind her, a creature stamped through the grass on her trail. She spun, grabbing at her knife. The mare trotted up beside her, wings furled.

"You warned me," she said. "I just didn't know what you meant."

The horse nosed in the grass. A surface glinted, and she crouched to investigate as the mare chopped at the earth. An ornament had fallen among the grass, frayed strands of silver ribbon caught in a tiny leather loop that had once fastened the ornament to another object. It was a cheap replica of a fox, no longer than her thumb and rendered out of tin: a poor man's year medallion, the kind of thing, like the eight ribbons, given out by the temples at the feasts dedicated to the year's beginning. The Year of the Silver Fox.

Maybe she was still dreaming.

The mare lifted her head, left ear flicking back. Her stance changed. She stared toward the tree line off to the north in the opposite direction to which the youth had fled. Clutching the fox medallion, Marit rose.

A spit of movement made the mare shy, and Marit jumped sideways. An arrow quivered in the earth.

"The hells!"

A punch jabbed her body. Gasping, she looked down to find an arrow protruding from her belly, low by her right hip. The mare spread her wings. Gagging at the sheer utter knife of red-hot pain, Marit snapped off the haft and tossed the fletched end aside. With a shout, to pour out a breath's worth of pain, she hauled herself into the saddle. The mare sprang into the air. Marit gripped the saddle horn, sweat breaking over her as she resisted screaming, as the point jabbed and ground inside her gut. Armed men ran into the meadow, bows raised and arrows rising in high arcs after her. These were the same sullen bandits who had first chased her, their ruthless captain identifiable by the lime-whitened horsetail ornaments dangling from his shoulders.

Then they were clear. Her vision blurred. Hills rose and fell on every side like an ocean spilling and sighing beneath her: highlands pine, vistas of grass and heath and bitter-thorn and later moss and lichen with no sign of the youth and his dogs and sheep. She concentrated on clinging to the saddle. Hold on. Hold on. Let the horse take its head and run the straightest course away from danger.

They will never stop hunting me.

"You're death," the lad had said.

Blood leaked down her belly and spilled over her thighs onto the mare's gray flanks, to drip-drop into the air like rain. Her hands went numb as feeling left them. The cloak wrapped her so tightly she could not even see the landscape passing beyond, shrouding her in the same way the white shroud of death drapes the dead. But she was still breathing, each breath like flame sucked into her body. The pain of burning kept her alive for a thousand years with each lift and fall of wings, and she hung on forever wishing that oblivion would claim her, but it never did.

With a jolt that made Marit cry out, the mare clattered to earth. She spread her wings, and Marit tumbled out of the saddle and fell hard on her back. Pain blinded her, or she was already blind with night suffocating her. She choked on air. Better dead than this. Desperate, wild, she fixed hands around the broken shaft and yanked.

A stink of blood and effluvia gushed free, warming her hands. The gods heard her pleas. A roaring like a storm wind battered through her. Rising out of that gale, the white cloak of death smothered her in its wings.

3

After a certain point death is a peaceful condition, but a bit uncomfortable if your one leg is twisted beneath you, and if your shoulder, pressed into rock, is beginning to feel the pinch, and if your hip aches. She shifted, because it irritated her that minor twinges must plague her when she had earned the right to rest. Once shifted, she realized she was awake and her mind was full with questions.

Why were those men hunting her? Why did Lord Radas want her? Was it not enough to murder Flirt? Must he torture and abuse her as well, as he had that poor Devouring girl? Yet he had not questioned her when she had claimed her name as Ramit. Did he seek Marit, the reeve, or Ramit, the unknown woman walking an altar? What had the shepherd boy meant when he had called her "one of them"?

So many questions, and not a single answer in sight.

She groaned and rose to her knees. A sticky dry substance flaked from her hands as she pushed up to stand. Blood stained her tunic and leggings; her hands were grimy with dried blood and slime, but the smell had faded. She raised her hands to rub her eyes, then recalled how disgusting her hands were, and looked around bleary-eyed as her skin went clammy with fear.

The mare had brought her back to a Guardian altar.

The cursed horse sucked noisily from a pool, tail swishing. The stupid beast paused to snap at a fly.

The hells!

Marit tugged at the stolen tunic, but the worn linen weave ripped right away. Below, her dark belly rounded in a curve dimpled by the Mother's Scar, her navel. A paler line, smooth along the skin but ragged in its journey, marked a scar just below and to the right of her navel. Had she earned that scar in her days as a reeve? Had she only dreamed the arrow that had punctured her abdomen? She probed along the scar, but felt no tenderness and no pain.

"What am I?" she said in the direction of the mare, who lifted her head at the sound of Marit's voice. "What has happened to me?"

The cursed animal gazed at her. What did she know about horses, really? Stubborn, unpredictable, skittish, narrow-minded, fixated on the familiar because the unfamiliar is a threat to them, they were prey, born to run from that which pursued them.

As she was running. She was no longer a reeve, bound to her eagle, free to hunt. She was the hunted. Like the deer, she fled the arrow meant to kill her, and when the next flight struck, she probably would not even have seen it coming.

"You'll give me warning, won't you?" she called to the mare.

The cursed beast flicked its ears.

"I'll call you 'Warning,' just to call you something. I'll hope you grow into your name." She dusted flecks of grime from her ragged clothing. "Why in the hells do you keep bringing me to Guardian altars?"

The wind hummed across the pinnacle of rock on which they stood. She was panting with anger, furious and scared together, but even so the rose-purple light of a setting sun caught her attention. She spun slowly all the way around, because when beauty awes you, you must halt and try to catch your breath and your staggered heart.

The wind was light this evening, a constant blowing presence but easy enough to stand upright in despite that she stood on the very top of a vast pillar of rock. Broken contours suggested that a low wall had once rimmed the edge. No craggy peak loomed above. No overhang offered shelter within. She stood a few steps from a sheer drop-off; she might easily stumble over tumbled stones and fall to her death because the ground was a long, long way down. There was no way down except to fly.

To the west, a range of hills was painted by the colors of the falling sun. Below the pillar, a ridgeline snaked out from the hills. The ridgeline terminated in a bulge where a ruined beacon tower stood, a complex of abandoned buildings arranged at the base of the spire on which she and the horse perched. To the east, the ground dropped away so precipitously that even a reeve with her experience of heights felt her breath taken away by the grandeur of the scene: A wide basin of land darkened as the eastern sky faded into purpling twilight. Clouds drifted like high islands above the land. Out there beneath the sea of night, a few lights glimmered, village watch fires lit against the gloom.

As twilight overtook them and the light changed, the twisting coil of the labyrinth came to life, marking the path to the center where the mare waited beside the pool. Water burbled up from the rock beneath. Marit licked her lips, smelling the moisture and craving its coolness.

She did not want to be caught out at the edge of the pillar once night fell, for fear of falling over the edge. That cursed mare had a knack for dumping her at the entrance to the labyrinth. She set a foot on the glittering path, then the other. Nothing happened.

With measured steps, she warily paced out the path. A pulse hummed up through her feet as the magic of the labyrinth came to life around her: a flat ocean pricked by the emerging milky-bright light of stars; a fallen stone tower rising above rocks barely visible above surging waves; the last rumbling footsteps of a thunderstorm over a tangled oak forest keeping time with flashes of blue light high in the sky; the sun drawing a golden road across a calm sea of water; mist shrouding a high peak; in a homely village of six cottages, farmers laughing together as they trundled their carts home.

For an instant she saw onto the place she actually stood: the pinnacle of rock beneath her feet, the vast bowl of land to the east, and the rose-painted hills to the west. She took another step and saw a dusty hilltop rimmed by boulders, the setting sun visible as a red smear. She faltered, chest tight as she sucked in air for courage.

When she had looked onto this place before, Lord Radas had spoken to her. Hastily, she moved on. She smelled the rotting damp of marshland but could see only the suggestion of a flat landscape against the swallowing night. As she moved through the path, she must smell and hear what lay beyond each turn because the sun had set and she was walking in layers of night, some too dark to penetrate and others still limned with the last measure of day as though she were leaping from east to west, north to south, and back again, randomly.

Not randomly. The pattern repeated. And if it repeated, she could learn it.

She took another step. Air iced her lungs. Her face and hands smarted in a bone-freezing chill. A tincture of juniper touched her nostrils. She halted, startled by the brush of that perfume, remembering Joss and how he had washed with cakes of juniper-scented soap sent twice yearly by his mother. Joss, her lover. The man she loved, even if she had never quite told him so.

Twilight is a bridge between day and night. On its span, the wind blows both into the whispering past and the silent future, and you partake of them both because you are in transition from one state to the next, a condition that recurs with every passage between night and day and night. Indeed, this condition occurs many times in the entirety of a life, which is lived out as a series of such transitions, bridges between what has gone before and what will come next.

Twilight is a presence, hard to know in its impermanence.

Twilight speaks to her in a soft foreign lisp, with a good-natured voice half amused and half cynical.

"Hu! There you are. They've been looking for you for a good long while now, since long before I came to them. They're getting irritated. If I were you, I would submit now. That's better than what will happen if you can't keep hiding from them. On the other hand, I don't mind seeing them wring their hands and stamp their feet a bit longer."

"Who are you?"

"I'm a ghost."

"A ghost! You don't sound like a ghost."

"What do ghosts sound like?"

"Aui! I suppose they sound like we do, I mean, that they talk no differently as ghosts than they do when living."

"So are you saying I can't be a ghost? Or I can be a ghost?"

"You're a flirt," she said with a laugh, because she liked his lazy, good-natured, and sexy baritone even if she could not trust him.

"It's been said of me before." Like twilight, he seemed not to partake completely of any one thing: he might be a good man coarsened by a bad situation, or a bad man mellowed by a good situation, or just someone caught in the middle with no way out but through.

"Don't trust me," he added, his voice darkening. "I'd give you over in an instant if I thought it would get me what I want. Who are you?"

"I'm not telling. What do you want?"

The lazy tone worked up to an edge. "Escape from this hell of endless suffering."

"Why are you trapped?"

His laugh scraped. "We're all trapped. Don't you know that yet? Wait where you are and submit when they reach you, or keep running and hiding."

The bitterly cold air hoarsened her voice. "Those can't be the only choices."

"How have you evaded them for so long? Neh, don't tell me. I don't want to know. But they're long in looking for you. They don't like that. They hauled me free at once. They made me what I am now."

"What are you now, besides a ghost, if you are a ghost?"

"A coward who fears oblivion and yearns for it. I have more power than I could ever have dreamed of. I wish I could die. I want to go home, but I never will leave this land."

"Who are you?"

For a long time he remained silent. Her fingers grew taut with cold until it hurt to bend them. Her ears were burning, and her eyes had begun to sting as though blistering from the cold.

He spoke in a whisper. "How I fear them, for they are sweet with the corruption that comes of believing they must do what is wrong in order to make things right. I was called Hari once, Harishil, the name my father gave me. Will you tell me your name?"

Marit had served as a reeve for over ten years. She'd learned to trust her instincts, and she knew in her gut that even if she might want to trust him, she must not. Anyway, what kind of person got a name from his father, not his mother? "I can't tell you. I'm sorry."

Had she been able to see him, she would have guessed he smiled. "You need not apologize for what is true. I'll have to tell them I saw you, but I'll say I didn't know where you were. There's one thing you need to know. We can see into people's hearts with our third eye and our second heart, but we are blind to each other. Remember that. It's your only weapon against them."

"Who are 'they'?"

"Nine Guardians the gods created, according to the tale you tell in this land. I think at one time they walked in accord, but now they are at war. Two rule, and three of us submit; five are enough to hunt and destroy the four who have not yet submitted to the rule of night and sun. They will find you in the end, and if you will not submit, they will destroy you and pass your cloak to another, one more easily subdued."

"The Guardians are dead. They've vanished from the Hundred. Everyone knows that."

"Guardians can't die. Surely you know that, now you are one. Hsst! That cursed worm Yordenas is walking. Go quickly if you don't want your whereabouts known to him! Go now!"

His urgency impelled her. She took a step, and a breath of fetid air washed her. She took another step into a spitting salt spray with the crash of surf far below, and another step to warm rain in her face amid the racket of crickets and the smell of damp grass. Her hands smarted as blood rushed back into the skin. The pulse beneath her feet throbbed with a third tone, hot and intense, the presence of blood washing down the path like an incoming tide.

She could not run within the confines of the labyrinths, but because she was compact she could negotiate the path's twists and turns economically, keeping ahead of the other presence. The muzzy confusion of earlier days had lifted and she felt both the widening focus and the pinpoint awareness of her surroundings from her days as a reeve when her instincts—right up until the last day—had served her so well.

She was back in the game, one step ahead of fear. Flirting with danger, the rush that her eagle had taught her to love. Wasn't all of life like that: never more than one step ahead until the day death caught you?

The path spilled her into the center of the labyrinth, where the horse waited, looking aggrieved, if horses could look aggrieved, as if to say: "Why did you take so long?"

Gods, she was thirsty. Hands shaking, she filled the bowl and drank her fill, the water blazing into every part of her body. She sank down cross-legged, panting, and rubbed her forehead. Night had fallen. Knowing a cliff plunged away on all sides, she dared not move, not unless the horse was willing to fly at night, something an eagle could not do because they depended so heavily on their vision. She'd heard tales of eagles who could be fooled or forced into flying at the full moon, but she'd never had such luck with Flirt.

But as she sat with a sweet breeze steady against her face, she realized the mare actually had a kind of sheen to it that might be described as a *glow*. Its coat was not so much pale gray as luminescent silver. Indeed, the horse had an unnatural look, a ghost in truth, if ghosts flicked their tails and tossed their pretty heads.

Why did the cursed mare keep bringing her to Guardian altars? Her chest was tight the way a person gets when they don't want to breathe for fear of inhaling where they know there will be a noxious smell.

A Guardian altar. A winged horse. A cloak. A simple begging bowl. Light from her palm, if she needed it, and a patterned labyrinth through which she seemed able to speak across distances to others like her.

She knew the tale. She could chant the words or tell it through gesture, as every child could.

> Long ago, in the time of chaos, a bitter series of wars, feuds, and reprisals denuded the countryside and impoverished the lords and guildsmen and farmers and artisans of the Hundred. In the worst of days, an orphaned girl knelt at the shore of the lake sacred to the gods and prayed that peace might return to her land.
>
> A blinding light split the air, and out of the holy island rising in the center of the lake appeared the seven gods in their own presence. The waters boiled, and the sky wept fire, as the gods crossed over the water to the shore where the girl had fallen.
>
> And they spoke to her.
>
> Our children have been given mind, hand, and heart to guide their actions, but they have turned their power against themselves. Why should we help you?
>
> For the sake of justice, she said.
>
> And they heard her.
>
> Let Guardians walk the lands, in order to establish justice if they can.
>
> Who can be trusted with this burden? she asked them. Those with power grasp tightly.

Only the dead can be trusted, they said. Let the ones who have died fighting for justice be given a second chance to restore peace. We will give them gifts to aid them with this burden.

Taru the Witherer wove nine cloaks out of the fabric of the land and the water and the sky, and out of all living things, which granted the wearer protection against the second death although not against weariness of soul;

Ilu the Opener of Ways built the altars, so that they might speak across the vast distances each to the other;

Atiratu the Lady of Beasts formed the winged horses out of the elements so that they could travel swiftly and across the rivers and mountains without obstacle;

Sapanasu the Lantern gave them light to banish the shadows;

Kotaru the Thunderer gave them the staff of judgment as their symbol of authority;

Ushara the Merciless One gave them a third eye and a second heart with which to see into and understand the hearts of all;

Hasibal gave an offering bowl.

All she lacked was a staff of judgment, whatever that was.

Really, a reeve who tallied up the evidence might suggest, against all likelihood, that these added up to an obvious conclusion:

Here sits a Guardian.

WAS SHE MERELY spinning and drifting on sweet-smoke, unmoored from the world around her? All she knew for sure was that she was being hunted by forces she did not comprehend, ones her gut—and Hari the outlander, if that was really his name—warned her never to trust.

She didn't know what precisely she was now, but she had been a reeve once. She could investigate. And it would help to figure out where the hells she was, where her enemies were, and what they wanted.

"YOU MIGHT WANT to turn back," said the old woman as she scooped nai porridge into Marit's bowl. They stood under the triple-gated entrance to a temple of Ilu, where Marit had come to beg for food. "Once you ford the river and cross through West Riding, you'll have left Sohayil."

"Merchants will trade, and beggars will beg, and laborers will seek work wherever they can find it." The nai's richly spiced aroma made Marit's mouth water; it was all she could do not to bolt down the food right there.

"In the old days that was certainly true, but not anymore. We can't be so easy about things in these days." Morning mist rose off the river and curled in backwater reeds. A last gust of night rain spattered on the waters, and stilled. On the grounds of the temple, an apprentice trundled a wheelbarrow full of night soil to the temple gardens, while a pair of children carried an empty basket to the henhouse. A trio of elders even older than the gatekeeper paced through the chant of healing from the

Tale of Patience, their morning exercise. From the round sanctuary rose the sonorous chanting of male voices. "I don't mind telling you, for your own good, really, that we've recalled all our envoys who've been walking the roads from here to Haldia and Toskala. Sund and Farsar and Sardia aren't truly safe, although some still make the journey."

"You must have envoys carrying messages to the Ostiary in Nessumara, to the other temples of Ilu. Not to mention your work as envoys."

The old envoy was spry, comfortably plump, and nobody's fool. "Think you so? Why are you headed that way? If you don't mind my saying so, your clothes and walking staff mark you as a beggar or a laborer down on her luck—and the gods know we've seen enough of them in these days—but your manner doesn't fit. The cloak's nice. Is that silk? Good quality."

Her interest was genuine. She was envious, in an amused way. She didn't trust Marit, not in these days with any kind of traveler out on the roads and every sort of awful rumor blown on the winds. The region of Sohayil remained a haven of relative calm probably only because of the ancient magic bound into the bones of the surrounding hills as a fence against trouble. But on the other hand, a lone traveler wasn't likely to cause much trouble unless she was a spy scouting for—

She glanced away, as if troubled, and the contact broke.

"For what?" asked Marit.

"Eh!" The envoy laughed awkwardly as she looked back at Marit. "For what? If I could find silk that good quality, I'd get a length of blue and make a wedding wrap for my granddaughter. But not white, like that. White is—White's not a color for weddings." White is death's color, but any decent person is too well mannered to mention that to someone who clearly has nothing else to wear against the rain.

"My thanks, Your Holiness. My thanks for your hospitality."

"Blessed is Ilu, who walks with travelers." Her smile remained friendly, but it was pitying as well: *Especially poor kinless women like this one, alone in the world. No one should have to be so alone.*

Shaken, Marit retreated from the temple gate and from its neighboring village of Rifaran. She walked back to the glade where she had concealed Warning. She slurped down the porridge, the spices a prickle in her nostrils, but the comforting nai did not settle her. She worked through a set of exercises with the training staff, but the martial forms did not focus her today. Even the delicate shift of the wind in trees flowering with the rains did not soothe her.

She'd never been a loner. She liked people. But perhaps she liked them better when she didn't have an inkling of what was really going on in their heads.

She sank down on her haunches, grass brushing her thighs. Red-petaled heart-bush and flowering yellow goldcaps bobbed as the breeze worked through the meadow. White bells and purple muzz swayed. Everywhere color dazzled, and the scent of blooming made the world sweet.

"Great Lady," she whispered, "don't abandon me, who has always been your faithful apprentice. Let me be strong enough for the road ahead. Let me be strong enough to stop thinking of Joss, to let what was in the past stay in the past. Let me be wise enough to know that what we shared then, we can no longer share. My eyes are open, and there are some places and some hearts I do not want to see."

Tears slid from her eyes. She wiped them away. "Hear me, Lady. I'll stay away from him. In exchange, please watch over him even though he belongs to Ilu. Surely we are all your children. I'll follow this road, wherever it takes me. I will always act as your loyal apprentice, as I always have. I will serve the law, as I always have. Hear me, Lady. Give me a sign."

Warning stamped. A red deer parted a thick stand of heart-bush and paced into the meadow. Twin fawns, tiny creatures so new that they tottered on slender legs, stumbled into view behind her. The deer stared at Marit for a long, cool hesitation, and then sprang away into the forest with the fawns at her heels.

Marit smiled, her heart's grief easing a little. The Lady of Beasts had heard her oath, and had answered her.

SHE NO LONGER needed much sleep, and anyway she didn't fancy the flavor of her dreams, which seemed to cycle between Lord Radas whipping hounds and archers in pursuit as she fled into a dark mazy forest, or her lover Joss aged into a cursed attractive middle-aged man except for his habit of drinking himself into and out of headaches and flirting up women at every opportunity. She'd never thought of him as a person with so little self-control.

She napped in the middle of the day, hiding herself and the mare in brush or trees. In early morning and late afternoon she worked through her forms diligently. She rode at night. Under Warning's hooves, the road took on a faint gleam that lit their way. It was funny how quickly you got accustomed to a piece of magic like that, when it aided you. She minded the night rains less when she was awake. They washed through and away, blown by the winds, and afterward her clothes would dry off as she rode.

One night, Warning shied and halted, refusing to go farther. Marit led her into cover just before she heard the tramp of marching men. They were a motley group; she could see them pretty well despite overcast skies that admitted no light of moon. They had torches, and all manner of weapons, and they were moving fast and purposefully, heading southwest. Their captain with his horse-tail ornaments had a ragged scar crudely healed across his clean-shaven chin, and he had the look of a real northerner, hair and complexion lightened to a pale brown by outlander blood. They all wore a crude tin medallion on a string at their necks, a star with eight points. In a cold moment, set against the misty-warm night, she recognized the men who had tried to capture her in the mountains.

She moved on once Warning was willing to go, but she could not shake the sight of those men. Most likely Hari had confessed that he'd seen her, and identified the Guardian altar where she had been standing. It seemed likely they were marching to the Soha Hills, hoping to trap her.

They'll never give up. They want me that badly.

She plotted a path in her head that would, she hoped, lead her to Toskala. She and the mare pushed north through Sund for days, begging at temples and farmsteads at dawn or twilight. She was always looking over her shoulder.

Warning, deprived of her favored sustenance at the Guardian altars, began to graze with the same enthusiasm a dog might display eating turnips. She deigned to water in streams and ponds as if the process disgusted her.

When they reached the region of Sardia, where the tributary road they were traveling on met the Lesser Walk, they turned east toward Toskala. Late in the afternoon they set out through woodland on a track running more or less parallel to the paved road. Just before dusk they began moving through managed woodlands, skirting an orchard and diked fields marked with poles carved at the peak with the doubled axe sacred to the Merciless One.

She found a copse of murmuring pine and left Warning in its shelter. Walking along the embankment between fields, she headed toward a compound lying in the center of cultivated land. From here she could not see the main road, but she knew it was close. She circled around the high compound walls, ringed at their height with wire hung with bells to keep out intruders. Drizzle spat over the ground as she stepped up onto the entry path and walked to the gate.

The doors were shut with the dusk, lamps hanging high on the wall. She ventured into the light and raised both hands to show she was holding no weapon.

"Greetings of the dusk," she called. "I'm a traveler, begging for the goddess's mercy by way of a bit to eat and drink. Maybe some grain for the road. Withered apples? Anything you have to spare." She held out her bowl.

"Go away," said a woman's voice from atop the walls. "Our gates are closed."

Among other things, Marit had been at pains to discover what day and month it was, now that she knew she had slept through nineteen years and by doing so walked from the Year of the Black Eagle, with perhaps a slight detour through the Year of the Blue Ox, directly into the Year of the Silver Fox.

"I'm surprised to hear you say so, holy one. I thought Ushara's temples kept their gates open all day and all night of the day of Wakened Snake. So it always was in my own village."

"The gates are closed, day and night," said the woman. "Shadows walk abroad. No one can be trusted, so we no longer let anyone in. Go away, or we'll kill you." Marit sensed the presence of five others along the wall.

"How can this be, holy one? The Devourer turns no person away. Her gates are always open."

She received no answer, and no beggar's tithe, and when they shot a warning arrow to stab the dirt at her feet, she walked away.

SHE HAD BETTER luck in the villages and towns set up as posting stations along the Lesser Walk. The folk there might be wary and reluctant to share with a mere beggar, but the laws of the gods were clear on the duty owed by householders and temples toward indigent wanderers.

"Greetings of the day to you, verea," said the shopgirl, a pretty young thing in a shabby taloos that was frayed at the ends. She tried a smile, but it was as frayed as the fabric, barely holding together. She looked ready to duck away from the hard slap her father would give her if she didn't close more sales this month than last month, even if it wasn't her fault that so few travelers were out on Sardia's main road, the principal route through this region to Toskala.

"Greetings of the day to you," said Marit. The girl's cringing attitude disturbed her, so anger gave bite to her tone.

"I'm sorry. How can I help you? I'm sure there's something here you must need. What are you looking for?" Desperation made the girl's voice breathy. She was trying too hard.

Marit forced a kinder tone. "I need a brush. For grooming a horse. And something to pick stones out of its hooves. It's a nice shop. You must get a lot of customers here, you're in a good stopping point along the road."

"Custom used to be better," admitted the girl, relaxing a little. She had a round face and a honey-colored complexion, smooth and unblemished. "Folk don't travel anymore."

"Why is that?"

The girl glanced at the entryway. Wide strips of hanging cloth, stamped with the gold sigil of the merchants' guild, were tied back to either side, so with the doors slid open, she could see straight down the road along which the posting town sprawled. The girl sucked in a sharp breath. Fear rose off her like steam. Marit turned.

She should have noticed the cessation of street noise, followed by the ominous slap of feet. A pack of armed men strode down the street, breaking off in groups of two and three to climb onto the porches of shops and dive through the entrances without even the courtesy of taking off their sandals.

The girl reached over the counter to tug on Marit's sleeve. "We have to hide!" She whispered, but her thoughts screamed: *They'll take me like they took Brother. Father won't protect me this time.* "Quick, duck down over behind the chest there, they won't look. Papa!" She opened the door to the back and vanished as she slid the door hard shut behind her.

Shelves lined the shop front, but pickings were scarce: a pair of used brushes polished to look new; a single piece of stiff new harness, and several neatly looped lead lines recently oiled. A few other refurbished items also catered to travelers whose gear might have broken along the road. The chest had the bulky look of a piece left behind by a prosperous merchant fallen on hard times; not many people could afford the weight of such an oversized container.

The door to the back snapped open.

"Cursed beggar!" A sweat-stained man slammed the door shut behind him. Marit realized she had let her cloak open, which revealed her ragged clothing still damp from the dawn's shower. "Get out of the shop, or duck down behind that chest. I don't want trouble from you! Beyond what I've already got!"

She dropped down into the narrow gap between the chest and a set of lower shelves. The space was so small she had to turn her head to breathe, facing into the open shelving. A pile of brushes and combs had been shoved back here, pieces missing teeth or with wood cracking.

A heavy stride hammered along the porch. A man's voice raised in the shop next door.

"You promised me eight new halters, but here are only four. I'll need coin to make up for the ones I'll have to purchase elsewhere."

A murmured reply answered him. Marit could not hear the exact words, but terror drifted like a miasma. Beside her face, dust smeared the lowest shelf and its discarded goods, and dust stirred in an unsettled swirl of air as the man stomped into the shop where she hid.

"Heya! What about it!" he shouted, although there was something insincere about the way he bellowed. "Where are those lead lines you promised us?" In a lower, more natural voice, he added, "What news, you cursed worm?"

The shopkeeper replied in a rapid whisper. "There's little to tell, Captain. The leatherworker is hiding the rest of his stock in the grain house in his courtyard. The woman who makes banners is hiding stock down by the mulberry orchard, in the old tomb of the Mothers, plenty of good cloth for tents and other such things. This is the third week the farmers have refused to come to market."

"We've taken care of the farmers." His voice had a snarl in it. Marit's skin prickled; it was like being close to a lightning strike, wondering where the next bolt would burst free.

The shopkeeper groveled. "The blacksmith left town. Thought he'd walk to Toskala. Hoped to be safe there."

"He didn't get far."

"Eh, hah, sure it is you'd not let such a valuable man walk out on you in your year of need."

"He's working where he can't argue so much, it's true. You've told me nothing I don't already know, excepting for the bit about the leatherworker hiding goods from us. I know you have a daughter as well as the lad. I need more than this in payment, ver." His tone was sly and nasty, drunk as much with the power he held as with the wine he'd been drinking.

Marit wanted to grab the slimy weasel and slam him against the counter until he begged for mercy and returned all that had been stolen, but of course this village had clearly lost far more than could ever be restored now. Anyway she had no weapon except the old knife, whose wooden handle was coming loose, and her walking staff, hard to use effectively in a crowded shop. She hated herself for what she could not do.

"A reeve came through," said the man reluctantly.

"Sheh! You know it's forbidden for you folk to talk or tithe to reeves."

"I know it, I know it," he gabbled. "But the reeve wore the Star of Life, like you folk do. He said he was flying down to Argent Hall, where a marshal was to be elected or murdered or some such. That's what he said. How can we stop a reeve from flying in, when all's said and done? Eh? Eh?" He was whining. "There's nothing we can do when folk do walk into town on their own feet. We can't stop them."

"Maybe so." The news had distracted the captain. Marit heard him scratching in the stubble at his chin. "Argent Hall, eh? Wish they'd made their move at Gold Hall, to get those cursed reeves up there off our backs, but there it is. The lord knows his business, just like you know yours, eh? The reeve halls will topple soon enough. What else? You've got that look about you, ver, like you're hiding somewhat from me."

"Neh, neh, nothing at all. Just a word I overheard the other day, a passing comment, you can't trust chance-heard conversation, can you? Anyone can talk and say anything they please, can't they? How can a poor soul know what's true and what is just sky-spinning?"

The captain's silence made the shop seem abruptly warmer, stuffy and hard to breathe. From the street came calls and cries, so remote they might as well have been meaningless: a woman sobbing, a man's triumphant giggling as with a fit of cruelty, a spasm of coughing and spewing. Marit heard, from the back of the shop, a murmuring like mice rustling below the floorboards, words exchanged between two people in hiding:

"He'd not betray her, would he?"

"Hush, girl. He'll do what he must to save us. Hush."

The words, sounding so clearly in her own ears, evidently did not reach the captain, who rapped a metal blade on the counter. "I haven't all day to wait! We gave you this chance to work with us rather than be cleaned out like the rest. I can burn down this shop if I've a wish to do so. Or take your daughter, like I did your son."

"Peace! Peace! Just a cricket in my throat got me choked." He made a business of clearing his throat. "There, it's gone now." Once started, the shopkeeper flowed like a stream at spring tide. "A merchant come through, a stout fellow headed southwest on the Lesser Walk and meaning to head onwards down the Rice Walk to Olo'osson. This was a few weeks after the new year's festival. He was still wearing his fox ribbons, all silver, very fine quality and embroidered to show how rich he was."

"I'm surprised a rich man chooses to strut his wealth these days. The roads aren't safe."

"Heh. Heh. You'd say so, ver, wouldn't you? Eh, he wasn't afraid. He was a cocky fellow, even if he did have that cursed sloppy borderlands way of speaking. He would sneer at our humble town, though he'd no reason to do so. He ordered me about when he could just have asked politely for the items he needed."

"What does this have to do with anything?"

"Oh, eh, it's just I notice such things, being a shopkeeper. We have to size up our customers. So when I went into the back to fetch out another lead line, I heard him saying to his companion that he had powerful allies in the north. That they were going to march on Olossi later this year. He did like to hear himself talk. He was indignant, said it wasn't his fault he'd had to make outside alliances. It was just that there were troublemakers in Olossi trying to elbow their way into power and push out those who had been good stewards for these many years, and he had to protect his clan."

It was a common saying among the reeve halls that some came into service possessed of good instincts while some learned good instincts during service, and that those who neither possessed nor learned did not survive. Marit had good instincts, and had learned better ones in her ten years as a reeve, although not enough to save herself from a knife to the heart.

But ever since she'd woken, she heard and tasted and smelled with cleaner senses, as if the Four Mothers—the earth, water, fire, and wind that shapes the land—had lent her a measure of their own essence.

The captain said, "Who else did you tell?"

He's going to kill him. The air told her because of the way his sour scent sharpened. The earth told her because of the way his feet shifted on the floorboards, bracing for the thrust.

The shopkeeper scratched his head, nails scraping scalp. She could smell his fear, but he wasn't afraid enough. He didn't see it coming.

"None but my wife, as a curiosity."

Because he thinks he can sell the information later. Because if no one else knows, then he can hoard harness and the used traveling gear he accumulates in the hope of making a greater profit off it later by selling to a mass of men on the move—an army—who need goods immediately and can't wait. The fate of the folk of Olossi concerns him not at all.

"If the troubles down south settle out," he added, "then maybe more folk will be on the roads, we'll see more trade. Trade's been scarce these past few seasons. Folk don't want to be out on the roads because they fear—"

She stood in the moment the captain drew his sword.

In the lineaments of a face shine the spirit; in the posture of the body speaks the soul. The tight set of a jaw reveals anger. A hand clenched around the hilt of a sword shows resolve.

Fear settles where a man leans back.

Shoulders hunching, a hand raised helplessly, the shopkeeper glanced toward Marit.

I am dead now, but at least I kept the secret. At least my sister will have escaped them. The shopkeeper's thoughts might as well have been words spoken aloud, they were cast like seeds in a broad spray, everything about him caught between his small, fatal victory and his simple fear that the blade, striking him, would hurt terribly as it cut and smashed his flesh.

We all live in terror of pain.

"You not least," she said to the captain. "You are one of those who will die in pain. You have sown with cruel seeds, and the bloody harvest will devour you."

His sword point dropped. She studied his face so she would remember it no matter how much time passed before they met again: a broken nose; a scar under his left eye.

His lips parted as he trembled. "You are death. Where did you come from?"

"Answer your own question. Go from this town. Don't come back. I know you now. I'll hunt you down if harm comes to any here."

His thoughts spilled as water over the lip of a fountain. *I'll be rewarded for this message, for telling them I've spotted one of the cloaks walking abroad in daylight. Or what if she is already acting in concert with them? What if this is a test? To see if I act rightly, follow orders? What if they punish me? Aui! Aui!*

"Get out," she said, wondering if she'd have to try and grab the sword out of his hand and kill him.

But he fled.

The shopkeeper began gasping, spurts of sobs punctuated by racking coughs. The door slid back. The pretty daughter stuck her head in, eyes seeming white with fear.

He spun, hearing the door tap against the stop, and before she could cringe back he slapped her. "Get back in the closet, you witless girl! Can't you stay where you're told?" The purse of his mouth betrayed his shame. He looked back at Marit.

An onslaught of thoughts and images tumbled: *She'll run away, find a temple, any place to take her in, but what if the soldiers capture her as they did Sediya*—? A young woman—his own sister—staggers into their humble house, sneaking in out of the alley and huddling in the chicken house until dawn. She's much younger than her brother, the last child of their parents. Like her niece, she's pretty enough, but haggard with misery. Her thighs are sticky with blood and she stinks of piss; she limps as her sister-in-law supports her into the house. She is crying, *"They'll come for me. I ran away. Please hide me."*

The shopkeeper jerked his gaze away from Marit.

"They'll kill us when they learn we've gone against them, that we're hiding one of the captives they took," he said hoarsely to his daughter, but she was too stunned to speak or move with her cheek flushed red from the blow. Her silence infuriated her father. He raised his hand just as the captain had raised his sword.

"Don't take your anger out on her," said Marit, "or she'll run and you'll have bartered away your honesty and your honor and your good name for nothing."

"Just get out, I beg you," he said, his movement as stiff as that of an aged elder as he kept his gaze averted. "Take whatever you want."

Reeves could accept tithes, receiving from those they aided the necessities that allowed them to live. She grabbed what she wanted: a feed bag, a pair of brushes one stiff and one softer, a hoof pick, a lead line, rope, and a bundle of tough rags.

She paused with the goods stuffed into the feed bag. What if a reeve became greedy? It happened; they took more than they needed, or they taught themselves to take what they wanted and told themselves they deserved it all. "He passed under the gate into the shadow." In every one of the Ten Tales of Founding, more than one man and woman crossed the Shadow Gate to the other side, where corruption takes hold in the heart. With each step, the path got smoother as you told yourself why it was acceptable to walk farther down this road. The tales of the Hundred told the story of humankind and the other children born to the Four Mothers. It was natural that some succumbed to the shadows.

Maybe it was unnatural that any did not.

"Where are the reeves who should be aiding you? Isn't Gold Hall patrolling? Isn't there a temple of Ilu nearby that can send an envoy to Clan Hall in Toskala to ask for help?"

He laughed recklessly. "The reeves can't help us. You can walk out of our town and never come back, but we have to live here. No matter what you said to him, they will come back. It's us will have to face them. Not you."

"That merchant," she said. "You said he was from Olossi. Did he give you a name?"

"Quartered flowers were his house mark. Is that enough? Will you go?"

Marit followed the sniveling girl into the narrow living quarters, tromping through in her outdoor sandals like the rudest kind of intruder. There was a single table and two cupboards, everything put away neatly except for a single ceramic cup filled with cooling tea set on the table. The floor was swept clean, and this homely indication of a woman doing her best to stem the shadows by keeping her home tidy made Marit hurt as if she'd been punched under the ribs.

She shoved open the back screen and clattered onto the porch and down three steps to the courtyard. The damp of night rains still darkened the ground. The gate that led to the alley was tied shut. She fumbled with the knot, her hands clumsy.

Where were they hiding the fugitive sister?

She paused to scan the yard: the squat house with scant room above the eaves; the small grain storage up on stilts; a pit house with the sticky scent of incense drifting; the henhouse, an empty byre, and the surrounding wall too high to see over. She clambered up the ladder to the grain storage and tugged out the smallest sack of rice, something easy to carry over a shoulder.

Stillness was settling over the village as folk assessed the damage and checked their injuries after the abrupt departure of the soldiers. There, after all, she heard the shallow breathing of a woman trying to make no sound: the sister was hidden in the henhouse, scrunched under the nesting shelf and by now smeared with fresh droppings and the filthy wood shavings strewn on the floor to absorb the waste.

Marit took a step toward the henhouse, mouth open to speak. But she said nothing.

She hadn't the means to support a traveling companion. It was difficult enough dealing with the cursed horse. A hundred other reasons aside told her she had to move on alone. This wasn't the time to try to save a woman here and a man there, like trying to hold your hands over one beautiful flower in a driving hailstorm while the rest disintegrate under the onslaught.

"The hells," she muttered. She said, in a low voice meant to carry no farther than the courtyard walls, "I'm a traveler, and I'm headed out of town. The soldiers have gone for now, but they'll be back. If you want, you can travel with me. I offer you such protection as I can, and insofar as I am capable, I will get you to a place of safety. If there is such a place any longer. I can't make you come, and I can't promise you much. There it is. Take it or leave it."

Her offer was met with a resounding silence. Thank the gods.

She turned back to the gate and fumbled with the knot, sure she had tugged on it the wrong way and caused what ought to have been an easy slipknot to jam into itself. She'd never been good with rope, not like Joss, grown up on the sea's shore where every child learned a hundred cunning knots . . .

"I'll go." The voice was soft and female, and not a bit tentative.

Marit turned. A woman crouched in the low entrance to the henhouse. Her hair had matted into clumps now streaked with white droppings; her face was patched with muck and dotted where wood shavings had stuck to the damp. The color of her cheap hemp taloos was concealed beneath a coat of red clay and paler mud, sprinkled with more droppings.

The woman looked right at her.

An assault of images: a weeping girl with hands bound; the ruins of a village smolder as the line of captives staggers past, but they're too exhausted to do more than cover their noses to ease the smell as the soldiers drive them on; an unexpected moment of laughter when eight of the captives, wary comrades now, splash in a pond; stumbling in mud while somewhere out of sight a baby cries and cries. She had lied about her name, because then all the things that happened to her were really happening to someone else, someone she was not.

Marit said, "Your name is Sediya."

Wearily, the woman said, "You're one of them, one of the cloaks who pin us. The soldiers are their slaves, and we're slaves to the soldiers. Now I guess I'm your slave."

"I'm not one of them," said Marit fiercely.

"You're not going to kill me? Punish me? Take me back to Walshow?"

"The hells! Did you walk all the way here from Walshow?"

"Not really. I was swapped out to a scouting patrol, to service them while they were ranging, cook their rice, pound their nai. We walked for weeks and weeks, and I was too scared to run away. Then I got to seeing places I recognized, and that's when I ran. They'll kill me when they catch me. That's the promise they make you."

Marit swiped a hand through her grubby hair, and cursed, the biting words taking the edge off her anger.

The woman had the numb gaze of a person who has learned to gauge how close she is to the next time she'll be hurt.

"Stupidest cursed thing I've ever done," muttered Marit as she turned back to the gate, but she thought of the Devouring girl in the temple up on the Liya Pass and she couldn't take back what she'd offered.

"Here, let me." Sediya had a funny way of walking, favoring both legs, trying to hide that each step pained her. But she had clever hands; the knot fell away.

The door to the house scraped open. The shopkeeper stuck his head out, saw his sister, and blanched. "Sedi! If they see you, if they know I sheltered you—you've already brought trouble down on us. Can't you think of anyone but yourself?"

Sediya wrenched open the gate. "I'm leaving." She bent her head just as Marit caught a flash of dull fear. "May the gods allow that you fare well, Brother."

Marit took a step out into the alley and glanced up and down the narrow lane. "No one's moving. Let's go."

4

When Sediya saw Warning, she sank to her knees and wept.

"The hells!" Marit knelt beside her. "What's wrong?"

The tears ended as abruptly as they had begun. Sediya wiped her cheeks with the back of a grubby hand.

"You're one of them after all," she said without looking Marit in the eye. "Are you going to kill me now, or after you've taken me back to Walshow, in the ceremony of cleansing?"

"I'm not one of them!"

She indicated the mare. "You ride one of the holy ones, the winged horses."

"These others do, too?"

"Yes."

"How many are there?"

Sediya glanced sidelong at her, then away, but Marit caught that awful need to believe that all might be well when after everything the woman had seen really it was a stupid thing to hold to but she couldn't help it. She couldn't help wanting there to be hope.

"I have seen four with my own eyes—twilight, sun, blood, and the one who wears green—but there's another they speak of, the one even the rest fear. They come and go out of camp. The one wearing the Sun Cloak is the worst, that was the rumor among us slaves. I used to smear my face with dirt." She faltered, staring at her hands. The two leftmost fingers on her left hand had been broken and healed crooked. "Are you the one others fear so much?"

"I'm not one of them," Marit repeated, teeth clenched. "What 'ceremony of cleansing' do you mean? I've never heard of such a thing."

Sediya sang in a thready voice a horrible desecration of a holy chant. " 'The weak die, the strong kill, and the cloaks rule all, even death.' "

"Sheh! That's not a proper chant." But seeing the woman cringe, Marit forced her shoulders to relax and her hands to uncurl, trying to appear less threatening. "How did you manage to escape?"

She brushed her belly, caught herself doing it, and winced. "After a while they get careless. They thought I was grinding grain over behind a tent. I just walked away."

Marit knew the signs. She could evaluate people quickly. "Had they just raped you? Is that what made you run?"

She started talking, fast and low, her shame like a rash. "After a while you get torn and you never heal. Now I bleed and pee all the time, it leaks out of me, there's nothing to hold it in. Maybe it would be better to be dead after all. What clan will ever want me as a wife for one of their sons? I have nothing to hope for. I'll go back with you. Please don't let them kill me." She never once looked up.

"We'll find a place for you to shelter," said Marit, so furious she had trouble tugging in air. "We'll go back the way I came, to the southwest. It's safe there."

Sediya heaved a sigh, then settled to sit crookedly along one thigh as if it were uncomfortable to sit straight down cross-legged in the normal manner. She plucked a strand of grass from the ground and wound it around her crooked fingers. "Where are you from?"

"I was born in a village in southeast Farsar. Very isolated, quite poor. My family was too poor to keep me, so they gave me a month's worth of rice and put me on the road. I walked to Toskala looking for work as a laborer. But I became a reeve, instead."

"Where's your eagle, then?"

The memory was still fresh. Marit shuddered. "My eagle is dead. She was murdered. By men under the command of Lord Radas of Iliyat."

Sediya showed no reaction to the name, her gaze still bent on the grass she was winding around her deformed fingers. At last she said, to the dirt, "I'm a Black Eagle. Born during the season of the Flood Rains."

Marit shut her eyes. "That's the year I—" But she could not say *That's the year I was murdered.* Ghosts didn't sit on the ground with the damp soaking through their leggings and have conversations with brutalized young women. "I'm a Green Goat."

The statement made Sediya's eyes flare as she murdered the earth with her gaze. "You'd be counting forty-seven years. You can't be that old. You don't look it."

"Did you serve your apprentice year with the Lantern?" asked Marit, laughing. "You sorted those numbers quickly."

"I did not, though everyone thought I should," said Sediya with a grin. The change of expression betrayed a friendly spirit with a lively manner, hiding beneath the grime. "I served my year with Ilu, because I liked the thought of getting to walk to the nearby towns and see a bit of the countryside. Afterward, the temple wanted to keep me for the eight years' service, and my brother would have tithed me out to them in exchange for freedom from the yearly tithings, but I wouldn't go." Her expression darkened, cutting to a dull gray bleakness with the speed of a machete hacking off a rains-green tree limb. "This is the gods' way of punishing me for not taking the service."

"What was done to you has nothing to do with the gods."

"Doesn't it? What are you, then? What are the others like you, the ones who see into your heart, who ride the winged horses? The cloaks are the Guardians, the servants of the gods."

"That can't be. Guardians bring justice. That's what the gods decreed."

"The gods turned their backs on us." She pulled the grass off her finger and pressed it into the dirt, pushing and pushing until earth buried that frail strand of green. "The Guardians aren't people. They're demons."

Marit remembered—felt to her bones—the poisonous air that swirled around the quiet voice of Lord Radas, speaking to her across a Guardian altar.

"Don't be angry, I didn't mean it. Don't hurt me."

We're both afraid, thought Marit. *Fear drives us.*

She rose. "We travel at night. Can you ride?"

Sediya rose awkwardly. A trickle of liquid slipped down her ankle, and shook out as a drop to vanish on the soil. "It's easier to walk." She drew the back of a hand over her eyes. Healed scratches laced the skin of her arms. Her right shoulder had a gouge in it, knotted with scar tissue. Using the movement as hesitation, she straightened her taloos, which had gotten twisted. She bit her lip, puffed out breath, found her courage and her strength.

"We're not going to Walshow," said Marit. "We'll go to Sohayil, try to find you refuge there, maybe at one of Ilu's temples. I know a place."

Sediya followed obediently, head down, mouth tight.

They walked in silence along the deserted road. Sediya stared at the glimmer that marked the horse's path, that gave them light to see by. She trudged along as if walking barefoot on nails, so clearly in pain that at length Marit called for a halt and found a sheltered spot to sleep.

The woman fell asleep, but Marit sat awake beneath the trees.

"I have seen four with my own eyes, but there's another one they speak of, the one even the rest of them fear."

She leaned her head back against a tree trunk, shutting her eyes, breathing in the sting of sharp night-wand and the odor of intermingled rot and growth.

She considered her options. To ride into the north, to make her way to Toskala through lands controlled by this mysterious army watched over by folk who wore Guardians' cloaks, was foolhardy. Most likely she would blunder into the nest of demons and get chopped up first thing. Even if she reached Toskala, no one at Clan Hall would have any reason to know and trust her. She'd been gone for nineteen years. There was no reason for anyone to believe she was who she claimed to be, or to believe her story of Lord Radas's treachery and an army led by five people pretending to be Guardians. No reason at all.

Not without proof.

An owl skimmed low. A night-flying insect whirred among branches that ticked in the steady wind. Water dripped. A creature rustled away through bushes heavy with damp leaves.

She opened her eyes.

Sediya was gone. Marit tracked her with her hearing. First the woman crawled—not a likely way to be creeping off to relieve yourself—and when she got far enough away from the night's encampment, she eased to her feet and trotted with an awkward rolling gait, now and again stumbling but picking herself up and going on with admirable determination.

Marit sighed. She stood. Sticks and scraps of vegetation tangled on her ragged clothes. She whistled. Warning came alert from her equine doze. She raised her hand and called light.

Sediya screamed when they caught up to her, and fell sobbing to her knees, beating her fists against the ground, praying, pleading, weeping.

Pain twisted in Marit's chest. *She's that afraid of what she thinks I am.*

"I meant what I said. I'm taking you to a safe place."

Sediya refused to answer.

AT THE TEMPLE of Ilu in the village of Rifaran, Sediya went mutely as an apprentice led her off to the baths. She did not offer a parting glance and certainly no thanks. It was likely that, whatever she said later, no one would believe her.

The envoys in charge gifted Marit with clothing in good repair in exchange for bringing one of their injured daughters to a place where she might find healing. The old woman who stood gate duty gave Marit a mended but otherwise stout cloak of a faded green color more appropriate to and practical for journeying.

For her own part, Marit thanked the envoys properly and retreated, alone, to the glade where Warning rested out of sight.

But when she unclasped the cloak to take off the rags and put on decent clothing, the cloak slithered back to clutch at her calves as if it were a living thing. She began to heave, sucking and coughing. She could not get air. The cloak poured up her body, wrapping her until she was too tangled to stand. She sprawled, vision fading . . . choking, she grasped the clasp and fixed the cursed thing around her neck.

She lay for a bit, skin clammy and hot by turns. After a while, she got to her feet. The cloak swagged around her like ordinary cloth, draping to midcalf.

An ordinary piece of cloth in every way, you might think, except it never became grimy. It never stank. The clasp did not rub raw her skin. Magic infused it. Death's cloak, she might call it, and it was true enough. Death's cloak had risen off a Guardian's bones to smother her that day up on Ammadit's Tit when she and Joss had broken the boundaries and invaded a Guardian altar. A day later, death's cloak had claimed her in truth, when the knife had pierced her heart in the woodsmen's camp. If she was dead, then it was appropriate that death's cloak wore her and would not let her go.

"*What are you, if you aren't one of them?*" Sediya had asked.

Maybe she was just asking the wrong question. Not "Why did the Guardians vanish, and where did they go?" but "What is a Guardian, after all? Therefore, what am I?"

SHE RODE TO Olo'osson and made her way via back roads and isolated irrigation berms to Argent Hall, the westernmost reeve hall, on the shore of the salty Olo'o Sea. She released Warning to fend for herself, as the mare had done for an unknown time before Marit found her. She hid the harness and saddle in an abandoned shack and walked to the gates to ask for work in the lofts as a fawkner's assistant's assistant. Remarkably, they took her on.

They assigned her to the most menial of tasks: sweeping, cleaning, hauling. Maybe later, they told her, if she proved herself, they might let her start working with the harness.

She had to keep her eyes lowered at all times, so no one could possibly suspect how much she could really see. She pretended to be a woman fallen on hard times who had become suspicious and unfriendly because of the beatings she had endured from an angry husband and his unsympathetic relatives. It was a situation she'd encountered all too often as a reeve. They accepted her odd manners because she did her work, and because they were so poorly supervised and understaffed that many of their long-term hirelings had recently quit. Because the reeve halls tended to attract people who didn't fit into the daily life of the village.

With her head hunched and her gaze lowered, and her cloak tied up out of the way and layered beneath the old green cloak, she observed.

Marshal Alyon was an ailing and ill-tempered old reeve poorly suited to manage such a roil. Half of the reeves stationed at Argent Hall had transferred here from other halls in the last few years, and they were malcontents and loose arrows to a man and woman, the kind of reeve Marit despised, the ones who kept taking more than they needed, the ones who got to loving their baton and the power they wielded more than the law they served. Marshal Alyon could not control them. There was at least one fist fight a day in the exercise yard. She kept her chin down and her eyes averted, but she saw everything. She heard their whispers. She knew how many stank of corruption, and how many fought for a restoration of the old order but kept losing ground. The newcomers were waiting, but she wasn't sure for what.

She'd not been there ten days when she woke one day to voices all aflutter.

"Garrard is back from Clan Hall. He says Clan Hall won't help us. We're on our own."

She washed her face and slouched to the eating hall. The nai porridge tasted particularly bland today, no spice at all, but as always it was filling. She sat with the other menials, who had learned to ignore her beyond a perfunctory greeting.

At the next table, the loft fawkners were whispering fiercely, heads bent together.

"Yordenas has returned, still with no eagle. I've never heard of a bird nesting for so many seasons. I don't like him. I don't trust him."

Heads went up as six reeves wearing gleaming reeve leathers sauntered into the eating hall. Marit shuddered; a red haze washed her vision, and the last smears of porridge turned as pink as if mixed with blood. She blinked, and after all it was only her eyes playing tricks on her. The porridge had no color at all, just a few grainy lumps stuck to the sides of the bowl.

She looked up, and saw a man wearing a Guardian's cloak.

He wasn't looking her way, or he would have known instantly, as she knew instantly. She ducked down, pretending to fiddle with her sandal's lacing. He sat down with his companions at a table well away from the one where she sat, because certain of the reeves strutted an attitude that they were better than the rest and certainly did not want to associate with the menials or even the fawkners, although the health of their eagles depended on the fawkners.

He sat with eyes downcast, listening more than he talked. His cloak was red as blood, somber rather than bright. It made her think of seeping wounds that never heal.

He did not eat, only made his presence and his allies known to all. Eventually, he left the eating hall. As he walked to the door, she bent down to let the height of those sitting at her table shield her from view. As soon as he was gone, the fawkners began whispering.

"Hsss! You see how the conflict will fall out. Yordenas means to become marshal in Alyon's place. He'll poison him."

"Poison Alyon! Even I don't believe that, Rena."

"You're a cursed fool if you don't believe it. It's going to get ugly, when Alyon dies, and he will die because he's weakening fast. Then it'll come down to a fight between Garrard and the outsiders, and that'll get even uglier. If we were any of us smart we would just up and leave like the hirelings keep doing."

"We can't abandon the eagles. They need us."

"That's right," the others murmured. The eagles needed them. For a dedicated fawkner, it was all the cause they followed.

The moment enough menials got up to go to work, Marit rose and kept within the pack of them, and with gritted teeth walked at their ambling pace along the aisle and out the door into the exercise yard. She slunk immediately to the barracks, where she gathered her few possessions and tucked them into the feed bag. Then she went to the pits to relieve herself, and afterward she hauled up two waste buckets and swung them on a pole over her shoulder and walked out the gates toward the dumping pit as if she had been assigned to clear out night soil. The dumping pit lay a good long way away from the reeve hall. The distance seemed even farther with that stench swinging to either side, always in your face. But it was far enough away that when she set down the buckets next to the stinking pit, she could keep walking because no one was likely to run out to question her or even notice her at all from the distant walls.

A man wearing a Guardian's cloak sat in a reeve hall, pretending to be a reeve. When she thought about it, it was a good strategy. If you want to build an army and terrorize the countryside, then corrupt the reeve halls first so they won't interfere. Yet what did Lord Radas want in the end? Was it greed that drove him? Perhaps it was as simple as lust for power, as it says in the Tale of Honor: *"The first man bowed before him, and at this sight his heart burned and his lips became dry, and then all the men must bow or he could not be contented."* Did he simply want to rule the Hundred?

She kept walking, lugging the feed bag. Storm clouds advanced over the Olo'o Plain, and a thunderstorm boomed, soaking her as she trudged. As the clouds spilled away toward the salt sea and the first cracks of sky appeared, firelings sparked in the heavens. She stared, raising a hand to shield her eyes from the last drops of rain, but the blue lights were already gone. Thunder rumbled in the distance, and she grinned, thinking of the time she and Flirt had flown through a massive storm like the complete and utter idiots they had been because they were young and full of glee. Thinking of how a fireling had winked into existence less than an arrow's shot below them, eyes afire and translucent wings a blaze of light. And cursed if Flirt hadn't stooped, and pulled up when the fireling had winked out before her talons struck. Only the blue light had flashed again below, and Flirt had stooped again, and then again and again, and for a brief wild insanely glorious passage she and the raptor had engaged in a game of chase with the one creature in the worlds no eagle can catch.

Eiya! Grief is a mire. She put her head down and kept walking.

Slowly, the skies cleared to a patchwork. After a day and a night she reached the abandoned shack and sank down, exhausted, beside the dusty harness. Her thoughts chased in circles. She was alone, just as the blood-cloaked Guardian had been alone even though he was sitting in the eating hall among reeves who identified themselves as his allies.

What is a Guardian? she might ask, and she had found one of her answers: A Guardian might walk among humankind, but she was no longer one of them. She never would be again.

MARIT WOKE AT dawn when Warning shoved her nose into her face and slobbered on her. The cursed mare's coat needed brushing, and her mane was tangled, but her hooves were clean of stones and debris and she was otherwise healthy. By all appearances, the mare was as happy to see Marit as Marit was to see her, curse it all, for there were tears in her own eyes.

"Here's your pay," said the stable master, holding out a string of vey. He cleared his throat, shifted his feet, scratched an earlobe. "You're a good worker, no complaints there. You don't make any trouble. But I have to ask you not to come back tomorrow."

"I see," said Marit to her feet. She knew what was coming. She had been through this conversation six times in the weeks she had been in Olossi.

He spoke quickly, to get through the distasteful job. "Custom is off, and that's besides it being the Flood Rains and fewer folk walking about this time of year due to the weather. Someone is causing trouble on the roads for carters and stablekeepers, for all us honest guilds folk, so we can't keep our hirelings as we might otherwise want in a better year."

"Custom does seem low. What do you think is causing the trouble?"

He cleared his throat. She glanced up, meeting his gaze.

Images and words churned: *she's got that northern way of speaking; what if she's a spy for one of the Greater Houses; I don't trust 'em; they're trying to corral all the trade for themselves and their favored clients; anyway, there's something about her that creeps everyone and no surprise . . .*

She dropped her gaze. He took a step away, as from someone who stank.

"Might be anyone," he said, backed up against the closed door, "ospreys diving for a quick snatch, criminals wandering down from the north, folk wanting to drive a wedge into the carters' guild and make trouble for them." His tone picked up confidence. "So there it is. Someone has to go. The other hirelings are, eh, well, it's your—ah—northern way of speaking. Makes them uncomfortable. I've had them on hire for years now, so that makes you lowest roll."

"First to go," she agreed with a twisted smile. She had replaced the old sandals she'd taken from the shepherd's hut with better ones, but after weeks in the city keeping her gaze down she had memorized every stain and nick in the worn leather. Her feet were dirty again, toenails black with grime from stable work. "My thanks. You were a fair employer, I'll give you that." She took the vey from his hand, trying not to notice how quickly he pulled his hand back, hoping not to touch her. As if she was a demon walking abroad in human skin.

Who was to say she wasn't?

Keeping her head down, she walked through the lower city of Olossi toward the baths she favored. Mud slopped over her feet. At the trailing end of the season of Flood Rains, every surface was layered in muck. The clouds hung low and dark, threatening to spill again.

She paused at the edge of Crow's Gate Field. In the dry season, commerce through the gate would be brisk, and the guards and clerks busy. Today, Sapanasu's clerks lounged under the shelter of a colonnade, seated in sling-back chairs, sipping at musty bitter-fern tea. They laughed and talked, teeth flashing, voices bright. One slapped another on the arm teasingly. A trio had their heads bent close, sharing se-crets. One dozed, head back and mouth open, and the others were careful not to jostle her. Their easy camaraderie reminded her of her days at Copper Hall among her fellow reeves. Those had been good days. She'd been happy there. She'd had friends, colleagues, a lover.

Some things, once lost, can never be restored.

Bear this grief, and move on.

She walked toward the river along the wide avenue that paralleled the lower city's wall, such as it was, more a livestock fence than a wall to halt the advance of an army. Her sandals shed dribs and drabs with each step. Aui! Everything stank. Everything dripped. Rich folk hurrying home before dusk made their way through town in palanquins carried by laborers whose brown legs were spattered with mud. The streets in the upper city were paved with stone, so presumably there was less Flood Rains filth there, but the one time she'd ventured past the inner gates she had felt too conspicuous. The lower city hosted all kinds: laborers, criminals, touts and peddlers, country lads and lasses come to make their fortunes in a trade, outlander merchants come to sell and buy, slaves and hirelings and shopkeepers and crafts-men and folk who would sell anything, even their own bodies, as long as they could grab a few vey from the doing. She might make folk uncomfortable, but in the lower city the watch would not drive her out unless she actually broke the law.

On a street on the river side of Harrier's Gate stood two ranks of bright green pipe-brush, ruthlessly cut back, which flanked an ordinary pedestrian gate set into a compound wall. A bell hung from a hook on the wall. She rang it, keeping her gaze on her dirty feet.

The door was opened from inside. "You again. It's extra for a bucket and stool carried to your tub."

"I know."

He held out a hand, and she pressed vey worth a week's labor into his very clean palm. He led her along a covered walkway raised above muddy ground and lined with troughs of red and pink good-fortune trimmed into mushroom caps. Water flowed smoothly alongside them through split pipewood. The attendant gave her a sour look when she bypassed the usual changing rooms and common scrub hall.

The private rooms were a series of partitions separating filled tubs heated by hot stones and stoked braziers. In the dry season, awnings could be tied across the scaf-folding of the tall partitions for shade. The smallest and cheapest private room lay closest to the entrance and the common baths, where everyone must tramp back and forth; the more expensive were larger and sited at the end of the walkway. The truly wealthy could purchase relaxation at one of five tiny cottages situated within the pleasant garden with its manicured jabi bushes, slumbering paradom, and flow-ering herboria.

He showed her into the smallest of the private chambers, and watched to make sure she removed her filthy sandals before she stepped up on the raised paving stones alongside the slatted tub. He left the door open until he brought back a bucket of water and a stool.

"You pay extra for pouring bowl, scrub brush, and changing cloth," he said.

She showed him the ones she had purchased from a peddler, items not too worn to keep in use but certainly nothing a prosperous clansman would carry. The attendant inspected the items, touching the cloth only at the corner, pinched between thumb and forefinger.

"You want the lamp lit?" he asked.

"No. I've light to make my own way out."

He tested the water with an elbow, sniffed to show it was satisfactory, and finally cut off a sliver of soap. When he shut the door, she had, at last, a measure of peace.

She stripped of everything except her cloak, scrubbed, rinsed, scrubbed, and rinsed, and climbed into the tub. The heated water was not hot enough to redden her skin, as she would have liked, but it was satisfactory. She draped the cloak over the rim, and sank in up to her chin.

The heat melted her. She tilted her head back to rest against the slats and let her senses open.

Someone lit lamps in other chambers, oil hissing as it caught flame. Folk passed clip-clop on the walkway, treading heavily or lightly according to their nature. Business increased at dusk, as the shadows gave cover to men and women who didn't want to be recognized.

She tasted the powerful scent of night-blooming paradom like cinnamon kisses on her lips.

A pair of lovers whispered in one of the cottages, words of longing and promise poured into willing ears. How fiercely they yearned! She sank into memories of Joss, made more bitter and more sweet because she knew he might well yet be alive, older than her now although he had once been younger. She had to let go of her affection for him. He had lived for twenty years without her, grown his own life without her. And anyway, was it even possible to love where there are no real secrets, where no part of your lover is thankfully hidden away from you?

She accepted the grief, and set it aside, because there was work to be done and she had never once in her life turned away from any task laid before her.

In these baths met merchants and guildsmen who desired privacy for certain delicate negotiations. She had come to these baths the first time because she'd heard she could pay coin for a private bathing room, an astounding luxury. Now she ate and drank sparingly of the cheapest gruel and watered rice wine, and slept in a boardinghouse little better than a rathole, so she could keep coming back for the conversation that her unnaturally keen hearing picked up.

She had learned a great deal about the city of Olossi: trade secrets and outside-the-temple dealings; petty rivalries pursued by narrow-minded competitors; militia men deep in schemes for the upcoming Whisper Rains games. Olossi's Lesser Houses and guildsmen were discontented, being ruled by the greed of the Greater Houses, and certain people in their ranks plotted an uprising. A group of reckless young men was engaged in smuggling, more for sport than for profit. A lad and a lass from competing clans who would never ever consider letting them marry made their assignation here, even though—as Marit knew—they were long since being followed by various agents from their own families.

She picked out voices like threads from a multicolored shawl.

". . . No one can know we are negotiating. I'll lose the contract if the Greater Houses suspect I'm going outside the official channels. I tell you, we in the Silk Slippers clan have been providing reliable river transport for generations, and what do the Greater Houses do now? They try to force us to lower our rates, greedy bastards . . ."

". . . If you take the cargo across the river after moonset, Jaco's boys will meet you just downstream of Onari's Landing with the knives . . ."

"If the militia continues to refuse to send out long-range patrols, then the carters' guild has agreed to cooperate with us. We'll send a joint mission to Toskala to appeal to Clan Hall directly, and ask them to intervene to improve the safety of the roads . . ."

"Eh. Eh. Yes, like that. Ah. Ah."

"I want you to kill a man."

Her breath caught in her throat as she strained to hear.

"That would be murder. Against the law." The other man's voice had a slight hoarse timbre, as though he had once inhaled too much smoke.

"Do as I ask, and no charges will ever be brought against you."

"How can you possibly guarantee that?"

"We control the council. It will never get past a vote."

"The council does not control the assizes if the reeves bring me in to stand trial."

"Argent Hall will not charge you. They have a new marshal, hadn't you heard? He'll not interfere."

"The hells. You sound certain, Feden. Considering what manner of crime you're asking me to commit."

"You haven't asked the name of the target. Or why he needs killing."

"I want to know first why Argent Hall won't interfere if it gets wind of the killing. Surely the dead man's clan will seek justice."

"Argent Hall is too busy looking for some manner of treasure that my allies in the North seek. Something valuable taken out of the Hundred years ago that they have reason to believe has been found and brought back."

The smoky-voiced man's laugh was sarcastic. "Silk? Gems? A rare cutting from one of the Beltak temples' Celestial Golds? A stallion for stud?"

"I don't know." This said brusquely. "It's not my responsibility, but if you want to keep your eyes open at the border crossing it wouldn't hurt to get word of such a thing before anyone else did. I don't mind telling you, I don't trust that new marshal, Yordenas."

The other man hrhmed thoughtfully under his breath. He seemed distracted, perhaps spinning out fantasies of treasure and wealth as the other man—*Feden*—went on impatiently.

"I don't mind telling you I think the entire cursed mob of them are hatching a plan to overthrow the Greater Houses."

"The reeves of Argent Hall?"

"Neh, neh, the Lesser Houses and those ungrateful guildsmen. After everything we've done to make Olossi prosperous and safe! If we kill just one man, one of the ringleaders, it may make the rest hesitate."

"Because they'll see you can get away with it?" asked Smoky Voice with sharp amusement. "Don't they already know that you in the Greater Houses can do what you cursed well please?"

Water splashed on rock and poured away as hands emptied a bucket over stone. A door slid closed with a slap.

"What if we ran away?" the youth demanded in a husky whisper. "We could go to Toskala, make a new life there for ourselves."

"Dearest," she replied breathlessly, still recovering from her drawn-out pleasure, "the roads aren't safe. Anyway, they'd send agents after us. How can we hide from them?"

That piece of practicality silenced the idiot, thank the gods. Marit wound a path past his unsteady breathing, past the chuckling of the young fools planning their latest smuggling venture for no better reason than the lark of evading the militia, pinched out the low-voiced argument of a man sure sure sure that the gift he had proffered to the Incomparable Eridit had been rejected because she thought herself unworthy of his attentions while his friends, lounging with him in the baths, assured him rumor had it she wicked anyone who was to her taste, so gifts were meaningless because she had rejected him merely because he was one ugly Goat.

There.

"I'll do it, then. But if you get any word about what the treasure is, you'll let me know."

"Don't tangle with the Northerners, Captain. Don't try to take what they want. You'll regret it."

"Only if they know I have it. If the Argent Hall reeves are so busy patrolling the Barrens and the Spires, who's to say they might miss what passes right under their talons, eh?"

"Do you envy the reeves, Captain? Is that resentment I hear?"

"I have a sword, and you have your coin and your clan's power. Don't think we're friends to share confidences. Just allies of convenience, that's all."

"You'll be glad enough I approached you, come the end of this Fox year. Mark my words. Come Goat year, you'll value this alliance. You'll thank me."

She hauled herself out of the tub and toweled dry with the changing cloth. She dressed quickly, and slung her bag across one shoulder; it was everything she owned and needed, the essentials of her life—or her death—pruned back to almost nothing. She waited, listening for the smoky rasp of his breathing, and followed. She did not need to stay close to keep track of him. She had been a good reeve in her day, able to sniff out trouble without knowing precisely where the rot grew, but she could now follow the odor of dishonesty and cheating and corruption and depravity straight to its putrid source in a venal heart.

The compound had half a dozen gates set at discreet intervals. He left by the one closest to Harrier's Gate, and by his gait and posture—and the rank his associate had given him—she placed him as a militia man, dedicated to Kotaru the Warrior and still in service to the Thunderer. He wasn't a fool. He felt an itch in the center of his back where her gaze had fixed, and once out on the street he paused to sweep his gaze along the passersby, most of them hurrying home with lamps to light their way. She halted some ways back, a nondescript traveler among many, but lifted her eyes to meet his.

As corrupt as they come, and willing to sell out his duty in exchange for wealth, yet even so, his were the shadows of a small heart ruled by the banal greed of a man pinched by jealousies and resentments.

He staggered, rubbing his head as if he'd been struck a blow. She stepped into the shadows. After a puzzled glance at the street, he strode to the closed gates and gave an order to the guards on duty. They let him out the postern gate and barred it back up tight, and she had no means by which to force an exit. She was not ready to draw attention to herself in a city whose masters had apparently allied themselves with the shadow out of the north. If they discovered her, she would find herself with wolves hard on her heels and a cloaked man called Yordenas ruling Argent Hall, not so far away.

As long as the others did not find her, she could continue her investigation. So she kept her head down, and worked gathering information in the same slow, circuitous way.

Master Feden she tracked to the merchant house marked with a quartered flower, just as the shopkeeper had described. But she could not reach him; he guarded his privacy too well and she never encountered him again at the baths. It was days before she identified the captain as a man called Beron, commander of the contingent stationed at the border crossing on the Kandaran Pass, which led southwest into the Sirniakan Empire. By then, a well-known merchant had vanished from town, and while gossip whispered that he'd been murdered, or decamped after a string of humiliating gambling losses, nothing could be proven.

She rode west on the trail of Captain Beron.

CARAVANS DID NOT travel in the season of the Flood Rains; folk tended their fields and stuck close to home. She traveled through the West Country, mey upon mey of empty road and sprawling vistas of uninhabited high plateau and stretches of shoreline. The majestic Spires thrust heavenward in the far distance. In an isolation that magnified one's daunting insignificance, it was easy to forget how difficult it had become to converse with ordinary folk in an ordinary manner because you did come to desire the simple everyday contact of one person chatting with another about the consequential and trivial matters of life.

Yet on every stop she made on West Spur to buy a bag of grain or a bladderful of ale, she was reminded all over again that people did not feel comfortable around her. To minimize these contacts, she spent more time foraging for food. Twice, Warning insisted on flying free, stranding her for a day each time in the wilderness but then returning. Marit had a very good idea that the horse was visiting Guardian altars. When she thought of the fountains that lay at the heart of every altar, her throat burned with a physical longing. Yet she dared not enter a Guardian altar, where the others could find her.

So the journey passed.

One evening, riding through a series of isolated valleys, she spotted a campfire in the trees. After dismounting, she led Warning under the cover of pine and tollyrake.

Alone, she walked forward alongside the road. Night wrens queried, cicadas buzzed, evening chats chivered. Her hearing had sharpened so much that it seemed she could hear every mouse creeping and night cat padding through the undergrowth.

Ahead, the forest was cut back into a clearing rigged out as a caravan rest point with troughs, hitching posts, fire pits, and a pair of corrals. She surveyed the open space. Aui! Two eagles slumbered upright on opposite sides of the clearing, talons fixed around logs mounted as perches. One wore a hood; the other did not, but its head was tucked against a wing.

The campfire burned well back in the trees. She approached cautiously. Because of her newly acute vision, she was able to step around clumps of thorn-fern and whispering thistle and avoid roots grown out from the earth or branches torn free in the recent storms.

A man and a woman sat on either side of a briskly burning fire, their faces in light and their backs in shadow. Short cloaks hung from their shoulders to keep off the rain, should it come. By the cut of their leathers and the tight trim of their hair, they were reeves.

The man gesticulated as he spoke, hands cutting circles in the air. "I say we abandon Argent Hall. There's nothing we can do, Dov. Nothing. Garrard is dead. We get out while we still can."

"We can't just abandon people. The fawkners will never go. They won't leave eagles with no one to tend to them. There must be something to salvage. Something left we can do."

He laughed bitterly. "We lost. Argent Hall is the playing ground for bullies, cowards, thieves, and murderers now. You would think that every crooked reeve has flown in and made himself a cozy nest in our lovely hall." He choked down a sob.

She reached out to touch his hand. "Garrard's death isn't your fault."

"If I'd called out sooner—" he whispered.

She slapped him under the chin. He reared back, and she jumped to her feet. "There's nothing you could have done! How many times do I have to tell you?"

He rubbed his jaw. "We could fly to Clan Hall, give them our report. Surely they ought to have sent someone to investigate. They should want to know why Yordenas swings the marshal's staff yet we've never seen feather or talon of his eagle."

The woman slumped down on the log. "Clan Hall! Didn't they authorize half the transfers of those criminals into Argent Hall? Maybe they're up to their beaks in the whole corrupt enterprise." She shoved a stick into the fire, then cursed when the edifice of burning scaffolding cracked and tumbled, spilling sparks and spits of red-hot wood everywhere.

They both leaped up, stamping and laughing in the way of old comrades who can down a mug of ale and enjoy a bowl of porridge after exhuming a rotting corpse from the pit where the murderer buried it.

"Eridit's Tit! That's burned my arm." The man brushed himself down. His face, turned into the light, had a grim pallor. "Eiya! Dov, what will we do?"

She sat back down, kicked a charred stick into the fire pit, and picked up a new branch to poke around until she rousted fresh flames. "See if it's true that this Captain Beron is in league with Argent Hall in some murky doings. I just don't get it."

"What's to understand? There's a larger conspiracy boiling under our noses. Yordenas is taking orders from the north. He's got his cronies hunting into the Barrens for this 'treasure' everyone is whispering of. Gold. Gems. Silk."

The woman shook her head. Like the man, she had the look of an experienced reeve not much older than Marit had been, in the prime of her reeve service. Tall and lean, she had a firm grip as she grabbed his wrist.

"Teren. Listen. Maybe it isn't an object. Maybe this 'treasure' everyone whispers of is a goal. Why take over Argent Hall with their thugs and their squirks if they didn't want the power to twist the hall and the eagles and the reeves to their own purposes? To rule the Hundred?"

"Neh. I think it's an object, all right. I think they're the greediest scum that ever mucked a pond, looking to make themselves rich. I think—"

"Hush."

She rose and drew her short sword. He eased back and picked up his baton from the ground behind him, held it under his cloak. They were not looking toward the place Marit had hidden herself.

The faint sounds of animals at their nightly rounds had ceased. Nothing moved. At first, Marit saw only the blink of late-season fireflies twinkling in the trees opposite her, but it was actually a woman stepping out of the shadows and blinking as her eyes adjusted to the firelight.

"I saw your fire," she said. "You're reeves out of Argent Hall."

"We are—" began the man.

The other reeve cut in. "How do you know?" She did not lower the point of her sword. "You don't mind my wondering why you're wandering out here in the wilderness alone, I am sure."

"Teren, son of Filava. Dovit, daughter of Zasso." She had a mild voice and a mild face, round like the moon and pleasingly dark.

Teren choked out a word and stepped back, stumbling over the root he'd been sitting on.

Dovit said, in a quavering voice, "Who are you?"

The woman wore an undyed linen tunic with leggings beneath, humble clothing that was also practical for a traveler. The cloak she wore was so black it seemed it might dissolve to become the shadows. Oddly, she carried a writing brush and a scrap of rice paper. Without answering, she bent her gaze to the paper and scratched a few efficient lines.

Like rag dolls let go by a careless child, they dropped: first Teren, and a breath later Dovit, her sword clanging on a rock as it fell from slack fingers. The pen ceased scratching. From the clearing, two angry squalls erupted. Wings beating, an eagle chuffed in distress. Afterward, everything settled back into an uncanny stillness.

The reeves lay with limbs asplay, Dovit's face pressed into the ground and Teren's hidden by the hump of root over which he had collapsed. Branches snapped on the fire. Flames hissed.

"Who is out there?" asked the woman in a sharper voice. It wasn't fear that edged her tone but a complex pressure of emotion rather like a cook who surveys her well-ordered kitchens with the sudden suspicion that a mouse is hiding behind one of the pots and means to nibble at the feast she has so perfectly prepared and laid out for her guests.

Marit sure as the hells did not reply, or move, or even breathe more than a shallow breath held, leaked out, and held again. She thought of how bright her cloak was, white as death, and she willed it to be as still and silent as the death that creeps unawares, never seen before it enfolds its unsuspecting victim.

How long that woman stood there Marit could not guess, but it might have been half the night. Cursed if Marit was going to reveal herself no matter how badly her legs ached from standing in one place. She could be more stubborn than anyone, and in the end she was.

Finally, the woman moved away into the trees, and Marit allowed herself to lean against a tree trunk, not a single step, until the world grayed toward dawn. She heard a crackling beyond the trees, and an eagle passed low over the forest. With a grimace, she popped the worst kinks out of her stiff limbs, then ventured cautiously to the dead fire.

The two reeves had no pulse and no breath, their spirits utterly vanished. They had flown beyond the Spirit Gate. She searched their bodies but could find no dart or needle that might have pricked poison in them. They had packs set on the ground and now crawling with bugs; inside she found a blanket, reeve's gear for tending harness, a set of clean and mended laborer's clothing for off-duty wear, and travel food: rice balls wrapped in se leaves, nai paste, a pair of sprouting yams, and a pouch full of nuts.

"May your spirits go gently under the gate," she whispered. "My thanks for this gift. I'll seek justice for you, comrades."

She hoisted the packs and backtracked cautiously until she saw Warning trotting toward her along the road. Well enough. She took the mare's lack of concern as a good omen. She scrambled up to the road and caught the reins. "Dead," she said to the mare. "I hope you don't mind the extra weight."

She could not get out of her mind the way they had both simply fallen, as though that woman was a demon in truth, a lilu who had sucked their spirits right out of their bodies even though she hadn't been touching them. Gods, that was a frightening thing!

Aui! And what of their eagles?

The hooded eagle lingered in the clearing, unable to fly because it was blind, but the other eagle had vanished. No doubt it was the raptor who had flown at first light. Eagles were not sentimental beasts. Reeves often joked that eagles jessed their reeves, not the other way around, since everyone knew that an eagle chose its reeve. Once a reeve had died, her eagle did not maunder or grieve. They departed for Heaven's Ridge, and in time—weeks or months or years—they might return to jess a new reeve.

The hooded eagle could not fly. It was in distress, calling out, wings extended, hackling and feathers flushed. Marit had lost her own eagle. She was not about to let this raptor starve or be slaughtered.

She balanced her staff in a firm grip in her left hand and fixed her knife in her right.

"Here, now, sweetheart," she said in her most soothing voice, but an unjessed eagle is a wild eagle. The raptor struck at the sound of her voice or perhaps a tremor felt in the earth. Marit danced aside. She lunged for and grabbed the slip. No time to strike the hood properly. She slashed with the knife, and cursed if the eagle didn't hook the plume with a talon and cast the loosened hood straight to the dirt.

They stared at each other, Marit standing stock-still and the eagle glaring with utter fury from under her ridged brows.

The raptor struck so fast Marit didn't even have time to scream.

RAIN POURED INTO her mouth, pounding the earth on all sides, hammering her flesh. She cursed and rolled over, spitting out a throatful of water. A big body appeared out of the storm, and suddenly the rain lessened because she lay in a rain shadow under the shelter of pale wings.

She sat up, opening and closing her hands. She sat in a puddle of slop. Her butt was cold, and her feet were bare. Several horrific rents had been opened in her clothing, and her skin beneath the ripped fabric was scarred. But she was whole. She was breathing. She was alive.

If she could call herself alive.

The eagle had flown.

The rain slackened, quieted, ceased. Wincing, she got to her feet. The eagle's hood lay on the ground about five strides away, covered with mud and scraps of vegetation but a good cleaning and oiling and a new slip would fix it. Her sandals were gone. She wiped water out of her eyes. Warning folded her wings and flicked her ears as though to say, "Can we go yet?" The two reeve packs remained fixed to the saddle where Marit had tied them to the feed bag. In the clearing, all the flowers were gone.

"Lady's Tits," she swore under her breath. She walked back into the forest, marking a forked tollyrake here and a tall pine there as landmarks to make her way back to the campfire.

"The hells!"

Animals and rain and wind had reached them first, but not even animals and the Four Mothers worked this quickly. Two greasy skeletons lay tumbled in the undergrowth, bits of soft tissue and fibrous muscle still attached but most of the flesh gone. One was headless, but she located the skull about five strides away. It was missing teeth, and she backtracked and found them beneath the neck of the remains. Their leather vests and trousers were in remarkably good shape, smeared with dirt and layered with foliage but otherwise intact. The woman's sturdy reeve boots still had foot bones—and scraps of desiccated flesh—inside them. Cursing, she emptied them and measured the boots against her own bare feet, and when she saw they would be a fair fit, she stumbled off to one side and vomited. The good ale in her drinking gourd had soured. The rice balls in the nai leaves had turned to mold.

"What is happening to me?" she cried, slapping a hand repeatedly against the ground, but her tantrum accomplished nothing except to make her hand hurt.

She rested her head against the bole of a tree, trying to get her breathing under control. The rain cleared off, and as night fell, a cold and bitter wind blew down off the unseen mountains to the southwest.

The season changes. Only late in the year do you feel the chill all the way down to your bones.

Marshal Alard used to say, "If you have to choose between what seems the most reasonable explanation, and what the cold, hard evidence reveals, go with the evidence."

The reasonable explanation was that she had slept through a day and a night recovering from the shock of what she had seen and from the eagle's attack.

When she thought it through, she had to believe that the eagle had killed her in its fury. The evidence of the corpses and the weather bore out the unlikely supposition that months had passed.

Guardians can't die.

They can kill, but they can't be killed.

Now, there was a recipe for corruption.

She rose to shake out her clothing. Why, in the tales, were the Guardians always honorable and upright, the upholders of a justice that is never disturbed by their own petty jealousies or grand descents into lust and greed? How honest were the tales, really?

What had Sediya sung? *The cloaks rule all, even death.*

Who would believe her, if she walked in off the street into Clan Hall and claimed to be a woman murdered nineteen years ago? Who would even remember her?

One man might.

PART TWO: CUPS

In the Year of the Red Goat

6

JOSS WOKE UP in his private chamber in Argent Hall to find a woman lying beside him on the sleeping mat, naked, tousled, and barely covered by the thin cotton coverlet. He sat up cautiously, rubbing his aching head. He had no idea how she had gotten there.

With a sigh, she rolled over, exposing a face he recognized and eyes that, opening, were clearly alert. She'd been awake for some time.

"The hells!" he muttered, staring at her in shock.

She sat up, exposing a pleasing, muscular figure ripped by healed scars. The worst ran from her left shoulder across the mauled remains of a breast and down past her ribs to pucker to a finish by her belly button.

"Regrets already?" she asked with a smile half of amusement and half of a woman thinking of giving an idiot man a slap to the face.

"Verena," he said, glad that at least he remembered her name and feeling ten parts stupid and ten parts hungover. Last night's activities surfaced in his memory as he woke up fully. Oh, yes, he remembered it all now.

She chuckled.

"No regrets at all," he said feelingly. "It was well worth the doing. I just suddenly realized that I am marshal of this hall now and you are a fawkner here, working under my authority. I'm not sure I should have—I'm accustomed to being a simple reeve—what I'm trying to say is—"

"That you don't want it said you took advantage of your position to get a woman into your bed?" she asked with a laugh. "Rest easy. You took a lot of coaxing, and an entire pitcher of cheap rice wine before I managed to talk you into it."

The chamber was strewn with clothing. This scene and its musky aftermath were nothing new, but with the weight of his new authority it didn't seem as carefree as it once had.

"Heya, Joss! Listen. We're of an age. I have living a twenty-year-old son and fifteen-year-old twin daughters, may the gods give me patience. My husband has been dead these ten years. It was a marriage arranged by the clan. He and I were never close. I have no wish to remarry, and since the clan got what it wanted from the match—my son has followed his grandfather into the guild—they have no further claim on me. My work and my life are here at Argent Hall. Still, I'm not dead. Yet. You're an attractive man. If you've a wish for this to end here, then say so. I'll swallow my aging pride and say nothing more of it."

It was true she wasn't a young woman with the breathtaking lithe charm granted by youth and worn by youth so carelessly. But women who had experienced the world possessed confidence and humor and wisdom, a sense of perspective that very young women lacked, so on the whole he preferred older women. She wasn't pretty, but she was attractive in every way that mattered: clear eyes, a good face, a love for her own body and its pleasures, and the strength of mind to match the rest. She knew what she wanted and she wasn't afraid to try for it. She reached out to find the dregs of the wine, poured him a tumbler, and handed it over. She'd been raked across the back, too, the wound treated so well the scars had remained supple.

"Where's that one from?" he asked.

"Which?" she asked, twisting to display first her back and then the horrible disfiguring gash across her front. "These are the two worst. The others—" She had a nick on her chin, another nick on her right shoulder, and a single white line running down one forearm. "These are like kisses. Sometimes those cursed eagles try to be affectionate and don't know their own strength. Even this one, the back, that's when U'ushu was trying to play and missed his aim. He's dead now, poor thing. He was a good bird. They all are, mostly, as long as you know how to handle them."

He gently traced what remained of her left breast. "What about this one?"

She said nothing for a moment, face pensive. She took the tumbler out of his hand and drained it. "Sheh! You need a new stock of wine. This is bitter even for being so cheap. Anyway, that's a gift from an eagle named Tumna. She's the worst-tempered raptor I've encountered, although I will tell you I put a lot of the blame on her reeve. He was an altogether foul character and he didn't care for her as she needed. He was one of those who transferred in during the bad years leading up to the days when Marshal Yordenas held sway here."

"Tumna?"

"Her reeve's name was Horas."

"Was?"

"She killed him. That same day you and Clan Hall and the outlanders rid us of Yordenas and his allies."

"Eiya! I remember now. That's a serious charge, when an eagle kills its reeve. When did she do this to you?"

She shook her head. "A few years back, when Horas first arrived here. She came to trust me later. We fawkners don't dwell on such things or we'd not be able to do our work."

He saw the warning look in her eyes, the set of her mouth and the way she had a breath half held in, but he couldn't quite let go. Maybe only because he wasn't sure if he'd betrayed her trust by allowing himself to sleep with her. "We all know the dangers of working with the eagles. But I'm only close to Scar, and he'd never hurt me. I don't know how you fawkners do it, training the young ones, treating the ones who are injured and in pain and most likely to lash out . . . teaching an eagle who's mauled you to trust you. Where do you find the courage?"

She slid a hand around the back of his neck and pulled him closer.

"It makes me feel alive," she murmured, and kissed him.

Amazingly, her breath was still sweet, although he was sure his was sour. A great deal more came clear about what had passed between them last night, indeed it did, and he wrapped his arms around her and settled her closer.

A hard rapping, tat tat tat tat tat, sounded on the outer doors.

"The hells!" he swore.

She cocked her head to one side to listen, then grinned and stretched. "Take your pleasure while you can, Marshal, for they will be clamoring for you as soon as you blink."

Didn't anything ruffle her feathers? Neh, surely not. She had more courage than he'd ever know. She'd faced the creature that tried to kill her, and won its trust.

She began to gather the clothing tossed here and there about the tiny sleeping chamber. He stood and caught her lightly by the wrist. She looked at him, studying his face.

"Listen, Verena," he said. "I thank you for what you offered me. I'm glad for it. But I'm marshal now, and I have to think whether it's best for the hall that I share such a relationship with a fawkner who works under my authority. I just don't know. It all came on me so suddenly. I'm not sure how to negotiate these currents, much less rebuild the hall after Marshal Yordenas tried his best to destroy it."

"You're honest. I appreciate that."

"I'm not saying that—"

"Joss. I'm looking for a pleasant way to pass the evening now and again, that's all. I think you're pretty well accustomed to women's admiration, so you have to believe me—even if it's difficult for you to do so—that I'm not looking for more than that. Nor will I sit around pining for you. And maybe this isn't such a good idea. We have enough complications as it is. It's true enough that Argent Hall needs us all to work hard and together if we mean to restore it to what it ought to be. We have forty eagles or more come home to the hall looking for new reeves, and a raft of hopeful candidates knocking at the gates—"

The pounding resumed, a thapping that made his head hammer right between the eyes.

She grinned. "I would have thought you held your wine better than this. Go on." She handed him the vest she'd unlaced last night, then tugged on her own pair of leather trousers.

"Marshal Joss?"

"I'm coming!"

He dressed, then tossed the coverlet back on the sleeping mat and decided to roll it up and store it away later. Verena picked up the empty pitcher and the pair of tumblers, slid the door open with a foot, and marched across the outer chamber of the marshal's cote to the outer door. Joss, trying to smear the muzziness out of his eyes, stepped into the outer chamber and slid the inner door shut just as she slid open the outer door. A pair of reeves and a fawkner in a linen coat stood on the covered porch.

The fawkner said, "Morning, Rena," as Verena stepped past him and hunted for her sandals by the stairs. "That cursed Tumna is still hanging about. We were thinking she'd fly on off to the mountains like any normal bird that's lost its reeve does, but maybe she's gone rogue. She's looking for someone else's head to rip off."

Verena turned to give the other fawkner a hard stare. "She's a good bird. Don't go thinking otherwise."

The two reeves watched this exchange with interest, grinning first at the fawkners and then at Joss. He ignored them and sat down in front of the cluttered desk that was the marshal's worktable, but all he could do was to stare in disgust at the hopeless disarray: two pots of unstoppered ink turning to sludge; a writing brush left uncleaned so its fine hair tip had dried into a twisted horn; a pile of paper needing a clerk to read to him; a mug filled with chits, each one marked with a name so he could resolve a long-standing dispute over duty rosters; a pair of blue and black glass-bead bracelets—what in the hells were those doing here?

"You didn't waste much time," said the older reeve, sauntering in when he hadn't been invited. "The story in the hall this morning goes that she got you drunk last night and hauled you off by the—Eiya! A new version of the usual tale, I admit, but with the same ending."

Joss squinted up at the man he thought of as "the Snake." "Volias. Greetings of the day to you, too. Why are you hammering on my door?"

"That was Siras, here." He gestured to the younger reeve, who was still standing at the threshold.

"Come in," said Joss wearily, beckoning to Siras and the old fawkner, whose name he had forgotten. Verena's footfalls crunched away down the gravel path. "I'm not awake yet."

"I'll fetch tea and soup from the cook," said Siras hastily and, without attempting to come in, he took himself off.

"Is the news that bad?" asked Joss, eyeing first the Snake's smirking face and then the old fawkner's serious expression.

Unexpectedly, the old man smiled. His was a sweet smile rather like a child's. "Neh, Marshal. It's a good morning when we wake up to know we're shed of Yordenas and the rest of his hateful crew."

"I admire you fawkers and reeves who stuck it out despite everything for the sake of the eagles and the hall," said Joss. "You did well. I mean that, Geddi." The name surfaced at last.

"Begging your pardon, it's Askar. Geddi is taller and about twenty years younger by my reckoning."

Volias snickered.

"Why are you here to plague me?" asked Joss. "Didn't I send you back to Clan Hall?"

"Commander sent me right back again. There's trouble everywhere, Joss."

"Wherever I see your ugly face. Aui! I recall now. You returned yesterday. High Haldia is fallen to an army larger and better-disciplined than the one that attacked Olossi."

"That's right," said Volias more soberly. "That we managed a victory here in the South and sent that second army into flight is by the mercy of the gods."

" 'By the mercy of the gods, and the cunning of the outlander,' " added Askar. "As it says in the tale. After you've had a sip of tea and a swallow of soup, Marshal, there's duty rosters to sort out. The fawkners would like to talk to you about the injured eagles. The senior reeves need to talk to you. The training master wants a word about how to sort out so many novices at one time. The hall steward needs your imprint to ask for a tithing increase since we're feeding so many new novices and eagles, with more to come. And besides there are a hundred new young hopefuls still waiting in the western parade grounds, each one eager to try for an eagle."

"Amazing how they will come," said Volias in a thoughtful tone, spoken in a way that made even Joss want to know what had provoked those words. Then he laughed scornfully, ruining the effect. "Eh! So this morning when passing out rice balls among them, Darga and Medard got to talking in loud voices about how that cursed eagle—Tumna—slaughtered her very own reeve. They did go into detail of what the remains looked like. A puncture wound in the chest big enough to slither through, which eels were doing. His head half ripped off, dangling by a few tendons, and one arm clean gone. By the time they were through talking, a good twenty of those bright-eyed innocents had slunk out the gates heading for home."

Joss grunted, feeling the headache reemerge. "Askar, have we a clerk who can read all these contracts and correspondence, and write replies?"

"Neh, Marshal. Marshal Alyon did have a good clerk on retainer from the temple of Sapanasu in Olossi, but when Yordenas came in he sent the man packing and kept that Devouring girl to read his letters for him."

"And read more of him besides, I am sure," said the Snake with his habitual sneer.

Joss felt his anger rising. Siras clattered up the steps, kicked off his sandals, and brought in a tray of tea and soup, which he set on the desk in the last cleared space.

"Well now, Volias," said Askar in his same serious tone, "you might think so, and many did think so, but I'm not so certain. I doubt the Devouring girl danced to Yordenas's melody."

The Devouring girl.

All memories of the sweet night he had spent with Verena vanished like so much chaff blown away under a stiff wind. Hoping his hand's tremor would be interpreted as exhaustion and wine-sickness, he sipped at the tea. The cook had kindly brewed thin medallions of ginger with a sprinkling of dried purple arrowroot flowers, good for hangovers.

"With your permission, Ruti will fly me into Olossi this morning so I can go to the temple of Sapanasu and see about them sending us a clerk for the work needs doing here," continued Askar. He went into detail about what needed the marshal's oversight and what usually ran well without his interference.

As Joss listened, he drank the spicy soup and drained the tea, glad to have the conversation move onto less volatile ground. Askar hadn't much of a sense of humor, but he knew what was needed for a reeve hall to run smoothly.

"I'm fortunate to have you," he said when Askar had done. He set bowl and cup on the tray, grabbed a knife, his short staff, and, after a moment's consideration, a pair of loose jesses. "How did you and the others manage not to lose hope while Yordenas ruled here, with those dirty, corrupt reeves gathered around him? They must have made life miserable, and dangerous, for the rest of you."

Askar shook his head. "We did what had to be done. Of course, now we know there was another mind, working at a distance to corrupt Argent Hall and the council of Olossi. That Yordenas was simply a tool."

"This battle isn't done yet," said Joss. "Our war is just beginning."

7

Standing in the shop of her Ri Amarah hosts, Mai studied the wares for sale: netted bags; varying qualities of linen and cotton cloth, from stands-up-to-hard-use to dainty-for-festivals; needles of varying length and thickness; and two shelves packed with thread and yarn of diverse luster, strength, and color. Behind the counter, Eliar's father presided over cubbyholes and shelves and baskets packed with medicinals.

"Isn't that oil of naya?" she asked Isar, indicating a display of vials containing a pale liquid.

"Oil of naya is famed for its healing properties, verea." Isar had Eliar's good looks, aged and mellowed, and Eliar's charming manners, but in other ways he reminded Mai of her own father: he liked tidy shelves and tidy rules, because he arranged them. "This is finest-quality water-white, useful against certain skin conditions and ailments. Crude oil of naya has the property that it burns even when water is thrown on it, so it is hard to extinguish."

Mai leaned against the counter to steady herself as the memory of living men engulfed in flame flashed in her mind's eye. Fifteen days ago, she had watched from the women's tower of the Ri Amarah compound as Anji and his troops, with the aid of the Olossi militia and the reeves of Argent and Clan Halls, had attacked the army invading the city. They had won a victory against a numerically superior force by dropping oil of naya on the army's encampment. Merciful One! Everything had burned, even flesh.

"Are you well, verea?" Isar asked. "If you'd prefer to go back to the women's quarters, you might find it more suitable."

She took in and released a measured breath, just as Priya had taught her, cupped a hand over the curve of her belly. After the battle, Anji had stayed with her for one night, and then he had ridden off with his troops in pursuit of the remnants of the broken army. He had his work. And she had hers. She would do what must be done.

"I am grateful to you for sheltering me, ver," she said a little hoarsely. "Your house has shown me nothing but kindness and generosity. But I find I miss the bustle of the market. It keeps my mind off those things I cannot change."

Isar seemed about to object when a pair of matrons entered the store and demanded his attention in their quest for an ointment to soothe abrasions and burns that men in their family had received while fighting the fires that had sprung up in the lower city during the attack. Mai sat on a stool reserved for customers, relieved she did not have to answer his objections, and watched the give and take. She never tired of bargaining. She could learn much observing how others conducted themselves. In addition to selling his wares, Isar acted as an apothecary might, refusing to recommend any tisane or ointment until he had led the women through an exhaustive list of symptoms to identify the severity and precise nature of each ailment. A pair of turbaned younger men entered from the back, bearing a tray with tiny cups. They offered this fragrant tea to the customers, but both women refused.

Several young women dressed in good quality silks ventured in, laughing together. As they spread out bolts of fabric, they glanced at Mai, whispering with heads bent together. The Hundred folk favored bold colors and patterns: stylized flowers too bright to be realistic, playful butterflies and bats representing day and night, handsome motifs formed out of ranks of green-on-gold vegetation. Their chattering, the strange patterns, the smell of unfamiliar herbs, and even the color of the dirt made her feel an utter outlander, tossed into a foreign land with no choice but to fight for her own survival.

She could not allow it to overwhelm her. She and Anji, and their company of about two hundred soldiers and additional grooms and slaves, had chosen to make their stand here, to carve out a life in exile.

"Verea, is there anything you need?" asked one of the young men hesitantly. When she smiled at him, he reddened and tugged at the cloth wrapping his head that concealed his hair, as if the action would deflect her gaze.

"No. I thank you." She rose.

Isar looked up from his customers, marked her exit with a creased brow, and offered a brief and possibly disapproving nod.

If only his daughter were permitted to accompany her, but of course that was impossible.

She pushed through the hanging banners stamped with the signs that signified to customers what was sold within, and emerged onto the porch. Every storefront had such a porch, set a few steps up from the street, on which folk left their street shoes before entering. Her attendants waited outside. Priya sat cross-legged on the porch, watching the passing traffic. Her lips shaped the words of prayers that she chanted to herself whenever she had a quiet moment. Chief Tuvi and four soldiers stood guard. Eliar, her chosen escort and local guide, was leaning against a wooden pillar chatting with O'eki, the mountainous slave, about wool.

As Mai bent to strap on her sandals, Priya rose. O'eki broke off his disquisition on the importance of a long and lustrous fiber to a carpet that would stand up to repeated wear.

Eliar grinned as he pushed away from the pillar. "Did my father talk you out of your reckless scheme, Mai?" he asked, as casual with her as if she were his sister.

Chief Tuvi gestured, and the soldiers fell into formation, two in the vanguard and two for the rear guard. "Mistress? What is your wish?"

She gathered her courage, let out a held breath. "Surely shopping must be the same in every town, even a foreign one. I am ready to go!"

THE MARKET STREETS in Olossi brimmed with ten times the wonders that even the twice-annual market fair in isolated Kartu Town could ever ever ever boast. Along one narrow street you could browse the stalls and shops of papermakers, with rice-paper lanterns, plain or painted fans, decorative paper for folding, and painted landscapes suitable for screens as well as ordinary white rice paper for windows and doors. An alley snaked between shops selling fabulous creatures carved from bone. She found mirrors backed with bronze lacework, braided cords to ornament jackets, and silk ribbons woven plain or patterned.

"You're dickering," said Eliar as they strolled down a rank of stalls that sold nothing but beads: wood, ceramic, stone, crystal, polished, unpolished, in so many colors she could not name them all. His silver bracelets jangled as he gestured toward the bustling shops. "But you're not buying."

"This is my first time out. I was fearful of venturing out, after the battle, with everything in disarray. Then your sister told me it was also the year-end festival with ghosts and such. So I thought it would be better to stay indoors. But now that's over—" She laughed. "You can see it wouldn't be wise to buy when I don't really know how bargaining works here."

"The same as any other place, I suppose." Eliar heaved a sigh that ought to have shaken earth and sky together. "Not that my father and uncles will let me travel to other towns and see."

"The roads aren't safe. Didn't a man from your house get killed on the road to Horn last year?"

"Yes. But they wouldn't even let me ride out with the militia during the battle. All I was allowed to do was fight the fire in the lower city after the army had already run!"

Mai shuddered, remembering the way buildings and tents and living creatures had burned and burned and burned. "People died fighting those fires."

"So they did. I shouldn't make light of it."

A girl scuttled up to the pair of soldiers standing rear guard. Ducking her head shyly, she held out a wooden platter of sweet rice dumplings. "My papa asks you take these as a gift, for fighting for the city. The Silver isn't permitted any."

Eliar's frown deepened.

"That's rude!" muttered Mai.

"Maybe not meant so," he said. "Best the soldiers be seen accepting the gift."

She gestured to Chief Tuvi. He strolled back to inspect the dumplings and the girl, who wasn't more than ten. He indicated she should eat one first, and when she popped one promptly in her mouth, he allowed the soldiers to share the rest.

"Even so, walking through the market is more than your sister can do," said Mai, mouth watering as she watched the soldiers devour the moist dumplings. She couldn't bring herself to taste them when Eliar was rejected in that way, but if he meant to let the slight pass, she would not mention it again. "She wasn't allowed to accompany me."

"She's unmarried. She's not allowed to walk in the market until she becomes an adult."

"Which I am, although I'm younger than she is? Just because I'm married? That doesn't seem reasonable."

Like his father, Eliar might smile and charm but there were things he would not joke about. "That isn't our way, verea."

"Forgive me. I had no intention to offend. I grew up selling produce in the market in Kartu Town. It seems strange to me that your sister lives so restricted."

"Let's move on," he said.

Even Miravia's absence could not ruin the delight of walking through the bright day and enjoying the sight of a city so rich they could build with wood as much as with stone and brick. So many colors and smells! Vendors sold oil by the ladle. At food stalls you could buy noodles, or mounds of colorful spiced and pickled vegetables.

A girl sat on a blanket under the shade of a canvas awning, fruit mounded in neat piles before her, crying her wares in a cheerful voice: "Sunfruit! Best and sweetest! Ghost melon for the new year! Strings of redthorn."

Mai wiped away unexpected tears.

Priya cupped Mai's elbow under an arm. "Mistress, are you well? Perhaps we should return?"

"Just remembering when I used to be that girl, selling fruit in the market in Kartu Town."

She bought several sunfruit, making only a cursory effort to bargain, and shared out the segments with the others. The moist flesh cooled her mouth, but it tasted a little sour.

The smell of fried fish made her stomach turn, so they walked on, past carpenters raising walls where a hall had just days ago burned, past roofers shifting broken tiles, past folk hauling water and pushing wheelbarrows piled with bricks, past men and women calling out their wares in a singsong that grabbed and held the ear. The rhythm of the marketplace truly was the same anywhere. And today she had no need to feel hurried, to grasp at trinkets in passing, to wonder if the coin she'd been given as a sign of favor by Father Mei might be pried from her hand by Grandmother Mei in a fit of pique. She could wait, see what appealed, how prices compared, and she could come back whenever she pleased, because she and Anji were wealthy. Anji's troop of Qin soldiers had saved Olossi. Acting as negotiator for their services, she had pinched the Olossi council for so much coin that she couldn't imagine how she'd had the audacity just days ago to manage it.

No, there was no haste to buy.

Not until they came to the street catering to those who knew how to write, with its brushes and inkstones and ink knives. In one shop, a dozen wretchedly preserved scrolls had been tossed into a dusty basket in the corner.

"Look here, Priya," she said to the slave, drawing her close, hand tucked into her elbow. "Don't those look like prayer scrolls? Whatever would such a thing be doing in this land, where they've never heard of the Merciful One?"

The shopkeeper hustled over. "Verea." He nodded at Priya, not realizing she was only a slave, and then at Mai, gaze shifting between the two to gauge their relationship. "How may I help you?"

"I'd like to look at these," Mai said. "What a curiosity!"

"Please, please." He was a short, broad-chested man wearing a sleeveless vest and loose trousers that fell to just above the ankle. He cleared a space on a table and carelessly dropped several of the frayed scrolls there.

A youth wearing only a kilt belted low on the hips was seated on the floor in the opposite corner at the rear of the shop, twisting hairs into brushes. His well-muscled chest was mostly hairless, quite smooth. He glanced up as if he had felt the weight of her gaze, and grinned flirtatiously right at her. She looked away, although not because she feared a lad's dazzling smile. The Hundred folk wore much less clothing in public than Mai was accustomed to, displaying a great deal of lovely brown skin. Perhaps it was no wonder Isar did not like his unmarried daughter to walk in the market.

Priya sucked in a sharp breath, a hiss of surprise. She had untied a ribbon and smoothed out the first few turns of a battered scroll, careful lest the ragged tears rip further.

"This is a copy of the Thread of Awakening," she murmured.

Was that a tear below Priya's eye, or a stray drop of rain? Priya had always a well-modulated voice, in which Mai heard only affection and wisdom. Tenderly the slave tied the scroll back and peeled open a second.

"Aie!" She sounded as if the sight pained her. "The Discourse on the Seven-Branched Candle. Ill handled for its pains. I cannot imagine how these holy books journeyed here."

"Yet here they are," murmured Mai as the woman mouthed the words silently and rocked side to side to the rhythm of the unspoken phrases.

The months-long overland journey with Anji's company had been hard on Priya, but she had never relaxed her care of Mai, never once spoken of her own fears and aches. Nor had Mai, in the seven years Priya had been her personal slave, ever asked. Anji was the one who had discovered that Priya had been kidnapped years ago from a temple where she served the Merciful One, and marched over high mountains to be sold into slavery far away from her homeland. Her only comment: *"I survived because of the teachings of the Merciful One."*

"Do these exceptional scrolls interest you, verea? They are rare. Outlander work. It was chance I was able to lay hands on them. You'll find nothing else like them in all of Olossi."

"Look how dirty and torn they are," said Mai with a kind smile. "How sad that those who handled them treated them with such scorn. Here, now, what can you tell me of these prints?" She indicated a set of pictures leaning against the wall. "How I love butterflies! So colorful they are! But is this a practiced hand? Or apprentice work? Please advise me, ver."

Distracted, he followed her to the ranks of prints on display. "It's very good work, although you might find Hoko's work more to your taste, she is a master artisan, the best in town. Here are Hoko's festival prints special for the Year of the Red Goat, which I can offer at a markdown since we scarcely had a festival this year due to the terrible events. See the detail of this wharf scene! The festival banners, the ghost ribbons, the food stalls. Here, the incomparable Eridit, and there a talking line of children from the Lady's temple dance the episode of the reunited lovers from the Tale of Change."

"It's very fine, but the colors here look a little smudged. Oh, I do like that one, but—"

She smiled brightly and spoke cheerfully, and wielded her "but"s like a trimming knife until the shopkeeper begged for mercy. "Your sweet tongue is as sharp as those swords carried by your soldiers, verea," he said, laughing. "I accept defeat! What is it you want?"

"It seems a high price for prints for a festival now over, for a year that won't come around again for—well—how can I even count that far? Many rounds of years, surely, before the Red Goat walks again."

"I can't lower my price, verea. My overhead. Surely you understand. But I could throw in something else. Is there something you have your eye on?"

She made a show of examining other prints, the brushes, the inkstones. He had an assistant bring tea. As she sipped, savoring the gingery taste, she entertained him with a long digression about needing to bind a new accounts book, as she must of necessity set up a household.

"So you and the outlanders are indeed staying, as it is rumored?"

"Is it spoken of?"

"Surely it is, verea. You must know every person in Olossi talks of little else. How could it be otherwise, since your bold attack saved us from ruin?"

She liked him, for his laugh and his praise of Anji and the soldiers, and because bargaining entertained him as much as it did her. Because he offered tea not just to her and Priya but also to Eliar and Tuvi and the four soldiers as they loitered under the eaves, waiting for her. "I'll need two accounts books. I am sure you can bind them with good-quality paper, something that will hold up better than those poor scrolls, and provide the necessary scribal tools."

In the end she purchased the prints and the accounts books, with the entire basket of dusty scrolls thrown in as a courtesy. The books and scribal tools and prints would be delivered, but Priya herself carried away the basket, clutched as tightly as a precious child. Mai could not have been more pleased.

"MISTRESS, HERE IS juice, just as you like it with lime and mint."

"Ah! That's very nice, Sheyshi."

"While you were gone, I washed the cloth just as you said. I folded the bedding. I cooked rice. The young mistress helped me."

"Very good, Sheyshi. Where is Miravia?"

"She went back through the gate, Mistress. Do you want your hair brushed, Mistress?"

"Yes, Sheyshi." Mai sank down onto pillows and sighed with pleasure as Sheyshi took out the combs and sticks that held her hair. Released, her hair fell past her hips. As Sheyshi brushed with steady strokes, Mai watched Priya examine the scrolls. The slave said nothing, but tears shone on her weathered skin.

"What have we found?" Mai asked finally.

"A treasure! Six of the scrolls are written in script unknown to me. They might be anything. But the other six are discourses and threads. I have not touched holy books since the day our temple was burned and we were taken away by the raiders." She wiped tears from her cheek. "I thank you, Mistress. This treasure brings me great joy."

Mai sniffled, wiping away her own tears. "We'll make an altar. You can teach me all the holy prayers."

"We will not build an altar in the house of the Ri Amarah."

"No," said Mai with a frowning laugh. "I suppose we will not."

The brush paused halfway down her length of hair.

"Mistress, what altar will you build?" Sheyshi asked. "Can I pray there? I know the words 'the Merciful One is my lamp and my refuge.' But that's all I know."

Priya touched each of the scrolls in turn, as if she could absorb their holy essence through her skin. "Of course you will pray, Sheyshi. The Merciful One hears the prayers of all people."

"Even women?" Sheyshi whispered. "Even slaves?"

"Especially women. Especially slaves." Priya sat back. She had grown thin. In Kartu she had been more robust, favored with extra food in her capacity as nurse-maid to the house's favored daughter, Mai. But the long journey had whittled at her flesh to expose the ridges and hollows of bone.

"You must eat more, Priya," said Mai, scooting forward to touch one of Priya's hands with her own. "And rest. I could not bear to lose you."

"I will recover, little flower. Do not fear for me. You are the one who must be careful to eat plenty, now that you are with child. Look. Here comes Miravia."

The guesthouse attached to the Ri Amarah compound was separated from the street by gates, and further separated from the main compound of the family by another set of gates.

Miravia entered, ran over, and kicked off her sandals before she dropped down beside Mai on a neighboring pillow. "Sheyshi, what a lovely brushing you've done!" The young slave dipped her head shyly, smiling at this praise. "Priya, you look tired. I will take Mai into the house for supper and afterward I will bring a tray of food for you and Sheyshi myself. That way you can rest."

"Let me put your hair up, Mistress," said Sheyshi.

Sheyshi braided Mai's thick black hair into the loose arrangement which she then twisted and bound up on Mai's head with combs and hair sticks, while Mai and Miravia discussed the shopping expedition and the scrolls.

"Don't mention that they are holy scrolls," said Miravia, with a look of alarm as if she thought invisible spirits might be eavesdropping. "They might make you get rid of them."

"Even if we just keep them here in the guest house with our other belongings?"

"It would be better if you did not mention it. Might you teach me the reading of the script, Priya?"

"Certainly," said Priya. "Must you ask permission from your elders?"

"I won't, for they would forbid it."

"Then not in this house. It would not be fair recompense for their hospitality."

Miravia sighed, and made no reply. She took Mai's hand. "Come, Mai."

They slipped on sandals and walked to the inner gate. "My mother is particularly keen to talk to you. She wants to know what you thought of our markets."

"I don't think it's right you're not allowed out to shop! Yet you visit the prison!"

"To bring food to indigent prisoners. That they cannot forbid me to do because of our obligation to act for justice and mercy where we can. But only adult women are allowed to go out into the marketplace."

"And even then, with a veil covering your face!"

"Mai, let it go, I beg you."

They had reached the gate. Mai embraced her friend as they waited for the mechanism to be drawn back from the other side. "I'll say nothing more. But I have my own plans. You'll see."

AFTER SUPPER, MAI accompanied Miravia on her lamp-lighting rounds.

"Do you miss him?" Miravia asked as she stood on tiptoe, pressing a lit taper to a wick. With a hiss, flame brightened.

Mai closed and latched the glass door. "Yes. But I don't like to think about him. What if he is killed? That would be too painful to bear, wouldn't it?"

"If you cared for someone, it would. Otherwise maybe it would be a relief, wouldn't it?"

Her voice had such a finely grained dark tone that Mai touched her hand, to let her know she was not alone. "When my uncle Girish died, I think everyone wept only because they were ashamed that they were glad he was gone. But people will feel relief, if a death lightens their burden."

Miravia wiped her cheek with the back of a hand, but she did not reply. She walked on to the next lamp in the vast rectangular courtyard of the women's side of the Ri Amarah compound. Older children not yet sent to bed played in the open space, shrieking and giggling as they dodged around benches and the twisting forms of pruned trees. A hearth glowed in the kitchens, and beside it a pair of old women prepared pots of steaming herbs. At a raised trough, chatting girls scoured dishes. Most of the married women had gone to the innermost apartments, leaving the supervision of the courtyard to the unmarried women and elderly widows.

"What if another's misfortune brings relief to you?" asked Miravia as she lit a lamp, keeping her face turned away from Mai. "If something you never wanted is made impossible through no effort of yours, only through trouble afflicting others?"

"What happened?" asked Mai as she latched the tiny glass door. They stood in shadow far from the running children, the clatter and laughter in the kitchen, and the intermittent cries and complaints of younger children being coaxed to bed in the sleeping rooms. "No one can hear us here. You know I'll keep secret any word you tell to me, Miravia."

A bench stretched below the lamp, the polished wood gleaming under the illumination. Miravia sank down, and Mai sat beside her, taking her friend's hands between her own.

"A courier came from Clan Hall to Argent Hall, a reeve bearing letters. One of the Ri Amarah houses in Toskala paid to have a message delivered to us. High Haldia is fallen—" Her voice broke on a caught breath.

"Yes, I heard that, too."

"I spoke once to you of the young scholar it was arranged I would marry. I should have gone a year ago but the roads weren't safe. To High Haldia. Where their house is."

"Oh, no," murmured Mai.

"A few survived the assault, and fled to Toskala with their news. But he's dead. Mai, he's dead. And I'm relieved to know it. I never even met him. It's just I didn't want to marry someone I never met and never knew. But you did."

"I always knew I would marry someone my father chose for me."

"He didn't choose your husband."

"No," said Mai with a strangled laugh. "He was very upset when Anji picked me. Father had no choice then. No more than I did. In Kartu, you could not say no to the Qin."

The lamplight made Miravia's face ghostly and vulnerable. "Where did you find the grace in your heart to accept it? And not fight it?"

"The only place to find happiness is inside. In the house I grew up in, the ones who fought to no purpose, who thrashed and flailed like Mei and Ti, they were the unhappiest ones. Even Uncle Hari didn't know how to be happy even though everyone loved him because he was so funny and charming. But a worm gnawed at him. He was dissatisfied. He never learned how to use his anger to build, only to tear down."

"How did you learn?"

Mai shrugged, amused at herself and saddened by Miravia's distress. "Maybe because I am like my father in wanting to control things. So if I can control myself, then no one can touch that part of me. That's my garden, where my spirit rests."

"My spirit flies in the mountains and fields and forests," said Miravia with a grimace, "or it would, if I could ever go there. They'll just arrange another marriage for me."

Mai felt her trembling. She kissed her lightly on the cheek. "Maybe you'll be fortunate, as I was."

"Maybe so," she said without meaning it. "But there was talk, before the scholar, of an old rich man who's already buried three wives, and needs a fresh young one. A lecherous goat!"

"Miravia!"

"It's true. You know how they talk around what they don't want said. Hearing nothing ill means there is nothing good. If a man is rich enough, he can buy what he wants. He has a daughter fit for Eliar, an excellent match for our family, but Eliar refused the match the first time it was offered two years ago because the agreement was for him to marry the daughter and I to marry to the old man. Eliar knew I would hate living trapped in Nessumara in a house said to be much stricter than our own. So he refused to make the bargain, knowing how I would hate it."

"How can a house be stricter than this one, with a men's court and a women's court?"

"Most everyone here is related, so we have more freedom of movement between the two courts than may be obvious to you. In a very strict house, all movement is regulated, and women who have married in especially are confined to the women's court and to a private family chamber where their husband meets with them. It's like a prison." The last lights in the weaving hall were extinguished, and the counting rooms went dark. "Even here, it was more informal when Eliar and I were little. But in the last few years we've had marriages, apprentices, and fostered girls brought in to complicate matters. And we absorbed a smaller cousin house from Horn that was driven out."

"Driven out?"

Miravia walked on to the next lamp, opened and lit it, and gravely regarded the light as it flared. "In fire and blood. Many in the Hundred still consider us outlanders although my people have lived in this land for a hundred years. We are honest merchants. Sometimes there is resentment, because we look different and don't worship their gods. Because we are wealthy, I suppose. Anyway, our house is now large enough that it will branch soon, sons and cousins splitting off to make their own house. Not like that rich old man in Nessumara, who clutches all the generations beholden to him in his fist."

"Maybe he found another wife when he heard you were betrothed to the scholar."

"Maybe he did." Miravia rose, shaking out her loose trousers and the calf-length pleated jacket worn over all. "Poor young scholar. I wonder how he died."

"In fire and blood," said Mai, remembering how the tents had burned outside Olossi, remembering the rising and falling whoops of men too weakened by burns for full-throated screams. She let her tears flow, knowing better than to suck them down. There was nothing shameful in sorrow.

"I've made you gloomy, too," said Miravia, hugging her. "How dare I! I'm sorry."

"It would be worse not to think about it. But we lived and won, and they lost and died."

"Thanks to Captain Anji and his company. And that reeve my friend Jonit cannot stop talking about."

"Marshal Joss is charming and handsome, I'll have you know, although he is pretty old."

Miravia laughed. In lamplight, the courtyard glowed. Mai brushed the last glistening tear from her friend's face. She wanted to assure Miravia that all would be well, but who could ever know? It was better to be honest, and remain silent.

Several women emerged from the weaving hall, walking the length of the porch around to the living quarters, where they disappeared inside. Girls carried heavy ceramic pots on trays across the courtyard and went in after them. Miravia tipped back her head and inhaled. "Ah! Can you smell it? Warmed cordial."

"It must be time for me to return to the guesthouse."

"Yes, it is, just when families gather in the evenings to exchange their news of the day." She snuffed out the taper. "I'm sorry you always have to go back to the guesthouse alone."

"Never apologize to me, Miravia. That you are here is what makes my days tolerable."

"A sad tale, to be sure, if listening to me complain is the best part of your day!"

Companionably, they strolled across the courtyard on one of the gravel paths, brushing against the waxy leaves and soft petals of night-blooming paradom.

Fumes from the hearth fires and the lingering smells of clove-spiced meats and sharp khaif roiled out as they passed the kitchens.

"Miravia? Is that Mai, with you?" The mother of Eliar and Miravia crunched toward them down an intersecting path. "Come with me, Mai, if you will. Miravia, please fetch warmed cordial and a pot of khaif and bring it to Grandfather's rooms."

Miravia gave her mother a startled look, but she released Mai's hand and hurried off.

Puzzled, Mai asked, "Isn't Grandfather dead?"

"So he is, but his rooms will go to Eliar when he marries."

"That's a notable honor."

"Eliar is Grandfather's eldest living male grandchild, although naturally my husband and his brothers hope for more sons. However, since Eliar has not yet married, the rooms remain unoccupied and therefore available."

Available for what? Her worst fears intruded. Barely able to speak, she choked out words. "Is there somewhat amiss?"

"Not at all. Your husband is back."

"Anji?" The drowsy languor of falling night vanished as quickly as droplets of water steam off a hot brick.

"This way. Your hirelings have already been informed that you won't be returning to the guesthouse tonight."

On the porch, Mai slipped off her sandals and found cloth slippers that fit well enough. Public rooms faced the courtyard. Beyond them lay a warren of inner chambers separated by papered walls, sliding screened doors, and corridors. Some rooms lay dark and quiet, or alive with the excited whispering of children who everyone pretends are asleep. Others rooms were lit. As Mai followed Miravia's mother, turning left and right and right again, she heard voices chatting in the companionable way of families catching up on their day.

They fetched up at a dead end, facing a pair of sliding doors. A narrow corridor extended to either side, ending in gates. The gate on the left had its top half slid open; beyond, lamps glimmered in the courtyard where she and Miravia had just walked. The gate to the right was latched shut, but evidently it opened into the men's court. Miravia's mother slid open one of the doors, and they mounted six steps into a narrow chamber lit by a single oil lamp. Polished wood planks gleamed, smooth and dark. The whitewashed walls bore no decoration save for a ceiling strip minutely carved with vines.

"This way."

This narrow room opened into another. Nearby, male voices rose in argument. In an alcove, a set of peepholes looked out over a bright chamber where men were talking and, by the sudden outbreak of laughter, not arguing but conversing in the intense manner Mai had always associated with arguments. She stepped inside the alcove and raised up on her toes, hoping to see, but Miravia's mother pulled her back and led her on. They passed a second alcove fitted with a bench and a series of openings like arrow slits in a fortification, and at the end of this series of small rooms found themselves in the vestibule to a square chamber fitted with mats, a wide sleeping pallet, a low desk, and a lit lamp hanging from a tripod. The chamber had a musty smell, and the merest twinge of sweet mold festering.

The woman sniffed audibly. "Eh, that mildew will have to be found and cleaned, wherever it's hiding. I'll be back in a moment. Remove your slippers before you go in."

She left, her footfalls ringing away. Mai fidgeted. She wanted to go back to the peepholes, to see if she could see Anji, but she dared not insult her hosts by eavesdropping on a conversation she had no right to overhear. The vestibule contained an empty table and a stand with hooks opposite, suitable for hanging articles of clothing.

Muted sounds drifted: more male laughter, and a burst of speech as several men spoke at once. Laughter again, after which a voice spun its tale uninterrupted. Was that Anji speaking? She pressed a palm to her chest, breath tight and heart pounding.

The soft slap of feet startled her, and she patted the creases and folds and twists of her hair, wondering if she looked worn or weary, but it was only Miravia's mother, bearing a tray with a pot of steaming khaif, a pot of warmed cordial, a pitcher of water, four small cups, a washing bowl, and a tiny bowl containing mint leaves. She set this tray on the vestibule table, laid out squares of folded cloth, and pressed Mai's hand between her own in a gesture meant to comfort.

"There, now."

She left.

Mai chewed on mint as the doors slid shut, and the quiet settled like dust, undisturbed but for the hearty festivities in the men's hall and, once or twice, a childish shout from farther afield. After a while, she crept back to the alcove, but even standing on tiptoe she could not see through the lowest slit. In the dim light she prowled the rooms until she found a pair of bricks, likely warmed in cool weather to place within the bed, and stacked them beneath the lowest peephole. She balanced carefully atop this, hands splayed against the wall to steady herself.

Ah! She peered into a high beamed hall. Mostly she saw the aura of light spilling from lit lamps, tangling with the darkness that pooled in the rafters. The mingled scents of burning oil and spiced cordial made her wrinkle her nose. The fierce conversation had died down. She saw a few turbaned heads, one crossing the hall and others lower, as if seated, swaying a little. Did that black hair belong to Anji? She pushed as high as she could, craning her neck—

"*What* are you doing?"

She shrieked, lost her balance, toppled back to be caught in strong arms.

"Anji!"

He was whole and unmarked, clean and smiling, perfectly handsome and entirely here, right here. She embraced him, pressing her face against his warm neck. He smelled of horses—he always did—and sweat and dust, the best scent imaginable. She knew she was crying, so she held on until she could draw up calmness and let it suffuse her. He talked in a voice as mellow as if their lives had not been turned entirely upside down, as if they had not been tossed into exile and then thrown into battle against an implacable enemy whose strength ought to have battered them into surrender but had not, because he was cleverer than they were. He was indomitable.

"My informants tell me that you are eating well, sleeping well, and have been out into the market despite their concern that I might find this behavior inappropriate in my wife. Which I do not. Our own endeavors have gone smoothly so far. The remnants of the invading army are fleeing north, but we're keeping on them, killing as many as we can although unfortunately some will escape and take news of our victory to their commanders. We can't know how long it will take the retreating soldiers to reach their base, or how their commanders will react. All these matters must be discussed and considered. I left Tohon and Chief Deze and most of the men on the hunt, with orders to drop back if our force gets too strung out. Reeve Joss has been named marshal at Argent Hall, which is excellent news. Meanwhile the Olossi council wishes to meet with me tomorrow on military matters. Isar has his sources, so I get advance notice of their complaints and fears and demands. It seems they want me to coordinate the entire regional militia, since the militia they have now is worthless."

She found her voice, still a little frail. She hadn't used to be so easily overset, but she remembered how the women in her father's house got irritable and weepy in early pregnancy. "Our soldiers need wives."

"Isn't it too early to be thinking of that?"

She could not hold him tightly enough. "If we wish to settle here and be accepted, the men must marry local wives. And the women they marry should have connections with local clans."

"Why would they not have such connections?"

"Many women will come who are destitute or without family, because their suspicion of outlanders will be overcome by their desperation. Such women will be grateful, and will work hard, but if there are too many kinless women, without clan support, then the rest of Olo'osson will not feel connected to us." He seemed perfectly able to understand her despite that she was speaking into his neck. She could not bear to release him, as if he would vanish if she let go. But even so, she had been thinking about these things for days and days, having little else to do. "We don't want to be seen as outlanders for generation after generation. We want to be seen as Hundred folk."

"Mmmm," he agreed, kissing her hair.

"Anyway, it will take months, perhaps years, to find fitting wives for all the men. Once children are born, then a transformation begins, the children become woven into the land, so it is less easy if the locals decide we have served our useful purpose."

"What do you mean?"

"To start agitating for us to leave, to feel we are not a part of the land, that they can't eat with us, to fear us or want to drive us out . . ." She pushed back, so by looking into her face he could see how serious the matter was.

Unlike every male in her family, he nodded to show he had heard her, that he considered her opinion worthwhile. "I do not think peace will come quickly, but you are of course correct in your assessment of the situation. You are in charge of the strongbox in any case. Do what you need to do, and I will do what I need to do."

"I want a house, a compound, of our own. A place Miravia can come visit me. An altar to the Merciful One where Priya and I can pray. I want—"

"Mai," he said softly. "Can this wait?"

There is a moment in every one of the thrilling story-songs she had grown up with and loved when the bandit prince clasps the young maid close against him, and devours her with his brooding gaze because he, never caught by those who pursue him, has fallen captive to her innocent charm. How foolish and naive are those who believe in such tales, none of which are true. That's what everyone always told her.

"Anji," she murmured, leaning forward to kiss him. "I missed you so badly."

He swept her up in his arms, carried her past the vestibule, and brought her to bed.

8

According to Siras, one hundred and two people hoping to be chosen as reeves had checked in at the gate over the last twelve days. Eighty-three remained when Joss called them to silence. Most sat cross-legged on the dirt of the parade ground; a few stood, apparently too anxious to sit. The majority were young men, a number of whom he recognized from Olossi's militia. A few young women and older men had made the trek as well, and he was surprised to see one stocky woman not much younger than he was standing in the back with arms folded and chin up. In the cloud-patched sky, eagles circled. That they appeared so tiny to the naked eye meant they were sailing very high indeed.

"I don't know why any one of you came to Argent Hall," he said. "Maybe you've always watched the reeves and wanted to be one of us. Maybe you want to know what it's like to fly. Maybe you're angry about what you see around you: injustice, crime gone unpunished, corruption in your village council or temple conclave with no other authority to appeal to. Maybe you watched that army march down on Olossi, burn villages and homes along West Track, and do worse besides, and you want to do something, anything, about it. Maybe you just want a baton of your own—" He brandished his baton. "—to whack people with."

The comment elicited a few chuckles, an elbow to the ribs, a snort of laughter.

"Most of you will go home disappointed. You can help us with our chores, you can share sex with any one of us, remind us that your uncle knows our aunt or your clan made a deal with one of ours years ago. You can share apprenticeship stories— I rode my year as a messenger for Ilu, by the way—but none of that will matter. The eagles choose. We don't. How they make their choice we've never known. Even with as many eagles as we have here now looking for new reeves, I can't even say that one of you waiting here will be marked and chosen by an eagle. You may all end up walking home. You may ask to stay on as assistant to one of our fawkners, who take on the difficult job of caring for the eagles and the lofts. You may hire on as one of the stewards and hirelings who do the day-to-day work of running the hall. Even if you do become a reeve, you'll discover that the training process is arduous and dangerous."

Restless murmurs began to rise. He raised a hand to quiet them. "Is there a question?"

An older man rose respectfully. "Marshal, thanks for hearing me. How long have you been a reeve?"

"Twenty-two years."

"And how long a marshal?"

"Twelve days." That got laugh.

A younger voice called from the crowd. "Is it true that eagles sometimes kill their reeves?"

"It's very rare, but it happens. If you don't like that answer, then leave now." He waited, but no one moved, nor did he expect any person to walk out while everyone else watched. "Hall eagles aren't as territorial as eagles in the wild. Perhaps the gods bred it out of them. But they are territorial, and they will tangle, and the routines of patrol and hall rest and mating cycles are carefully calibrated so the halls can function smoothly. Eagles are our partners, not our servants. Their needs come first. There's one other thing you may not fully understand. Once chosen, you cannot change your mind. You are a reeve for life. You can't leave. And if your eagle dies, you will die with them."

"Do you regret it?" called the older woman suddenly. "Do you regret being chosen as a reeve by your eagle?"

Joss grinned. "Never."

He put his bone whistle to his lips and blew a note no human ear could hear. From elsewhere in the compound, dogs barked. Scar appeared, huge body seeming monstrous as he flew in low over the walls. Folk shrieked in alarm. The big eagle braked with talons forward and wings wide, and whumped down onto one of the big perches. Most flinched, or jumped back. A few, to their credit, did not. Scar dipped his head and turned it upside down to stare at the assembly, making many laugh nervously. Joss walked in under the cruel beak, within reach of the killing talons.

"You'll need the courage to stand here, knowing your eagle can kill you. You'll need the courage to imp her feathers, cope her beak and talons, and a hundred more things besides. You'll need patience to build the trust that jesses the bond between you."

Scar opened his wings like great sails. He flirted. He squawked with that funny chirp the big eagles had, so at odds with their size and magnificent beauty.

"We're bringing a training master down from Clan Hall, by the name of Arda. The senior fawkners are Askar, Verena, and Geddi. Now, Steward Govard will assign work duties and sleeping billets to those of you who wish to try your luck."

He stepped from under Scar's shade, and whistled. The eagle thrust and with a hammer of vast wings beat aloft, caught the wisp of a current, rode it to a better thermal, and shot up into the sky. Govard took his place, and Joss retreated to the marshal's cote. Askar had left for the city, but others filed in with a thousand tasks left undone that needed his sanction. The morning wore on and on. He downed another two cups of rice wine, poured a third, but set it aside untouched.

Siras stuck his head in. "Marshal? The bell rang for meal. Will you want to eat in the hall or have me bring you a tray here?"

"Gods!" He stared longingly at the third cup of wine. "Can someone clear out these writing things? Who is meant to straighten this chamber?"

Siras shrugged, looking embarrassed. "I'm assigned to you for the moment, Marshal."

"Surely you should be patrolling, Siras. Don't you have a young eagle?"

"Fortune is his name. He vanished just after you and the outlanders drove out Yordenas and his crew. The fawkners told me Fortune's overdue for nesting, so they think he's flown to Heaven's Ridge." He wore the optimistic vigor of youth easily, but when he thought of his eagle, the line of his mouth cut downward and his gaze tightened. "Wouldn't I know if he was dead?"

"The fawkners here know their business," said Joss. "Heaven's Ridge it is, and so you're assigned to me for the interim, I take it. No doubt you'd rather be patrolling."

The lad grinned winningly. "They do say it's the best way to learn. That is, to follow around a more experienced reeve." His gaze drifted to the full cup, and flashed away, and Joss wondered if someone had told him to monitor the new marshal's drinking. It was the kind of thing the commander out of Clan Hall would happily command; she had a gift for sticking the salted knife into an already open wound.

He sighed. "I'll go to the hall and eat with everyone else. That's the custom."

At first the senior reeves who were left hesitated to join him at the marshal's table, but he waved them over with a pleasant smile to cover his irritation. In his short tenure as marshal, Yordenas had corrupted the traditions of the reeve hall even down to so small but significant a habit as the marshal taking his meals with the reeves so he could gauge the temper of the hall through hearing the complaints, troubles, gossip, and good tidings that circulated around the tables where everyone ate.

"What's our strength today?" he asked when the senior reeves had settled onto the benches around him with their gruel, salted fish, and soft goat cheese.

Medard was a young man—by Joss's estimation, that meant anyone under thirty—with a mean streak a mey wide. "Get rid of Toban. That hells-rotted vermin walked hand in hand with Yordenas and the worst of his bootlickers, and now he whimpers that he'd no choice but to cozy up to them in order to spy for the sake of the rest of us, those of us who suffered. Or the ones like Dovit and Teren who just disappeared."

"I didn't see you leading the resistance," said Darga, an older woman with a blade of iron in her gaze. "You went running Yordenas's errands up in the Barrens every chance he gave you."

"To stay alive! I tell you, that cursed Horas wanted nothing more than to murder me, with the blessing of his sniveling comrades. He would have done it, too, if I hadn't kept myself away from the hall. I ran no errands for Yordenas!" He was flushed with indignation. "You just ask in some of those villages up in the Barrens, who was it who presided over their assizes when no one else would step in? That was me!"

"Here, now," said Joss. "What's past is past. As it says in the tale, 'no use trying to build with a charred log.' Toban will be given a chance to do the duty assigned him. If he scants it or neglects it, then we'll censure him what the dereliction has earned. We have lost too many reeves as it is, some dead and others flown off."

"Where does a rogue reeve and his eagle make their perch?" Darga asked. "Who will take them in?"

"I don't know," said Joss. "That's why we need Toban under supervision, doing such tasks as he can be trusted with and thereby freeing up other reeves for patrol. We're dealing with a desperate situation in the north. We have to find out what is happening, who these people are who are attacking throughout the Hundred. We have to maintain constant communication with Clan Hall, and the other halls if we can. We must be prepared for anything."

A girl with the slave mark tattooed at her left eye ran into the hall, sweating and out of breath. Every person there hesitated, with spoon half raised to mouth or cup to lip, sentences cut off, laughter choked down. They were like dogs and children who have been kicked once too often: expecting the worst.

She grabbed hold of her braid as for courage, and quick-stepped up to the head table. "Marshal." The squeak of her tiny voice made Medard snort and folk at nearby tables titter.

Joss rose to survey the hall until every voice was stilled and no one moved. The girl wasn't much more than ten or twelve, a fawkner's assistant's slave by the look of her clothing, someone to sweep the floors and fetch and carry.

"Go on," he said, trying out a kindly smile. "Do you have a message for me?"

She whispered in that scrap of a mouse's voice. "An eagle's dropped in. Carrying a—" Her voice faded, and he barely caught the last two words. "—Qin soldier."

"Aui!" He straightened.

"The hells!" muttered Medard. "I don't trust those outlanders with their funny eyes and their strut. I hope you're not going to make us eat with one of them."

Joss laughed, although he wanted to slug the horse's ass. "That's funny, I recall one of the Qin soldiers remarking the same thing. I wonder why that might be."

With a grin to point the sting, he left before Medard could decide whether a retort was worth the risk of insulting his new marshal. Siras scrambled after.

As Joss walked alongside the girl, he considered his position within the reeve hall as an outsider brought in to restore order. He couldn't decide if the night's dance with Verena would earn approval or disdain from the hall at large, and so far no one was ready to challenge him to his face. Medard's carping seemed of a piece with his personality, nothing serious. So far.

Out on the parade ground, a fawkner and his assistant had raced up to take charge of the newly arrived eagle on its high perch. The reeve was unhooking a Qin soldier from the harness that allowed a reeve to haul a passenger hooked in front.

When he saw Joss approaching, the Qin soldier spoke a word to the reeve and then came over. "Marshal Joss!"

"Tohon, greetings of the day to you. I'm surprised a man of your position among the Qin was chosen for messenger duty." He grinned, because the other man was a little white about the eyes, like a panicked horse.

Tohon was a man willing to laugh at himself, as well as being a superb scout. "I was the only one brave enough to volunteer. Hu! A good horse under me is all I need! Not wings. Still." He eyed the eagle, whose feathers were ruffled as it decided whether to settle in or take off. He glanced heavenward, to the eagles circling above. "It's amazing how much you can see from up there."

"True enough. A man of your skills can truly appreciate it. What's your report?"

"We are tracking down the remnants of the Star army as it runs north. We need more reeves out on patrol. They can spot soldiers hiding, or those lagging back. I will tell you this." He scraped a hand through hair mussed by the wind. He was a man somewhat older than Joss, stocky, fit, and as tough as they came. Entirely ruthless, Joss suspected, when it came to the honor and safety of his captain. "There are refugees everywhere. They wander down the roads, they get in our way, they beg for help or throw rocks at us. What do you want us to do with them?" He paused, and when Joss did not reply right away, went on. "We cannot restore order when so many landsmen wander away from their homes. Also, soldiers from the army can walk among the refugees and pretend to be what they are not."

Joss rubbed his forehead. "Eiya! A heavy list of complications. Let me think on it."

Tohon's grin flashed. "My boys need me back by evening. I thought I would piss myself, I was so scared at first, but then I got to staring so much I forgot where I was. Hu! The land looks different from up there."

"That it does. I'll not keep you longer than I have to. Meanwhile, if you go to the eating hall, a reeve named Medard will get you something to eat."

BACK AT THE marshal's cote, Joss sent Siras to fetch Volias. While he waited he downed the third cup of wine, then composed himself with a satisfied smile, having hatched his revenge.

Volias slithered in with a smirk on his ugly face. "Medard's spouting. You gave him a real kick in the ass by sending that Qin bastard in to ask for food. Especially that one fellow, their special scout. That cursed smile of his makes me nervous, and I swear to you he figured your angle the moment he walked into the eating hall, he's that canny, and it amused him to tweak a few ears. He pretended not to know how to use a spoon! I don't think Medard likes you better for making his ears red."

"Medard doesn't need to like me," said Joss equably, just barely able to suppress a smile.

Volias glanced suspiciously around the chamber, which was no neater than it had been this morning. And the wine cup was empty.

Joss slid an unused cup—there were four more on the tray—over to the ceramic bottle. He picked it up and tipped it. There was just enough to fill a new cup. He set down the bottle and pushed the cup toward Volias. Siras, hovering by the door, made a move toward the desk, as if to take the bottle away for refilling, and then with the graceless charm of a young man who hasn't learned to disguise his thoughts, made himself stop and sit down beside the open door. No doubt they had given him instructions: Don't let the marshal drink too much.

"For me?" Volias picked up the cup, held it briefly beneath his nose to take in the aroma, then downed it in a gulp. Setting the cup down, he licked his lips. "Not bad. I trust I'm about to hear something I won't like."

"Sit down." Joss indicated a pillow.

"I'll stand."

A sense of glee filled Joss, but he kept his voice level. "The most significant problem the Qin and the militia have encountered seems to be refugees. There are far too many folk uprooted and displaced by the recent incursion. Disruption will lead to trouble if order isn't restored. I need you to get out there, identify a few collection points, and arrange for the militia and the Qin to send refugees to those points. We'll need a temporary assizes at each one. All these people out wandering on the roads will merely create more trouble."

Volias snorted. "That came out smoothly. Getting your revenge on me?"

Joss felt the sweetness of this petty victory. He smiled, as at a woman he was seeking to win over. "I wish it were so, but the truth is, you've the experience to do a proper job."

"Smile that pretty smile all you want," said Volias, "and I hope you end up sucking on it for a cursed long time, because I know it will turn sour. Still, I admit I'll be glad to be out of this pus-hole."

Siras grunted as though he had swallowed a nasty-tasting grub. Out in the marshal's garden, voices rose as two men laughed at a shared joke; they were coming closer. Siras glanced out the crack in the door that let him see outside, but he shrugged and did not rise, so with no great surprise Joss watched as the door was slid open and Askar walked in with the informality of a man accustomed to his voice being heard.

"Heya!" Askar looked at the table as he wiped his hands on a linen scrap. "Any chance there's wine, Marshal?"

Siras leaped up, grabbed the ceramic bottle, and left.

"No surprise but that the mess this place is in, it builds a strong thirst," remarked the fawkner, ignoring Volias's smirk. "And I do have a tale to tell."

He patted his lips with the cloth, then wiped his brow. "I'm back from Olossi. Cursed merchants and guildsmen running around like ants with their hill smashed. So it happens, Marshal, that I went to the temple of Sapanasu, and explained your situation, and cursed if the hierophant didn't tell me they would be best pleased to send a clerk to be at your disposal."

"Surely that's good news," said Joss.

"Wait for it," murmured Volias, who had the instincts of a stoat when broken eggs are about to be revealed.

"Which they did say they would do as soon as they have cleared all the contract work to do with the burning of the outer city and the tangle of contracts and legal claims that the siege has brought to Olossi's assizes."

"That could take weeks!"

"Sure enough. They were quick about dismissing me, too, leaving me with my hair on fire, I don't mind telling you. I had to go cool my head with a few drinks."

"Too bad the marshal couldn't have joined you," said Volias with a foul smile.

Joss curled a hand into a fist, but he let it go. "Then we'll wait a week, to be polite. I'll go next week myself, once the worst of the disorder in Olossi is put to rest. They'll not be so quick to push aside my request if I come in person."

Volias opened his ugly mouth, no doubt to make a retort about some attractive clerk being taken with Joss's charms, but Askar cut him off in the manner of a man who hasn't heard a thing.

"So there I was, drinking in the Demon's Whip, which is not the kind of establishment you might think it is from the name, and a hierodule walks right up to me and says I'm to come to the delta, to Ushara's temple. She says the Hieros has a message to be delivered personally to a representative of Argent Hall so I can bring it personally to the marshal. Naturally, I went. The Hieros is not a woman to cross, and it seems some crossing has been done. She wants to see you immediately." He scratched his neck.

Volias snorted. "I would think Joss here is one of the foremost devotees of the Merciless One. I can't imagine how he would have come to offend the holy Hieros, as he never seems to turn down any offer made to him."

Cursed if the old fawkner wasn't the finest kind of fellow, able to sail right past that idiot comment by Volias as if it had never been spoken.

"It's about that Devouring girl who tended to Marshal Alyon in his final illness, and then stayed and kept house—or so some claimed—for Marshal Yordenas during his vile tenure. But perhaps you don't know who she is."

"I know who she is." Joss was amazed at how cool his voice sounded. He picked up his cup and shook it, hoping there were a few drops to wet his throat, but he was dry.

"It's like this," said Askar, sketching gestures in the air as folk did to start a tale. "The young woman was sold to the temple as a girl, as happens, and was trained as a hierodule. Then just before the northerners besieged Olossi, her brother bought out her debt. I wasn't told the particulars, but the Hieros was forced to accept the payment he offered and therefore to let the girl walk free. Any fool with eyes could see the transaction made the Hieros unhappy, that her hand had been forced. Now it transpires the payment the brother offered didn't belong to him at all. She had to give it up to its rightful owner, and so she wants her hierodule back. And the brother punished for cheating the temple."

"What's this to do with me?" asked Joss, as his thoughts tumbled. When had he seen her last? About two weeks ago, twenty-four days. She'd been riding away from Olossi with packhorses and gear. By the Herald! What were the last words she'd said to him? *"Had I known you were so full of yourself, I'd have known I need only wait until you fill up with the poison of self-love and strangle on it."*

Desperate, he found the teapot and poured cold ginger tea into his empty wine cup. The powerful flavor—it had been steeping all day—made his eyes sting.

She'd done her part in saving Olossi from the army that had marched out of the north and east. She'd earned the reward she'd asked for: to leave Olo'osson with her brother before the battle was fought. But it seemed she wasn't a free woman after all. It seemed she still had obligations here.

"What's it to do with you?" mused Askar. "That I don't know, Marshal. The Hieros wants to talk to you particularly. She's not so willing to bring the council of Olossi into the matter, maybe due to this outlander, Captain Anji, who stands so high among them now. Anyway, our eagles can search quickly for the woman she's wanting back."

"The Hieros wants me to find her." The taste of ginger still buzzed on Joss's lips.

"There are reeves here who could recognize her," said Askar. "No need for you to go out on patrol."

"I'll go to the temple, and see what the Hieros wants. There's the pursuit of the northerners to keep on eye on, and this matter of refugees. Knowing that the marshal of Argent Hall is himself out in the field overseeing the efforts may help the locals feel something is truly being done for their security. You fawkners and stewards have things well in hand here. I can't do much more with my office until a clerk is released by the temple of Sapanasu." He drained the tea and set down the cup.

Volias stared at him, eyes wrinkled with puzzlement, and it was clear the Snake could not figure out where to prod. It all made too much cursed sense. Joss grinned. Rising, he grabbed a knife, his baton, and after a moment's consideration a pair of loose jesses. Siras came into the room with a full bottle of warmed wine, the smell enough to make you sigh with pleasure.

"Siras, can you see that a light travel pack is made up for me? I'll be out for some days. Volias, too, for that matter."

The young man looked startled. "Yes, Marshal. I'll tell the factors at once."

Joss walked out to the porch, Volias trailing at his heels while Askar remained inside to pour himself a cup. The sun was out, bright with the morning, but the headache that had been trembling above Joss's eyebrows was receding as he walked into the marshal's garden and looked for flowers to present to Verena as a thanking gift. An eagle skimmed low, shadow shuddering along the ground. He bent his head back, shading his eyes to see at least twenty eagles gliding high above: reeveless eagles come to choose a new reeve for themselves. And there were more out there.

Two weeks ago Argent Hall had been ruled by a marshal whose very breath "was like the taint of corruption," as it said in the tale; whose presence had driven reeves out of Argent Hall and halted the return of eagles seeking new reeves. Two weeks ago the town of Olossi had been besieged by an unstoppable army of criminals, bandits, and despicable outlaws who wore cheap tin medallions stamped with a sigil they called the Star of Life.

Now that army was on the run, with a troop of excellent soldiers and their doughty allies in pursuit, and Argent Hall was free of the corrupt marshal and reeves who had tried to poison it. Joss had been perfectly content to remain a simple reeve, as content as he could ever be with the demons of grief and reckless anger that had chased at his heels for half of his life. He hadn't wanted to be named marshal of Argent Hall, but sometimes you didn't get what you wanted.

He thought of the glorious Zubaidit, whom he had met briefly in the course of these troubles. Not that she had necessarily returned his interest. It was difficult to tell with a woman like that, although he was certain she would not be pleased to hear that the Hieros, and the temple, had reclaimed her life and her freedom.

She had walked north with her brother straight toward the advancing army. He did not know if she had even survived.

9

"ARE YOU SURE it's safe to light the lamp?" Keshad asked his sister.

"That's the third time you've asked. If I didn't think so, I wouldn't have lit it."

Keshad stood beside a stone pillar, the only one left standing atop Candra Hill. In ancient days, according to the tale, the beacon fire had roared in times of trouble, but all that remained of the old tower complex was fallen walls and the bases of seven other pillars. From the treeless height, he stared over the town of Candra Crossing. The main district massed in the center; homes, shops, gardens, temples, fields, and refuse pits stretched east and west along West Track until woodland took over. The River Hayi widened here to make a good ferry crossing in the rainy season and a passable if dangerous ford in the dry season.

He had already seen everything he needed to know, but he could not stop looking because the sight so unnerved him: The town was deserted. Emptied. Swept clean.

"I know the main force of the army passed us already, but what if there are outriders coming up behind? Sweeping for stragglers? Looking for more villages and hamlets to burn? Women to rape? Children to bind into slavery? Hands to hack off?"

"Kesh! Get hold of yourself!"

He sucked in a breath and let it out, shaking.

"There's no one here," she went on. "The townsfolk have fled. The army is marching on Olossi. We're safe enough tonight to light a fire. Do you trust my judgment, or not?"

He shuddered as he turned away from the view. Someone could easily creep up the hill's steep slope under cover of night. Maybe it was best to get killed from behind, not knowing death was stalking you. That way it would come as a surprise. No fear and no anticipation meant no pain, surely. But it was already too late. As he looked across the ruins of the old tower complex at his sister, he was already afraid.

A single lamp illuminated the tumbled stone walls and dusty ground. Most likely, the folk in Candra Crossing had experienced relative peace for so long that no one had thought they needed to repair the beacon tower. No one had thought an army would appear from the east, devastating all the towns and villages in its path.

In the remains of the ancient tower, Zubaidit had discovered a fire pit, sheltered from the wind, that had seen recent use. A stone slab protected an old cistern, which was half full of reasonably fresh rainwater. It was a good place to camp.

As he came up beside her, the fire she was making kindled and caught. She sat back on her heels and waited until the fire took hold, then pinched out the lamp and set it beside the saddle bags. The two ginny lizards, Magic and Mischief, were dozing side by side on a strip of cloth. Bai grabbed the cloth by two corners and gently pulled them closer to the heat of the fire. The ginnies stirred, giving Kesh indignant looks as if to accuse *him* of disturbing their rest, but settled as Bai scritched them. The three horses were already watered, fed, and hobbled for the night, penned within the higher walls of an adjoining chamber, heard and smelled but not seen. Their presence, at least, was a comfort.

Bai unfolded a small iron tripod and hung a pot over the fire. Firelight softened her face. "I'm brewing khaif," she said, without turning to note that he had come up behind her, "so stop complaining."

When he did not reply, she rose easily; every movement she made seemed effortless and powerful. Beside her, he felt clumsy and weak.

"Kesh, what is bothering you? You've scarcely spoken ten words together since we escaped that skirmish on West Track days ago. And those words were mostly to question my judgment and, if I must say so, to whine. Just as you're doing now. This isn't the big brother who gave me courage, who pulled me out of the water when I fell in over my head. We're free, because of you. Free to walk where we want, free to start a new life."

"Unless the Hieros sends someone after us, hoping to get you back into the temple's clutches. Unless Master Feden concocts an excuse to question my debt payment and tries to chain me back into his service. We made them our enemies when we bought our freedom because they didn't want us to go."

"Are you still afraid?"

"Yes."

"Of what?"

Afraid of a little sister who had grown up to become someone more frightening than death.

"Nothing." He picked his way around the ruined wall, felt for the fallen gate, and sat down on the stones blocking the passage. Past this gate stood the horses, drowsy and calm. Their big bodies soothed him. Horses liked familiarity. They liked to know where they fit in. But Bai, born in the Year of the Wolf, had become a wolf in truth: Everyone knew that wolves will gladly tear apart a man even if they aren't hungry. You never knew when they might strike.

For a short while there was silence, then he heard her moving about.

"I'm going to make the prayers for a safe night. You want to help me?"

"No." He touched the blessing bowl that hung at his belt, but he did not pour water into it and murmur the proper blessings for day's end. At the edge of the firelight, she stamped the rhythm with her feet and sketched the story with hands and body as she sang.

> *"The Four Mothers raised the heavens and shaped the earth,*
> *and then they slumbered.*
> *and then they grew large.*

and then they gave birth.
The seven gods are Their children,
who brought order into the world.
who built the gates that order the world.
who sawed the wood and split the wood and planed the wood and carved the
wood and dug the iron and forged the iron and hammered the tools and put
piece into piece to form the arch and gathered the harvest and bled the sap
and colored the resin and coated the lacquer and sprinkled the dust of gold
and the dust of silver into the base and polished the surface.
and thus Shining Gate rose and Shadow Gate rose.
and thus day and night gave order to the world.
Look! Look! Look at the horizon! A voice calls.
Shadow Gate rises.
Night is come."

This late in the year it was still hot even with the sun set and the night rains coming in. Her skin glistened. She brushed moisture from her eyes and swiped the back of her neck. She glanced toward the gate, where the shadows hid him.

"You don't pray with me. You carry one of the bowls that the slaves of the southern god carry. It imprisons their souls. But you don't pray their prayers, either."

Uncomfortable, he shifted to ease the pressure on his seat.

"If you truly believe in the southern god, Kesh, then you should pray to him. If you don't, you shouldn't carry that bowl."

She strolled back to the fire, poured a sludgy mix of khaif and rice porridge into their cup, and held it out to coax him out of the darkness. "Aren't you hungry?"

He slouched into the light. She waited until he took the cup, then spooned gruel for herself straight out of the pot. They ate in silence. The khaif went straight to his head. As always, the buzz made him feel reckless and irritable.

"Why should I pray to any gods? What have the gods ever done for me?"

"Sheh! For shame! How could we be here, without the gods? How could anything have come into existence? The gods ordered the world. But it is our prayers that hold it together."

"You have to believe that because you served in the temple."

She lifted the spoon to her lips, sucked in the gruel, then licked clean the spoon. All the while she stared at him. He didn't like that look.

"What are you accusing me of?" he demanded.

She gestured, and he handed her the cup. She measured out another portion and returned the cup to him. Then she removed the pot from the tripod and scraped out the leavings.

"Well? Say something!"

She finished eating and set the spoon into the pot with a gesture of closing. "We'll ford the river at first light."

BEFORE DAWN, THEY led the horses down the path into Candra Crossing. The ginnies, riding on Bai's shoulders, were drowsy and irritable. In the heavens, the boldest stars still shone, while a blush lightened the east. Birds twittered. No wind stirred. It was already hot.

They approached along a dirt path that ran parallel to West Track behind the riverside row of buildings. Trampled fields marked where a large host had camped, and animals had grazed. The army had left shallow ditches stinking with refuse and offal, still swarming with bugs many days later.

A few buildings had burned down. The doors of the temple dedicated to Sapanasu had been smashed, and the counting house was singed. The compound dedicated to Kotaru, the Thunderer, was stripped of weapons and stores. Bai paused outside the gates of the temple to the Merciless One, carved with Her sigil: the bloom of the lotus pierced by a dagger. Like the rest of the town, the Devourer's temple was abandoned. When Keshad peeked through the half-open gates, he saw only dust and dead plants, and a solitary stone bench where a single passionflower had fallen, its color withered to a pale pink.

Was that a noise? The scuff of a foot? A voice, speaking soft words?

Magic lifted his crest and hissed.

"Keep moving," whispered Bai.

Kesh kept glancing back over his shoulder as they walked away. Surely those noises had only been rats scrabbling through the leavings or birds fluttering in the abandoned buildings. There was no one here. No one at all. The army had poured past Candra Crossing, and the town's population had drained away after them, dead or fled or taken captive.

"Careful, now," said Bai as they approached the River Hayi. "Listen."

A shallow river sings with a different voice from one at flood: water babbles over smoothed rocks along the bank, purls above barely submerged sandbars, shushes through a backwater of reeds. Through the gaps between houses he saw the ford. Where the water rippled and lightened, poles had been hammered into sandbars that almost breached the surface. Where the current dug deep, the water ran dark and swift, and from this bank that gap looked wide and dangerous.

"I wonder where they came from," said Bai as the ginnies bobbed their heads.

Four people stood on the bank, two adults and two children.

Kesh choked down a yelp. "You said no one was here."

"Those are refugees. I'm surprised they're not running. Here, now, fetch those skiffs pulled up on the bank. I'll take your leads."

"What do we need a skiff for?"

"Those children can't swim the ford."

"We're not going to slow ourselves down by *helping* them?"

Bai called. "Do you need our help getting over the water?"

She strode away. With a curse he trudged over to the skiffs. Most were dragged well up onto the shore, but two had been shifted down to the waterline and left there, sterns rocking. He checked around nervously but saw no sign of a struggle, of any poor townsman struck down while attempting to escape, of goods and possessions abandoned midflight. He grabbed the towline of the smaller skiff and shoved it around until the water lifted it; here in the shallows the current wasn't overwhelming and he could haul it upstream toward Bai.

What was she about? She had halted a prudent distance from the ragged group: two young women not much more than girls with dusty clothes and hair matted with leaf and twig, and a pair of grubby children. The littlest, likely a girl, was very young, old enough to walk but small enough to need carrying most of the time.

The young boy's piping voice raised as Kesh splashed within hearing. "They can't be thieves," he was saying indignantly to his elders, "for no person can steal the holy ones. She must be a holy one, too. Maybe she ran away from a temple to get away from the bad people."

Bai laughed, rubbing the jowls of the ginnies. "The offer is sincerely meant, but I can see you've had trouble, so if you've a wish for us to move on without bothering you, we'll just ford the river and leave you be."

"Where are you going?" demanded the elder of the young women.

Magic lifted his crest and opened his mouth to show teeth, a mild warning. Bai's smile sharpened, just like the ginny's. "We're going away from the place we came from. Where are you going?"

"Our village was burned down. We'll take your help. I'm called Nallo. These are my children: Avisha, Jerad, and Zianna."

"We'll take your help with *thanks*," said the pretty one, Avisha, as she flashed a hesitant smile.

"Can I touch them?" asked the boy.

Mischief tilted her head and gave the boy a keen and almost flirtatious look. There was no accounting for the taste of those animals.

"These two are Magic and Mischief, and yes, if you move slowly, and follow my directions, you can greet them. I'm Zubaidit. This is my brother Keshad. Kesh, get the boat in and load it. Put our gear in as well. The horses will do better without the burden."

"Those can't be your children," said Kesh to the elder girl. "You're far too young."

"I'm the second wife. Their mother's dead three years past. Died bearing Zianna, or how else do you suppose the poor little girl got such a name?"

She was the kind who bit first!

"Where's your husband, then?" he retorted.

As soon as he uttered the words, he felt shame. Avisha looked at the ground, a spasm of grief twisting her expression. The cursed ginnies eyed him, as if saying *Kesh, you stupid idiot! Change the subject, already!*

The boy said, "I want to touch the holy ones!"

"Keep your mouth shut!" snapped Nallo. She flicked a glance at Bai and then, oddly, flushed. "Here, now, Jer," she added in a voice meant to be kindlier but which only sounded curt, "just get in the boat."

Cursing the wasted time and his own stupid mouth and the pointless bother of stopping to assist useless refugees who were no doubt doomed despite whatever help they might receive, Kesh untied the others' gear and settled it in the skiff. Their possessions seemed to consist of an impressive coil of heavy-duty rope and a single large bronze washtub carefully packed with scraps and oddments: cloth tied around a scant tey of rice; a few scraggly bundles of herbs; a stand for making cord; a pot of sesame oil; an iron knife with a charred wood handle; an iron cooking pot; and two whole leather bottles grimy with ash. He peeked inside a singed leather case to find, within, a dozen untouched first-quality silk braids, colorful work suitable for fancy cloaks, festival jackets, or temple banners.

In they all must go. The little girl woke and cried, then subsided. The boy trembled with excitement. Bai peeled the ginny lizards off her shoulders, introduced them to the boy, and draped them over the mound of gear. They chirped, and Jerad, in imitation, chirped back. Zianna scooted to the bow of the boat as far away from the ginnies as possible; she sucked on her thumb, her gaze troubled.

Bai said, "We'll need to string rope along those poles to give us a handhold. That's what they're there for. The water's come up some with the rains, I'm guessing, so with everything we've got to get across I want that rope for a safe hold."

"I can swim," said Nallo. "I'll help you. We've got enough rope to string across the ford."

Bai grinned at her. "Good. You can strip down if you don't want your taloos wet. Although it'll dry quickly in this heat. And you might be cooler afterward for leaving it on."

The young woman blushed again. "I'll leave it on. Vish, put my pack in the boat."

"You're limping. What happened?" Bai asked.

"Turned my ankle on the road."

Bai glanced at Kesh and shrugged. She waded into the river with the coiled rope. Reaching the first pole, she tied a loop and placed the line. The sun's light flooded the horizon as true dawn raised. The two women plunged into the deeper current.

Avisha sidled over to Kesh, where he waited beside the horses. "Do you know who those soldiers were? Those locusts swarmed into the village one morning. We were lucky to escape."

"They marched out of the north, that's all I know," he said reluctantly, not wanting to be drawn into this conversation.

"We hid in the woods." She hesitated, as if waiting for him to reply, and then went on. "Our house was burned down. My father's dead. We're going to the Soha Hills where Nallo's family comes from, only she doesn't think they'll want to take us in because they never liked her much anyway because of her bad temper. She does have a bad temper, not like my dad. He never loses his temper. He's the kindest and gentlest man. Everyone said that's the only way he could stand her, Nallo that is, my mother talked a lot but she never lost her temper at anyone."

"You'll want to consider how much you tell to strangers, who might not have your best interests at heart. That army was taking slaves. You're a good age for it. Pretty enough to be of interest. Worth a few cheyt on the open market."

She stepped away, then looked at the little children, measuring her chances to run. "Eiya! My sister was a hierodule. She'd never go against the law."

A woman shrieked. In the deepest part of the river, where the current ran hard in chest-high water, Nallo had lost her footing.

"Nallo!" screamed Avisha. She choked out wordless yelps and started to cry.

"Here, now. Bai's got her."

Bai hauled her into shallower water. Nallo sputtered, coughed, spat, and both women began laughing. Bai looped the rope around the farthest pole and with Nallo's help tugged it taut, then tied it off. Holding on to the rope, they crossed back.

"That's good-quality rope," Bai was saying as they dripped up onto the pebbled shore beside Kesh and Avisha.

"My husband made it," said Nallo with evident pride. "He only made best-quality rope, and for the temples, too, and for festival banners and all manner of ornament. Everyone said he was the best ropemaker on West Track."

"I was so scared when you slipped," said Avisha in a gulping wet voice. "I thought we lost you."

"Well, you didn't!"

There was the temper. It made even Kesh stand up straight.

Bai said sweetly, "Kesh, you swim the horses across. I'll take the boat. You two follow. Best we get moving in case anyone else is on the road."

The crossing went swiftly and without incident.

While Kesh slung panniers and bags back on the packhorse, Bai and Nallo waded back into the river to recover the precious rope. On this side of the river, someone had abandoned a pile of refuse since battered by wind and rain. Avisha ripped through the pile, but except for sodden cloth and a bronze bucket she found nothing worth keeping.

"Where are you two going now?" Avisha asked as she rolled up the cloth.

He shrugged, hoping she would leave him alone.

"It's true what you said," she added with a catch in her voice. "We walked a long way to get to Candra Crossing. It's the only place you can cross the river for days and days. We had to hide a few days after we left the village because there was a group of soldiers, marching Hornward on West Track, back the way they'd come. They had tens of children roped up like beasts. Eiya! Just like beasts." She grimaced, wiped her eyes and her nose, and sucked in breath to keep talking. "We could see from where we were hiding. There was one child who stumbled and another child who helped him up, and then the soldiers come and beat that child to death, the one who helped."

Kesh had seen such a company of children being marched away as slaves, and he had no desire to relive the memory. If only she would stop talking!

"Just for helping, you know. Just for helping." She began to rock back and forth like a sweet-smoke addict.

Kesh grabbed her wrist. "Listen! If you want to survive, you have to keep walking. There's nothing any of us can do for those children."

A glance from fine, tear-filled eyes could make the world bright, if you were the kind of man who liked pretty girls made tense by a touch of fear. He'd worked as a debt slave in Master Feden's house for twelve years, and he'd seen men, and women, who did enjoy forcing sex on reluctant slaves. He'd hated them especially. He released her arm as though it burned him and turned away, but the cursed girl would keep talking.

"I thought Nallo was going to abandon us, too, when we got back to the village to find my father dead and everyone dead—you know Dad and the rest, they ran out with their shovels and hoes to try to hold off the soldiers so us children could run away. Afterward, the landlady wanted to sell us as slaves. Nallo wouldn't let her."

"Can you tighten that rope for me?" he asked, to shut her up. "We need to get moving."

Bai splashed through the shallows and jogged up the slope, Nallo limping behind. He recognized the grim look on Bai's face.

"Get moving." She slung the rope over the packhorse's neck, fixing it to the panniers. "Kesh, put the girl in the basket, and tie the boy up on the mare. Nallo, you'll ride the gelding. Avisha, you'll either have to leave the washtub or carry it at the pace we'll set. There's something coming into town. I want everyone out of sight before it gets to the riverbank and spots us. Move! I'll meet you." She settled the ginnies into the sling tied to her saddle.

Nallo mounted awkwardly, stomach over the saddle, then pumping her legs until she got the left one over. Thanks to the gods, the horse remained quiescent despite her obvious lack of experience. Swearing under his breath, Keshad lashed the horses into a line and set out at a brisk pace. Avisha hurried after, lugging the washtub. On the mare, Jerad was grinning at the ginnies.

As Bai crossed the river back into town, all Kesh could think of was his old friends Rabbit, Twist, and Pehar, the worst companions a man might fear to have. He hoped they were all dead now, but he was sure they weren't. How anyone could defeat the army that had been descending on Olossi he couldn't imagine, which was why he and Bai had left and more honorable or foolhardy people had stayed behind. Like she was doing now. The road cut into the woodland, and he lost sight of the far shore.

"What about your sister?" said Avisha with an anxious look.

"Shut up. Keep moving."

No one spoke as they strode along. For the longest time he just walked, thoughts shut down. The horses were obedient, the children quiet, the girl steady.

After a long time he heard hurried footsteps pattering on the earth, coming up from behind. He drew his sword. Avisha started to cry.

But it was Bai, loping like a wolf chasing prey. She was wiping her hands on a scrap of cloth, and although she threw away the cloth before she reached them, he was sure it was bloody.

10

Nallo knew the tales, how the persistent, fortunate, clever child fought past obstacles and won through to a good life in the end. But she'd never believed in them. She'd watched three older brothers die, too weakened with diarrhea to do more than stare mutely at those tending them. She'd been sent to Old Cross market with her uncle and littlest niece, both girls meant for debt slavery, but although her little niece's labor had been bought up quickly, not one soul had bid on Nallo. Too thin, too sour-looking, too tall, too old, not pretty. There were plenty of desperate folk on the roads, farms failing, laborers out of work, too many children and not enough food to feed them all. The folk who could afford to purchase the labor of those unfortunate enough to be selling had the leisure to be choosy.

Her husband had made the contract with her family through intermediaries. He'd needed a wife quickly; there was a newborn to care for. Everyone had told her she was fortunate. It was the best life she could hope for.

He'd been a gentle man, patient and kind. Everyone in the village had said so, reminding her again and again that she was fortunate. And it was even true.

She wasn't gentle or kind or patient. Everyone had said so, and it was true.

She had no obligation to stay with Avisha and the little ones. But she had nowhere else to go. That had been her husband's last, if unwilling, gift to her: a reason to keep going and not just walk into the hills, lie down in the grass, and die.

THEY WALKED FOR half the morning, and at length halted to let the horses water at a pond ringed by mulberry trees. The children peed, and got a scrap to eat and a swallow of old wine. Then they walked on.

Avisha moved up to walk alongside the man. She tried to draw him into conversation. When he wouldn't talk about himself, she talked about her old life, about her father, about her mother; she chattered about plants and their uses.

"She's a pretty girl," remarked Zubaidit over her shoulder, addressing Nallo. "She seems knowledgeable about herbs."

"Her mother taught her."

"That's a good piece of knowledge to have. She's old enough to think of marriage."

"We're too poor to think of marriage. We've no kin. We've nothing."

"Perhaps you can find a man willing to look no farther than youth and herbcraft."

"One who is desperate enough to take on a destitute girl with no marriage portion and no kinfolk to sweeten the net of alliance? It was hard enough for my family to find a man willing to marry *me.*"

"Why is that?"

"I've got a bad temper. I say things people don't want to hear. I ought not to, but they just slip out."

"Which god took your apprenticeship service?"

"The Thunderer. After my year was up, my kinfolk asked if the temple would take me on for an eight-year service, but they didn't want me either." She hated the way she sounded, like a child whining for a stalk of sweet-cane to suck on. "Never mind. It wasn't so bad. My husband treated me well. The work wasn't so hard. We didn't go hungry."

It had been a good life. She saw that, now it was gone.

"It's a hard path to walk, away from what you can never go back to."

"Is that how it is for you and your brother?" Nallo asked boldly. Since she could not see the hierodule's face, she watched her walk instead.

The woman wore a plain linen exercise kilt, tied with a cord at the waist, and a tight sleeveless vest. Her limbs, thus displayed, were smooth, sculpted, and strong. "I'm not sure where this path will lead us."

They hit a steep stretch, too difficult to climb while talking, and afterward Nallo could think of no way to resume the conversation. Up ahead, Avisha had started in again.

Late in the afternoon they halted for the night near the dregs of a stream. They shared out a leather bottle full of vinegary mead and finished off a sack of dry rice cake and mushy radish, although these scraps could not cut the hollow feeling in their stomachs. Avisha got the little ones settled to sleep while Nallo went to wash in the stream, to take a little privacy to do her business. Coming back, walking slowly because her ankle ached, she came up behind the sister and brother where they had moved away from the camp to talk between themselves. She paused in the cover of a stand of pipe-brush, too embarrassed to reveal herself.

"What is wrong with that girl? She won't shut up."

"You'd be more agreeable if you'd look at people with a little compassion. I worry about you, Kesh. You aren't happy."

"We were slaves for twelve years! In what manner am I meant to be *happy*? Or does the goddess have an answer for that as well?"

"The gods have an answer, if you take the time to pray."

"I pray that we get rid of them. We're moving so slowly, Bai. Why did we have to bring them with us?"

"We had to get everyone out of sight, because if that lot marching into town saw these on the far shore they might think to cross and grab them, and then they'd find sign of our passage. I don't want any trouble."

"We've got trouble enough with these refugees. How long will you let them burden us? Or do you mean to hand out our coin to them, too, until we have nothing left for ourselves?"

She chortled, but it was a bitter laugh. "We have plenty of coin, Kesh."

"Stolen from Master Feden's chest! I'd have liked to have seen when you grabbed those strings right in front of his fat face. Aui! What do you think is happening in Olossi?"

"Captain Anji has found a way to defeat them, or he's dead and Olossi is overrun."

"Then best we not drag our feet helping every sad traveler on the road. We can't help everyone."

"We can help these."

"Nallo?" Along the track from camp came Avisha.

The brother muttered a complaint under his breath while the sister laughed softly and said, "I'm going to make the prayers for a safe night. Do you want to help me?"

"No. I'll go take a piss."

"As you wish."

"Aui!" That was Avisha, meeting them on the trail. "I didn't see you here. Did you see Nallo?"

Nallo rattled the pipe-brush, then moved into view as if she'd just come walking that way. Keshad pushed past her. Nallo noticed what had been staring her in the face all along: the man had the debt mark tattooed at the outer curve of his left eye. Twelve years a slave. He had said so himself. He wore no bronze bracelets to mark his status as a slave, but those were easy to take off. Zubaidit's face was unmarked, but that wasn't unusual in those dedicated to the gods, which was a different form of servitude and obligation than that taken on by those who sold the rights to their labor or their debt on the auction square.

They were runaway slaves, who had brazenly raided the master's strongbox. Wasn't there a penalty, assessed at any assizes court, for those who aided or abetted slaves running away from their contract?

At dawn, Nallo took the children and their few possessions aside. She saw, in the man's face, a rush of relief at the thought of being rid of them, and she supposed that Zubaidit's complicated frown disguised relief as well.

"Our thanks for your aid," Nallo said politely. "May the gods watch over you and grant you the same courtesy you have shown others."

Zubaidit snorted, and her brother looked alarmed.

"Can't we go on this way together, Nallo?" Avisha asked plaintively.

"No. We'd just slow them down."

"Let's go." Keshad was already looking up the path as the sun rose.

The hierodule's gaze was a terrible thing; she might see anything with such a stare, that pierced right through you as though she could read your every thought just in the way you scratched a bug's bite in the crook of your elbow because you were uncomfortable and embarrassed. How could you ask two armed and strong adults if they were runaway slaves? It was better to remain silent.

Zubaidit nodded. "It's true we'll make better time not burdened with you. Yet are you sure?"

"We've been traveling on our own for days now," snapped Nallo. "I know the Soha Hills well enough. There won't be many folk traveling, if there are any traveling at all in days like these with so much trouble on the road. We can take care of ourselves."

The brother left without more than a barely polite fare-thee-well. The hierodule offered them a pouch of food, another bottle of old wine, and five precious leya, just as if they were beggars, which they were, so Nallo took it and with thanks. Jerad wept to see the ginnies go.

As soon as the horses were out of sight, Avisha burst into tears. "Why did you make them leave?"

"They're runaway slaves, and thieves in the bargain. We'll get fined if we're caught with them, and that will throw us right into slavery. Is that what you want?"

The little ones hunkered away from her temper.

Avisha sniveled, wiping her eyes, but the tears kept flowing. "Eiya! The slave mark on his face. How he was so anxious to get on. He wouldn't talk to me. You're so clever for seeing it, Nallo."

But she wasn't clever. She was angry, and embarrassed, and she couldn't stop thinking about that woman. She couldn't stop hating herself for never having once in three years as a wife looked over her kind and patient husband with the kind of unexpected and thrilling desire that had hit her smack between the eyes the moment she had seen Zubaidit. Who had treated her with respect and courtesy, but nothing more. Nothing more.

"Where are we going, Nallo?" Jerad asked.

She swung Zianna up onto a hip. "Just walk!"

*   *   *

THAT WAS THE day everything began to go wrong. Not that it hadn't gone all wrong from the day the army marched into the village and killed her father, but Avisha had begun to hope they would escape, find a safe refuge, and make a new life. Keshad and his sister had appeared, as though sent by the gods, to help them across the river. He was so handsome! But not very talkative. Burdened with doubts and concerns, most likely. Why should he want to hear the chatter of a dreary, irritating girl who couldn't keep her mouth shut? Avisha was so ashamed of herself, knowing she had prattled on trying to impress him, when after all a man as goodlooking and intense and experienced as him couldn't possibly be interested in her.

Then Nallo realized that their two companions were runaway slaves, and thieves in the bargain, and therefore dangerous to travel with. Isn't that what Papa always said, when he scolded her for being vain of her looks? A sincere heart is better than a pretty face.

So they set off on their own, again, tramping along the road at a snail's pace with Jerad sullen because the ginnies were gone. The wind picked up, and it started to rain, a big gusting downpour that soaked them through. It came down so hard and fast that the road churned with muddy water, but they had to keep going. They walked in the rain all morning, and rested where they could find shelter. Midday the rain slackened and ceased. Soon after, the sun came out between shredded clouds, and they walked in the steaming heat until Jerad could not go one step farther.

Ahead lay a village, surrounded with a fence to keep livestock in and wild beasts out. Stands of fruit and pipe and mulberry trees broke the expanse of field, and in the distance rose denser woodland not yet cleared.

It had been so many days since they had seen folk walking about their daily lives that it seemed strange to Avisha to see it now. Men sowed rice in seedling fields. Younger men guided their draft animals, plowing furrows through the larger fields, mud and water splattering until they and the beasts were coated. A pair of young women stood on the raised earth that separated the fields, holding trays with drink and food for the working men; they were chatting and laughing as though they'd no idea what had happened to Candra Crossing not three days' walk away. Seeing the refugees, the young women splashed away into the cover of trees.

Two young men hurried over along the raised berms and confronted the travelers with spears and sour faces. The way they looked Avisha up and down made her shiver, for it wasn't a nice look at all but an ugly one. "You're not allowed to stop here."

Nallo placed herself between the armed men and the children. "We can offer what news we have, of Candra Crossing, in exchange for a meal of rice."

"We already know about Candra Crossing. You're not the first travelers to come through. So you just move on."

"The gods will curse you!" Nallo spat on the dirt.

The brawnier of the young men pushed the haft of his spear right up against Nallo's chest. "Don't threaten us. Take your ugly face and your pretty sister and your little brats and get moving before we make you wish you'd never walked this way. We'll protect ourselves."

Nallo grabbed Zianna and swung her up onto her hip. "The gods will judge the worth of your hospitality. Come, children. No need to linger here. It's a gods-cursed place, as they'll soon discover."

Her stare sent the men back a few steps, and Nallo walked past, not looking to see if Avisha and Jerad were following. Those hostile stares scared Avisha, but she could only walk so fast and keep the washtub balanced on her head, and anyway Jerad was lagging. But he stuck it out, and Nallo—who wasn't as oblivious as she sometimes seemed—called a halt as soon as they discovered a Ladytree on the far side of the village, just off the road. Under its spreading branches they found shelter from the drizzle. In a recently used fire pit, Nallo got sticks smoldering and cooked up two handfuls of rice, not enough to fill their stomachs but enough to cut the ache of hunger.

"I wonder what happened to Keshad and his sister," Avisha said when the little ones were asleep, wrapped up in the blanket, and she and Nallo lay on the ground sharing the cloak against the damp night air. "They should have been ahead of us on the road."

"They've gone off the road. There could be a dozen trails, a hundred, leading through the fields and woods. We should take to the fields, too. If an army marches, it'll be on this road."

"You said we'd be safer going this way than east on West Track and walking into Sohayil by the Passage."

"Safer. Not safe. I'll decide in the morning."

In the morning, Nallo identified a trail that ran more or less parallel to the main path, seen as a berm beyond fields and coppices. Walking on this trail, they spotted clusters of buildings that marked hamlets or villages, but they kept their distance.

That night, they camped under a scrawny Ladytree growing at the edge of a meadow. Its canopy was dying. Bugs ate at them all night, a cloud of annoyance. A nightjar clicked, so that she'd start dropping off to sleep and then startle awake. Late in the night it rained again, dripping through the branches.

By morning, Zianna was sniffling. They slogged through intermittent rains all day, drying out when the sun shone.

By the next morning, Zianna had started to cough. Although Nallo explained that they had not yet begun to climb into the Soha Hills, this was rugged country, sparsely inhabited, and rough walking on a path that sometimes was smooth and easy and sometimes little more than a gouge barely wide enough for one foot. Several times Nallo stopped and, pointing aloft, marked the passage of an eagle high overhead.

After some days they reached the outlying hills and began climbing. As they toiled up the first slope, slick from the rains, Avisha slipped. She lost her hold on the washtub, and it slid downslope and spilled its contents every which way on the wet hillside among trees and scrub.

She scrambled down through thornbush and prickleberry to retrieve their belongings and the precious bag of rice while the others huddled under such cover as the woodland gave them. Her father's cordmaking stand—the one special thing of his she had salvaged from the ruins of the house—had broken in half. The fire had weakened it, and the fall snapped it. Just like her life. She sobbed, holding the pieces. Papa had handled this so gently, and now it was gone. It couldn't be fixed. None of it could be fixed.

"Vish! What are you doing down there?"

Of course Nallo had no idea how sharp her voice sounded.

"Almost got everything," she called back.

A length of bright orange cloth, not theirs, had gotten stuck among prickleberry. She pushed over to it, careful of thorns. The cloth was stained, wet, torn. Below, tumbled into the bush, lay the corpse of a young woman, freshly killed: blood stained her thighs and belly. She'd been raped and had her abdomen cut open in a jagged line.

"Vish?" Nallo's voice drifted down to her, but she might have been a hundred mey away for all it mattered.

Flies crawled in and out of the gaping mouth. Her fingers had been eaten away, and her eyes were gone, two empty pits. Abruptly, her belly stirred, the skin rippling. A bloody face popped out of the cut. Black eyes stared at Avisha. She shrieked. A small animal darted away into the brush.

"Vish!"

Her throat burned. Her eyes stung. She backed up, tripped, fell rump-first into a tangle of bushes. Her hands brushed a trailing branch of prickleberry, and blood bubbled up on her palm. Scrambling back, she found the washtub. But as she climbed the slope, dragging the washtub behind her, she kept losing her footing and slipping backward. The ghost of that dead woman was trying to drag her into the shadows. Claws bound her ankle, tugging at her. She whimpered, but it was only a vine caught around her foot. She wrenched the vine loose, and climbed. After an eternity she reached the road. She was scratched, soaked, caked in dirt. Blood dripped from her palm. She wiped her hair out of her eyes.

Nallo wasn't even looking at her. *She* was staring up at the sky, mouth open, rain washing her face.

A huge eagle swooped low over them. Avisha ducked. Jerad wailed. Zianna hid her face in her hands, sobbing. The creature banked around and, flaring its wings, struggled to a landing in an open space above them, beside the path. It stared at them with eyes as big as plates and a beak large enough to rip open a poor girl's belly so every manner of vermin could crawl in.

"Is that blood on its feathers?" said Nallo. "Look how it's holding its wing. It's injured."

"Look at that beak!" sobbed Avisha. "Those talons! We can't walk past it."

"Have you ever heard of a reeve's eagle killing a human being?" Nallo picked up Zianna and began walking up the path.

"Nallo! I'm afraid!"

Jerad burst into tears. "Won't go. It's so big!"

"Stop it, Vish! Look how you've got him blubbing! That bird isn't going to hurt us."

That bird was staring at them, deciding which was plumpest. "How can you know?"

"Stop shrieking! Look how it gets your brother and sister scared."

"C-Can't we just wait until it leaves?"

"No! No! No! No! No!" sobbed Zi.

Nallo set the little girl down roughly. "We'll stand here in the rain until the cursed bird flies off and we'll all be dead by then anyway." Abruptly, horrifyingly, Nallo, too, began to cry.

The rain pattered over them as they wept. Avisha's clothes were wet, her feet were cold, and her face was muddy, smeared with dirt. Her hand hurt, and that girl down there was dead and mutilated and abandoned, just like she was going to be. Everything was the worst it could be. She wished Papa was alive because he could have fixed it all but he was dead. Why did Papa have to die? Why did everything go so bad? Why couldn't they just all be at home in their good little house all dry, sitting on the porch like they always did when the first rains came and watching the wet over the other houses and over the fields and woodland and sipping on the last of the year's rice wine that Papa always held over for the first day of the rains and the promise of a new year? Now there would be a new year without Papa in it, nothing good at all, everything torn and broken and bloody and hopeless.

She kept gulping, trying to stop crying, but the sobs kept bursting out, shaking her whole body. It wasn't fair. It wasn't fair. It wasn't fair. Why did any of it have to happen?

The eagle chirped, a delicate call at odds with its size.

Jolted out of her misery, Avisha turned to look. The eagle flapped, rose awkwardly, then dove along the path, talons raised and ready to hook them.

Avisha shrieked. She grabbed Jerad and threw herself flat, Jerad squirming beneath her. The heat and roil of the eagle passed over her body.

Below, men yelled out in a panic. Then they screamed.

She lifted her head to see men scattering away from the eagle's attack. The eagle had plunged into a group coming up the path. With talon and beak it slashed and cut and tore.

Avisha pushed Jerad's head down. "Don't look!"

Nallo cried out. "Vish! Those are soldiers like the ones who burned the village. Run!"

Like the ones who burned the village.

Like the ones who could rape and murder a girl in the woods.

She bolted, slipping, cursing, weeping with terror, sprinting into the woods where she might hope to hide. Glancing back, she saw the batting wings, the slash of talons, the flash of gold that ringed its beak. The men's screams drove her on. She ran with trees clawing at her, until her sides heaved and she fell to her knees spitting and retching. Her chest was aflame.

Nallo leaned on a tree, gulping air, holding Zianna. "Where's Jerad?"

Avisha lifted her head. Jerad was not with them.

The ground dropped out from under her. She fell, dizzy, tumbling, helpless. But she was kneeling in the dirt with rain drizzling over her. She hadn't fallen at all.

Nallo said, *"Did you leave him behind?"*

Between one ragged breath and the next, the rain ceased falling.

Jerad wasn't with them. She had left him behind.

11

Someone had to go back and find Jerad. So Nallo didn't wait. She pried Zianna off her body as the girl whimpered and clung, shoved her into Avisha's arms, and stumbled back the way they had come.

She'd recognized what those men were the instant she had seen them. What a fool she'd been! Avisha had stood there blubbering on the path, when they should have kept going despite the eagle. That was how those outlaws had walked up from behind without her hearing.

Eiya! She must watch, observe, keep her eye on the trail they'd tramped through the woodland so she could find her way back. She must listen, to make sure she didn't stagger out like a flailing drunk onto the road, an easy target. The rain gave her cover; the vegetation was damp enough that instead of snapping it merely bent, squooshed, sucked. She marked how the canopy altered where the path cut along the slope as it moved sidelong around the hill. She slowed down, grasped the slender trunk of a pine tree, trying to quiet the surging pound of her heart in her throat and ears.

She heard no sound of men talking. She heard no sound of footfalls, nor press of branches swept aside as they searched into the woodland for the runaways. She eased forward into the cover of a stand of pipe-brush. Her ears stung as the wind picked up. Still nothing. Crouching, she tipped to hands and knees and crawled through the muck to the shelter of a bush from which she could see the path.

Six bodies sprawled on the ground, limp and torn, several still twitching. She forced herself to scan the path.

The eagle chirped.

She slunk along the line of bushes until she could see where the path pushed onward. With wings spread and head raised, the eagle waited. A bundle of clothing had fallen to the ground beneath it.

It wasn't clothing. The eagle was standing over Jerad, cruel talons fixed on either side of the boy and its gaze pinioned on the dead men it had ravaged.

She found a stout stick on the ground, tested its heft. With this pathetic weapon, she walked onto the path.

"Jerad!"

The eagle flared its wings wider. She halted. Like the eagle she, too, was panting, angry, scared, injured in her own way. When it looked at her, she returned its fierce gaze without fear.

"We're friends, not enemies," she said, a little testily.

Its mouth gaped, showing its tongue. Was that a good sign, or a bad one? She took another step and a third, by stages moving closer until she could see that Jerad was alive. The eagle was guarding him.

"You saved us," she said, hoping to sooth it with her voice.

It swiveled its head, measuring her.

"N-Nallo?" His voice was so soft she barely heard it. "I'm scared, Nallo. Did you see what it did to those men? Is it going to kill me?"

"Hush!"

At her agitated tone, the eagle flared again, and Nallo said, more harshly than she intended, "Stop that! He's just frightened! You're scaring him."

He sobbed, so she grasped the stick more tightly and held it a little above and across her head as if that flimsy stick could ward off the eagle should it strike. She walked at a measured pace right up to the huge eagle. Under its wings and the vicious-looking beak, she knelt beside Jerad and coaxed him to his knees.

"Come on, now, Jer! If the eagle meant to kill you, it would have done it already."

"It's going to eat m-m-me."

Really, the boy was impossible. "No, it isn't. Get up."

"They play with animals, and then eat them alive."

"Get up!"

He clung to her as she dragged him away from the eagle and off the path. "It tore that man's head off. It stuck that man right through the chest with its claws. Did you see?"

"It protected you, Jerad."

She shoved the boy down into a heap of sodden leaves ripe with smells released by the rains. Turning, she examined the eagle. The heavy feathered brows made its stare more intense, and naturally the hooked bill with its pointed tip looked daunting. The top of its bill was colored a bright yellow, and yellow rimmed its mouth behind the bill. Its feathers had a golden sheen, shading darker along the wings and breast, patched with white. Its legs, too, were feathered, shaped like leggings. Its talons were skin and claw, big enough to enclose her chest.

As she watched, it began to clean blood and bits of flesh from its bill with one talon. It had a fussy touch, comical until you thought of what the eagle had just done.

Where had the outlaws come from? Were there more of them?

"Jerad, hide in the woods. Take this." She picked up, and handed to him, the pouch she had dropped in the first steps of their panicked flight.

"It's too heavy."

"Take it into the trees. I'm coming."

She found the washtub where Avisha had dropped it. When had that happened? The series of events blurred in her mind: the washtub tumbling down the slope and spilling its contents every which way; Avisha hauling it up again. The eagle had come, and then the outlaws, and she realized that the eagle had surely come because it had seen armed men moving up behind them. It had deliberately saved them.

It lifted its head, looking past her. She heard men tramping up the path, moving in haste. She lugged the washtub off the road, and just in time she and Jerad dropped behind a stand of pipe-brush. She left the washtub beside the boy and shimmied forward on her belly through the brush until she could look over the path. The wind was rising again, rippling in the clothing of the dead men as if the cloth had woken and meant to abandon the mutilated husks.

Two men trotted into view. They wore the same leather coats and molded leather helmets she'd seen on the armed men who had marched into her village. One of the men carried a red banner marked with three black waves enclosed in a black circle, similar in cut to the banner she had seen that terrible day, although the banner those men carried had had four stripes.

The soldiers scented death before they saw it. They moved hesitantly forward, then spotted the dead men and, last, the waiting eagle. Backing up hastily, they called to unseen companions. One man hoisted his bow and, hands shaking, fitted an arrow.

Fly. Fly.

As if it heard her thoughts, the eagle spread its wings, thrust, and beat hard. It rose agonizingly slowly, and the archer loosed an arrow. But the shaft went wide, and the eagle was aloft, out of range, as Nallo sucked in a breath, dizzied, her pulse thundering in her ears.

The men shook fists at the sky, then split up to investigate the scene of the battle. As they prodded the corpses, another dozen men came up behind, a straggling, undisciplined line that collapsed into commotion with a lot of shouting and cursing.

"Get on! Get on!" they cried, hurrying forward as if something more dreadful than an eagle was chasing them.

She and Jerad hid as the afternoon wore on, while groups of men passed at erratic intervals, fleeing northeast into the Soha Hills. Those who staggered into sight panting and exhausted found strength to move on when they spotted the dead. She grinned. They were beaten, whipped, frightened and disoriented, a beast without a head to lead the way.

"Did you see Captain Mani? He was burned alive. I saw the bones in his face while he was still screaming. . . ."

"Captain Mani's dead? Then who's in charge?"

"We have to reach Walshow. There'll be captains there to tell us what to do. . . ."

"We've not going fast enough. If they catch us, they'll kill us. They're demons."

"Is the lord dead? Can he be dead?"

"Did you see the tent burning? The fire stuck to it. Water wouldn't put it out. No one could escape such sorcery."

"They promised us! Said nothing would stand in our way."

"Neh. This was a test. Those who didn't truly trust the lords' power, died. But we survived, didn't we?"

"Heh, so we did. We spoke the proper prayers and offered the proper sacrifices, not like the others. We'll be admitted to the real army—"

"Aui! Look! Eagles!"

Three eagles swooped past. Shouting, the men ran. The eagles rose higher into the sky with an eerie glide, wings not beating. These eagles carried reeves slung into harnesses that dangled beneath, leaving their arms free to hold weapons. Trapped in the brush, she lost sight of them, but she heard the hammer of hooves as a company of horsemen approached at speed.

"Run! Run!" the men cried.

It was too late.

Up the path swept a score of horsemen, black wolves on the hunt. They harvested the fleeing soldiers with swift strokes. Half rode on, up the path, while others spread into the woodland on the trail of men who bolted into the trees. She dared not move; she scarcely breathed. Men screamed as they were cut down. The mounted soldiers called to one another with calm shouts. One dismounted to survey the corpses killed by the eagle. He was an older man, somewhat older than her husband, although it was difficult to tell his age. He had an outlander's look, with a broad face and pronounced cheekbones, a mustache but no beard, and noble eyes that flicked restlessly over the scene. She held her breath as his gaze passed over the pipe brush, but he looked away. He walked to the spot where the eagle had stood guard over Jerad. He knelt, touched the ground as if the ground could speak to him, then rose. Briskly, he walked directly to the stand of pipe-brush, halted, and spoke.

"Come out." His words were strangely accented and a little difficult to understand.

She didn't move.

He sighed. "Come out. You are in there. With you is another one."

Maybe he was only guessing.

He hacked through the pipe-brush above her head, shearing it off. Leaves showered her. Stalks rattled onto her body. He stepped back and waited.

He might still go away.

He tilted his head, rubbed his chin, and took another step back. She heard crashing in the brush, male laughter, and—like a stab in the heart—a woman's sobs. Two black-clad riders emerged onto the path within her line of sight. Using their spears as prods, they were driving Avisha in front of them. She had Zi clutched to her chest. Her eyes were red from weeping, her hair tangled in disarray. She shivered with terror as the men looked her over.

"Pretty girl," said the older man, measuring her.

Nallo rose and pushed through the brush, splintering stalks in her haste to get to the path before they could do anything awful to Avisha. She flung herself to her knees before the older man. "Don't kill us, I pray you. We've done you no harm. Don't kill us. Take me if you must, but leave the girl alone."

The laughing soldiers fell silent. The older man pulled off his helmet. He had a pleasant face, even if he did look and talk like a foreigner.

"The pretty girl, she is your sister? You not look alike."

"She's my husband's daughter."

"Your husband, where is he?"

"He is dead."

She cursed herself silently the moment she said it, but the man nodded as he looked from her to Avisha and Zianna, then past them. Jerad came running, and he flung himself at Avisha and hid his face against the fabric of her tunic.

"You are walking from your house to your kinfolk, maybe?"

"That's right. They're expecting us."

He rubbed his chin again, looked over at the younger soldiers where they guarded the children. "Maybe they are dead, also."

Three soldiers appeared on the path above and studied the scene, grinning as they spoke to their companions. Farther away, a man's shriek cut off abruptly.

"Please don't hurt us." Her mouth formed soundless prayers.

He shifted his sword to the same hand that was also holding his helmet, and with his free hand wiped sweat and maybe blood from his eyes, careful as he cleaned his brows, rather like the eagle in his fastidiousness. One of the younger men spoke in rapid words she could not understand, and the older man laughed and, with a friendly smile—or perhaps a mocking one—turned back to her.

"My young comrade wants to know if you and the pretty girl are looking for husbands. We are looking for wives."

Why had they to suffer all this, and now more besides? Anger boiled over, and words spilled out. "We can't stop you from doing what you want. But don't mock us by calling us 'wives'!"

He laughed, face crinkling. "Whew! My ears are burning. You remind me of my wife, may she find peace."

"Then if you have a wife, you can't be looking for a wife."

"She's dead many years. I am not mocking you." He offered an affable grin. "Maybe I am having a little fun. We could rape you and kill you. This is true. But that gives pleasure for a moment, and not much pleasure when you come to think of it afterward. Maybe we are wanting something different. We are new to this country. We intend to settle in lands west and north of Olossi. So, if you are looking for husbands, I know where some can be found." He indicated the five mounted men.

Startled by this speech, she really examined the soldiers. They looked different from Hundred folk in having broad cheekbones and scant beards, but she could tell them apart even with the helmets covering their hair: one had a long, dour face and small eyes, and another a big grin and two missing teeth. One had pox scars and a thoughtful gaze, while the one with the roundest face had a markedly reddish-brown complexion. The one with pretty eyes and regular features kept glancing at Avisha in the way men had when they were thinking more of their strut than their manners. Not that these men need have manners. They carried weapons.

"Are you hunting down the outlaws?" she asked.

"Yes. We hunt them and we kill them."

"Good!"

"Perhaps these are the ones who kill your husband?"

Grief caught her unexpectedly. Tears blurred her vision. "Or ones like them."

Three eagles glided past, and one turned in a great loop that took it out of sight over the trees before it dropped back and came to earth with a thump on the path, just where the eagle that had saved them had first landed. A reeve unfastened from the harness and picked his way down the muddy path. He looked over Nallo, Avisha, and the children, shaking his head as he halted beside the soldier.

"What have you found, Tohon?" he asked.

"Maybe these strong young women will agree to be wives to the Qin soldiers."

"It seems you saved them from a gruesome fate. That might persuade them, if your charms can't." The reeve was a good-looking man, with handsome features and a sympathetic expression as he nodded by way of acknowledging her. "I'm called Joss. I'm a reeve out of Argent Hall. You and your sister and the little ones look like you've been traveling for a while. That can't be good, not in these days."

"It was an eagle killed most of those soldiers, not these men," said Nallo irritably. "I'd think that you being a reeve, you'd have seen it at once."

"Would you? Aui! I am found out as a man with little wit and less observational skills." But his smile took the sting out of the words, and anyway he seemed at ease laughing at himself. He seemed at ease, despite the brutal nature of his task, scouting for soldiers on the hunt for outlaws so they could kill them. If she hadn't recognized the men who were on the run as similar in dress and look to those who had overrun the village, she wouldn't have known who to distrust most. "Listen, verea. We haven't much time, for as you can see we've urgent work at hand hunting down this army of outlaws. We can leave you on the road and let you go your way, or we can direct you to a sheltered spot where you can wait for the Olo'osson militia to escort you to a place of safety."

"Does that include the offer of marriage?"

He looked at Tohon and laughed again. "Are you making that offer to every woman you meet on the road?"

"No harm in asking," said the other man. "The young men will want wives. A man isn't complete without a woman. Nor can he fill his tent with children, and what is a man after all without children?"

"He might be something like me," said the reeve without heat, "so I think your point is well taken. What will it be, verea?"

Belatedly, Nallo realized that Reeve Joss was surely only a little younger than her husband, only he did not seem old as her husband always did. She said, "I'm called Nallo. This is my husband's daughter, Avisha, and her brother and sister. My husband's dead."

"Yes, I suppose he is. I'm sorry to hear it. Where are you from?"

"I'm born and raised in the Soha Hills. But the village where we lived lies along West Track, or it did, anyway, before it was burned down and half the folk murdered."

None of these words surprised him. "I've heard this tale too often."

"Best we be moving." Tohon sheathed his sword and gave Nallo a wink. "These are good young men. They have discipline. They will treat you in the proper manner, with respect." He fastened his helmet on his head, mounted, and called the advance. The young man with the pretty eyes raised a hand, in a parting gesture to Avisha, then followed the others up the path on the trail of the fleeing army.

"What do you mean to do?" asked the reeve.

"I would marry," said Avisha suddenly. "If they meant it. If they would take the little ones in, and raise them as their own. What other hope do I have?"

"Eiya! Don't go leaping before you've looked."

"Are you saying they're not looking for wives?" asked Avisha desperately. "Maybe they need a marriage portion. No matter what Nallo says, we have nothing and no hope for anything except to walk until we're starving and willing to sell ourselves into slavery. Or until we're caught on the road and raped and cut open and left like refuse in the brush."

"It doesn't have to end that way. They're as good men as any others. Tohon meant what he said. There's two hundred or more, all looking for wives. They're far from home and hoping to make new homes here in the Hundred. Just . . . you're a pretty girl, and you're still young. If you'll trust me, and wait in the shelter I've promised, I'll see you get escorted to Olossi. There, you can see what the Qin will offer you to make a marriage with one of them. Just don't go making a bargain before you've seen the goods."

Avisha began to cry. Nallo fumed, thinking of how the girl had boxed them in with her thoughtless words. To say differently now would sound heartless, not that she didn't have a lot of experience with being called heartless. The hells! Avisha was right. They had no better prospects in Sohayil or Sund, if they could even walk that far with outlaws everywhere.

"How long have you been on the road?" the reeve asked Nallo.

"I don't know. Fifteen or twenty days."

He sighed. "We're not just hunting outlaw soldiers. We also have a commission from the temple of Ushara by Olossi. We're looking for a man and a woman, a brother and sister as it happens, who cheated the temple. We're hoping to bring them back to face the Hieros."

She examined her dirty feet, caked with wet slop over dried mud over dirt, layers on layers, like deceit. She owed those two nothing. Then she happened to look over to see Avisha staring at her, lips pressed together to urge her to keep her mouth shut.

Nallo had never felt much allegiance to the gods because the gods had never been particularly kind to her, and because most of their priests were buffoons. Even the Thunderer's ordinands she'd spent her year's apprenticeship with had been self-important imbeciles, or tiresome bullies, or bored slackards going through the motions. Only the Merciless One had shown her kindness. She'd been welcomed into the arms of Ushara, the Merciless One, at her temple in Old Cross. Many a youth went there at the age of choosing, wearing a necklace of flowers, and was sweetly introduced to the embrace of the goddess. She held those tender memories close. She owed a debt to the Merciless One.

"We saw them down at Candra Crossing."

"Nallo! How could you!"

He glanced at Avisha, curious at her outburst.

Nallo continued. "They did us a good turn, helped us across the ford with the little ones. Otherwise we might not have made it. We didn't realize they were runaway slaves until after we had crossed."

"How did you find out?"

"I overheard them talking. So they went their way, and we went ours. They must be days ahead of us. They had horses."

"Many refugees walk the roads in troubled times."

"He had the debt mark by his eye. Her name was Zubaidit."

His eyes flared. Then he smiled. "That's right. They were traveling on this track?"

"They walked the road out of Candra Crossing that leads into the Soha Hills. We walked that road for a few days, but I thought it would be safer to stay away from the main road."

"You were right to do so. These outlaws are running scared. They've attacked villages and done worse."

"Then we'd be foolish to keep traveling rather than taking an offer of shelter. The outlanders you're hunting with, they can't possibly kill all the outlaws, can they?"

"No."

No decision she made now could possibly be a good decision, only the least bad decision. Although the reeve glanced now and again at the sky, and at his eagle, he otherwise showed no sign he was impatient to go. "How do we know we can trust you?"

He winced, just a little, and laughed, just a little. "Once, you would have trusted me simply because I was a reeve. But we no longer live in those days, do we? You must know that Tohon and his company could have done what they wished to you. I have an eagle at my back and companions aloft, watching for trouble. So either we are telling the truth, or we are more deceitful than you have yet imagined, devising a sport in which we lure you into trusting us only to abuse you later."

He twisted to take a long look at his eagle, a watchful bird with a noticeable scar. Then he walked down the path and made a quick circuit of the corpses, pausing to study the sprawl of limbs, the trajectory of blood as it had spattered, the cuts and gouges, the manner in which each man had met his death. Circling back, he halted in front of Nallo. With his gaze narrowed, he looked much less friendly. She stood her ground.

"How do you know an eagle killed these men?"

"Aui!" That was an easy question. "We saw it."

"You saw it?"

"Yes. The outlaws were coming right up behind us. They would have caught us and killed us, but an eagle attacked them."

"An eagle? With a reeve?"

"No, just an eagle. One of its wings seemed injured."

The scarred eagle chirped.

"The hells!" He looked into the sky.

It was as if her words were a summoning. Her eagle—she thought of it as hers, in a funny way—glided down, hitched up as it overshot his eagle, and thumped hard on the path below them. It raised its big head, and chirped.

The reeve stared at the eagle, looked at Nallo, looked back at the eagle, and then again at Nallo. "The hells. Do you know what this means?"

Whatever she had seen in him before—geniality, charm, a gaze that made you feel he was looking at you alone with no thought for anyone or anything else— vanished as he thought through some deep conundrum, as he frowned and made a move as though to grasp her arm, then withdrew his hand and fixed it awkwardly in the straps of the harness he wore around his torso.

"You *have* to come with us now."

"The hells I do! Why?"

"No need to snap at me." He flared. He wasn't one bit cowed by her temper. "Didn't you wonder why that eagle dropped down right here, right then, only to aid you?"

"The gods fashioned the eagles to seek justice."

"So they did, but a lone eagle without a reeve flies to the mountains and lives in solitude, in their ancient hunting territories. Only with a reeve does an eagle seek justice. And you'll note that particular eagle carries no reeve."

She didn't like the probing way he examined her. She wiped her dirty chin with the back of a hand. "I'm not blind!"

"I know that eagle," he continued, ignoring her outburst. "Her name is Tumna. Her reeve is dead. I thought she'd flown to the mountains, to mark the passing as eagles usually do, but I see she's already chosen a new reeve."

Nallo looked at Tumna, at her ragged unkempt feathers, her injured wing, her angry, impatient gaze. Here was an eagle who was irritated that her reeve was dead and she had so much to do and no partner with whom to accomplish all those tasks. How annoying people are! Why can't things fall out without so much trouble and incompetence muddying the waters?

"Who?"

He took hold of her hand, gently, as would a relative when offering condolences.

"You, Nallo. This eagle has chosen you to be its reeve."

12

Keshad stood beside a stone pillar, staring nervously over the darkening vista. After days of hard traveling, they'd pushed through the rugged Soha Hills. Tonight they sheltered in ridgetop ruins that overlooked Sohayil, a wide basin with hills rising on all sides. The valley floor blended into the darkness as daylight faded. "Bai, if outriders from the army stumble onto us, they'll kill us."

"Kesh, on all those caravan runs you made into the Sirniakan Empire when you were Master Feden's slave, were you as likely as this to jump at your own shadow? The approach to these ruins is narrow, along the ridge. No one is going to try to navigate that track at night without a light. If they come with a light, we'll see them. As for whatever folk live down in Sohayil, even if someone down there happened to see our light all this way up here, they'd most likely think the ruins are haunted. So we can rest easy for one night. Why don't you trust my judgment?"

He shuddered as he turned away from the view, clutching his bowl of gruel in his hands. Someone *could* crawl up that long steep slope, even at night, testing each handhold, moving slowly, using feel and the texture of the air to make his way. Someone who knew the hills well.

A single lamp illuminated the stone walls and dusty ground. The old beacon tower had collapsed untold years ago. Most likely, the folk in Sohayil had experienced relative peace for so long that no one had thought they needed to repair it. Just like in Candra Crossing, no one had thought an army would march through, devastating every village in its path. Maybe in the valley of Sohayil they still didn't know. An army marching down West Track could have entirely bypassed Sohayil.

A spire of rock, its sheer face impossible to climb, thrust up behind the ruined beacon tower. It had a flattened top, and if you looked at it from the right angle you might imagine those contours were the remains of an old wall, all the way up there where only someone with wings could reach. Probably it was an old Guardian altar, long since abandoned.

Was that a light—a lamp's flame—winking up there? No. It was only a trick of the light, catching in the angles of rock as the sun set behind them.

From the the tower's ruins, beside the campfire, she watched him. "You've never told me."

"Told you what?"

"Obviously since my debt was bought by Ushara's temple, I was apprenticed to the Merciless One. All those years we were slaves, I never saw you more than once a year. You never told me where you served your apprentice year. Which of the gods you served."

His stomach was aching, and his head hurt. He gulped down the last of the gruel, walked back to the fire, and took hold of the pot's handle. "I'll scrub this clean."

She grabbed his wrist and held it. "I'm just curious."

"Let me go."

Her hold tugged on him, like a river's current dragging you in the direction you don't want to go. "Are you telling me that Master Feden broke all custom and holy law, and did not let you go for your one year when you were fourteen or sixteen? He could be fined for that! Even children sold into debt slavery must be allowed to serve their apprentice year to one of the gods. Why didn't you complain?"

"Do you think any of the temples in Olossi would have listened to me? Master Feden rules the council. A word from him, and the tithes to the temples would have dried up like a dry-season channel in the delta. A word from him, and any merchant who tried to mention his lapse to one of the temples would have lost her license to trade and been ostracized in the bargain. You are so naive, Bai."

She released him. "Maybe so, but when I was in Olossi twenty days ago, Master Feden was in deep trouble. He's the one who made a dirty alliance with the northerners, the same people who burned villages and murdered innocent village folk just for whatever sick pleasure they took in the doing."

"Don't forget I had to march with that army for an entire day."

"The council in Olossi now knows what Master Feden did. We needn't fear Master Feden any longer."

Having to remember the twelve long years he had served out his debt slavery to the man made him want to kick and punch and destroy some helpless object, breaking it down until it hung in splinters. Wasn't that the way his and Bai's life had been destroyed, when they'd been orphaned and their aunts and uncle had sold them on the block rather than raise them? The life they might have hoped to have had been smashed to pieces, and here they were, remade into people he no longer recognized.

She went on, a wolf gnawing at cracked bones. "Once we reach a place we can stop, you have to apprentice to one of the gods. It's not unheard of to come so late to your year of service. It's better than carrying around that prison bowl, where the southern god sucks in the souls of his worshippers."

"You don't know anything about Beltak!"

"A Hundred man should not be praying to a god from the empire."

"I only took up the bowl because it gave me an advantage in trade. That way I didn't have to pay the fines the empire men levy in the market on merchants who aren't believers."

"I thought their priests burned anyone who didn't sacrifice to their god."

"They do, but they have to accept merchants from other countries, at least in the market, or they'd have no trade, would they? But they can charge them extra, and forbid them to build temples of their own or to say prayers to other gods."

Her lips, pressed together, made a tight line.

"I did what I had to! I got us free, didn't I?"

"You did," she said as the line of her mouth softened. "It's not too late. The gods will not abandon you. You only need stand before them. It's just . . . I can't look at you and easily see to which god your service is best suited. Kotaru the Thunderer? You're not obedient enough nor do you get into fights just for the fun of it. Ushara the Merciless One? You can't give up your very self to the heart of the goddess. Atiratu the Lady of Beasts? No, for hers is a caring and selfless heart, and you have trouble looking beyond your own troubles. Taru the Witherer? He who waxes and wanes? I think not, for you have remained constant all these years, and that's a fine thing, since we're both free now because of your efforts. Ilu the Envoy? You've traveled, but you're just not talkative enough. You're observant, but only when you're toting up things to your own advantage or disadvantage. Sapanasu, the Keeper of Days? It's true you're an excellent accountant, and you've made good use of those skills in acquiring the coin to free us. But I just can't see you being willing to shave your head on the day you enter through that gate. You're too vain of your lovely hair."

He glared at her, thinking she was teasing him, but it was obvious she was perfectly serious. The hells! She was right, of course: Although she'd been glad to leave the temple, she was nevertheless sworn to the goddess in her heart in a way he could not fathom. No doubt she considered herself a hierodule still, even if she no longer served at the temple of Ushara, the Devourer, the Merciless One.

"That leaves Hasibal, the Formless One. Eh!"

He jumped, spinning around to see if anything was sneaking up behind him, but there was nothing except shadows.

"You might have been walking Hasibal's path all along," she continued, because the exclamation had been merely a grunt of consideration. "Still, you know what they say."

"Must you drone on with this annoying prattle? When you were little, you were so quiet. The temple ruined you."

"Our souls are bound to the land through our service to the gods. At birth we enter one of the twelve years, which determines much of the character of our heart. With our naming, we are linked to one of the Four Mothers, which determines the texture of our mind. Without service to the gods, we are as a boat without an anchor: adrift in stormy seas."

"I survived twelve years adrift. But I might expire if I have to hear any more of this. Can't we go to sleep now?"

"A difficult path to follow, but the deepest."

"Sleeping?"

"Hasibal's path."

"Won't you stop?"

"No!" Rising to face him, she seemed larger, brighter, fiercer, a wolf about to lunge. "Don't mock the gods, Kesh. Don't turn your back on them. We are what the gods make us."

"We are what we make ourselves!"

"How can you separate the two? You only think you can."

"You don't know anything!"

Her weight shifted forward. Her shoulders stiffened. He thought she was ready to rip out his throat. She could kill him. He knew it. She knew it.

Then she smiled, and relaxed. Raising both hands, palms out, she nodded briefly. "You must walk your own path, Kesh. That's truth. But there's another truth you don't want to hear and must hear: You must walk a path, or you'll always be lost and wandering, as in the wilderness."

"Aui! Can't we—"

"Go to sleep? Yes. Scrub out that pot. I'll check on the horses."

He scoured the pot with a handful of gravel, then rinsed out the grit with water from the cistern. Bai took the pot and hauled more water for the horses. He wrapped himself in a blanket, in a walled corner where he'd get shelter when it rained during the night, and closed his eyes.

But he was restless. Their argument had robbed him of the ability to sleep. The words of the evening prayer to Beltak, Lord of Lords, King of Kings, the Shining One Who Rules Alone, whispered in his head.

Rid us of all that is evil. Rid us of demons. Rid us of hate. Rid us of envy. Rid us of heretics and liars. Rid us of wolves and of armies stained with the blood of the pure. He touched the sacred bowl tucked against a hip. "Teach me to hate darkness and battle evil. Teach me the Truth."

Yet what is truth? Master Feden had prayed to the gods of the Hundred, and paid his tithes to the temples at the proper times and in the proper amounts. But he had cheated his own slaves by padding out their debts so they remained in perpetual servitude to him, never able to buy themselves free. He had made common cause with a mysterious commander out of the north, whose army included the worst kind of criminals and sick, twisted men. Feden had done all that to consolidate the power his faction already held in the council of Olossi.

Still, any Hundred-born-and-bred man must admit that the situation in the Sirniakan Empire was unpleasant, with lords and priests able to kill any man they wanted at their whim, with helpless folk born into slavery and never able to buy themselves free, with women trapped like animals behind high walls. When Kesh had hired a Sirniakan driver named Tebedir to cart his trade goods north from the empire on the very last trading journey Kesh had taken as a slave, Tebedir had made all kinds of awful remarks that struck Kesh's ears as offensive or cruel. And yet, Tebedir stuck by his oath to stay with Kesh even when they'd been attacked by bandits in the village of Dast Korumbos. He could have run, but he'd said himself that honor was more important than death.

So who was a better man, Feden or Tebedir?

"Peace. Peace. Peace," he whispered. A wind soughed up from the basin. Rain pattered through the stones. But he was not soothed.

When bandits had attacked, threatening to rob him of the precious treasure that would buy his and Bai's freedom, he had prayed to Beltak, Lord of Lords and King of Kings, the Shining One Who Rules Alone. And after that, the black wolves—Captain Anji's troops—had ridden as out of nowhere to save their caravan from the ospreys who sought to pillage it. So maybe Beltak had answered his prayer. Or maybe it had just fallen out that way. Maybe he'd just been lucky that the right people had come along at the right time. Maybe it was only that Master Feden had abused his power and gone against the law because he wanted to enrich himself and squeeze the throats of others more than he wanted to do what was right in the eyes of the gods.

On Law Rock in Toskala, the laws governing the Hundred were carved in stone. *When a person sells their body into servitude in payment for a debt, that person will serve eight years and in the ninth go free.*

But laws mean nothing, not really. They only mean something if people agree they do, if people walk in obedience to the law, or are forced to comply. If your heart had turned away from the law, then your heart would not restrain you when you violated it. Long ago the Guardians had stood over the Hundred, to guard the law, while the reeves had enforced the law. But the Guardians vanished, and while some of the reeves were turning their back on their duty to enforce the law, the others were losing their power to do so even if they wanted.

So who was a reeve to talk of justice? Who was anyone to do so? Anyone could be lying. Anyone could be speaking words out of the right side of her mouth and acting opposite them with her left hand.

Aui! His Air-touched mind could not quiet. He must turn and turn things, flit from one thought or memory to the next. He must wonder what was happening in Olossi. He must wonder what would happen to Nasia, who had been his fellow slave and lover for four years even though he had abandoned her the day he'd returned. He must wonder what would happen to the treasure he had obtained far to the south through simple good luck. He had handed off the ghost girl without a second's regret, trading her freedom and her life in exchange for Zubaidit's freedom.

He must wonder about the envoy of Ilu he had met on his last journey over the Kandaran Pass. That amiable man had conversed cheerfully with him, had laughed kindly at him: *"Goats are inconstant and unstable, prone to change their thinking, especially if they're Air-touched and liable to think too much. Still, they can survive anything!"*

Kesh suspected now that the envoy had been looking for the ghost girl with the demon-blue eyes. It should no longer matter. The envoy was dead, murdered in the bandit attack, yet his face and voice haunted Keshad. How was it that you might meet a person and spend only a day with them, and yet have them imprinted so deeply on your heart and your mind that they could never be forgotten?

The rain eased. The wind stilled. He slipped into a state drifting between a waking dream and a restless doze.

He woke abruptly, but he wasn't sure what had broken his sleep. Listening, he heard nothing except the whisper of wind through the stones and the irregular drip of water onto stone. Some night animal had been out on the prowl and wandered away, that was all. Yet the night's unease had returned, and along with it the memory of that last trip over the mountains out of the south. The envoy of Ilu was dead. He hadn't even known the man's name, but he could still remember vividly the look of his face and sound of his voice and the effortless way the man had negotiated the twisting paths of life.

*　*　*

AFTER THE TWILIGHT rains washed through, the waters of the wide Olo'o Sea calmed to become a mirror in whose depths burned those few stars visible between tattered clouds. The moisture soaking into the earth woke a sweet scent that permeated the air. Long ago, an unknown hand had planted a stand of thorn trees in a crude semicircle, with the open side facing the inland sea. A traveler's shelter, four poles and a low thatch roof, was tucked away within that protecting fence. A man uncovered the fire pit and blew on its coals until flame rose along fresh wood. By its light, he sat back on his heels and busied himself with raking stray embers into the center, where he'd built a frame of kindling. Light flared as the embers caught in the wood.

He was a slender man of mature years, no longer young and not yet elderly, and dressed in the gaudy manner of an envoy of Ilu: baggy pantaloons as dark as plums, a knee-length tunic woven of a cloth as pale as butter, and a voluminous cloak that in daylight would be seen to be the same color as the cloudless sky, a pure, heavenly blue.

He hummed softly, hoping the sound of this wordless melody, like the rains upon the parched earth, would soften the girl's hard shell.

She said nothing. Silence, like night, is a cloak that conceals.

She was young, no longer a girl and yet not entirely a woman, and startlingly, disturbingly, horribly pale with a ghostly complexion and hair colorless as straw.

She seemed to be staring at the ground, not even lifting her gaze to the lovely dance of fire. So be it. He was patient.

He tended the fire. Waves slapped the tumble of rocks in the shallows before hissing back into the sea. She sat on a large rock that some thoughtful soul had rolled into place untold years ago, a homely act to benefit strangers from whom the builder could never hope to gain thanks, or profit.

"It is hard to know whether we will meet with brutality or kindness in the world," he mused aloud. The fire popped. A spark dazzled, spinning into the air, then flicked out. "Or indifference. I traced the tracks of your passage to the temple of the Merciless One by Olossi, and there indeed I did find you. I admit you were not what I expected. I thought you would speak your name and know at least something of where you came from. That's usually how we awaken. But, in truth, how is life ever what we expect? We are constantly surprised. I suppose it is those who wish never to be surprised who cause most of the trouble. I wonder . . ."

She did not rise to the bait. He rose, returned to the shelter, and picked up one of the torches that a passing traveler had bound and left for those who would come after. A small courtesy, one of many in the fabric that weaves society together. He thrust the knotted end into fire. Flames licked up the torch to reveal their surroundings more clearly: The outline of thorn trees was softened with white flowers folded against the night. The grass in the clearing was cropped short. A red flag was tucked into a corner of shelter, one flap loose, and bound by a rope that could be used to tie it atop the roof as a signal to any passing reeve if travelers found themselves in trouble.

He walked toward the shore but halted where the last thorn tree held its ground. A treasure was caught in the branches. Using his free hand, he eased it free, then walked back to the fire holding a huge feather mottled brown and white. The feather was as long as his arm but so light it was like holding air in his hand.

"A tail feather. See how the quill runs right down the center. You'll learn to know the shape of any given type of feather, whether it is a tail feather, or the leading edge of the wing, or the rear edge, or a contour feather grown close to the bone . . ."

Even the precious eagle's feather did not attract her attention. She stared as into a void.

He sighed. In the days since he'd found her, he had not touched her in any manner, fearing that even a reassuring pat might be interpreted as violence. It was so hard to tell with this young thing, caught as she was in the whirlpool of awakening and trapped as well in a deeper stream whose currents he could not fathom. Some other trap was strangling her voice. She must emerge of her own will, by her own choosing, in her own time.

Yet leisure was the one thing they did not have. Now that he—and she—were back in the Hundred, those who wished to destroy them would seek them out swiftly and without mercy. Days and months and years they had in plenty, given what they had become, and yet a measure in which to pause and breathe, they had not at all.

"We can't stay here long," he said.

Mindful that the molt feathers of the giant eagles were sacred to the gods, he anchored the feather within the bristling hedge of thorn trees. The gods must watch over that which they deemed sacred. Another traveler would come, and find it, or no one would.

He stood beside the shelter with the torch still blazing, his gaze turned toward the dark sea. He mused aloud, as had become his habit over the years. He was not a man who liked to be alone, but he had learned to endure solitude when he must and enjoy company when he could. Anyway, he supposed that the sound of his voice, kept low, might soothe her.

"After so many years and such an arduous journey, I expected further trials of a very different sort." He chuckled. "So I am paid in my own coin, being given what I had hoped to avoid. Yet it did seem to me that you recognized something, that there was a spark of knowledge, a moment of trust, when we first came face-to-face in the temple of the Devourer. You gave me a question, and a decision. You asked me, 'Who are you?' You told me, 'I will come with you.' And here you are, and here I am." He smiled, amused by his own consternation. "Aui! Now it seems you cannot speak, or will not speak. I love conversation above all things. Shelter over my head, a dram of cordial, a well-laid table, and a few cheerful companions with whom to pass the evening! I like to think of myself as a man who makes few demands, and is easy to please, and content with little enough, but I see the gods have chosen to test me in the manner meant to make it hardest for me. So it goes."

Her torso expanded and contracted as she took in and released breath, that was all.

"I remember my own awakening—a long time ago now, to be sure! It took the patient coaxing of a pair of cloaks—like you and me—to instruct me. Twilight was one. Strange that I can't now recall the other. Yet there is more to your silence, for it's not the usual way—not that there's anything wrong with it, mind you! What brought you here? Where did you come from? How—why—did the cloak of mist reach to you? What is your name? I have a name, too, although no person has called me by name for a very long time. I was born in the Year of the Blue Rat, which is what makes me what I am. We Rats are known for being acquisitive, but Blue Rats don't grasp after money but rather after company and conversation and secrets. Then I was dedicated to Ilu, the Herald, because I was always restless, seeking, wandering. And named by my mother in the honor of the Water Mother, whose fluid nature thereby enhances those other qualities. It's a wonder I can keep silence at all! Nothing like you. I suppose we're well matched in that way. I talk, and you— heya!—maybe you listen and maybe you're hearing some other voice entirely, one I can never hear. Maybe you're tired of voices."

The wind has a voice, light and airy, full of promise, but sometimes cruel and rough. So does the rain have a voice, and the waters of the sea lapping the shore with their constant motion, never entirely quiet, able to choke and drown those the sea swallows. Fire has a voice, first crackling and impatient and later fading into a soft burn that may spark again when least expected. The earth's voice seems to slumber, but she, too, speaks in her slow, measured way and she may crack when none expect her temper.

Even demons and ghosts can speak, if one has the ears to hear.

She raised her head.

He smiled gently, to encourage her.

She was looking beyond him. He turned. The two horses had wandered back into view. They differed from ordinary horses in several ways, two of which were obvious now: they possessed uncanny night vision, and they had wings, at this moment folded tightly over their backs and flanks. She rose, walked past him, and went to the horses.

She didn't approach too quickly but held back, waiting for them to invite her. They let her know they'd allow her to approach. She stroked their ears and noses. She had a treat for each, shriveled pieces of fruit he'd not seen her hide in her sleeves.

He must coax her as one would a skittish, abused, anxious horse. Her scars ran deep, certainly, but she hadn't run away from him. Or maybe it was just that she hadn't run away from the horses. He must be patient. He had time in plenty, after all, as long as their enemies did not catch up to them before he had won her trust and taught her the terrible truth about what she had become.

13

The surviving militiamen from various villages and towns in the eastern Olo Plain had been hastily organized to patrol the roads and tracks and to guard safe havens. In these havens, folk who had fled their villages or lost their homes could gather, catch their breath, reassess their situation, and decide what to do next. That was the idea, anyway. In practice, it wasn't so easy.

After a day searching the Soha Hills, Joss and his eagle returned to the staging camp at the southwestern edge of the hills. In ancient days, a refuge had been constructed on a pair of hills joined by a narrow ridgeway path. Farmers still worked the terraced fields, but the walled fortifications had been uninhabited for as long as anyone could remember. Both hilltops had been stripped of trees and substantially leveled, although the taller hill retained a rocky protuberance on the northern edge of the steepest slope, a perfect landing and perch for the big eagles. Leaving Scar up in these rocks, he scrambled down to the open ground and walked straight into an assault of petitioners.

"Reeve! I have a complaint! This man's cart blocked the trail. . . . When will there be an assizes? Two men got in a fight. How are we to make provision for—? What's this I hear about people burying the dead—?"

He raised both hands to show he'd not be answering questions yet. Much of the crowd moved away, but perhaps a dozen followed him across the summit. They just would not stop talking. He walked past women cooking over fires and men hoisting canvas awnings to make shelters against what remained of the old walls. Bedraggled hierophants paced out the proper dimensions for a temporary foundation temple to Sapanasu, the Lantern, while in the distance a cadre of young ordinands cleared stray rocks from a section of ruined wall so they could patrol on top of it.

He turned on the petitioners. "Enough! Give me time to take a drink and eat something. I'll hear your petitions at the assizes."

They backed off. He cut over to the ordinands, climbed onto the old wall, and shaded his eyes as he surveyed the countryside. The landscape rolled away westward into the Olo Plain. On the road, a dozen wagons and many people moved toward the haven. From up here, they looked so small, but you could never know how big their problems were.

The sergeant of the little group approached him diffidently. The hells! The lad was so young he had scarcely any beard along his jaw. "Reeve. If I might—?"

"Yes, what is it? I'm Joss."

"I'm called Gani. Out of Sund."

"You're a long way from home."

"I am. I was sent to the temple in Westcott to do my year's service with Kotaru. I made a pledge for the full eight years of obligation. They sent me on to the temple in Candra Crossing. We had to flee for our lives."

He was a quiet lad, not at all belligerent, with a humble manner that Joss liked.

"How can I help you?"

Gani scratched his forehead, rubbed his chin, and looked back at his cadre, who were all watching him intently.

"Go on. I won't tear your head off, whatever you might be thinking."

"Is it true you're the marshal at Argent Hall?"

Joss sighed, feeling the weight of responsibility settle back on his shoulders. "I'm Marshal Alyon's successor."

"There was another man serving as marshal before you."

"He wasn't a real reeve. He had no eagle that anyone ever saw. Anyway, he's dead."

"Ah. Eh. That's it, you see. There came a pair of Devouring priests, a kalos and a hierodule, with a message from the Hieros of the temple in Olossi. It's said there was a conclave of all those holy ones in charge of the temples in Olo'osson. They agreed that any of the men from the army that attacked Olossi and who are dead now are to be . . ." He stiffened.

"You haven't been sergeant long, have you?"

"I am most senior of those left," he admitted, but the comment gave him courage—or made him ashamed of his hesitation. "It's like this. We've been told to dig ditches out of sight in the forest and to—to bury those dead men and cover them with dirt." Having started, the rest poured out in a rising voice. "But if we do that, then they can't rest. They can't pass the Spirit Gate. What if they turn into demons? Or haunt us? Their ghosts will be angry, and trapped! I know it's meant as a punishment for them, but what will happen to us who are assigned to complete such a task?"

"That's not reeve territory, lad. I can't help you." Thank the gods! Still, it was shocking. A brutal, calculated impiety. "Yet the army that invaded us has done terrible things, rape and murder, desecrating temples, defiling corpses."

The lad looked at his companions. They were silent and uncomfortable. They didn't want to talk about it in front of him.

Such talk made Joss uncomfortable, too, and he let his gaze wander. Six children worked the slope leading down to the terraces, picking petals of the baby's-delight that flowered with the first rains. The pale flowers brightened the slopes, which evidently had been recently cropped short by industrious sheep. He met the lad's gaze with a stern one of his own.

"It's an ugly thing to contemplate. But I saw the army marching Olossiward on West Track. I saw what they left behind. Maybe it's best if their spirits are crushed beneath earth. They're already corrupted. This is a pollution that must be buried before it consumes us. But that doesn't mean you have to like it. That it bothers you means your heart and spirit are clean."

"Very well, Marshal." The lad nodded, so tense it made Joss sad to think of what he must have seen in the last two weeks to cause him to look angry and worn down. "We'll do as we've been bid. Perhaps you'd come at dawn, to where we've been assigned to dig the ditches. By that stand of ironwood." He pointed toward a dozen mature ironwood trees towering above the edge of dense scrub forest that flowed away over the nearby hills. "Just in case any folk see what we're doing and make trouble. You could let them know the temples gave the order."

"That's fine. I'll be there at dawn."

Below, a crowd had gathered, waiting on Joss. He assured himself that Scar was at rest, preening as dusk settled. Then he clambered down and waded into the roiling waters.

A temporary court had been set up within the compound. Who had he assigned here?

Ah. The Snake.

"I don't care if your son is younger than the other man," Volias was saying to a particularly persistent woman whose face was flushed. "Every witness says they were both drunk. That makes them both culpable. Why these young idiots should make themselves free with wine in times like these is more than I can understand. Haven't they anything better to do, with folks living under canvas and desperate for water and food, and babies sick with diarrhea? Well, they will have something to do now, since I've assigned them both to dig and cover night-soil pits for the rest of the month."

"You can't—!"

"I can. Now get the hells out of my face or I'll ask my militia escorts here to drag you away and toss you into the pits. The ones that are already full with the same crap that's coming out of your mouth. Gods! Let someone else have a turn."

He looked up, sensing the crowd that approached. Seeing Joss, his ugly scowl turned into a sneer. He waved away the next petitioner, rose, and strode over to Joss.

"You gods-rotted rutting ass! These people are impossible."

"Such a good match, you and them." Although he knew better, he grinned because he did so enjoy seeing Volias suffer.

"You'll drown in your milky self-love someday. And I hope I'm there to watch and not throw you a rope. Listen, can we talk with some privacy?"

The crowd refused to give them up. They pressed around, everyone talking at once. "What about the theft from my cart? I've nothing to feed my children. We've no shelter. We were told we could return to our village, but it's not safe to go back. Is it true the outlanders are looking for women to marry? Why aren't there more reeves here? One isn't enough."

Joss raised both hands to get their attention. "Heya! Listen!" At length, they quieted. "We've got business to talk over between ourselves, and then we'll open the assizes for another session this evening. There are other reeves, at other refuges. But in the end you'll have to either go back to your homes and rebuild, or go to Olossi. If you're thinking your lives will be easier in Olossi, be aware that much of the outer town was burned. The folk there have all they can do to rebuild. Go back to your own homes."

"Why shouldn't we go to where walls and numbers will make us safe?" shouted one man.

Joss identified the speaker and noted his close-cropped hair and broad shoulders and the plain leggings and jacket commonly worn by farmers. "You'll get safe passage in a few days. I expect the roads from here back to Olossi to be as safe as we can make them in the time we've had. I can't promise safety on the Hornward road, but patrols will continue to range as far as East Riding. You must take responsibility for local patrols. Each village must set up a militia of able-bodied adults. There may be a few outlaws left hiding in the woodland. You'll need to capture and turn over to the Olossi militia every straggler you find. Meanwhile, the single most important thing any of you can do, ver, is to plant fields for the coming year while the season is ripe for planting."

"Can't Olossi's militia protect us? What of those black wolves who rode through here a few days ago, chasing the invaders? The tale says that an outlander will save us!"

His questions were echoed by others, all pressing forward so eagerly that Volias actually took a step back. Joss held his ground.

"We were aided by the outlanders. Captain Anji's company served us well. But another army, a stronger one, may attack out of the north in the months to come. Don't give the responsibility to protect yourselves to someone else, lest you forget how to defend yourself when there is no one to lend you a sword or bow. You've faced that day already, and lost your homes and kin. Best we don't walk this road again."

He nudged Volias's elbow. Before the crowd could recover, he and Volias moved back behind the table set up to mark the assizes court and into what had once been a house. The upper courses of the stone walls were gone, but the sections of wall that remained served as a barrier. He leaned against stone and scratched at a watering eye.

"Dust everywhere," he muttered.

The Snake paced. "You get all puffed up with your hectoring. Half the women in the audience were eyeing you, hoping for a glance from those pretty eyes."

"Enough! What do you have to say to me?"

"There's a solo eagle hanging around, comes and goes. No reeve. She favors one wing, a recent injury."

"Tumna?"

"Is that her name?"

"Yes. She's out of Argent Hall. Her old reeve's dead. It seems she's already chosen a new reeve."

"How could she have done that? No one's stepped into the circle."

"I don't know. But it happened. Hasn't the girl made herself known to you? No, maybe she isn't here yet. It'll take her days to reach here, and she has small children with her."

"Married?" asked Volias with surprise.

"Widow. They're stepchildren. The father must have been a lot older."

Volias leaned on the wall, propped on his elbows, and stared over the darkening hills to the northeast. Their personal feud had gone on so long that Joss rarely saw on Volias a neutral expression, but the man had borrowed one now, and it softened his features and made him appear almost likable. "You weren't just putting her on to try to get a taste of her, her being thankful for the attention?"

"Gods! For sure that's a likely thing for a newly appointed marshal to do. And in such times as these! The hells, Volias! Is that really what you think of me?"

"Heh. Got you." There it was: a grin. Not precisely friendly, but not quite bitter and mocking either. "I'll keep an eye out. What do I do with her?"

"She'll have to go to Argent Hall to train. Tell you what, when she comes in, you fly her back to Argent Hall, or delegate another reeve to do so. Yet I'm not sure she'll be willing to separate from the children until we can get them settled in some other way. There's an older girl, old enough to marry. I'm hoping she might be persuaded to marry one of the Qin soldiers."

"Whew! It's a cursed shame, us encouraging good Hundred girls to marry out-landers. You can't trust foreigners. Everyone knows that. Maybe they don't even have eggs. Maybe their members have thorns on them, like it's said in the tale about the wildings. Best if our lasses stick to their own kind."

Joss wanted to slug him, but refrained. "We have over two hundred unmarried men who have weapons, who know how to use them better than our militia do, and who might expect a little gratitude after saving Olossi and Argent Hall. I'd rather these outlanders marry good Hundred girls and have a reason to settle down and ally with us than go riding after someone who'll make use of them. Like the North-erners."

"I don't like their slanty eyes. They look at us like they think we're so much smaller than they are. They remind me of you in some ways." The sneer was back.

Joss pushed away from the stone. "Is there anything else? I'd like to eat and drink before I sit down at the assizes for the evening."

"Are you going to allow this order that came from the Olossi temple conclave? To bury the corpses of the dead soldiers?"

"I am."

"The hells! You can't mean it. It's going against the laws of the gods."

"You saw what those criminals did in the villages. We must bury such spirits."

"And become as impious as they were."

"Maybe so. But young men—and debt-bound slaves—will think twice about running away to the north to make their fortune robbing and raping and murdering, won't they? Anyway, it's the punishment spoken of in the Tale of Fortune, isn't it? That must be where the temple ruling comes from. That's all I have to say. Make sure Nallo—that's the new reeve's name—gets to Argent Hall. If she won't leave the children, then make sure some provision is made for them, else she won't cooperate. Otherwise, you're in charge here at this haven until everyone has dispersed. Then you can return to Clan Hall."

Volias was still stewing. Joss took his silence for assent and went to find something to eat. A scrap of bread, sour wine, and the leavings of watery soup were all that was available, and even that must be eaten with folk rudely trying to get his attention while a trio of young militiamen out of Olossi did their best to hold back the crowd. He set up afterward at the makeshift assizes court, and the petitioners kept coming to him and Volias for hours. A woman needed a healer for a broken hand. Every small child in one corner of the sprawling encampment had diarrhea. A dispute had broken out between two families over the contents of a wagon full of goods salvaged from their burned village. A lad and a lass wished to sit on the marriage bench, but both their clan heads forbade it, while the hopeful couple claimed that they had already received permission from clan elders who had, alas, been killed in the recent trouble.

He heard numerous accusations of petty theft, and four serious accusations of assault. Twelve children had vanished since reaching the haven, there were nine abandoned children no one would claim, and one chubby infant girl that two clans both swore on all the gods belonged to their house. He finally sent an exhausted Volias to rest but was himself up half the night, and the demands never slackened. Nor, when he made a judgment, were the petitioners satisfied, but would want to keep arguing for a different outcome.

Finally a new watch came on, headed by a vigorous old woman who took one look at his face by the light of her lantern and, turning to the crowd, declared the assizes closed for the night. She had a hard face and a bullying manner, and he'd never been so grateful for either.

"Get you some rest, lad," she said in her country way. "You can't make good judgments when you're so tired, and them too tired to listen to what you do have to say. They'll not pester you if you take your rest now."

"No, truly, they won't. If you'll lend me a light, or someone to escort me, I'll sleep by my eagle."

She chuckled. "Eh! You'll get no petitioners bothering you there, I'm thinking." Then she winked at him. "Although you're the kind might want bothering."

He laughed for the first time in days, it seemed. "Truly, I need to sleep."

A burly man escorted him most of the way, humbly silent out of respect for Joss's exhaustion, or perhaps exhausted himself, for he had a stiff gait and favored one leg. Only over by the rocks, atop which Scar perched in his night drowse, did the man venture a question.

"Think you that northern army will attack a second time?"

"We have to prepare."

"It's said the soldiers wear a talisman, this 'Star of Life.' I saw one for myself, a starburst sigil hammered out of cheap tin. But what do they want? Where did they come from? The tales tell of war and trouble in the days before the Guardians came to stand at the assizes. And now—well—begging your pardon and no disrespect to you reeves, but it seems that with the Guardians vanished from the Hundred, bad times have fallen again."

They were honest questions, and deserved an honest answer.

"I know not much more than you do, ver. I've heard tell that a man named Lord Radas commands another army in the north, likely larger and better disciplined although we don't know for sure. We do know that the city of High Haldia has been overrun. What do they mean to do next? That I don't know. March on Toskala? Or march again on Olossi? We'll fight. Don't doubt that. As for you and your people, you must return to your homes and fortify them. And plant your crops, else we'll have famine on top of all else."

"Are the Guardians gone forever? Or is it true, as some whisper, that they'll return? I've heard it said that the Guardians never left the Hundred, but that they became cloaked in darkness and now mean to kill us all and rule those who are left behind. I heard it said that the man who commands this dark army is a Guardian."

"That can't be." But perhaps he said the words as much to convince himself. A number of Captain Anji's men had seen, and shot at, a man riding a winged horse. They had no reason to lie, and on the whole Joss had found the Qin soldiers to be temperamentally disinclined to exaggerate. Zubaidit had claimed to have seen winged horses, and so for that matter had the Hieros. The gods had created the Guardians to bring justice to the land, to stand in judgment at the assizes. The Guardians could not die.

And yet they had all seemingly vanished.

"Who else could raise an army?" the man asked. "Who but a Guardian would have the authority?"

"Why would the Guardians vanish, leaving the assizes without their oversight, and then reappear at the head of an army that has committed nothing but murder and mayhem, the worst kind of injustice? Everything that goes against why the Guardians were created by the gods in the first place? Why?"

The man bent his head, as though listening to another, softer voice. He scratched his beard. "Why does anyone lie or cheat or steal? Or do worse things, which we've all heard of and you, reeve, have surely seen plenty of in your time. When the Four Mothers shaped the world, they set all in balance. Afterward, the gods ordered the world, but it is our prayers that keep all in balance. But what if balance and order are lost? In one man, in one woman, that loss may give rise to a lie or even a murder. Yet that is only a single act. In many men, or in one with the power to sway men, the loss of order means chaos will rise. Then greed and fear will rule. That's what I fear. That the shadows have risen, that order is lost."

"What's your name, ver?" said Joss, for he was struck by the man's sober wisdom. "I'm called Joss, as you may have heard."

"Heh!" He had a modest way of chuckling, and a friendly grin. "I'm called Pash,

Fire-born like you. I grow rice and nai in a village on the plain, not far from here. We were fortunate. We gave shelter to a few refugees, and thereby knew to take flight ourselves with our most precious goods. We hid in the woodland. Some men then come ten days past, those running from the battle by Olossi, but they hadn't time to burn anything for they were in such haste to flee north. They only stole a few of our stores, nothing we can't replace."

"Wise heads prevailed. I'm glad to hear it."

"Let me ask you another thing, for I know you had a hand in the battle by Olossi." Pash favored him with a close gaze, as if trying to sort out if his heart was in balance, or in chaos. "I have five daughters, ver, and not enough land to parcel out between them if each one hopes to make a living from it. There aren't enough lads with decent portions nearby to make husbands for all of them. I saw the Qin soldiers. Is it true they're looking for wives?"

"They made a bargain with the council of Olossi that if they could drive off the army, they'd be allowed to settle in this region."

"I heard, too, that they're cursed rich. That they've a canny merchant among them, a real Rat, if you take my meaning, who flayed the coins off those fat Olossi merchants and filled the outlanders' coffers."

"She's an Ox, not a Rat, and a very beautiful woman, but, yes, that's more or less how it happened."

"Ah. You've an interest there?"

Joss laughed. "Not I, ver. She's married to the captain. And she's very young."

"Good fortune for him. So these young soldiers, any one of them are well set up? Likely to be well endowed with land and coin? Worthy of one of my good daughters?"

Joss grinned. "As worthy as any man could be, ver."

"Heh! You have me there, for I don't think much of most men when it comes to my good daughters. But tell me true, reeve. If it were your own daughter, would you be willing to marry her to one of these outlanders?"

"I suppose they're no different than other men in most ways. They held to their side of the bargain. They mean to settle here, and make their way. I'd seal no bargain until the lass had looked them over, but it's worth a look."

"My thanks, then." He shifted his staff and, with a slight grunt as he bent one knee, seated himself on a stone wall. Scar's shadow loomed above them, at the summit of the rocky promontory. "I'll settle here to keep petitioners away, ver, if you've no objection and if your eagle won't tear my head off."

"My thanks."

He picked his way up through the ruins. Dressed stones gave way to true rocks where the ground was too rugged to tame into architecture. At the crest, he paused to catch his breath. Behind lay the busy encampment, lit with watch fires, itself inhaling and exhaling with so many frail lives huddled in what fragile haven they could find. Before him, the hillside plunged down a steep slope impossible to climb. Because of the clouds, it was too dark to see anything. He felt out an open-sided overhang in the rock that offered a little protection from the night rains.

Above, Scar had roosted for the night. After wrapping himself in a blanket, Joss lay down and closed his eyes.

THE DREAM UNWINDS itself in a veil of mist, rising into the heavens as if the rocks exhale the breathe of life, which has in it the essence of all those spirits killed in the recent attacks. The dream is familiar, well remembered. He is walking through a dead countryside of skeletal trees and scorched earth. He is himself dead, yet unable to pass beyond the Spirit Gate. The mist boils as though churned by a vast intelligence. For years, at this point in the dream, he would see her figure in the unattainable distance, walking along a slope of grass or climbing a rocky escarp-ment, always in a place he cannot and must not reach because he has a duty to those on earth whom he has sworn to serve.

But this night he finds himself sitting up, still sheltered beneath the wide over-hang. Scar drowses. The rains haven't yet come. Mist billows in the air, and she emerges from it. A death-white cloak spills from her shoulders, enveloping her. She rides out of the air as if the air is a path. She can ride on the air because the horse has wings. Its hooves ring on rock as it halts a short distance from him and furls those impossible wings, tips hiding the length of her legs.

"Joss," she says.

"Marit!" To hear her voice is agony, because he still misses her although twenty years separate them. "You're dead," he adds, apologetically, because it is after all a dream.

"Yes." Her smile is sad. "Don't carry this burden. Don't mourn me, Joss. Let it go."

"Is that you telling me, or me telling myself? Why do you haunt me?"

"I bring you a warning. At dawn, they'll try to kill you. The guards you've agreed to meet by the ironwood trees are not guards but outlaws who have infiltrated this haven to murder you. Beware!"

"They're just lads!"

"Look into your heart, Joss, and you'll see their story doesn't hold water."

"Everyone is talking about how the temples have ordered it done. As it says in the Tale of Fortune: 'Their spirits were buried.'"

"That's not what I mean. You're a reeve. Investigate!"

"Yes, and you're a reeve, too." The only woman he had truly loved, his first and only lasting passion. She was the only woman he had truly betrayed, and in the worst way: He'd never meant to abandon her to her cruel fate. "So why do I see you in the form of a Guardian, with a death-white cloak and a winged horse? What are the gods trying to tell me?"

"I don't know what the gods are trying to tell you, Joss."

"I wish you were here to tell me where that cursed woman Zubaidit and her brother are got to. Taken some side trail into the Soha Hills, but Scar and I haven't found them."

She looked away abruptly, breaking eye contact. "There's a black tide trickling north and east through the Soha Hills, the remnants of the army."

"Is it true a Guardian commands this 'Star of Life'?"

"Lord Radas commands them."

"Lord Radas of Iliyat?" He remembered the lord's strange behavior, years ago, on the Ili Cutoff. Then he shook his head. "Maybe so. That doesn't make him a Guardian."

"How can any of us know what a Guardian is? They walk abroad, hiding themselves in plain sight. I see with my third eye and I understand with my second heart that they are corrupted, so I dare not approach them. They will destroy me if they find me."

"Because you are a Guardian, or because they are? You speak in riddles."

She looked back toward him without truly meeting his gaze. "I'm alone, Joss. You're the only one I know I can trust."

He tried to make sense of her words. "A man appeared before the Hieros in the Merciless One's temple by Olossi. He demanded she turn over to him a slave, a 'ghost girl,' they called her. He was dressed like an envoy of Ilu, but he claimed to be a Guardian, and the Hieros believed him. He had with him two winged horses, and when he spoke, she said, 'Every heart listened.' As it says in the tale."

He knew Marit as well as he knew any woman, though that knowledge was twenty years' gone. For months, each least variation in her expression had been his most intense study. That cast of face—mouth slack, gaze drawn inward as thoughts raced—and the tension in her shoulders marked surprise and shock as a clever, powerful mind reassessed what it thought it knew.

"A man dressed in the manner of an envoy of Ilu, claiming to be a Guardian? On the trail of an outlander? Seen at the Devourer's temple in Olossi?"

He nodded, but she was already turning her horse, moving for the edge of the promontory. She looked back over a shoulder. "I saw a woman and a man, traveling together, with three horses, camped in the ruins beneath a Guardian altar right where the Soha Cutoff begins its descent into Sohayil."

"Marit!"

The horse opened its wings and sprang into the sky. A gust raked through the overhang, and he woke to find rain spraying over his blanket and boots.

"The hells!" He scrambled out from under the overhang, right into the teeth of the wind. Rain spat into his face, and he wiped his eyes as he stared into the darkness, but there was nothing there. By the time he crawled back into the shelter, found a brand, lit it, and searched the ledge, the rain had wiped every track away. He knew he would have found nothing anyway, no mark of a horse's hoof. It had only been a dream.

The rain passed, the last drops splattering on stone. Scar chirped, rousing, and Joss saw distant objects in the east, evoked by the lightening that presaged dawn. He shook his head like a dog shedding water, and shook out his cloak, then rolled it up. In the dim light he picked his way carefully down the slope. There, sitting on the stone where he'd left him, was the farmer, Pash.

"Greetings of the day," Joss said.

"Morning is coming on," agreed Pash, who seemed remarkably alert for a man who had, presumably, stayed awake all night. "Whether it will bode good, or ill, I can't say. You're up early."

"Where did you say you came from?"

"A little hamlet, you wouldn't have heard of it. We call it Green Water for the particular color of a pool there, a holy place dedicated to the Witherer. It's a day's walk from Candra Crossing."

"Know you anyone here in the haven that's out of Candra Crossing? In particular I am looking for any person who might have served, or be serving, in the temple of Kotaru there."

He chuckled. "Why, indeed, the old battle-axe who took command of us is a captain in the Thunderer's order. You met her. Whew! She hasn't the strength of arm I'm sure she had once, but she has that manner about her that is as good as a blow to the head, if you take my meaning."

"I'd like to see her right away."

She was awake, with the night watch, getting ready to turn their duties over to the day watch. She introduced herself as Lehit. It was true she was old enough that her youthful strength was gone, no great threat when it came to arm-wrestling, but none of the militiamen doubted her authority: A look is as good as a hammer, as the saying went.

At his question, she shook her head. "No youth named Gani apprenticed at the Thunderer's temple in Candra Crossing since I've served there, and that's been forty years. Best we send a party down to the ironwood grove with you. Or better yet, if you'll give me a few breaths to sort things out, set an ambush. If they see us all coming, they're like to flee. I'd like to capture them."

So it happened that, somewhat after dawn, he walked alone along a track through muddy fields toward the grove of ironwood. The tops of these green pillars swayed in the dawn breeze. A lone figure stood beside the massive trunk of the closest tree, waving at him to draw him closer. Just out of what he judged to be bowshot, Joss bent as if to shake a stone from his boot.

Shouts rose from the trees. Joss straightened. The figure had vanished, but a moment later Gani burst from behind the tree and sprinted toward Joss with sword drawn.

The hells! Joss drew his sword. In recent days, he'd felt that weight too often in his hand, for as the old reeves who had trained him had always said, "If you have to draw your sword, you've already lost control of the situation."

Halfway to him, Gani staggered, stumbled, and fell facedown in the dirt with a pair of arrows sticking out of his back. He thrashed a moment, got his head up, and began crawling toward Joss with a grimace of determination on his beardless face. He was still holding his sword. A pair of militiamen jogged out of the trees, bows in hand. As Joss stared, they ran to the lad, tossed down their bows, and stuck him through with their spears as if they were finishing off a wild pig.

Joss trotted over to them, but it was too late. Gani lay with body slack and blood leaking from his mouth. "I thought we were going to capture them."

The two militiamen—one a heavyset young woman and the other an older man—had fury etched in their expressions. Both spat on the corpse before turning to Joss.

"You'll see," said the woman. She tested her right leg, then groped at her right knee.

"How bad?" asked her companion.

"Eh. It'll bruise, but nothing was cut. Now I understand why the holy ones ordered their spirits buried. Fah!" She spat again, wiped her mouth, and kicked the corpse.

"Here, now!" Joss hadn't yet sheathed his sword.

"We'll lay offerings at the Thunderer's altar so his blood doesn't corrupt us," added the woman. "Come on." She limped back toward the trees. Joss and the other man followed.

The settlers in this region had left the rank of ancient ironwood alone, but the woodland behind it showed all the signs of being second-growth, trees and shrubs sprouting where once a mature stand of forest had stood. His companions hacked a way through. He pushed past bushes whose crests waved above his head. His feet squelched on debris soaked by the rains.

A tiny campsite had been cut out of the middle of a particularly labyrinthine architecture of interlaced tranceberry bushes. It was wider than he expected, although still in shadow from the foliage all around it, and covered with a carpet of recently downed branches and the mulch of last year's leaf litter. In this small clearing, eleven ordinands lay dead and two militiamen were wounded. Lehit had her back to him; she was hectoring some poor soul. She saw him, and limped over.

"What happened?" he asked. "I thought you wanted to capture them."

Shock showed in the way she stared at him, as if she could not comprehend words. She shook her head, but was only trying to get strands of hair out of her eyes. She brushed them away with the back of a bloody hand. "Once we suspected they were here, it was easy to track them. We crept in on three sides, and attacked just as we said. They wouldn't surrender. Once they saw they'd lost and that they couldn't escape, they fought to make us kill them, or killed themselves rather than be taken prisoner."

"A frightening sense of purpose. That lad crawled at me with two arrows stuck in his back. He meant to kill me."

"Yet none of that is the worst you'll see." She gestured, and he walked with her over to a sliver of an opening in the pipe-brush.

They had dug a pit into the ground, deep enough that a tall man standing upright could barely touch the rim with outstretched arms. The walls of the pit were slimy with moist soil, worms, and bugs, and the stink of excrement and urine was strong in the depths. Into this pit they had flung children. One was a headless corpse, still dressed in the ragged remains of an everyday short tunic now smeared with dirt and spattered with blood. The rest were alive, staring up fearfully. He counted twelve.

"Are these the missing children?" he asked Lehit, feeling sick. "Do any of you recognize them? Here, let's get them out of here."

They were too afraid to reach up their hands to be pulled free. They didn't know the guardsmen, and it quickly became apparent some had been raped. Coming out of the pit might bring a new round of horrors. One boy began to cry and, after a moment in which they watched the stunned and horrified guardsmen for their reaction and saw that nothing was to happen to the crying boy, the rest began to weep as well.

With an effort, Joss found his voice. "Lehit, send a couple of your guards and ask members of the families who are missing children to come out here."

Two were sent. Lehit stayed, scratching her chin, while the heavyset woman jumped into the pit. The children shrank away from her, but she crouched and began talking in a singsong voice, telling the tale of the Swift Horse, a familiar and soothing bedtime story that every child knew by heart. She didn't look at them or try to engage them; she just talked.

Joss moved back from the edge of the pit. In the clearing, the guardsmen were dragging the bodies to one side, while the older man and Pash knelt beside the wounded pair, stanching and binding.

"Bad enough to kidnap children," said Lehit in a low voice. "But we all hear such stories, when a family becomes desperate without young ones to carry on the line. But to brutalize them in such a manner, and them not even having celebrated their Youth's Crown to be of age! While meanwhile, the Devourer gives freely to any person willing to walk through Her gate. How could any decent person choose this over what the gods have ordained?"

The familiar throb of a headache was beginning to build. Joss rubbed his eyes. "They'd not been here long. It doesn't smell bad enough."

Lehit leaned close. She'd had a bit of rice wine; its sour brack perfumed the air briefly. "How did you know this camp was here? That these youths were part of the enemy's army? We're so overwhelmed with all the folk up in the haven that we'd never have known. I sent out a few patrols to search for the missing children, but . . . how did you guess?"

He thought of his dream. "A reeve asks questions when things don't look right."

"That other reeve didn't ask. Seems to me you've better sight than most."

He shrugged.

Pash walked over, wiping his hands on a bit of torn cloth. "Best we carry the wounded and the young ones back to the haven quickly, for a miasma dwells in this place that would corrupt the healthiest man." He glanced toward the pit.

The woman's voice drifted up, the tale unfolding in a soothing patter of words. The other guardsmen waited in silence.

"How did you know, Reeve?" Pash asked Joss. "We'd have never found them if you hadn't guessed. Them so young to be so foul. Sheh! It's beyond my understanding."

Joss remembered words spoken twenty years ago. He still heard Marit's voice as though she was speaking into his ear. " 'Make them ashamed of themselves and they will not betray you,' " he said, " 'because they will know they have stepped outside the boundaries and made themselves outcast by their deeds.' "

"As the captain's wife said in the Tale of Fortune," mused Pash, shaking his head. "True enough words. Thank the gods I kept my good daughters close beside me."

"No wonder the temples want their spirits buried," said Lehit. "Such corruption must be crushed beneath earth and never allowed to rise. We'll bury them in the very pit they dug. Then we'll lay offerings on the Thunderer's altar so their blood doesn't corrupt us."

In the pit, the young guardsman's voice flowed on. She'd gotten to one of the funny episodes, the encounter of the horse's ass of a merchant and the horse's ass itself, complete with a steaming pile of horse manure always calculated to amuse a child of a certain age, and sure enough there came a tiny childish chuckle, a sound so unexpected that Joss thought he might have dreamed it. Branches snapped, and a pair of young men loped into the clearing with their bare arms scratched up and their faces sweaty.

"We checked all around, Captain, but we saw no evidence that anyone got away."

Lehit nodded. "Good work. No doubt once they'd murdered the reeve, they meant to run. Yet with the children, as well? It makes no sense. They'd be a burden to them. And that poor child—the hells! what do you suppose happened to its head? Why did they want to murder the marshal of Argent Hall?"

"Because we killed the one who came before me, who we have reason to believe was set in place by those commanding the northern army."

"Will you be going back to Argent Hall, then? The hall might be the safest place for you, now you know they're stalking you."

Argent Hall awaited, and he had plenty to do there. "Not yet. There's one last task I must accomplish out here. One last person to track down."

SCAR WAS WELL rested and eager to go. Where the hills shouldered into the plain there were plenty of thermals. They rose, and glided far above the Soha Hills. This range was rugged although not high. Many a narrow valley and densely wooded vale offered shelter to fleeing men. Twice he saw cadres of Qin soldiers on the road, easy to mark because of their distinctive dress and manner of riding and also because one reeve was assigned to each cadre to scout for ambuscade or refugees in the lands along the Soha Cutoff.

Just after midday, they hit the shifting currents that marked the abrupt end of the hills where the land fell away steeply into the wide basin of Sohayil. In the distance, seen as green smudges, he saw hills to the north and east. These slopes were cut by the gaps of West Riding and East Riding, although in truth those gaps lay more to the north and south.

He banked low, spiraling down. Maybe his dreams spoke true, granted him by the gods. Maybe that really had been Marit talking to him, however impossible that might seem. Or maybe it was just a good hunch, filtered through his sleeping mind. For there they were, the pair of them with their three horses, plodding down the switchback trail from the height of the Soha Hills into the deep basin below. They were easy to spot, right out in the open on the bare slope, and they had nowhere to hide here in the afternoon with the rain holding off and no one else on the road. He recognized her the moment he saw her, for no matter how small she might appear there was something in her shape and posture he could never mistake for another. The fugitives paused to look up as he circled overhead, and although he was riding the thermals and quite high above them, he was sure she knew what reeve had tracked her down.

He sent Scar to earth at the base of the trail. The tall grass was greening under the onslaught of early rains. He unhooked from the harness, dropped to the earth, and strode forward to the road. Not too long after, they trudged into sight. It was obvious even from a distance that they were arguing, and soon enough he heard their conversation.

"Bai, we can't just give up—"

"What do you intend to do? Turn around and toil up that damned steep road? It's better to face what's chasing you than to keep running."

She was close enough that he could raise his voice and hope to be heard. "Good advice, verea. For here I am."

Her gait shifted subtly, enough to make him catch in his breath as she sauntered in full swing toward him. She looked him up and down in a measuring way that made his ears burn. "Yet I must be wondering why you have come after us and, apparently, alone but for your fine eagle there."

He grinned. "Reason enough."

"So I imagine, by the look of you."

"Bai!"

Joss spared a glance for the brother, then looked again, surprised that he recognized the young man. The intricate architecture of causation and consequence unfolded before him: he'd met this young man for the first time in the village of Dast Korumbos, when they were both standing over the body of an envoy of Ilu who had been mortally wounded by the ospreys—the bandits—who had invaded the village.

For a moment he was speechless; he'd known, but it hadn't really occurred to him that so many of the players in this tale were linked so neatly. Then they halted in front of him, the horses blowing and stamping, eager for water and yet nervous of the eagle, the woman amused and the man irritated and anxious. Two holy ginny lizards stared at him. Their gaze was unnervingly disapproving, so he shifted his attention.

"Keshad, isn't it?" he asked.

"So it is. We're clear of our debts. We're free to go."

"As it happens, you aren't."

The young man had an expressive, passionate face, although his features were marred by a sense of perpetual impatience and anger. "That bastard Feden—"

"Master Feden is dead. His heirs, indeed all the Greater Houses of Olossi, are in disgrace. You're safe on that count."

"What does the Hieros want?" asked Zubaidit.

She was a truly magnificent young woman, handsome without shallow prettiness, built with the strength of a woman who knows how to labor, forthright, bold, unbelievably attractive. Her black hair was pulled back from her face, but a few thick strands fell over her shoulders. Her sleeveless vest was short enough to show a bit of belly; her kilted wrap left most of her long, muscular legs showing. The hike had made her sweaty; her brown skin glistened. Whew.

"What are you thinking?" she asked with a laugh.

"Just thirsty all of a sudden."

"I can see you're the kind who drinks a lot."

"Eiya! I'm hit."

"Maybe. You clean up well, I'll say that."

"Bai!" protested the irritable brother.

Joss chuckled. "Did I ever thank you for rescuing me?"

"Likely not. In my experience, men so rarely do. They get what they need, and they leave."

"How can I thank you, then?"

"Not in the way you're hoping."

"How can you possibly know what I'm hoping? Verea, I fear it's your own thoughts have taken charge of your lips. Not that I'm complaining."

"Enough of this!" cried the brother. "Make your claim, or let us go on."

"Yes," she agreed, smirking in that maddening way that made Joss hotter than the day warranted. The larger ginny opened its mouth, showing teeth. "What claim are you making?"

The flirtation played between them lost its power to amuse. Whatever his expression showed, she caught his change of mood at once. The smaller ginny hissed.

"What?" she demanded.

He raised both hands, showing empty palms, the old gesture for "it's out of my hands." "I've been sent by order of the temple of Ushara in Olossi, by order of the Hieros with the backing of the Olossi temple conclave, to return both of you to Olossi. For breach of contract. For theft."

She looked thoughtful.

Her brother was not so patient. "I delivered property to the temple, which the Hieros accepted as compensation for Zubaidit's debt. The accounts book was marked and sealed. I have it here in my possession." He patted the strap of the pack he had slung over one shoulder.

"New information has come into the light. That's why I'm here."

"What I offered, the Hieros accepted," said the brother. "The payment was ample compensation for Bai's debt to the temple."

Bai turned to look inquiringly at Joss, as if to say, "How will you answer that?"

He shrugged. "What you offered in payment for your sister's debt was not yours."

"Of course it was mine! If I find a precious stone on the riverbank, it's mine. That is the law, that any item which has no other claimant can be taken and owned by the one who finds it."

"There was another claimant."

"How can there have been another claimant? I found the girl abandoned and dying in the desert so far south of here that I wasn't even in the empire, much less the Hundred! Am I to understand that now any person who likes can just claim whatever he wants? I claim your eagle, then. Or your sword. Or the temple itself! I'll claim Master Feden's storehouse, if I've as much right to do so as another person who dances in after me to claim what *I* found and *I* transported and *I* fed and cared for and I *sold to pay off my sister's debt*!"

"Kesh," said Zubaidit in a soft tone. "Let him speak."

"A man, mature but not yet elderly, came to the temple some nights after you made the exchange," said Joss. "According to the testimony of the Hieros, and corroborated by every hierodule and kalos I interviewed thereafter, he was dressed in the manner of an envoy of Ilu but claimed to be a Guardian."

Kesh snorted. "Guardians! There's a man who knows how to dance a fraud. The Guardians are gone. Vanished. Dead."

"Kesh! Let him finish." The teasing manner she'd had before had fled utterly. This was not a woman you wanted to cross.

"The man went on to say he was sorry if the treasure came into her hands in any manner which led her to believe she could own it."

Kesh was really angry now, puffed up as certain animals fluff up fur or feathers to try to intimidate the beast that has cornered them. "I admit the girl's coloring was odd, her skin as pale as a ghost's and her eyes demon blue and her hair an unnatural gold-white color. But when has it ever been said that no one can own a slave? Except among the Silvers, I grant you. Heh! Did he claim that she was a Silver? None of us have ever seen the faces of their women, although the men don't look anything like that."

"The man claimed that the girl, like him, was a Guardian."

"How can anyone have believed that?"

"The Hieros believed it. She let him take the girl."

"To sell for a tidy profit elsewhere! I didn't know that woman was a fool."

"She's no fool," said Zubaidit.

Joss glanced at Scar, who watched the interaction with his usual uncanny alertness, ready for trouble. At the foot of the hills, the basin still sloped away, and from this vantage one could see the vista rolling into a heat haze. Clouds covered the sun, and the recent rains had softened the air and made it bearable, but it was still hot. A man still sweated, thinking of how much he did not understand about the world. "He came attended by two winged horses."

"Winged horses!" blurted out the brother. "What kind of child's nonsense is this?"

"So my eyes were not cheating me after all. I saw a winged horse in the camp of the army."

"So you told me," Joss said. "I didn't believe you at the time."

"No, you didn't. What happened at Olossi?"

"Captain Anji and his troop, two flights of reeves from Clan Hall, and the newly elected council master of Olossi using the local militia combined forces to drive the northerners away."

She nodded. "There are two of us, and only one of you," she continued amiably enough, but Joss's instinct for danger crawled like a prickling on his skin. Like a fine steel sword, she was a honed weapon. "Even with the eagle, you can't force us to go with you. You can't carry us both."

He braced with the haft of his reeve's staff fixed on the ground, ready to move with a mere tightening of his grip. "I can track you until the Qin soldiers who are hunting down the remnants of the army catch up to us."

"Ah." She nodded with a faint smile. "I concede this match."

The brother fumed, and the glance he loosed at his sister betrayed other emotions struggling beneath the surface.

Joss said, to her, "You truly saw a winged horse at the army's encampment?"

"Yes, on West Track, a few days before the army reached Olossi. Even so, I find it difficult to believe I saw what I did. Do you think this supposed 'envoy' who approached the Hieros could be in league with the dark spirits that attacked Olossi?"

"Dark spirits, indeed," said the brother with unexpected heat. "I've seen what they're capable of. But now I'm wondering about that envoy. I met an envoy coming out of the south, but he was killed by ospreys in Dast Korumbos."

"Ah." Joss nodded. "You remember."

"I'm scarcely likely to forget that day, or that we've met before, ver. The envoy was a man of mature years, not yet elderly, now that I think of it. And he was looking for something. I think he suspected I had the ghost with the demon eyes. Yet he died, so it can't have been him who spoke to the Hieros, can it?"

"It's difficult to see how it could have. Although the descriptions match. It does seem we're talking about the same man."

"Anyway, I cannot see that envoy—such an amiable man!—as being in league with those corrupt soldiers." But, as if struck by a new thought, Keshad sighed sharply.

"What is it?" Bai asked.

"I did meet a different man, with a shadowed manner, and an odd accent. He said nothing of being a Guardian, but I was sure—then I thought I had dreamed it—"

Zubaidit grabbed his arm. "Sure of *what*, Kesh? You never told me this!"

"That hurts!" He pulled his arm out of her grasp. "I was sure he was riding a winged horse. He seemed to leap down right out of the sky, but it was night, and then I thought afterward I had mistaken it. Wouldn't anyone think so?"

"Where did you see this?" she demanded.

Reluctantly, the brother spun a halting tale. He'd been marching with the army, forced to do so because he and his sister had been overtaken by the strike force on its march toward Olossi and it was the only way he could save his own life. By his unfeigned disgust as he related the tale, Joss believed that he'd had no part of the army before or after that encounter. While at their night's bivouac, a man on a winged horse had arrived in the encampment. Keshad had been sent in to speak with him. "He wanted to make sure I wasn't there to betray his company. He gave me such a look, I thought my insides would be torn out. I said I cared nothing for him and his, and it was true anyway, and thankfully he believed me and sent me away. That was the last I heard or saw of him."

"The hells!" said Zubaidit, laughing again. "Say something, reeve. For I think that's shocked you as much as it's shocked me."

Joss eased an itch that had sprung up on the underside of one wrist. "The Hieros also said that the envoy of Ilu told her that there has not been peace in the Hundred for these last many years." He remembered the clipped, forceful way in which she had repeated the words. "That the war for the soul of the Guardians had already begun."

Zubaidit dropped the reins and crossed to stand directly in front of Joss. She stared into his face, as if daring him to look into her heart—or at least, to not drop his gaze down to the swell of her breasts under her tight vest. It was a struggle, but he managed it.

She took hold of one of his wrists. Her fingers were strong, her skin cooler than his own. "Every child who's listened closely to the tales knows the Guardians can't be killed. That's part of what gives them their power. What if more than one Guardian has survived? Or if some are aligned against the others?"

Maybe he swayed, because her grip on his wrist tightened as if to stop him from falling. Marit was dead, but walking again in his dreams, claiming to be a Guardian. Was he crazy?

She released him and walked to the horses.

"We'll go back with you," she said, over her shoulder.

"Bai!"

"Kesh!" Her rejoinder was almost mocking. Her brother winced. There was a passionate quality in the young man's heart that seemed about to burst out over the merchant's chilly façade. "Keshad, what's at stake here is greater than our freedom. We'll go back and face the Hieros. Then we'll seek out the truth about the winged horses people have seen, and the truth about people claiming to be Guardians."

"Why do *we* have to do it?" he whined.

"Because you cheated the temple." Between one breath and the next, Joss's headache returned. "That's a crime."

"I can't have known a mute girl I found at the edge of the desert in foreign lands was—"

"Kesh! We have to do it because it's the right thing to do. Because it has to be done. Because we have an obligation to the gods, and to the Hundred. Now shut up." She turned to Joss, all business now. "Is the road safe?"

"It should be cleared by now. The Qin are efficient and effective."

She cocked her head to one side. "So they are. Let's hope that wolf doesn't bite back."

She took the reins of her horse and, without a backward glance, began the long climb up the switchback. After a glance at Scar and a roll of dark eyes that girls might find pretty, the brother grabbed the reins of the other two horses and followed.

Joss watched them go. They had a hard trudge ahead, and he was already exhausted. Scar chirped an inquiry. Like their reeves, the best eagles learned to judge to a nicety danger and mood in any situation, and they were very smart birds, but they were birds all the same.

And yet what did he really know about the origin of the Hundred's eagles? No more than he knew about the Guardians. He'd encountered strange things in his life: He had seen the eyes of a wilding at the edge of the deep forest where they hunted and lived; he had spoken to one of the rare delvings who walked out of the caverns of Arro into the sunlight; he had traded information with the nomadic lendings in the grasslands through a series of hand signs and stones; he had even heard the rippling voice of a fireling in its brief passage through the sky. He'd dealt with every manner of human greed and generosity, cruelty and kindness, anger and calm acceptance. He'd memorized the law, because it was carved in stone. He'd dedicated his life to serving justice.

Now he wondered: Was it all for nothing?

If it was true the Guardians still walked in the land, and if it was true they warred among themselves, then what could justice possibly mean? How could any ordinary person hope to live a decent life if those the gods had raised to establish and maintain justice in the land had fallen into the shadows?

A shadow fell over him from behind. Scar's big head lowered until the eagle was able to look him in the eye. Joss stroked the curve of the beak offered him.

"We're not beaten yet. Not as long as you and I have anything to say about it. Now go on." He tugged on the leather cord hanging around his neck and pulled his reeve's bone whistle out from under his vest. Raising it to his lips, he blew the set to signal to Scar that the eagle was free to hunt.

The raptor huffed, raking the ground with its talons. Joss walked out of range, and the eagle thrust, beat, and flew, then found a thermal along the steep slope and rose swiftly into the sky. Joss scanned the road. Sister and brother hadn't gotten far. Zubaidit paused to watch the eagle's ascent, then bent her gaze down to where he stood at the base of the trail. With a grin, Joss slung his pack over his back and walked after them.

14

The man long known as an envoy of Ilu stayed too long at the thorn tree shelter on the shore of the Olo'o Sea. He enjoyed the hiss of rain over the wide waters and the smell of the first buds squeezing into the air as the rains woke the drowsing vegetation. He watched the ceaseless spill of clouds as the change in air currents between land and water shredded them. But when one day became three and three became five, their enemies caught up to them.

He never slept, not anymore, but he had learned to slip into a drowse similar to the long interlude before awakening, when he had drifted for untold days weeks months years in a state between waking and sleeping. He liked to think of himself, in this state, as similar to the condition of trees during the season of drought: not dead but held in abeyance.

Change will wake them.

He startled into awareness. First he smelled sweat and fear. Then he heard a branch snap and a whispered exclamation.

The sun nosed up in the east. To the west, the band of the inland sea remained dark, speckled with the last bright stars fading into the rising of day. The girl sat beside him. She had fallen back into her stupor, eyes open but unseeing, mouth lax and hands loose on her thighs.

A pair of unsavory-looking men burst into the clearing, pursued by the bay mare, who had her wings tightly furled along her flanks. She was a biter, mean when she wanted to be, and they edged away as she circled. But they had spotted the two cloaked figures under the shelter. One of the men swung with his spear, and the bay shied away, although she was only playing with them.

With a sigh, he rose and walked out to confront them. They shrank back to the edge of the trees, where an unbroken fence of thorn at just that spot made them hesitate. One was taller, one shorter. He caught the gaze of the shorter man.

The flood of images and thoughts never got any easier to absorb. A man might as well be kicked and beaten, for all that the surge of emotion bruised him.

Gods! Is that a ghost, or a demon? I wonder how she tastes, and if she cries when—

The power we wield over others brings us power. Take pleasure, take pain, take life, and you'll gain strength. Otherwise, you are the victim.

And why should I be persecuted, eh? The Daped clan lied about me cheating them and shamed me in front of the entire village as the hot sun burned and burned

"Stop!" The man's shrill voice rang in the quiet dawn. He tossed aside his spear to fumble with his bow, loosed an arrow that spent itself harmlessly in the dirt.

"The hells!" cursed his taller companion, loosing an arrow in reaction, so careless that the missile wobbled to earth. Then his gaze was caught.

As reward, they give me more coin. With the coin, suck more sweet smoke. Need the coin. Need the smoke.

The bay mare snorted. The gray mare trotted into view from around the far edge of the thorn tree fence. She halted, looking things over with her usual pragmatic consideration. She was even-tempered, but not a horse to mess with. She stretched her neck, then partially opened her wings and charged.

"Shit!" The shorter man lost his anger and his courage, and tossed his bow aside. With his short sword he hacked into the thorn, yelped as the thorns tore at him although no more sharply than his own sour thoughts.

"Eh! Eh!" The taller one stumbled in his wake, too muddled to make his own decisions.

The envoy shuttered his eyes. He let the taste of the breeze moisten his parted lips. He let the scents drifting on the air tickle his nostrils. Others hid in the brush, six in all, a cadre on the hunt.

He heard whispers pitched too low for ordinary ears to hear.

". . . Can't face him . . ."

"Sniveling whiner. No wonder they keep passing you over for promotion. Harbi and I will go."

"Let's just get out of here."

"Then he'll move on and we'll have the hells of a trip tracking him down again. Or you want someone else to get the prize money and the promotion? A chance for the lord's favor?"

"I'm not going back out there. Those horses are cursed demons."

The girl rose. She walked over to the spent arrow and fallen bow, picked them up, examined them with a frown. The envoy caught a glimpse of dark cloth where the men peered out through green branches.

"What is that? A lilu?"

"A demon!"

"A ghost."

"I thought we were just after the sky cloak. I didn't come here to hunt demons!"

She fitted the arrow to the string; tested the pull; swung the bow around to aim into the trees. Loosed the arrow.

A scream—a hit!—surprised him. He heard a shout of pain, then the rustle of undergrowth as they retreated through the undergrowth. Men argued:

"We're six, they're two."

"The horses!"

"Not that easy." That was taller's voice, startled out of his dream of sweetsmoke. He spoke in a mumble that quieted the others. "He'll kill us just by tearing out our insides, just with a look from him. You know it's true. Best we hurry back and report. Maybe he won't chase us if we go quickly."

Eyes narrowed, she spotted the second arrow and fetched it.

In the brush, the whispered debate went on. "You fools. Two of them, six of us."

"Best we saddle the horses, if you will," the envoy said to her.

For the first time, she was listening to him. She walked back to the fire as casually as if no man had just tried to kill them, as if they were not in danger of a second attack coming at any moment.

She whistled, and the horses trotted over to her. He held his staff at the ready, his senses trained on the thorn tree fence and the woodland scrub beyond it, on the noises of the cadre as they crept out of arrow range, debating what to do next, no one able to take charge. He didn't fear them, and if they attacked, he'd have no choice but to kill them. Perhaps they instinctively guessed it, for the taste of their living essence faded entirely. They had chosen retreat.

A weaver bird flitted within the thorns, its wings a faint stutter. Branches ticked against each other as the breeze stirred them. A bud breathed into a trembling petal as it struggled to unfurl with the same slow majesty as wings.

She walked up beside him, leading the horses. He slid back into himself.

She had saddled them, tied on his few possessions. She said nothing; she didn't even look at him but kept staring at the break in the thorn fence where the short man had cut his way out. She was ready to go.

He took Telling's reins and swung into the saddle. He didn't trust the bay mare, and because the girl tolerated her easily, he let her ride the bay.

He turned Telling's head toward the sea, and the girl, on Seeing, followed his lead. He urged the gray to a trot, to a canter, to a run, and as they reached the shore, they unfurled their wings and skimmed over the water, rising on slow wing beats. The sea fell away beneath. As the shelter shrank with distance, the thorn trees could from the height be seen quite obviously to be planted by hand, while the scrub grown beyond them had a wilder scumble.

He was accustomed by now to riding almost everywhere, but he still preferred to walk. You saw things when walking—the blade of grass, the bee's feet tickling a flower petal, the last tear of a wronged woman who has resolved to seek revenge—that the height and power of a horse might hide from your senses. She was at home in the saddle. Aloft, her aspect changed. Her eyes opened wide, watching every-where as they winged over the sea. Even after all this time, each least bobble or hole of turbulence in the air made him gulp and grip and hope he did not tumble. She simply rode.

Eiya! What to do? Where to go? He dared not take her to one of the altars, be-cause there they would easily be spied out. And once she touched her staff, she would likely be out of his control. Yet it wasn't safe to give the staff into her hands until she understood what she was. It wasn't safe to give it into her hands until he was sure she would walk the path he had chosen and not the easier path, the path that begins in light but soon enough crosses under the gate of shadows into cor-ruption.

*   *   *

"WE TELL STORIES to make the time pass between birth and death," Bai was saying.

"I thought the gods gave us stories to help us understand the world," Joss replied.

"So we are taught in the temples," she agreed. "But think about it. What is a story?"

She would chatter on so, flirting with that cursed reeve. Even huffing and puffing up the switchback trail that, incredibly, they'd had to climb back up, those two had talked and talked in the way of people showing off for each other. Kesh wished they would shut up.

"It's not the truth, and yet there's truth in it. It's a way of ordering the truth, just as we order days and weeks and years, as we order guilds and colors and the Hun-dred itself. Did the gods create the tales? No. People like you and me made the tales and told them to others. Even so, the ten Tales of Founding are not like other stories. We made them because the gods commanded us to. Because they help us order the world, just as worship does. And what is the world except that time between when we enter this place and when we leave it?"

They reached the ruins where he and Bai had sheltered last night. Here, Kesh thought, they might decently pause to rest, but the other two would keep talking.

The reeve answered her. "As it says in the Tale of Discovery, 'Where did we come from, and where do we go?'"

"That's right," she said with such a flattering smile that Keshad actually gave a disgusted grunt. She glanced at Kesh and for an instant resembled the child she had once been, his little sister, as she rolled her eyes at him to say, *Don't ruin this for me.*

The reeve didn't notice. He walked to the ruins of a stone wall and jumped up atop it, right at the edge of the drop-off where most men wouldn't dare to stand. Shading his eyes, he gazed across the basin now turning a hazy purple-blue as day-light faded. He was breathing hard, as was Kesh, face suffused with blood. Bai watched the reeve when he wasn't looking at her. This was a side of his sister Kesh had never seen. Sisters weren't supposed to have such feelings, nor to flirt with men so much older. The hells! Bad enough they should flirt at all.

He took a few steps, closing the distance between them.

"Bai, he's old enough to have fathered you. What can you see in a man like that?"

"The horses need water, Kesh. Make sure they don't drink too much."

Stung, he grabbed the reins and led the exhausted horses to the trough while, naturally, she sauntered over toward the reeve.

"Not many men would stand right there at the edge of the cliff," she called to the reeve.

"I've no fear of falling," he said without looking at her. "Or did you think I was afraid of taking the plunge—"

Halfway across the open space, she paused beside a scatter of faced stones long since tumbled from their place. She turned. She raised a hand and, seeing the gesture, Kesh stepped back from the horses. The reeve turned, alerted by her stillness, and when she waved a hand, he started talking again.

"I never feared climbing trees when I was a child, or standing at the very top of the watch tower in Haya, but even so, after years with an eagle, you get used to surveying the land from very high up."

Bai prowled past Kesh, circling the horses and the cistern, and vanished behind the remains of a round building. The reeve nattered on, but as he spoke he drew his short sword and shifted sideways on the wall, ready to move.

"Some people can't abide heights. That's a strange thing about the eagles. They never choose a person who fears heights so much he can't bear to go aloft." He gestured meaningfully at Kesh. *Your turn.*

"Eh, emm, how do reeves get chosen?" Now that he thought about it, he wondered. "I always thought it was other reeves who picked out likely candidates."

"Not at all," said the reeve in a lively voice, although he wasn't smiling. As he spoke, he scanned the ruins. "Eagles choose, not reeves nor any other person. Some do try to put forward certain young men or women. We've been offered bribes. But it makes no difference to the eagles. They will choose at their own—"

A man shrieked. An object slammed against stone, and metal clattered. The reeve leaped from the wall, dashed across the open space, and ran out of sight around the building. Kesh grabbed the horses and pulled them away from the trough.

The reeve backed into view, retreating against the attack of two desperate men. One slapped at him with a staff, while the other cut wildly with an axe. They were not well-trained fighters; the reeve punched away their strokes easily, but he could make no leeway because they were crowding him.

Kesh drew his own sword, but before he could step into the fray, Bai slipped around the other side of the building, climbed over the trough, and raised an arm. She flicked her hand. A blade winked. The man with the axe staggered, fell forward onto his face with a knife lodged in his back. The other man yelped, and the reeve broke inside his guard and twisted the staff out of his hands.

"Down! Put your hands out to the side!"

The man dropped to his knees, ripping at one sleeve, clapping a hand over his mouth as if stifling a scream.

The reeve slapped his shoulder with the flat of his blade. "On your face! Hands out where I can see them!"

Bai nudged the axeman with a foot, yanked out the knife, and rolled him over.

"He's dead." She turned back to the reeve, who stood over the prisoner. "Kill that one, too."

"He's surrendered to my authority. We are not judges, or Guardians, to render a verdict. He must be taken to trial at the assizes."

She shrugged. "Do you mean us to escort him and feed him the entire way? He'll eat our food, and try to kill us. It's a cursed long walk back to Olossi, I'll have you know. I haven't the luxury of eagle's wings to take me in two days what a earth-bound person must walk in ten."

"It's the law," the reeve said.

"I agree with Bai," said Kesh. "Bad enough we have to keep watch for these bandits, but to have to nurse one along who just tried to kill us. . . . The hells! How many were hiding here?"

"Five."

"Where are the other three?"

The prisoner shuddered, seemed about to push himself up. Bai's intent gaze fixed on him, but the reeve placed a foot on the back of the prostrate man to hold him down.

Bai wiped her knife's blade clean on the dead man's tunic, then opened the pouch the man wore at his belt and tossed its contents onto the ground beyond the pooling blood. "Vey. A spoon. A needle with thread. A razor for shaving. Flint. Not much to show for himself."

"They abandoned their supplies when they fled Olossi," said the reeve.

She laughed, a startling sound. "It's a story good enough for the tales. The few against the many. Oil of naya, and rags set alight. Eagles swooping down from the sky."

Kesh was still staring at the dead man. He'd seen death in plenty, walking the roads as a merchant's factor. There are many ways to die, and in time all people do die, even if Beltak's priests talked of a garden where believers dwelled after death on this earth. That place had sounded a better fate than the hells that greeted most folk, but Kesh wasn't sure he believed in hells or gardens. Certainly the sight of a dead man, and a prisoner lying so still as if pretending to be dead, made his stomach hurt. The reeve looked angry. Bai glanced toward the path.

"Here come Qin horsemen," she said, shading her eyes. The sun's westering light fired the Soha Hills. "You sure you don't want me to kill that one?"

The reeve had not slackened his control of the prisoner. His frown made Kesh smile and Bai look twice. "If we allow the law to be altered for our own convenience, then we will have murdered the law anyway."

"There comes a time when change overtakes the traveler, as it says in the Tale of Change."

"Not so great a change as to abandon the law," he protested. "You're the one who agreed to return to the temple because of your respect for the law and the gods."

She lowered her hand. "It's true we can't abandon the law for our own convenience. But I serve the Merciless One, not the reeve halls. Anyway, we can't know how great a change we face. We can't know what may happen next. We must be ready for anything."

Sometimes people talked with words, and sometimes they spoke with looks, and sometimes the way their posture altered communicated their emotion and the words they hadn't uttered. Kesh watched Bai and the reeve, and he knew they were talking but in words and meanings that excluded him. He was alone, as always. Rescuing Bai had not brought him a companion. She had her own path, and it seemed to him that she treated him little differently than she did the horses, as a beast she needed for the time being to make her way.

"Kesh," she said. Hearing his name, his spirits lifted. "Taking the horses to drink at the trough made the bandits think we hadn't noticed they were hiding there."

He twisted out a smile. He'd had no idea bandits were hiding here, and he had a good idea the reeve hadn't either. Only Bai had. Ushara trained her hierodules and kalos in the art of love. But the Devourer was also called the mistress of life, death, and desire, the Merciless One, and in the inner precincts of her temples another sort of acolyte was trained.

Riders appeared on the path. Dust settled around them as they halted. One man dismounted and walked across the ridge path to meet them in the fort. He greeted Joss casually as the reeve sheathed his sword.

"Tohon, this is Zubaidit," said Joss, "and her brother."

"I recall you," said the Qin soldier with a respectful nod and the flash of a grin directed at Bai. He paid no attention to Kesh at all. "I'm Tohon, chief of this small company."

"Yes," she agreed. "I remember you and your captain. Your soldiers did good work in that battle, and better work later, so the reeve tells me."

"We accomplished what was needed," he said, a statement neither modest nor boastful.

"How is the road?" the reeve asked.

"There are others fled ahead of us, but we are now strung out far from our lines. Better if they escape than if we push out too far north and get cut off."

"Yes," the reeve agreed. "It is time to turn back. We've done as much as we can for now. If you will, Tohon, escort these two back to the temple of Ushara outside Olossi. I must return to Argent Hall. Send a messenger ahead of you, and I'll meet you at the temple."

Tohon scratched his chin. "Is this temple the place where a man can walk in with no coin in his hand and a woman will have sex with him? And there is no shame in it?"

"How do folk sate their desires in your country if there is no Devouring temple?" Bai asked. "Or do the Qin imprison women in cages as it is said they do in the Sirniakan Empire?"

Tohon had an interesting face, of the kind of man Kesh did not mind bargaining with: He knew how much he wanted to pay and would bargain without malice until a deal was struck.

"Our daughters and wives are not so free in what they will give to others," he said to Bai, "But neither are we barbarians. We are not like the Sirni."

"Then come to the temple, and be welcome." She finished wiping her hands. With a gesture, she called Kesh. "Let's go. We've got a long walk before us." She looked at the reeve. "Will we meet there, Marshal Joss?"

He looked troubled as he examined the dead man and the living prisoner, now silent and still. "I suppose we will. Here's a prisoner, Tohon."

"That one? He's dead."

"The hells!" The reeve jostled the man with a foot. When he got no reaction, he knelt and turned him over. Sightless eyes stared. Brown foam stained the mouth.

"Poison," said Bai.

"Did you see him take it?"

"I saw him die. Didn't you?"

Without replying, the reeve walked to the wall, and lifted his bone whistle to his lips to call his eagle. A hot wind rose out of the basin, humming among the stones. The sun beat down. Kesh wiped sweat from his brow as he tugged the horses forward.

"He lives too much in the past, and can't see how change is overtaking us," said Bai in a low voice, but her gaze stayed on the reeve.

"I'm just glad the man poisoned himself and spared us the trouble of guarding him. Bai! Must you stare like a lackwit at the very man who's destroyed our plans for a new life?"

"He's a fool," she added, but her eyes said something else.

*　　*　　*

THE ENVOY AND the girl flew north along the shore of the Olo'o Sea, halting during the day to rest and water the horses. The rich farmlands of the Olo Plain gave way to sparsely settled drylands. Irrigated fields and tidy villages became separated by tracts of pastureland and finally by the wilds of scrub grasslands as the land rose steadily toward the foothills. They did not fly high enough to see the peaks of Heaven's Ridge, the mountain range that ran like a huge stockade all along the northwestern border of the Hundred. By late afternoon he began to seek a place where they might shelter for the night.

In a place where a silver stream spilled into the sea, she indicated by gesture and action that she wanted to make camp. Trees crowded the stream's banks, spreading upstream and along a gully. Thickets of assertive chamber-bells in flower spilled into the scorpion grass that carpeted the far hillside. Spiny broom mingled with carob bush.

She took the horses. He walked a wide circuit from the shore, tasting the air for threat. He allowed his sense of the world to expand until the smallest things touched him: the snuffling of a red deer through a stand of pipe tree; the rattle of a pair of yellow caps within the cover of the prickly-branched chamber-bells; the respiration of blue tranquillity flowers, petals quivering with each touch of the breeze. The gasp of breath as life, and spirit, escape a living creature.

He stood, turned his head, listened.

Footsteps crashed through brush. A mouth panted. There came a branch-splintering tumble, a grunt, and then a cough of triumph. The salt heat of blood spilled onto the wind. He ran back to the camp, his face hot and his hands cold with fear.

With the other arrow, she had killed a small red deer, slit its throat, and hung it from the branch of the largest nearby tree, hindquarters up and head down. She had filled his good bronze cup with deer's blood. Her lips were stained as red as a jarya's as she looked up and, seeing his hurried approach, offered him the cup.

"Neh, neh, I am sure I do not care for any of that," he said, swallowing a bitter taste in his own mouth. To drink blood fresh from the animal was a barbaric custom known among the lendings or the herdsmen in the Barrens but not among the civilized city folk where he'd been bred and raised. Yet as the thought struck him, his revulsion vanished as he paused to watch what she would do next.

She drained the cup and set it aside. With his machete in hand, she wandered into the trees. He followed her, taking the cup, which he rinsed out in the stream. She tested first this tree, then that. She tore off strips of bark and twisted them; she chopped down saplings and bent them, testing their spring and strength. With a quickening of breath, she saw what she wanted: the tree known as silver-bark, which usually preferred higher ground and a cooler climate. Somehow, a scattering had taken root in a damp depression where the stream had made its bed in former years. She measured, then cut down one that was more than a sapling but not yet truly a tree. This together with two saplings she dragged back through the undergrowth to their camp.

He watched, not wanting to interfere, although he set up a shelter against the rains that might come in the night. She took out every item he possessed and sorted them: The iron pot and tripod legs she kept beside her, the cup and leather bottles she set aside. Flint and knives and awl and shovel she set beside the pot. He caught in his breath when she examined the writing box, but she placed it unopened back in the saddle bags with the small brass lamp and strings of vey and leya. Needles, leather, cordage and straps she recognized; the scissors she puzzled over.

First, she cut three long strips of wood, like backbones, out of the trees she had felled.

Dusk interrupted her, but in the morning she set to work. While bark boiled in the pot, she skinned the deer, then butchered it. She carefully pulled and scraped off the glistening sinew from its back and neck and legs. She cleaned and washed skin, sinew, and membranes. She rendered fat and boiled glue stock, cooling it in hollows in bare rock. She cut down saplings and shaped them into arrows. She practiced with the captured bow.

Her industry silenced him; he had not before seen her work to such purpose, and he did not want any word he uttered to distract her, for what she did now revealed much about what she was and where she might have come from.

15

They reached Olossi at last, and in the temple dedicated to Ushara, the Merciless One, the All-Consuming Devourer, Keshad scratched along his jaw into the fresh growth of new beard, trying to get out the dust that chafed his skin. A dozen Qin soldiers sat on a bench in the courtyard while Bai scolded him in a low voice as Magic hissed.

"You have to wait here with them. Explain the way things go. Make sure they don't insult any of the hierodules or kalos."

"Why not just let them wait outside the temple while you attend the council? Outlanders can never be properly respectful in the temple. You ought to know that."

"If the Qin truly intend to settle here, they must learn our ways. Since they have to wait for me anyway, this is a perfect opportunity to begin. So, you're responsible for their behavior."

"*Me?* They don't even like me!"

"Stop whining, Kesh."

Mischief parted her mouth in a brief, mocking smile.

With the ginnies on her shoulders, Bai sauntered to the white gates that led into the garden of the Hieros, the innermost sanctum of the temple. The Qin soldiers watched her go, but Kesh couldn't tell if their interest was sexual or a more masculine form of comradely respect. Certainly during the long ride here she had joked and sparred with the soldiers in the most casual manner. She was not as physically strong, one to one, but she was quick, fearless, toughened to pain, and well trained in every kind of dirty trick. The soldiers had liked that about her. Of course they had ignored Kesh.

The white gates opened a crack, and Bai slipped inside. A hush settled over the Heart Garden where Kesh and the Qin sat. Men shifted, toying with their hands or shuffling their feet. One rose, turning toward the entry gate, ready to leave.

"Shai, sit down," said Tohon.

The young man sat.

The glorious blue and violet stardrops of Kesh's previous visit had been stripped bare by the rains, but the rest of the garden had bloomed, and the woozy scent of flowering musk vine overlaid everything. It made you open your eyes and look around, aware of the sharp, bright beauty of the world.

"Heya! Zubaidit's brother! Where are the whores?" asked Chaji, the soldier with pretty eyes and the features that most passed for good looks in the Hundred.

As if his words were a summons, the gates of gold opened without a sound. Four young women and one young man strolled out to look over the foreigners. The kalos was dressed in a kilt and vest, while the four hierodules wore taloos draped fetchingly around their figures.

One of the hierodules was a tall, lanky girl with a teasing grin. "I'm Walla," she said to Kesh. "Do you remember me?"

He tried not to stare at the swell of her breasts under the tightly wrapped taloos. Every part of him remembered her, although he'd never touched her.

"You're Bai's brother. You thought you were so smart, but you two are in deep trouble now. Hah!"

Chaji stood and grabbed Walla by the forearm. "I take this one."

The look she turned on him should have killed him; he didn't even notice as he tightened his grip. The other holy ones became very quiet and very still. Even the breeze seemed to falter and catch its breath. Tohon rose. The younger soldiers watched with steady gazes.

"Eiya!" Kesh made a show of getting up with a hefty sigh. "That's not how you do it! There are customs to be followed. If you offend the holy ones you'll never be allowed to pass the gate a second time."

Chaji, despite his pretty eyes or perhaps because of them, had a spoiled temperament. He stared blankly at Kesh and did not remove his hand from Walla's shapely arm.

Tohon said, "This is a brothel. We choose one. Coin changes hand with the mistress of the place. We get our pleasure. She gets the coin. We leave. Neh?"

"There are times I wonder why the Merciless One opens her gates to all," murmured the kalos to Walla as the other three rolled their eyes, looking disgusted. "They're such savages. In their lands, those who should be allowed to offer pleasure freely are slaves forced to the work."

"No," said Kesh to him, "those who might offer freely aren't allowed to. It's considered shameful. Those who are slaves are forced to the work whether they wish it or no."

Now he had shocked them. Here in the southwest, where they entertained the most traffic from outlanders of any of the temples, the holy ones ought to have known better. By their horrified expressions, they did not.

"The customs of your country are not the customs here," said Kesh to Tohon. When he looked at Walla he received for his pains another mocking smile that made him sweat. "This is not a brothel. No coin changes hands. This is a holy temple. The holy ones give freely because they serve the goddess Ushara, the mistress of war, death, and desire."

The Qin looked at him blankly, not understanding.

"Never mind," said Kesh impatiently.

He closed a hand over Chaji's wrist and yanked to dislodge his grip. He barely shifted Chaji's arm, but the soldier sucked in breath with an audible hiss, then released Walla and slugged him.

The blow landed on his shoulder, and he staggered back with a yelp. The holy ones shouted for the warders, Chaji grabbed at Walla, and Tohon strode into the breach with angry words that sat Chaji down on the bench as though he'd been shoved. Everyone quieted. A pair of broad-shouldered warders, easily spotted in orange sashes, showed up from the outer court.

Walla examined Tohon and, then, Chaji with his petulant expression but obedient seat on the bench. She made a sign with her left hand, and the warders stepped back to lounge watchfully by the gate.

"Maybe we get tired of explaining ourselves to grasping, rude, horny outlanders," she said to Kesh. Her stare made him self-conscious in a way both irritating and provocative.

"When you come to the temple, you are offering yourself at the altar of the goddess," Kesh said to the Qin. "The hierodules and kalos choose you if they are willing to, ah, worship with you." He brushed a hand over his curly hair, aware that he was blushing. Not that any of it was at all shameful, only that Walla was bullying him. He wondered if she hated Bai, and if this was payback for an old rivalry.

"*They* choose us?" Tohon tugged at his ear, obviously wondering if he'd heard wrong. Of all the Qin soldiers, this middle-aged man was the only one Kesh respected. He ruled his cadre firmly but without cruelty; he conversed pleasantly with Zubaidit, treating her like a comrade. The worst Keshad could say of him was that he seemed genuinely to like that cursed reeve, Joss.

"The hierodule or kalos makes the offer. You can refuse it, if you wish, and hope to receive another offer. Which may come, or may not. Men walk through the gate of gold and women through the gate of silver, to the gardens, where the acolytes of the Merciless One wait. Then it's up to you to accept or refuse what is offered."

"What of these four here?" asked Tohon, indicating the four hierodules and ignoring the young man.

"These *five* acolytes," said Kesh, "all reside beyond the gate of gold, which admits men to the inner precincts. They came here to the Heart Garden because you're outlanders, and they wanted to see if you could behave according to the temple rules. Not all outlanders can."

"I can behave!" said one of the young soldiers, Jagi, with a grin, and Walla looked right at him, seeing something in his smile that interested her.

The one called Pil looked sidelong at the kalos, then away quickly before anyone could notice, but the kalos marked the look and yet hung back.

Tohon was still stroking the nub of his ear. "Huh. What else are we to know?"

"You'll all need baths." Walla bent her gaze on Jagi, whose grin widened. "But you won't mind that. Whew! You all do smell. How often do you wash those heavy garments?"

"Take a *bath*?" cried Chaji. "In *water*?"

"Here, now," said Tohon, beckoning to Kesh. "Is that necessary?"

"I should think so." Even the heady smell of blooming flowers could not cover the rancid odor of the men and, in particular, their clothing. "Folk in the Hundred bathe every day if they can. Don't you have bathhouses in your country?"

This word brought blank looks.

"Water weakens a man," said Chaji.

"It's not what we're accustomed to." Tohon had given up on the ear and was now twisting the few whiskers that grew, like a wraith's beard, from his chin. "There are evil spirits in water. Everyone knows that."

The bold and brave Qin soldiers shuffled their feet and looked toward the gate to the outer court, as if seeking escape.

"The baths lie just beyond the gate," said Walla, "and you can advance no farther into the goddess's body without cleansing." She beckoned to her companions. They sauntered back to the gate and went in, leaving the gates ajar.

"Baths aren't bad," said Shai hesitantly, and the others looked at him, and away. "They never killed anyone, eh?"

Released by the sun's heat, fragrance poured off the flowers until it seemed to drown them. Birds flitted within the lush arbors of musk vine with their bright red passion flowers.

Jagi jumped to his feet. "I'll try it!"

That was enough for most of them. They trundled forward cautiously, leaving

Kesh sitting on the bench beside Shai, Chaji, and Tohon. Tohon gestured to Shai, and the young man sighed but, obediently, stood and followed the others.

"It can't be right, this story about the whores picking and choosing and turning a man down if he wants them," said Chaji after Shai was gone. "They're just saying that to take advantage of us."

"Best you go in after them," said Tohon to Kesh. "Make sure the lads do what is fitting. We have to learn to live in this land."

He might as well have been in collusion with Bai! With a grimace, Kesh rose. "You're not coming?"

Tohon slanted a gaze sidelong toward Chaji. "Anyway," he added, "I have an old feud with the water spirits. I'm not sure about these 'baths.'"

"There are bathing pools, it's true," said Kesh, "but you can also just wash yourself out of a big basin. You just have to strip down and wash your whole body with a cloth and soap. You have to clean yourself before you can get in the pools anyway. And, honestly, you might want to—well—wash your clothes."

Chaji rose, both hands in fists. "What makes you think you can insult us? You're no better than a naked rat, a worthless—"

"Chaji-na," said Tohon sharply. The young soldier sat down, shoulders heaving.

Kesh was shaking, but he kept his voice cool. "I was born in the Year of the Goat, Gold Goat, as it happens, not that you would know what that signifies."

"No need," said Tohon mildly, "to keep talking, lads. I'd recommend you both to shut your mouths. Keshad, go on, as I told you."

Chaji lifted his gaze just enough to let Kesh know he was looking. Those pretty eyes didn't impress Kesh; glaring, he crossed his arms.

"Go on," said Tohon, voice like the snap of a whip.

Kesh grabbed his small pack; everything else they'd left at a stable in the village of Dast Olo, by the pier where they'd taken boats to the temple island. Behind, he heard Chaji murmur, his words too faint to understand, and Tohon's curt rejoinder. He reached the gate, set a hand on the painted door, and paused before stepping into the garden of gold. From inside, he heard the spill of water into a basin; he heard laughter. A woman was singing a familiar song in time to the beat of a hand drum and the rhythm of shaken bells: *I paused inside the gate and beheld the garden.*

"Keshad!" A youth wearing the casual kilt of the off-duty acolyte stood over by the white gates, beckoning to him.

The hells! Kesh walked over to the youth, where Tohon met them.

"It seems you and I are called to the council," said the soldier to Kesh. "Chaji waits here. The rest—hu!—let's hope they behave."

Back on the bench, half concealed at this angle by the arbors and flowering trees, Chaji sat in sullen silence, fists pressed in his lap.

"The Hieros wants you right now," said the temple lad impatiently.

Kesh and Tohon followed him through the white gates into a courtyard filled with a tangle of vegetation. A narrow path littered with petals and old leaves cushioned their steps.

"Hu!" muttered Tohon. "What a thick forest! I can see nothing." His gaze darted this way and that, and once he stopped and abruptly brushed at his face. Then he stared into the shadowed branches. Draped on a limb, a ginny stared at the Qin with a look Kesh recognized as amusement.

"Huh!" grunted Tohon. "That's the male Zubaidit keeps. She let him go."

"They're the goddess's acolytes," the lad called over his shoulder. "They belong here, truly. Anyway, the Hieros doesn't like to be kept waiting. She's got many more things to accomplish today, and wants this business finished and closed."

Kesh wiped his brow and scratched his chin. The shade gave relief against the sun, but the overwhelming scent of green growing things oppressed him. They strode out into the open space in the center where the fountain splashed, water tracing the strenuous curves of a man and woman intertwined in the act of devouring.

Tohon actually blushed, and looked away, gaze fixed on the back of the lad, who kept walking without a glance at the sculpture to another path on the far side of the clearing. This path wound through a jungle of spiky orange and yellow proudhorn and falls of purple muzz and white heaven-kiss, their scent almost too sweet. Tohon walked as if expecting an attack.

A steeply slanted tile roof rose from the greenery. They ascended a flight of stone steps, pressing through uncut shoots of musk vine that groped at Kesh's body. He staggered into a pavilion of surpassing beauty: the pillars painted in gold leaf designs; the benches upholstered with rich fabrics so expensive that immediately his mind toted up their worth in days of labor and the price of slaves; the floor inlaid with a complicated pattern of precious woods. The lad threw out an arm before Kesh or Tohon could actually step onto the floor, and indicated that they must remove their shoes and then sit to one side on a pair of plain silk pillows.

Four waited in the pavilion, sipping wine. Zubaidit looked perfectly comfortable seated cross-legged on a pillow, ginnyless. Beside her, that cursed reeve flirted with a smile on his smugly handsome face as he made some quip meant for Zubaidit's amusement. Captain Anji sat quietly. Bai marked Kesh's arrival with a glance but did not acknowledge him. The reeve kept talking, attention fixed on Bai. The Qin captain noted Tohon, then Kesh, and gave each a crisp nod before turning back to the conversation.

The fourth person sketched a greeting. Master Calon was the head of a well-to-do merchant house whose faction had never before held power in the city, although today he wore the crossed sash of a seated council member with the red braid of power fixed to his right shoulder. In the aftermath of the battle, a huge change had swept the city and council of Olossi. The Greater Houses, who had held power for untold generations, had fallen to the machinations of the Lesser Houses and the guilds in alliance with Captain Anji and his troop.

A pair of elderly hierodules—by their age, lifelong slaves to the goddess— mounted the steps and with a tinkling of bells announced the arrival of the Hieros. All rose, Kesh last of all. How he hated this woman!

Her attendants helped her sit on a particularly fine pillow covered in a heavy damask of an intense jade green that set off the pale pipe-sprout of her rich silk taloos. For such a delicate, frail, elderly little woman, she had a stare that hammered you. And she was gloating. He could see it in her smirk as she addressed the gathered company.

"That man, the Qin sergeant. The stink of his clothing offends me. Have your people some objection to bathing, Captain? Yet by all report you are yourself perfectly happy to indulge in the baths in the city."

"I see you have a network well placed to bring you all manner of reports, holy one," said the captain with a faint smile.

"As you will yourself in time, I expect," she retorted. "You haven't answered my question."

Captain Anji looked at Tohon, gave a nod.

Tohon's expression remained calm, his voice untroubled. "I can answer for myself, holy one. As a man who has earned respect, I ask to be treated with respect."

She looked him over. His gaze, on her, was not challenging but it was also not submissive. "I will listen to your words."

He acknowledged her reply with a nod. "It is well known among my people that the water spirits hate human beings. They are kin to demons, and therefore there is a long war between us. We Qin know better than to trouble the spirits. Maybe you folk have a better understanding with them than we do. Anyway, my daughter drowned, and my wife died of grief from losing her to the water spirits."

Kesh expected the Hieros to scoff at this ridiculous story. There weren't any spirits in water except for strong currents and unexpected eddies. The merlings lived in the sea, but they were living, material creatures like humans and delvings and firelings, not spirits. Even demons were living creatures with powers beyond human understanding. The only spirits abroad in the world were ghosts. Everyone knew that.

The Hieros touched fingers to her right ear and then her forehead, the gesture of hearing and understanding. "Very well. If you wish to walk in the temple, then come to me personally. Like all hierodules, I am trained in the act of cleansing a body in preparation for the act of worship. I am powerful enough to protect you against anything, within these walls, that might wish to harm you."

The temple lad whistled under his breath, Bai looked baffled and Joss and Master Calon amazed, but the elderly hierodules made no comment at this remarkable offer. It was impossible to know what Captain Anji was thinking.

Tohon tugged on his left ear, blinked, and then met the Hieros's steady gaze. "My thanks to you, holy one."

Kesh hadn't known the old bitch could smile in a friendly way, but she did so now, like a flirting girl all lit up when a boy agrees to meet her family. "That's settled, then. Now to our other business." The smile vanished. She turned a cold shoulder to Kesh quite deliberately, drawing attention to his disgrace. "Marshal Joss, you've fulfilled your duty and brought me these criminals. Zubaidit I absolve from fault, although naturally she will have to return her accounts bundle and resume her service with the temple. She can't have known that her brother would use a stolen object to purchase her freedom. He, on the other hand, must pay full forfeit and be prosecuted for his crime of buying out the contract of a temple slave under false pretenses. He tried to cheat us. The temples cannot allow such behavior to go unpunished."

"The girl came into my possession by finder's right, which none of you can dispute," objected Kesh. "How can I have known some envoy of Ilu would come along to make a claim on her? How do I even know you're telling the truth? You could be trying to cheat *me*, to get Bai back into your claws."

She continued as if he hadn't spoken. "How the assizes choose to deal with any complaint in the matter brought by his former master, matters not to me. Master Feden is dead and his house disgraced—"

"I bought out my own contract with trade goods! Nothing illegal about that!"

"—so it may be that the heirs of the House of Quartered Flowers will bring no claim against him. But the temple certainly means to take back what is rightfully ours—"

"Only because you'd been cheating her all along, you old bitch—"

"Keshad!" snapped the reeve. "Be quiet!"

"I won't be quiet! I've been found at fault without being allowed to speak in my own defense, or have any kind of representation at the assizes. She means to tilt the judgment against me before I ever stand up at the rail. What kind of justice is that? Or do the reeves simply stamp as justice what's the wish of those in power?"

Ha! That stung!

The reeve examined Kesh with a look that hadn't the hammer of the old bitch's look but which was just as annoying, like someone poking into you to see what would make you squeak. Kesh shifted on his pillow and rubbed his throat. Tohon coughed into a hand. Bai watched the Hieros much as the ginnies had watched her.

The captain broke in. "If you will. It appears the dispute rests on whether this man, Keshad, brother to Zubaidit, had a legal claim on the individual whose body he used as payment for his sister's freedom. He exchanged a girl he found in the south for the outstanding balance on his sister's accounts book, the unpaid balance of which kept her as a debt slave to the temple. Am I correct?"

"You are," said the reeve.

"I accepted the female as payment because of her obvious value," said the Hieros. "I would have been a fool to let such a treasure pass out of the temple's hands. However, it appears she belonged to someone else."

"This is the part I do not understand," said the captain. "A man came to the temple, at night, and claimed the female. Did he have a contract? Proof of ownership? He might himself have been a thief, a clever con man, who cheated you and left the blame to fall on Keshad."

There is a silence that soothes, and a silence that frightens. Silence can conceal, or reveal. It can make you stop and think, or it can be a warning. The garden lay quiet behind them, smothered in green growing things. Clouds scudded overhead, piling up over the Olo'o Sea. Kesh smelled rain coming, but it hadn't reached them yet.

"He was a Guardian," said the Hieros, "and so was the girl."

Nine simple words, coolly spoken. A cold thrill woke in Kesh. Guardians walking the land again! He could not imagine what it might mean for the Hundred. Or for him.

He got up clumsily and glared all around. "Maybe it's true, maybe it isn't. But how would she ever have gotten to the Hundred, eh? Many months' journey! She could never have made it alone, a naked girl, with nothing and no one, starving, mute, lost. *I* brought her here."

"You have no idea what Guardians are capable of, or why she might have been walking in the south," began the Hieros in a cruel voice. "You are the worst kind, making excuses for your crime, refusing to accept responsibility for the acts you have committed. Don't think I don't have reports of what you did as Master Feden's factor, how you treated those in his employ, how you treated your fellow debt slaves, how you used them and discarded them—"

The captain broke in, politely. "I beg your pardon, holy one. It seems to me that, while you are perfectly reasonable in your assessment of the young man's faults, they are not among the concerns that trouble us most in these days."

"That he cheated the temple is of no concern to you?"

Captain Anji had a pleasant smile that deflected anger. "It is of greatest concern to me, although naturally you understand that as a newcomer to the Hundred, I do not worship at the altar of your gods for I do not know them. But I am aware that every land is tightly woven with its gods. This dispute is a matter to be judged carefully, and thoroughly. My concern is that you may have no chance to do so if other events overtake us in the meantime."

The old bitch counted her temple and her authority higher than any cursed thing in the Hundred, that was obvious. But when she looked at the captain, she raised a hand, wristlet bells tinkling like whispers, and touched ear and forehead to show respect.

"Captain Anji, your actions in recent days saved Olossi, and this temple. You've earned the right to speak. Kass, pour wine around."

The lad poured gracefully from a silver pitcher into goblets adorned with intricate silver patterns and tiny pearls: the Hieros first, of course, then the reeve who as marshal of Argent Hall deserved special respect, then Master Calon, then the captain followed by Tohon. Zubaidit and the two attendants were served last, and the lad took the pitcher away without offering Kesh anything.

They drank. Tohon nudged Kesh. The pressure jarred his aching shoulder. He hissed pain through his teeth. Tohon tapped the cup, still half full of wine, against Kesh's arm. Gratefully, Kesh took the cup and drank.

Anji set down his own cup on the floor beside his right knee. "I'll make short work of my accounting of events. Our company rode into the Hundred as guards for a caravan, but we were also looking for a place to settle and begin a new life."

"Because there is a succession dispute in the Sirniakan Empire," said the Hieros. "The current emperor, Farazadihosh, considers you a rival because you are his half brother, sons of the same father, Emperor Farutanihosh, now deceased. Meanwhile, his cousins—who are also your cousins, the sons of your father's younger brother—dispute Farazadihosh's right to the imperial throne and title."

"You have good sources of information, holy one."

"I do. It may be that your relation to the imperial court will cause trouble for us later, but for now I am content with matters as they stand because I do not see we have any choice. Go on."

"The Hundred is no longer a peaceful land, that we can all agree on. There is trouble in the north. A city called High Haldia has fallen to an army commanded possibly by a man known as Lord Radas. Toskala and the lands of lower Haldia lie under immediate threat. The commander of all the reeve halls sits in authority in Toskala, and there also many of your ancient traditions have their heart, although I understand that the largest city in the Hundred is called Nessumara and lies farther south, on the delta of the River Istri."

"You've grasped a great deal of the Hundred in your short time among us, Captain."

"I have good sources of information," he said with a smile. Was he sparring with the Hieros, or dancing to her chant? It was hard to tell. "A second army marched south and west on West Track to attack Olossi. Too late the people of Olossi discovered that some among the Greater Houses had made a pact with this army, to consolidate their hold on the Olossi council. Too late, these same members of the Greater Houses discovered that the leaders of this army had no intention of honoring that pact but meant to burn and pillage Olossi as they did the villages lying along West Track. Together with Marshal Joss and the reeves of Clan Hall and the support of Olossi's new ruling council and their militia, my troop managed to rout the besiegers. We then pursued those who fled, and have killed as many we can. However, many have escaped back into the north and east whence they came. It is obvious to me, and I hope to everyone, that if they could attempt this attack once, they can regroup and try again. They have numbers, coin, wagons, weapons, and horses in plenty. And it seems to me that they have something more difficult to defend against, some manner of sorcery."

He picked up his cup and drained it, set it down with a thap that made Kesh start. "I have come to the Hundred to make a home for myself in a place where I may know peace, and to raise children with my wife. That is all I hope for."

"Where is your wife?" asked the Hieros. "I have heard many speak of her, but she has not come to the temple."

"Nor will she."

"Ooosh!" murmured Kesh.

The reeve coughed, while Master Calon gasped at the implied insult.

The Hieros pounced. "Why is that? Here today you are come to the temple."

Captain Anji opened his mouth to speak, and then he closed it and said nothing.

Marshal Joss said, "Surely an outlander who worships another god is not expected to visit the temples of the Hundred."

"What gods does your wife worship, Captain? Surely not the god of the empire, for that god does not look kindly upon women. Or so my sources tell me."

His mouth twisted in annoyance. He picked up the cup, noted it was empty, and set it down again, but now his expression was neutral and his voice smooth. "The Lord of Lords and King of Kings rules each person as befits his nature, men according to what is proper to men and women according to what is proper to women. But you are right. My wife is not of the empire. She prays to the Merciful One, whose mercy is known all along the Golden Road and past the southern desert even into the lands beyond the Sky Pass and the towering heights of the Heavenly Mountains."

"Ah," said the Hieros. "The orange priests. There's an old hut far up on the Kandaran Pass where an orange priest once lived with his begging bowl. It's said he would give aid to travelers without regard to their station or their gods. Then he died. Gone altogether beyond, as they say in their prayers. Such a strange phrase, 'gone altogether beyond.' What does it even mean?" She was still holding her cup. She handed it to an attendant, her wristlet bells chiming softly with the movement. "So, Captain, it is true that a shadow has grown in the north, a shadow we cannot name. By your efforts and those of the reeves of Clan Hall, many of us were saved. Yet this war is not over."

"It is assuredly not over."

He had a whip, which he'd been allowed to keep on the temple grounds. He played with it now, pulling its length through a hand as he considered what he meant to say. At length, he turned an inquiring gaze on Master Calon.

Briskly, Calon said, "I am here as representative of Olossi's ruling council. This man has accepted as a temporary measure the responsibility to oversee the defense of the city and the surrounding region of Olo'osson. We ask for your cooperation and the cooperation of all the local temples in our efforts to live in peace in our own homes."

Now Kesh understood. In the region of Olo'osson, long overseen by the town of Olossi, the Greater Houses had ruled until the battle two weeks ago, when a cabal of Olossi merchants and guildsman, a troop of outlander mercenaries, and that cursed reeve from the north had defeated the invading army and overthrown the Greater Houses. The Hieros was the most powerful temple official of any of the temples in Olo'osson. Joss represented the reeves, Anji the militia, and Master Calon the Olossi council. The four of them met now to decide what action they would take next.

So much for the vaunted council of Olossi, with its warring factions and voting members and raucous assemblies! So much for village elders and local authorities and temple priests. Here Kesh sat, witnessing the only council that mattered. He was here by accident, because he was a bit of flotsam that the Hieros wanted to sweep up, being the kind of person who didn't forgive anyone who defeated her in even the smallest way. Yet as long as they didn't kill him, he could find a way to exchange knowledge for coin or something even better: freedom and the right to be let go without interference. They hadn't beaten him yet.

"When I make a plan," Anji said, "I prefer to know as much about my enemy as possible. I have heard the Tale of the Guardians, but surely there is more you can tell me about the Guardians."

"The gods formed the Guardians out of the land to serve justice. The gods sustained them as they went about this duty. Yet they vanished from the Hundred when my grandmother was a girl, so we had come to believe they were gone forever."

"Anyone may claim to be a Guardian," said Joss suddenly, "and maybe they are, and maybe they aren't."

The Hieros turned her proud gaze on the reeve, making him glance away before he had the courage to meet that stare. " 'You will know the Guardians when you meet them,' " she quoted. "Can you doubt it, Marshal Joss? Do you doubt it?"

He said nothing.

She said, "I do not doubt, nor should you. I have seen the truth with my own eyes. I have touched the truth in my heart. The envoy told me that there is war among the Guardians. Fear this, for even as he spoke the words, I knew them to be true in my heart and in my spirit. Where the Guardians war, the Hundred falls into darkness and chaos. The tide of that war has swept over us once. If we do not resist it, protect ourselves, and push back, we will drown."

"What you're saying, holy one," said the captain, "is that in truth you know very little about the enemy we face."

"Captain," murmured the reeve warningly.

Master Calon fluttered a nervous gesture with a hand.

The Hieros smiled coldly. "That is indeed what I am saying. The Guardians withdrew from the affairs of ordinary men many rounds of years ago. We who are mortal were never privy to Guardian councils in any case. Now their wars have spilled over the land, but we are as ignorant of their plans and feuds and their network of influence—always hidden from us!—as are newly born infants just waking to the riot of life."

"Ignorance will kill us," said the captain.

"Yes."

He nodded. "This is my proposal. We send scouts into the north."

"To what end? The reeves already spy out the northern army, scout troop movements, mark which villages and towns are under threat, and report back."

"They do their work well," he agreed, nodding at Joss, "but they and their eagles are targets when on the ground. They cannot walk into the heart of the enemy and hope to learn their plans."

"Any such venture is likely to end in death," she said.

"Perhaps. But without good intelligence, and careful observation of the lay of the land and the discipline and organization of the army, we can't hope to confront, much less defeat, a force so much larger than our own. Tohon is a scout of unsurpassed excellence, whose observations I would trust with my life. He can bring one of his own men to carry a message back to us, if necessary. If I had my way, your servant Zubaidit would go as well. We must seek every opportunity that offers itself. If anyone can assassinate the army's commander, she can."

Kesh gasped aloud. He hadn't finished the wine; it spilled now, the dregs staining his tunic. Tohon grasped his wrist and tightened his grip until Kesh sank back passively. But he'd already lost the battle. A grin tugged at Bai's lips. Her shoulders straightened, and her chin rose.

"Eiya!" said the old bitch. "You're quick to throw my best weapon into the worst battle."

"The battle will be upon us whether we wish it or not, holy one. The only question is, on our terms or theirs? You know she is the best choice."

She knew it, so she refused to acknowledge him.

Bai said, "I'll go, but on condition that Keshad is cleared of all charges against him."

"Yes, indeed," said the Hieros scathingly, "cleared of charges, let to go free, and you'll hare off and join him once you've walked out of Olo'osson, no doubt."

"He can remain under house arrest under my guard until Zubaidit returns, or her death is confirmed," said the captain.

"Do you think you're bargaining over a loaf of bread or a bolt of silk?" demanded Kesh. "I refuse—"

"Enough!" said Marshal Joss. "Shut your mouth, you self-regarding idiot! You've got no rights in this negotiation. If you're fortunate, you may benefit from it, so just be quiet."

"You've got no call to talk my brother that way!" cried Bai.

"You've come to me to set the seal on your plan?" asked the Hieros of the captain.

"You stand highest among those who sit in authority over the temples of Olo'osson," said the captain. "You know it must be done this way."

" 'A sharp blade can cut both ways,' " she said.

"I beg your pardon?" demanded Joss. "What has the Tale of Change to do with the matter at hand?"

"Do our weapons serve us well, or ill?" Raising both hands, she traced phrases from the tale with graceful gestures accompanied by the tinkling of her wristlets. She need not sing the chant, for all they knew the words by heart. *In he rode, the one meant to save them, the handsome one, with his sash and his kilt, his sash and his kilt and his garland of sunbright. But the gods embrace silence. The gods turn away, they avert their eyes.*

"This is not a language I understand," said the captain.

"No," agreed the Hieros. "You are an outlander. It is the language of our heart, we who live in the Hundred. Very well. It is true that if we cut off the head of the snake, the body might die. The price Zubaidit names for her cooperation is not too high. I will consult with the other temples and we will choose a second candidate as well, someone suitable for spying. What about the council, Master Calon?"

"I think it's a fool's errand," said Master Calon with a heavy sigh, "tried once before and ending in utter failure. But my voice was overruled. The council wishes to make contact with clan members in the north, restore alliances, and so on. Three have been chosen to go, well-connected sons and nephews, alas. That cub Eliar pushed and pushed."

"The Ri Amarah wish to send one of their young men as part of the scouting group?" asked the Hieros. "To see what profits can be reaped?"

Kesh snorted. "In what way are they different than the rest of the merchants, then?"

The captain said, quietly, "the lives of the Ri Amarah are at risk, just as ours are."

"The presence of a Ri Amarah man would give away the scouts immediately," said Joss.

Calon raised his hands to signal a stop. "The cub's father forbade it before I was forced to point out that a Silver would be spotted a mey away. The three men we're sending are at least good fighters. However, anyone seeing the Qin soldiers will know them at once for outlanders."

"They'll pose as runaway slaves," said the captain.

Kesh touched the raggedly healed scar beside his left eye.

The marshal said, "will you tattoo them? That's how debt slaves are marked here. The enemy will have heard tales about the outlanders who aided Olossi. They'll be suspicious."

"I'll take Shai," said Tohon, "for he looks nothing like the Qin. No one need know we are any relation. Anyway, Shai has family business up by this town called Horn. Captain?"

At first, the captain looked ready to refuse, but then his expression changed as he thought of something he did not share with the others. "Yes," he said with narrowed eyes. "Shai might prove very valuable. But let me tell my wife that he's to go."

"We are agreed, then." The Hieros clapped her hands. Her attendants helped her stand, although Kesh doubted she needed the aid. For such an old woman she was limber and vital, perfectly at ease. Before she stepped off the pavilion, she turned back. "So, Captain, what does your wife do now, while you sit in the councils of power?"

"She is not absent from the councils of power. Her skills are of a different constitution than mine. I would suppose that right now she is settling matters of land, title, and business."

"Ah." She acknowledged Master Calon and Marshal Joss with a nod and Bai with a critical stare that, strangely, softened her eyes. Kesh might as well not have existed, but at length she smiled at Tohon.

"Hu!" He laughed. "Don't mind if I do. Captain?"

The captain nodded. As Tohon followed the Hieros into the garden, Anji caught Kesh's attention with his gaze. "You'll come with me," he said, no argument about it.

Kesh looked helplessly at Bai, but she shrugged. The hells! She was already thinking about walking into the shadows. Walking into death, it might as well be. He'd bought her freedom with tainted goods, and now they'd been thrown back into slavery, as if the simple act of daring to grab for freedom had cursed them to worse than what had come before.

She'd be dead and he . . . It hit him as in the gut, a blow that made him double over with fear and grief. He'd be alone, without purpose, for that was all that had sustained him during the twelve years he'd labored as Feden's debt slave: the hope of freeing his beloved younger sister.

"Kesh?" Leaping up, she crossed to kneel beside him. "Is it something you ate? The old bitch didn't even offer you wine, just for the spite of it!" Her hand warmed Kesh's shoulder.

"I'm all right." He forced his fear under control like a hand pressing billowing cloth back into an open chest in a high wind. "Do you have to go?"

"Of course I have to go."

"You're just going to abandon me? And the ginnies, too?"

"They can't come on such a mission. They'll be well taken care of." She turned to confront the captain. "He'll be well taken care of, Captain. That's what I expect." She swiveled her head to glare at the reeve. "All the charges dropped, just as I said, Marshal. Is it agreed?"

She was a wolf, ready to lunge for the kill, but they were predators, too. Joss was a proud, handsome eagle. Folk had started calling the Qin soldiers "the black wolves" for their manner of dress, and even though Captain Anji had not been born in the Year of the Wolf as Bai had, he might easily be mistaken for that beast.

Anji's smile showed teeth, a threat. "Are you questioning my honesty, or my honor?"

She grinned the reckless grin Kesh had come to distrust. "You're still an outlander, Captain Anji. So we'll see."

Anger burned in his expression, a tightening of the eyes.

"I expect to be judged in the same manner," she added. "Yet you've held a hostage for my honor."

His shoulders relaxed. "True enough. I'll treat him as my own cousin." His wolf's grin flashed. "By Qin laws of hospitality, I assure you, for in the imperial palace of Sirniaka, any male cousin or half brother of mine is dead by now."

"I'll see Keshad is well treated," said Master Calon. "I know his worth."

Kesh offered him a grateful nod.

Bai embraced him. "Courage, Kesh. Keep your eyes open and your heart bold."

She released him. Let him go.

"I never had anything to do with the charges brought against your brother," said the reeve to her, "and I'll thank you not to imply I had."

Kesh put on his shoes and, with the captain and Calon, descended by the stairs behind Kass. Bai remained in the pavilion, and it appeared she had fallen into a roaring argument with that cursed reeve.

"Whew!" said Kass with an appreciative look toward the pavilion and the pair under its roof. "She really fancies him, doesn't she? She'll chew him right up, and I bet me he'll love every minute of it. I never saw her go after a man like that before."

"She's a respectable woman," said Anji repressively. "It's ill-mannered to speak of women in such a way."

Kass laughed merrily. "You outlanders!" He looked around for someone to agree with him, but Kesh couldn't be bothered and Calon was lost to sight down the path. Kass glanced back a final time. "Heya! She's slapped him! I knew she had a temper, but—"

A thick curtain of patience cut off their view.

"Slapped him!" yelped Kesh, shifting to go back, but Captain Anji caught his wrist.

"If she didn't fancy him, she'd have slugged him and been done with it," said Kass. "That's foreplay for certain folk."

"I've heard enough," said the captain.

Branches rattled. Bai appeared on the path, flushed and breathing hard.

"He wouldn't lie down quickly enough, eh?" said Kass.

Her hand darted out.

"Ow! That hurt!" A mark reddened on the lad's forearm.

"You pinched him!" said Kesh.

"Nothing the little pest hasn't earned twelve times over!"

Grinning, the lad rubbed his arm.

Her glare did not cause the flowers to erupt into flames, but it was a close thing. Kesh remembered the woman who killed so skillfully that she couldn't possibly be his timid little sister. He remembered the way the reeve had stared at her after the ambush. Troubled, Kesh had to admit, rather like Kesh was troubled. He wanted to hate that cursed arrogant reeve, but at the moment he wondered if they shared something in common, wondering what kind of person Bai had become, an assassin sent into the north to kill.

"There comes a time when change overtakes the traveler." Bai pushed past Kass and Kesh, and skirted the captain more politely. "If you don't mind, I'll walk a little way with you. Where do you go now, Captain?"

He was an odd man, seeming such an outlander one instant and then, with an unexpectedly charming smile, such a familiar one. "Where do I always go, to find my heart's ease? To my wife, of course."

16

A trio of hirelings unshackled and dragged open the doors before retreating to the courtyard to await further orders. Sunlight poured a path into the dark interior. Mai ventured a few steps into the empty warehouse, smelling dust, the loft of air above her head, and a faint sweet rotting scent.

Chief Tuvi cut in front of her. "Let the lads go in first."

She stepped back beyond the threshold as four Qin soldiers entered the building while outside the hirelings took down wooden shutters to reveal rice-paper windows. Each stripe of light revealed more of the warehouse, a long building with a bench built along one side and windows set above, a row of cubicles on the opposite side, and a complicated structure of roof beams visible all the way to the shadowed cleft within the peak. When the soldiers had checked out every corner, they gave the all-clear and she walked into the hall.

"What was this used for, and why was it closed up?" Mai asked Eliar.

"This warehouse is owned by the House of the Embers Moon. Thirteen years ago they fell into a dispute with the Greater Houses. I need not tell you that the Greater Houses went out of their way to ruin the house's fortunes and destroy its reputation. In the end, the last adult member of the house made public what the gullible thought was a wild accusation: that the Greater Houses were involved in a conspiracy, that they'd allied with unnamed villains out of the north."

"Which is true."

Eliar snorted, flashed a grin, then sobered. "Yes, all too true, which I tried to tell everyone a thousand times for all the good it did. When he vanished, some said he'd been arrested by the militia and sent to the assizes prison. Others said he'd been murdered."

"He's the one Captain Beron murdered, isn't that right? Master Feden ordered the murder done on behalf of the Greater Houses. And then the temple ordered Captain Beron's murder when they discovered he'd carried out an assassination without their imprimatur. Are the politics of Olossi always this convoluted?"

Eliar heaved a passionate sigh. "Olossi got off easy. Thanks to Captain Anji. And to you."

He smiled his charming, flirtatious smile. Chief Tuvi eyed him skeptically. As if Tuvi could possibly think an untested youth like Eliar compared to Anji!

"Anyway," Mai said, waving Priya and O'eki forward for a look, "what's that sad tale to do with this warehouse?"

Eliar's gesture, indicating the echoing space, made the silver bracelets on his forearms jingle. "With no adults remaining to stand in authority over the house, the business was shut down by order of the Greater Houses. All their stock and their contracts and slaves and real estate were placed in administrative hold until the case be resolved."

"There are child heirs? No adults at all?"

"Eight under-age children. No adults except for hirelings under contract and debt slaves. Many of the hirelings were naturally released from their contracts, and of the slaves, some were sold to pay for maintenance expenses." Frowning, he glanced at Priya and O'eki.

"Hu! That's one way to rid yourself of business competition. What merchandise did the House of the Embers Moon deal in?"

"Oil, of course. For as the moon wanes, you've more need of lamps, do you not?"

She smiled. She liked Eliar. He had a mind like hers in many ways, he treated her with a respect she'd never experienced in the house where she had grown up, and of course his clan had shown her nothing but gracious generosity. Most importantly, he was Miravia's beloved brother.

And he was still talking. "Cooking oils, spiced oils."

"Rose oil? Other perfumed oils?"

"I suppose so."

"Oil of naya?"

"They would have had access to the trade route, since seeps lie in the western Barrens beyond the Olo'o Sea."

"Nut oils? Thatch-tree oil? Mu oil?"

He smiled. "Oil is not my specialty, so I don't know. This particular warehouse is set up to store their stock in storerooms depending on type and grade."

She counted the narrow cubicles, opening doors and testing latches. "Each of these can be separately locked shut."

"Mistress, I'll check the rooms, take a count, and measure space," said O'eki.

"Yes." At the far end of the warehouse a single room ran the width of the space, with heavy braces and tripods for lamps and a pair of elaborately carved low writing desks beside two wide cabinets with numerous small sliding drawers to store parchment and scrolls. "The main office. What is through those doors?"

"The public receiving rooms of the house. There are private living rooms as well, accessible through a hidden door. This was the clan's headquarters, their main compound in Olossi, so it's an elaborate compound. They own two warehouses in the outer city and a small estate on West Spur where they grow olives. They stored their best product here, under the watchful eye of loyal guards. The head of the household lived here while residing in the city."

Mai was tired, her feet hurt, and she had constantly a bad taste in her mouth. She touched her belly, and with a blush drew her hand away in the hope no one had noticed.

Priya was there in an instant, hand under her elbow. "Mistress, do you need to sit down? I saw trees beyond the walls of the main courtyard. Perhaps there is a garden where you might rest." The slave looked at their escort.

Eliar nodded. "I have the keys to the living quarters and gardens as well. Shall we go in?"

A pall of dust had settled over the living quarters. Mai shuddered, finding the vacant quarters eerie in neglect with the furniture left neatly in place and one cabinet door ajar as though someone had meant to get something and then left before closing the door. She kept expecting a stranger—or a ghost—to walk into the chambers.

The compound included two gardens, one an intimate herb and flower garden and the other a larger enclosure with a dozen fruit and nut trees ranked on either side of a pair of tiled basins filled with water and the scattered debris of fallen leaves and withered petals. Priya brushed windblown scraps off a bench under an octagonal pavilion sited between the long pools. Mai sank down gratefully. Several roof tiles had smashed on the paving, and an iron lamp stand listed on one broken leg.

"This is very pretty," she said, because when she talked she could ignore the bile creeping up the back of her throat.

"It hasn't been maintained." Eliar surveyed the garden with a critical eye while Chief Tuvi paced the length of the basins and back, counting steps under his breath.

Mai coughed, and swallowed.

"Mistress?" Priya knelt beside her.

"Nothing I shouldn't have expected."

"Would you like to go back to my family's compound?" Eliar asked, looking pink and embarrassed.

"No." Louder and more firmly, she repeated herself. "No. If there are no adults remaining, then who can negotiate for use rights for this compound?"

"The council has appointed a temporary factor to oversee the clan's interests. Usually in such matters a hierophant from one of the temples of Sapanasu is hired until the estate is settled or a child reaches legal age. In this case, as I happen to know . . ."

Mai pressed a hand to her collarbone as Eliar's words blurred away into meaningless noise.

Chief Tuvi trotted back. "Mistress?" he asked.

Priya said, matter-of-factly, "Just the usual sick."

Mai said, "Oh, no."

She stumbled down off the pavilion and made it to a patch of bare earth before vomiting. The wet soil stained the fabric of her gown, and her hands came up dripping crumbs of earth. Yet even with the taste of vomit in her mouth, she felt better.

"Grandmother would say, 'Now you have fertilized the garden, you must plant in it.'" She wiped her mouth with the back of a hand.

Eliar flushed as though he'd been burned. Tuvi laughed.

A door slammed shut with a sharp report. Footsteps raced on stone flooring.

Tuvi drew his sword, swearing under his breath. "Move behind me," said the chief.

Mai had never forgotten the armed men who had burst into her private chamber in an inn in Sirniaka. She could still see their pragmatic expressions, men bent on killing with no feeling but of business that needed to be concluded. Not again! She ran over to the grizzled soldier, while Priya placed herself between Mai and the house.

Mai's young uncle barged out into the garden. A pair of Qin soldiers followed, not hiding their grins.

"Shai!" cried Mai on a burst of expelled air. "You frightened me!"

"What's this, Seren? Tam?" Tuvi's glare jolted all three young men to a halt. "With all your clattering, I thought the Red Hounds had found this house."

Shai said nothing, as usual.

Seren was first to speak. "This one"—he gestured to Shai—"was in a hurry. Sorry, Chief. Captain Anji is in the warehouse talking to Mountain."

"His name is O'eki," said Mai, more curtly than she intended, still panting from the scare.

"Shai calls him Mountain," said Seren with a shrug.

"I'm going after Hari," said Shai.

Now that Mai's heart could slow down and with her stomach settling, she saw that Shai was holding his entire body as though ready to leap. "Uncle Hari? He's dead."

He hauled her out of earshot of the others. Tuvi grunted, but did not otherwise react.

Shai bent close, whispering in an urgent voice. "It's my chance to prove myself, Mai. They're letting me go on a scouting expedition into the north, with Tohon and some others."

"How many of you?"

"Seven."

Seven sent to scout the trail of a marauding army now in retreat! Already she imagined their violent deaths, just like in the tales, cut to ribbons and the pieces dropped into a dry ravine.

Shai was still talking. "Father Mei sent me to find Hari's bones and return them to the family. Now I have a chance."

He glanced over his shoulder toward the waiting Qin as they both heard voices from the inner rooms. His hand tightened on her wrist. She gritted her teeth because he was strong from years of carpentry, and he was anyway more passionate now than she had ever seen him in all the years they had grown up together in the same clan house in faraway Kartu, where she had been everyone's favorite child and Shai had been the youngest and least-favored of Grandmother's seven sons, only two years older than she was. They had played together more like siblings than niece and uncle, and she knew him as well as anyone did.

His round face glowed, and maybe it was sweat but maybe it was determination that animated him. "I have a chance to prove myself to the Qin."

More Qin soldiers poured through the doors into the garden. When Anji appeared, still talking to O'eki, Shai released her. She rubbed her wrist as Anji marked Chief Tuvi and Priya, greeted Eliar with a nod, and walked over to her.

"You'll have heard," he said to Mai. Shai dropped his gaze to the paving stones. "The scouts leave tomorrow at dawn." He narrowed his eyes and leaned closer. "You are sick?"

"I am well, just the usual trouble."

"What trouble?" demanded Shai.

She made a sharp sideways gesture with her head, and mercifully he took the hint and moved away, then halted to watch them.

"Why does Shai go?" she asked in a low voice. "He isn't a soldier."

"It's true he's not ready for the rigors and subtleties of such an assignment, but it would be dishonorable of him not to seek out his missing brother at Horn."

"He could easily die!"

"Tohon will look after him. There's another reason. You know and I know that for whatever reason, both Shai and I can see the ghosts of the newly dead. He can even hear their voices, which I cannot."

"Yes, and in Kartu, people who saw ghosts were *burned*."

"That may be true, but among the Qin, they were honored as holy ones, and in the empire, such boys were taken away to become priests."

"You weren't."

"Because I was the son of the Sirniakan emperor, and nephew of the Qin var through his sister, who was my mother."

"Yet both your father and your uncle betrayed you in the end."

He shook his head curtly. "Leave it, Mai. My point is, we don't know how such people are treated in the Hundred, whether honored or hated. But what matters right now is that a man who can hear the voices of newly-made ghosts makes a valuable scout."

"What if he doesn't come back, Anji? He's my only kinsman here."

"Then it has fallen out as it will fall out."

Further argument was useless. Anji was determined, and anyway Shai did have to try to find Hari's bones or he would dishonor the Mei clan. She nodded her acquiescence. Shai, seeing her nod, smiled brilliantly at her, a rare gift from a young man usually frowning.

Anji went on. "I am thinking it is time for me to ride a circuit of the countryside to survey possible settlement sites for us and the men."

Anxiety fluttered within her chest. So might a bird react, finding itself caged. Anything might happen. It already had. But Mai knew from long practice how to quiet her fears. She put on her market face. "Ride west, and survey the estate of the House of the Embers Moon. They also own this compound."

Anji looked closely at her, rocked back on his heels, and forward again. "You are interested in renting from the House of the Embers Moon?"

"No. We should acquire the entire house, which has no living adult members, and its assets. I'll have to look through their accounts first. Their specialty trade was in oil. Their primary olive estate lies on West Spur. That road gives access to the trade route for oil of naya."

"King's oil. Very good, Mai. King's oil saved us."

"So I was thinking. If we mean to establish ourselves in this country, then it seems to me we should make sure we always have king's oil in our possession." She frowned.

"What troubles you, plum blossom?"

"West and south lies the empire. I thought today—even Chief Tuvi thought it— what if the Red Hounds follow us here?"

He did not often touch her in public, but he did so now, a delicate touch as light as a bird's as he brushed her hand. He did not smile to placate or reassure her. He never played that dishonest game. He knew the risks, as did she.

"Sometimes you have to fight where you stand," he said, reminding her of her own words to him. He lifted his hand to show the wolf-sigil ring he had taken from her hand as a sign of the gamble they had mutually agreed on the night they had decided to make that stand, to build a new life in the Hundred. "We can pre- pare our ground, so any fight we enter is under circumstances and in the place of our choosing."

17

The Barrens were a dry and brutal place, thoroughly unpleasant. Keshad winced as he walked down to the shore of the Olo'o Sea. The air stank, and his eyes watered, but the tears came mostly because of the stabbing pains in his buttocks and thighs.

"You're not accustomed to riding." Captain Anji halted on a slick shelf of rock lapped by oily water.

"I was a slave," said Kesh irritably. "Slaves walk, or at least they do in the Hun- dred."

"Yet you walked south over the Kandaran Pass many times in order to trade, and returned safely each time. That suggests you are hardier than you act, and smarter than your sulks and dagger's tongue make you appear."

Kesh eyed the Qin captain in the last light of the day, with the sun pouring light across the calm salt sea. Anji was a man of medium height, with the coloring and broad cheekbones common to his Qin tribesmen but a sharp-hooked nose more usually seen among the Sirniakans of the empire. He intimidated Kesh far more than his old master, Feden, ever had, because while Feden had been a tyrant, a man of pouts and rages, he was also a man whose pouting and raging made him vulnerable. As he had been in the end, for the price he had paid for selling out Olossi to the northern army was his own life.

Anji had none of those weaknesses. Kesh was sore not so much because they had been traveling for ten days but because they had pushed on, with a string of mounts for each man, at such a blistering pace. He was rubbed raw in places he did not want to think about. But in this group he would never dream of complaining. Under Anji's leadership, no one complained. They just got on with it.

Now they were many days' ride west of Olossi, having rounded the southern limit of the Olo'o Sea and ridden north into the Barrens with the land-locked sea stretching away to the east and the jagged Spires rising abruptly in the west. Broken tableland bridged the transition between mountains and water.

"You can't farm this land," said Kesh. "Not like that estate on the West Spur we stopped at. At least that had a substantial olive grove." He crouched, drew a finger across flat rock, and tasted the substance on his tongue. It was oily, salty, and entirely nasty. He spat. "But there are unexploited seeps of oil of naya everywhere in this region, if hard to reach and transport."

"There's enough grass for sheep and goats to graze. Streams coming down out of the mountains, and other sources of water to be channeled. There may be water and forage enough for horses and even cattle, maybe even fields." The captain scanned the landscape. "Maybe a spring is hidden out there."

They had left West Spur days ago and ridden north-northeast on a cart track past a few villages and hamlets so isolated that everyone had come to stand at the side of the track to watch fifty Qin soldiers ride past. The locals had been wary, but not scared; as the local experts in oil of naya and pitch, they didn't expect trouble, even from foreigners.

More fools they, thought Kesh. The Qin could have slaughtered them without breaking a sweat.

"There's no one living this far out," added Anji. "I haven't even seen herdsmen with flocks."

"All the villages we passed trade in oil and pitch. There are enough seeps and sinks south of here to keep them in livelihood. I'm sure traders send expeditions into this region occasionally, but it's difficult to transport." Kesh shaded his eyes. "If you keep riding north, if there's a path, which I doubt there is, you'll eventually reach the valley of the River Ireni. Ten or twenty days' walk, I'm not sure."

Anji indicated the sea. "Has no one thought of sailing from here to Olossi?"

"Trade over the water is expensive to maintain, and anyway there's nothing much to trade. There's a route that runs overland from Olossi around the eastern shore of the sea and then north through the valley of the River Ireni, that I just mentioned. Heaven's Ridge and the Spires meet northwest of there. It's possible to travel over the hump from there into the land beyond the Hundred, the white-grass plains, but it's so dry out there that no one goes that way except to trade with the barbarians—eiya!—that is, the folk who live on the plains."

"Like the Qin." That quirk in his lips was Anji's way of showing amusement.

Kesh found himself smiling. "Like the Qin. Horses, hides, steel, gems, slaves."

The wind off the mountains brought a chill that crawled along his shoulders. He shuddered, thinking of the ghost girl he had brought out of the southern desert. "I heard there are tribes of demons on the plains. You can tell them by their blue eyes and white-grass hair."

Anji looked away from Kesh, and something about the way his shoulders stiffened and his jaw moved slightly, as though he was swallowing hatred, made Kesh wonder what the Qin captain was thinking. "Plenty of demons. We Qin have battled demons for generations."

Caution stilled Keshad's tongue. The oily film oozed and bubbled on the rocks, and the smell hit so hard it was like tasting. Then a wave of salt water washed the edge of the shelf, changing the composition of the liquid, and the stink eased.

Anji said, "You know a great deal about the trading routes in and around the Hundred."

"How much I know might depend on what it's worth to me."

Anji's smile made Kesh shiver. "Your sister's life and freedom, perhaps?"

"You have no control over that!"

"Is that so? The Hieros placed you in my custody, and in my custody you'll remain until the transaction is complete. Yet what can you do? You're not a soldier, a farmer, a herdsman, a craftsman, a poet to weave songs and tales. A man who contributes nothing to the tribe is worthless. If he has his own tent and herd, he may survive on his own, but if hard times come—and they always do—he'll need the support of his kinsmen. You and your sister are alone, without tent or herds. That leaves you vulnerable."

"Do you want something from me? Just say so!"

The sun set behind the mountains. A fire burned where the Qin soldiers had set up camp. Two guardsmen waited close by, arms crossed and shoulders slumped in a posture that to the untrained eye might appear as boredom, but Kesh knew from experience that the men who guarded Anji never relaxed.

Nor did Anji.

"You may carry an accounts bundle that marks you as a man freed of this debt obligation you Hundred folk call slavery. But a man is not free if his heart is not free. It seems to me, Keshad, that you are always carrying your chains. You trust no man because you cannot trust yourself." He began to walk carefully along the rock shelf toward drier ground beyond.

Kesh hurried after him, sliding once, arms flailing, and righting himself. "Why should I trust any man? What man has ever done right by me, or tried to do anything but exploit me?"

Anji's boots crunched on gritty earth. He flashed a grin over his shoulder for no reason Kesh could fathom. "That's the first sensible thing I've heard you say since we rode out on this expedition. Trust no man. No man except one who holds honor higher than his own life."

"Where can I find a man like that?" demanded Kesh.

A cool wind chased down from the heights. The fading light cast a warm glow over peaks whose ragged contours were softened by the change of light. Over the sea, scraps of cloud drifted into shadow, but here there was no rain.

"Where, indeed? 'How?' is the question you should ask."

A spark can touch off a conflagration. Kesh boiled with anger, not even knowing why. "What makes you think there is a single honorable person in this world?"

The press of darkness swept over them, the bright fire their only beacon in an empty land. Anji spoke in a quiet voice that was nevertheless perfectly clear.

"Because I am married to her."

18

No one disturbed their encampment in the wild lands bordering the northeastern shore of the Olo'o Sea. As one day passed into the next, the envoy of Ilu figured out how to help the girl in her work. He'd not grown up in the country, with country ways and country skills. He was a city boy by birth and training, accustomed to buying what he needed from the shops and artisans and craftsmen of Nessumara. Yet after so many years of wandering alone, he'd learned to survive.

He cleaned hide, a task he detested. Really, it was so unpleasant to get one's hands so slick and stinking. He wove a crude shelter of green saplings, and built a fire of greenwood to smoke the deer meat. He spent an entire afternoon scouring the stench of glue-making out of his precious iron pot, which had accompanied him for so many years he sometimes thought of it as a congenial friend. He left the horses to stand guard—for they would be sure to alert him if they sensed an enemy approaching—and ranged wide, gathering edible plants. He walked the shoreline until he found a place where salt pans had formed. The deer's hooves were boiled, and antlers polished. When she vanished one day with Seeing, he took from Telling's calm manner a message, and he waited for her to return, which she did late in the day bearing the deer skin wrapped around a slimy collection of cattle parts: four horns, raw hide, intestines, sinew, heart, and the best cuts of meat. He asked no questions. She volunteered no answers.

She carved and shaped hooks and drills and points from bone; she chewed sinew to make it malleable, then rolled it into thread. She glued side strips of a denser red wood to the backbone of silver-bark, and in the shallow channel along each face, glued strips of horn. She carved out and smoothed a ring of bone to fit her right thumb.

He sat beside her. She showed him with her hands what she wanted him to do, and he did it: scraping, polishing, grinding, twisting, oiling. Talking, for he could not bear the lack of words.

"As it says in the Tale of Beginnings, 'We tell ourselves stories to make the time pass between birth and death'. But it's more than that. We tell tales to try to understand the world, the gods, and ourselves. Let me tell you a tale."

He told the story punctuated by the most basic of gestures, enough to suggest the tale's outlines. As he spoke, she measured and she glued and she shaped, but he was not sure if she listened.

"Long ago, in the time of shadows, a bitter series of wars, feuds, and reprisals laid waste to the countryside and impoverished the lords and guildsmen and farmers and artisans of the Hundred. In the worst of days, an orphaned girl knelt at the shore of the lake sacred to the gods and prayed that peace might return to her land . . ."

The tale unfolded easily, but then, he had always found it easy to talk.

". . . Now it so happened that the girl had walked as a mendicant in the service of the Lady of Beasts, and when the other gods departed, the Lady of Beasts remained behind.

" 'They are content,' said the Lady of Beasts, 'but I see with the sight of eagles and I listen with the heart of an ox. For this reason, I know that in the times to come the most beloved among the guardians will betray her companions.'

" 'Is there no hope, then, for the land and its people?'—"

He broke off, smiling humbly as he watched her hands.

At last he saw it take shape.

She was making a bow.

She looked up. The feverish gleam of those demon-blue eyes, touching his own gaze, startled him.

"A good bow demands patience," she said, challenging his stare. "This one—" She touched the bow at her right hand. "—I'll reflex on a form and store in a dry place for many months. Then maybe after two winters it will become a good bow. This other, if the glue sets properly and I give it more time, maybe it will serve until the other is properly cured. I'll make a pair of simple bows from staves. But a cured bow is best if you want to reliably kill a man."

He gaped, speech squeezed out of him by the force and content of her words. Her speech was fluid and easy although her vowels were clipped, very short, and she coughed certain consonants and slurred others. Had she known the language of the Hundred all along, or had it poured into her when her destiny enveloped her?

Telling neighed. Seeing raised her head to look upstream.

The girl rose, grabbing the captured bow and a handful of crude arrows, shafts with sharpened points. She pushed her cloak back over her shoulders, to leave her arms unencumbered. He stood, too, gripping his staff.

"What cursed use is it," he muttered, "to wait so patiently, to spend these days in silence so the child wakens a little more—with such triumph!—only to be caught yet again by those hells-bitten criminals?" He was shaking, even angry, really just entirely twisted dry of the good humor he prized most of all as a Water-touched Blue Rat sworn to serve Ilu the Herald.

Dusk had crept over them without his noticing. The gleam of their cloaks gave them an aura, and made them targets. The horses, of course, could barely be seen. He saw an inconstant pattern of light fading and waxing by the nearest thicket of chamber-bells; their delicate tinkling caught in the wind.

A woman stepped into view, wrapped in a bone-white cloak. He knew that cloak. Once, he had known the man who wore it.

"Who are you?" she demanded. "What are you?"

The girl nocked an arrow and drew back the string with thumb and forefinger.

The woman shifted, not moving closer but not retreating. "Nay, that was ill-said.

I am here to talk with you, nothing more. Do not think I am here to threaten you." Yet her tone was that of a woman accustomed to ordering people about. "I would know who and what you are, for others have spoken of you, and I think you are not what you seem. Oh, the hells!"

Almost he chuckled, to hear the voice of authority break with frustration.

She continued. "Are you Guardians, or are you not? I beg you, tell me what you know so I can understand what has happened to me."

The girl glanced at him as a soldier looks to her captain for the order to loose, but he shook his head, yet raised a hand to show that she must stay ready.

"Show me your staff," he called, "and we can talk."

"I have a walking stick." She held out a trim pole. "I can defend myself, lest you believe otherwise!"

His disappointment was sharper than he expected. Also, he recognized the stab of fear that pricked his breast, but he smiled to show a bland face. "No need to quarrel with me. I am a peaceful man, camping here in the wilderness where I had hoped to bide undisturbed."

"You don't trust me!"

"It seems you are standing a long way from me."

"I want to trust you. But I don't know who to trust. I have seen others . . ." She glanced at the girl with a shake of her head. Then she clucked, and a pale shape moved out of the shadows: a horse.

Telling snorted, as in greeting, and the other horse replied with a whinny and a toss of its head. Seeing flicked her ears dismissively.

"What others?" he asked, because, alas, he knew now what she was. She belonged to his opponents, her staff held by them as hostage to keep her a prisoner to their will. They had sent her to hunt him down.

"There's no point in loosing that arrow at her," he said to the girl, "because even if you hit her squarely, you cannot harm her."

She nodded to show she'd heard, but her gaze, and the arrow, remained fixed on the target.

"There are others like us," said the woman.

"How do you know?"

"I have spoken to them within the labyrinth."

"Have you approached them, as you approached me?"

She smiled, an ironic quirk that made him want to like her. But he must not succumb to congeniality; he had made that mistake a long long time ago.

"No, for it seemed to me that they smelled sweet with corruption. I am a reeve— that is, I was a reeve—so I knew better than to trust them."

"Tell me your story. Don't come any closer. I can hear you perfectly well from here."

She laughed bitterly. "There! I'm told by your words what you think of me. Yet what choice have I?"

Her horse nuzzled her arm. She fished in a sleeve and plucked out a turnip. This delicacy the mare peeled daintily from her hand. Telling and Seeing watched the exchange with interest; was that an accusatory gaze Seeing turned on him, as if to say *Where's my treat?*

She went on. "My name is Marit, if indeed I am still who I once was, which I at times doubt. I was a reeve, out of Copper Hall. My eagle was called Flirt." At the name her voice hardened, choking down anger. "I believe I must be dead. I was stabbed in the heart twenty years ago when I was taken prisoner by men under the command of Lord Radas. It surprised me then, for I'd seen Lord Radas stand in authority over the assizes in Iliyat some months before that day, and he seemed a man like any other. I understand now that he had changed to become something other than what he was before."

"He had become a Guardian."

She covered her eyes with the back of a hand, then lowered the hand. "Yes, that's what I have had to come to believe. For a long while after I was stabbed I was not awake, not aware, but not asleep either. Dead, yet I never passed the Spirit Gate. I have been alone since that day."

"Why would you trust me with this secret?"

"You don't have the stink of corruption that the others do. You know what I am, don't you?"

"In some ways I may, but in more ways I do not. Therefore, alas, I cannot trust you. She has been trying to find and destroy me for years, but I have so far eluded her."

"Who is *she?*"

He waited, to see how she would answer herself, but she only watched him with a hard stare. Eager to hear. Desperate to understand. Aui! He wanted to like her. It was true there was no taint to the air, no vile taste on his tongue, nothing to suggest that she had turned on the path away from the lit road and walked into the shadows. That she was what she claimed to be was inarguable. The cloak at her shoulders gleamed with the pallor of bone. The horse—he'd not seen this mare before, or if he had he did not recognize its markings and face—tolerated her; maybe it even liked her.

Taking pity, he said at last, "If you don't know who *she* is, then I will not tell you."

"What then?" she demanded, goaded to a burst of temper. "How can I gain your trust? I need allies. And I am guessing that you do, too, for you speak of opponents. Meanwhile, not all the Guardians are accounted for, are they?"

He began shaking, exhausted by the long years of running and hiding and by the terrible hope that this precious ghost girl would not turn away from him on the day she came fully awake.

"I'll tell you this," said Marit. She wasn't one to give up easily. "Myself, that's one. I heard of your existence from others, not from others wearing the cloak but from a reeve who spoke to a hieros, who spoke of how you came to the temple and claimed that girl. That's why I sought you out, and how I found you. You're two more. That makes three Guardians. Lord Radas makes four. And I have encountered three others who I believe are allied with Radas. One is called Hari, one is Yordenas. The third is a woman wearing a cloak of night. That makes seven. But there are nine Guardians. Where are the other two? What are we, if we are not the

Guardians spoken of in the stories? If we are not the Guardians who sit in authority at the assizes, who guard the law on which the land is built? What happened to the real Guardians? Why did they vanish, and why are you and I here now? Do you know the answers?"

For once it was easy for him not to speak. Without trust, there can be no free exchange. Without trust, there can be no answers that have a hope of sounding out the truth.

"What can I do to earn your trust?" Her gaze burned, but he would be veiled to her just as she was veiled to him. The third eye granted to the Guardians by Ushara the Devourer allowed them to see into the hearts of mortal men, not into the hearts of other Guardians.

"Kotaru the Thunderer gave each Guardian a staff," he said. "Where is yours?"

"I don't know. I never had one."

Maybe she was a very good liar. Maybe she was as ignorant as she seemed. He had no way of knowing, and no way of finding out.

How sad, really, that he sought to teach the girl to trust him, while refusing to trust this woman who was, after all, asking of him nothing more than he was asking of the girl. If she was what she said she was, then they might join forces. There was strength in numbers. There was hope in numbers. Alone, he and the girl could do nothing but run. Here she came, offering the thing he desired most. No doubt his enemies knew that. So easily they could tempt him, snare him, and destroy him. Take the girl for themselves. And plunge the Hundred so deep into the shadows that he couldn't see how the land could ever recover.

"The hells!" she said at last. "Can you not help me? Will you not?"

Weary, he remained silent.

"Eiya!" Then she laughed. She wasn't a fragile creature, one crushed by a single blow. He could well believe she had been a reeve. She had a reeve's confident physical stance, and measuring, deliberate stare. A good reeve was stubborn and observant. "Aui! The man I loved—and love still—now thinks of me only with regret and pain, while it's another, younger, woman who he burns for in his thoughts with passion and longing. While you won't talk to me at all. So be it. I've wandered too long hoping to find someone to tell me what I am and what I must do now. You've taught me something, ver, by just standing there with your friendly smile and wishing me gone. I have to find out the truth where it lies within myself. I must walk into the shadows, and see if I am strong enough to come out unscathed, with the truth fixed in my heart and my duty carried in my hands."

She waited a moment longer. When he did not answer, she led the mare away into the trees. The rattle of their leaving faded. The wind sighed in the underbrush.

Seeing whinnied, and the other horse—now out of sight—called in answer.

"Have I made a terrible mistake?" he said to the air, to the sky, to the earth, to the water.

The girl looked at him, her gaze a question, perhaps even an act of trust.

He nodded. "We must pack up. It's time to move on. Quickly now, lass. Quickly."

19

After the gates were unlocked, the women who had been waiting all morning on the hot Olossi street were herded into a courtyard surrounded by high walls. Avisha trudged in, carrying Zianna and holding Jerad by the hand. Their keepers, a foursome of militiamen hired to maintain order, kept up a running patter of crude jokes.

"Heh. I wonder if those Qin soldiers have swords or prickles, eh?"

"Sharp as their swords, eh? I wouldn't want one swiving me."

"This lot hasn't much choice. Heya! Rufi, look there. Isn't that your mother? Eihi! No call to go hitting me, just a joke."

Avisha kept her head down. Fortunately, she was not the only woman here burdened by children, so perhaps that wasn't an immediate disqualification for marriage. Her arms were numb from the weight of holding Zianna. Jerad was sniffling.

She pushed him over toward a small door set into one wall where the tops of pipewood rising on the other side of the wall offered a silver of shade. A beggar in a red cap and ragged kilt who was leaning against the door in that shade kindly moved away as she and the children approached. She sagged against the door, wiping sweat from her neck as she looked around.

The court's stone pavement and high, whitewashed walls suggested it was either an unloading ground for wagons, or an open space for people to work. She had no idea how things worked in a city as big as Olossi, with its crowded streets and aggressive inhabitants as likely to shove you out of the way as wish you the blessings of the day. Her eyes watered from all the cook-smoke and from ash that still drifted off the burned sections of the lower city. Clouds were piling up in the east, and she was sure that on top of everything, it was going to rain.

"Vish." Jerad's voice threaded into a whine. The sad little sprout sagged against the wall, his legs crossed.

"You have to be patient, Jer." She shifted the sleeping girl, Zianna's weight aching her shoulder. The little girl's naming-day clothes—the nicest garments anyone in the family had ever owned—were dirt-stained and stinking from being urinated in more than once; the once-precious orange silk was probably beyond salvaging after all those days on the road. "Just a little longer. See those double doors, there?"

She pointed with her free elbow.

The women pressed forward to cluster around the impressive wooden doors that gave access into a building bigger than Sapanasu's temple hall in the village. There was a door in each wall of the vast courtyard. To the east, gates led to the street. The warehouse entry doors carved with elaborately twined salamanders were set in the western wall. To the north stood a gate trimmed in iron, big enough for wagons. The small door against which Avisha and the children huddled was the kind of entrance regular people passed through. The trees rising on the other side of the wall meant there was a garden beyond, filled with cool shade and, perhaps, a fountain. She licked dusty lips with a parched tongue.

"Don't crowd!" shouted one of the militiamen as he reined his horse in a mincing circle, whip raised.

There were about fifty women, with perhaps twenty children in arm or in tow. Most of the women were young; some were older. Most were wrapped in a plain cotton taloos or dressed in the linen tunic and trousers worn by farmers and artisans and laborers. Poor clans desperate enough to send their daughters and sisters to make a marriage with outlanders; impoverished widows eager to find a home with their children. The beggar shuffled through the crowd, trolling for alms among folk likely as poor as he was!

A pair of elegant city girls passed him a few vey and returned to their conversation.

"My uncle told me to demand nothing less than forty cheyt as a marriage portion. They can afford it. They took the whole treasury. Greedy bastards."

"Forty cheyt? Whew! You could never hope to see that much coin in your whole life. Who's being greedy?"

"It's fair payment for having to marry a dirty outlander."

"Best make sure they don't find out about—" Their voices dropped to a whisper.

A girl with a bright red birthmark splayed over one cheek kept lifting a hand to cover her face. "Auntie, don't you think they'll turn me away the instant they see me? Can't we just go home? I'd rather go to the temple than be scorned again."

"Quiet! The dowry the temple is demanding is more than we can afford. We'll offer you to the outlanders with no request for a bride price at all. That might induce them to take you."

A middle-aged man fussed over two girls dressed neatly in farmers' best, each in a cotton taloos, one dyed a calm sorrel green and the other a reassuring bracken orange-brown. "Be polite. Be respectful. It's a good opportunity but there's no need to sign any contract unless you're truly willing."

"Papa, you've said this twelve times."

He smoothed down the hair of one, twisting the end of her braid, and tugged out a wrinkle in the cloth draped over the shoulder of the other. "They have to prove themselves to you, girls, in the same way you have to prove yourselves to them. They're folk just like any other, even if they look different than we do and have different ways."

Avisha wiped her forehead again. Taru have mercy! It was so hot. Thunder rumbled, but the clouds hadn't yet gotten to the city. Her hair felt stringy and tangled, however much she had tried to keep it combed and clean. She'd washed out her one good taloos a day ago, in a stream, but it had gotten stepped on and there was a big smudge of red clay dirt smeared across her hips. She hoped her face was clean, but Zianna would keep rubbing her hands in the dirt and then patting her big sister's cheeks.

"I have to pee." Jerad's body was jiggling as he tried to hold it in. Tears dribbled down his face. "I don't want to wet myself out here in front of everyone."

If only Nallo were here!

But Nallo had been marched off to the reeve hall. They'd probably never see her again.

A shout from the gate startled her. A troop of grim Qin soldiers dressed in black rode into the courtyard from the street. She'd seen them during the long march from the Soha Hills to Olossi with the other refugees, but except for the day she and Nallo had encountered them on the trail, she'd not spoken to one. Every gaze shifted to stare with fear or apprehension at the newcomers.

If Nallo were here, Avisha knew what she would do.

"The hells!" She grabbed the boy by the wrist. "Come on." She jiggered the latch and found the door unlocked. They slipped through while every eye in the courtyard was fixed on the Qin soldiers.

She closed the door behind them and sank against it, breathing hard. A stand of hatmaker's pipewood screened the door. Jerad fumbled at his trousers—she'd made him put on his only pair so he would look respectable—and with a snivel of relief let go of his water. The spray rattled so loudly Avisha thought the whole city must hear, but the clamor of horses in the courtyard drowned him out. Her arms ached, and she looked around to see if there was anywhere she might put down Zi.

They stood in the shadowed corner of a walled garden. A larger garden lay beyond a second wall, green with fruit and nut trees, but this modest garden was laid out in a square with beds and troughs for medicinal plants, now overgrown and neglected, and stands of pipewood or shrubs of rice-grain-flower and purple-thorn and other such useful plants set against the walls. In the corner opposite her hiding place, a second door stood ajar. Just a few steps from it, a young woman sat on a bench. With her shoulders bowed, she was weeping too softly to be heard, but weeping nonetheless, wiping her face with the back of a hand as she lifted her head.

She was an outlander! She didn't look like the Qin, with their flat faces and broad cheeks. She was some other breed of outlander. She wore sumptuous silks, the kind of cloth only a rich woman could afford or that, if the stories were true, a rich man would lavish on a valuable bed slave. A broom lying slantwise across the walkway and a hem of dust on her silks betrayed that she'd been sweeping.

Avisha gaped. How could she risk dirtying such magnificent silks by wearing them to sweep in? What manner of person was she? Had she tried her luck at a marriage contract only to be rejected? Or did she live in this grand compound?

Jerad coughed as the river slacked to a trickle, and ceased.

"Who's there?" said the girl in a cool, firm voice. You'd never have guessed she'd been crying.

Avisha stepped out from the pipewood, trying to keep her voice calm and her hands from shaking. "I'm sorry, verea. I was just waiting out in the courtyard with the others when my little brother had to pee. He's just nine, you know how it is, and tired from all the waiting."

The girl examined Avisha and the sleeping Zianna critically. "Where is he?" she asked with a pretty smile but a searching gaze.

"Here, Jer, come out," said Avisha.

The boy stumbled out to the open square, still tying up his trousers. He saw the other woman, and his mouth dropped open. "Her eyes are pulled all funny. Is something wrong with her?"

"Hush! Don't be rude! I'm so sorry, verea. He's just a sprout. We've never been to the city before. We don't see outlanders where we come from."

"No offense taken," said the girl as her shoulders relaxed. She squeezed back the last of her tears and sniffed hard, then wiped her nose with the back of a hand. The more she spoke, the more you could hear the funny way she had of speaking, the sounds squished tight so it was hard to understand her. "What is your name?"

"I'm called Avisha, verea. This is my brother Jerad, and my little sister Zianna."

"You are here for the interview?"

"Surely I am. There's quite a few out there, truly."

"That's a surprise. In the first five days after the announcement in the markets, only fourteen women came to the gate. I do not know why so many crowded in to-day."

"Do you live here?" Avisha gestured to the peaked roofs that marked the build-ings of the greater compound.

"I do."

"Sheh! Whoever is gardener of this place should be hauled out and whipped. No one is taking care of these valuable plants!"

"It has been neglected, that is true." The girl examined the garden as if she was really getting a good look at it for the first time. "Why are they valuable?"

"To start with, that's a nice stand of hatmaker's pipewood, although it needs thinning. My mam would crush the seeds of purple-thorn—there—to kill insects in the storeroom. You can perfume clothes with the rice-grain-flower . . ." Now that the girl's flush of tears had faded and her face was more at ease, Avisha saw that she was lovely despite her odd features. She had lustrous black hair bound into a long tail with a ribbon; the tail hung to her hips. "Or you can put a spray of the flowers in your hair, like an ornament."

All at once, she felt sorry for the other girl. No one rich enough to wear silks of such quality would also wield a broom. She knew the tales as well as anyone. A rich merchant house could afford foreign slaves, and of course a life slave had no rights at all. Nothing about them belonged to themselves, not like a debt slave, who might hope to pay off the debt and walk free of all claim. No wonder the poor girl had been crying. "You're from the south, aren't you?"

The girl had been scrutinizing the rice-grain-flower, brushing at her hair where an ornamental flower might adorn her, but she turned back to Avisha. "I am, that's true."

"You have a funny way of pronouncing things." The idiotic words sounded worse now that they hung in the air, awaiting an answer, so Avisha stumbled on. "I'm sorry for your trouble. I saw you were crying. We didn't mean to interrupt. It's just the boy had to pee so badly and didn't want to wet himself."

"Vish!" hissed Jerad indignantly.

"No, I'm glad you came." The girl patted the bench. "Sit beside me. I am glad of a girl my own age to talk to." As Avisha approached, the girl indicated a shady spot in one corner of the paved square.

"Ooof!" Jerad stopped short with a squeal of outrage followed by a childish gig-gle. "Did you see what she did?"

"What did I do?" asked the girl, alarmed.

Avisha wanted to slap the runt, but he didn't know any better. "Nothing, verea. It's just rude to point with your finger like that."

"Ah." The girl stared at her for a moment with her mouth open in a smile that wasn't quite sincere and wasn't quite false; anxious, maybe, or embarrassed. She had all of her teeth, and they were as white as the landlady's string of precious pearls, so perfect that Avisha felt a stab of ugly jealousy for the careless beauty she would herself never ever possess. Then the smile faded, and the girl rose, with dignity, revealing a shawl that she had draped over the bench and on which she had been sitting. This she spread in the shade. "The little one can rest here."

"My thanks!"

It was such a relief to have Zi's weight off her arms and back that Avisha almost wept, but instead she sank down on the bench beside the outlander and rested her head wearily in her hands. Still suspicious, Jerad sat down cross-legged beside Zi. His head drooped, his eyes closed, and he dozed off.

"Why do you want to marry one of the outlanders?" the girl asked. "Most Hundred folk don't seem eager."

"There's a good group waiting out there today."

"Good, or numerous?"

Avisha laughed. "There are a lot of them. There were two women there, dressed as fine as ever I did see, in city fashion, nothing like we'd ever see in my village. All they could talk about was how much coin they mean to demand in exchange for marrying. I didn't think that was nice. But there was a nice father, telling his daughters they'd best be polite, and that they could look things over and make their own choice if they wished to wed an outlander. That was kind of him, for usually the clan gives you no choice. You know how it is."

Only what a stupid thing to say to a slave who was no longer her own person!

The girl smiled softly. It was hard to tell if she was happy or sad. "Truly, sometimes a person isn't given a choice."

Impulsively, Avisha reached toward her, but drew back before she touched the other girl's arm because the gesture seemed so intrusive, so bold, so intimate. "Eiya! I shouldn't chatter so much. That's what Nallo says."

"I don't mind your chatter. I like it. You remind me a little of my sister. Maybe it's only that we're of an age."

"I was born in the Year of the Ox."

"Why, so was I! Who is Nallo?"

"My father's wife."

"She's not your mother?"

Avisha looked at Zi, sprawled on the shawl and snoring with toddler snuffles in the blessed shade. "My mother is dead. My father remarried soon after. That's Nallo."

"A second wife! Is she kind to you, or awful?"

"She's got a murderous temper, and she slapped me once! But then Father got angry at her, and he never loses his temper, so she apologized and she never did it again. How I wish she was here. She's very tough-minded. Nothing scares her."

"Where is she?"

"They took her to the reeve hall. They said she was chosen by an eagle and she has to be a reeve even though she doesn't want to be one."

"Is that how it goes? You get chosen by an eagle? Even women?"

"Of course even women," said Avisha. Really, outlanders were so ignorant! "If an eagle chooses you, then you have to be a reeve. Isn't it that way where you come from?"

"We don't have reeves where I come from. Although I suppose that's not true anymore. I come from here, now." The girl's expression brightened momentarily, then darkened as she recalled a bitter thought. She sighed heavily. "Hu! Enough of feeling sorry for myself. What of your father, then? Where is he?"

It was like being slapped in the face.

"My father's dead, isn't he?" Avisha snapped.

The girl flinched, and the echo of the words—not the sound but the ugly anger in her own voice—made Avisha cringe with the vivid memory of the ruined village, the swarming flies, the sweet stink of rotting flesh, and the acrid stench of burned houses. Of the way the mellow green cloth of her father's jacket and trousers had rucked up around his corpse. She mustn't bring that anger with her now, or she'd never save herself and the children. She heaved in breaths, shaking.

The outlander draped an arm around her shoulders. "You're safe here."

"How can we be safe?" Avisha sobbed into her hands. She'd hammered it in for so many days. "We've no close kin. We owe rent to the landlady, so she wants to sell our labor, so we'd have to become slaves. All I can hope for is that some outlander I don't know might want to marry me because people say I'm pretty, and that counts for something, although you must wonder what I'm frothing on about thinking too well of myself since I must look like a field hen with my feathers all every-way for I haven't had a bath in days and our clothes must be stinking, and all torn besides. And I have the little ones and I can't just let them go. I wouldn't anyway, and it would be a terrible dishonor to my father's memory to sell their labor just to save myself. Now what will we do? Who will want us all? Why would anyone agree to take us in?"

Her voice became brisk and competent. "Priya, bring me a cup of sweet ginger cordial."

Avisha gulped down sobs and raised her head, but there was no one else in the garden. The little ones still slept. They were so very tired. She was all they had, now that Nallo had been dragged from them. She hadn't leisure for weeping. She was an artisan's daughter, accustomed to working hard, not some city-bred girl lounging in elegant fashions and thinking she could get forty cheyt—whoever had forty cheyt altogether except maybe the temples!—from some outlander to marry him.

With a fierce scowl, she rubbed the tears from her cheeks and swallowed her fear and her anger. "Eiya! I don't know what came over me. Best I leave you, verea. I'm sure you have your duties to be about. I wouldn't want you to get beaten for shirking."

"No, I wouldn't want that either. Here is Priya and she's brought some ginger cordial. Won't you taste it? It's very good. It's my favorite right now, for it settles the stomach. Priya, maybe some juice for the two little ones, although I don't think we should wake them yet."

A woman with amazingly dark skin and round outlander features offered her a cup with a kindly smile. Dazed, she took it and sipped the most glorious sweet ginger concoction, sharp but light on the tongue. Its bite rose to her eyeballs, making them water.

"Eihi! That's good!"

The girl stood, her expression transforming as she smiled. The older woman took several steps back. Belatedly, Avisha turned to look behind her.

"Here you are, Mai."

A man walked into the garden, wiping wet hands. He wore black, like the Qin, and he was accompanied by a middle-aged Qin soldier with the typical round face and merry eyes of the foreigners and by a huge man with a slight slump and a complexion rather like the pretty girl's. Outlanders, all. The man was not handsome but not ordinary. He halted with his hands out in front of him, registered Avisha's presence, and looked around the garden as if expecting a tiger to leap out and devour him. Of course he noticed the sleeping children. He looked back at her. Really, he was a fearsome man with a commanding stare, a sword swinging casually at his hip, and a way of looking at you that made Avisha feel she had done something very wrong.

Then he looked away. The older woman handed him a cloth and he finished wiping dry his hands.

"You are returned." The young woman used that same cool voice Avisha had noticed when she and the little ones had first stumbled into the garden, but Avisha thought she understood it better now: It was the voice of a woman holding her emotions in check.

"We are returned, and we have seen much to interest us. Who is this?" He pointed at Avisha. "Who are those children?"

"Don't point with your finger, Anji. It's considered rude. This is Avisha. And that is . . . ah, Jerad, and the little girl is Zi'an, I think."

"Zianna," said Avisha reflexively. "Zi'an would be a boy's name although that would be very old-fashioned."

"Thank you," said the girl. "Avisha, this is Captain Anji."

Avisha rose hastily and brushed off her horrifically rumpled and dirty clothing.

"Where did she come from?"

"From the courtyard gate." Mai indicated the stand of pipewood. "Now that I think of it, Chief, how will I ever convince the Ri Amarah to allow one of their daughters to visit me if I can't promise a secure house?"

The middle-aged man narrowed his eyes. "That door was secure at dawn, for I checked it myself." He trotted over to the gate.

The captain's gaze assessed Avisha. He was like the temple clerks, toting up numbers that might not bring them any personal benefit but needed accounting because that was their job and one they were accustomed to doing well. "Who is she? Certainly not one of the Red Hounds, for they don't admit women to their ranks. An assassin from the temples, perhaps?"

Mai seemed amused. "She's a girl from a village. These are her siblings. She hopes to find a husband among the troop."

"Ah." He handed the cloth to the older woman and turned to look through the open door, into an interior Avisha could not see. "Nothing I need concern myself with, then. Mai, I have an idea Keshad might actually be useful."

The older soldier walked back to them, shaking his head in disgust. "When I find out who left that unsecured, I'll whip him myself."

"Tuvi-lo," said the captain. "Where did the prisoner go off to? He was right behind us."

Inside, a familiar voice rose. "Don't touch that! Don't you know a priceless vase when you see one? What kind of five-burned fool are you?"

The splintering crash of ceramic meeting floor answered the question. Gales of laughter followed this assault, accompanied by a few choice swear words that genuinely shocked Avisha, for the only person she had ever heard say such rude things was the disreputable village drunk.

"Who did that?" demanded Mai in a voice meant to carry indoors. "If that vessel was truly valuable, then the owners of this house will have to be paid its value out of your own portion. What a waste!"

Her words cut short the laughter. Three young men filed into the garden. One was smirking, one was still stifling laughter, and the third was fuming with such intensity that Avisha expected steam to rise from the top of his curly black hair. Eiya! He was the man with the handsome eyes and the overbearing sister who had rescued them at Candra Crossing and gotten them across the river.

The law had caught up with him.

His gaze passed over her, and she found herself smiling stupidly only he had already looked away without any flicker of recognition. He glanced first at Mai, then looked at the captain and, flushed, glared down at the paving stones.

It hurt to be dismissed so easily. Avisha was used to being known as a pretty girl in her village, but she also knew perfectly well that her village wasn't very large and that the world must be populated with women twelve times more beautiful than she could ever hope to be. And yet those two young Qin soldiers were looking at her in a gratifying way even if she did wish it was Keshad who found her of interest. In fact, the soldiers were staring as if they recognized her, and all at once she remembered the one with the pretty eyes. He had been part of the cadre that had intercepted them on the road in the Soha Hills. His teasing grin made her grin shyly in return, and his grin widened.

"Which of you did it?" asked Mai in her cool voice.

Keshad's head came up. "It's not just these two. They were all jostling and making jokes with no respect for the possessions of others! They all need a lesson in good manners!"

"You're called Keshad, aren't you?" asked Mai in a kind voice that would have killed most men and made Keshad shut right up. "I need to hear from these two men what they will say. I thank you."

He gulped down a couple of breaths. Poor man! He felt things so deeply. But even as she thought it, Avisha saw Priya and the big man exchange an intimate glance, and the big man rolled his eyes and mouthed something that made Priya look at Keshad and smile with unconcealed amusement.

The clip-clop-clap of hooves on stone clattered in the courtyard; a buzz of women talking in low voices droned under. The sounds of hooves faded, shuttered by a clang of closing gates. Chief Tuvi walked over to the children and gently tipped Jerad so he could rest comfortably on the ground beside Zianna. Then he returned to stand by the captain. Everyone looked at the two Qin soldiers.

The soldier with the pretty eyes spoke first. "It slipped out of my hands."

"I told you!" muttered Keshad.

Mai said, "Chaji, why did you drop the vase? After he said it was valuable?"

Chaji shrugged. "How could I have known he knew what he was talking about? I only meant it as a bit of fun. I didn't mean to drop it. It slipped."

"You may go, Chaji," said the captain. "You'll continue to ride with the tailmen until I say otherwise."

His eyes widened; his mouth twitched. Yet as quickly as anger flashed, he controlled it, tightening his lips into a straight line. He nodded obediently, spun, and left the garden. The other Qin soldier began to follow, but Anji raised a hand.

"Hold on, Jagi. What do you have to say for yourself?"

The soldier's gaze shifted toward Keshad, who was still glaring at the pavement. Then he looked back at his captain.

"Chief Tuvi," said the captain, "place Keshad in a private chamber with guards."

"Come on," said Chief Tuvi with a cough that was almost a laugh.

When they were gone, the captain nodded at the remaining soldier. "Jagi?"

Jagi scratched his pock-scarred chin. Like all the Qin, he had a mustache but no beard to speak of, just wisps of hair on his chin. Captain Anji alone had a neatly trimmed beard.

"Speak," said the captain.

Jagi sighed. "Captain, none of us like him. That's the truth. First, some of us journeyed many days with him and his most excellent sister. Now we've traveled with him again to the barren lands and back. He's arrogant. He's unfriendly. He treats us with no respect. He never shared wine or ale but hoarded his own cup. So I suppose I thought he had it coming. I admit I enjoyed seeing the way his mouth frogged open and his eyes bugged out." His grin made his eyes wrinkle and look merry.

"An honest answer, but yours was the behavior of a boy, not of a man."

The smile fled. "Yes, Captain."

"Furthermore, you know what situation we find ourselves in. We must establish ourselves as settlers in this land, respected and accepted by those we mean to live among, while at the same we know that a dangerous threat remains, one we do not understand nor know the extent of. I need my tailmen to become men, so I can assign each one of you to stand as sergeants over recruits. To survive, we have to protect ourselves. To protect ourselves, we need what our enemy already has: an army. You may go."

"Yes, Captain." He left.

Mai said, "Anji, after the battle, you told the council of Olossi you were not minded to accept the post of commander of the militia of Olossi."

"Because the commander of the militia of Olossi can accomplish very little. This whole region needs a militia, not just the city. *We* need a militia, plum blossom, so our children may grow up." He shifted, reaching to take Mai's hand, but before he touched her he caught himself, glanced at Avisha, and withdrew his hand.

Mai rested a hand on her abdomen. "You think the army wearing the star will attack again."

"I am sure they will."

Avisha sank onto the bench.

Trembling, Mai sat beside her and took hold of her hands. "Don't fret. You'll be safe."

"I would attack, in their place," he continued. "But I would also assign new commanders, get better discipline in my troops, and most importantly I would send—" Looking at Avisha, he broke off. Paused. And started again. "I would do what I have already done."

"Shai is not ready for this," Mai whispered, and Avisha thought she did not mean the captain to hear, but he did.

He said, " 'If you do it, don't be afraid.' "

She smiled wanly. "I will not falter. It's just that sometimes it seems so hard."

He nodded. "Mai, we'll get the land we need. We'll build a stronghold and set up our perimeter. While you run the business, I'll teach the people of Olo'osson how to fight. Between us, we can survive."

"Of course," said Mai faintly as her expression twisted. She swayed, covering her mouth.

He said, briskly, "Priya, can you fetch her some of that sweet ginger cordial she likes?"

"Here's my cup," said Avisha.

The older woman whisked the cup out of Avisha's hand and knelt beside Mai. "Just take a sip, little flower."

It seemed unfair that the woman had ripped away her chance to give a kindness to repay the kindness shown her. She glanced at the children; their ragged clothes and dirty faces wouldn't help her cause. But she had been rehearsing speeches for days now, making lists of reasons she would make a good wife. "My mam taught me a tincture, steeped herbs, that helps settle the stomach of pregnant women. I can make some for you."

Mai was still sipping, looking almost cross-eyed with nausea, trying to hold it in.

Avisha looked up, straight into the gaze of the captain. Finally, she had caught his interest, and she straightened her shoulders and lifted her chin and felt that her ears were going to burn off, only they didn't. "For instance, you've got a nice stand of tallowberry over in that corner." She pointed with her elbow. "Mama would say, 'Inedible, good tallow for candles, oil pressed from the seeds good for varnish or paint and can be used as lamp oil although poor quality, residue of dry cakes with oil pressed out is good for fertilizer, also soap.' The wood carves well, and can be burned for incense. The leaves produce black dye if boiled in alum . . .'"

He smiled so suddenly it made her heart jolt.

"Choose wisely," he said, transferring his gaze to Mai. "They're not all of equal worth."

Avisha flushed, seared as though by lightning. He had already turned his back, and anyway, a man like him was far beyond her reach. While Priya fussed, he went inside, followed by the big man talking about sheep and wool.

"That's better," said Mai, sitting back with a sigh. "I thought sure it would all come out."

Priya set down the cup, then examined Avisha. She had a dark gaze so deep it seemed to go on forever. When she touched Avisha's hand, tears stung in Avisha's eyes although she didn't know why.

"You'll stay with us," said Priya. "Won't you?"

Tears spilled, and she began to laugh as much as cry, for it was raining finally, a mist that smeared the dirt and pattered among the leaves, presaging a fiercer storm to come.

"You'll want a bath," added Priya with a kind smile. "Once you've gotten it all out."

"I just didn't think—"

"There, now," said Mai. "I have to interview all those women. Later, if you feel able, maybe you can point out to me the ones who were talking about coin."

"O-Of course." She gulped several times and found she could swallow, she could breathe, she could think. She fixed her jaw, braced herself. "I'm so grateful. B-But I'll need a contract. So I have a chance to choose a husband from among the s-soldiers—" Or Keshad, if he would have her. Thinking of him made her skin scald with heat because she was so stupid, but she was alone, the only one the little ones had left. She had to proceed as she knew Nallo would, by being forceful and bold. "—and that I'm assured n-no one will change his mind and throw me out. The children have to come with me and be treated as full kin, not debt slaves having to work to offset the expense of keeping them."

Mai laughed. "I do like you. Is there anything else?"

To think of her father was to yearn for him, to wish the gate might open and he, with his gentle smile and with a half-braided cord in hand, would walk in to greet her. The grief of knowing he was truly gone had not lifted, and she supposed it never would. Yet she had hope she could raise the children, and honor their father's memory by doing so.

"It's just a small thing, and I don't think it would be too hard . . . it's just . . . I would like know how Nallo is faring."

*   *   *

"I DON'T LIKE you," said Nallo. "So quit bothering me."

"Eiya! I was just trying to be nice." The young reeve took his bowl of soup and his inane banter, obviously meant to impress her, and walked over to another table in the eating hall where he was greeted with friendly cheers.

She thought herself shed of them, able to eat the spicy cawl-flower soup in peace without a bunch of chattering pleasantries, when another cursed reeve plopped down beside her.

"I don't like Siras either," said this man. "All that glad-handing talk, like a cursed entertainer." He placed his bowl on the table, nudged it to the right, and stared at the dumpling floating in the center surrounded by limp cawl petals and specks of bright red pepper. "Did they replace the cook? This looks more appetizing than the last meal I ate here."

"I wouldn't know. I only got at here yesterday. And I plan to leave tomorrow."

He chuckled. "Don't you remember me? I'm Volias."

"Yes, I remember you. You made me leave the children I'm responsible for and come here to Argent Hall, where I don't want to be. And since I'm not planning to stay, I don't see why I should have to remember anyone's name."

"You're very irritating and rude," he said appreciatively. "Will you promise me you'll be this rude to the marshal?"

Nallo wasn't used to people smiling at her. It made her suspicious. "Why do you want me to be rude to him?"

"Because I don't like him. Not enough people are rude to him, just because he's charming and good looking. How like them not to see past his handsome face to the insufferably smug and self-righteous man beneath!"

"Will being rude to him help me get out of here?"

He laughed. She wasn't a good judge of laughter. She couldn't tell if he was laughing sympathetically, or if he was laughing at her, and that made her bristle.

"Why are you so ill-tempered?" he asked.

"I didn't say anything!"

" 'A look's as good as a hundred words,' as it says in the tale. Have you always been this way?"

"So they tell me!" She turned her attention back to her soup, sipping cautiously, but it had just the right sting of pepper to really make your eyes open as you swallowed the rich broth.

He tried his own.

"This is good," he added, as if she weren't ignoring him. "Listen, Nallo. The gods marked you the moment that eagle chose you, or the eagle chose you because the gods marked you. It's hard to know how that works. You can no more walk away than you can expect to see your dead husband walking among the living. Keep your ill temper and your rudeness if you wish. It'll intimidate people, once you get out into the world as a reeve. But the sooner you accept that you can't leave, the better it will be for you. Although why I bother to tell you, I don't know. I'm leaving tomorrow anyway, to return to Clan Hall. I won't have to deal with your sulks and outbursts, although I'll miss them. I like you."

She was finding it hard to breathe because the air had gotten so thick and the pepper in the soup was stronger than she'd realized, making her eyes water. "No one likes me."

"That sister was bawling her eyes out when you took your leave of them—"

"She's my husband's daughter, not my sister. I don't have any obligation toward them now their father is dead."

"Which is why you are mad at me for taking you away from them. Hrm, that makes sense. Anyway, presumably your husband liked you."

"He tolerated me. He needed a second wife quickly because the first died in childbed. I'm the prize he got!" Her voice had risen. Folk seated at other tables looked at her and quickly away when she glared at them.

"Here, now," said Volias with a sneer. "If you feel a little more sorry for yourself, even I might begin to dislike you despite your wonderful ability to say cutting things to people deserving of a cut like that idiot, Siras, who fancies himself a future marshal just because the fawkners here pet him so and signed him up to run errands for the marshal. So how many people do you suppose are dead already, and how many more do you suppose are going to die, with the way things are these days? Maybe we need reeves right now. Maybe we need the work reeves can do. Maybe the gods are desperate enough to touch you, or maybe you're just someone who could be a good reeve. Think about it."

Now he did ignore her, working at his bowl in silence. The hum of other conversations surrounded them. The hall had windows open to a courtyard. Rain pattered on the pavement outside. Lamp flames trembled under the breeze raised by the twilight rains. The hall easily sat two hundred; truly, Nallo had never in her life been under a roof so large because not even Sapanasu's temple in her village had been anywhere this big. She might as well be outside as inside because there was so much loft hidden by darkness up in the open rafters. And yet it did smell like indoors: the shavings that covered the floor to keep down dust and mess had been mixed with herbs to sweeten the air. The scent reminded her of home.

Home.

Not the house where she had grown up, which had smelled of goats, but her husband's house. His was not a violent or expansive temperament. He was quiet and kind, and he liked things to be tidy and pleasant, and yet unlike the landlady, he didn't fuss unnecessarily to make a point that it must be done his way or not at all. He was a good ropemaker, a true artisan, because he had an eye for detail and a real love for doing things right just because that's what satisfied him. She had respected him, but she had never loved him.

Overcome with feelings she did not understand and could not explain, she slumped forward with her elbows on the plank table and covered her face with her hands.

"Making the women cry again, Volias?"

"I'm the only one she'll talk to. She probably saw you coming. It's enough to make me weep."

She lifted her head. Volias lifted his bowl to his lips and slurped down the last of the broth. The marshal was standing behind him, holding the short staff carried by all reeves. He was a good-looking man; you just couldn't help noticing that every time you set eyes on him. When he saw that Nallo had looked up, he smiled, a look calculated to melt people's hard hearts.

She scowled. "I don't have anything to say to you."

Volias set down the bowl with a clunk. "My heart, have I told you recently that I love you?"

This was not worth replying to, nor did her harsh words have the effect she hoped for.

"You two are well matched," said the marshal in such a genial way that she wanted to slap the good humor off his handsome face.

"She and I?" said Volias. "I'm flattered you think so."

"No, I meant her and the eagle. A worse-tempered raptor I've never encountered in my life, which is why I need to talk to you right now, Nallo. You'll come with me." Under that charm lay an implacable temper, maybe worse than her own once roused, and she knew all at once that she dared not cross him. She shoved the bowl away and got up from behind the bench.

"That just goes over to the table, there," said the marshal helpfully, pointing to a table where other bowls and utensils had been stacked. All of the other people in the hall—reeves and fawkners and hirelings—had turned to watch the encounter. Aware of their scrutiny, she stalked to the table and set down the things before walking to the door, where he waited for her. Volias came with him, the two men talking in low voices.

"—I think it's a risk with that eagle," Volias was saying, "and I'm surprised you—"

The marshal nudged him.

He broke off.

"I'm here," said Nallo needlessly. Sometimes she didn't even know why these griping phrases popped out of her mouth. "What do I have to do to convince you I'm not the right person to be a reeve? That I don't want to be here?"

"Oh, you've convinced me you don't want to be here," said the marshal. "But as you'll discover, how you feel about your situation doesn't actually matter."

"There's no sign of that eagle."

"*That* eagle's just flown in, and she's in no better temper than you are."

"The hells," swore Volias.

"That's right," said the marshal. "Quicker is better. Come on."

Rather than walking across the courtyard through the rain, he skirted the edges of a quadrangle of wooden buildings: the eating hall, the fawkner's warehouse and shop, the barracks, and the back wall of one of the high lofts, like a byre for beasts, where eagles quartered. Eaves sheltered them from the rain but the wind sprayed moisture over them. She welcomed the cool spatter. The Flower Rains at the beginning of the year were her favorite, a cleansing draft to cool what burned and tore at her insides. Angry, she followed the marshal through a narrow alley between two buildings and halted on the edge of the vast parade ground.

Four fawkners stood against the far wall of the north loft, under the eaves. One clasped her right hand to her left arm as though she'd been raked. Another held a hood, ties dangling, as they all stared despairingly toward the center of the parade ground. The yard was cleared of all eagles save one, who clutched a perch and stared belligerently at the fawkners. The idiots hadn't even gone in to examine her wound; dried blood and fresh glimmers discolored one wing.

"She's really angry," said Volias. "You know what she did to—"

"Let me finish," said Joss to Volias. "Nallo, do you recognize that eagle?"

"That's the one that protected us on the trail. Can't you see its injury? Why isn't anyone helping it? I thought these fawkners knew everything about eagles."

"They need to hood it first."

"Why don't they?"

"She's really angry," repeated Volias.

She did look angry, with her neck feathers puffed out and the rest of her slicked down.

"They need that hood on so they can treat her injury," said the marshal. "She'll settle down then."

Volias frowned. "You can't mean you'll send Nallo out—"

"If that injury isn't treated properly, the eagle will not survive. If the eagle dies, Nallo dies."

"You're saying that to scare me. To get me to agree." It was ridiculous the way they were all scared of the big eagle, not that she wasn't a frightening sight when you really compared how puny the humans looked compared to the magnificent size and weapons of the raptor. But Nallo had sheltered under that vicious beak before; the bird had saved Jerad from the bandits.

With a grunt of disgust, she strode over to the huddled fawkners. "Give me the hood."

Blood stained the skin of the woman clutching her arm. "She's favoring her right leg," she said, calm as you please, "which is what saved me from worse. If she strikes, she'll strike with her left. Watch for the talons."

A man handed her the heavy leather contraption.

"How do I get this on?"

"That part fits around the beak," said the injured woman. "Just get the eyes covered. Once she settles, we'll do the rest until you've learned more."

One of the other fawkners, a short, fine-boned man, whistled under his breath and shook his head, but the rest simply watched as she took a step back.

"Oh, I see," she said as she opened it out. The leather was soft and pliant, heavy because there was so much of it, and there was an obvious hole for the beak. She'd grown up dealing with goats. This couldn't be that different.

Yet as she approached the eagle, whose fierce gaze fixed on her, her heart raced until her ears throbbed. That beak was big enough to rip off her head.

The eagle moved, a swipe with her talons. Nallo leaped back out of range as, behind her, a man groaned and many voices gasped.

"Just keep going." That was the marshal, calling encouragement. "If she'd meant to hook you, she'd have made contact. You're much slower than she is."

"Isn't he the cheerful one," said Nallo to the bird, taking courage in irritation. What a prancing idiot that marshal was! "Although by the look of you, I suppose it's true. Or I hope it's true." If she kept talking she didn't have to think about how scared she was. "If you really wanted to bite my head off, I don't see how I could escape you."

Taking a deep breath, she stepped forward. The eagle raked again, but she was slow and jerky.

"Stop that!" She was on her toes ready to bolt with a knot in her throat she had to squeeze the words past. Even so, feeling stuck between all those cursed reeves and fawkners expecting her to do what she didn't want to do, and the huge raptor looking furious with everyone, made her temper rise even more. If that was possible. But not at the poor bird.

"Here, now, you recall me. We met up in the Soha Hills. You gave the boy shelter, didn't you, and I appreciate it as I think I said then so I don't know what you're slashing at me for now. I never did you any harm!"

It drew up one leg. Its neck feathers eased.

That seemed less threatening. She went on.

"So if you want that wing looked at, you'd best be cooperative. Not that I can't see that you dislike all of them, and I surely can't blame you for doing so since they seem an unlikable lot to me, too."

It lowered its head. A feathered brow ridge gave her a grouchy look, as if she were saying, "What took you so long?"

The hood was bulky, and Nallo tried to sling it over. The eagle lifted her head, and leather spilled off and flopped to the dirt with a thump.

"Be still! Do you want that injury tended to, or not?"

As she bent over to grab the hood, she heard a sharp hiss, a whispering, the shifting of many feet. Rising, she swung around.

All kinds of folk had crowded under the eaves to watch. There were a dozen more fawkners, some armed with staves and long padded spears and hook-bills, and too many reeves and hirelings to count. The eagle lowered her leg to get better purchase on the perch. Nallo sensed her contempt and impatience and pain.

"Yes, may they all rot in the hells, idiot gawkers! Just let me get this thing— oof!—" She heaved. "—up over your head and—" Tugged awkwardly, one leather thong briefly clamped in her teeth to keep it out of her face. "—sheh! keep your head down!—and you won't have to look at their ugly faces anymore. There!"

The eagle was hooded, although the straggling ends needed tying off. Nallo beckoned to the fawkners. "Don't just gawp there! How do you fix this thing so she can't scrape it off?"

Three started forward, including the woman with the torn arm. They grabbed the leather ties at the back of the hood and, while the eagle still had her head lowered, tightened them.

"These ties are called the brace," explained the injured fawkner. "You stayed calm."

"Best get that arm tended to, Rena," said the small fawkner, taking charge. "Aras, can you run and get the salve? I'll need the imping needle and—Eiya!—just bring the lot of it. What's your name again?"

When no one answered, Nallo realized he was talking to her. "I'm called Nallo."

"Well done. Tumna's famous for having an uncertain temper at the best of times, but you handled her well. Better than Horas ever did."

"Who is Horas?"

"Her last reeve."

"What happened to him?"

Tumna dipped her head, huge beak probing the air as the marshal and Volias walked over.

"Keep talking," said the small fawkner. "She likes the sound of your voice."

"Tumna, don't fret, they're coming although I must say they're slow about it and why all these staring fools have to stand here and stare so rudely is beyond my understanding. How badly is her wing injured?"

The fawkner was grinning, although she couldn't figure what he thought was so funny. "She can fly on it, so that's one thing. But we've got bleeding even after this long because she's not resting properly. As you can see, she's still in pain and not healing as she ought."

"Volias," Nallo said, "can't you just chase these people off? Don't they have anything better to do?"

He said, to the marshal, "You're a hard man, Joss. I didn't know you had it in you. I thought sure the cursed bird was going to rip—"

"Shut up, Volias," said the marshal in a flat voice.

"I'll take it from here, Marshal," said the small fawkner in the manner of a man rushing to fill a gap.

"What was he going to say?" Nallo demanded.

"Rip off the hood," said the marshal. "They're trained to accept the hood when they first come to the hall. An eagle like Tumna or my Scar is accustomed to it. It eases them, helps them settle if they're injured or exhausted. An eagle tumbles quick from keen-set to frail-set."

"If you don't mind," said the fawkner, "we'll get her settled."

Thus dismissed, she had no choice except to walk with the marshal out of the parade ground and down an alley between storehouses. The reeve hall was a prosperous place, with plenty of impressive buildings to house its reeves, fawkners, assistants, hirelings, slaves, and eagles, and to store the provisions necessary to maintaining the hall.

"What happened to her other reeve?" she asked as her feet kicked up chalky dirt.

Volias coughed.

The marshal said, "Dead in the recent battle."

"Do eagles mourn their reeves when they go?"

"Hard to say. We like to think so."

"Do reeves mourn their eagles?"

He sighed as he looked at her. "Reeves don't survive the death of their eagles."

"You can't mean it. How old can an eagle get?"

"Hall records show that the longest known life span of an eagle encompassed six reeves, although only one of those reeves lived to old age."

"Do you mean if I agree to become a reeve and that eagle dies, that I'll die?"

"You already are a reeve."

"Is this how you force people to agree to become reeves? Because they think they have to? We're no better than slaves. I'd have better luck walking to Olossi and trying to get a husband from those foreigners. At least I'd be my own mistress, able to do what I wanted."

"Who knows what disgusting customs those outlanders have," said Volias with a smirk. "You're better off with us. Not that you have a choice."

They walked into a garden so fancy that Nallo gawked. It had its own pool, with fruit and nut trees along either side, reflected in the still water. Aui! There was even a fountain of burbling water, just like in the tales! Avisha would have gushed over the many herbs and other flowering plants burgeoning out of troughs and terraces. A pavilion overlooked the far end of the pool. That pest Siras was seated on the steps leading up to the covered porch, and when he saw them he leaped up and brushed his hands on his trousers as if he'd been eating.

"I guess Tumna didn't rip your head off, then, eh?" said Siras with a big grin as they reached the porch. "Not like she did to Horas. Not that he didn't deserve it, mind you. He was rotten all the way through."

"The hells!" said Volias. "Siras, you're a bigger horse's ass than even I thought."

Nallo halted with a foot on the porch and one on the step below. The marshal turned, balancing on one foot with a sandal half pried off the other. He grunted with irritation, a man who has just been caught out in a lie.

Rain spat through the pretty garden. In the distance, thunder rolled and faded. *Rip your head off.*

They had all known that the eagle was a killer who had murdered its own reeve.

When she got really mad, her tongue lit and she couldn't stop herself. "That's why everyone came to watch. Was it a good show? Or is everyone disappointed she didn't rip my head off, too? Does it happen often? Because if I were an eagle, you three would all be in little pieces by now, but I wouldn't eat a single scrap of bloody flesh because your foul taste would make me cast it all back up."

Her heart was sucked dry, and her blood was raging. She walked away.

Volias called, "Here, now, Nallo—"

The marshal interrupted him in that smoothly dishonest voice she should have distrusted from the first. "We didn't say anything because we didn't want you to fear her before you had a chance to understand eagles. And Tumna in particular."

"No one *told* her?" yapped the young one in a tone that couldn't have made him sound stupider if he'd been a novice entertainer acting a part.

Ignoring every soul who tried to talk to her, she strode through the compound until she found the cot she'd been assigned. She grabbed her bundle of useless odds and ends, the worthless rubbish of her life, and walked out the gates of Argent Hall, never to return.

20

The arrival of the seventh Guardian, wearing the cloak of death, forced his hand.

He and the girl flew west across the Olo'o Sea, heading for the isolated western Barrens and its mountainous desert high country where few folk traveled and fewer lived. With Argent Hall no longer under the hand of one of his enemies, they might be able to walk an isolated labyrinth without falling into the custody of the others.

After that burst of speech, while shaping the bow, the girl again ceased talking. It wasn't fear that closed her mouth, he thought. She liked to fly. She enjoyed the wind and wide waters below. Nothing frightened her.

They flew a night and a day and into the next night, a steady pace that would eventually exhaust the horses, but he had no more time to wait. At length, in the glimmering twilight before dawn, they flew into the swirl of currents that marked the western shore. South of them a pair of campfires burned, so far away they appeared like candle flames. But the salty air and fine grit on the wind told him no sour tales of the folk camping in this wilderness. He would have to take his chances that they were no threat.

They crossed over briny pools and streaks of dried salt and minerals that marked the shoreline, and beat crosswise up tableland that rose in stair steps to rugged highlands beyond, the massive foothills of the Spires. Peaks glittered as the first edge of sun out of the east caught on their icy crowns. Antelopes and gazelles nibbled on grass on broad terraces. Wild goats bounded alongside coursing streams as dawn's light scattered them from their night's stupor. The sun pushed into the sky. The horses labored, but they struggled on. They knew where they were going.

This altar was hard to find if you didn't know where to look. Unlike many of the others, carved into cliff faces or sited atop granite pinnacles or bare peaks or breathtaking spires of rock, this altar had a humbler position nestled in a rocky saddle between two forested peaks. A homely place lacking magnificence, but one where he felt sheltered because of its immense isolation.

The horses clattered onto the open space. The rounded peaks rose to either side. The saddle linked the two high spots but was itself pretty much impossible to reach because of unstable slopes falling away to either side. Boulders lay in shattered heaps at the base. Pieces of broken rock like so many discarded roof shingles littered the slopes, piled in frozen waves at the bottom.

The girl dismounted and paced the rim, careful to stay away from the entrance to the labyrinth just as a canny animal shies away from a trap. The horses abandoned him, making straight—as only the horses could—for the pool at the center where they could refresh themselves.

He gripped his staff of judgment, knuckles white. He tried to relax but could not find calm within. With his free hand he parted the pocket sewn into his sleeve and grasped the mirror he had carried hidden within it for so many years. Three times he tapped his staff against the rock. The third time she looked at him. He beckoned. Hesitantly, she crossed to him.

"Come." He tried to gentle his voice, but he could hear how tightly coiled ran the thread of words. "Walk with me."

He set first one foot, then the second, on the glittering entrance to the labyrinth. That which is cut may heal, but if it scars, then the flesh loses its flexibility and can easily tear itself open. Her ability to trust was scarred.

But on this day, she was willing to trust him.

He had not walked for many years, because it was too dangerous to reveal himself. Yet even after so long away, he knew the path as well as he knew his own hands.

Needle Spire, a slender thread of rock thrusting out of the ocean beyond Storm Cape; Everfall Beacon now in ruins on the South Shore; Stone Tor in the midst of the Wild; Salt Tower on the dead shore of the high salt sea; Mount Aua; the friendly environs of humble Highwater and its tumbling stream; the Pinnacle above the crumbling archon's watchtower overlooking the basin of Sohayil; the dusty Walshow overlook; the deep swamp within Mar-lake-swallows; Horn Vista; the Dragon's Tower; Thunder Spire; the Five Brothers; the Seven Secret Sisters; the Face, whose sheer cliff overlooked the first mey post on the Kandaran Pass. He knew the name and location of every one; he had walked them all, at one time or another: the hundred and one altars sacred to the Guardians, scattered throughout the land.

He walked quickly, although at intervals she slowed as if wanting to look through onto one of those faraway landscapes. Passing through the turn of Hammering Ford, the river overlook north of Westcott, he scented blood, tainted with the sweet-sour smell he had come to associate with those of his brethren who had crossed under the shadow gate into corruption.

"Who are you?" an unfamiliar male voice whispered from within the maze. "Where—?"

The girl hissed, her shoulders tensing, but they moved beyond the taint. Finishing the path, they fell out into the center.

In a basin hollowed out of rock, clean water bubbled up from a crack in the ground. With a cry, she fell to her knees and cupped her hands. She drank, sucking in the clear liquid until it dribbled down her chin. The horses watched her with patient gazes. He slid the mirror out of his sleeve.

The bronze openwork backing curved with the shapes of twining dragons rising out of a stylized rendition of layers of mist. The silver-white finish of the actual mirror flashed where sunlight caught in it, like the flicker of a soul.

She looked up, gasping from the bitter drink, blinking like a sleeper coming awake.

"This belongs to you," he said, holding out the mirror. "This is your Guardian's staff, which you must carry."

Her hand extended, but whether she chose to reach or the mirror pulled her to it, he could not say. She took it from him, drew it toward her body. Turned it. Stared into its polished face, seeing her own face hovering ghost-like.

Her mouth opened, and closed. The smooth lines of her face cracked as she hunched her shoulders. For the space of a breath he thought she would scream, or faint. Then she moaned, a low sound of despair, the worst cry in the world for being so weak.

"She lost her mirror, so she is dead. Don't make me remember her." Although she trembled, she could not release the mirror. It would swallow her, and she would awaken in truth.

How he hated himself for what he had done, even knowing he had no choice.

The trembling in her hand passed into her body, a palsy shuddering through her. Grief is an anvil on which you are beaten, beaten, beaten. We cry for many things, but there are sorrows that lie beyond tears. Sometimes it is easier to look away, and when you are forced to recognize the hammer as it descends, all you can do is wait for the impact that will shatter you.

"Let her stay dead!" she cried.

The hammer fell.

PART FOUR: GIFTS

In the Western Grasslands Beyond the Hundred
(Four Years Earlier)

21

ONE NEVER KNOWS what gifts a stranger brings.

"There's nothing of interest in our lineage or possessions or grazing lands to cause a man of his tribe to wish to marry into ours," said Kirya to her cousin, but as soon as the words left her mouth, she was sorry she had said it that way.

Mariya dabbed at teary eyes with her free hand. Three tiny beautiful beaded nets were cupped in her other palm.

"Nothing besides you, I mean," added Kirya hastily. She looked away, toward the eastern horizon, measuring the curve of the sun's back as it rose.

"He didn't have to give me this gift," said Mariya. "He told me his aunt would speak with my mother at the confluence."

"Mari, be practical. In our entire tribe we have nine hands of sheep, four hands of goats, and five horses. Three proper tents. He's born to a daughter tribe of the Vidrini lineage. Who are we to even think of bringing a son of that lineage into our tents? We can't possibly pay the marriage price. We've no son of our own tribe old enough to make a marriage across the lines in exchange, if they would even take one."

"You don't know anything about his tribe, or his mother and aunts. Or what they want."

Kirya took the beaded nets out of her cousin's hand and twisted them onto the tails of Mariya's three dark braids, a seal binding the loose ends. "There, you look very pretty."

Mariya unhooked her polished bronze mirror from her belt and regarded her blurry reflection with a frown, a piece of vanity that made Kirya sit back on her heels. "Mother will scold me," she said, heedless of the impiety of admiring her looks in the holy mirror.

"She scolds everyone. We'd best get moving, or we'll miss our chance." She took the mirror out of Mari's hand and hooked it back on the belt.

Mariya rolled up the blankets they had shared while Kirya saddled the gelding and the piebald mare. The tribe lay a day's ride behind them, and she wasn't surprised it had taken Mariya this long to reveal even to her beloved cousin the gift a Vidrini boy had given her, since as a stranger and a male he ought not to be giving her gifts at all. It had been at least six nights back that the two tribes had happened to share temporary grazing lands by a watering hole on their way to the summer's confluence on the Targit River.

Kirya scanned the landscape: The long slopes, never quite hills, were scantly covered with yellowing grass or brown scrub growing low to the ground. A hawk circled above. More crucially, a pair of vultures glided over the land toward the southeast, where Kirya guessed the two hunters would find the herd of fleet-footed gar-deer she had spotted yesterday. Such deer didn't venture into the dry eastern grasslands often, and these had looked plump and juicy.

"At least demons didn't eat us last night." Mariya tossed a rolled-up blanket to Kirya, then tied her own gear onto the back of the mare's saddle. "I thought they would. Did you hear them howling?"

The gelding was surly this morning, as always. He gave a halfhearted nip at Kirya, who shoved him with her shoulder to remind him who was boss. "That was the wind."

"You can't be sure! I don't know how you can be so brave!"

Although their mothers were sisters, they looked nothing alike: Mariya had thick black hair, a pretty face, and the darker complexion that was rare among the tribes, while Kirya had the bland white-blond hair and round face common especially in the northern-roaming tribes of their people. Their looks were not the only way in which they differed.

"Mari, I will never understand you," she said finally with loving exasperation. "You're the best archer in our tents. Even at night, you would pierce any demon that tried to get close."

"Demons can't be killed," said Mariya ominously. "Arrows would just go right through it. Then it would devour us."

"That's why we have the two arrows the Singer blessed. Those are proof against demons. Or we can capture their hearts in our mirrors. Then they would flee."

Lips pressed tight, Mari surveyed the land. Despite being a child of the plains, she felt most at ease among the tents.

"I don't want to miss that herd," Kirya added. "I want something to bring to the confluence so we won't be shamed in front of the other tribes."

"Do you think he'll be there?" Mari asked. "He said his aunt would talk to my mother."

"Maybe. Don't you want a good haunch of meat to offer when folk come to call?"

Kirya set a brisk pace in the direction of the circling vultures. The hawk moved away toward the north, but the vultures hung steady. The wind was hot and dry, blowing out of the eastern deadlands, but posed no threat to their hunting, as it would blow their scent and the noise of their approach into the west. The skin of the earth had a sandy color, bleached like the cloudless sky, and the summer heat had turned the green of spring grass to a brittle gold-brown. They'd had decent rains this spring, enough to keep their usual watering holes usable all summer. Twin lambs, both female, offered hope that they might begin to increase the tribe's paltry herd. Now she had in her sights this unforeseen herd of deer, strayed out of their usual territories like a portent of prosperity glimpsed and pursued.

"But who ever feels that way after just two days?" Mariya could not stop chattering. "I know that Mother has already spoken with the headwoman of the Oliski tribe about a match with Laoshko Oliski, but—oh, Kiri!—he's so old, with two wives dead already."

"Young enough to father children and keep the herds, especially if it's true he has some special knowledge of husbandry, as they claim."

"You marry him, then!"

Kirya laughed. "If this Vidrini boy convinces his aunt to make the match, despite all the reasons for his tribe to speak against it, that's probably what will happen. You'll get the young one, and I'll get the old one."

"You won't be angry at me afterward? You haven't even had your Flower Night yet."

"How could I be mad at you, Mari? The men who look interesting to me are always following after you. Like Orphan."

"Mother would beat us if she heard you talk about Orphan that way."

"Never mind, it isn't your fault. You're just so much prettier and livelier than I am."

"I'm being stupid," Mari muttered. "I'm sorry. I'll stop going on and on. Look. No, over there. Just past that notch in the slope. There's a deer."

"Where?"

"It's gone below the horizon." Mariya slid her strung bow out of its quiver and rested it across her thighs, four arrows bunched in her left hand. Out on a hunting trip, they kept their gear ready at all times. Her aspect had shifted, as swiftly as lightning struck. She was foolish and silly and all too often scared of the ripple of her own shadow, but she also had keen sight and the gods' kiss on every arrow she loosed.

They pushed along the slope, Mariya leading them sidewise as they approached the distant rise.

"Men fall in love faster," said Kirya in a low voice. "Everyone knows that. Women are more practical. Like in the story of the daughter of the Sun. The war leader fell in love with her the moment he saw her, but she didn't like him at all. Not until she thought he would die."

Mariya was no longer listening. "Tss! There."

She gave the signal for Kirya to swing wide to the left before pulling her own horse toward the right. They separated, moving in a wide circle. The gelding flicked his ears and picked up his pace; like Kirya, he loved being out in the grass. Coming up the rise, she shifted her path to make sure the wind would not carry any hint of her presence to the deer. At length she dismounted and, leaving the gelding with reins loose to the ground, crept through the grass until she could look into the hollow beyond where the beasts had spread out around a sink. The swale was moist enough to nurture a coat of grass and scrub ash. Tails flicking against flies, the deer foraged.

Mariya eased down one of the western slopes to take a position where low ground offered an escape route for startled deer. Kirya scooted back to the gelding, mounted, and made her approach, coming over the rise. A few deer raised their heads, but she kept the horse to a steady walk as she nocked an arrow to the string. On the far slope, Mariya signaled.

With a shout, Kirya whipped the gelding forward into the swale. She took aim as the deer scattered. Her first arrow struck the flank of a springing deer; her second vanished into the bolting herd. They raced along the low ground, seeking the easy route.

With two clean shots, Mariya brought down two deer, but her third arrow missed and a gust of wind caught her fourth and sent it spinning. The gar-deer were already through the gap, the injured buck staggering at the back of the group.

Kirya waved at Mariya as she rode in pursuit.

It was a strong beast, young and healthy, and had the fierce will to preserve itself that animals must have to survive. At first it managed to keep up with the tail end of the herd, but step by halting step it slipped behind. Kirya closed the gap as they raced up one long slope and descended another on the trail of the fleeing herd.

The pair of vultures, which she had thought marked the position of the herd, were now almost above her, circling. A third glided into view from the east and joined the vigil.

The buck stumbled and collapsed. Kirya brought the gelding up beside it and dismounted, flipping the reins over the horse's head. She drew her knife, unhooked her leather bowl from her belt, and knelt by the young deer's head. It struggled briefly, but she caught its head in her arm, holding it down. She sang the brief prayer to Uncle Grass, thanking him for this offering, and cut its throat. Most of the blood poured into the bowl; the rest blessed the soil. The deer jerked a few times in its death throes. She unhooked her mirror and studied the reflection of the animal in the polished surface, seeing no mark of demon corruption.

With a sigh of relief, she drank the hot blood, emptying the bowl. They hadn't eaten since yesterday. Mariya would be enjoying the same feast from her own kills. It was a good kill, a strong spirit, fat and prosperous. A portent, she hoped, for the coming prosperity to be hoped for by their tribe. Maybe her aunt would negotiate a marriage settlement with the mother of that Vidrini boy. Sometimes prosperous tribes had such an excess of boys that they were willing to marry some into lesser tribes. The youth would have a chance to prove himself as something more than the least man in a large warband. It might work out.

One of the vultures dropped out of sight. She wiped her blade dry on the grass, tied a blue string on the dead buck's ear to mark her kill, then rose. The gelding grazed, ignoring the smell of freshly spilled blood. He'd seen worse than a slain deer. She walked up the slope with an arrow loose against the string, cautious as she edged to the crest. Beyond, the land flattened as it stretched into the eastern dry-lands. Grass had dried to a golden pallor under the summer's heat. The sky whitened at the zenith.

A vulture perched on the ground, staring at a stubborn knot of mist pooled within another of the sinks where spring's rains had collected and slowly were dry-ing out. A second landed a short distance from the first. Both fixed their gaze on that insubstantial clot.

At first she thought it might be an animal, shifting as it struggled. But it was not. The misty silver substance was cloth so fine it appeared as light as air, and rippled in the wind that blew out of the east. She crept closer, pausing at intervals to scan the horizon and the heavens for threat. The vultures, seeing her, kept their distance. She kept her bow held ready, arrow taut against the string. Grass crackled under her steps, but as she moved into the sink the crackling faded to a softer sound where the grass had enough moisture to bend without breaking. At a stone's throw out, she halted.

It was cloth of a fine silken weave, precious fabric trapped by a weight wrapped within it. A body, but whether living or dead Kirya was not sure. By the behavior of the vultures, they were unsure as well, and she trusted them to know better than she the presence of the breath of life in any creature left lying on earth. Demons haunted the shadows that bridged the gap between the living and the dead; it was dangerous to pass too close to the edge.

But such fabric, shimmering and rich, was worth the risk. Anyone must fear demons; it was only prudent, especially here so close to the eastern drylands where demons haunted the night, and where their more human enemies, the dreaded Qin, hunted in summer and autumn. But the daughter of a poor tribe must brave dangers that would chase away the less desperate daughter of a more prosperous tribe.

She slipped the arrow into the quiver and unhooked her mirror. The reflection showed her nothing different than what she saw with her eyes. She drew her knife. With her bow in her bracing hand and the knife in her strong hand, she approached. She hesitated a body's length from the body, seeing coarse black hair fluttering at one end and the fabric twisted so tightly around the rest that only a single bare foot could be seen. Brown-skinned. This was no tribal woman, but a stranger.

The vultures watched as she knelt beside the body. The unstained heavens cast no cloud shadow. Perhaps this was a demon pretending to be a dead woman, hoping to snare her. Perhaps the vultures were its cousins, in bird form, luring her in.

Her iron knife, blessed by a Singer, would protect her.

She studied the wrapped body, the layers of finely woven cloth. Its color was magnificently subtle, more silver than gray, shot through with the delicate light that is mist rising off the earth at dawn. She touched the cloth with the blade.

Death can overtake life between one breath and the next. A man may blink, and find a sword in his gut. The deer may leap, and be dead before it falls.

The wind on the plains is a constant. A violent gust tore the cloth free. It billowed into her, choking her as it wrapped her body, pressing into her face until she could not breathe.

Theirs is not just a poor tribe but a dying tribe. No one will say so out loud, but the end will come soon. Estifio and Yara will ride off on their own with their boy; the Tomanyi cousins will eat their oath-bound words and seek the shelter once offered them by distant cousins in the west, hoping to make marriages for their young daughters. That will leave the cripple, the old uncle, and the orphan boy as their war band, the four young children, and three adult women, one of them gravely ill and one slow of mind . . .

The Vidrini boy will never be allowed to marry Mariya. Never. Their tribe is already dead, just twitching as animals sometimes do after the spirit has fled.

Gasping, she clawed herself free from the horrible thoughts. Her hands stung. Her lips smarted, and when she licked them, motes of skin flaked loose to dust her tongue. She slapped the cloth down with the knife, got it fixed under her knees. The wind died as suddenly as it had come up. With the mantle torn loose, the body lay uncovered.

The woman wore foreign clothing, spun from flimsy cloth that could not withstand winter's piercing winds. One sleeve had torn and been mended with a darker thread. Her face was brown and her hair was black. Her hands, lying lifeless on her belly, were scarred with many tiny white lines as though repeatedly cut by a stone scraper. She looked as if she were sleeping, not dead, but her chest did not rise or fall, and when Kirya held her mirror in front of those lips, no breath misted the mirror's surface.

Those without breath are without life. Yet she smelled no decay, nothing putrid. No bugs crawled. No vermin had begun to feast. And the vultures had vanished.

Air pulled in her lungs as she sucked in, then exhaled. Her own breath made mist smear the mirror's surface. She was still living, then. She had not been devoured.

She scanned the heavens, but saw no birds, no messengers of any kind from the gods. The sun had shifted higher. Somehow it had become midmorning.

The cloth rippled under her knees as wind pressed through the grass. Both her hands hurt: Blisters bubbled on her skin. This was demon cloth's, dangerous to mortal kind, and thus doubly valuable. They could actually hope to trade it for what they needed most: life for their tribe. Husbands. A tribe without women cannot be called a tribe: It loses its name and its heart and must be cast to the winds in the manner of a lost spirit. But likewise, in different manner, a tribe without brothers and uncles and sons and husbands cannot hang together; it will unravel, fabric that cannot keep its binding.

"Kiri!" Mariya stood at the crest of a hill, holding the reins of both horses.

Kirya gave the hand signal for her cousin to keep back.

The mantle clasped just below the hollow of the throat. The brooch had a complicated design, a set of interlocking circles molded of silver, and it radiated heat. She dared not touch it with her bare skin. She cut away the sleeves of the dead woman's tunic and wrapped her hands in the cloth. When she touched the clasp with wrapped hands, it did not burn her. Simple cloth, it seemed, was proof against demonic sorcery. She unhooked the clasp and pushed the halved parts to either side, revealing a throat deeply bruised at the hollow.

A drop of blood beaded on the skin. The body shifted. She started back, but it was only the movement of limbs slipping as the lifeless hands that had been resting on the belly of the corpse fell to either side. It was only a stray drop of blood that had been confined by the pressure of the broach.

Her hands still wrapped, she tugged the cloth free, then folded it in lengths and rolled it up, tying it with a strip of cloth. The blisters on her skin rubbed painfully, and her hands, lips, and face stung with the pressure one might feel when she steps too close to fire. Sweat ran cold and hot in waves. But she had captured the demon in the cloth. She had taken a treasure so precious that it could alter the destiny of her tribe.

There was nothing else worth taking. The dead woman wore a belt of mere hempen rope, a poor woman's garment and in any case very worn, and no rings, no necklace or armband, no anklet. She didn't even carry a mirror, as all proper women did.

Kirya paced a spiral around the corpse, opening the path out sunwise until she found a spot where grass had been trampled. A horse had stood here, hooves leaving their print, grass torn where the animal had grazed. But the hoofprints vanished as abruptly as the vultures had, as though it had taken flight. There was no trail she could follow to pursue so valuable a prize as a stray horse. No doubt the woman's other belongings had been slung on the horse as well. Somehow, she had fallen, and the horse had run away. Perhaps she'd been overtaken by a demon and her breath devoured out of her while she struggled. It was too bad they'd lost the horse.

"Kiri!" Mariya was not patient. Daughter of the tribe's leader, she expected to sit in authority over the tribe in time. This knowledge had made her impulsive and anxious rather than persevering and pragmatic.

Kirya bound the mantle with strips of plain cloth until no part of it could touch skin. She fashioned a loop out of the ends. She whistled—wheet wheet whoo—and Mariya released the gelding. He trotted up and nuzzled her. Hands still smarting, she grabbed the saddle and swung on. With the bundle slung from her quiver, she rode back to her waiting cousin.

22

Kontas was a good boy but absent-minded for all his eleven years. When Kirya had done the morning milking, she had to call for him. He was playing dice with his cousins Stanyo and Danya.

"You should be helping with the chores, not playing. You two boys take the herd off away from the tents to graze." He grinned at her, never one to take a scolding to heart; she gave him an affectionate clout on the head. "Pest! Go on! Danya, go help Feder with the turning. I'll send Asya over to help you."

Danya ran off. The boys chivvied the bleating sheep and goats farther into the grass. Four of the six dray beasts followed with placid amiability, while Nimwit and None-in-the-Skull kept ripping up the grass where they stood, oblivious of the movement around them.

She hooked the stool under her arm. With the leather sack sloshing with warm milk over a shoulder, she trudged through the scatter of tents that marked their tribe. Her cousin Estifio sat cross-legged on a threadbare rug outside his wife's tent, embroidering the sleeve of a man's shirt. He grinned as she paused to admire the intricate line of vines wound around dainty flowers.

"A wedding shirt," she said. "For Mari?"

"I was thinking for trade. But I'm down to my last needle."

They looked at each other. Thread they could spin, and plants collect for dye, but they had no blacksmith nor any tribe obliged to offer them the services of a black-smith.

"Uncle Olig can make you a bone needle," she said.

He shrugged, his way of passing off disappointment. "His bone needles are very fine, but not fine enough for this delicate work."

"If you finish it before the confluence ends, you can trade for needles and the best dyestuffs."

"Yes, I suppose."

Estifio's wife Yara, together with Uliya Tomanyi, knelt on a mat, pressing felt into the distinctive linked-circles pattern passed down through their tribe for genera-tions. They were talking intently, heads bent together. Yara's son slept in a sling on her back. Uliya's two little girls tied knots beside Asya, Uncle Olig's granddaughter, who was concentrating so hard that she was biting her tongue. Kirya sighed. They were good girls, very serious, but she could not imagine how Uliya would ever get husbands for her girls, or what Asya could expect as the last descendant of her tent, with no aunts or mother to bargain for her.

Yara and Uliya glanced up to see her, and started as if they'd been caught whis-pering secrets. What were they plotting?

With a grimace, she hitched the heavy sack a little higher, walking on. Uncle Olig sat on a rug under the awning of what had been his sister's tent, she who had been cousin once removed to Kirya's aunt and mother. Wood shavings littered the rug as he planed the inside length of a shaft of wood.

"Kiri, that gelding kicked Manig again."

"I don't know why Manig keeps going near him. Is he hurt?"

Not far away, Manig Tomanyi was stewing glue from the deer she and Mariya had killed.

"It was just a warning kick. If that bad-tempered beast had meant to cripple him, he'd have done so. Here, little one, come try this now."

She set down her burden. Grasping the wood at the center, she set one tip on the ground and leaned into it as the old man examined the way the lower limb bent.

"Would you take off more wood?" he asked her.

She flipped the bow and leaned on the other end. "This end is stiffer. Who is the bow for?"

"Asya is ready for a bow with more draw. That one there—" He pointed toward a composite bow braced into shape and curing.

"Yes, I know," she said with a laugh. "Mine will be ready in a few months."

He smiled. "A good bow demands patience."

"Let me get this to the churn and I'll come back," she said to the old man, hand-ing back the stave.

Little Danya was twisting the rope that turned the drill, and Feder the Cripple bent over the wood he was shaping into a bowl, whistling in time to the rhythmic whoosh whoosh of the turning. He could sing, too, and his ancient winged kur with its horse head, stylized wings along the neck, and two strings sat in its place of honor in the small wheeled cart on which he got around. He had been a fighter before the incident that had crippled him; his saber rode in a sling alongside the precious kur.

He didn't look up as she passed. He didn't need to. "Ei, ei, Kiri! Here's a tune for you today. I can hear it coming out of your ears!" He swung into a new tune. With a smirk far too knowing for her tender age, Danya altered the pace of her twisting to match the words. " 'Who is that handsome youth walking through camp? His sister is looking at me, but he pretends not to see me.' "

Her ears burned.

Orphan was scraping the last hide, stripped to the waist, skin gleaming. He was a very good-looking youth, a few years older than Kirya and Mariya, but of course to even think of an orphaned lad who did servant's work was impossible.

" 'Why is that handsome youth hanging around camp? His sister brings cheese and boiled meat, but he pretends not to see me.' "

Orphan had showed up at the edge of camp about two years ago, silent and empty-handed, and at first they hadn't been sure if he was a demon because although he was black-haired and dark-complexioned like Mari, he had twisty eyes, pulled at the ends as though drawn like a bow, a sure sign of demon blood. But he spoke their language in the same way they did, and he asked what work he could do in exchange for a bit of food and worked so hard day after day and month after month that eventually they simply accepted that he belonged to them now. After all, what other tribe was desperate enough to take in an orphan?

" 'Why do the flowers bloom so, everywhere around camp? If I offer the flowers at the entrance to his sister's tent, will he pretend not to see me?' "

Orphan glanced at her, and away at once, since it wasn't proper for any man not related by blood to stare at a woman. She forced her gaze away from the rippling muscles of his back and swung around behind her aunt's big tent. Feder's song faded to whistling.

Her aunt was weaving in the shade of the awning. Seeing Kirya, she set down her shuttle. "There you are, Kiri. Take that milk to Edina. Then you and Mari take an offering to the holy Singer's tent and get his blessing for the marriage. Then go round to see if the Oliski tribe has come in. I want to talk to Mother Oliski as soon as she is ready to negotiate."

"Yes, Aunt. Can I take the little ones? They'd like to see all the different people."

"There'll be time for that later."

"What about just Kontas, then? He's old enough to—"

"No. I don't want them underfoot to get in your way or say the wrong thing. We need the blessing of the Singer if we hope for a marriage."

Mariya had her head down, polishing the silver necklaces, bracelets, and headpieces that made up the riches of the tent.

"The cloth I found might be a powerful gift, Aunt. We can expect something better than the Oliski tribe's castoffs."

"Did I ask for your opinion, Kirya?"

"No, Aunt, you did not."

"Then do as I say."

"Yes, Aunt."

Beyond the shelter of the awning, her youngest aunt, Edina, was hanging strips of meat to dry in the sun, singing the first verse of a child's counting song over and over because it was the only verse she knew. The churn had already been set up for the sheep's milk. Kirya poured the milk into the churn, savoring the rich aroma. She unhooked the ladle from the churn and dipped out a portion for herself. After drinking it down, she licked her lips. Wind sighed in the canvas of the tent, inhaling and exhaling. She carried a ladleful of milk into the tent.

Mother lay on her side, propped on pillows, but she was asleep. The illness had ravaged her, a nest of agony inside her bones. She so rarely fell into a true sleep that Kiri couldn't bear to wake her even for a sip of strengthening milk.

Back outside, Mariya had gathered up a leather bag with the best haunch of meat inside, as well as a length of backstrap sinew suitable for presentation to the holy one. Defiantly, she wore the beaded nets, and she gave Kirya a strong stare to warn her not to say anything, so Kirya said nothing, just slung the bag along her shoulders and headed out toward the distant smoke of gathered fires. Mari hurried along behind.

In any confluence, tribes sited their camps according to an unspoken order. A tribe as weak and poor as theirs had to set up their tents on the fringe of the confluence grounds, well away from the well-connected and rich tribes around which the councils and settlements and marriage offers would pool. They had to tramp through tall grass for quite a ways, passing well-guarded herds of sheep and horses, before the sprawl of the major encampments came into view, and then they had to trudge through the lesser granddaughter tribes and the tribes losing position owing to raids or famine in their herds and inward to the positions of greater importance.

Each tribe had roped off the ground it claimed for its own, leaving wide strips of grass separating camps. They circled in spiral-wise, to get a good look at the banners and rugs and young men of the many tribes assembled so far. There were plenty of banners, and beautiful rugs, and attractive young men laughing and joking and embroidering and practicing with their sabers and whips. Showing off, as young men did in such company.

Of the Vidrini tribe they saw no trace.

Young men kept their eyes lowered as the two girls passed, but masculine gazes brushed them, and heads turned after they had gone by to track their passage. Mariya had that effect on men. Kirya smiled wryly, aware that she was like a stone point placed next to an iron-tipped arrow: serviceable enough, but not the first thing you would reach for.

Two Singers had traveled to this confluence, their presence marked by tall poles wound with streamers. They dared not approach the Sakhalin tribe, whose headwoman's tent stood at the center of the huge encampment. The least of the Sakhalin servants might count herself higher than the Moroshya headwoman. But the Singer out of the Konomin tribe had a humbler station, and anyway they had made offerings to him before and gotten blessings from the holy man for two of their arrows. He was old, no longer in the full flush of his power, and because all of his sisters were dead, he lived in the tent of a niece, its awning visible from here.

They approached the gap in the rope where a pair of jaunty young men stood guard with sabers swinging casually at their side, and took a place at the end of the line already formed by folk fortunate enough to have less far to walk. Everyone carried offerings. A good-looking man wearing a beautifully embroidered shirt swaggered to the front of the line. After a muttered discussion with the guards, he and his armed followers were admitted into the camp.

"I like that," said an old woman, bent and weary, who stood in front of them. "That's the Vidrini for you, eh?"

The man strode up to the awning, made his courtesies, and was offered a pillow to sit on while his followers hung back with arms crossed. From this angle, Kirya could not see the Singer, but at least a dozen people stood or sat in attendance under the awning.

"Was that the war leader of the Vidrini tribe?" Mariya asked, a little too eagerly.

The old woman raised an eyebrow, looking over the two girls with a gaze that measured their worth and station. With a snort, she turned her back on them.

Mariya leaned into Kirya. "I told Mother I should wear jewelry. Then people wouldn't treat us as they do."

The haunch weighed too heavily on Kirya's shoulders for her to shrug. "It doesn't matter. Aunt means to marry you to Oliski."

"I mean to put her off until I discover what's become of the Vidrini," muttered Mari with a black look. "I don't want to marry an ugly old man!"

"Women have no choice in marriage, you know that. You can take lovers afterward, if you're prudent about it. Or I'll marry him."

Mari was close to tears. "Mother says they asked for me specifically. We're so small in their eyes that even an old, useless man can demand to marry the next headwoman rather than her cousin. It's hard to imagine what manner of man Mother believes we can find for you if that's the case!"

Kirya winced.

"I didn't mean that as it sounded."

"The bruise doesn't get any less sore if it keeps getting poked. Let's just leave it, eh?" She was used to having nothing much to expect, not even a Flower Night with a decent fellow, someone she could choose. Maybe this confluence would be her only chance to taste a piece of joy just for herself, not for the sake of the others, before the cold truth blew over them like winter's blizzard. But the thought of offering her Flower Night to a stranger who would not otherwise look at her twice was too grim to contemplate.

"Hey! Hey!"

Mariya grabbed her elbow, shaking her back to earth.

Four armed men crossed out from the Konomin camp, pointing at them. "Yes, you two! Get out of here."

Under the stares of every woman within earshot, Mari began to snivel.

"Are you talking to us in such a rude way?" asked Kirya. "We're here to make an offering to the Singer."

"The Singer doesn't want you here. Says you're cursed. Now get out."

The old woman spat on the ground by Mari's feet and pointedly moved away, as did everyone else in the line. By now, all movement within eyeshot had come to a halt. The men did not threaten them directly; that would have gone against the gods' sacred laws. But words were enough, even if no saber was drawn.

Kirya knew her face was hot with shame. People in the distance were whispering and pointing. "How can we be cursed? How can the Singer even know we are here, or who we are? We only came with an offering to ask for a marriage blessing."

" 'Ghosts of a dead tribe, be gone,' " said the man in the lead, without looking them in the eye. " 'The gods have cursed you. You've been touched by the breath of demons.' The Singer's words have been spoken. There is no taking them back."

Mari tugged on her sleeve. "Let's go, Kiri. Please!"

The gathered people parted to make a path for them to retreat. No one wanted to chance the taint of demon's breath spreading from their nostrils. Head bowed, sucking down sobs so she would not disgrace them further, Mari strode back the way they had come, but Kirya, following behind, kept her head high. What did the Singer know, anyway? Yet when she thought of the cloak, and the dead woman she had touched, she shuddered.

Coming at last into their own camp, sweating and hot, they passed a woman who strode past them without a greeting. Aunt sat in the shade of the awning, shoulders bowed and face so wan and weary that Kirya choked down fear, wondering if the sickness that had struck down her mother had attacked her aunt.

"Mari! Kiri!"

Beyond the tent, Yara and Uliya were whispering, and the men stood in a huddle like sheep, Feder's cart pulled out to join them. The children cowered at the entrance to the tent, Kontas with his head in his hands.

"What did you say to insult the Singer?" demanded Aunt. "Now Mother Oliski has sent word that under no circumstances will she consider the marriage. We're ruined!" Her words were punctuated by the rhythmic slap of Edina whipping the churn. Cheese and butter could not wait on disaster.

"We didn't even have a chance to talk to the Singer." Kirya heaved the leather sack to the ground and stood there, panting.

"I knew that orphan was trouble!"

Mari said, "Orphan?"

Kirya clenched her hands. "Orphan? What has he ever done except work hard to please us?"

"His eyes are demon eyes!"

It was true enough, but Kirya was too angry to keep silence. "This isn't his fault. How the Singer could even have known we were coming to see him I can't imagine."

"The gods see everything." She looked old, broken. "We have to leave at dawn tomorrow. Orphan cannot come with us. That's the end of it."

"Just one more day, surely—" cried Mariya. "Just one more day."

Aunt turned a cold gaze on her daughter. "Do you think I don't know your hopes about the Vidrini boy, Mariya? Put them aside. We must go quickly. Trouble is coming. We must run before it catches us."

Mari covered her face with her hands.

"Maybe that cloth I found is the trouble," said Kirya hesitantly.

"Pack up everything. Orphan may take some meat, a pair of wooden bowls, some sinew, a sack, and knife with him. He's a strong young man now. He can find a place in a war band."

"Not as a kinless orphan, Aunt. He's done nothing wrong."

"His family is dead, and he survived. That is enough wrong for one person. We should never have taken him in. A demon's child can have a handsome face as easily as an ugly one." Her eyes were stones, the line of her mouth a closed tent. "Take some milk to your mother."

Her mother was awake, but only semiconscious, too weak to sit up but able to swallow milk spooned into her mouth. Her eyes were the same intense blue as Kirya's, and with these she gazed at her daughter, her only way of communicating since she could not speak. Such torment. Such trouble.

Kirya said, "It seems we'll be moving on, Mother. Don't worry, I'll be with you always."

Gently, she turned her to the other side, arranged the pillows around her, took away the pad of soft grass that caught her urine and loose feces and replaced it with another. The smell wasn't too bad; she was used to it. Maybe if her mother could talk, she would ask to be left behind on the grass, to die in the proper manner, but the illness had taken her voice as suddenly as her ability to walk, and in the eyes of the gods to abandon her without her consent was no different from murder.

Anyway, Kirya did not want to lose her. "Kontas," she said, calling to her brother. "Pack our things, and sit by mother. Sing to her, will you? She likes your voice. Mine is such a croak!" She made frog sounds, and that got him to smile a little, but his serious face troubled her as she went out to help Uncle Olig with his gear.

"What did we do wrong, Uncle?" she asked in a low voice as she bound a dozen green staves and placed the bundle in the wagon. "It doesn't seem right that Orphan is punished for it."

"His eyes are demon eyes," said uncle, but no force animated the words. Like all of them, he was too sick at heart to fight Aunt's proclamation. They could not confront the Singer. They had no choice but to leave.

AS TWILIGHT SETTLED over the grass, Kirya slipped away to a tangle of late-season wildflowers that the sheep hadn't trampled. She plucked a handful of pinks and whites, humble flowers, nothing special, just like her.

Sometimes your position is so bad that the worst thing you thought you could do no longer seems bad at all. Clutching the flowers, she went in search of Orphan. He'd had his talk with Aunt and been given his sad bundle and banished from camp, but he hadn't gone far. He'd hunkered down within sight of their tents.

He saw her coming but did not move or speak. She sank down on her haunches beside him, slung her quiver off to one side, and offered him the flowers.

Ei!

He swayed back, visibly startled. He did not open his clenched hands.

"It's rude not to take them," she said, not sure whether to grin or to slap him.

He stared at the flowers. "You don't want me," he said in his hoarse voice.

"Aunt forbade me, not in so many words, but you know how she is. But I've changed my mind about obeying her. It's my Flower Night. The gods say I can choose who I want. Now are you going to take them?"

As though they were precious, he took them from her. He brought them to his face, inhaled their scent. Then grinned, twisting a finger into the tangle and pulling out a green stalk with triple-pointed leaves. "These sour-root leaves are edible. Did you know that? Orphan's food." He sank back onto the ground, one leg crossed before him and the other with knee up so he could prop an elbow on it. He plucked the leaves, chewed several, and touched the rest to her lips. "I've been teaching the children to recognize which plants they can eat."

The idea of Kontas eating ground-digger's food made her flush with shame. "Like we're no better than—?"

"They're sweet."

His hands were warm, and his smile warmer. She parted her lips and licked at the leaves. The leaves had a snap, but a sweet aftertaste that lingered in her mouth. He chuckled. She leaned toward him, brushed his cheek with her own. She blew softly at his ear, and he cupped her neck in his hand and pulled her closer.

"I'm only an orphan." With her head turned, and his lips pressed close to her ear, she could not see his expression. "I'm not worthy of your Flower Night."

The twilight darkened, brushed by rose like fire along the western horizon. To the east, fires burned where the encampment sprawled, a place they were no longer welcome. Exiles all. Yet maybe none of that mattered. They had good green staves for new bows that could be traded; twin female lambs as well as not one lamb lost to wolves or mouth fever; Feder's precious kur, on which he could sing for favor from the gods.

"Who is worthy?" she said to the heavens. "We'll follow the gar-deer. We'll ride to new pastures, somewhere they don't know the Singer who cursed us. You'll follow, and in a month or two Aunt will relent and let you back. Things will get better."

She lay down in the grass and he lay beside her, and as she caressed him and he caressed her, the drumming of her heart quickened and the blood thrummed in her ears like galloping hooves. She unfastened the loops on his tunic and slid her hands beneath, tracing his muscled chest and smooth back. The small noises he made as she stroked him made her crazy; she could could not hear or see anything, nothing but the presence of him pressed close against her and the warmth that spread through her body. She fumbled with the loops on her own tunic.

His hands gripped hers, crushing her fingers. She grunted with pain. He bent close.

"Listen."

That drumming was not her heart.

"It's a raid," he added. "Stay down."

"How can you—" She struggled, trying to sit up.

He rolled on top of her to pin her, with the tall grass still concealing them in a conspiracy with the falling of night. His whisper was harsh in her ear.

"How do you think my kin died? I was out looking for a lost lamb. I hid, but I heard it all."

"Oh, gods," she whispered.

Hooves drummed on the earth, felt through the soil. Orphan stayed on top of her, nothing of love or lust in his position, only desperation. He had heard what she must hear now.

The *shing* of steel drawn, shouts and screams, the hiss of flame, the wailing of children, the bleating of panicked sheep. The sounds shuddered the air until she could bear it no longer. She shoved him so hard he toppled sideways, and she sprang up to see a tent spurting flames as riders raced away into the night laughing and howling. Stars blazed above, fire below. She ran. Orphan overtook her and tackled her.

She screamed at him, "My mother's in the tent!"

Swearing, he leaped up and ran with her.

It was too late.

In the ruins of the camp, Uncle Olig and Feder the Cripple lay dead, cut down despite being too old and too infirm to fight. Cowards! The tent burned, and Aunt had burned hands as they dragged her back from the flaming canvas while Mari sobbed.

"Where are the children?" Edina ran in circles, keening and shouting by turns. The tents were alight, burning crisply. "Where are the children?"

They shouted and they called, and Kirya whistled—wheet wheet whoo—over and over again. All night Kirya and Orphan and Edina searched in the grass while Mari held on to her mother to stop her from throwing herself into the burning tent where her beloved sister lay.

The Tomanyi cousins and their daughters, as well as Estifio and Yara and their baby son, had fled or been taken.

The children—Kontas, Danya, Stanyo, and Asya—were gone.

Stolen.

23

At dawn, they knew what was left: the gelding and the piebald mare, who had trotted back into camp late in the night followed by two skittish goats and a dozen confused ewes; the chest Edina had salvaged with cloth, utensils, and Aunt's weaving kit; the churn, ladle, and whip; Feder's overturned cart with his saber hidden under one of the wheels; some scattered bundles and gear not taken out of the wagon, which Kirya had helped load the afternoon before, the remains of Uncle Olig's workshop. Nimwit and None-Skull had refused to budge during the night's excitement and grazed stubbornly nearby, having moved away only enough to get out of the trouble zone. As for the rest, they possessed three bows and two quivers and the meager goods belonging to Orphan.

Weary beyond measure, Kirya poked through the remains of the burned tents with one of the green shafts. She scraped odds and ends out of the wreckage. A rolled-up felt rug had its ends and outer layer scorched, but the interior could be salvaged. A belt buckle formed in the shape of a deer and a pair of copper bracelets inscribed against the evil eye need only be cleaned to be wearable. A leather case had burned black, but the precious porcelain cup nestled inside it and belonging to Uncle Olig remained intact. A small leather bucket set inside a larger one emerged unscathed. She raked harness buckles and a stirrup and a valuable axe head from the ruins.

"There's nothing in the Tomanyi tent," said Kirya to Mari. "It's as if they had already packed and were ready to run."

Mariya kept raking. Now and again she glanced toward her mother, who sat on a rug Mari had saved from the fire. Her hands and arms and face were red and blistering. Orphan had set himself to milking the ewes. Edina paced around the camp, still looking for the children. They did not try to stop her. Once fixed, she could not change direction.

Rays splintering off the rising sun caught a gleam within the wreckage of the main tent, and Kirya jumped back, fearing she had uncovered her mother's bones, although she had tried to keep away from the area within the tent where her mother had died. But this had a more silvery shine than bone. It fluttered as if a rat crawled beneath it. In its shimmering, restless billow, mist breathed out of the dead hulk.

"Gods," she breathed.

Mariya set down her rake. Her face was drawn with pain, aged by grief. "The demon still lives."

"No, it's just the wind." Kirya scrounged for scraps of cloth and wound them around her hands, then cleared a path for herself into the hot ashes and grabbed for the cloth. She heaved it up, skipping backward, and the cloak unfurled like a great wing, ash and flakes of soot spinning away from it.

Even caught in the fire, unprotected, it had not burned. It showed no stain at all, no soot, no blackened edges, no discoloration where the heat should have browned it.

She looked at Mari. Her cousin straightened, squaring her shoulders. Now the accusation would come: the demon cloak had brought this down on them. They were tainted, and Kirya had been the cause.

"Did you see the raiders?" Mariya's voice was hoarse from shouting and crying all night.

"No."

"They wore the Vidrini patterns. That boy made eyes at me, and flattered me with trivial gifts, and then went back to his tribe's council and told them everything there was to know about what an easy target we'd make. Then maybe some woman talked to Uliya or Yara, and that is how we were betrayed. But I took the first step, wanting a pretty boy to smile at me even if I did know a Vidrini boy couldn't possibly be serious about me." She touched the lapis-lazuli beads that bound the ends of her hair, meaning, perhaps, to fling them to the ground. But she lowered her hand, leaving them in place, and glanced toward Orphan, seated on their last milking stool, working with quiet efficiency.

"I know what we have to do."

"IT'S THE WAY of things when a tribe is dying," said Mother Oliski, come to survey the ruins. An amazing number of people had walked out from the main encampment to survey the aftermath of the raid, all those people who had refused to look at them yesterday. "The stronger takes what it needs from the weaker. The wolf picks off the diseased. It's for the best."

Aunt stared straight ahead, not speaking, not hearing. Mariya confronted the visitors.

"We no longer have anything you want, Mother Oliski. Why have you come, except to pick at the bones?"

"Tssh! You should be grateful for any offer you get, girl. We'd be willing to take your remnant into our tribe as servants. Your mother is a good weaver, if her hands aren't ruined. If you're obedient and work hard, we might allow you to marry Laoshko despite your low position. It's the best a girl like you can hope for."

Edina hissed.

Kirya began to speak, a bleat of anger more than a true word, then bit her tongue. Mother Oliski was right. She was only glad her mother had been spared this final dishonor.

Mariya stood beside her mother, squinting as though trying to identify an unpleasant flavor. "What makes you think, Mother Oliski, that we are interested in negotiating with you?"

"Hah! You have nothing with which to negotiate, girl. A wagon, a pair of broken-down horses, a straggle of a herd, a single chest of poor possessions. You have no man in your tribe, not even sons who can grow."

"Kiri," said Mari in an undertone. "Fetch Feder's saber and give it to Orphan."

"Heh?"

Mari threw her a stinging look. Kirya was so startled by the intensity of that gaze that she obeyed. She scrounged in the wagon as Mari kept talking, raising her voice so everyone who had gathered to gloat could hear her.

"You can all go back to the confluence unless you have come in good faith to negotiate. The Moroshya tribe is departing today, so if you wish to speak to us, be quick about it."

Some laughed, while others scoffed. They were vultures, waiting for the dying corpse to stop twitching, only there was nothing holy about their intentions. Kirya walked around behind the wagon, where Orphan hovered well away from Aunt and the other women. She offered him the saber. He stared first at the blade, then at her. She indicated Mariya and pressed the saber against his arms until, reflexively, he took it from her.

Mari said, in a loud voice, "You may all as well witness. That you rodents all scurried over here to sniff for food interrupted my betrothal."

She turned to look at Orphan, whose eyes grew almost round as he stared at her in surprise. Women have no choice in marriage, of course. While any man, however powerful or poor, could walk up to any woman, however well- or ill-connected, few marriages were founded on such unstable earth as sexual desire or the impulse of a moment.

Mariya could be silly, vain, self-centered, and vague, but the desperate gamble she threw now made her entire body seem larger and more imposing; she was a daughter of the gods, loosing the last arrow left in her quiver.

Orphan caught the shaft at once. He frowned mightily, but his body became taut with expectation and joy. He unsheathed the blade and, like steel taken life, cut past the onlookers to stand in front of Mari with blade extended. She lifted her chin expectantly. Kirya wept silently, and she did not know why.

In the gathered crowd, some tittered, while others drew back as though they could not bear to witness the shame of an orphan marking a headwoman's daughter, even in a tribe so cast out that it now consisted merely of two adult sisters, a daughter and a niece, and what remained of their paltry herd.

Orphan rested the tip of the blade on Mari's cheek. She stiffened, preparing herself, and he sliced a short mark, not too deep, into the skin. Blood drooled, sliding to her jaw. He did not smile. If anything, he looked more grave.

Mari said, through the pain, "Now you see we have everything we need. A headwoman, her daughter properly wed, and our own herds intact. We may be a poor tribe, but we are not dead. If you have nothing further to say to us, then go."

Kirya would not have expected every onlooker to depart. After all, there might be a great deal of entertainment in watching them load their solitary wagon and lumber off shrouded in the tatters of their doomed pride. But the taint of demon's breath rested heavily on the scene.

When the last of them was out of earshot, Mari shook herself, although she did not touch the mark on her cheek or the blood on her skin. "We have to get the children back."

"How are we going to do that?" Kirya twisted her hands into her belt. She didn't know whether to slap Mari, or embrace her.

"This is how we're going to do it," said Mari in a calm voice, just as if she were headwoman. "I have to remain separate from Orphan now anyway, and I've no tent to go into seclusion. You and I will ride after the raiders. We'll take anything possible to ransom back the children. We'll claim kin-right to the things they've stolen, like Feder's winged kur."

"We have no power to make them give anything back."

"We're going—you and I—and that's all there is to it. Orphan will stay with Mother and Edina and the herd. They'll travel to that swale where we hunted the gar-deer, and wait for us there. He knows how to survive, and he can do anything that Feder and Uncle Olig could do, maybe not as well, but he learned from them."

Orphan was a clever youth, always learning, the hardest worker Kirya had ever met. That he was a good-looking boy always off-limits to her, and now married to her beloved cousin, must not cloud her judgment. She did not want to become a servant in another tribe where she would be assigned the most arduous or tedious tasks like churning and cleaning skins and smoking meat and hauling night pans out of tents every morning, given the worst cut of meat at mealtime and the last curdled ladle of milk, and left to sleep at the edge of camp under a wagon no matter the weather.

Reluctantly, Kirya nodded her agreement. "If we can get the children back, we can stay far from the other tribes. With Orphan's skills and our hunting, we can survive until the children are grown. But I don't know how our tribe can grow."

"I do." Mari's gaze slid over to rest on Orphan. In Mari's look Kirya saw a softening that abruptly spoke its secret: Mari had also long admired the handsome orphan the gods had tossed into their midst, but she had feared her mother's anger too much to do anything about it.

Now she had him. And Kirya didn't.

"Why shouldn't we take in other orphans?" asked Mari.

"It's bad luck to take in orphans."

"Bad luck?" Mari gestured to the wreckage surrounding them. "What does that matter now?"

OUTRIDERS MET THEM before they came into sight of the Vidrini camp. That one was the youth who had gifted Mariya with the lapis-lazuli nets was evident from the way he jeered with more blustery force than his young comrades as they galloped in circles around the two girls but did not, of course, make any move to touch them.

"What are those? What are those? Beggars and servants, beggars and servants. Orphan, orphan, will you come out to play? Pick up my boots, grease my harness! Here's the scum from the broth for your licking."

Kirya and Mariya had ridden for five days on the trail of the Vidrini tribe, and Kirya was too hungry and too exhausted from grief to shout back in kind. Mari kept her gaze fixed forward, ignoring the youths. She might have been a daughter of the Sakhalin, with that proud gaze and contemptuous expression.

People stared as the two girls rode into camp. Here were fine tents, and a blacksmith's portable foundry pouring its rich offerings of smoke to the heavens. The Vidrini had no Singer, but they had churns fitted with copper trimmings, weavings hanging in profusion, men strutting around in brightly embroidered shirts, and women wearing everyday jewelry like bracelets and silver necklaces because they were wealthy enough to show off their riches even as they went about their daily chores. Or perhaps because they had servants to do the chores for them.

Mari's glare cut a passage right up to the awning of the headwoman's tent. Mari dismounted while Kirya remained in the saddle, scanning the camp for any sign of the children.

Shockingly, the Vidrini headwoman was a foreigner. Like Orphan, she had demon-scratched eyes, not round but slanted as though a demon's claws had raked them into her face. But she had a much more foreign look than Orphan, a real Easterner with hair as black as soot, eyes as black as night, and flat features marked particularly by a cruel mouth. Seated on a plush pillow, she did not rise to greet them. Feder's winged kur was propped on a stand beside her, and a small girl child with similar eyes but lighter hair sat on a pillow next to the kur, dressed in unspeakably rich silk robes.

Mariya marched to the edge of the carpet, and spoke in a clear, carrying voice. "It is easy to steal servants from tribes that cannot defend themselves. No wonder you Vidrini have become rich."

Many folk, both male and female, had gathered, but it was women who hissed at Mari's bold insult.

"That which is dying is prey," said the headwoman, her words clipped off by a foreigner's way of speaking. "What do you want?"

"My kinsmen returned to me. My tribes-folk released."

"Those who came of their free will cannot be 'released,' " said the headwoman with the scorn wielded by the powerful. A man sauntered out of the crowd and ducked under the awning, to kneel behind her. He was the war leader they had seen at the confluence. He whispered into her ear, and she nodded without taking her gaze off Mariya.

"Then the Moroshya tribe claims compensation for their migration into the Vidrini tribe."

The Vidrini headwoman laughed mockingly. "How do you mean to enforce your claim?"

"I am here as representative of the headwoman of the Moroshya tribe, who is my mother. I negotiate on her behalf for the return of two sons of the Moroshya tribe. Furthermore, you have taken two daughters of the Moroshya tribe against their will. That is a grave violation of the laws of the gods."

"You say so only because yours is the weak tribe, and mine is the strong. Do you mean to trouble me longer, or will you go, so I may be at peace?"

Mounted, Kirya was able to see over the heads of the crowd. Trying to hide around the curve of a tent stood Yara, the bitch, looking anxious as she surveyed the assembly. Over a distance, two gazes may meet. Yara jolted back, vanishing behind the tent.

Betrayed by their own tribesmen.

"The gods will judge in the end," said Mariya.

"So they will. Are you finished?"

"We have brought ransom."

The war leader snorted, and people guffawed and chortled.

The Vidrini headwoman smiled. "Do you mean to return to my cousin's nephew the pretty baubles he gifted you? I see you wear them still. I gave them to him myself, when he told me of his plan."

Mariya ignored the laughter and gaily spoken taunts. She waited for a proper response.

"What can you offer us? We relieved you of everything of value, except the piebald mare. I hear it bolted when the gelding broke free." The headwoman ran a covetous hand over the belly of the winged kur. Kirya found her teeth on edge, her jaw tight, wanting to crush that hand and knowing she could do nothing to get Feder's kur back.

Mari said, "We have cloth worth the ransom of the children. We'll trade it to you, in return for them."

Her proud expression grew cunning. "Hu. I doubt it, but let's see. I'm willing to bargain. It would amuse me."

The man smirked, and Kira had a sudden idea that these two were lovers, even though the headwoman of a tribe and her war leader ought not be engaged in such a way. Desire clouded judgment, everyone knew that.

"I need to see they are safe and unharmed before I make my offer," said Mariya.

"Very well. Go get them." Her war leader did not move, but a ripple stirred the assembly as someone else hurried off into the camp. While they waited, Kirya examined the man boldly, knowing he had no right to look directly at her. He was a very good-looking man, with golden-white hair and light blue eyes, an arresting face, broad shoulders, and lean hips. Although not as handsome as Orphan with his black hair and leaner face, he was a man in his prime. Had he lured the foreign woman into the tribes with the promise of power and position? Or had she followed him out of lust, and ripped the leadership of the Vidrini tribe away from whatever hapless woman had held it before her? Feeling the pressure of Kirya's gaze, he glanced toward her and, with a frown, looked away.

"Kiri! Kiri!"

Kirya rose on her stirrups. The gelding sidestepped, sensing her spurt of joy and relief. "We're here."

Three children came running, sobbing as they saw Mariya, and tumbled to a halt beside her. Her grim expression never wavered from the Vidrini headwoman.

"Three children," said Mariya, without acknowledging them. "Where is the fourth? The older boy?"

Oh gods. Kontas.

The headwoman's smile was meant to wound. "We traded him away yesterday. Got a good offer for him from an eastern merchant who was passing on the Golden Road, south of here. They liked his gold-silk hair and pretty face."

Kirya was off the gelding in an instant, but Mari's curt command slapped her.

"Kirya, stop there. Don't move!"

Shaking, Kirya found an arrow in her right hand and her bow gripped in her left. Men had pushed forward. She was not dead only because she was female; a man would have been cut down for the impiety.

"You must have known it was likely we would come after the children to redeem them. It goes against the laws of the gods to trade him away so quickly."

"You are a foolish, foolish girl. We would have traded away the other boy, too, but the merchant only wanted the blond one. Now, take your complaining and depart, or make your offer and I will consider it."

"The gods will punish you," said Mariya, so gray that she looked half dead. But wasn't their tribe already half dead, thrashing about blindly as the lifeblood drained out on the ground? Oh, gods, how terrified Kontas must be! And their mother dead in the fire—an honorable death, sent to the gods, certainly, but dead is dead. Kirya could not speak for tears, knowing herself half an orphan already although she had cousins to succor her. And yet what did she have to look forward to? Orphan was taken. What man would accept her Flower Night, now that her night with Orphan had been interrupted in such a ill-omened manner? The gods had cursed her. What did she have left?

Nothing.

"Mari, it's as she says, take it or leave it." She had worn gloves as a precaution, and she unslung the quiver from her back and untied the bundle, heedless of those edging close to shield the headwoman, whom they all obviously feared and obeyed even if she was a foreign monster with demon eyes. She grabbed the cloak with her gloved hands and shook it free.

They shouted with dismay when the silver cloth snapped out like the unfurling wings of one of the gods' holy steeds. Only the headwoman and her war leader did not shrink back. The silk-adorned girl child covered her face and began to cry. Her mother grabbed the girl's wrists, pulled them down, and slapped the little thing in the face.

"Never snivel! Don't show fear." She looked up at Mariya. "Give us the cloth. Take the children. It's a fair bargain. They're worth nothing to us, just more mouths to feed."

"What of our other goods? The winged kur belonging to our war leader? The worth of those of our tribe members who have crossed the lines to join your tribe? We're owed something in recompense."

"You're owed nothing. You are fortunate I am in a generous mood today."

"Give the cloth to her, Kiri," said Mariya without looking toward her cousin. "Children, start walking out of camp. Stanyo, Asya, keep Danya between you, as she is smallest. Steady."

Words filled Kirya's heart, but they would not climb onto her tongue. The cloth subsided against her legs, and she folded it, in halves, and halves again, until it was a manageable bundle that she wrapped in a scrap of dirty hide scrounged from the ruins of the burned camp. She took her time, so Mariya and the children could walk out of camp.

Deliberately, she tossed the bundle to the dirt. A young man had crept up behind her. The gelding kicked, hard, and he yelped and hobbled back. Ears laid back, the gelding sidled around, looking ready to clip anyone who had the temerity to approach. Kirya began walking in Mari's dust, hand on the reins, the gelding behind her.

The assembly remained silent for a few breaths, then burst into a babble of voices and exclamations and laughter and arguments. A man leading a horse pushed into her way, confronting her. She glared at him. When he did not move, her grief-blinded gaze finally saw him.

Estifio held the halter of the bay mare, the prize of their tiny herd. Without a word, he shoved the reins into her hand and slid away into the tribe. The mare settled in beside the gelding, content with this familiar place. Kirya kept walking, and somehow no one noticed because they had all crowded up to see the precious cloth the headwoman had acquired. Who cared about one more horse among the many the Vidrini owned? Who cared about the straggle of useless children, who were just more mouths to feed?

Precious mouths.

By the time they reached the grass beyond the camp, out of sight of the tents, Kirya was fighting sobs as rage and grief squeezed her. The gelding breathed hot on her neck.

Mariya halted. The children ran to her, huddling around, crying until she cracked stern words over their heads. "None of that, or we'll never get home! Hush now!" She looked up, and saw the bay mare. The piebald greeted her companion with a friendly snort.

"Kiri! The mare!"

"Estifio handed her over to me while I was walking out. He ran away. I didn't talk to him."

"He's not the one who betrayed us," said Mari. She turned to the children. "Asya, you'll ride the bay. You're skilled enough to manage the trip bareback. Stanyo, you'll ride with Kiri. Danya, you'll ride with me."

"No," said Kirya. "I'm going after Kontas. You heard what she said. They traded him away just yesterday. I can catch up. The gelding is good for it. He's the toughest horse we have."

"What will you offer this eastern merchant? He'll not care about the laws of the gods."

"Neither did that motherless hag!"

"Hssh! Kiri! Of course she did. She doesn't dare spit on the laws of the gods. A foreign woman sitting as headwoman over one of the tribes! She had to make the trade, or be seen to scorn the laws of the tribe that took her in. What could we truly have done to her? Nothing! So she didn't have to give us anything, or even make the trade. That she feared looking like an outsider in the eyes of her tribe is the only reason we have the children back."

"Maybe you're right. But she wanted that cloth."

"They took Kontas." Asya tugged on Mariya's arm. The girl had a black eye, and the grime of tears and dirt smeared on her face and arms, as if she'd been pushed into the ground. "I tried to hit them, but I couldn't stop them from taking him."

"I know, dear one," said Mari. "I know you did what you could. Now we're going home."

"I'm going after Kontas," said Kirya. "We can't abandon him, Mari. I can't. How will my mother ever rest at peace among the gods?"

Mariya rubbed her forehead, pretty face creased, and Kirya saw suddenly how much effort it had cost her cousin to endure the taunts of the youth she had lain with, who had whispered endearments and promises which had all along meant nothing to him. How much courage it had taken her to stand in front of that crowd as if their sneers and scorn did not touch her, who had been taken so thoroughly for a love-struck fool and had her foolishness announced to everyone.

"Oh, Mari." She dropped the gelding's reins, and hugged her beloved cousin fiercely. "I have to go."

Mari glanced in the direction of the camp, but no one had come after them, not yet. "Asya, you'll walk with me. Stanyo and Danya will ride the bay, but we'll saddle it first. Kiri, you'll take the piebald, in the halter. Trade the gelding if you can, although why anyone would take that misbegotten beast I don't know, not once they've seen his temper. Trade the piebald if you must." She tugged the three lapis-lazuli nets off her braids, and wept as they kissed. "I don't need these. Maybe they'll be worth something. We'll wait four days for you at the pond where we camped last night. Otherwise meet at the gar-deer sink. Now go. Go."

24

Kirya's tribe had never ridden south to see the Golden Road, but she had heard tales of a path on which foreigners traveled east and west along the southernmost range of the vast grasslands roamed by the tribes. East lay the brutal Qin, and south lay the mud-feet, people who stank from living in their own garbage all year around. Sometimes the tribes raided them, taking what they could grab. Sometimes the mud people marched into the grass to take vengeance, but any tribe could simply pack up and move; even a child like Danya could outride the mud-feet's boldest warriors.

She paced the gelding, switching off to ride bareback on the piebald at intervals. South of the Vidrini camp, the hills flattened and the grass changed variety, turning brittle with heat. She had a pair of filled leather bottles, but anyway she knew the signs that revealed sinks of water waiting a short dig beneath the surface; she could smell a swale or rivulet before she saw it. Now that she thought about it, Orphan had taught them a lot about surviving in the wasteland. Poor tribes were always driven off the best pasturelands, pressed toward the deadlands, and maybe Orphan walking into their tribe two years ago had been the gift of the gods after all.

Midway through the afternoon, a long upward slope brought her to a tipping point in the landscape, beyond which lay a dry lake bed so wide she could not see the far side. Clumps of brush dotted the flat. She searched for the golden gleam that must mark the road, but saw only ruts in the hard ground running east and west, so many crisscrossing the dead lake that they tangled like a child's unsteady weaving.

To the east spun a thread of dust.

To the west, a huge herd of sheep spilled over a distant rise, hounded by riders and dogs. Somewhere, west and north of here, a tribe had set up camp. A moment later, a pair of outriders galloped into view. The two youths circled her at a prudent distance and raced back to their tents. She debated whether to ask for shelter within their camp for the night, but she dared not stop. She had to follow what trail she had, lest she lose Kontas entirely. Turning the gelding, with the piebald in tow, she rode down onto the dead lake and turned east.

Hooves kicked up a fine dust, making her cough. Her eyes watered as particles stung her face. Sound echoed oddly, magnifying the fall of hooves into many more than two horses.

She looked over her shoulder. Four riders followed her, three male and the fourth dressed in female garb, long felt jacket reaching to her knees and a quiver slung by one knee.

"What do you think?" she asked the gelding. She wasn't in the sanctity of camp, but after all, what would they do to a lone girl? The laws of the gods forbade any insult done to women; that was how it had always been among the tribes. What if they had news of Kontas, or the eastern merchant?

She reined over and waited for them to catch up.

The males—two she recognized as the youths who had first scouted her—pulled up and let their companion approach, as was proper. She was not much older than Kirya, with her golden hair divided into a trident braid and a headdress adorned with silver atop her head to mark that she was married. She wore necklaces of gold and silver and bronze across her chest, displaying her family's wealth.

"Good riding, stranger," she said, greeting Kirya. "I am cousin to the headwoman of the Orzhekov tribe. Are you one of the Vidrini?"

"No, I'm Moroshya."

"I don't know you," said the other girl in the formulaic way that meant she'd never heard of that tribe. "This is dangerous ground, between the grass and the border of demon lands. Why do you ride here?"

Kirya saw nothing to distrust in her open face. "The Vidrini raiders stole my young brother. I've brought a horse to trade for him, if I can catch the eastern merchant who took him." She indicated the east and the dying thread of dust spun up from the darkening horizon.

The other one smiled with a twist that made Kirya uncomfortable. "Your tribe doesn't trade down here, does it?"

She shrugged, realizing how foolish she was, blabbing her errand to these strangers.

"You've seen your mistake now, haven't you? We might track you, and once you have the boy, what's to stop us from stealing him and trading him again to the merchant?"

Kirya indicated her quiver and bow. "I am not unarmed. Would your riders attack a woman?"

"Don't insult us!" The girl's hard expression softened to one more thoughtful. "That's the kind of thing the Vidrini might do, now they've raised a foreign woman to be their headwoman. They might do anything, with a hard-hearted Qin woman having put her claws into their hearts. Still, it's a rash choice on your part, to ride into demon lands."

"They're not so far away. I can catch them by tomorrow, surely."

"Take only one step into demon lands, and anything might happen. If you die in demon lands, the gods will never find your spirit and bring you home."

"He's my younger brother. Our mother is dead."

"Yes, I can see you are obligated to retrieve him, although I wonder why your war leader has not—well—" As Kirya sucked in a sharp breath and tightened her hand on the reins, the girl broke stride and changed course. "The Easterners speak words smeared with honey, but you can't trust them."

"How do you know?"

"My people trade with the *caravans*. The Easterners are not people, not like us. Yet I suppose you can do nothing else, not if you want to keep your honor. May the gods ride with you, cousin."

She signaled to her companions and rode back the way she had come, back to the familiarity of tent, herd, and grass.

KIRYA CAMPED THAT night on the lake bed, staring up at the stars, the campfires of the gods' tribe. Beside which of those fires did her mother now shelter? She could not tell.

She moved out at first light. Not long after dawn she began to taste the caravan's dust. Soon after that, she rode past the disturbed ground where they had camped. Soon after that, she saw firsthand the ponderous creature that foreigners called caravan. This ungainly beast was made up of a tightly controlled herd of sheep and unsaddled horses, a line of grindingly slow-paced wagons dragged by worthless dray beasts a toddler could have outpaced, and various human figures—maybe some demons, although from here it was difficult to tell—walking alongside and within the ranks. Between two wagons, six ranks of boys and youths, most blond, trudged along. She scanned the rows. Was that Kontas? He had his head down, so she couldn't be sure.

Swinging wide, she rode parallel alongside the caravan. She willed Kontas to look up, and the pale head shifted, face rising to look at the heavens . . . even from this distance, she could see it was not Kontas. She felt as if she'd been kicked.

The caravan guards saw her, but for a while no one seemed to react. The caravan lumbered forward like a beast staggering on its last legs, while her horses made it known they couldn't understand why they must walk here when it was obvious they did not like the bones of the dead lake and the smell of demon lands. It was getting hotter as the sun rose swollen and fat. She licked chapped lips.

"Hoy! Hoy!"

A fat man on a sleek mare rode out from the wagons, waving at her. She kept riding at the same steady walk, and eventually he pushed up beside her. He had a funny complexion, like clay, and he was perspiring and licking moist lips and looking her up and down in a bold way that made her think he must be a demon, since men knew better than to look directly at women. Therefore, she ignored him.

He said, in labored and very precise speech, "You are a tribeswoman, are you? Never before see I one tribeswoman so close. Whew!" He wiped his dripping forehead with a cloth. "Why ride you here?"

"I will only speak to a man, not a demon," she said, trying to shame him by meeting his gaze deliberately, but of course demons cannot feel shame. He did not look away.

"Whew!" He said words in demon language, then thought better of mumbling on in words that only proved he was not a man. "I say good things about your blue eyes. Very pretty! Your hair! Very pretty! I am a man. I am not a demon. I am obligated to say I am only a—" He spoke a word she did not know. "For this reason my—" Another demon word. "—sends me out here to speak at you."

Despite the demon words, he spoke human speech well enough to make her wonder if he might be a human person after all, just a very ill-mannered one.

"I have come for my brother. He was traded to an eastern merchant. I want him back."

Without turning, he indicated the caravan behind him. "One of the boys, eh?"

"Yes."

"Hrm." He scratched his bare chin. "I go ask my *sarvar* if he negotiate with you. You ride here, meantime?"

"I will ride here."

He rode back to the caravan. He had a heavy seat that disturbed his horse's natural grace. She was trembling as she considered her options. She had two horses. If she could get Kontas up onto the piebald, she and Kontas could outrace them. They wouldn't know how to track her in the grass.

Six armed guards appeared from the vanguard of the beast and rode back to get a look at her. They were Qin, with demon-scratched eyes, coarse black hair pulled up into a funny knot, and broad faces, part human and part demon. Circling her with the easy grace of men raised on horseback, they called to each other in their barking language. They stared rudely, not civilized men at all.

She ignored them. But their ugly faces made her think of the Vidrini headwoman, who might as well be their sister for all that they looked so similar. The Qin were a brutal-hearted, demon-tainted people, always happy to hire themselves out to fight for whatever foreigner paid the most. She doubted she and Kontas could outride these.

"Hoy! Hoy!" The fat man returned, bouncing awkwardly on his trotting horse. Two riders followed him.

The Qin soldiers rode away toward the rear of the caravan.

"Greetings, greetings," called the younger of the two men. He had a dark face that looked reasonably human, and kept his gaze averted in a mannerly fashion as he kept talking. "Greetings, tribeswoman. My *sarvar* say to me, you desire to trade for a boy."

His companion was wiry, sour-mouthed, and funny-looking, his features mismatched. This old man looked her up and down as impertinently as if she were a horse he meant to acquire.

Nervously, she glanced toward the retreating Qin soldiers. "I will trade this horse for the boy. That is good value."

The younger man grinned at his hands, cast a glance at his narrow-eyed companion.

The old man said, "These horses are shit, ugly as my wife's face." He scratched at his groin. "We no take them for the boy. Not worth the boy."

"Both horses, then," said Kirya desperately.

"No," said the old man. "The horses are shit. No boy."

The younger one smiled as a man smiles when hearing a pretty melody that reminds him of a lover. "We offer a better trade," he said. "For you, five boys. You pick, any five boys from the herd."

"For the two horses? What about my brother?"

"No, no," said the younger man, chuckling now, although Kirya could not see what anyone might find funny in this situation.

The old man said, irritably, "You trade your person, for five boys. Including the boy you say is brother to you."

Dumbfounded, she could not fathom what they meant. "Trade what?"

"You. You are girl," said the old man. "With the ghost hair and the demon eyes, and a female, you are worth five boys. Worth plenty. You want the boy, the brother? Or no boy, and we ride on? We will not wait. Weather changes, hot days comes, we cannot wait. We ride far, go fast. Decide now, or ride away with nothing. Now, now. Decide."

Now. Now. Decide.

On the caravan rumbled, lurching forward like a wounded beast. A pair of wagons stuck in an irregularity in the track, and the ranks of trudging boys staggered to a halt behind it. One boy, at the end of a row, stumbled, fell to a knee, and hastily jumped up just as a guard closed in with whip raised to strike him on the shoulder.

"Kontas!" she shouted.

He raised an arm to shield his body from the blow. He didn't hear her, and as the whip came down he jerked back, knocking into another boy, who shoved him into yet another, and the guard slashed at their heads with the biting whip until all cowered and wept.

Kirya said, "Ten boys. I choose them, and another three horses. Also, provisions for their trip. One year I work in servitude to you. Then you release me to return to my tribe."

It was a desperate gamble.

The younger man laughed.

The older said, as swiftly as a snake striking, "Done. You hand yourself, of free choice, into our hands. Ten boys of your choosing, and three horses we release of our choosing, in exchange."

"I serve in your tribe for one year only. No pursuit after the boys. No raid on them. They ride free to the grass."

"Done, done," said the old man, his gaze as hard as stones and his mouth pursed as if to keep secrets.

The younger man whistled as folk do at a narrow escape. Then he giggled, an odd sound coming from a grown man. He turned to bark orders at the fat man.

Commands shouted up and down the caravan brought the beast to a jerking halt. The six ranks of lads were chivvied out like so many baffled sheep, about sixty in all, and all but a handful having light hair and blue eyes, like hers. Kontas ducked out from the group and ran to her, and when a guard struck out after him, the old merchant called the man back. The boy was crying as he halted beside the piebald mare, but he grabbed the mare's halter and, looking up at her hopefully, said,

"Are we going home, Kiri?"

"You are going home, Kontas. Now I need you to listen to me, very close and very hard. Any boys there were kind to you? Any were mean? Any who admitted they were orphans? Point them out to me."

So many faces stared at her, confused, calculating, frightened, tearful, dejected. Some called, asking what was going on. Most remained silent, for those who were traded away by the tribes and handed over to foreigners knew by this token that no one wanted them, or that their own kin could not save them. To be marched into the demon lands was to be damned. You might as well already be dead.

Older boys might turn on Kontas, steal the horses, and run. Younger boys would be a burden to feed until they could do more work themselves. Did Mariya want nine more boys? How would she get them wives? Could Orphan mold them into a war band that could protect the Moroshya tribe?

Did it matter? For one year she would walk into demon land in servitude; she could churn their milk and grease their wagon's axles and scrape their hides and carry buckets of their stinking night soil if indeed they bothered to keep clean. She could eat their leavings and sleep under a wagon instead of in a tent. In exchange, Kontas and nine boys would not lose their souls.

She searched the young faces who turned to look at her, a woman of the tribes like their own sisters and mothers and aunts and cousins. That one was scratch-eyed, that one was snot-nosed, and that youth had too much anger in the set of his shoulders and ugly fresh whip scars on his face to show he got into trouble frequently. There, a hopeful one, begging pitiably with his stare. There, two little blond boys holding hands, like brothers, looking helpless and frightened. Beside them, a bigger boy, maybe Kirya's age, rested a protective hand on the shoulder of a younger one. The younger was an especially pretty child no older than Danya, one of the few with dark hair.

"Those two were kind to me," Kontas said suddenly, pointing at the mismatched pair, blond and dark. "They're orphaned cousins. The Vidrini captured them months ago when they raided the remnants of their tribe. They were traded at the same time as me."

Those two, then, and the two little blond brothers, who upon being brought across told Kirya that the angry youth had been beaten five times by the guards for helping boys who were faltering, which is why he had those scars. So she must indicate him as well, and he wasn't eager to come until she spoke to him in a low voice and told him what she hoped for, and then he didn't want to believe her because it is fearful to hope for the very thing that is about to be ripped from your hand, but she was a woman of the tribes after all, willing to walk into demon land to free her brother. Once started, he told her a great deal quickly: He had walked with the merchants for many days; he had watched them bargaining for horses and hides and flesh; he had seen them desperately trying to coax girls, especially blond girls, out of the tribes, but of course not even the Vidrini would hand females over to foreigners.

"Swear to me that you and this other youth will help my brother sneak past the Vidrini and reach my cousin," she said to him. "That you'll obey Orphan, who is the war leader of our tribe. Swear to me that you'll become Moroshya."

"I'm an orphan," he said. "I'm ill-fortuned. The gods cursed me and left me alive when my kin died. No one wants an orphan except the demons, and they are cruel, and they hate us."

"You're not an orphan. You are Moroshya."

He was a fierce boy, with bright eyes and so much anger, which she saw now was strength, not a bully's weakness. "I am Moroshya, then. I swear this oath: Your tribe will never die, because you are our mother, and gave us life."

"What is your name?"

"Ilia. What is yours?" He had a western twang to his speech, but he was as human as she was. He was a lad she might marry.

"I am named Kirya. Four more boys I can choose. Hurry."

Hurry.

Too quickly she assembled the little war band. The fat man brought saddlebags crammed with provisions, dried meat and also slabs and balls of tasteless grain that the boys assured her were edible. She approved three horses; with five all together, the ten boys might ride doubled-up. With some coaxing and after one frustrated kick, the gelding agreed to accept Kontas and Ilia. In an odd exuberance of generosity, the old merchant gave them leather bottles filled with foreign drink, which anyway could be used for water later.

"There, now," he said, "give the boy back his weapons and let them go."

What was this demon yammering about? "The boy has no weapons. He is too young to be a rider."

"You carry his bow and quiver."

"They are mine."

The young merchant laughed. "How can a woman say so?"

She did not see what was so funny, but the old merchant looked thoughtful.

"Servants cannot carry weapons. We take, or you give to the boy. Your choice."

"No woman gives up her bow!"

"No man touch you," said the old man.

What a strange thing to say! What man would dare to touch a woman of the tribes without her permission? None would! Once a tribe was marked by such a shameful act, they were condemned to death and every neighboring tribe would certainly do their part to make sure their name was nevermore spoken and all their goods and innocent children taken into a tribe whose people obeyed the laws of the gods.

Yet if she wanted to save Kontas, what choice did she have? She handed quiver and bow to him.

"And the knife," said the old man.

And the knife. "Remember everything I told you, Kontas," she said in a choked voice. "Now go. Be quick."

He was an obedient boy. He wept, but he rode away nonetheless with the band moving tightly behind him as the angry youth turned to shout, "We will keep them safely for you. I swear it."

The old merchant cackled, and the younger merchant smirked. The Qin soldiers trotted over. When they were up on their horses and she was standing down on the ground, she trembled. This fear had a sharp tang that ran through her entire body and into her groin and made her shudder as if with desire only it was more like having a knife at your throat.

The old man stopped laughing abruptly, patted his hands a few times as though wiping off dust, and said, "Good, good." The young one burst into a passionate demand in demon language, and the old one stepped right up into his face and slapped him so hard it made his dark cheek red. The fat man bawled out orders, and the caravan by stages jolted into forward motion until the entire sluggish beast shambled eastward. The younger man sulked to his horse; the soldiers trotted away to oversee the rear guard.

The old man snapped his fingers, and the fat man rode away and returned with a pretty mare already saddled and caparisoned, a handsome horse fit for a head-woman's daughter.

The old man indicated the horse, to show she should mount.

She would stay strong. She could hold on to her soul for one year. Careful to show no emotion, she took the reins and mounted.

25

"Forbidden you talk to these ones," the old man said, taking hold of her mare's reins and drawing her away from the herd of captive boys before she could question them about their names, their tribes, their circumstances.

He set strict rules. She must ride in the front beside the old man and his younger associate all day as they plodded through the flat lands of the old lake bed. What grass there was snapped clean, and the vegetation bristled with thorns. The soggy swales where they watered stank of mildew and sour breath. Mostly the old man did not speak to her, letting her ride in silence, which suited her bleak mood. He made cursory attempts to teach her words of demon language, although she wondered what the use of that was, since he could speak human speech.

Each evening when the caravan laid up for the night, he had his servants heat water in a copper tub—a most remarkable and luxurious item—which was set into a corner of his traveling tent and concealed by curtains. There, she must strip naked and wash herself by lantern light. That wasn't so bad, since dust settled everywhere and she liked to be clean.

The third night, hearing soft, grunting noises, she realized someone was watching her through a gap in the curtains. She splashed out of the tub and yanked the curtain aside.

There sat the old man, sitting relaxed on a stool with a look of calm appraisal on his face, and the young one, who was disheveled with trousers down by his knees and his left hand clutched tightly around his hard red member. Which spurted its milk, just then, as he groaned and gasped and grimaced, staring at her with a bold gaze that made her skin creep.

So stunned was she by this bizarre behavior that she stood there and gaped until the fat man, who was fussing with a pot by the entrance, gave a deep sigh and hurried over to push her back into the little alcove.

"Don't touch me!"

He snorted, a curt laugh. "I am cut. No man parts." He gestured to his groin. "I not touch you. No love desire. Now, be good girl, be quiet. Be finish. Or the old *master* hit you."

THE NEXT NIGHT, she was led again to the curtained tub.

"I won't do it! It's demeaning."

The old man slapped her so hard it staggered her. "You my servant. You do it."

Shaking, she stripped off her jacket, then halted, because he still stood there. "Go."

He said, "No. You do what thing I say." He raised the hand he had hit her with, showed her the reddened palm.

The Orzhekov girl had been right to warn her. In demon land, anything could happen, the laws of the gods turned onto their heads, made mock of, stripped and demeaned. How had she been so stupid as to believe it would be otherwise?

As she took off her clothes, he watched her not with sexual desire but with a different and no less intense desire, one she saw on the faces of small-minded women who saw their rivals wearing more golden jewelry than what they themselves possessed. When she was naked, he studied her as if she were horseflesh. He examined her rump, sidled around to scrutinize her flower, and frowned, and smiled, and rose, all without touching her.

"Now you bathe." When he parted the curtain to go into the other section of the tent, she saw the younger one waiting there, already untying his trousers, and two other men beside him, their eager faces greasy with lust.

Furious, she stood in the tub and bathed herself, and this time she heard the grunts and their release clearly, as if the men had nothing to hide.

THAT NIGHT, SHE scraped away dirt to open a gap under the taut hem of the staked tent. She rolled off the pallet on which she slept, pulled what gear was left her against her torso, and squeezed into the open air. She squirmed on her stomach between tents and under wagons to the horse lines. It was easy to pick out the pretty mare. She whispered and coaxed her way along the lines without disturbing the other horses, and whispered and coaxed her way beyond the lines with the mare trusting her enough to come along after. The guards had fires lit at the van and rear, but the center remained murky. She led the mare out without being noticed, and for a long time they walked. Even out of the sight of camp they walked slowly because there wasn't much more than a quarter moon shining over the pale earth. The mare was uncomfortable walking in such poor light, but she trusted Kirya enough to attempt the journey. Anyway the ground was so flat that mostly they had only to avoid the occasional snackling stand of thorny brush and the seams and cracks that rutted the earth.

She heard the horns before dawn. There was, of course, nowhere to hide, so as soon as the landscape turned from night to gray she swung up on the mare and pushed westward. Dust soon coated her face and her tongue. The mare had a strong disposition and an eager heart, and for a while Kirya thought she might manage her escape, but the old man sent the Qin soldiers after her with spare mounts, and if anyone could ride as well as a tribeswoman, it was their old enemy, the Qin.

In the end, when they caught up and surrounded her, she was too proud to weep or struggle. They did not laugh or show any sign of triumph. They kept their distance and offered her some dignity, that she might ride the blown mare slowly back to the caravan.

When they rode up to the tail of the caravan, every man there who could, turned to watch as the old man rode out to meet them. He had a whip in his hand. He slashed her across the shoulders so hard she screamed from the shock as pain cut deep. But even dizzied and stunned, she did not fall from the mare's back.

Not until he brought the whip down a second time, and a third and fourth and fifth and more. The pain of lashing washed her entire body and her hands went numb and her legs lost all feeling. She tumbled to the ground, and struck her head.

A silver mist, sparkling with bright flecks of burning ash, swallowed her in its pale wings. She blacked out.

VOMITING, SHE CAME to, the vile liquid spitting down her chin. She was splayed on her stomach on the hard floorboards of one of the wagons. Sun shone in her eyes, making her gag and retch.

The young man was yelling at the old man. "Yah yah yah! Yah yah yah!"

The old one shouted back. "Yah yah yah! Yah yah yah!"

The wagon shifted as the young man clambered up and tugged at her felt jacket, then grabbed the waistband of her trousers and yanked.

She kicked. The old man connected with the whip, and the crack made her wheeze with fear and pain, only it hadn't hit her. The young one shrieked, gabbling, and the old man yahhed furiously. The curtain dropped, cutting off the painful light, and she was left alone. Her head throbbed so badly. Men yelled in the distance, echoing and buzzing.

The wagon lurched forward. She coughed and spat, and her insides clenched. Bile spewed. Ashamed of her weakness, she wept.

SHE SLIPPED OUT of sleep in a drowsy half-awareness. A wagon rocked beneath her with the comforting rhythm of home. Except the air smelled wrong, too dusty, too bitter. Iron braces shackled her wrists. Tugging, she came up short like a hobbled horse. What nightmare was this?

When she opened her eyes, a sea of cloth billowed around her. Her stomach roiled. Dizzy, she retched until nothing was left to bring up, and then kept retching because her body would not stop trying to cast up its leavings. Or its heart. Or its soul.

She was trapped in demon land.

SHE SMELLED THE place before they reached it. The air stank of manure and urine, of an overhanging mildew and the rotting sweet corruption of garbage left in the sun. The dust tasted as if it had been crushed too many times beneath the haunches of dogs and the thighs of dirt-stained women who never were allowed to wash.

She heard such a clamor beyond the accustomed tromping and scraping of the caravan that she wondered what battle they had wandered into, but from within her cage she could see through only a slit in the canvas that widened and narrowed as the wagon jounced. A tent wall. A child's dirty face. More tents, oddly textured and aligned, not proper tents at all. A woman walking with a basket balanced atop her head. A flowering tree splendidly clothed in stark white blooms, a thing of rare beauty that made her close her eyes because it hurt to see beautiful things in demon land.

They rattled to a stop. Men shouted in tough, argumentative voices. A whip cracked. She flinched, but no cord struck her.

She tested the limits of her chains, pushing with her feet, pulling and tugging while careful not to make the sores at her wrists worse than they already were, for they were raw and weeping. The peg fixing one chain shifted, like a breath let out. She jerked with all her might.

The wagon lurched forward, pitching her onto the floorboards. She tasted blood on her lip, licked it, savoring the flavor. What lives, bleeds. As long as she bled, she had not lost her soul.

She counted back days, so she would not forget. Probably the eastern merchant meant to cheat her; he could not be trusted. One year held eighteen passages of the moon, and each passage of the moon held twenty-four dawns. She had been careful to keep count as the caravan rumbled east out of the lake bed and up into new country.

Twenty days she had been chained in the wagon, allowed out at dusk to walk around under heavy guard. Three days before that she had watched her brother ride away. Today was a new day, the end of her first month of being a servant. If she had survived this, she could survive another seventeen months.

They passed into shadow, as though night had fallen. Then they emerged into light, and through the slit she saw they were in a confluence more crowded than the assembly at the Targit River. Stiff tents raised out of wood were packed one up against another. Truly, who ever thought there was so much wood in the world? Other tents were built of stone, just as it said in the tales, or of a clay-red rock with squared corners. No one raised proper tents here.

Folk moved along the open spaces, thoroughfares packed with people trudging and carrying and pushing wheeled carts and barking dogs and crying children until her head hurt. The howl never let up, only muted when they came around several corners and thence past a wall and into a quieter enclosure. The wagon halted. The dray beasts were unhitched; they crunched away over dirt to slobber at a trough. The smell of water was like sweetest honey on her tongue, for she'd had nothing to drink that day.

She set to work on the peg, bracing her feet against the wagon, straining, pulling, until she was sweating and in a rage with frustration. Her left wrist had begun to bleed.

Blood means life.

She heard the old man's voice, answered by that of a woman. She swung around to face the approaching threat. The entrance flap was untied and swept back.

An old woman with a commanding bearing stared belligerently in at her. She was dressed in such an astounding wealth of silk that Kirya knew she must be a headwoman of great consequence. The old one grunted with displeasure, and another woman clambered into the wagon to unlock the chains. Cautiously, Kirya crawled out of the wagon. She stood in a space surrounded on all sides by high walls. Dusty green trees shaded the trough at which dray beasts watered. A boy swept fresh droppings into a pan, but when he saw her, he stopped working to stare with mouth dropped open. Grooms turned, pointing and whispering. A girl half hidden in a doorway stepped out into the sun to squint at her.

"Yah yah!" yelled the old woman at the loiterers.

Folk abandoned the open space. Only the old merchant, the headwoman, and a trio of cousins remained. The women in their embroidered caps and bright silks looked very much alike with broad faces and reddish-clay complexions.

"Are you human, or demon?" Kirya asked.

The old woman grabbed her hands, clucking over the sores on her wrists as she scolded the old man in a withering harangue which he ended by throwing up his hands and walking away. This impertinence toward the headwoman passed without comment. Kirya found herself led to a long wooden tent with a narrow door guarded by two men holding staffs and barred by wooden beams that must be shifted before the door could be opened.

Inside was a confusing mash of walls, women, cloth, and doors, and beyond it a space surrounded by a high wall. Girls and young women pressed forward to touch her as she was led through their ranks into a place with a pair of vast copper tubs. Now, again, she must strip and bathe, only this time twenty or more females, mostly young but some old, sat on or stood behind benches and stared with eyes wide and whispered comments but not a breath of laughter. The tub soon muddied, and she stepped out to stand dripping on cold tiles. A child brought a cloth, and she dried herself. The old woman fanned herself on a stool as she examined Kirya with the implacable gaze of a headwoman who considers the impact of a stranger come into her tribe.

She gestured. A girl hurried forward to collect Kirya's discarded clothing. Kirya grabbed for it, but the old woman slapped her on the wrists with a quirt—right where the sores made them most raw—and Kirya yelped and withdrew her hands as she was left naked.

A girl brought perfumed soap, and indicated the other tub, filled with clean water. While Kirya washed herself again, and washed the grime out of her hair, the old woman searched through the soft leather pouch that held Kirya's mirror, her comb, her cup and spoon, and the beaded nets Mariya had given her. The old woman handled these things and set them aside as of no value. No doubt she could not respect a woman without bow and knife.

Silks were brought, and their colors held up against Kirya's body, and comments made—yes or no by the swaying of heads and clatter of hands and excited whispers. They dressed her in silk of unspeakable softness, underclothing so smooth it seemed to have the weight of a cloud; loose trousers and a knee-length overtunic slit for walking in a cloth the color of the sky before dawn, more gray than pink. The old woman brushed a gooey salve onto the sores that circled her wrists. It stung, but then the spicy scent relaxed her. The old woman gestured to show she must sit on a stool with arms extended, so the salve could dry.

Giggling, three girls approached her. One had black hair and black eyes, one brown hair and brown eyes, and one hair streaked with a reddish-brown color that matched her complexion.

"Mima. Mima," said the black haired girl, tapping her chest. She pointed to the others. "Ebba. Ebba. Noria. Noria." Then she pointed to Kirya. "Yah? Yah?"

Kirya knew better than to give her name to demons.

Mima smiled kindly. "Yah yah yah," she added. She displayed a metal comb and mimed combing hair.

Behind, the other young women and girls hissed and hooted, or coughed and sneered. Several girls just sat there staring blindly at nothing, and one girl rocked obsessively side to side, but she sat away by herself, no one close by her. Yet none of them left. They wanted to watch as when, the only other time Kirya had seen a foreign person in the tribes, all the children had followed the foreign person around the entire time that person had walked within camp.

Kirya shrugged, to show acquiescence. Anyway, Mima's pretty smile reminded her of Mariya. Was it so bad to want a person to be friendly with, even if it was a demon?

Hesitantly, Mima reached for Kirya's hair, but withdrew her hand without touching it. The old woman snapped out words. Mima fixed a nervous smile on her face, and tapped the hair as if it might burn her. Her companions squealed, and giggled, and Kirya grinned, just a little, because they were so funny.

"Yah yah yah," said Mima with a giggle. She began to work through the long tangles. As she worked, the place quieted while every soul there, except for the girl who rocked side to side, watched and exclaimed as if they expected the color to change with every stroke, only of course it did not.

They were dark, some like Mima handsome in the manner of Mariya and some demon-scratched like the Qin, while others had a clay-red complexion or a pleasing brown one, and one pair of girls had skin so black that Kirya wondered if the color had been painted on. But no one else was like her, a woman of the tribes with pale hair and pale skin.

A low clang shivered through the air. The old woman clapped her hands, and the girls and young women hurried away, some gabbling but most silent. Several girls lifted up and then pushed along the girl who had been rocking side to side; she was like a sleepwalker.

The attendants closed in on either side of Kirya, gripped her elbows. They steered her down a long narrow place fenced by high walls and a roof, and into a big place, like a headwoman's spacious tent, only this tent with its unmoving walls had benches set on a raised platform and other places to sit heaped with pillows. Lamps hissed. A sharp perfume smoking up from piles of incense made her eyes water and her nostrils sting.

They sat her on a stool on the platform. An attendant tucked a startlingly beautiful white flower between Kirya's hair and ear. In twos and fours, the other girls and young women filed into the room, some with eyes cast down and shoulders hunched and others with bold, hard laughter and snatches of song. So much bright silk dazzled Kirya. This was a rich tribe, indeed, that all its daughters and even a servant like herself were dressed in precious cloth.

Wood clappers snapped out a staccato rhythm. A pair of older women pulled back the purple curtains to reveal doors. A pair of stocky men armed with staffs came out of the shadows and opened the doors. Twilight swirled in on a dusty breeze, and on its wings tramped a horde of jabbering men who, as they settled inside, fell quiet suddenly and stared at her so brazenly that after all they were not proper men who knew better than to stare but must be demons, even if they looked mostly like men.

There came the old merchant from the journey, and the young one flushed and drunk in his wake, scratching at his groin again, that itch having come back. What animals they were!

The old woman strode to the dais and gave a lengthy speech which every man there followed with avid attention. Then she raised a hand. At once they began shouting at her and shaking pouches at her, one overtopping the next. The young merchant cursed in a loud voice and stormed out; the old merchant faded to the back to watch. The clamor looked a lot like haggling at a confluence when one tribe was trying to get more hides or saddle blankets in exchange for dyestuffs or a particular stud.

A shout of triumph from one of the men. A groan from the others, and suppressed if intense whispering among the girls as the triumphant man strutted forward and dropped a heavy bag at the old woman's feet. An attendant counted out bars of silver from the bag he'd tossed down.

The behavior of demons made no sense at all, so Kirya was relieved when the attendants pulled on her elbows and made it known she could get out of that unpleasant, crowded place and go away into a different one. They led her past a curtain into a cave of tiny places like narrow cages with high walls. They pressed her into one of these narrow places. A lamp burned on either side, hanging from the low ceiling. She stood on a strip of worn carpet, nothing special; she'd felted better patterns as a little girl. A cot set against one wall filled half the space.

The attendants backed out, and the man who had thrown down the bag of silver bars sauntered in, grinning. He was a burly, middle-aged fellow dressed in a silk robe belted with a polished gold buckle. A curtain slipped down behind him, cutting them off from everywhere else. They were alone.

"Whew!" he said in a friendly way. He plucked the flower from her ear.

Abruptly, it all made sense. He thought she was offering him her Flower Night.

"No!" She took a step back. "You are not my choice!"

He laughed. "Yah yah yah," he said jovially as he walked to her, driving her back until she bumped into the wall and could retreat no farther. His heavy hands settled on her shoulders. He fumbled at her hair, bringing strands to his face, closing his eyes, and taking in a breath. She wedged her arms up between them, and shoved.

"Oof! Heh!" He stumbled back a few steps. He chuckled at first, but then he frowned, and then he furrowed his brow, and then he called out in an annoyed tone.

The old woman appeared, mouth pressed tight.

"Yah yah yah," he complained, gesturing and grimacing.

She grunted, went out past the curtain, and returned with a quirt in her hand. This she raised threateningly. For that first instant, Kirya was so greatly relieved that the headwoman of the tribe had come to teach this outrageously behaved man some manners. As if he could just walk in and demand her Flower Night, when it was hers to offer, not his to take!

The quirt whipped down onto her forearms. She yelped, more angry than hurt. Again, it slapped down, and this time she kicked out to defend herself. Her foot met flesh, and old woman shrieked. The quirt thwacked into the side of Kirya's head, staggering her. The man was scolding in a loud voice as shouts and questions flew from outside, and the quirt slapped into her calves so hard Kirya fell. She hit, hard, on her back, breath punched out of her lungs, dazed and dizzy and utterly confused.

He was taking his clothes off.

She struggled to sit, but the quirt slapped her down again, and this time she shouted with rage, coming up fighting. Attendants swarmed in, bound her raw and aching wrists and her ankles with rope, and tied her to the cot, and then they departed, not even angry about her kicking and punching, as if tying down a screaming, struggling girl who was about to be forced against her will was something they were accustomed to doing every day.

After that, there was nothing she could do to stop him. Or the next one. Or the next one. Or the next one.

26

The long night begins.

It is not night always. She counts the days and polishes her mirror. She accepts a name, Azalea, a white flower. She might laugh with Mima and Ebba and Noria over a joke as they are scrubbing floors, or during a song they are teaching her while they grind kernels to flour in big stone bowls, or when she makes a mistake speaking a word, saying "I comb my chair" instead of "I comb my hair." She might sit on a bench with her friends in the shade of a tree and drowse in afternoon's lazy heat. She might appreciate the melting sweetness of fruit in her mouth. She might close her eyes with the pleasure of perfumed soap and warmed water coursing down her skin.

But after the twilight bell she pretends her body does not exist. The *customers* don't like her to close her eyes. She gets whipped for that. If her eyes are closed, then it's like she is dead, a pale corpse, and while there are a few demons who might like to imagine they are rutting into the empty shell of a corpse, mostly they imagine other things and those other things mean she has to keep her eyes open to show she is alive.

But that doesn't mean she has to see. After long enough, she can be blind with her eyes open.

ONE MORNING, SIX months into her servitude, they woke to discover that the girl who rocked side to side and never spoke had thrown herself into the well and drowned.

Twenty-three days after that, Ebba stabbed with an embroidery needle one particular customer who was trying to do something to her the old woman would not speak of afterward, and as the days passed the bleeding from her flower wouldn't stop and turned into a horrible infection that killed her.

Fourteen days after the dead girl was hauled out of the compound to be thrown into the waste pits, eight of the girls got a flux, maybe from eating tainted meat, and five died after days of agonizing cramps.

The best-earning girl, after Kirya, got pregnant, and died from a bad batch of purgative.

The next day, the old woman took Kirya to the market and sold her to one of the masters of a passing caravan, handing over the girl, the mirror, and the beaded nets.

"Bad ghost," she said, in a rare moment of honest assessment. "Demon eyes unlucky."

But the men could not take their eyes off her pale hair and pale skin and blue eyes. They had a long journey to make, many months traveling east on the Golden Road across the Qin pastures and farther east still through the fabled wastelands of the bone desert. It was good in such circumstances to have entertainment and, really, you could do anything you wanted to a demon because it wasn't human.

WHEN SHE TRIED to run away, the guards caught her, and after they were done with her, the master whipped her, and after he was done with her, he chained her to the whores' wagon so she couldn't run.

SHE LOST COUNT of the days.

ONE OF THE guards took her mirror and gave it to another of the caravan whores, and when she tried to get it back, the master whipped her.

WITHOUT HER WOMAN'S mirror to show what is truth and what illusion, she might as well be dead, her shell an empty vessel that imitates the motions of life. Maybe it is better that way. Maybe everything that came before was the dream, and she is after all a demon and the ones who torment her are human, just as they say they are.

THE CARAVAN WAS plagued with bad luck. Dead birds littered the path they followed. A way station where they usually picked up water and supplies had been abandoned. A guard crawled away into the night, raving, and was never seen again. A water hole known as safe proved to be tainted, and everyone got sick with a flux that felled a number of sheep and three grooms and left the rest trembling and weak. Which was a respite for her.

A company of Qin soldiers clattered past, in a hurry to get to the border on some military errand, so they only stole what they could easily carry on their horses— wool thread, vials of western spice, saddle blankets, silver bars—but when they ripped open the canvas entrance to the whores' wagon and saw her, they made warding signs, hurried back to their horses, and cantered off as if fleeing from an approaching storm.

Which hit several days later.

The sandstorm raged for an eternity. When they dug themselves out, two wagons and a pair of dray beasts had vanished beneath the shrieking winds and blowing sands, and four drovers trapped in shelter without water had died of thirst.

Outside her wagon, the master said, "We sell the demon in the next town. The old bitch spoke true: Demon eyes bring bad luck. So, take your turn now if you still want."

THE NEXT FIVE days were the worst she had endured even after everything that had come before.

IN THE TOWN, the master took the precaution of bribing a priest to certify her as human even though everyone in the caravan knew she was the demon who had called down the storm and poisoned the spring. Then he sold her in a private auction.

Before he handed her over to her new master, he slapped her, and said, "Now I hope you will suffer as you made us suffer."

HER NEW MASTER examined her with the ugly lust she had come to recognize in male faces, but he did not touch her even after the merchant collected his coin and departed. He made her hide her hair and face under a draped cloth, and led her out of the private room in the merchant's hostel into a courtyard where two other persons fell into step beside him as they crossed under the hostel gate and out into the town.

"For Girish?" asked one.

"For Girish. Better a slave than a wife."

"Yes, Brother. Girish cannot be allowed a wife."

She was surprised, because they spoke the same kind of demon speech Mima had taught her. It was the speech all the merchants and guards knew, but in the towns, people usually used other words if they weren't speaking to the merchants.

She walked three paces behind them through the confusing babble of what she now knew was called a street. This one stank as usual but besides that twisted and turned and changed direction, yet since she kept her face shrouded and her gaze fixed on his feet, she saw nothing except the red-clay earth on which they walked, the well-made leather sandals he wore, and the occasional piles of steaming manure from dray beasts which they must avoid. The person he conversed with had soft, dark feet encased in good leather sandals. The third person, with big hairy callused bare feet, remained silent.

Once the master paused to talk to another man, making elaborate greetings in babble words but afterward slipping into the speech she could understand.

"A good harvest, eh, Master Firah? We drink plenty of wine next year from your grapes."

"If we have any wine to drink! What think you about the meeting with the Qin commander? I like not the new regulations, and the high tax. What think you, Master Mei?"

"I think we obey, or the Qin kill us. For me, an easy choice. For you, a different choice?"

"Heh heh, no, not at all. Just talking."

"My brother Hari got arrested and taken away for 'just talking.' "

"Sorry to speak of it. My apologies, Master Mei, for reminding you of your family's ill fortune. Any news of your daughter, eh? I hear talk from my wife that maybe now the girl is old enough, a marriage may be arranged. We have a good, strong son, sure to inherit the business. If you are interested, come talk."

The master grunted irritably. "I do not speak of my daughters out on the street."

"My apologies. My apologies."

They walked on.

The sandaled companion said, "Brother, Firah has much coin and a good vineyard."

"Not for my orchid."

"True. True. We can do better for her."

"She is too young for marriage!"

"Heh, Brother! She is old enough, fifteen now. Plenty old. And maybe we can offer that teakettle as part of the bargain."

The master's voice was his whip. "Enough!"

"Pardon, Brother. Pardon. I mean no disrespect. So, eh, ah. Is the slave a pretty one?"

"It is a slave."

"I hope it was cheap. He'll damage it soon enough."

"Maybe not this one."

After more turns, they walked under a gate into a dusty courtyard that smelled of dusty water and dusty leaves.

"Take it into the storehouse," the master said.

He went away. The barefoot one led her into a building. As soon as they walked into the dim confines she began to shake, for here exactly were cribs like the cells of the brothel. She was afraid to cry, because crying got her whipped. They walked to the end of the corridor and into a room with a window onto another courtyard shining so brightly green that the colors made her eyes hurt. A fountain splashed, moisture tickled her nose. She clutched the cloth tightly around her head, but kept a slit open toward the window so she could see the beautiful green foliage and the flowers, orange and white and pink, nestled along the branches. Four young children played beside the fountain; a woman seated on a stool nearby mended clothing.

The door opened.

"Look it over," said the master. "You'll see why I bought it."

A hand tugged on the cloth, and she released it and cringed as she saw five people staring at her: the master and another man who looked enough like him to be his brother, two women, and a huge barefoot man. All but the master made warding signs.

The two women were likely cousins or sisters. They stared at her for a long time, then looked at each other, as sisters and cousins will, sharing stories in the tilt of a head and the shift of a mouth and the way an eyebrow lifts. Then they looked at the master and his brother, at the stiff way the men were standing.

The older of the woman said, "Mountain, take its clothing off. I don't want to touch it."

Reluctantly, the big man minced forward and began the difficult task of removing her clothing without actually touching her.

"It's a demon, husband," said the younger one. "Look at those blue eyes! Just like cornflowers. Bad luck! Why do you bring a demon into our clan?"

"For Girish."

"Grandmother won't like it," said the brother.

The master snorted.

The older woman said, irritably, "Grandmother has been letting Girish do as he pleases. I've already been put to the expense of purchasing and training new slaves. She's blind to his habits—"

The master's expression darkened. "Do not speak of my honorable mother in such a tone, Wife!"

She flinched. "Pardon, Husband. Pardon."

The younger woman broke in, "What if it is diseased? It could infect everyone—"

The slave tugged off her dirty undertunic. She stood naked before them. The master's hand strayed low, but with a deliberate shift he reached up and scratched his jaw instead. The brother had no such control. Her pale skin and pale hair and blue eyes never ceased to excite and horrify. That was what demons were: an evil lure to tempt people into the wastelands where they would be devoured down to the bone.

The older woman's horror receded as her gaze narrowed with calculation. "No other man in Kartu can claim to own a demon. It might content Girish, now that he's clamoring for a wife."

"An allowance, and the demon," said the brother. "That might shut him up."

"Pardon, Husband," said the younger woman to the master, "pardon me that I speak out so boldly, but if you perhaps might be willing to tell Girish also that you will take the demon away from him if he molests the slaves." She hesitated, dipping her head submissively.

"I am not unaware of the trouble Girish has caused you, or of his disordered and repulsive habits," said the master with a stern frown that squelched conversation. "Let us see if this contents him."

27

"It's so ugly," said Girish with his habitual giggle as he hauled her into the smoky interior of the narrow house and shoved her toward a stained couch hidden behind a screen. "I don't know what you see in it, Ramda." His hands were shaking with excitement as his voice rose in a petulant whine. "What do you have for me today? You promised me something new."

Ramda was a thin, nervous man who never looked directly at her. He flicked a hand toward the curtained entrance to the back rooms, not watching as Girish pushed past the curtain and vanished.

"Here." Ramda handed her a lit smoke.

She brought it to her lips and sucked. Warmth spread from tingling lips down into her throat. She sighed, taking another suck as the warmth spread throughout her body. When Ramda limped over and dropped his trousers, she took another suck and let him press her back onto the couch with its lumps and damp spots. After a while he finished. Other customers came and went in the main room, and sometimes after coin changed hands a man might step behind the screen and lie down on top of her, breath hot against her face. The ceiling of the hall was half obscured by threads of smoke that traced patterns along the wood. She followed their slow dance with her eyes, the way smoke crawled up the slope of the eaves or pooled beside brackets and beams. Coin jingled. Men laughed. Dice rolled. A child's thin scream penetrated the smoke, and for a moment all fell quiet.

Then they started up again, gaming, drinking, smoking, talking. She drowsed in the warmth.

An argument erupted in the main room. The warmth was beginning to wear off as the smoke lost its hold. Ramda never gave her more than one for herself, and every time the ache of its leaving prodded her like a fresh wound. She fumbled with the ties of her long jacket, closing it over her naked body. Shoved from the other side, the screen clattered down on top of her. She fell off the couch, found herself sitting on the loose trousers slaves wore, her thighs sticky.

"Come! Come!" Girish shouted at her as he wiped blood from his hands with a cloth. She struggled clumsily to get the trousers on, unable to remember having taken them off.

Ramda shuffled in behind him. "Get out!" His hair was mussed as if he had combed it with his hands. "That's the second one this month you damaged. I don't want you to come back."

"You cheating dog! You said it was a new one, but I saw the same one last week over at Nonku's chop. I wanted a fresh one. One that will really be scared." He grabbed her by the braids and tugged her. She tripped over the trousers, which she hadn't gotten up over her knees. The long jacket bunched and tangled around her hips. He slapped her once, twice, a third time. "I hate you! I hate you!" He spat at her. "You're the cause of all my trouble, demon!"

"Here, now," said Ramba, hands trembling as he picked up the screen and set it aright. "No need to hit it. It's just a slave."

"It's a demon. I wanted a wife, and they gave me a demon because they are pigs and scorpions, my own relatives! They're just jealous because Mother loves me best."

"You're drunk, Girish. Would you get out?"

"If you don't let me come back, you'll not get to poke her again, eh? And what of the other men? I know you sell her stinking flower while I'm inside, heh, heh." He rubbed his fingers together as if he was feeling the texture of a coin. "Don't think I don't know that you're padding your sleeve with a little coin on the side, selling the demon while I'm busy elsewhere, eh? Heh."

She wrestled her trousers up and tied them, then tugged down the long jacket.

Ramda stared mournfully at her, remembered himself, and looked away. "If you damage my goods, you can't come back, Girish. I can't keep replacing the things you break."

Girish handed him coin. "You can replace it. Here. Get some new ones this time."

Ramda sighed, taking the coin. "You're rich, suddenly. Did Father Mei increase your allowance?"

"My brother?" Girish dropped the bloodied cloth to the ground, spat on it. "He begrudges every copper."

He hooked the leash to the slave bracelet she wore on her right wrist and yanked her after him, out the door and into the alley. The sun's light staggered her; its heat was a blow. When she stumbled, he whipped her with the end of the leash.

"Come on! Come on!" He whipped her again, and again, smiling as she cowered. "Put your hands down. Put your hands down."

So she did, and let him strike her across the torso and shoulders, shuddering under the lash, until he grew tired of the sport of seeing her cower submissively before him.

"We're late. Stupid demon. Why do you always make me late?"

She walked behind, her gaze fixed on the ground, as he hurried onto a side street and through town to the market. Now, seeing acquaintances, he was all gracious smiles, smooth greetings, heartfelt inquiries after aged relatives and promising children, and unctuous agreement with whispered diatribes against their Qin overlords. Women in the marketplace flirted with him as he browsed their wares, because he was a good-looking young man from a respectable clan. But there was still a speck of blood on the palm of his right hand. There was always blood on his hands; she just pretended there wasn't. The smokes Ramda gave her hid her aches, but they couldn't hide the blood. They couldn't hide the screams.

"Eh, there is the lovely Mai. How are you faring, Niece?" He fetched up before a fruit stand. "Have you sold your quota today? Ensnared a wealthy husband, eh?"

Father Mei's eldest daughter sold fruit in the market, and she stared placidly at Girish from under the shade of a parasol. "Uncle Girish. Here you are. Sales are good today, although the peaches are a little underripe. Of course Father Mei will choose a suitable husband for me. Maybe next year."

"You are such a stupid stupid girl, Mai," he said with a grin. "Here, give me a peach."

He grabbed, but the girl snatched up a peach and pressed it into his hand before he could topple her neatly stacked pile. He sulked, then spotted a pair of young men strutting down another lane. "Hei! Hei!" he called.

As he turned to go after them, Mai slipped a peach into her hand. "Here, Cornflower. Something for you."

Horrified, she tried to hand it back, but he was already trotting toward his friends, and the leash, tugged taut, forced her to stumble along after lest he whip her for slowing him down.

His friends greeted him with lively expressions of joy—obviously drunk—and they fell to talking about some race meant to be held out beyond the walls in a few days' time, not that any of the locals were allowed to ride horses on penalty of death, but they could bet on the Qin soldiers who would be racing for the honor of their individual companies. Glancing back, his smile twisted and a flare of anger widened his eyes.

"Did you steal that, demon?" He snatched the peach out of her hand. "Whew! A nice ripe one. Here." He offered it to his friends.

"Not after the demon touched it!"

He shrugged. "Eh, you're right. Tainted now. Probably make any of us sick." He squeezed it until juices began to run, then gave it a heave up over the rooftops. They walked on, chattering, as she trailed behind, grateful she had not been beaten. At length the friends left him, and he made many twists and turns through back alleys and arrived at a tavern's back entrance. Slipping inside, he was stopped by two Qin soldiers lurking in the corridor.

"Chain the demon up outside," they told him. "The commander does not want the creature anywhere close."

"Chain her outside, and anyone who sees her will know I came here and wonder why."

They grunted, and settled on shoving her into a tiny storeroom. She sank down between two barrels, head resting against the wall. It was nothing more than a thin barrier of wood, and through it she heard Girish's whine and the calmer rumble of a man speaking with the Qin way of chopping off *k*'s and swallowing *r*'s.

"This man said this, this man said that. . . ." Names and complaints rolled off Girish's tongue as the Qin officer questioned him for details of the most incriminating and treasonous remarks made by the inhabitants of Kartu Town.

She shut her eyes. If she did not think, she would not hurt. How many days until he went back to Ramda's? He usually could not afford to go more than once a month, so she had another passage of the moon to hunger for the smoke. She could still taste it in her mouth, but the warmth had drained out of her.

"Hei! Hei! Lazy demon!"

The leash flicked so hard against a breast that she gasped. Hurry. Hurry. She scrambled up, and he hit her a few more times as the Qin soldiers watched impassively. When he pulled her past them, they stepped back so as not to touch her. An open door revealed a man dressed in a golden tabard, sitting on a pillow as he sipped from a cup. He glanced up with his demon-scratched eyes. Seeing her, he made a warding sign and gave a signal, and an unseen servant closed the door.

Out on the street, folk stared as Girish strode past with her on a leash behind. The Mei demon, they called her. Girish liked their whispering and pointing. Today he hummed under his breath, always a bad sign. He rarely used her, and then only at night when he was particularly restless and couldn't sleep. His brothers, and the other males in the house, eyed her when they thought he was not looking, and their desire pleased Girish, who dragged her everywhere with him on the leash so he could gloat that he held what others lusted after. Everyone knew what he was, but they stared as at the smoke on the ceiling and pretended not to see and hear, not as long as the blood did not touch them.

Despite its orderly environs, the slave and livestock market stank of piss, fear, manure, and despair. Giggling now, he strode to the open corrals behind his favorite warehouse.

"Master Girish! So nice to see you. Please, please, this way. What are you looking for?"

"Ah, eh, yes. My mother desires a few children, pretty ones, to decorate her chamber and wait on her. What do you have that's fresh and new, nothing damaged."

She stared at her feet, browned by the sun. Long sleeves covered her pale arms, and loose trousers covered her pale legs, the jacket buttoned up to her neck. A cap shaded her face; he whipped her if she forgot to wear it. But her feet and hands might turn brown, resembling the color of human skin. She wondered that if she were to turn brown all over, if she would become human, but maybe a demon could never be human, no matter what it once had believed it was.

"Cousin! Cousin!"

Her ears puzzled over the strange word. Her mind made a funny twist, and suddenly she was staring at her feet in the middle of a dusty, stinking, filthy pit of demons wondering why she was hearing true speech again. She looked up. In the fenced area in front of her huddled about twenty children, very young, dressed in little more than rags and looking thin and dirty. She saw him immediately because his dark hair and coloring and features were instantly familiar. He was a boy of the tribes, no more than eleven years of age, someone like her taken as a slave and sold away into demon land.

"I like the look of that one," said Girish, following her gaze. He pointed at the boy. "Where's it from?"

The merchant shrugged. "Western tribes. There are so many of them out there, and they're all savages. I bought it on the Qin borderlands. You can see it's not a demon, not like that one you have there. I'll purchase her from you. Female demons are rare, I don't mind saying."

"Not for sale." Girish had a hefty pouch of coin in his hand. She'd never seen him with so much coin. He was usually begging for more, but not now. With a satisfied smirk, he counted out silver into the merchant's open hand. "Send that boy and the other three I indicated to Ramda's house. You know the place."

The merchant frowned uneasily, scratched his ear with his free hand, and sighed as he closed his hand over the payment. "If you say so, Master. It's just that Ramda's house is known for—"

"Eh? What's that?"

"Nothing, Master. I hear you can get a good smoke there. I'll have them there by this evening."

A small voice trembled from the huddle of child slaves, speaking words no one but she could understand. "Cousin! Can you hear me? Aren't you of the tribes?"

Girish yanked so hard on the leash she fell onto her buttocks. Laughing, he dragged on her so she had to scramble backward on heels and forearms trying to get turned around as he cut back through the slave market. Eventually he tired of the joke and let her clamber to her feet.

"Come on, come on." He took a brisk pace, humming and giggling, until they reached the Mei compound.

"Mountain!" he shouted. "Mountain! I want a bath. Right away, you fat oaf!" He slapped her. "Demon, brew me some tea. You know how I like it." He strode off.

She remained in the family courtyard, shaking as with a fever. The boy's hopeful, frightened, desperate gaze burned in her mind's eye.

One never knows what gifts a stranger will bring. She touched the beaded nets that capped the ends of her braids. The memory of the boy's gaze was enough to make her remember Mariya and Orphan and Kontas and the tribe, when after all this time she had forgotten.

"Cornflower?"

The master's youngest brother paused while walking across the paved courtyard. Shai was the worst of them, because he stared the most at her when he thought no one was looking.

"You look like you've been dragged through the dirt," he added. Mercifully, he looked away. He had thick arms and strong hands, these clenched now as he muttered. "Why does everyone look away and say nothing when they know what is happening?"

She said nothing.

After a moment, with a mighty sigh of frustration, he walked into the house.

She knew what was happening, no matter how much she stared at the smoke curling along the ceiling. Enough. She would not give that boy to Girish, not him and not the others.

In the compound of the Mei clan, slaves padded silently about their tasks. Compared with the misery of the brothel and the nightmare of the caravan, it was not a bad life as long as you did not ignite Father Mei's legendary temper or get in the middle of a dispute between jealous wives or aggravate one of Grandmother's petty grievances. As long as you ignored what Girish was, and what he did.

She went back to the servants' court and washed her hands and feet and face. Afterward, in the kitchens, she brewed tea and padded with a cup and a tray to Father Mei's office. No one noticed her as she slipped inside, head bowed, to stand by the door waiting to present the cup; she had lived in the clan for many months, and although they would never be used to her, she no longer startled them. He was making accounts, something he did with a stick marking a tablet, and after a bit he raised his eyes and frowned.

"What are you doing here?"

The door opened and his two wives hurried in, shut the door, and began to squabble.

"You just think the Gandi-li clan isn't of great enough consequence for Mai."

"I think the lad is more suitable for Ti, yes. If he can stand to hear her spout all day!"

"How dare you say Ti is worth less than Mai—!"

Father Mei slapped a hand on his desk. "Why have you barged in here to disturb my peace? I did not send for you. And who sent *her* in?"

The two wives turned, saw her, looked at each other in the way of enemies who have just become allies, and took a big step away.

He said, "what are you doing here, slave?"

She did not use her voice often. It was hard to find, and certainly it was easier to understand the words of the demon tongue when spoken by others than to get them to come out of her own mouth. "Father Mei. Pardon, I beg you. Master Girish is a bad man with a bad heart. He hurts children to make them cry. He ruts with them to make them cry—"

He rose, his expression hardening.

The younger wife hissed in fear and grasped her sister's hand. Yet the older wife pressed her lips together, looking first at her husband and then at Girish's slave.

"Do not speak of this again. You are a slave, and a demon. You do not have a voice." Glancing at his elder wife, he frowned to see on her face an emotion he did not like. "Get out!" he commanded, and they fled the room, the door snicking shut behind them. In the room lay silence. Beyond the door, no footsteps pattered away, as if they had paused to listen.

He moved around the desk, took the tray out of her hands, and closed one hand around her pale throat, his palm coarse and warm against her skin.

"If you speak of such things again," he said, "I will kill you."

IN DEMON LAND, anything can happen. In every meaningful way, she is already dead. Except for the one last angry spark that has reawakened.

THERE WAS A shrub whose name she did not know but that produced beautiful five-petaled pink flowers to adorn most every garden in Kartu Town. The old woman at the brothel had taught the girls to brew it for a purgative that would loosen their wombs if they inconveniently caught a man's seed. It had to be brewed in just the right proportions: too little, and you would just vomit; too much, and it would kill you, as it had killed the second-best-earning girl in the brothel, the one whose death had precipitated her sale to the caravan.

They were accustomed to her presence in the kitchens. Late in the evening, it was easy to take Girish a cup he was too drunk to recognize as different from his usual tea. Because the brew sickened and weakened him, he suffocated on his own vomit as she held him down. But his thrashing death throes woke others. Her back was to the door of his chamber when it opened, and a woman screamed in a panic. Holding a lamp, Mountain stamped into the chamber while she sat beside the dead man and the half-empty pitcher. He blocked the door, so she could not escape. When the master's wives arrived, staring in shock and horror at the scene, she turned a calm gaze on them and, raising the pitcher, drank the rest.

PART FIVE: MIRRORS

28

IN THE HUNDRED, in the season of the Flower Rains, the rains bloomed and withered in erratic patterns that depended on the topography and how far west or north or east or south you stood. If you knew your geography, you could anticipate the weather. In the Barrens, a person could lie in a stupor out in the open for days, and still not get wet.

When at last the girl roused, she stared at the envoy of Ilu with a changed look. Sometimes a person knows who they are and wishes they did not. Ignoring his tentative greeting, she saddled Seeing and rode away without saddling Telling in turn.

"The hells!" By the time he got Telling saddled, she'd flown out of sight into the wispy clouds crowding the mountains.

He flew in sweeps, even near enough to survey the campsite where outlanders and local hirelings were digging a ditch and berm around a pair of hills. He searched but did not find her. Long after the light failed, he returned to the altar. With fumbling hands, he cared for the horse and released it. He collected firewood to augment an old stack piled here by another reeve, possibly himself. Disturbed by this activity, rodents and spiders fled.

He had failed her. He sank onto the sitting stone beneath the overhang and stared as the red coals faded to ashes.

SHE WOKE HIM by touching his hand. As he started into awareness, she pressed an irregular oval object into his palm.

"Here, Uncle. It's sweet."

He studied the fruit. The morning light described its lumps and hollows, the way its smooth skin gave slightly. Delighted, he laughed. "I haven't tasted a sunfruit for years! My favorite! Where did you find it? They don't grow in the Barrens."

She gestured further into the foothills. "There's a valley with many trees, and water. Someone was hiding there, but all I saw were threads like silk blown in the wind. The fruit is good. Try it."

The sweetness cooled his dry mouth, and an odd expression creased her face: She was trying to smile, to show she was pleased that she had pleased him.

"What is your name, lass?"

She backed away, unsaddled Seeing, and busied herself grooming. Ox-footed fool! He had shouldered in too quickly. He finished the fruit, wiped his hands and, because he had to do something lest he start jabbering again, began whittling.

After a while, still brushing the horses, she said in a low voice, "What is the twisting path? When we walked on it, I saw other places."

He kept up his stroke with the knife. "There are a hundred and one altars spread across the land. Any Guardian, at one altar, can speak to any Guardian at another altar at the crossroads where our paths meet. You and I must beware, because the others who are like us wish to do us harm."

She paused to look at him. "The horses have wings."

"Yes."

"We are demons, aren't we?"

"No. Ghosts of a kind, perhaps. But alive in our own way."

She resumed brushing. "When I was a human, I had a mirror. Every girl is given a mirror when she comes into her blood. A mirror is a woman's strength. But they took mine." She dropped the brush. Seeing sidestepped away from her as she fumbled into her sleeve and brought out the mirror and stared at her ghost face. "Why did you make me look? Why did you give me this mirror?"

He set down the knife and rose. "The mirror is your staff. Each Guardian has a staff, each according to the nature of the cloak that Guardian wears. I have a staff, as you see—" He picked up his stout, beribboned staff from the ground. "—although I admit I am the only Guardian with a staff that is actually a walking staff. You have a mirror. Death—you saw her—should carry a sword, appropriate to death, I am sure. The sun with his fiery arrow. The earth with her deadly snake. And the others, so on. There is a great deal to teach you, lass. Tell me when you are ready to hear more."

The weary despair in those demon-blue eyes made him wish to weep for whatever misery she had endured. "Why did you make me remember?"

"The altar made you remember. And the mirror did as well, by strengthening your connection to the altar. A Guardian's staff has many uses. One is to aid a new Guardian in awakening. By fully knowing what you were, you can perhaps accept what you are now, what is right and what is wrong, and where your duty lies."

"I want to go back to my tribe."

A rising wind rumbled over the saddle, promising rain. He tasted its sweetness on his lips.

"I want to go home," she said as the first falling raindrops slid down her face.

"Come, lass, take cover." He indicated the overhang.

But even after the horses wisely broke for shelter, she remained out in the open while the rain hammered her, as if she were praying for obliteration.

*   *   *

THE RAIN SLACKENED to a drizzle, which faded to drips, and a ray of sun lightened the blooming terraces of veil of mercy and hundred-petaled butter-bright until the colors dazzled. In Argent Hall, Joss sat cross-legged at his desk, looking out through the open doors at the marshal's garden and the two reeve hopefuls who had been put to work weeding. The young men talked together in the way of new acquaintances who have discovered they like the same things: the best kind of hook for catching white-mouth, the best weight of stick for a casual game of hooks-and-ropes, the best fertilizer if you wanted a better yield from your jabi bushes. Farm boys.

"Marshal?" The clerk sat with hands folded in his lap. He was a slender lad with a narrow face, dark eyes, and a freshly shaved head with a healing nick over behind the left ear. "Was there more?"

"Neh, not if you got that lot of correspondence complete. You can go, Udad."

"Yes, Marshal." He hesitated, not gathering up his supplies.

The lad had an inability to ask questions directly that Joss found exceedingly tiresome. "I meant you were free for the rest of the day. Do you want to go back to Olossi?"

"Not if you need me, Marshal."

Joss surveyed the neat stacks of correspondence ready to be carried by eagle to their intended recipients, and the striking lack of mess in the chamber. A cupboard divided into shelves and cubbies was organized according to subject matter and sender or some other arcane system Joss hoped he would never have to decipher. "We've done enough. Take a pair of free days, if that's what you'd like."

"If you're sure it's not too much trouble, Marshal."

"If I did, I wouldn't offer," said Joss dryly. "Be back by twilight on Resting Snake. That'll give you three free days in Olossi."

"Thank you!" Still, he did not rise.

"Is there something else?"

Siras was sitting by the door, idly chiseling patterns in a broken plank. Without looking up, he said, "I think Udad is hoping a reeve can ferry him to Olossi."

"Of course! You'll go with the correspondence. You can deliver it yourself to-night. Otherwise, you'd spend your three days' leave walking there and back." With an eagle always at his disposal, it was difficult for Joss to remember how long it took other people to get around.

"Thank you, Marshal!" Flushed, but grinning, the lad unrolled his work cloth and set the drying inkstone in its box, the brushes and other scribe's tools in their sleeves. Joss watched, caught between admiration and an intense relief that he himself need not be so tidy.

As soon as Udad clattered down the stairs, Siras said, "If you had him tending your sleeping chamber, it wouldn't be such a wreck."

"If I were another man, you'd be whipped for your impertinence."

"As you say, Marshal." He grinned without looking up from his work.

"What *are* you doing?"

Siras set the chisel aside and displayed the plank, salvaged from an outbuilding that had collapsed during Yordenas's brief tenure as marshal. A row of flowers bloomed across the top of the wood.

"That's quite good."

Siras laughed. "Didn't think I had any talents, did you? Both my mother and father are woodcarvers. That's what I always thought I would do."

"How did you get to Argent Hall?"

Siras gestured toward the men working through the herb bed, hands plucking and tossing the always verminous weeds. "Came to try my luck, same as many do. My clan didn't want me to go, but my mother told them to let me try. Thought when I spent my months here and nothing came of it, I could come back to my true work."

"A wise woman, your mother. Was she quite irritated it didn't work out as she planned?"

Siras smiled, but instead of answering he swept up the bits and dust of wood and scattered this debris in the flower beds, to the laughing protests of the farm boys. A bell rang, signaling the end of drill.

"Bring tea, will you? The fawkners and trainers will be here shortly. And tell those lads they're finished for the day."

Siras tucked the chisel into his sleeve and the plank under his arm. Joss heard him exchange words with the youths outside, who—like the responsible farm lads they were—said they'd finish the one herb terrace they were on before they left it for the day, thank you.

Light shimmered on the flowers. A haze of aroma and color seemed to rise out of them, and out of that incandescent blaze might walk Marit, to chide him for his faults. The hells! Was that what he had reduced his memories of her into? A lilu who wished not to seduce his body but to improve his character? She hadn't pinned him down that very first time, years ago, because she was interested in his character.

Fawkners and trainers arrived in a flood of chatter and complaints, with Volias slithering in their midst.

"Didn't I tell you to return to Clan Hall with a report?" Joss asked, singling him out as everyone else settled on pillows and mats.

"Going at dawn tomorrow," muttered Volias, his usual snarl subdued. "Just did another few sweeps looking for that cursed woman, Tumna's reeve."

Joss was so surprised to hear this that he answered as he might any other person. "She can't have got far. I don't believe she had any kin to turn to, or any place to go, really."

"Yes," agreed Volias. "Which is what worries me."

"Tumna's healing in the lofts. She'll do her own hunting once her wing is better."

"If Nallo survives so long."

When Volias glared at him, waiting for the sarcastic retort, Joss felt shame for snapping at the other reeve just because he himself was brooding. "Everyone should be keeping such a close eye out for her, it's true. Nevertheless, if she's gone to ground there's not much we can do. She's stubborn."

Volias sat, elbow propped on bent knee and forehead resting on the back of a hand as he gazed out the open doors, as if hoping to see her walk in.

Aui! This was something.

Joss sat.

Verena rubbed an arm, smiling wryly. "You look tired, Marshal."

"So do we all, I am sure. How's your shoulder?"

"Healing more quickly than Tumna's wing."

"What's new since this morning, then?"

"I am at the end of my wits," said Askar. "So many unjessed eagles descending all at once, looking for new reeves. Who must all spend months being trained. We can't do it all in this one place."

"It's true," said Verena. "It's never happened before. Some of those eagles must have spent years in the mountains waiting to return." She turned to the other two fawkners. "Did you see Sweet? That sly old bird! I thought sure she was dead. I last saw her eight years ago, if a day."

"Marshal Joss," said Arda, the trainer sent from Clan Hall. She'd lived in the hall all her life and knew nothing but eagles and reeves. "We must set up a camp elsewhere to keep the raptors out of each other's way until they're settled in and their new reeves have finished training. Until we get the rest of the eagles jessed."

"We don't have the resources," said Joss. "And what about the safety of the new reeves and their eagles? How can we protect them until they're trained?"

"Three or four months for basic training," said Arda. "At last count we've got twenty-two new reeves—"

"—and at least forty more unjessed eagles passing by every day," added Verena.

Askar said, "Some of the eagles will simply *not* come in with so many other unjessed raptors, and with such a mob of folk churning about. We need that temporary camp, Marshal."

Arda had known Joss a long time, and had besides never shown the slightest sexual interest in him, so it was easy for her to slip into the hectoring ways she had felt free to use when they'd both been at Clan Hall. "It's not as if we haven't been telling you for the last many days. I admit, I hoped the eagles would choose faster, but there's no reason to think they haven't looked over this crop and taken what suits them. Can't you get rid of these useless hangers-on?"

Govard, the steward, broke in, rubbing the short hair atop his head with a hand. "And if I may speak to that, Marshal. I don't have room for all these cursed lads, the wrack and leftovers that have washed up in the hall. The young ones are the worst. Two fights today! Perhaps if you'd encourage them to give up and go back to their homes."

"And leave us in peace with the overwhelming task we already have!" added Arda, in case Joss hadn't gotten the message.

Joss raised both hands. "Calm down. Don't think I haven't been considering this."

"Heya! Heya!" Running footsteps crackled on gravel. "Marshal! Come quickly!"

Volias was already on his feet. The rest of the group crowded onto the porch as Siras sprinted up. Overhead, a thick spiral of eagles had massed.

Three Qin strode out of the alley that led between storehouses and lofts from the marshal's garden to the parade ground. Joss pushed past the others, slipped on sandals, and jumped down the stairs to the path, then hurried over to greet the visitors beside the fountain.

"Captain Anji. Greetings of the afternoon."

"Greetings of the afternoon, Marshal. If you will come with me, I need to show you something."

As Joss walked beside the captain, the others maintained a gap between themselves and the pair of dour guards who attended the captain everywhere he went. They passed into the shadowed alley.

"You came sooner than I expected," said Joss.

"I have my own difficulties." Anji scanned the storehouse doors, all tightly shut against the rains, and the freshly painted braceworks. "The Olossi council is reluctant to grant me the resources I need to build an effective fighting force. Will you come to the council meeting on—" Joss could almost track the captain's thoughts as he picked through unfamiliar words to pluck the right one. "Wakened Rat, the last day of the month. Ten days from today."

"How can I help you?"

"I've scouted out lands in the Barrens, on the western shore of the Olo'o Sea. Good pastureland, sufficient water, and mostly uninhabited. Familiar territory for Qin seeking to make new homes for themselves."

"Unaccountably close to sinks of oil of naya."

Anji smiled. "So it is. We will put forward our claim to the land at the next council. Meanwhile, I tell them they must expand the militia to an army on a permanent footing, but they don't want to hear. I refuse to waste my efforts on this—this—" He struggled for words. "Rags and scraps hastily tied together do not make a fine gown any more than rags and scraps hastily placed in marching order make an army. Here we are. Now you'll see."

They strode into the parade ground, where five horses were being held by two grooms in the shade. The perches were empty; all the eagles had flown, as they were likely to do when things got too exciting. Every person there meanwhile was crowding the landward ramparts and staring toward the fields. Without pushing or saying, indeed, a single word aloud, the two Qin soldiers opened a path for the captain and the marshal to a steep stair that led up to the rampart walk. Joss clambered with the ease of long practice, fawkners crowding up behind him. Everyone was talking, exclaiming, and a few of the newcomers, young men who'd come with the hope of jessing an eagle and gotten no satisfaction, were mumbling complaints.

"There," said the captain, shouldering aside an onlooker—a hireling by the cut of his threadbare tunic—to give Joss room.

Joss did not have a great deal of experience of horses, but he had ridden them for about a year during his apprenticeship as a messenger to Ilu, the Herald. He had an idea that the stout Qin horses were the most phlegmatic, and toughest, equines known to humankind. But they were definitely scared of the big eagles.

The company of thirty men Anji had ridden in with had scattered to a safer distance, although all had bows at the ready, waiting for the command to shoot. One poor fellow had been thrown from his panicked horse and left on the road facing down a handsome female eagle. Joss had to admire the way the lad stood his ground, not sure whether to bolt or brazen it out, but sticking with the latter course of action in the face of the imposing head and wicked talons.

"What do you make of that?" Anji asked with the same admirable calm.

"Does anything shock you?" Joss asked him.

"It might, if I had noticed you were worried, but since you are not, then I assume you know what is going on. That's one of my tailmen, Pil. What do you make of it?"

"The western shore of the Olo'o Sea is not all that far as the eagle flies, if she flies, as she can, from Olossi across the sea rather than being forced to walk roads and tracks the long way around the shore and through the wild lands. There are boats that usually ply the eastern shore, that could haul supplies to the west. I'll argue before the council in favor of your claim, if you'll help me build a temporary reeve hall in the Barrens for my flight of new reeves. Like that lad, there. What did you say his name was?"

Ha! Now he had surprised Anji.

"Pil? What are you saying, Marshal?"

"You live in the Hundred now. If you mean to make this your home, then you have to abide by our laws. That eagle has made her choice. She's chosen one of your soldiers."

29

The envoy of Ilu did his best to track the girl on her journeys around the Barrens without hounding her. Sometimes she hunted, or practiced her archery at a target she set up at the base of the hill, where the winds weren't so strong. Sometimes she returned to the hidden valley, with its unseasonable harvest of fruits and nuts and the strange, glittering threads drifting in the air. Sometimes she scouted the outlanders' building activity, and the nearby hills. He kept his eye on her from a distance, because he knew absolutely that to try to force her to accept what she had become would be the ruin of his hopes.

One day she returned in the late afternoon in the teeth of an unexpected cloudburst. This time of year, an unusual pressure of storms boomed out of the Spires, strong weather pushed over the mountains from foreign climes. Under the overhang, he coaxed the coals into a brisk fire, and after she had cared for the horses she sat down on a rock opposite him.

"The fire will dry out your clothes," he said. "Not that you can precisely catch your death and die of a fever," he added as she turned her mirror to catch the flames in its reflection.

Moisture rose like mist from her clothes. "Could you see what the mirror forced me to remember?"

"No. Guardians are veiled each to the other."

She looked up sharply. "Tell me the truth, Uncle. Am I still a slave?"

He studied the half-finished carving he held in his right hand, a sinuous otter with laughter carved into its curves. "Now, there is an interesting question. What is a Guardian, if we were formed by the gods to serve the land?"

"Why should I be forced to serve your land?"

"Why were you chosen? There is a question I cannot guess at, unless you tell me your tale."

She said, to the fire, "There are men not so very far from here, building a compound. Did you see them?"

"I saw them. They don't know we are here. In any case it's unlikely they can climb to an altar even if they would be bold enough to break the boundaries of what is forbidden."

"There are eagles, too. Huge eagles."

"Yes. I've seen them. The eagles will ignore us, but their reeves might spot us. It would be prudent to move on."

"Some of men there are Qin. I recognize them."

"The Qin are outlanders, pasture-dwellers like the lendings here in the Hundred, only unlike the lendings the Qin look perfectly human to me. What do you know of the Qin?"

"They are my enemies. They call my people demons. But that's not what I mean. I mean, I know those particular Qin. Because I traveled with them."

"You've surprised me!" He set down the half-carved otter and picked up his staff, resting it on his thighs. The wood was as smooth as silk under his hands from untold years of handling. "When did you travel with them?"

Addressing the restless flames, she began to talk. "One never knows the gifts a stranger brings. My cousin Mariya and I were out hunting. She showed me the gift a lad from another tribe—a lover—had given her, even though he ought not have done so. It was bold of him, not proper. Little nets woven with lapis lazuli, very pretty, to bind the ends of your braids. . . ."

A STORM PASSED, and night fell with sheets of rain as she talked. Later, the clouds parted, and the Embers Moon rose late, a stroke against the sky.

". . . MASTER GIRISH WAS dead. They knew I killed him. When a slave kills a master, then the slave must die."

"So you drank the rest of the poison."

"I drank the poison." It was remarkable how calm she sounded, but her hands were wrapped tightly over the mirror, hiding her reflection.

"Is that when you died?"

She blinked. "I died when I walked into demon land."

"When did the cloak return to you?"

She lifted the fabric to the wind and watched the air flow silver within the night. "How do you know it is the same cloak?"

"I knew the Guardian who wore it before you. She walked out of the Hundred because she wanted to die in a place far away from our enemies where they would never find her. Or, if her cloak passed to another Guardian, then she hoped I would have a chance of reaching the newly awakened one first. To that end, she left three things with me. The first was the mirror."

"What are the other two?"

"An offering bowl, the gift of Hasibal, the Formless One. Also I have for you the gift of Sapanasu, the Lantern. Look." Beyond the fire's light the darkness crowded them, creeping closer when the flames subsided and slinking back when he placed more sticks on the fire. He raised his right hand, clenched it, opened it. Light shone from his palm, illuminating the rocky curve of the overhang above and the dusty ground with its neat piles of gear below.

"Aui." It stung. He closed his hand, and the darkness leaped back in.

"I like that! How can I do that?"

He caught a smile before it betrayed him. "I know a bit about these particular Qin. I heard the tale of how they saved Olossi."

She opened and closed a hand, then looked at him through narrowed eyes. "Is the light demon's sorcery?"

Rats were known as good merchants because they weren't afraid to bargain. "How do the Qin enter your story?"

She remained silent for so long he thought she had decided not to answer. This late in the night, sliding toward dawn, the wind's moan took on a eerier tone, or perhaps the angle of shifting winds just made it rub up against the slope of the rock differently.

"After Girish died, the women of the house took pity on me. The men did not." Abruptly she was panting, as if running from a beast that meant to rip her apart, and she shut her eyes and fought down memories until she breathed normally. "The women took pity on me, anyway. They hated Girish because they had no power to stop him. It was their idea to send me away with Master Shai."

He had questions, but he dared not interrupt.

"When the sandstorm came, the Qin captain saw his chance to be rid of me. He hated demons. He pulled the beads off my hair and threw them to the ground like they were poison. He told me he would not let me destroy his troop, because everyone knows demons bring ill luck. He made me walk naked into the storm."

"Eiya!"

Her gaze was a thousand mey away. "I was happy to do it. I could hear their voices."

"Whose voices?"

"My mother and my father and my older sister, my cousins, Uncle Olig and Feder the Cripple, all the dead ones from my tribe. They called me. They asked me to come home. So I was happy to go to them."

"Perhaps they were demons," he said kindly.

She rocked side to side. "Are there demons? Or is it just a story we tell?"

"Eiya! Certainly there are demons in this world. Some are human, and some are not."

She jumped to her feet. "I am a demon! Everyone said so!"

"You are not a demon, lass. You never were. You are a Guardian."

"What is a Guardian?"

"Heh." His Rat's mind was pleased at this small victory. "A difficult question, one that in the end must be answered by what you do, not by what I tell you. The Guardians were placed in the Hundred by the gods to bring justice to the land. To preside at the assizes, the local courts, so that those who commit crimes are punished properly and those who are innocent are not wrongly charged."

"I want justice."

"Of course. We become Guardians because we sought justice—indeed, gave our life in seeking justice on behalf of others. As you did for your brother and the other children."

She looked away.

"What is your name?" he asked gently.

She turned back. "I want the offering bowl, and the lantern."

Her bold demand pleased him. Something of the self-sufficient girl he had glimpsed in her tale sparked in her expression as she regarded him with hand outstretched.

So be it.

"Here, the bowl." He handed it over. "There's a loop to fasten it on your belt. I will place a stone in your palm. I can't predict how it will affect you. I fainted for days, but Mist—who came before you—told me she merely felt a sting."

"I'm not afraid," she said, by which he suspected she meant: I'm not afraid of that kind of pain, having endured something much worse.

He fished in his sleeve and drew out the black stone, as smooth as a river pebble and smaller than a warbler's egg. "Which is your strong hand?"

"My right."

"Hold out your left, then. Palm up." She watched him. Those demon-blue eyes were unnerving, if you stopped to think about their watery pallor. But that did not matter. She was part of the Hundred now, and if he did not teach her properly the others would find her and corrupt her, and he would be the last one left.

He placed the stone in her palm.

Light flared, so bright he shut his eyes.

When he opened them, she was still sitting there, hand clenched in a fist. The fire crackled as if nothing had happened.

"Ouch." With beads of sweat on her upper lip, she cautiously opened her hand. Light pierced the darkness, and she giggled unexpectedly, sounding like a girl.

Of course, she was just a girl.

"Do you know in what year you are born?" he asked her, not sure if demons counted the years as humans did.

"I'm a Hawk!" She grinned, fisting her hand and opening it to see no light, and then fisting and opening to bring light.

"There is no Year of the Hawk."

"Of course there is! The hawk flies after the deer and before the ox."

"Ah! A Crane, then." With the turn of the year, she had made nineteen years.

"What is a crane?"

"The crane is a bird. She is orderly, cautious, honest, and kindhearted. Yet once Cranes have developed an opinion of somebody, it is difficult for them to change it. What is your name, lass, so I may call you something?"

"Kirya," she said, still playing with the opening and closing of her hand, the word tossed carelessly.

"Kirya, eh?" It was a workable name; so many foreign names were simply impossible. "Dedicated to the Fire Mother at birth."

"Not fire!" Fragile lines of confidence deepened as she frowned disapproval. "Fire is sacred to the gods. It is not for us to claim we are part of the gods."

"How can we be separated from the land, and the land from the gods?" He had lost her. "Maybe so, yet in our country the name Kirya will be understood as partaking of fire."

"Why?"

"Because it's a Fire-born name. If you don't like it—eh, had you a pet name your family called you?"

"Kiri."

"That's a man's name. Water-born. Yet what of this? Water-born, you would be Kirit. How do you like that?"

"Kirit." She rolled it on her tongue as she might test the flavor of spiced barsh.

"A Water-born Crane, orderly in its nature but made adaptable by its heart of Water. Born in the Year of the Red Crane, which adds energy and intensity to your nature, and also—well, let's leave that for another time. The Red Crane is known to be passionate in its opinions, and ruthless in its quest for justice if an injustice had been done."

The wind soughed and the fire slumbered, popping once, ash settling. The clouds were shredding to bits on the peaks, and in the east the stars began to fade into a gloom presaging day.

Blinking, she said, "Why do you talk so much?"

He laughed. "Because I am a Water-born Blue Rat, dedicated to Ilu, the Herald. Also, there is so much to say. Here, now, let me tell you the Tale of the Guardians again. That is the best place to start."

But she rose as the twilight before dawn, mist-silver cloak flowing around her. She paced along the rim of the height, below which the slope was so slick with rubble that a single step would send you plunging. With her head turned eastward, she scanned lands broken by furrows and gullies and the occasional tabletop plateau, that sloped to the mantle of darkness marking the distant sea. Returning, she saddled Seeing. When he realized she was loading all her gear into the saddlebags and leaving his particular things behind, he scrambled to pack.

"Kirit. Where are you going?"

The girl who had ridden into demon land to redeem her brother was not about to let one useless man's blithering objections rein her in.

"I want justice."

OF COURSE HE was such a cursed fool just as the others had always teased him, a city boy born to luxury who hadn't the wits or skills to make do outside of the salons where expensive jaryas gathered to declaim their poetry and scions of rich families gossiped and intrigued and made behind-the-curtain deals. Not that he had done any dealing, famous as he had been, in those days long ago and in his limited circle, for being too proud to gamble; that had been their way of saying they thought him too naive to understand what was actually going on.

He had missed some important gesture or shading of her mood. Oblivious as the moon in love, thinking he had awakened her and finally done something right all the way through, he had let it tromp right past him. He thought he had actually fulfilled the pact he had made with Ashaya, who had worn the cloak of Mist and walked into the shadows because of the persuasion of the others but who had the strength in the end to turn her back on corruption, when in truth he was the least of them, really, too stubborn to fall into the shadows but not strong enough to fight.

Mostly he was able to walk through the world cheerfully enough; it's just that some-times the façade was stripped away by an unexpected setback.

Where would Kirit go?

Was it the view she had seen when she'd walked along the height that had jolted her into action? Was it the sea, or the dawn, or the sky? Or night's shadowed sky calling to her?

Far in the distance, if you had quite good vision, could be seen the flare of human-made fires.

I want justice.

Too late, he knew where she had gone.

IN A SHORT span, an exceptional degree of construction had flowered on a pair of neighboring hills situated to overlook a bay where the Qin were building a settle-ment. When the wind shifted to blow in from the sea, the stink of bubbling oil tainted the air, but it rarely lasted long. Eagles glided above. Young men drilled in military order at dawn and dusk, their shouts carrying in the dry air. Between drill, these hirelings and debt slaves shaped bricks and dug ditches and heaped dirt into what would, when completed, be an impressive stretch of berm encircling both hills and the narrow valley down which a shallow five-seasons river ran. Also, laborers cut a well. At night, the workers slept in tents.

A cadre of men and seven women trained as reeves; not that he knew the drills and technique, but it was obvious who had an eagle at hand and who did not. Shallow-drafted cargo boats beached on the shore within the shelter of the bay. La-borers hauled logs from the boats to build crude lofts for the eagles: At least forty raptors were gathered in the greater span of this territory, a phenomenal number to be seen outside the reeve halls. Some were willing to share close quarters while oth-ers kept their distance in the Spires.

As for the fifty or so Qin, they ranged wide as they scouted the lay of the land un-til, he supposed, they knew it as well as a farmer knows his fields. They kept watch over lads who shepherded flocks of sheep and goats, and several of their number stayed with the herd of horses grazing the slopes. They supervised a contingent of debt slaves who were digging an underground irrigation channel farther inland. They hunted antelope and black deer through the tableland, not unlike the eagles. They explored the long-abandoned hilltop ruin in pairs, harvesting from sinks of naya near the ruins.

Every day they drilled the hirelings in weapons and formation. Those who could ride they brought hunting with them, although none could ride as well as the Qin.

Rats are known to be impatient, quick to become restless, eager for a change. But he had to think like a patient Crane. She was but one small pale young person. And yet she was born and raised on the grass, as the Qin were: She was a hunter. As animals re-turn time and again to a watering hole, so did the Qin keep going back to the ruins.

HE APPROACHED THE ruins on foot just before dawn. Long-abandoned build-ings leave a footprint: buried and broken walls; sunken lanes where folk once walked; scatters of potsherds and broken masonry. He almost stumbled into a well, half filled in with debris. At intervals, he heard hissing, and although he watched for snakes he saw only birds, rodents, and the ubiquitous thumb-sized flying roaches. He passed between the collapsed ruins of an old gate and climbed a ramp of stone now buckling and mostly covered by earth. Who had built all this?

A bewildering maze of ruins greeted him at the crown, whether residences, temples, storehouses, or courts of justice he could not tell. He heard snatches of a gulping sound, like a man's exaggerated swallows. The hiss had returned, and the sulfurous smell grew stronger as he pressed toward a craggy bluff. He kicked through heaps of shattered pottery and broken figurines, fragments of stone carved with staring eyes that had no face, mouth with no eyes, a long-fingered hand, a bare foot—a woman's foot, surely, for its delicacy. The ruins of an octagonal building and its pillared courtyard lay before him.

As he came to the crag's edge, the rising sun spread a glow across the waters, several mey away but nevertheless striking as they shone with coppery-pink light. She had crouched beneath an intact archway cut low to the ground. She watched a pair of Qin soldiers who were riding toward the ruins.

Cursing, he ducked through another opening, crawling over rubble to get inside. He saw her form limned by the light. She did not acknowledge him. Within, steps carved out of the stone led down into the rock. A stink, rising from the depths, was strong. Cautiously, he edged down, stepping over fallen bricks, until he came into a wide underground chamber lit by shafts. He sneezed at the dust raised by his feet. In the center of the chamber rose a round platform with a cleft struck through its center, and in this cleft a disembodied flame burned. Its hiss echoed like a thousand whispers, a story told in a language he did not know.

For all the years he had walked on earth, he had never known of this place nor heard tale of it. With a shudder, he retreated back up the steps.

With her back to him, she said, "If you go back outside, they may see you and come up here to investigate."

"Think you so?" he said, pleased by her words.

"Just to the west lie bitter springs. Mostly the Qin ride there to collect pitch. I hear them talk. They will bring a company of slaves to harvest the pitch and store it. The pit frightens them because the flame burns without fuel."

"How long have you been hiding here?"

"Three days."

"Why are you here?"

"I am waiting."

It was like teasing splinters out of skin! "What are you waiting for?"

"What is a Guardian?"

With a sigh, he sank down a few steps from her and leaned against the wall. The smell made his eyes water, but he didn't notice it as much. He brushed dust off his palms.

"I don't know," he admitted, "what the Guardians truly are, or what they were meant to be. The gods awakened the first Guardians during a time of war, when every clan fought for itself and every clan did as it pleased. Without law, there is no order. The Guardians serve the law."

"They are slaves, then. If they must serve."

"If you serve only yourself, lass, then to whom are you really a slave? Even in the place you come from, you serve the customs of your tribe and do your work and marry and bear children and die in your time, all without considering yourself a slave."

She was silent, her back a wall.

"The Guardians serve the law, and by serving the law they serve the land and the gods. Whereas in the days of chaos any person with power might dispense justice according to her whim, now the assizes courts were established in every city and town and the chief villages. The Guardians journeyed from one assizes to the next to the next. They stood over the court and heard witnesses and made judgments. They hold in their hearts Ushara's gift: the second heart and the third eye, with which to see into the hearts of all. It is not so easy as you might think to seek truth within the hearts of women and men. At first, I thought I knew everything, but then I discovered that my own nature caused me to make assumptions and misread what I learned. I have become more cautious in passing judgment."

"Who was the woman whose body I found on the grass?"

He nodded, although she did not turn to see him do so. There was so much to tell her. It was like running, and tripping over your own feet. "Yes, yes. You see, it is this way. Naturally, there is a risk. The powers the Guardians hold are also a temptation. Within the council of the Guardians, five—a majority—may judge one of their own who they feel has passed under the gate of shadow into corruption. They can strip the cloak from that Guardian and allow it to pass to another person, as it—the cloak—chooses. So you may possibly see the problem that confronts us. What if a Guardian succumbs to the shadows, and yet has the outward countenance of light? What if such a Guardian bides her time, out of fear, out of greed, out of anger, and in her turn corrupts one by one her fellow Guardians until four others walk at her behest? Five in all. Five, who can control the council and rid themselves of those Guardians who will not do as they demand. What is the handful who remain loyal to the gods meant to do?"

The tale came hard to his lips. He had not rehearsed it. To think of the long years in which, slowly and in secret, the corruption had eaten away at the council was too bitter to endure. It was "a knife in the heart," as the tale said, a well-worn phrase but true enough when you felt the stab of pain. How blind might a trusting soul be! How foolish and naive!

"Ashaya was corrupted by promises and sweet words and reasonable explanations. She was corrupted by fear, since fear, beyond all things, brings with it the shadow. But in the end, she fled corruption. She knew if she passed on the burden of her cloak while still in the Hundred, that the others would find and control the newly awakened one. Instead, she walked out of the Hundred. And I waited for you—obviously, I did not know it would be you, Kirit—to return."

"Because the cloak would bring me back."

"By one means or another."

"A cruel master," she observed.

"Neh, neh. Not a master. It is our charge. Our responsibility. Our obligation."

It was hard to meet those pale eyes because they did not look human, but her face was so young and vulnerable that he recognized the humanity in her, that which is capable of both compassion and malevolence.

"Where are the assizes courts?" She stumbled over the unfamiliar words.

"Typically you find them in the cities, towns, and chief villages. But an assizes can be held wherever a Guardian chooses to stand."

She rose. "Then it is time to make a judgment."

THE QIN SOLDIERS were using fronds to scoop scum from one of a series of bubbling pools sited just beyond the tracery of the outer wall. Their horses took no notice of Kirit as she walked toward the two men, holding her strung bow and an arrow in her right hand but her mirror in her left. As he feared.

The soldiers leaped up and, in turning, brought their bows to the ready with arrows already nocked.

"Demon!" spat one man.

The other's face was a mask of fear. His arrow slipped out of his hand to the dust.

The envoy sensed their fear and consternation as much from their posture and expressions as from his second heart and third eye. And since neither looked at him, only at her, he could not see into their hearts.

"I remember your names. Eitai. Sayan." She gestured to the man who had spat. "You did not harm me, Sayan. Go, if you wish. Or if you want to be judged for any other crimes you may have committed, I will hold up the mirror, for the mirror reveals the heart."

"We are Qin," said the first soldier scornfully. He marked her companion and dismissed the envoy, unarmed as he seemed to be, as no threat. "We do not dishonor ourselves by abandoning our comrades. How has Eitai harmed you?"

"He raped me."

Eitai lunged for the fallen arrow and, rising, nocked it. "I paid! It was perfectly legal! Your master made the offer, and I accepted in good faith. How was I to know your demon's ghost would return to haunt me!" He loosed. The arrow shot true, punching her so hard in the left shoulder she staggered back two steps. But she did not fall.

She said, "In the tribes, such a crime is punishable by death."

Sayan loosed an arrow and hit her in the belly. She grunted, but despite her evident agony, she did not go down.

"Stop this!" the envoy cried.

They ignored him.

"A man cannot do only as he pleases," she said in gasps as blood soaked through her tunic. "Otherwise there is no law. Did you commit the act?"

Eitai's answer was soundless, a sideways look through narrowed eyes, the tilt of his head as he leveled his bow.

"You cannot kill me," she said hoarsely. "I will return again and again, and the next time I will kill you. See your fate in this mirror, that shows the heart of those who are guilty and those who are innocent."

She turned the mirror's face toward the men. Light caught and flashed. Sayan screamed with fear. Eitai collapsed in silence, his spirit taken.

Eiya!

The living soldier dropped to his knees and pressed a hand to the dead man's neck, but such efforts would be in vain.

She stumbled forward. The living man shrieked. His gaze skimmed the envoy's face, the blast of his terror like a cold wind out of the mountains. He bolted for the horses, and galloped away as Kirit dropped to her knees beside the dead man, grunting as the impact jarred the arrows stuck in her body. The fall had loosened the soldier's topknot. Strands of black hair spread a delta of fine channels on the dirt.

She held her mirror a hand's breadth above his parted lips. Breathing raggedly, she watched the mirror's surface. "Is that his spirit? Caught in my mirror? How did he die?"

He had to speak, although he feared the consequences. "The Guardian's staff—"

"It can kill. I killed him!"

"Vengeance is not justice."

Her face was sheened white under sweat. She grinned, showing teeth. "The wolf pack picks off those in the herd who are diseased. It's for the best."

"We are not wolves. We are human beings, and we serve the law, not our own impulses. We do not bring down death with a casual flick of our hands. Death is the most severe sentence. It was long ago agreed that in death sentences, the council must be unanimous, all the Guardians must investigate such a serious case and agree, not just take matters into their own hands at their whim. The hells! Let me get those arrows out of your body."

"Go away! I am not your slave!"

She grasped the arrow that protruded from her belly and, with a shrill yaaah!, yanked it out. With less difficulty, because it had already punched mostly through the meat of her shoulder, she pushed the second arrow out through the sinews of her back and, reaching under her arm, pulled it free. Weeping, coughing, mewling, she rested on her hands as blood dripped onto the dusty earth. The sinks of pitch burped like foul cauldrons.

He had no idea what to do now.

"I am not your slave," she said, as if to the land itself. She rubbed a hand over the sticky patch of blood, smearing it into the dirt. Already her body would be healing itself, knitting what was severed, although the pain, naturally, was staggering. He tried not to think about the last time, when he'd been pierced by arrows and trampled by horses. That was the hells of it: The price you paid for your unnatural life was to learn to live again and again with the agony of dying.

She raised her head. Her demon eyes leaked water, which some might call tears.

"They cannot kill me, but I can kill them."

"That's not what the gods intended."

She hissed, an attempt at a whistle. Sucking in more breath, she managed a sharp trill. Unlike him, who preferred to do his stalking afoot, she had hunted with her mount nearby. Obedient to her call, Seeing trotted into view, skittish at the smell of blood. The girl heaved herself over the mare's back, groaned and, with another grating yell, dragged a leg over to sag into the saddle, clinging to the horn.

"It's not what the gods intended," he repeated helplessly.

As Seeing spread her wings, Kirit looked back, face white, lips as bloodless as a ghost's, tunic blotched with red.

"They are not my gods."

30

Just because Edard had to show off to impress Eridit, the scouts got in trouble as they rode east toward Horn.

"I'll scout point today," the ordinand said at dawn, then looked at Eridit to see if she made a comment or gave an encouraging look. She yawned, stretching in a way that made a man think of—

"Shai," said Tohon. "You'll ride rear guard, with me."

Eridit flashed a smile their way, measured Shai's expression, and arched her back which of course just made her breasts more prominent beneath her thin shift. Shai flushed and looked away, stumbled up to his feet as the militiamen, Ladon and Veras, laughed.

"You'd think you'd never seen a woman before," said Veras.

"Outlander men and women live separate, didn't you know that?" said Ladon. "Never touching. Eiya! Maybe they only do it with sheep."

"Shut up," said Edard. "Finish saddling the horses. Tohon, you take rear guard today."

"As you say," said Tohon with a genial smile. "You ready yet, Shai?"

They slung packs from their saddles, Eridit last of all.

Zubaidit appeared on the path, already kitted out. "What's taking so long? Aui!" She prowled over to Eridit, just now bending over to tie up her pack while every man stared at her making a display of the curve of her rump beneath low-slung trousers. Shai turned away, afraid he was going to embarrass himself. Tohon started sweeping the ashes out of the fire pit.

"Doesn't it bother you?" whispered Shai, but the scout just chuckled.

Bai said, "Eridit, I am so overcome with lust for you. Do you want to lie down right here now and get it over with? Or will you get the hells moving? Why did the temple council send you? Were you screwing them all? And if so, why did you bother to come?"

Shai looked up.

Even Eridit's scowls were sexy. "I'm good at what I do."

"In truth, I've seen you perform the tales at the arena. You are good."

"My thanks," she muttered grudgingly as she hoisted her pack over the saddle.

"Good at your *art*. Don't be an ass, Eridit." Bai slapped her on the rump.

Shai jumped, and so did the other men, all except Tohon, who shook his head as if wondering how he had ever had the misfortune to end up on this deer track carved through woodland country, riding east into the heart of the enemy. If they ever got there. Eridit laughed.

Shai and Tohon hung back as the others set out in single file, soon hidden in the woods although he could track their noise. Tohon ruthlessly tightened the girths on both saddles, shaking his head. "Those lads are strong enough, yet not only the lass but even the horses play them. Hu!"

He paused, tilted his head back.

Shai looked everywhere, but saw nothing.

A shout rang out.

"Draw your sword. This is a good trail for an ambush." He handed Shai the reins of all four horses. "Come up behind them. I'm going around."

He slipped into the woods, and Shai stood there like an idiot while more shouts and cries broke. Then he got the horses strung on leads, mounted up, and pushed along the trail. A crashing in the brush alerted him. He swung in the saddle, glimpsed movement to his right, felt a kiss on the breeze, and slashed down, just missing a man who lunged at him brandishing a crude spear. With a hoarse gasp, the man fell across the path with an arrow buried in his back. Shai kept riding, the horses jumping over the body as they caught his tension. Ahead, Ladon had plunged into the trees and was hacking at a person on the ground, while Veras crashed through the forest in pursuit of unseen others.

Edard was swearing, clutching his right arm. "I didn't see them! They jumped right out at us!"

"There's four or five more," said Zubaidit, holding a bloody sword. A man had crawled off the trail and collapsed. "Best we catch them. We can't chance being recognized later."

"Let's go!" Eridit had a short sword, one of those common to Olossi's militia, and although she'd drawn it, she held it as if in gesture, a way to look dashing and brave, not as if she had the least idea how to kill. But wasn't that what she did as a professional entertainer? She chanted and acted tales in front of an adoring audience, they'd told him. She grinned at Shai, and he thought it would be better to die than to feel this way when he needed to be concentrating on the trouble at hand.

"Where's Tohon?" asked Bai.

The scout appeared as she spoke, grabbing the reins from Shai. "If they escape, they might recognize us later. Veras is on their trail, good lad."

Edard spurred after the young militia man, Eridit right after him and Ladon pushing past as Bai hung back.

"I'll do a circuit," said Tohon. "Make sure we've missed none. You go ahead with Shai."

Bai nodded, and Shai followed her. But the soldiers they were chasing were on foot, made swift by desperation, while they were impeded in the woodland by having horses. They pushed south, yet their quarry remained just out of range all day, and they had to switch out walking and riding lest they blow the horses. Only Tohon and Shai's Qin horses were tough enough to keep the pace.

As afternoon settled into twilight, the woodland cover became more scattered and the land sloped steadily upward until with night falling they reached high plateau country. The fleeing soldiers pushed on into a sea of grass. Where they crossed a shallow stream, Tohon and Bai handed out their horses to the others and jogged into the darkness.

"The hells!" muttered Edard. "Do they think we can't manage? A cursed outlander, and her, not much older than my own eldest daughter? Do they think they're going to kill them all?"

Shai watered the horses, careful they did not take too much. Then he led them by turns in cooling circles, Ladon and Veras walking the others, while Eridit washed and bound Edard's wound by lamplight.

"Do we wait here for them to come back?" Eridit asked. "Or go after them?"

"At night?" Edard clucked irritably. "Ouch!"

"Sorry. It's not too deep. I don't think you'll die."

"Didn't say I thought I would."

"He's a prick," muttered Ladon to Veras, and Veras grunted agreement. Shai could tell these two knew each other well, and he had to admit they'd handled the skirmish decently and, like Eridit, kept up today's hard pace without complaint.

Eridit was murmuring close beside Edard, asking him to tell her about himself and his famous clan, the river transporters who wore the badge of the silk slippers, like in the tale. He looked like he wasn't feeling any pain from his injury as long as she was petting him. Ladon and Veras walked with heads bent together, checking the horses now and again but mostly talking in low voices and occasionally peering into the darkness.

Shai offered them the leads. "I'll take watch."

That sent them over to Edard. "Here, Edard, are we staying or not, because either we should get moving or we should set out sentries. We might be attacked at night, taken unawares, like you on the cursed track today sizing up Eridit and not paying attention to—"

"I said, shut up," said Edard. "Anyway, she was behind me."

"I was," said Eridit. "You two were the ones sizing me up."

A long slow slithering drag like a heavy weight through grass hissed in the darkness. They all shut up. Faintly, in the distance, rose screams and shouts and afterward silence.

Eridit shuttered the lamp. Since they had no cover and nowhere to hide being exposed there by the stream, they circled the horses and set up positions to sight in all directions, not that their night vision was any good. The land was flat. Grass sighed as the wind blew. Shai's ears itched, and he slapped at clouds of tiny bugs rising like mist around their bodies. Everyone began waving hands in a vain attempt to drive them away.

"The hells!" swore Ladon, and Veras echoed him.

A light bobbed out in the grass. The horses neighed, pulling at their harness, and were answered. Out of the darkness rode a swarm of riders, veiled men covered head to toe, only their eyes and hands showing. Bai and Tohon staggered in at the point of spears as the riders spread out to encircle their group. The cloud of bugs sank into the earth as though banished.

"Did you lose the cursed men we were chasing?" demanded Edard. "Now look what trouble we're in!"

Bai looked at him sidelong, unwilling to take her gaze off the riders. "We didn't lose them. These folk killed them, all five. Why they didn't kill us, I don't know, for I fear we have trespassed where we are not wanted."

"Where is that?" asked Tohon as he scanned the picket of riders, seeking any weak link and shaking his head when he found none.

"We've strayed into the Lend. A wide and mostly empty land, to be sure, but it looks to me as though we've violated a tribal boundary."

"Eiya!" muttered Edard. "They'll execute us for sure."

BUT THE LENDINGS did not kill them, although they ignored all overtures of friendship or bargaining. If they spoke to each other, they did so out of earshot. They watered their horses at the stream, and the next morning a leather blanket laden with tart cheese, creamy yoghurt, boiled mutton, and a flavorless flat bread appeared beside their camp.

"Good food," said Tohon, eating the last two boiled sheep's eyes.

"Folk don't like to murder folk they've shared food with," said Bai.

Tohon scratched an ear. "Good horses, too. Big, elegant, and strong. Captain would like a herd of those. I wonder what we can trade for them."

"If they mean to kill us," said Edard, "I wish they would just cursed do it and not make us wait."

After the first day, Shai and the militiamen exercised the horses as well as they could, and afterward paced out training drills. Even Eridit joined in, although she hadn't enough strength to damage anyone. Bai fought dirty and would not share her meanest tricks no matter how hard Ladon and Veras tried to wheedle them out of her. The lendings appeared to ignore the drill, but it was hard to say with them having veiled faces. One morning Eridit began to pace out the measures of a chant, and the lendings abruptly and deliberately turned their backs. She stopped immediately, looking truly frightened for the first time.

Two days turned to four. Three times Tohon tried sneaking out and three times got himself prodded back, politely but firmly. Four days turned to eight. Bai led the others in the prayers that welcomed dawn and night, but they kept their voices low and their gestures modest. At these times, Tohon and Shai sat apart. Tohon was not a praying man, although Shai whispered supplications to the Merciful One.

On the morning of the eleventh day three new riders appeared, faces unveiled. Shai thought they looked like women, although their long robes were cut so cunningly to hide their bodies while making it easy for them to ride that it was hard to tell. Their dark skin looked human enough, but it was mottled with a strange green color, like something was growing on them. They reined in their horses out of arrowshot, dismounted, walked four paces forward, and waited with arms crossed.

Edard walked forward. "Greetings of the dawn, honored ones. I am commander of this small party, which—" They turned their backs.

He retreated, looking flustered.

"What in the hells does that mean?" he muttered to Bai as the others gathered around. "Do they mean to just let us sit here and grow old by this cursed stream with this cursed grass and sky driving us to cursed madness, eh?"

"Let me try," said Eridit.

"They turned their backs on you before," he warned her.

"If I have to die, I'd rather do it quickly than wither away any more days in this cursed prison! I don't even dare have sex for fear it will violate their invisible boundaries. I don't know about you, but this is the longest I've gone without since I celebrated my Youth's Crown and started in on my Lover's Wreath!"

Shai covered his eyes. Bai laughed. Tohon sighed.

"Back me up, Bai?" Eridit asked.

"I'm game."

Eridit sucked in a deep breath. Shai watched her cross the open ground to stand before the three women who, hearing their steps, turned to face them.

"Greetings of the day, honored ones," said Eridit, her gestures emphasizing the words. She had a clear voice that carried easily. "We are come peacefully, with honor held in our hearts, having strayed out of our own land in pursuit of certain criminals who had broken our laws. We beg humbly your pardon for our transgression, and we request humbly that you allow us to continue our journey, out of your territory."

"You must pay," said the woman standing in the middle. "For food, you must pay. For transgression, you must pay."

Eridit looked to Bai, and Bai leaned over and whispered. Nodding, Eridit addressed the lendings. "Perhaps we may offer trade goods in exchange as an expression of our goodwill."

"What in the hells do we have to trade to the likes of them?" muttered Edard.

"Hush," murmured Tohon as, at the sound of Edard's voice, the lending women again made a show of turning their backs.

After a moment's silence, the three turned back and displayed empty palms to Eridit and Bai. "You possess nothing worth the weight of transgression. But one of your tales, we'll hear. If it is worthy, then you show yourselves to ride with honor, and you may walk free."

A tale.

"Sit down," whispered Ladon. "This could take a while. I've seen her perform."

The four men sat. The veiled lendings turned their backs, a ring of dark cloth stretched across broad shoulders. Every man carried a bow and quiver slung across his back, and leaned on a spear. A haze spanned the heavens. Clouds piled up in the east, as though a hand were holding them back. Shai shivered, not cold but disturbed by strange vibrations within the earth, and he thought one of the unveiled faces bent its gaze on him, but she was too far away for him to be sure.

Eridit crouched, head bent. As she rose, her posture changed so her body seemed larger not in size but in spirit, as though she was inhabited by others as well as herself.

"My nose is itching. Many whispers have tickled my ears these many nights, but this is the tale that speaks. Listen! To the famous tale, the most famous tale, of the Silk Slippers."

Shai had heard snatches of song and chant in the streets of Olossi, seen folk punctuate a line of melody with graceful gestures made by their hands or by the bending of elbows or knees. He had not seen a tale fully chanted, complete from beginning to end.

The brigands raged in,
they confronted the peaceful company seated at their dinner,
they demanded that the girl be handed over to them.
And all feared them. All looked away.
Except foolish Jothinin, light-minded Jothinin,
he was the only one who stood up to face them,
he was the only one who said, "No."

It took her half the day, pausing four times to drink water Bai brought in a bowl. By the end, she was sweating and triumphant, shaking with fatigue and yet standing proud.

"Hu!" said Tohon. "Impressive."

"I'm in love," murmured Veras.

"No, I am," whispered Ladon.

Edard glared. "I don't know why either of you think the likes of her would take a second look at your callow hides, despite your rich clans and good connections."

Shai had no words. She would never look at a mere tailman, a Kartu lad, nothing-good Shai.

The three unveiled lendings raised bows and each loosed an arrow. The arrows raced high and then, tumbling, were incinerated in gouts of flame.

"Demons!" Tohon leaped to his feet.

Eridit sank exhausted to her knees, Bai squatting beside her. The lendings whistled, and just like that they mounted and cantered away, still whistling. Cursed if their own horses didn't tug at their lines, break loose, and gallop after. Everyone ran in pursuit, even Eridit.

"Gods-rotted savages!" swore Edard when they had straggled back empty-handed, panting and heaving and having lost every horse. "They stole them!"

Eridit hid her tears. The lads kicked up clumps of grass.

"They must be demons, to have such magic," said Tohon.

"They're not demons," said Bai. "They're lendings."

"The tale was payment for the transgression," said Eridit through her tears. "But they also said they wanted payment for the food we ate."

"Aui!" Bai shook her head in disgust. "That's why they took the horses!"

"We've got half the day left to get off this cursed grass," said Edard as he surveyed the heavens. "We'll have to go back to Olossi and get refitted."

"And lose more days?" said Bai. "Neh. We'll redistribute our goods, and we'll walk. We've come too far to go back now."

"The hells you say!" He puffed up in that way men have when they are trying to intimidate others. He was a fit man, one of Kotaru's ordinands, physically imposing.

"The hells I do," she said so calmly that he stepped back. "Over long distances, we don't make that much better time with the horses, and they'll attract attention. I say, we cut along through the grass at the edge of the Lend, making straight for Horn. We'll make decent time, and we've been left with our own provisions, at least. What do you say?"

But she wasn't asking Edard, although he had been named commander of the expedition. Tohon nodded, and therefore, it was decided.

31

Life wasn't too hard in the Qin compound in Olossi, not for a marriageable girl, anyway.

"I help you, Avisha," Chaji said with a grin, unhooking the full bucket and swinging it over the lip of the well. He set it down on the paving stones. Water slipped over the side to darken the stone.

"I thank you." Avisha blushed, flattered by his attention.

"That one, too?" His smile crinkled his very pretty eyes as he nudged a second bucket with a booted foot. "I fill. For a kiss."

Avisha giggled, but she pressed a hand over her mouth and then, seeing the frown that darkened his face, wished she had not. If she made herself disagreeable, none would want her. Behind, footsteps slapped on the paving stones.

"Hu! Chaji, you don't do it for a price." Jagi elbowed his comrade aside and slung the empty bucket onto the hook.

Chaji muttered, "Like saying you want no meat when you eat it up with your eyes."

Avisha felt her ears go hot, but Jagi pretended not to hear, muscular shoulders working as he turned the crank. The bucket splashed into the deep reservoir below, and he hauled it back up while Avisha kept her head down, Beneath half-lowered lashes she surveyed the two men—Chaji with his pretty eyes and pretty grin and Jagi with his broad and rather homely face—her own smile fighting against a fear that it would be unseemly to show how much she enjoyed being the center of their attention.

"I carry them for you," Jagi said. "To the kitchens?"

"That's right. Thank you."

She followed him as he headed for the open gate. The well and the cisterns stood in a courtyard beyond the two gardens, at the highest point in the compound. A complicated system of troughs and pipes brought water from two large cisterns to the pool, the plantings, and the privies, an astounding display of wealth that Avisha still marveled at after weeks living in Olossi. This compound by itself was bigger than the temple complex in her village.

"So, you will marry *me*, yes?" Chaji paced alongside, hand tapping the ranks of damp cloth in all their bright colors hung on lines to dry. By the smaller cistern, two women pounded wet clothes on stones, pausing to eye Chaji. "You are the prettiest of the girls. You are young. You work hard. The mistress favors you."

Ahead, Jagi grunted under his breath, but he kept walking through the gate into the passage that separated the open-to-the-air kitchen from the living quarters. He turned left, under the kitchen's tiled roof, where hirelings standing at long tables plucked chickens and chopped up haricots, onions, and apricots. In the kitchen yard, steam rose from pots of rice and fragrant barsh set over hearths. Ginger tea was brewing.

Avisha stepped up into the shade of the porch and slipped off her straw sandals, while Chaji bobbed on his toes on the walk.

"Yes?" he asked, not coming after her. "That is your answer? Yes?"

Looking back over her shoulder at him with just, she hoped, the right amount of promise, she pushed through the curtained entrance and promptly tripped over the handle of a broom. She sprawled, hitting her chin on the plank floor. Sitting up, she saw Sheyshi lazily pulling the broom straight.

"You bitch! You did that on purpose!"

The other girl stared at her with dull, angry, stupid cow eyes. A heap of swept dirt was piled by her dainty feet.

Avisha grabbed for the broom. "I'll show you!"

Sheyshi yanked the broom away and backed behind the ranks of rolled-up bedding.

"Merciful God, gift me patience!" Priya walked into the room. Under her quelling gaze, the two girls looked away from each other. "What happened here?"

"Nothing, verea," said Avisha as she got to her feet. Although Priya was a slave and therefore not actually deserving of the respectful form of address, Avisha saw perfectly well how the mistress trusted her. "I just tripped. The water buckets went to the kitchen. I can get more."

Priya examined first her, then Sheyshi. "Sheyshi, finish sweeping, then fold the mattresses properly and hang out the bedding. I'll have no bugs. Avisha, come with me."

Rubbing her throbbing chin, Avisha followed Priya into the inner chambers, each one ornamented with painted scrolls hanging on the walls and a few well-chosen pieces of polished black-lacquer furniture that had, as it happened, belonged to the previous owners. They had been rich enough to own five chairs, and the mistress sat in a padded chair now as she regarded a pair of merchants seated in visitor's chairs. Mai received favored business associates in the chamber known as six-seasons-of-the-crane because of the six-paneled screen set against one wall.

Avisha waited beside the entrance as the mistress completed her business. She never got tired of studying the beautifully painted screen, with cranes dancing in a field of early-blooming pink-heart on one panel, or a bachelor flock staging for their journey to the drowsy swamps of Mar beneath white-petaled wish-vines symbolic of hopes of finding a good mate on another.

"Meanwhile, ver," Mai was saying, "it has come to my attention that your factor has changed the unit of measurement from a unit by log to one of standing timber."

The man she addressed was considerably older, plump, with a primly pursed mouth. He glanced toward Chief Tuvi, who stood behind Mai's chair. "It's the usual standard of sale, verea."

Mai had a pleasing, cheerful voice, quite innocent of malice. "Yet the original contract was made by unit of log. I can't help but wonder if standing timber may produce less log depending on defects within the trees themselves, which may not be detected until they are split and sawed for building. Really, ver, you have given us such fine quality and quantity of wood, that I would hate to have to ask my factor to begin negotiations with another house." She smiled. Like the masterly painting of cranes on the screen, you could not help but admire beauty.

"Eh, ah," said the merchant, stumbling over his tongue. Avisha was sure he had never had such a cold threat delivered so prettily. "I am sure my factor made a mistake, verea. I'll speak to her at once."

His glance toward the clerk would have scalded skin. And, indeed, Avisha could smell, from the kitchens, that the plucked chickens had been dumped into a pot of boiling water.

"You may speak to my factor in the office on your way out," said Mai kindly.

"That would be the young man, who once was Master Feden's factor?"

"He serves our house. Was there something you wanted to say, ver?"

"Neh, neh. We'll be on our way."

They sketched the formal farewells.

"I'm hungry," said Mai once they were gone. "I'll take cake and tea in the pavilion, and interview more women."

"Perhaps you should rest, Mistress," said Priya.

"I'm not tired. Just so hungry! I feel I ought to have some marriages arranged now that the settlement is rising in the Barrens." As she rose, she turned a warm gaze on Avisha. "What about you, Vish?"

"Oh, I don't know," Avisha answered as her gaze skipped to the curtained entrance where Keshad might, if he left the office to consult the mistress, walk in at any moment. But Mai beckoned, so she followed her into the large garden where they sat on benches beneath the repainted pavilion and laughed and chattered as they ate bean curd buns so sweet Avisha could not finish even one while Mai devoured two without apparently noticing that she had done so.

A pair of girls watched over a dozen small children, the offspring of women Mai had hired to work in the compound. Their babble lightened an otherwise cloudy day as they, Zianna among them, splashed in the long pools or played throwing-sticks on the stones. Chief Tuvi stood on the porch that ran the width of the garden. Mostly he scanned the garden, the walls, Mai, her attendants, but at intervals he paused to watch the children's play with a smile.

Jerad was slumped on a bench beneath the branches of a butternut tree. He slouched over to the pavilion and waited at the base of the steps.

"What is it, Jer?" Avisha asked.

"I want to go home."

This ridiculous statement embarrassed her. "Don't be ungrateful," she said in a low voice, leaning down toward him. "We're fortunate to have been shown so much favor."

"You just like the pretty silk and the soldiers smiling at you. You don't care about Papa at all anymore, do you?"

"How dare you!" That Mai should overhear this only made it worse. She raised a hand, threatening a slap.

"Jerad," said Mai. "I'm going to cut the rest of the buns into pieces. Can you take them around and see that every child gets one? You'll have to make sure the greedy ones don't take more than one. They'll try. Especially that little Nanash. He's quite a sneak."

"I don't like him," said Jerad stoutly. "He pinches when he thinks the adults aren't looking."

"Well," observed Mai as she sliced up the buns with a knife, "I think he saw some very bad things, so naturally he is frightened all the time. Just like you did, Jerad, only it seems you are able to treat others kindly instead of taking out your fear on them. That shows a good heart and a good nature." She offered him the platter.

Eyes wide, he took it gravely. "Yes, Auntie." Shoulders straight, he marched off to distribute the sweets.

"Thank you," mumbled Avisha, thoroughly ashamed.

"Hu! I grew up in a clan surrounded by siblings and cousins. You think that wasn't anything I didn't hear ten times a day?" She slurped her tea, set down the delicate cup—more fine than anything Avisha had ever handled in her life but everyday ware here—and called out. "Chief! Another round of interviews now."

"I'll separate out fourteen, Mistress. No more."

"You'll need a rest afterward, Mistress," added Priya.

"I am overwhelmed by superior numbers." Mai smiled.

In the weeks she had lived in the household of the captain and his wife, Avisha had learned that Mai's smile hid more than it revealed.

Mai continued in a murmur meant only for Avisha's ears. "Don't they see that the interviews are the worst part? I'd rather have them all done than drawn out over weeks."

"More will keep coming," said Avisha. "Until all the Qin are married. As women hear, or decide to try their luck, or see how bolder women have fared."

Mai sighed.

Priya leaned over, resting a dark hand on Mai's belly. "Are you weary, Mistress?"

"Yes, but not tired!"

"Here they come," said Avisha.

The Qin soldiers were never really off-duty, although as far as Avisha could tell they had a fair bit of leeway in going about their tasks. Rather more than a dozen men filtered into the courtyard, in addition to the guards who were on duty, as a group of hopeful women were herded into the far end of the garden and then cut out in family groups when it was their turn to come forward.

A pair of cousins dressed in gaudy town fashion wanted to know how much coin they would be paid to marry the outlanders. They were dismissed.

A poor widow who would soon be too old to bear children was given a string of vey and sent away.

A nervous girl came forward with her even more nervous uncle, and had little enough to say for herself, but when Avisha questioned her she relaxed enough to admit she could tailor.

"Come back tomorrow with samples of your work," said Mai. "If you are willing to set up housekeeping in the settlement we are building in the Barrens on the western shore of the Olo'o Sea, your skills will be useful. Think about it."

Several of the Qin soldiers marked the girl with interested gazes as she and her uncle left.

A frowning woman strode forward, dragging a young woman pretty enough except for the splotchy red mark across her right cheek. "This is my daughter. I would be happy to see her wed without any bride-price—"

Tuvi leaned down to speak in Mai's ear. "With that demon's mark on her face, none of the men will take her."

The girl saw, and interpreted, his expression, and hid her face with a hand.

"What will happen to her, verea?" Mai asked the mother.

The woman's disappointment was easy to see in the way her hand had tightened on the poor girl's wrist, as if the girl had been rude. "Some of the clan have suggested selling her labor as a slave, but it would shame our family to have it known we'd been forced to do so. We haven't the dowry for her to go to the temple."

Mai fished in her sleeve and pressed a gold cheyt into the woman's hand. The woman stared, too shocked to close her hand over it. "See that she goes to the temple, for the sake of your clan's honor."

An audible murmuring rose from the crowd of hopeful women. They shifted, moving back as Keshad pushed through and trotted up to the pavilion ahead of the next supplicants. He mounted the steps with a handsome frown on his face as he sketched a greeting to Mai. He did not even look at Avisha, but why should he? She was nothing to him! Nothing at all.

"Greetings of the day, verea." A woman addressed Mai with the confidence of a person whose position is secure. She was dressed in a taloos of elaborately embroidered silk that proclaimed her wealth and station. "I am Bettia, of Seven Fans House."

"Greetings of the day, verea," said Mai politely. Her gaze drifted to the young women standing behind Mistress Bettia. "Who are these?"

The prettier girl was staring at the ground, but the other, eyes wide with shock, gaped at Keshad as her lips moved, forming his name. Avisha glanced at him, but he was fiddling with his factor's staff, a short wand about the length of his forearm whose narrow end was crowned with a band of ribbons and a pair of seals fixed to leather cords. He looked like he wanted to lash something, or someone.

"I'm a merchant, as you are, verea," said Mistress Bettia in the manner of a confidant, "but in the recent troubles two of my house's warehouses burned down with our stock inside. I find we cannot afford to keep the number of slaves we're accustomed to. I thought you might wish to purchase the remaining debt of these two. They're hard workers. They would make good wives."

Avisha was pretty sure that Bettia was thinking, "good wives for *outlanders*." She wanted to knead her heel into that proud merchant's gold-slippered foot until the woman squealed for mercy.

Keshad bent down between them, a faint aroma of cloves wafting from him. Probably he washed and dressed his hair with an infusion of clove oil and other herbs. She wondered what it would be like to wash those lustrous curls.

"Don't take them," he whispered.

Mai smiled. "Mistress Bettia, I fear I cannot say yes to such a proposition. I have made a policy not to accept the entanglements of debt. Only free women need apply."

"Had you advertised that before, and I missed it?" said Bettia with a shake of the head that brought attention to the cunning ornamentation of ivory combs and beaded braids that no doubt took her attendants half the morning to prepare. "Yet I see here Master Feden's slave, now serving you as factor." She made a crude show of looking surprised as she addressed the slave who had mouthed Kesh's name. "Why, Nasia, you came from Feden's house, did you not?"

The slave mumbled something.

Chief Tuvi made a business of coughing, and Mistress Bettia looked at him. She blinked first, smiled as if she was in pain, collected her slaves, and retreated.

"What was meant by that performance?" Mai asked.

"She hopes to set spies in your midst." Keshad's lovely eyes narrowed as he brooded. "She's known for trading information as well as fans, screens, scrolls, and lamp shades. Eyes and ears placed inside the house of the outlanders would be valuable, indeed."

Mai considered this with no apparent change of expression, stroking the smooth silk that covered her bulging abdomen. Avisha, who knew her own face shouted every least thought and emotion, envied her that smooth countenance. "Would it not be prudent to accept such a person into the house? Better to know who will be spreading tales than to have one sneak in who we do not know of."

"There's truth to that," said Tuvi. "Let them think we don't know."

"Maybe so," said Keshad. "If we don't give ourselves away. Also, verea, if you hand out charity in such a public way, you'll cause everyone to come just to eat out of your hand."

"I felt sorry for the girl, knowing no one wanted her."

"They will take advantage of your good nature, verea," said Keshad passionately.

Chief Tuvi glanced at Kesh, and made a show of clearing his throat. "Are you growing tired, Mistress?"

"No. Let's go on with the interviews."

Jerad crept up to the edge of the pavilion and tugged at Avisha's arm. "Vish? Can I go to the stables?"

The chief signaled a new family group to come forward. Mai smiled at the party of humble farmers—a father and daughters by the look of them. Keshad was pretending to look at his hands but was in fact studying Mai under lowered eyes.

Did Kesh love Mai? And why wouldn't he? Mai was beautiful, and kind, and well-mannered, and very clever.

"Vish!"

"No!" she whispered, wishing she could tweak one of Jerad's ears to make him stop bothering her at always the wrong moment. "You'll just get in the way."

He rolled his eyes as he tugged at a fold in her taloos. "No, not by myself. Jagi said I could go with him and learn to groom a horse! Please."

Jagi was standing by the small gate painted with a winged horse. He touched his forehead, saluting her. She flushed. "All right," she muttered. Jerad dashed off without replying, cutting so close past the new supplicants that they halted, trying not to look fools and yet also chuckling to see a child so free to run about the garden, which was a reassuring thing when you thought of it: a local boy at ease among the fearsome soldiers.

Chaji was not in the garden, maybe because he had already chosen her. A few matches were already being spoken of, and one girl was supposedly pregnant, a thing that had infuriated Chief Tuvi so much he had beaten the soldier who admitted to the act and demanded the girl be sent away for being a bad influence. Mai had intervened, though, and instead the pair had been carted off to the settlement in the Barrens to begin married life together.

The Barrens did not sound like a nice place, dry and brown, but they could be no more barren than a place where both her mother and father had died and where she had no hope of building a home for herself and the children no matter how much she missed the ash swales, the song of water rushing over the pebbled river shore, the call of the larks that nested in the third lintel over the gate to the temple of Ilu. She did not want to go back without her father braiding cord in his shop and telling her the tales of the Hundred, which he so loved.

"That's done," said Chief Tuvi. "Will you rest now, Mistress?"

Mai walked down the garden to the porch and, pausing in its shade, accepted a cup of tea brought on a tray by Sheyshi. The stupid girl had a smudge on her nose.

"Thank you, Sheyshi," said Mai, more kindly than the ill-tempered little tramp deserved.

As Mai moved into the house with Sheyshi padding at her heels like a devoted dog, Priya touched Avisha's arm. "Sheyshi has not a lively spirit, as you do, Avisha. It is not surprising the mistress prefers your company to hers. That does not mean she cannot feel excluded. For so long she and I were the mistress's only female companions. She feels the loss of that intimacy. If you make an effort to be kind to her, it would speak well of your nature."

Avisha hung her head, too shamed to reply, and Priya was too wise to keep beating that stake into the ground. They followed Mai into the spacious reception chamber with its mirrors and its painted rat screen, a lighthearted series of scenes of taloos- or jacket-clad rats at work counting coin and at play flying kites.

"I'm going to the livestock market," said Mai to the chief.

He looked resignedly at Priya, and Priya shrugged. Caught by the reflection in one of the mirrors, Avisha saw Keshad standing behind the others but looking at Mai. Avisha shivered. If only he would look at her in that way!

But he did not.

"Will you come, Avisha?" Mai asked.

She hesitated.

"Keshad, I would like your opinion as well. The sheep market is today, is it not?"

"It is, verea. This late in the day the best animals will already be sold."

"I'm not buying," said Mai. "I want to see what the lesser quality of animal looks like."

"I'll go." Avisha glanced at Sheyshi's sour expression. "Maybe Sheyshi would like to go, too."

So it was arranged. Avisha went back into the garden to tell Zianna she was going out, but the little girl was napping. A contingent of guards was assembled, the big man pulled from his counting frame to accompany them, and another of Anji's senior men, Chief Deze, left in charge of the compound in Tuvi's absence. Sheyshi brought straw sandals suitable for a trip to the market.

They left the house through the warehouse, where women and children sat on the long benches, waiting their turn to be interviewed. The supplicants carried baskets and bags with rice balls and se leaves to eat during the long wait. Children dozed on the floor. Women looked up as they passed, eager to speak, but the escort of Qin soldiers intimidated them.

The sheep market lay down the hill outside the gates of the inner city, on open ground untouched by the building that consumed Olossi's outer districts. Mai was fascinated by the sheep. She and O'eki asked interminable questions of the herdsmen and farmers who had brought their lots to market. Keshad stuck next to the mistress.

It was odd to walk in public accompanied by the Qin. Chief Tuvi had detailed a dozen soldiers, and while they did not swagger or push, they cleared a path for Mai simply by being armed and alert. Avisha dropped back to where Chaji walked as part of the rear detail. He smiled briefly and then ignored her as his gaze roved the crowds.

Many glances were cast their way, not all kindly ones. A pair of men garbed in the homespun of farmers bent close over a ewe. By the way their eyes watched the Qin, they might have been whispering about the condition of her mouth or they might have been muttering complaints. A woman dragged her daughter out of the path of the Qin, as if she feared they would kidnap the girl.

"A blessing on you, verea. A blessing!" A beggar wearing a greasy red cap and ragged kilt trolled for alms, holding out an offering bowl.

The forward group reached an intersection. Avisha hurried to catch up as Tuvi shouted an order. The soldiers halted, blocking the intersection. Mai turned. Then she smiled.

Captain Anji and four soldiers strolled up the other avenue, which was lined with pens and booths selling songbirds, chickens, crickets in miniature cages. The crowd melted away to give them room. Conversations faded to silence as the two groups met, and merged.

"Will you attend me, husband?" Mai asked with a smile that made the captain grin, even though he was in public, and caused Keshad to look away.

"Of course," the captain said. They went back the way she had come while she described to him the characteristics of the local breeds and the wet season problems with foot rot.

"If I know something, it is about sheep. I was meant to marry into a sheepherders' clan."

"Where you would have been wasted."

"They were wealthy."

"I assure you," said Anji with a smile that made Avisha blush even though it was not directed at her, "they did not have as many sheep as my Qin clansmen. That our estate will have, if we acquire the core of a strong herd."

"I am interested in this herd." Mai indicated an extensive pen mostly emptied by sales. They entered into a protracted discussion with a clan that herded extensive flocks near Old Fort.

Avisha sidled up next to Keshad. She glanced toward Chaji, to see if he was watching her, but like the other soldiers he was scrutinizing the passersby, the farmers deep in conversation, a pair of laughing laborers carrying axes on their shoulders, the skulking dirty children.

"That was well done of you to spot those spies that merchant wanted to place in the house," she said to Keshad.

He flicked a glance at her, as if surprised she could talk. "Eh. Yes."

"Eh, do you know, if you and your sister hadn't helped us over the river, I don't think we would have survived."

"Probably not," he said without looking at her.

"Have I made a proper thanks?"

"A hundred times over."

"Oh. Ah. Have you news of your sister?"

He made a brushing motion with his hand, as at a pesky fly. Abruptly, he stiffened, and she took a step back, afraid he was going to say something cutting, but he was looking past the soldiers into the crowd.

"Avisha." Mai touched Avisha's arm. "It's best if you return to the compound." The company had re-formed, ready to move on. "We're going now to take afternoon cakes and tea with the Ri Amarah in their compound. They'll tell me today their decision, if Miravia can visit me in my own house. But since you're not allowed in the compound, you would just have to wait outside, so you might prefer to go back home."

Avisha wondered if this was what Sheyshi felt like, pushed to one side. "Are you sure you want to go? The Silvers cover their heads to conceal their horns!" When Mai laughed, Avisha went on determinedly. "That's what everyone says."

"The women don't have horns."

"That doesn't mean the men don't have them. Everyone knows they do!"

"Every ignorant villager," said Keshad over his shoulder.

Captain Anji had waited throughout, standing patiently behind his wife. "Have you seen their uncovered heads, Keshad?"

"No."

"Then you are only speculating. If you will, Keshad, return to the office with Avisha and have one of the clerks ink a contract, something I can take with me when I ride out to examine the herds. Come, Mai, I'll escort you personally. The Ri Amarah are honorable and trustworthy friends."

He nodded at Avisha, who wished herself dead and her bones picked clean for having spoken so stupidly. Who was she to mock Sheyshi? At least Sheyshi kept her mouth shut.

"Open your mouth and prove yourself a fool," she muttered as the company moved off en masse, the big man's head towering over the rest. They were talking about sheep again!

"Do they really have horns?" Chaji came to stand next to her. He indicated Keshad, who was fulminating, staring toward that same poor beggar with offering bowl held out in trembling hand as he limped through the crowd in the same general direction as the Qin company. An odd-looking man under the grime, and oddly familiar.

"Avisha," said Keshad under his breath, "here's a vey. Keep walking, split away from me. Then go say a pretty word to him and bend close and put it in his bowl, and afterward tell me if there is a mark in the bottom. Wait until he is out of our sight before you meet up with me."

He had spoken to her! She did as she was told, angling away, pretending to be walking by herself, a simple village girl come to the city for the first time. Men smiled at her, in her pretty clothes and well-kept hair. Women eyed the cut and quality of her taloos.

"May the gods grant you blessings, holy one." The beggar was old, thin, with a beaky nose and dark rodent's eyes that had an unpleasant glimmer. Then he moaned grateful noises, a few mumbled words that could have been anything. He reeked, as if he'd been sleeping in a smokehouse after having been rolled in dung. Whew!

She remembered where she'd seen him before.

She caught up with Keshad by the gates to the inner city, where he had paused to wait for her with the four Qin soldiers assigned to guard him.

"Well?" he demanded.

"It's a wooden bowl. There was a mark painted in the bottom, crossed knives linked under a circle."

Keshad pressed a fist to his mouth, then lowered it.

"What means that?" asked Chaji, very serious now.

"That's what empire folk call a blessing bowl, for the god Beltak. Now, maybe he stole it, or maybe he found it, but maybe he didn't."

Avisha bit her lip. "Heya." She hesitated. When Keshad gave her a look of barely veiled disgust, she blurted out the rest. "The very first day I came to the compound, I saw a beggar in a red cap in the courtyard. I'm sure maybe it was him."

"Maybe he is a spy," said Chaji. "The captain warned us, maybe Red Hounds from the empire follow us over the mountains. You want, we kill him right now." He grinned at Avisha. "You want to watch? Very fast, we kill him."

"You can't kill a holy beggar in the public street!" Keshad surveyed the street traffic, the gate guards staring at the Qin soldiers and factor and girl loitering in the sun, the laborers and market women pausing to whisper. A pair of raggedly dressed young men watched the Qin soldiers with what looked like admiration. "Even if this one is a spy, no one seeing the impiety would know that. They'd only see outlanders killing a holy beggar."

"The captain must know," said Chaji. "I send Seren and Tam to follow the spy. Avisha, return to our own compound. Tell Chief Deze what we saw. You and I—" He indicated Keshad. "—we go to the Ri Amarah compound, find the captain."

Avisha admired the swift way Chaji took control of the situation, but Keshad balked. "Are you perhaps overreacting?"

The Qin were not in general demonstrative men. Chaji's look of scorn flashed quickly, and was hidden at once. "From the empire, there is always danger to the captain. Even a tailman knows this. Avisha, you go quickly, yes?"

"Yes," she said breathlessly, not sure if his dazzling gaze was offered in praise or just because he was tense.

"Eiya!" muttered Keshad. "We'll do as you say, but I know the city better, I'll be able to retrace the spy's trail. Send the others to follow the captain. You and I follow the beggar."

"You try to escape, maybe?" Chaji said with a grin. "You try, I enjoy chasing you down." He sent Seren and Tam off after the captain, then grabbed Keshad's elbow and dragged him through the gate with Umar trotting behind, leaving her alone, the center of stares, a girl who consorted with outlanders and accepted their smiles.

"Trying to get a husband?" said a young laborer, passing her with a long-handled adze braced across his broad shoulders. "I'll interview you, lass. They say the Qin soldiers have nubs instead of good sharp tools. Don't waste that pretty face on them. Come by the carpenters' guild house. Ask for Keness."

"Leave her be," said his older companion. "Don't insult the lass. Anyway, the outlanders saved us, in case you forgot."

"I don't like the way they look. Cursed proud, if you ask me. Still, I suppose the coin is good, neh?"

She ran away into the crowd, tears burning. Of course the Qin didn't worry she would run away from them: The coin was good; she had no better option. No use crying about it. She was protecting the children and doing what she must, and it wasn't as if the Qin were so bad. Mai had been good to her. She was fortunate to have fallen in with them.

When she stopped sniffling she realized she had gone the wrong way and stumbled into a secondary market where men, women, and children were roped into lines. Labor gangs, being pressed into service. Half of them had fresh debt marks carved into the flesh by their left eyes, some still dribbling blood from a hasty job.

Their hard luck made her realize just how fortunate she was.

As men and women jostled her, she stopped, trying to remember in which direction lay the inner gate. Stunningly, an anonymous man groped her breasts. She shrieked, slapping out, but hit instead a woman carrying greens in baskets hanging from a pole balanced across her shoulders.

"Clumsy bitch! Sheh! And you a rich clan's daughter in such silks. Not that you'd know what hunger is."

Babbling apologies, Avisha crouched, careful to keep her hem from dragging in the mud, and plucked the thick se leaves one by one out of the muck. The woman cursed at her until she shrank back, red-faced and sniveling, looking for a place to get out of the fray and catch her breath, but there was nowhere that people weren't moving, shoving, blustering, shouting.

"Heya! Ready to move, now! We march to the docks. No falling behind." A factor brandished a whip as, from the saddle, he addressed a pathetic gang of laborers, young women and men with fresh debt marks and freshly shaven heads that made them look like Sapanasu's clerks, only in homespun, not the robes worn by the Lantern's hierophants.

She would not have recognized Nallo with all her hair gone, if the woman standing in the second rank of the gang had not blanched and tried to cover her face.

"Heya!" The whip cracked a warning in the air. "Look sharp! Stay in line! You'll find you're well treated in your new work if you keep discipline and remain orderly. Don't disappoint me, or your new masters."

They marched off toward the docks down the main avenue, feet shuffling on churned earth. In their wake, the market traffic resumed, but Avisha stood as with feet planted, folk bumping into her, cutting around her, cursing her for getting in the way and would she please move on move on. She began to cry.

Nallo had sold her labor. She was now a slave

*　　*　　*

KESH THOUGHT THAT probably the old man was just a beggar, fallen on hard times, a Sirniakan carter stuck in Olossi because his team foundered and afterward reduced to begging. It happened. But Chaji's urgency infected Kesh. It was odd that the girl had seen him hanging around the Qin compound weeks ago.

Their biggest problem was in how to move through the city without drawing attention, because of course everyone noticed two armed Qin soldiers. They would have to hope that the beggar's attention would be fixed on the large party he was following, which was certainly roiling the waters. And not just because of the Qin soldiers and the huge slave. Everyone must stop to stare at beauty as it passed.

The red cap slid sideways to the side of the thoroughfare as, far up ahead, the company stopped at a merchant's stall. From within the crowd, he could not see what the merchant was selling, but then the object she held in her hand caught sunlight and flashed.

Mirrors, for the vain to stare at their pretty faces.

The beggar loitered. Keshad glanced at Chaji and Umar, and they nodded. Very suspicious!

The company moved on, the black-clad soldiers opening a wedge through the crowd not so much by forcing it as by simply being there. For a moment, the crowd thinned in just such a pattern that he saw her lustrous black hair arranged in a complicated set of falls held up by combs and hairsticks. She was speaking to the captain, laughter in the lift of her chin.

He was not a fool. Compared with the Qin captain, he could be of no interest to her. He didn't even want anything from her anyway. It's just she was clever and lovely and close at hand to stare at, when his heart was already torn in half and thrown to the wild beasts to savage because he had lost his sister and his purpose in life in one dreadful change of fortune. Because Nasia, the slave-woman who had been his lover, had stared at him with recrimination in her face, even as he told Mai to turn Nasia away from her only hope of freedom.

"Lost him," said Chaji as he shoved Keshad to get him moving.

"There he is," said Umar, behind them. "Beyond the gold awning."

As they cut past noodle shops, the singsong of the flirting ladle girls drifted alongside appealing smells: "hot and spicy! for the rains!" "best qual-i-ty, best qual-i-ty," "mushrooms and leeks, here's your mushrooms and leeks." At a plank table, two men chopped radishes and purple-heart; over a brazier, a girl slip-fried them with pipe-shoots and salt in smoky sesame oil.

Chaji grabbed his elbow. "There's Chief Tuvi, walking rear guard. Get moving."

The larger party was walking up the shoemaker's lane, the long way around to the district where the Silvers lived if you didn't know the city as well as Keshad did. But the beggar's red cap moved past the shoemaker's lane and cut up the tailor's lane, so they climbed after him, pretending at intervals to look at fancily embroidered festival jackets selling cheap because in the wake of the attack the city had not mustered a festival this year.

"The captain is actually the half-brother of the Sirniakan emperor?" Kesh asked.

Chaji gave a curt shake of his head, which meant Keshad had stepped out of bounds by asking an inappropriate question, and kept walking.

"Lost him," said Umar. "Hu! There he is."

They hurried through the bone-carvers' alley, in shadow under canvas slung between buildings. The carvings were polished to such a high gleam that they seemed alive in the dim light: winged horses, dancing lions, writhing salamanders, swimming dragons. Hugging the corner, they ventured onto a wider street. Uphill, Chief Tuvi's broad shoulders vanished around a sharp turn where the street split into three. A red cap slouched behind a pair of matrons.

"There," said Umar, starting forward, but Chaji caught him by the tunic and tugged him short as a barrow filled with bricks rumbled by, pushed by a sweating man wearing a linen kilt and an unlaced sleeveless vest flapping back from his torso.

"He's working with a second man," said Chaji. "That one with a rag tied around his left arm, standing beneath the green awning, behind the rack of sandals. He's seen us."

"The hells!" swore Keshad. "Two of them!"

"Maybe more. Where are Seren and Tam? Why haven't they caught up with the captain? It isn't like he's moving fast."

A whistle blasted above the street noise. Chaji bolted, Umar at his heels, shoving past anyone in their way as they sprinted after the company. Keshad found his way blocked by the barrow-man, who was swearing as he struggled to stop the unbalanced barrow from spilling. Kesh grabbed the lip and pulled, and the man thumped it down on its legs with a curse.

"Sheh! Cursed outlanders!"

The red cap bobbed past, flowing downhill. Keshad pushed past the same pair of well-dressed matrons and followed the cap down the street. The beggar ducked behind passers-by, then twisted into an alley. Kesh sprinted after him, but negotiating the confines of the alley of combs was not so easy because the artisans recognized him, Master Feden's household having spent a good deal of coin on fancy combs and lacquered sticks and clasps. A small girl seated with legs dangling from a second story balcony watched his progress, her round face solemn as she tracked him.

Panting, he came out into the tailor's street. He scanned up the angling terraced steps and down toward the sprawl of the outer city seen through gaps in buildings. A red cap bobbed in the crowd, then stilled as the man stopped and looked back.

To make sure he was being followed.

"Aui!"

Although similar in stature, this was a different man. He wore a subtly different twist of dirty kilted rags and had less of a bandy-legged gait, a man who had spent less time on horseback than the first beggar. Now that Kesh thought of it, where did a beggar get bandy legs from riding horses so much, unless he was an outcast fosterling raised and later discarded by the lendings?

Where had they lost track of the first beggar? It could have been at any time after Avisha had tossed two vey in the man's bowl. Maybe down by the gold awning amid the clamor and slurp of the noodle stalls. Easy enough to slide one red cap in the place of another.

"Guards! Murder! Murder!"

The red-capped head was still turned to watch him, and Keshad knew absolutely that to run down past that man would be idiotic. He plunged back into the alley of the combs and halted in front of the stall of a woman he'd dealt with a hundred times.

"Where's your mistress?" he asked the lad overseeing the wares. "Mistress Para!"

She was an attractive woman, her taloos wrapped around advanced pregnancy. But she was remarkably light on her feet as she emerged onto the porch with a cup in one hand and a tiny chisel in the other. "Keshad!" She smiled. "I heard you left the city."

"Heya! My apologies. Can I cut through your house to the alley behind?" Beyond the bright opening of the alley, traffic passed on the tailor's street.

She was Air-touched like him; it gave them a measure of kinship. She stepped aside, and he sprang up the steps in his outdoor shoes and raced through the workshop while a pair of apprentices paused in their work to gape. He ran down the long corridor that fronted the living quarters. Emerging finally in the narrow kitchen yard, he pelted through an open gate into the fetid confines of the back alley.

He cut back toward the tailor's street and hurried down the terraced steps toward the commotion below, where men were still shouting for the guard. He hadn't meant to cut so close to the incident, but when he saw Seren leaning against a wall, holding his side as though injured, he shoved through the traffic and fetched up beside the young soldier, who was red-faced, breathing raggedly, and doubled over, barely able to keep his feet.

He didn't touch him. "What happened?"

Seren was vomiting, his face gray with pain. The hand he had clutched to his stomach was slick with blood.

Beyond a gold awning where fry-ups were sizzling ran an exceeding narrow walk between three-story buildings, accounting houses topped by apartments. A young militia man appeared in the gap. Seeing Kesh, he beckoned him over.

"Weren't you one of the Master Feden's slaves? Aren't you hired now by the outlanders? Best you come see."

Back here the buildings were a maze, walkways barely wide enough to let a bar-row pass. They turned a right corner, then a left, and in the center of a stone drainage ditch awash in spilling sewage and flowing blood lay the other Qin soldier, Tam.

He was dead.

32

From a ridge, Marit looked over a substantial valley, green with the season. Far below, a lake and river sparkled in the afternoon sunlight. The Orator and her Three Daughters formed a bulwark to the southeast, snow dusting their heights and clouds threatening behind. To the east rose a sheer line of cliffs running almost due north and south, ends lost in haze. The uneven patch of lifeless brown scarring the lake's shore near the confluence with the river marked the town of Walshow.

Here on the northern frontier of the Hundred, where many weather systems met and mingled, the wind blew in changeable eddies. Vultures drifted along currents of air right where the foot of the long ridge met the valley floor. Far above, a speck circled, almost certainly an eagle, although it glided too high up for her to be sure.

She led Warning along the ridge trail to the road, a graded avenue that, having cut through the hills that separated the valley from upper Haldia, now switch-backed down the grueling slope into the depression. This late in the day, she had the road to herself, no traders, no casual traffic moving up or down. She might have flown it, but now that she had traveled all this way through the wild lands of Heaven's Ridge, keeping out of sight, she found herself reluctant to hasten into the belly of the beast.

And no wonder.

Where the road bottomed out on the valley floor, poles had been erected at in-tervals as trees are planted to shade a thoroughfare. Corpses in every stage of decay dangled from the posts, hoisted up by their arms and left to rot. Where the soft tis-sue had pulled free, remains had fallen into heaps on the dirt. Some of these bones had been weathering here for years, when they ought to have been offered release at a Sorrowing Tower. The impiety—the sheer scale of executions—was meant to in-timidate anyone approaching Walshow. Where had all these dead people come from? She remembered Sediya's chant: *"The weak die, the strong kill."*

She rode on through the drowsy afternoon.

Most of the trees in the valley had been cut down. Sheep and goats grazed among stumps. After about two mey, the scrub and pastureland spilled into fields being worked by men and women who kept their heads down, glancing at her swiftly and getting straight back to work. Threads of smoke rose from the town. It was too quiet. Chains rattled when the wind caught them just right. Skulls leered at her from the ground, tilted back to make their unhinged jaws open in a wide grin.

The poles with their corpses were, evidently, the first line of defense. The second was a stockade ringing the outermost neighborhoods of the city; beyond that rose an actual city wall with gates and battlements. Strangely, the stockade gate lay open and unguarded.

Beyond the gate, the outer town had the look of a place ransacked and left to recover. Ramshackle hovels sprouted beside sturdier row houses with shops in front and living quarters in back. Children ran away into shacks. A man trundling a barrow took a sudden detour, and a trio of women carrying washing in bundles atop their heads turned right around and hurried back the way they had come. She dismounted by the first relatively clean inn, chickens scattering from Warning's hooves as she walked the mare into the unswept yard.

A woman appeared on the porch, tying her black hair up into a bright linen kerchief in the northern style. Her eyes were darkly lined with cosmetics, and she smelled of sour milk. Within the inn, soup boiled, a thin broth flavored with smoky sesame oil. Her gaze flashed away from Marit, a tangle of startled wonder at seeing the sacred winged horse so close that she could distinguish each silver feather, and anticipatory fear because after all how could anything good come of one of them walking into her humble yard and maybe after all now she would get the news of his death because she knew it was coming eventually however much she dreaded it. A child cried in one of the back rooms. She bowed her head and hid her face behind her hands.

"Shardit, are you coming?" called a man impatiently from the interior.

"Shardit," said Marit, recalling the name. "Is your man with the army? Is that him in there?"

"Just a customer," she said into the space between her face and her hands. "I haven't seen my man for months, have I? What else am I to do?"

"Do what you must," said Marit hastily, thinking of Joss. "You have to go on with life. I'm not here to judge you."

The awkward silence dragged out. Inside, the child's crying faded to a grating whimper. A weight was shoved over a floor, like furniture being moved. Beyond the yard, a dog yelped; the steady stroke of someone chopping wood rang.

"Where can I find the commander's hall?" Marit asked.

"In town, in the old Assizes Court."

"In the Assizes Court? Where is the actual Assizes Court held, then?"

Marit heard Shardit's tone alter, because really even a child ought to know this. "Lord Radas runs the Assizes Court, him and his underlings."

"So that's where I'll find him?"

"Him?" The woman was surprised enough that she dropped her hands and looked: a shuddering memory of a man cloaked in sun riding a dazzling winged horse in the vanguard of a mass of armed men. "Neh. You're come too late. They've already left."

"Left?"

The hands came up to shield the face, like an act of obeisance. "They marched weeks ago. They're gone."

Gone.

"Where did they go?"

Shardit shrugged. "High Haldia first, then Toskala, and after that Nessumara.

Not that we were told anything, not folk like me, but the soldiers have a song about it. 'The cloaks rule all, even death.' The Star of Life will rule the Hundred. That's what they say."

"And then what? Will the soldiers who lived here come back?"

She hunched a shoulder, seemed about to turn away in shame but did not. "I have to hope they do. If there's no one to sup from my kettle, then how will I feed my children?"

"Did you live in Walshow before, or were you brought here?"

"Oh," she said, and then, "oh." She began to cry, not sobs but simply tears trickling down her face, the taste of their salt like sorrow.

"Can you go home?" Marit asked more gently.

The man called from inside. "Shardit! How long do I have to wait?"

"Why do you torment us?" Shardit whispered. "Teach them to kill, who were peaceful before? Isn't it enough to rule us?"

The hells!

"Don't give up hope," said Marit, and knew it for a stupid thing to say the instant the words left her mouth. She tugged on Warning's reins and rode out of the inn yard without looking back. There's only so much a reeve can do. But she swore under her breath the entire walk back to the outer gate, as if her words were knives to cut away the bonds that confined people like Shardit.

Guards had meanwhile shown up at the gate, two elderly men who raised hands nervously to shield their faces as she approached. Their rustic spears, little more than sharpened tips, leaned against their frail bodies to leave their hands free for the obeisance: the hiding of their eyes.

"Where's the army gone?" she asked them.

In stumbling words, clearly frightened, they told her the same story Shardit had. By the look of these broken-down men, Lord Radas had sucked the town clean of all able-bodied men and left the leavings to fend for themselves.

"Is Walshow abandoned?"

"The commanders pulled everyone out, Lady. By your leave, Lady. Is there aught we can do to serve you, Lady?" They cringed away from an expected blow.

"Nothing," she said furiously, which only made them cringe more.

Outside the gate she mounted, and gave Warning her head. Near here, surely, she would find a Guardian's altar. The horse must walk, then trot, then gallop and lift. She liked the horse, but the slow rise into the sky had none of the thrill of an eagle's thrust or soaring glide. It was more as if the horse paced out a road of air invisible to all others and rode it above the ground.

She surveyed the earth as well as she could, with the wings beating wide and, together with the body of the horse, blocking her view. An archer could loft an arrow into the horse's belly and she never see it loosed. From an eagle, you missed nothing.

She saw no rice fields, but a few agricultural strips recently plowed and planted. Orchards and pastureland made up the second ring, and beyond that—as she had seen before—the valley had once been forest, but it was all hacked down, leaving gouges in the earth and serious erosion where the rains had cut unprotected dirt into a hundred destructive channels. Charcoal heaps smoldered under caps of dirt.

They headed for the bulwark of the Orator. The stony peak lay directly ahead, her three daughters clustered close. The sun's last rays glinted on the spires, and as the disc slipped below the western horizon, the shadow of twilight grew. A wind out of the northeast thrummed in the spires like a voice too deep for its words to be understood.

Although the sun had set, a dazzle glimmered atop the rounded head of the shortest daughter. There they trotted to earth on a dusty top ringed by boulders any one of which might topple from the peak and crash down the steep face to the tree line below.

They had arrived at a Guardian altar.

She released the mare before setting her own feet on the labyrinth's entrance. She paced its measures, seeing how the different landscapes passed through late afternoon all the way into night and back again, depending on how far west or east they lay in the Hundred. She paused, recognizing the overlook onto Sohayil.

Twilight lingered in the west, surprise evident in his tone. "You're above Walshow!" he said through the crossroads that linked them.

"Hari! I hoped to find you."

"Why are you in Walshow? Just where you shouldn't be."

"The army has moved out. There's no one here but the folk they've left behind."

"Lucky for them."

"Maybe for the locals. There are others who are little better off than fish left to gasp on the shore. You're on the western edge of the basin of Sohayil."

"So I am. Lost and lonely and, fortunately, not with the others. Although I must soon join them. I have made of my assigned task an utter fiasco for which I will suffer, I guarantee it. Lord Radas sent that pervert Bevard to gather up the dregs of the broken army, and has called me back to him. Thus I linger in the west, and travel as slowly as I may." He laughed as he spoke, but the edge in his voice was sharp. "Where will you go now?"

"I'll ride the Istri Walk south, on the army's track."

"Why go after them?"

"Because I must. Just like you."

"Eiya!" But the lament sounded sweet spoken in that slurred foreign accent.

Saying no good-bye, she left him behind. She walked the labyrinth to its center, where she found Warning had already drunk her fill from a basin chipped out of rock, clear liquid seeping out of the stone to form a pool so still that she saw her own face as in a mirror.

She looked the same, brown face, brown eyes, black hair clipped short so it wouldn't get in her way. But she was no longer the reeve who had partnered Flirt. She was someone else now, a stranger with a face and heart she recognized but whose purpose remained in shadow.

She knelt, filled her bowl, and drank until she thought she would burn up from the inside. But she knew it now as the nectar that demons crave, the clear milk of the gods. She could exist without it, hiding from the others, but to drink it made her strong. It gave her the clarity she needed for the path ahead.

33

In the Qin compound in Olossi, in the center of the living quarters and sur-rounded by a porch backed with rice-papered sliding doors, lay a square courtyard. Lamps set on tripods burned with a particularly bracing flavor, purple-thorn seeds crushed in with the lamp oil, that mostly cleared the twilight air of insects. On a brick platform surrounded by troughs of flowers, Mai sat cross-legged on a pillow, happier than she had been in many days, because her dear friend had at last been al-lowed to visit.

"Anji has forbidden me to go to the market—to go out at all!—until they've tracked down everyone involved with the attack."

"If such people can be tracked down," said Miravia, "which I doubt. Really, any-one might have killed Tam. A Sirniakan spy posing as a beggar, as your husband be-lieves. A discontented laborer. A sweet-smoke addict. A thief."

Mai shook her head. "Only a trained assassin like one of the Red Hounds could have lured two Qin soldiers into such circumstances, and then taken them by sur-prise like that."

"Perhaps Olossi's sweet-smoke addicts have surprising talents."

Mai laughed, and then was ashamed she had done so, thinking of Tam, a polite young man who had never said more than ten words to her in all the time she had been with the Qin.

"It isn't funny, is it?" said Miravia as she picked up her ceramic cup and exam-ined, with half her attention, the egrets in flight painted around the white finish, brushstrokes of gray and black suggesting the movement of the wind. "Nor do I suppose a common thief or disgruntled laborer could have managed such a skillful murder, or known to put such a deadly poison on his blade. Your husband is correct in being cautious."

"Surely any attack is directed against him, not against me."

"Because of his connection to the Sirniakan throne?" She set down the cup. "But it has always been true that one way to strike at a man is to strike at what he values most."

"Must I live forever trapped inside the compound?" Mai rubbed her belly. A flut-ter like butterfly's wings startled her. "Oh! Here, feel it. It moved."

They sat in silence as Miravia pressed her hands over the curve of Mai's belly. Then she, too, gasped, and laughed. "I felt it!"

Priya looked up from her seat on the porch, smiled, and resumed her discussion with Miravia's brother, who naturally had to act as escort to make sure his sister was at all times isolated from the men of the house, although Mai suspected that he had also been tasked to make sure that Miravia behaved according to other more subtle strictures. Miravia's attendants remained beyond the doors, the veiled women in a private sitting room and the male guards relegated to duty beyond the private rooms in tandem with the regular Qin guard.

"It will be a healthy boy," said Miravia.

"That's what everyone says. Naturally I am required to desire a son first and second, and a daughter third."

"No, I meant that Grandmother says it will be a boy, so it will be." Miravia sipped thoughtfully at her tea. "Grandmother has been against my coming all along, of course, but Mother said you must be lonely in circumstances to which you are unaccustomed."

"So poor Tam, by getting murdered, made it possible for you to visit me?"

"Perhaps. But Grandmother herself tended that other soldier."

"She saved Seren's life."

"Yes. I never saw him, of course. That would never be allowed, as I remain unmarried." Miravia's tone slid toward a darker edge. "He was very polite to her even when the poison was at its worst. Since he was in unspeakable pain, she determined that even the lowliest Qin soldiers had sufficient good manners and proper notions of propriety as well as discipline to be trusted not to barge in and discover me unveiled. And trusted to guard me, in this house, since of course no household in the Hundred can be trusted to safeguard the dignity of women."

Mai picked at the tray of cakes and fruit. She was hungry all the time, nibbling constantly. "Even at home I was never confined like this, and certainly my father was strict about the dignity of the women of his household. It's just that I'm accustomed to being in the market. It's so dull, being stuck inside the walls all the time."

"You have plenty of company."

"That counts for something, certainly, but many of the women will marry and go off to establish their own households. So we must hope. Priya is always with me. And there's a sweet girl my age among the ones we're hoping will marry the soldiers. I like her, she reminds me of my sister Ti, but she is not a deep thinker, Miravia, if I may say so. As Ti would say, I think I would die die die if I couldn't see you."

Miravia pressed her hand softly.

In pregnancy, Mai's thoughts had begun to wander down strange paths unknown to her before, or perhaps it was the long journey she had undergone, from being Father Mei's favored pet in Kartu Town across months of travel through desert and hills and mountains to the fragile peace she had grasped for herself in this new land. Her thoughts, once confined by the limits of Kartu Town, had roamed into a wilderness she did not at all comprehend.

"Is it strange to say," she said hesitantly, "that even so quickly, I felt when you and I met that we knew each other already?"

"Not strange at all. Souls are reborn, and in their new lives they move toward the souls they have loved in previous lives."

"Is that what the Ri Amarah believe?"

"What we believe? It is the truth. Perhaps you and I were sisters in another time."

"I hope not among your people, for I think I will go mad with these restrictions!"

"Yes. Your husband is out on his own business."

Growing up in the Mei clan, where her father ruled with a whip hand and his wives by turns quarreled and cooperated, had not prepared Mai for her own married life. Nothing could have prepared her for Anji. He was indeed the very prince both dangerous and lovely who walked through the sentimental stories she had loved as a girl. The songs hinted of stolen pleasure, the sensuous delights of the bed, but in the Mei clan she had observed discontented or quietly abused women who had to accept every whim or cruelty laid on them by their husbands and masters. She had supposed her own husband would offer a similar service, the Gandi-li boy of whom she had never heard a bad word except that he was an obedient son of a wealthy family determined to increase its stature in town.

Anji was nothing like the colorless, uninteresting men of Kartu Town.

"You're blushing," said Miravia with a smile. "Is he very good to you?"

Grandmother Mei, disappointed throughout her life, had had sharp words for any person who admitted to happiness. She would crush a flower before she would see a child rejoice in its fresh beauty. Yet why allow Grandmother Mei's bullying ways to dictate her own path? If boasting was bad, surely it was because it demeaned the hopes of others, and embittered your own modest spirit.

"He is good to me. So is it wrong of me to be a little angry that he gets to go out, and I must be confined?"

"He's out on militia business." She gestured toward her brother. "It's not only women who aren't allowed to go where they wish."

Priya, wearing a humble cotton robe, and Eliar, with his butter-yellow turban wrapped tightly to conceal his hair, were bent over a scroll. Eliar was holding the ends open while Priya used a hair pin to point out the words as she followed them from top to bottom.

" 'To arrive on the far shore. Six virtues carry you, as ships ferry passengers across a turbulent sea. Generosity, which is communication. Discipline, which is openness. Patience, which is space. Energy, which is joy. Contemplation with the inner eye, which is awareness. The highest of these is knowledge, a sword with two edges to cut through the knot of confusion and trouble, the obstacles that confine us and stand as barriers to our liberation.' "

Miravia continued as Priya paused in her reading. "Eliar wanted to join the militia, but he was consigned to escort me, since he is my only brother of age, so you can see there are strictures laid upon men as well. Eliar is wild to go on some adventure. But no one will let him. It would be easier for me to go." She made a face to show she didn't mean it.

"You can conceal yourself under the veil and go anywhere you wish," said Mai, "and no one would recognize you. We could go out together, veiled in that way."

"Everyone who saw us knowing we were Silvers!" She spoke the common word for her people with a biting lilt. "Afterward we would have to face my grandmother, and your husband, dear friend. I do not have the courage to attempt *that.*"

The glamour of twilight passed; night settled, and with it the daytime sounds of rumbling cart wheels and casual traffic. Water burbled through the complicated system of pipes that fed the fountains of the compound. Now and again they heard the fire watch clapping through the streets, or a swell of singing from one of the temples, and once they heard a man's startled shout.

Eliar said, "The waters represent death? And the far shore is the existence we hope for after death?"

"No," said Priya. "To arrive on the far shore is to follow the path of awakening."

"There was still a light burning in your office when I came in," said Miravia.

"That was Keshad. He never stops working. I don't think he sleeps."

"Your factor?"

"One of them. He's young, but knowledgeable. I don't know if any of the Ri Amarah ever had dealings with him. He was a slave to Master Feden."

"Any merchant in Olossi knows better than to send slave factors to deal with my people. It would be terribly insulting."

Mai glanced again at Priya. Would Miravia hate Mai if she knew Mai had slaves of her own? Surely Miravia already knew, and looked the other way. And yet, Mai could not see the harm in it. Everyone kept slaves, who could afford to do so. Slavery was what happened to people when they had lost everything. Yet that did not mean slaves were not human. When folk mistreated their slaves or forced themselves upon slaves who had no recourse but to accept unwanted attentions, that was cruel.

"Cruelty is always wrong," she said.

"Yes, of course," said Miravia with a surprised look. "Slavery is cruel because it deprives a person of their own life and of their honor. It is always wrong to permit slavery."

This was treacherous ground.

Mai said, "Anji means to take a boat across the sea to look at the work being done in the Barrens, on our new estate, which I might remind you I have not seen—"

"Not that it isn't a hundred mey away from any kind of lively markets!"

"Don't remind me!" Mai laughed. "I will visit there twice a year to check on the herds. It sounds very much like Kartu Town, all dust, only with no market to liven the day. Many women who hope to marry the soldiers will be sent to live there the year around. Can you imagine!" She took a segment of sunfruit and considered its moist flesh, then popped it in her mouth and sighed as the sweet juices cooled her throat. "After the attack on Tam and Seren, Anji decided to increase the recruitment for the militia on the Olo'o Plain. He rode upriver with a company. He is sure another attack will come."

"From the empire? Or the northern army? Surely the leaders of the northern army know who was responsible for their defeat."

"Anji has many enemies." So the hero always did, in the tales and songs. Sometimes he won and lived, and sometimes he lost and died. And often he won, and died anyway.

"Captain Anji is a very clever man, I am sure from everything you and Eliar and my father and uncles say, not that I will ever be allowed to speak to him conversationally. I am sure he knows what he is doing."

"I am also sure of it, but that doesn't mean he isn't in danger. And it's doubly worse because Seren did not see who stabbed him, and was then overtaken by the poison so he never saw what happened to Tam."

She shuddered. Anji had arrived in time to see Tam's ghost, but of course he could not hear the speech of ghosts, and the spirit had departed with the setting of the sun. If only Shai had been here!

A dog barked, answered by another. In a nearby district, drums beat a rhythm uncannily like the thunder of hooves on a hard road, but the pounding faded away into silence. A light flared in the sky.

"What was that?" Eliar released the scroll, stood, and stepped into the open. Miravia looked over her shoulder, her brow furrowing with puzzlement as she stood and bent back her head, the better to stare. Twisting, Mai could see nothing above the curved roof.

Nearby, many voices joined in shouting, the noise expanding outward like the clash of bells. From the courtyards, at their stations, guards cried the alarm.

A door slid open, and Sheyshi came onto the porch carrying a tray of fresh tea. Oblivious of the others, she got to the steps before she responded to the outcry. She raised her eyes to stare along the peaked roof and, with a shriek, dropped the tray. The pot shattered. Miravia reached down to pull up Mai, but by now there was nothing to see in the sky. Yet shouts and curses from the gardens grew louder, more intense. Priya hurried down off the porch without putting on outdoor sandals.

"Mistress, come quickly. Back inside."

"What did you see?"

"A demon," said Priya. "Come quickly, Mistress."

"A ghost!" Sheyshi collapsed beside the shards of the teapot, weeping noisily. "It will eat us!"

"That horse had wings!" cried Eliar as he clattered up to his sister and gripped her shoulder.

"It is a Guardian," said Miravia breathlessly, her face alight with wonder. "A Guardian has entered your house, Mai."

The household alarm bell began to ring.

*   *   *

O'EKI SET ASIDE his counting frame and accounts book and rose from his desk. "Master Keshad, you've done plenty. I think you can quit for the night."

"No, thanks."

With a shrug, the big man padded off, remarkably quiet-footed given his size, slid open the doors that led in to the public receiving rooms, and left Keshad alone in the office.

When Keshad worked, he did not have to think. Tallying accounts focused his mind. Scraping ink from stone and mixing it with water into a fluid state calmed his trembling. The firm tap tap tap of beads, flung one into another on his counting frame, soothed him with its impersonal pattern. The hiss of lamp flame eased the raging of his heart.

Would he ever see Bai again? Even if she did return, what *was* she now? Did he mean anything to her at all? Or would she natter on at him, trying to force him into an apprenticeship to one of the seven gods, when in truth the gods meant nothing.

He scratched tallies onto paper: rates for timber bought by the log, hire for carpenters who would bring their own tools, and hire for tools to be used by the gang of debt slaves recently sent to the Barrens.

Why had that bitch Mistress Bettia paraded in with Nasia in tow? Only to stab at him? But maybe she didn't even know that he and Nasia, when slaves of Master Feden, had been lovers. She likely didn't know how he had rejected Nasia out of hand the day he had bought himself free from Master Feden's service. Why should Nasia have thought he would clear her debt, too? There was no way to prove that the pregnancy Feden had rid her of had grown from his seed. Surely Nasia understood that everything he had ever done, he had done to free Bai from the temple's clutches? Not because he loved Nasia.

He dipped brush to ink. While he could not write, having not been trained among the hierophants of Sapanasu, he had learned the tally marks and basic ideograms necessary to do business, to account, to recall. Anyway, it impressed the mistress when he announced he had done the tallying himself. Yet her two older slaves could write, and so could Captain Anji. There was nothing special about him, nothing anyone would notice or care about.

Why think about the captain's wife at all? Really, a man could bear her smooth expressions and pleasant smiles and doting looks for only so long. Her even-temperedness would become cursed tiresome.

Chisels and awls and files, on hire; straw bought for matting, and matmakers to do the work; extensive negotiations with the blacksmithing guild, since the captain hoped to entice a smithy to set up shop in the cursed forsaken Barrens. All dust, no markets. Keshad could think of few worse places of exile. Why would anyone want to live there?

He smiled, feeling the curl of irony in his gut. Anyone, that is, except a person who wanted to control the trade in oil of naya, now that it had been proven as useful in war as in healing and lighting.

More acquisitions for the house, coin drawn against the household treasury: a bronze alarm bell; breeding ewes and a pair of rams; homespun for the eventual bridal portions of twenty women who had agreed to travel to the Barrens and set up household shops there.

To marry Qin soldiers, and raise children of their own. All that time, when he was Feden's slave, he had slammed closed his thoughts any time folk discussed marriages of people they knew. Better not to hear about the things you could never have. A debt slave could never marry.

A bead of ink dropped from the brush to splatter on the finely grained rice paper. Aui! He was clumsy, distracted despite his best efforts, an Air-touched Goat whose mind could never rest but must skip from one thing to the next. He could not find peace, not even in prayers said over the prayer bowl he had received in the Sirniakan Empire when he had taken the oath of Beltak: *Accept my obedience, you who are Lord of Lords, King of Kings, the Shining One Who Rules Alone.*

Peace! Peace! Peace!

What did any of it mean? What did any of it matter?

Shouting broke the silence of his empty chamber. Doors, slid sharply open and shut, gave a series of reports like stick-fighting. He rinsed the brush and set it on its stand, untied his sleeves as he rose.

The alarm bell clanged. The very one purchased in the wake of Tam's death! The vibration shook through his feet. Who would protect Mai?

He unlatched and opened the secret door behind the scroll cabinet, and ducked into a narrow, lightless corridor that buffered the office from the main house behind. He felt along the brackets on the low ceiling above: one, two, three, four. A latch unhooked another secret door, and he slid into the crane room. By the light of a single flame, the white cranes gleamed like ghosts.

The shouting turned into a roar of confusion as doors drummed open and shut. A woman screamed. Mai!

Mai was in the inner chambers, entertaining the Silver girl she called friend. Of course he had never been in the innermost chambers, but he knew where they were. He ran through the rat room and into a featureless chamber with bedding rolled up against one wall and a door gaping. Two Silver guards with hair concealed beneath turbans had their backs to him as they stared out the other side. He shoved past them.

"Hey, there!" One grabbed for his shoulder. "You can't go in there."

With a splintering crash, a wall shattered. Both guards shouted in surprise. Keshad leaped across the corridor, slammed open a door, and dashed through a small room fitted with an altar at one end, draped with cloth and adorned with wilted flowers and the stubs of candles. Men shouted after him. He shoved the next door aside, and stepped onto a porch surrounding a squared courtyard open to the air. His foot touched ground just as bodies smashed through the doubled doors to his left: Qin soldiers in desperate fighting retreat. Wood cracked, spun in the air; scraps of rice paper floated.

In lamplight, Mai stood with mouth agape. Priya stepped in front of the young mistress. One of the soldiers—Jagi—loosed an arrow from his taut bow, but he was shaking so hard its flight went wild and stuck quivering in a beam. The Qin spread out in a half circle to shield Mai, Chief Tuvi at the apex. The chief's normally imperturbable face was creased with shock and—yes—*fear.*

A woman rode out of the house, ducking under the lower eaves of the porch. Her wings flared silver, only they were not wings but rather the flowing cloth of a gleaming cloak doubled over the paler silver-gray wings of the horse. She was a ghost, with pallid ghost skin in a round ghost's face, and ghost hair pulled into three braids like cords of straw. Her eyes burned with the blue fire of demons. If there was any doubt that she was a ghost, she had an arrow still quivering in her left shoulder and one that had caught in the fleshy skin of her neck, and although blood pulsed from the wound, she did not falter. Her gaze swept the courtyard, and when it flickered over him, he staggered, barely caught himself on a wooden pillar.

The hells!

She was the ghost girl he had found at the edge of the desert. When he had found her, she had been naked but for that silk cloak, mute and unresponsive. Whatever stirrings of sexual desire her white skin and pale-gold hair and demon eyes might have aroused in him when he had stumbled upon her, curled up behind a rock at the side of a dirt path, were nothing compared with the greed she had enflamed when he had realized an instant later that she was a treasure of incomparable worth. He had brought her, in hiding and at great expense, all the long journey north through the empire and over the high mountain pass, just so he could exchange her for Zubaidit's freedom.

Her gaze passed on as she dismissed him. The Silvers cried out with garbled words, like men waking into nightmare, and ran into the house, crashing into furniture in another room. Nearby, a female sobbed as in agony.

The big man stumbled into the courtyard through another door. "Priya! Where are you?"

The bold Qin soldiers were struck as into stone by the power of her demon gaze. She raised a hand, holding a mirror with brass fittings, chased in the old style. She turned the mirror to catch a reflection.

"Umar is now dead, like Eitai," she said in her dead, flat voice. She pointed to Chaji, who cowered among the soldiers. "You are the last one, Chaji. The wolf must cut out those who are diseased, to keep the herd strong."

Lamplight flashed in the mirror, a doubling and tripling of flame.

Chaji collapsed to the paving stones as though the strings to a dancing doll were sliced through and the wooden body clattered to the floor. None moved to attack. They were utterly terrified.

The demon gaze shifted, and halted on the big man, who cowered for all his hulking size. "You took the coin, and pushed me into the house, to let the others at me."

Mai stepped forward, around Priya, and pressed the older woman behind her.

"What do you want, Cornflower?" she asked, her voice alive in the air like the scent of flowers. "You are dead. Why do you haunt us? How can we help you rest?"

The two girls were of an age, Kesh thought idly and at random, both barely past girlhood and venturing cautiously into the bloom of young womanhood. But where Mai was sleek and cared-for, a well-tended garden showered with the constant rains of affection and admiration, the demon girl was all edges, no different really from the splintered doors hanging in tatters behind her.

She said, in her emotionless voice, "You did not harm me, Mistress."

"Neither did O'eki. He is a slave, as you were. He must do what his master commands. You cannot hold blame to him for that. Please do not harm him."

The mirror, still raised, shifted as the girl twisted it. Priya groaned, but the demon lowered her hand, hid the mirror's face, and stared at Mai. "What the master commands. Where is Master Shai? Tell me where he is. Then I will go."

And kill him were the words she left unspoken.

"Shai never touched you."

"He was my master. He took coin into his hand in exchange for three to rape me. How is it different to murder a man with your own hand, or step back and allow another to do the deed for you?"

Chief Tuvi struggled to raise his bow, and she fixed her gaze on him until he wept. She looked at each of the others to cow them likewise.

Mai took another step forward. "Shai is not your enemy. He was foolish, perhaps, but he did not hurt you. You don't know how many times he spoke to his brothers, asking them to take you away from Uncle Girish for fear and disgust at what Girish might be doing to you—"

The ghost girl gazed deep into Mai's face, and Mai's smooth façade crumpled as she moaned in pain.

"You suspected, but you did not know," said the girl. "Girish tried to hurt you, too."

Rubbing her belly as if it hurt, Mai said in a ragged voice. "Girish was a bad man, but Father never allowed him to touch any of us children. Shai tried to have you taken away from him because he pitied you. He pled your case—he did you no harm—I beg you—"

"North," the demon said, as if the word had been spoken aloud. "He went north, with the scouts."

She reined around the horse and rode away into the darkness of the house, broken lattices and shards of ceramics cracking under hooves.

Chief Tuvi shook himself, staggered upright, and loosed an arrow after her. Its thunk—burying itself deep in wood—woke everyone else.

Keshad's gaze drifted, seeing now the outlander slave Sheyshi curled beside a lacquered tray as she scratched at her own face with her nails until she drew blood. Seeing now Priya sobbing disconsolately as she staggered over to embrace O'eki. Seeing now a young Silver man reeling backward as from a blow, hands groping at the turban wound tightly around his head as if he feared that the cloth had unwound to leave his hair naked to the sight of all.

One other person stood in the small courtyard, shaken more with wonder than with fear, an oddly joyful expression infusing her exotic features. The Silver girl had not feared the demon! She had a handsome, if serious and somewhat square face, full red trembling lips, and eyes like a brushstroke, dark and mysterious and bold as her gaze slid to meet his.

She stared at him until he could not breathe, and found his knees giving way beneath him.

Then she smiled, grabbed a fold of cloth off a pillow and, shaking it open, threw it over her head to conceal her face from all those forbidden to see her.

34

Joss had never seen the Qin captain lose his temper, and it made him cursed uncomfortable the way the man did not shout or gesticulate but rather grew still and cold.

"Mai could have been killed."

"Here, now," said Joss, with hand raised, as he might try to calm an angry eagle with the gestures used as signals to train the birds. Hoods worked best, but not on humans. "It was a shock to me, as well, when I first heard. I came myself to find you. I wouldn't let anyone else deliver the news."

Joss had tracked Anji well north of Olossi, to the village of Storos-on-the-water, where lay a temple of Kotaru. Anji was attended by his usual pair of guards, Sengel and Toughid, and by Chief Deze. The rest of his company—about forty soldiers— waited in the outer training yard with several hundred locals. Three Olossi men had accompanied Anji on this expedition, a militia captain named Lison and a pair of merchants, one an older Silver man wearing a full set of bracelets and the other a robust woman representing the council, whose names Joss had missed. These three had invited themselves into the sanctuary courtyard to hear the news Joss brought. Two local officials—the censor of the temple and the village council mistress— waited also, looking torn between uneasiness and confusion.

"You did not witness the attack yourself," said Anji finally.

"I did not. Chief Tuvi alerted the reeve stationed in Olossi, who flew to Argent Hall at dawn and brought the matter to my attention. I returned to Olossi immediately and interviewed a number of people who were in the compound at the time as well as townsfolk who reported seeing a light and a winged horse above the city. Then I came to find you."

The temple of Kotaru stood on high ground between road and river; the creak of wheels as wagons rumbled along the Rice Walk melded with the flowing song of the River Olo. With towers raised at each corner of the square temple, it was a good place to oversee both river and road traffic. A good place to station a significant contingent of armed men.

"It's bad enough," said Anji, "to suspect Red Hounds from the empire are hunting me. To imagine that even after my mother cut my ties to the palace when I was twelve and sent me for safekeeping to her kinfolk among the Qin, my brother—and cousins, I suppose—still wish to kill me. Yet they are human, and might be reasoned with or outwitted. Nowhere is safe from demons."

"If it was a demon," said Joss.

"It was a demon," said Anji. "The person you describe was the slave. She died in the desert. No human could have survived such a sandstorm. You're sure the horse had wings?"

"The testimony comes from your own men. And from others in the compound who witnessed, the servants of your household as well as Ri Amarah guards. In addition, as I said, there were independent sightings from elsewhere in Olossi."

"Why were Ri Amarah guards at the compound?" asked the Silver. The man stood aloof from his Olossi comrades with his arms crossed and his slanted eyes giving him a suspicious expression.

What was the cursed man's name? Isar sen Haf Gi Ri. "Your son and daughter were visiting, in the private garden."

This statement surprised everyone except Anji. Isar muttered, skin suffused with blood. The hells! He was cursed angry, if Joss was any judge of expression. But he said nothing more.

"You do not think it was a demon," said Anji.

"If you have to choose between what seems the most reasonable explanation, and what the cold, hard evidence reveals, go with the evidence. It was a Guardian."

"The Guardians have vanished," said the temple censor, called Guri.

"A Guardian," said Anji, "who according to your tales hold an exalted position as guardians of justice. Yet a creature matching the description of these Guardians has murdered two of my men. Now that I think of it, it would explain Eitai's death some weeks ago in the Barrens. Sayan's report of the incident was so disjointed that we thought both men suffered a sun-sickness from heat and lack of water, and that Eitai died of it, but perhaps we were mistaken. Which means the Hieros was also mistaken in her assessment of the envoy of Ilu she thought was a Guardian, the one who removed the demon from her care."

"I would not lightly dismiss the testimony of the Hieros," said Joss. "She is no fool. He likely was a Guardian, but considering the subsequent behavior of the outlander girl, she was already corrupted."

"Or bringing what she thought was justice," said Isar.

Joss was surprised to hear him speak; the others regarded him as if his horns were suddenly visible.

"What do you mean?" asked Anji.

"My people do not sanction slavery. According to the testimony of the witnesses, the demon—the Guardian—the girl—accused three of your soldiers of rape. Those who are slaves have no right to say yea or nay over what is done to them. Therefore, a slave woman who is in that condition made to have relations with a man has no choice. That is rape."

"Not according to the laws of the Hundred," said Censor Guri. "We are not ruled by Silver laws."

Anji frowned. "She belonged to Shai. He sold her services to certain of my men one night only, which was certainly his right. When my wife objected, he ceased the practice."

"Your wife is an honorable woman," murmured Isar.

"I agree, although that is not the issue at hand. It would be easy enough to ascertain if the three soldiers who died are, indeed, the three who used her on that occasion." He indicated Joss. "But that does not explain how she killed them without leaving a mark on them."

Censor Guri stepped forward. He was a burly, muscular man in the prime of life, vigorous and a bit aggressive, a typical adherent of Kotaru the Thunderer. "Every Guardian carries a staff. So the tales say. Their staff 'measures life and death.' What if the Guardians walk the land to take vengeance, not to bring justice?"

Joss shook his head, his throat too tight to speak.

"Just because you don't want it to be true doesn't make it false," pressed the censor. "Just after the turn of the year, a family of refugees walked through Storos on their way to relatives farther north. They'd escaped from their village on West Track. They said folk saw a man riding a winged horse with the invading army."

"Which doesn't answer how it was done." The fury that had scorched off Anji earlier had subsided, to Joss's relief. "Is it sorcery? A sword has an edge, and can be met with other weapons. What weapon protects us against another attack such as this, whether demon or—as you say—Guardian?"

"Nothing," said the censor. "The gods set the Guardians over us, to serve justice."

"We cannot raise our hands against the Guardians," said the Storos councilwoman, Volla. "They possess a second heart and third eye, to see into the heart of every woman and man."

Anji looked skeptical. "That being so, I should think they would be frightening to meet. Who among us wishes his innermost thoughts flung open?" He tilted his head, considering his own words. "Although it might explain Chief Tuvi's lapse, which I can comprehend in no other way."

"No, indeed, Captain," said Chief Deze. He was a thin, phlegmatic soldier, tough as best quality rope. "Tuvi would die before he would fail you."

Joss wondered. If the Marit he had met at the refuge had not been a dream, as he imagined, then she had seen into his innermost heart. Now that he thought of it, she had often looked away while talking to him, as if she did not want to see the truth of what he had become. Aui! Blindness between lovers was a blessing.

"Marshal Joss," said Anji, calling him back to the muggy courtyard under cloudy skies. "I'd like to see for myself that my wife has weathered this storm before I continue my efforts here on the plain. Can you convey me to Olossi?"

"I can, and I will. My eagle needs rest, and meat. We've been a full day searching for you, and in any case he can't fly at night. We'll leave at dawn."

Anji turned to the censor and the local official. "That being so, we should finish our business. I have a proposition to make in my capacity as commander of the Olo'osson militia."

They walked back to the training ground, Joss falling to the rear. Every temple of Kotaru was arranged in four quarters, with four gates and four corner watchtowers. This temple had prospered and been requartered in the past. The walls of the original temple now constituted the barracks quarter, and new quarters for the sanctuary, workshops, and training ground extended from the old square, careful to keep a strict north-south and east-west axis despite irregularities of ground.

As they passed through the central crossing gates between the four quarters, Isar dropped back to walk with Joss.

"You said you interviewed everyone at the compound for their story of the incident. I trust you were not allowed to speak to my daughter."

"No, indeed, ver. That had all been settled before I arrived and everyone returned to their place. But I did receive written testimony from her hand, which was read out to me by your son, Eliar. I must say, hers was a forthright and clear-sighted account, very useful to me."

By his tightly clenched mouth, Isar was as angry, in his own way, as Anji had been earlier. And even less likely to be placated. "It should not have been allowed."

"That she give testimony, in such circumstances? Every free person who witnesses a crime is required to give testimony."

Everyone said the Silvers were cunning merchants. The look in those dark, slanted eyes was angry, certainly, but calculating in its own way. "But not slaves? Still, I was speaking to myself, Marshal, not to you. Forgive me for showing a father's vexation.

I knew such a reckless scheme would come to no good. Grandmother and I argued against it, but Eliar twists his mother around his heart, and likewise several of the uncles could not say no to the pleas of the captain's charming wife, for which I am sure I do not blame them." He nodded toward Anji, who was walking beside the censor, deep in conversation. "But it is to be understood that the virtue of a Ri Amarah woman is only safe within her own household. Now my daughter is compromised."

"Compromised, ver? For visiting the house of a friend?"

"You Hundred folk cannot understand."

"It is your people who live in the Hundred, not ours who live in a land of your making."

"So it may seem," he agreed. "Forgive me for speaking intemperately."

"Neh, think nothing of it. We are all upset to hear such strange tidings."

"Do you really think it was a Guardian, Marshal?"

"Not as we know of Guardians from the tales and the records of the assizes kept by the Lantern's hierophants. We hear no accounts of summary execution. But the other elements—the light coming from no visible source, the winged horse, the cloak—how are we to think otherwise?"

"The tale of the Guardians speaks of corruption: 'I know that in the times to come the most beloved among the Guardians will betray her companions.'"

"I fear the evidence suggests that such a terrible shadow has indeed consumed some of the Guardians," said Joss, feeling the weight of the words in his heart.

On the training ground, as the light deepened to a hazy gold in the last drawn sigh of afternoon, about two hundred persons had assembled: mostly young men with a few women and older men among them. Most were seated cross-legged on the ground, listening as a Qin soldier recalled the battle of Olossi in some detail. The soldier's precise descriptions, rendered without the gestures and chant usual to tales, brought a stark power to the narrative and held the locals quite fascinated. The rest of the Qin stood at the back of the group or had taken watch positions on the walls, keeping an eye on road and river.

Anji hung back, evidently not wanting to disturb the flow of the story. The censor bent his head close; the two men were still talking. Joss fell in beside them.

"I am aware," Anji was saying in a low voice, "that your militias are organized into cadres, companies, and cohorts. If you have experienced men to serve as sergeants, I am prepared to leave as many of my own men here to serve as captains, over companies, as you have companies to fill. How many companies can this area raise?"

"Who would command these gathered companies?" asked the censor.

"Naturally they will serve under your formal command and oversight, since you know the region best. Consider, if an army marches out of the north, it is likely they will use either West Track, as they did before, or Rice Walk, to approach Olossi."

"Having used West Track once, they might try Rice Walk the second time. Better forage, too. More paths to Olossi, won't be confined to the one road as they are on West Track."

"Exactly. Therefore, we must be prepared, and we must have trained, disciplined soldiers to face them. If I learned one thing from the battle at Olossi it is that the army—however large—that marched against us did not have good discipline. They expected that brutality and fear—and sheer numbers—would win the day for them. But it did not."

"How many soldiers do you want?" asked the censor, scratching his beard.

"Can you raise six companies?"

"A full cohort? The hells! That would be over six hundred men. Maybe in the tales you could gather so many. We're moving into transplanting season. Folk are needed in the fields."

Volla said, "How will these soldiers be fed and clothed?"

"Taxes, both local and regional. In kind and in coin. You are paying to protect yourselves."

Volla was about Joss's age, with a healthy girth and healthy color in her brown cheeks. Not a woman, Joss supposed, who dismissed danger lightly in the hope it would flit away. "We have seen refugees on the road, and resettled a few families in this area in the months since the year's beginning."

"You know what is at risk," said Anji.

"A standing army." The censor shook his big head like an ox dealt a blow. "I don't like it. Seems like too much. What do you think, Marshal Joss? I hear tell you came out of Clan Hall, before you was appointed marshal at Argent Hall. Not a day too soon, if you ask me, for there was trouble at the hall."

"There'll be worse trouble sooner than you dare think," said Joss. "There was confusion within our enemy's forces after the defeat in Olossi, but the northern army has redoubled its efforts to bring Haldia and Istri under its control."

"Haldia and Istri?" asked Volla. "That's a lot of country."

"Clan Hall sends reports that a huge army is marching south down the Istri Walk toward Toskala. If they take Toskala, and after that Nessumara, what's to stop them from striking against Olossi? Do you want to take the chance that they won't?"

"They might kill themselves, trying to do too much," said Guri. "Wear themselves so thin, they break."

"They might," agreed Joss. "I hope they do."

"Eiya!" said Guri. "I catch your drift. Well, then, Captain Anji, you're saying you'll leave a few men here to do the training, whip these colts into shape, and maybe keep the captaincies of what companies I can raise?"

"Trained men can go home to their farms once they're no longer needed," said Anji. "As I hope they can all do in time."

"I doubt I can raise an entire cohort, but I'll fling my net wide, as it says in the tale."

A delighted shout rose from the assembly as the soldier reached the part where the eagles had dropped ceramic vessels filled with oil of naya over the army. Yet the memory of what Joss had seen when oil burst into flames gave him no delight.

"We'll have some trouble raising taxes, in coin or in kind," said Volla. "Folk will want protection, but they won't want to pay."

"Do what you can," said Anji, "and apply to Olossi's council for additional supplies of rice and cloth if necessary."

Guri grunted, frowning as he narrowed his eyes. He glanced at Joss. "Giving Olossi's council another rope around our necks."

Volla nodded, but she looked skeptical. "Marshal, there's another thing, since you're here. We've need of a reeve to preside over our assizes. We have a number of cases to settle."

"I'll sit this evening, if that will help you. What I cannot clear, I'll be sure to let the stewards at Argent Hall know needs attention. They'll send a reeve out."

"I thank you, then. I'll see an assizes table is set up after supper."

"I have one other request," continued Anji. "If there are respectable young women available, looking for husbands, I'd ask that the men I leave here be allowed to marry according to the custom of your country and set up a household. I could have women sent up from Olossi, but it might provide my men with more stability within the local area if their wives come from local families."

"Outlanders." Volla eyed the dour Qin soldiers as they listened to the tale of their bravery and bold counterattack. "That won't be easy."

"Any woman who marries one of my men will live well, and be treated properly."

Guri shook his head. "Why is it necessary? They can visit the temple of Ushara, if that's what you're worried about."

"My understanding is that any man can visit a temple, or other such establishment," said Anji, "but that is not how a man would propose to conduct his entire life. Is that what you would want for your own sons, censor?"

"I have no sons. I've never married. I'm dedicated to the Thunderer." He chuckled as he looked Anji up and down. "I'm not fashioned in the same way you are. I like the same flesh Volla does."

She slapped him on the chest, in a jesting way. Joss smiled. These two trusted each other, which meant they could probably work together effectively in dire times.

Anji had a way of marginally tightening his eyes that revealed, to Joss, that the captain, however clever he undoubtedly was, had not worked out the meaning behind the exchange.

"Dedication to the gods is a worthy service," the captain said finally, "but nevertheless, my men want to get married. The temple is not part of the custom of the land we come from. No man of my people will feel himself complete without marriage. That's just how it is."

"Did none of these men leave behind wives in your old country?" Volla asked.

"Some did, but since we are exiles and can never return, those women may as well be dead to them."

She pressed him. "How can we be sure they will not mistreat a woman here? No offense intended, I'm meaning, just we hear stories about how badly the Southerners treat women."

"We are Qin, not Sirni," said Anji. "However, it's true not every mating is a happy one. It is dishonorable for one party to leave another without proper negotiations. If there is trouble, you may bring the matter to the attention of my wife, in Olossi. I can assure you she will not allow any woman to be mistreated. If any of my men does so, I will whip him myself."

This coolly delivered promise satisfied Volla. "I suppose a woman who marries one of your men will be assured a decent house and furnishings, utensils, clothing."

"The opportunity to set up a workshop of her own, if she has a trade, which is a condition my wife insisted on. I only insist that you deal fairly with my men in this issue, that only hardworking and healthy women come forward, not leavings that no other clan would take. If you would prefer negotiations on these matters to go through my wife, you will find her better prepared to answer your questions and deal wisely with your concerns."

Volla examined the captain, then gave a swift and rather admiring once-over in Joss's direction, enough to sweeten his grin. "I'll see what I can do. Guri, what do you think?"

"I think he's not your type," said the censor, tilting his chin toward Joss. "I don't trust them when they're that handsome *and* they know it."

She chuckled as Joss felt himself redden. Then she sighed. "It isn't only rumor that discontented lads have walked north looking for adventure and never come home. That debt slaves in greater numbers than usual have vanished up country as runaways. Villages have been burned. The roads aren't safe. Trade is hurting. We must be prepared. I just don't know why we need outlanders to raise and train companies. What's wrong with the likes of Censor Guri, here, and Kotaru's ordinands, and the local militias? No offense meant, Captain Anji."

Captain Anji had a tough hide, able to take these repeated slings without showing their impact.

"No offense taken, verea. Your militias and ordinands are sufficient for local traffic, but in terms of disciplined troops who can act in concert at range, and under severe conditions, you need a different sort of training, a thoroughgoing element of toughness. That's what my troops can provide. We are the skeleton of a new fighting force, one that will protect Olo'osson. Every man willing to take up arms can receive the same training."

"I don't see we have a choice," said Guri. "It's true enough that Kotaru's legions are trained to serve local matters and local manners, not to march in cohorts under the command of a single general. But this is my question. Put our men under control of the city, then what's to say the city doesn't decide it controls us? Neh, Marshal?"

"The man's got a point," said Volla.

"It's a fair enough question," said Joss. "But these aren't ordinary times, Censor Guri. If the Northerners attack again, having learned from their last attempt, we can't fight back as a scatter of small units. We'll be crushed."

"Let me tell you something about my mother's people, the Qin," said Captain Anji. "Our ancient enemies are demons who live in the west. There are a lot of them, I assure you. They steal young men and women from our people when they can." His gaze drifted to a point somewhat above his listeners' heads, and for a pair of breaths he stared pensively into the sky. By the way his jaw tensed, he was thinking about a matter that displeased him. Then he blinked, relaxed, and continued.

"Why have the demons not overrun us? Because we have a var—a king—while demons always fight among themselves. They have no leader, no general. So we ride as a united people, and they scatter themselves into tribes." With a half smile, he nodded at Volla. "Not that I'm comparing you folk to demons."

She snorted, pleased with his turnabout joke.

"But bear in mind," he went on, "that those who lead the northern army don't care about niceties of Hundred custom. You can take your chances with an army in which you have some say, or you can take your chances with the invaders, who won't stop to ask your leave. That's how I see it. I came here to make a home for myself. I don't want to ride to war. I want to live with my wife and raise my children—if I have many children, as I hope—in peace. So I'll do what I must, to get what I want."

AT DAWN, JOSS rose after too little sleep, washed his face, dressed, and slouched out to the gates of the temple. Thank Ilu that Volla had kept the assizes polite, swatting down witnesses and offenders who threatened to become unruly or loud. She had kept him supplied with a good stock of decent wine. His head ached, but so far it was a dull throb.

A number of locals, some he'd heard from yesterday evening, had gathered at the gates of the temple, come to purchase vials of oil of naya—best-quality water-white—from the Silver merchant before the troop rode on. Anji finished delivering instructions to the five soldiers he was leaving behind in Storos, then walked over to Joss.

"If one of the reeves can return me to my company after I've assured myself all is well with Mai, I'd be doubly appreciative," he said, pulling on gloves.

Joss rubbed the back of his neck, hoping to to find the root of the ache and smooth it out. "Your company is not riding straight back to Olossi?"

Anji shook his head. "We must set up additional training camps and muster in as many recruits for training as possible, immediately. Just as you're training reeves—and I'm training more soldiers—in the Barrens."

"Ah, yes. In the Barrens." Joss nodded toward the gate. "Do you have an arrangement with the Silvers?"

"With the Ri Amarah? What do you mean?"

"Isar is selling oil of naya. A precious commodity, found within lands you've now claimed, in the Barrens."

"King's oil—that's what they call it in the empire—is renowned for its healing properties. The Ri Amarah concentrate on physic and ointments, items easily carted in small amounts and used for healing. Which they sell at a fair price, and make available to all, not just the wealthy."

"Captain," said Joss with a laugh, "was that an answer?"

Anji's smile when it came was full with real amusement. Aui! The man had dimples. Who would have thought it!

"Better to speak truth to the man on whose harness my life will be dependent, eh?" he said. "Lest, like an arrow, I be loosed to fall to earth."

"I'd not loose you for anything less than, say, stealing your beautiful wife."

That was the wrong thing to say. Anji's grin vanished, but after all he was still looking at Isar. The other Olossi merchant was talking to various local men and women, but she hadn't brought anything to sell to the villagers.

"I've been betrayed three times, Marshal. I don't give my trust easily. The Ri Amarah have dealt honorably with me, and given sanctuary to my wife."

"I was joking about stealing your wife," said Joss hastily.

Anji raised a gloved hand as a customer dismisses an offered cup of cordial at an inn. "I know it. You're an honorable man, and you're too old for her anyway."

The silky way the words slipped out made Joss wince.

"And there's your weakness," added Anji, a wicked gleam sharpening his straight-lipped expression. "You're vain of your good looks and your ease with women."

"Ouch. So what's your weakness, Captain?"

"Not for me to say."

"Your love for your wife?"

"Not at all. She is my strength. It's not my place to go naming my weaknesses. That would be like showing my enemy where I'd placed my most inexperienced tailmen."

Joss laughed. "You're a hard one to catch out."

"I trained in a hard school, the palace school of the imperial palace in Sirniaka."

"Would the Red Hounds who serve the emperor really track you into a foreign country?"

"Track the emperor's half brother? Especially now that the emperor is facing a revolt from his cousins over whose claim to the throne is most legitimate? My brother considers me a danger to his position, and my cousins likely more so, as I am the only other surviving son of Emperor Farutanihosh, who was their father's older brother. Or do you think Tam was killed by the demon you're calling a Guardian?"

"He was murdered with a poisoned knife. And your other soldier poisoned as well."

"Seren's life was saved by Ri Amarah healing, I remind you. He and Tam had nothing to do with the demon girl, ever. Indeed, Seren complained bitterly about her traveling with the company. Many of the men did. They wanted no demon to bring ill luck down on us." He stroked his tightly cropped beard. "Listen, Marshal. The local militia has looked into the death of Tam. But if the deed proved to be of local origin, some malcontent, would the Olossi militia hesitate to turn on one of their own?"

"You don't trust them, even though you are—as I believe—their new commander?"

"I'm an outlander in their eyes, however appreciative they might be that my men saved them. That's another reason I must recruit more widely. I mean to create an army out of men drawn from all over the region who will be trained under banners, not with their local cousins but with strangers. They will learn to be loyal not to their village but to Olo'osson."

"A dangerous thing, an army," said Joss. "As Censor Guri pointed out."

"As you must all know by now, seeing what havoc an army can wreak on an unprotected population. Nevertheless, if your reeves might investigate, I'd be grateful. I want justice for my dead soldiers, as any captain would."

Joss nodded. "We have our ears and eyes open. Are you ready, then? I'll call Scar."

"I'm ready."

Joss raised the bone whistle to his lips, but lowered it before he blew. "You never answered my question about the Ri Amarah, and the oil of naya."

The dimple flashed again. "Marshal, don't you know that I leave all trading arrangements to my wife?"

*   *   *

MAI PLACED FLOWERS on the altar, a table raised on bricks and covered with a red cloth. An image of the Merciful One gazed upon them with a gentle, almost detached expression of compassionate enlightenment, an upraised hand to signify awakening and another hand cupped at the belly to signify comfort. The colors in the painting glowed, not quite yet dried. The features and robes had more straight lines than curves, reflecting the style of the Hundred, but the artist had done a decent job in a short time with an unfamiliar subject.

"I offer these flowers at the feet of the Merciful One. Through the merit of offering may I walk the path of awakening. The color and fragrance of flowers fades, so does the body wither and disintegrate. Receive this with compassion."

She sat on the floor beside Priya. Sheyshi and several of the younger Qin soldiers sat behind them in the small room, while at the open doors several soldiers and a few of the local women watched. Priya led the chanting.

"I go to the Merciful One for refuge. I go to the Truth for refuge. I go to the Awakened for refuge."

As Priya chanted on through the Four Undertakings, the Five Rewards, and the Six Virtues, Mai heard voices elsewhere in the house punctuated by the clack of doors slapped open and shut. Men shuffled by the entry, rustling and murmuring, and she lost track of the thread of Priya's prayer. A little annoyed, she looked over her shoulder to see who had the audacity to disturb them.

The onlookers made way as Anji stepped into the room. With only the barest flicker of a glance in her direction, he knelt at the back of the room, sitting with hands open on his thighs. He closed his eyes. The disturbance raised by his entrance stilled. Priya had not faltered, and she worked on through the Seven Candles, lighting each stick of incense, and the Eight Truths, while Mai struggled to regain the momentary peace she had felt when she placed the flowers before the image of the Merciful One.

"Merciful One, your wisdom is boundless. Excuse me for the transgressions I have made through thoughtlessness, through neglect, through fear. May the rains come at the proper time. May the harvest be abundant. May the world prosper, and justice be served. Accept my prayers out of compassion. Peace."

Mai rose and walked out of the chamber to her private sleeping chamber where no person but Anji or Priya would dare follow. As Anji did. She turned to face him as he slid the door closed. He remained by the door, she by the wide pallet and its neatly piled coverlets.

He studied her with a frown. "You are well? Unharmed?"

As with a cloudburst, the sky opened. "She had only to look at me, and it was as if she ripped free every terrible memory I ever had. There was one time I was not more than six or seven, and Uncle Girish wasn't more than thirteen, and he sat down beside me in the garden and started stroking my hair in a way that made me feel dirty. When I tried to get up he dragged me back by the wrist to sit beside him. Then Father came out into the garden, and he beat Girish until his nose bled and one of his teeth cracked, and told him that if he ever touched any of the household children again that he would kill him. Afterward when Grandmother saw Uncle Girish's bruises she went crazy yelling and screaming at everyone because she never liked Father even though he was her eldest. He was Grandfather Mei's favorite so she hated him because she hated Grandfather Mei, and anything Grandfather Mei liked, she hated. It was an arranged marriage, but the matchmakers weren't careful enough, and it poisoned her. So because Grandfather Mei thought Girish was too fussy and spiteful, she loved Girish best even though it spoiled him until he fermented. Well, she loved Hari, too, but everyone loved Hari. And then after Grandmother's tantrums, Girish tried to lord it over Father, and Father made all of us little children come into his office and then he choked Girish until he blacked out, and then he said to us, if he ever touches one of you, tell me. So Girish left us alone except to say ugly things to us, but of course now I see he must have gone elsewhere where folk weren't so particular about what he did to children. Cornflower poisoned him, and then tried to poison herself, but the poison didn't kill her. Mother and Aunt wanted to sell her, and Grandmother was delirious with grief, but the men refused to sell her away. They couldn't let her alone. In a household like that if there is one female who gets special attention from all the men, then usually the other women are jealous of her, but no one hated her. They wanted to be rid of her—which is how she got sent with Shai—but they didn't envy her. Maybe they were grateful to her for killing Girish." She was in a sweat, mouth dry. "Merciful One! I'm babbling."

"No, you're making a good deal of sense." Still, he did not approach her. "She is a demon, Mai. That you resisted her testifies to your strength. Chief Tuvi says you saved O'eki's life, when everyone else was helpless. Let us hope she has taken her revenge and will leave us alone."

The knot that weighted her heart unraveled in a scalding explosion of tears. "B-B-But she's going north to kill Shai! Because of what I said."

She sobbed so hard she was only vaguely aware of Anji drawing her down to the bed, sitting with arms around her, holding her close as she wept. As the storm faded, he wiped her running nose with a cloth, pressed a cup of juice to her lips. She sipped, and hiccoughed. He wiped her eyes with a finger, kissed her, explored the curve of belly with a tentative touch.

She hiccoughed again, and blew her nose. "Isn't there any way to warn Shai? Couldn't the reeves look for him?"

"The demon has to track him down first. I'll talk to Marshal Joss." He startled, sitting straight, and pressed a hand against her belly. "What was that?"

She shifted his hand to a lower spot. "Did you feel him move?"

"A boy? How can you be sure?"

"It's what the Ri Amarah women say. Oh, Anji, now I've gotten Miravia into all sorts of trouble. The men came crashing into the courtyard—breaking everything—the new doors aren't in place yet—and Keshad came running from the office, not to mention the Ri Amarah guards and O'eki. All those men who aren't her kinsmen saw her unveiled. That won't be forgiven, you know. They'll never let her come here again. Because of you, and the oil of naya, they've let me visit her once there. She's so unhappy."

"We cannot interfere with the customs which the Ri Amarah hold among themselves. There, now, Mai." He flicked a finger against her chin, smiling softly. "Did you get it all out?"

She took in a shuddering breath and let it out as a shuddering sigh. "I suppose so."

"I will stay in Olossi for a few days. The marshal and the Hieros mean to call a council meeting to address this business of the demon. I've words to speak about the formation and disposition of the militia."

"Then you'll leave again?"

"I will."

"Why must you be gone so much?" She hated the way her voice sounded, and with an effort, finding her market face and her market voice, she pressed two fingers to his lips to silence his reply and went on in the tone she would use toward customers, light and cheerful. "I know you must. It's just that I miss you. I got accustomed to being with you every day."

He kissed her fingers, grasped her wrist, and drew her hand away. "I'll keep you beside me every waking and sleeping hour while I am here. But these matters will need my attention for some time. We have to prepare. You're going to the Barrens."

"I don't want to go to the Barrens!"

"It's the only way I can know you are safe. We've seen it's impossible to guard you here. I don't know who killed Tam, or who sent the demon to kill Chaji, Umar, and Eitai."

"Demons walk on their own feet, as it says in the songs. They have volition, and thought, and they can hate and love, just as humans can. Maybe no one sent Cornflower. She walked on the trail of her own grievances. Anji! If I'm sent to the Barrens, there'll be no market, nothing but grass and sheep like out on Dezara Mountain back home. I won't be able to see Miravia!"

He released her, stood and, after a moment, extended a hand. She considered pleas and protests, but discarded these useless thoughts at once. She knew better. Taking his hand, she allowed him to pull her to her feet.

"I will do what I can," he said. "This is a temporary measure, but I have decided. There will be no more discussion."

35

Despite living for twelve years as a slave to one of the most prominent men in Olossi, Keshad had never set foot inside the council hall. As a lad he had often waited outside in Fortune Square for half the day, slumbering in the heat with his master's umbrella tipped over him to keep off the sun, waiting for Master Feden to emerge so he could shade him on the walk back to the clan compound.

Situated at the city's highest point, Fortune Square offered a view over tile rooftops and the steep peaks of raftered halls, over narrow alleys and broad avenues, courtyard gardens and humbler courts where washing was hung out. The noise of construction rose out of the lower city, where buildings were rising in the gaps where the fire had eaten holes. The light was muted today, pearly beneath clouds. No one was carrying shade umbrellas.

A pair of militiamen stood guard at the door to the stone watchtower with its open roof and fire cage. A line of supplicants, rain cloaks slung over their shoulders or draped over an arm, waited with varying degrees of patience in front of the council hall. Here a free man could bring a grievance, although no slave ever could. In Captain Anji's company, Kesh walked past the supplicants and up the steps. The soldiers took up positions on the porch as he followed the others inside. An entry chamber stretched the width of the hall. It was empty except for a clerk sitting at a low table among a disorganized scatter of tablets and scrolls. Looking up, she spattered ink from her brush onto the table.

"Marshal! Captain. Verea." She offered Kesh a puzzled nod, not sure how to place him, then bent to wiping up the stain. She was a bit older than he was, nicely curved but nothing special to look at even if the cursed reeve flirted with her.

"I'm glad to see you well, Jonit. You and your family survived the assault unscathed, I hope." The grin flashed.

The woman blushed. "I did, thanks to the Qin." She smiled nervously at Captain Anji.

Mai smoothly interposed herself into the breach. "Jonit! We've met once before, in the guest house of the Haf Gi Ri. Aren't you a dear friend of—" She hesitated, glancing at the men. "—Master Eliar's sister?"

Keshad knew that her name must never be spoken aloud. He still did not know it. He closed his eyes, and at once recalled her face, the subtle smile, the moist red lips, the searing gaze that had cut right through him until he could see nothing else.

"Keshad. This way."

The captain's voice was as good as a yank on a chained man. Kesh stumbled up another rank of steps, looking over his shoulder at the chamber they were leaving behind. The central screen depicted a lovingly painted Ladytree beneath whose branches lay a pair of abandoned orange slippers. How appropriate! Every council hall ought to ornament its entry hall with the tale of the Silk Slippers, which featured much lying and conniving and brutality, even if the innocent girl did triumph in the end. They crossed under a stone archway that opened onto the council garden. Here council members might while away the heat of the afternoon before an evening council session. Here allies might plot among the troughs and terraces of flowering shrubs and ornamental trees ruthlessly pruned back. Here enemies might agree to agree as they undertook to stab a third party.

He knew what he had to do.

Their allies waited under an open pavilion. The three Silvers—two old and one young—turned toward the approaching company. With punctilious courtesy they greeted Mai, Anji, Marshal Joss, and Jonit. The resemblance between the young Silver man and his sister was noticeable, the same straight brow and full lips, but the brother lacked the intangible boldness of spirit that animated the young woman. Eliar cast a look at Kesh as venomous as the snarl of an enraged lilu thwarted of her prey, so Kesh hung back on the steps, using one of the pavilion's pillars as a shield. The older men pointedly ignored him, but he knew who they were because they worked with Mai on various mercantile pursuits: Isar, and his elderly cousin Bethen, both with forearms entirely ringed with silver bracelets.

On the other side of the pavilion, across from the Silvers, a curtained palanquin rested across two benches. A youth dressed in vest and kilt bent to tie back the curtains, revealing the Hieros sitting on pillows within. The old bitch greeted Anji and Joss, acknowledged the Silvers with a polite gesture as cold as it was correct, nodded at Jonit to include her, and paused to look at Keshad and then deliberately away. The slight did not disturb him. Nothing disturbed him now, except the memory of *her* face.

Last, she examined Mai. "Captain, is this your wife?"

Before the captain could reply, Mai stepped forward with a smile and a courtesy. "You are the holy priestess, the Hieros, who presides at the Ushara temple outside of town. I give you greetings, holy one. I am Mai."

"Prettily spoken," said the Hieros. "You have not come to the temple to worship."

"No offense is intended, holy one. I pray at the altar of the Merciful One, who is not known in these lands."

"Gone altogether beyond. An odd philosophy, if you ask me, but there is no accounting for the thinking of outlanders. There was an orange priest who lived for many years on the Kandaran Pass, begging for alms. He also dispensed healing and—so folk said—wise advice on the topic of household troubles. But he is gone now, to wherever his kind go after their spirit departs the world."

"You have heard of the Merciful One!"

"Do not look so surprised, verea. It is my business to keep my eyes and ears open. That is why your husband and I must meet. To exchange information."

"Of course, holy one."

"There, now, Captain Anji. I have satisfied myself as to her beauty and her good manners. You are a fortunate man."

He lifted both hands in a gesture of surrender to the inevitable.

"When I was a child, folk would talk about me as if I wasn't there," said Mai in a sweet voice.

"And with a bite, too," added the Hieros. "You may come to visit me, verea, if you wish it." She smiled, seeing the captain's expression transform from a pleased smile to a sharp frown. "Come directly to me, I mean, without walking in Ushara's garden, Captain. I have no hidden motives. You outlanders have peculiar customs, binding to yourselves what is meant to be shared freely according to the will of each person. But in any case, I am merely interested in talking to a outlander woman who walked into these lands of her own free will. The few outlander women who come here, come as slaves. They are often ill used. While I accept that those with debts must sell their labor to survive, I agree with my Ri Amarah colleagues, even if they remain suspicious of our gods and of the Devourer in particular. Those who have no choice in the act of devouring are being abused, not honored. Indeed, I say so especially because it is my life's service to honor the path of the Merciless One, the All-Consuming Devourer."

"I would like to visit you, holy one," said Mai, the words so sincerely meant that it seemed she was oblivious to the undercurrents swirling through the pavilion.

"Best we discuss this at another time," said Captain Anji, looking cursed grim.

The Silvers wore sour expressions, their trim little noses out of joint as if someone had suggested one of their hidden women dance naked at the festival.

With a burst of feeling as strong as being up to his neck in an outgoing tide, Keshad knew where he belonged: on the side of those who thought young women ought not to be locked up in their father's brother's house, or bound into years of unwanted servitude to the temple. Yet those who owned the chains would keep binding what they found useful, or desirable.

"I have something to say!" He leaped up the steps.

The captain set a hand to his sword's hilt, and the marshal gripped his baton. Eliar cocked a first, ready and eager to take a swipe. The Hieros's attendant stepped in front of the old woman, his body her shield.

But Kesh plunged on. "You said yourself you meet here today to exchange information. About the goings-on in Olo'osson and the city, I am sure. Yet you also sent a group of scouts into the north weeks ago to see what they can discover about the Star of Life."

"We have," agreed the captain, removing his hand from his sword. "And not heard word back. Where are you going with this?"

"No doubt the reeves will be searching for the demon who killed the Qin soldiers, who may also be a Guardian, whatever a Guardian is, since obviously the tales are mistaken."

"I admit the incident took us by surprise," said Marshal Joss, "although we're not agreed on what it all means."

"If the Guardians have become demons, best we be prepared," said Anji.

"That envoy wore no shadow," said the Hieros. "Of that, I am determined."

Joss nodded toward her. "As it says in the tale, 'He wore no darkness, not even a shadow to follow him.' Meanwhile, we're keeping our eyes open. I've sent reeves out to see if they can track the demon." He nodded at Mai, whose face lost a little of its luster to anxiety. "We'll try to warn those people who may be in danger, including your uncle."

"So," continued Kesh. "All this you have encompassed. But what about these ones

Captain Anji calls the Red Hounds? What about men in red caps and their accomplices who stalked the Qin through the streets of Olossi? Who Captain Anji believes came from the Sirniakan Empire in search of him? The ones who murdered Tam?"

He had their attention.

"We have no good sources of information in the empire. I am sure, Your Holiness, that your hierodules and kalos comb what bits of gossip and hearsay they can from those outlander drovers who visit the temple. I am sure everyone in Olossi interviews every merchant who returns from the south."

"We listen," said the Hieros. "Anyone would."

From this angle, he could see across the garden and through the archway, glimpse the figures of men and women passing through the entry way to the council hall, folk who had a stake in Olossi's prosperity and well-being.

"Advance me coin to purchase trade goods. I'll go south as a merchant. I'll investigate this civil war between the emperor and his cousins. I'll look for traces of the Red Hounds. I'll keep my eyes and ears open. I'll be your spy."

"You'll slip your bonds," said the Hieros. "Run away. You are our surety for Zubaidit."

"Do you think there is a life for a man like me in the empire?"

"A merchant can live in the caravanserai in Sarida," said Anji. "Live well, if his chief concerns are food, drink, and luxurious furnishings."

"Always as an outlander. But that is the risk you will take, in the hopes of gaining the intelligence you want. I might take the coin, and never return, that's true."

"Your sister will be angry if you aren't here when she gets back," said Marshal Joss.

Kesh wanted to say, Not as angry as you'll be if you can't get her in your bed, but he did not. "If I'm not here. If she returns. You can't guarantee she'll return. She'll probably get herself killed, and then where will I be? Working as a factor for the Qin."

"Do you have complaints of your treatment in our house?" Mai asked with every appearance of genuine concern and a smidgeon of indignation. Or perhaps she had simply the best disingenuous market face he had ever encountered. "You are not being held in any manner of slavery."

"A chain is still a chain. I live on the sufferance of those of you who are making the plans. Give me eight months' parole. There's still time to make the crossing before the snows set in. I'll gather what news I can, and return to you by the end of the year. Any profit I make after repaying the cost of the goods, will be mine to keep."

"A bold offer," said the Hieros. "And a dangerous one. Worthy of your sister, if you can pull it off."

"Why do you want to do this?" asked the marshal. "For your sister's sake? To act in service of the captain? Of the Hundred? Or the gods?"

"No." Kesh glanced at the Silvers, but of course they had no idea of the riot of confusion that raged in his heart. "I act purely on my own behalf. For my own selfish reasons."

"We have sent spies into the north," said the marshal. "It's true we'd be wise to send them into the empire as well. If it can be managed. Keshad knows the territory. But the council must approve the expedition."

"Wouldn't it be better if no one else knew?" asked Anji.

"I agree," said the Hieros. "If too many know, it will jeopardize his mission. Word will get out. Whispers will spread. If these Red Hounds are as skilled as you say they are, Captain, they'll find out the truth and murder the lad." She looked not at all distressed while considering such an outcome.

Anji nodded at the Hieros. "It must be assayed in absolute secrecy. Although I don't like to think of Keshad attempting this alone. I can't send any of my soldiers with him, either to aid him or to prevent him from running away and cheating us all, or selling what he knows into the hands of our enemies."

"I'll go," said Eliar. "Even with him."

"Impossible," said his father.

"Imprudent," said Anji. "Your way of dressing betrays you. Nor would I ask you to dress in another way to disguise your heritage."

Opportunity is an open gate. Kesh saw it clear. "Why should he not come along? I am also a foreigner. I might dress the part, but no one will ever mistake me for a Sirniakan. If he draws attention by his looks and clothing, more may overlook me. As it says in the Tale of Plenty, 'While everyone watched the barking dog, the carter crept into the storehouse and retrieved the stolen rice.'"

"Are you comparing me to a dog?" demanded Eliar.

Keshad smiled spitefully. "It is the custom in the Hundred to ornament our words with our sacred tales. The barking dog is a bold and clever hero."

Eliar stepped forward, fist raised, jaw clenched.

"Enough!" Joss stepped between the two young men. "I have no patience for young men preening and bumping in this tiresome manner. If you cannot work together, I will not be persuaded of Eliar's fitness for the expedition. In any case, according to your own laws, Eliar, you must obtain the permission of your elders."

Scenting victory, Keshad bit back a triumphant smile as he lowered his gaze modestly. The floor of the pavilion boasted a mosaic of tiny tiles cemented together in a stylized pattern of light and dark, fortune falling and rising.

"Let me do this," said Eliar passionately to his father, "and I will agree to all the demands you've made."

"Even both marriages, your own and your sister's?" said his father.

Surprised, Kesh looked up.

Eliar flushed, his expression twisted midway between grief and shame. "Even both marriages. May she forgive me."

The two older Silver men glanced at each other, caught by surprise. "You're sure, Eliar? You have stood fiercely in opposition to her marriage."

"I'll take an oath on it," he said bitterly, "and hate myself after."

"Do not make a mock of it, boy," said his father. "The negotiations with the house in Nessumara are badly damaged, close to falling through, because of your objections and the recent impropriety." There was a dull anger in Isar's eyes that Kesh found frightening, although he thought it was not precisely directed at him, the stranger who had glimpsed the face of a daughter of the Ri Amarah, who must walk veiled in front of any man not her kin.

"Is it decided, that they'll go south as spies?" asked Joss. "I am not sure I approve."

"I think it's an interesting plan," said Anji. "Although I hold out little hope they'll discover much of interest. If the Red Hounds scent their intentions, they won't survive. You must understand the risks, Isar."

The talk of marriage had settled Isar's mind. "We'll put forward the coin for the expedition."

"I want my own share," said Keshad. "My own profit."

Marshal Joss pressed a hand to Kesh's shoulder, forced him to look into his eyes. For the first time, Keshad shrank back. The Silvers were strict, everyone knew that. Captain Anji was a soldier, a dangerous man who knew how to kill. But Joss, for all his careless charm and his flirting ways and—so it was whispered—a tendency to drink too much, had the gaze of a man whose honesty could not be bought or bargained with. He would walk with you every step of the way, until you crossed his line.

"Are you sure you're doing this for the right reasons? That you want to proceed?"

"I'm doing this," said Kesh. "And you can take my offer, or leave it."

"Bold words," said Joss. "Spoken passionately."

"Eliar," said Mai, "are you really going to sacrifice her happiness in exchange for being allowed to go, when if you would only wait and be patient—?"

Eliar turned away, bracelets jangling. Shoulders heaving, he stamped down the steps and strode off into the garden.

"Mai," murmured the captain, "this is Ri Amarah business, not ours."

Bowing her head, she hid her eyes behind a hand.

Kesh knew. They all did. It might as well have been shouted. In exchange for getting to do what he wanted, run away—the best phrase for it!—on an adventure just to scratch his own festering itch, the cursed Silver would acquiesce to forcing his sister into an unwanted marriage no doubt with some old goat of a lecher eager to seize on her astounding beauty. No one would squeak, because that was what people did: They married off their young ones according to what benefited the clan.

Not if he had anything to do with it. The roads to Nessumara were not safe, and might not be safe for many months to come. They couldn't haul her off yet. He had time.

One way or another, he would find a way to save her.

36

They camped on rough ground several mey outside the city of Horn where, years ago, a battle had been fought. An overhang sloped deep into an outcropping of rock, giving enough shelter that they dared build a fire and boil rice. Shai whittled. Zubaidit cleaned se leaves with a scraper. Tohon fed the fire one dry stick at a time to keep the heat even under the pot. Edard was on watch. The other three had crept away to another nook in the outcropping, but even so, Shai thought they were being awfully noisy, all that giggling and enthusiastic panting.

"I have a question," said Tohon, twisting his ear as he studied the flame.

When he faltered, Zubaidit looked up. "There's little you could say that would offend me, Tohon."

The scout probed the fire with a green stick, maneuvering a hot flare under the belly of the pot. "Sometimes it is hard to know what I am asking. Among the Qin, we are not so—well—so free with all this."

"I'll talk to them. What possessed them to get into it now, I can't imagine. I thought they had more self control. We could be attacked at any time, as they know, and they're—"

Tohon coughed.

She chuckled. "Sorry."

He raised a hand to show no offense taken, and glanced at Shai. But Shai had nothing to say; he was more concerned with stifling the signs of arousal in his own body, because it was difficult not to pay attention to the whispered encouragements, the moans and groans. Whew! He bent his knife to the wood and shaved away a rough bump.

"You are a whore," said Tohon.

"A hierodule," corrected Zubaidit without heat. "A whore takes coin. I serve the goddess, and give freely in the act of worship. Eridit's all right otherwise, it's just she's got a compulsion to get every male she meets chasing her ass. It's cursed tiresome. Anyway, she's one of Hasibal's pilgrims, so don't think this is part of the Devourer's worship."

Ladon staggered out of the darkness, tying closed his jacket. "Aui! I didn't know anyone could be so *flexible!*"

Tohon and Zubaidit broke into laughter. Shai covered his eyes just as Veras, in the nook, came to climax on a series of rising yips. Everything seemed very hot. He ached.

Edard stomped into the light, bow in hand. "I'm of a mind to send you three back to Olossi. Could you be any stupider after what we've already been through? Eh, Ladon?" He raised his voice. "Eh, Veras? As for you, Eridit, you deserve a whipping."

"Promise?" came her bright voice. "I can tell you just the way I like it."

"What the council was thinking I don't know, since you two lads are as worthless as any rubbish I've stuck my foot in. I guess your clans paid them off, eh? Eridit at least is useful as a spy, and for impressing the cursed savages, and for that matter, now we know she can shave every cursed soldier in the enemy's army until they beg for mercy and surrender. Get your ass in here, Veras. You can't even report for watch duty on time, too busy getting your sword sheathed."

Veras hurried in, wiping his mouth. "Shut it up, you canting ass. She sheathed you a few days ago, didn't she? You angry you're not enough for her?"

Tohon scratched at his ear, he and Zubaidit exchanging a glance.

"Don't give me any of your piss, Veras. You were given explicit instructions when you volunteered for this expedition. I'm in charge."

"Bet you wish I was like Shai, here, and never said a word, eh?" He mumbled a rude word under his breath.

Eridit sauntered in, wearing a cotton shift that left little to the imagination and loose trousers slung low around her hips Hu! Even knowing she strutted around that way on purpose, he could not look away.

"Is it my turn?" asked Tohon.

Zubaidit grunted with choked-down laughter.

"Ouch." With a rueful grin, Eridit got her hair twisted up and fixed with a comb, then lowered her hands to splay on her hips as she surveyed the unhappy fireside scene. "I earned that, didn't I? Sorry. I should have known better."

"This is not an entertainment, and we're not your audience." Edard was red-faced and stewing. "You three could get us all killed. We've stayed one night too many out here, hoping to find some cursed leavings from the battlefield to console our mute friend there. I've had enough. Time to move on. And once we're past Horn, the more likely we are to run into trouble. Gods help us all if you three have your trousers down when those bastards find us. Can you two lads get that through your ass-crazed heads?"

"Rice is done," said Tohon.

Smelling sweaty and salty, Eridit sank down beside Shai. He eased away, making her smile. In a huff, Veras grabbed his sword—his fighting sword—and stomped out to take the watch. The scrape of his feet as he climbed the outcropping serenaded them while Tohon spooned out rice onto se leaves. They ate in silence. Shai tried not to look at Eridit, but she was magnificent with her lustrous black hair, her glowing brown skin, her sleek curves, her inviting smile and coy glance. Zubaidit made him nervous; Eridit made him hard.

"I guess I wasn't thinking," said Ladon suddenly. "I'll do better. I know I was fortunate to be chosen. It's just—" He looked at Eridit, and chuffed out a breath between closed lips. "Aui! That was something! Do they do it with three at the temple, Bai?"

"Did you ever ask?" retorted Zubaidit.

"You'd be surprised what's available at the temple if you think to ask," said Eridit with a purr that made Shai's whole body shudder. She crept a bare foot over to rub against Shai's, and with his ears burning and his face aflame, he jerked his foot away.

"Leave the lad be," said Tohon quietly. "He's not accustomed to the ways folk have here."

"You outlanders are a puzzle," agreed Eridit good-naturedly. "Is it true you've no temples to the Merciless One?"

"We do not."

"How do young people meet the goddess for the first time, if they can't go to the temple? How do folk married by their clans get their pleasure if their partner's not to their taste, or if one is not fashioned that way? Even if they do like each other, how do they learn new tricks, keep things fresh, eh?"

"It's not our way," said Tohon. "A man marries."

"That's it?" Edard pulled a comical grimace. "Only to have relations with the person your clan chose for you? Never to worship the Merciless One?"

"A man may have more than one wife, of course. If he can afford her. Keep them satisfied. A mistreated wife can appeal to her family and raise a feud. Everyone knows that."

"And a woman can have more than one husband?" Eridit asked with a teasing grin. "Like they say the lendings do? That sounds fun."

"That would not happen. Also, a man may go to the brothel for relief. Or buy a slave for a concubine."

Eridit frowned. "What about women? What are they to do? For relief?"

"Women aren't so free," said Tohon. "If you were my daughter, or my wife, I'd have to whip you for such behavior."

"The hells you would!"

Tohon had a sweet smile. "We are not in my country. Now we are Hundred folk."

"I'm going to sleep," said Edard.

Rain spattered the rocks. On the outcropping above, where he was keeping watch, Veras swore as he scrambled for shelter.

"This smoke is getting to me," said Ladon. "I'll go over where we—eh—anyway, it's dry there." He walked out, hunched under his short cloak as if he was still embarrassed. Edard followed him. Zubaidit strolled to the mouth of the overhang, where she leaned against the rock and stared into the night, her head tilted at a pensive angle.

Tohon hooked the pot's handle and lifted it off the fire, setting it on the dirt nearby and covering the mouth with a lid. "If I may say so, lass," he said to Eridit in a pleasant voice, "you do yourself no honor by teasing the men so they are set against each other. You may get attention, but you do not get respect."

She crossed her arms over her chest. "You don't intimidate me, Tohon. I get masses of respect, flowers and gifts heaped at my feet."

"Have you ever killed a man?"

"I've slain many! They fell at my feet. And wept with pleasure." She looked Shai up and down with such a pressure of sensuality that he wished he had the courage to beg her to stop. Her dark eyes and thick lashes were beacons. Her hips slid sideways as she leaned toward him.

"Shai's a good boy, but he's young and untested and likewise raised in a town where a lad like him hasn't much chance to meet a woman like you. Anyone can kill a man who is unarmed and unprepared."

She shifted away from Shai, her gaze fixed on the scout. "Aui! Are you saying I can't seduce you, Tohon?"

"You can't. Marry me, maybe. But I don't think we'd suit."

She laughed so hard that Zubaidit turned from her contemplation of the rain and walked back to the fire. "I'll win this duel. I'll wager you on it."

"When I scout, I don't play games." Despite the even tenor of his voice, the words were a warning that cracked her so hard she got to her feet and stamped outside into the rain, pouting.

He studied his palms in the light of the fire, unaffected by her outburst. "What think you, Zubaidit? Split up Ladon and Veras, and they will get smarter. Together, they goad each other. If one is reckless, the other must be, also. Edard is strong, but he is no leader."

"He's well connected. Branches of his clan run river transport all over the Hundred. If anyone can hauls soldiers by boat or move oil of naya in bulk to combat the northern army, they can."

"I see his value. But he needs a guiding hand, and he will not take one. As for her, she should be at home birthing healthy children."

"Are you saying a woman has no place on this expedition?"

"You are a woman. Eridit is skillful at disguise. She collected useful information in Horn three days ago. And that tale she sang had real power. But she has never actually killed a man. We cannot know if she is prepared for what will come. Why did the temple council send her?"

"And the Hieros agree to it? I don't sneer at her ability to disguise herself, ask questions, and chant tales. She's proven herself more valuable so far than the militiamen and the ordinand. Because truly, I ask myself if those four are the best Olossi could put forward for such a crucial expedition. Have we become so ill prepared, all of us?"

"We soon find out."

"So we will. I'm going to sleep."

He nodded. "I will take first watch. I wake you later." He began scraping clean the used se leaves. "Shai," he added, without looking up, "best you catch some sleep, also."

"And I wish you would stop talking so much, little brother," said Zubaidit from her blanket.

Stung, Shai sheathed his knife and wrapped up the carving in a strip of cloth. "Better to keep your mouth shut and be thought a fool, than to open it and be proved one."

"Wit to go with those brawny arms!" Chuckling, she yawned and turned over.

He settled against the rock wall, where even if it rained hard, he'd be sheltered. When he closed his eyes, he thought of Eridit. He was hot all over. Impossible to sleep in this state. He herded his thoughts to cooler pastures. Stuck without horses, they'd trudged east-northeast for many days, careful not to stray into the Lend. Edard had suggested again and again that they return to Olossi and get new gear, but Tohon and Zubaidit had refused. Horses were useful, but not necessary. Like himself, he thought as he drifted off to sleep.

SHAI DID NOT like to think about things that bothered him. If he did, then he felt as if they nipped at his heels wherever he walked. As Eridit was doing this morning as he trudged a final time over the remains of a battlefield.

"It has to be the battle where your brother was lost," she was saying. "Everyone I talked to in Horn agreed there had been a cadre of outlanders with the troop. No one had seen anything like them. The time is right, if you think he could have died three years ago."

He stooped to turn over a rock. Bugs swarmed over white roots, like thoughts hiding from the light. He settled the rock back in place.

She went on. "The odd thing is, no one knew where the outlanders came from, or where they were going. Or who the men were who attacked them and wiped them out."

They reached the highest point in the tumble of rocks where they had made their camp. Shai halted in the shadow of a huge rock to survey the grass and scrub growing in the hollow beyond. There were remains scattered all the way from the banks of a distant stream cutting down the far slope to these outcroppings, as though the men fighting had done it on the run.

"The folk I talked to said everyone died in the battle. But I think a few of the outlanders were still alive. From what folk let slip, the Horn folk came through afterward and slit the throats of the wounded rather than try to heal them. The other group ran away."

"Folk lie."

"It seems likely." She rested a hand on his elbow.

He shifted away.

"Don't tell me you've never had sex."

He turned away so she wouldn't see how red he was. "I went to the temple in Olossi."

"One time, I hear."

"I've been to brothels in Kartu Town." Only twice, but he needn't say that! Anyway, the girls there had been glazed on sweet-smoke, unable to distinguish one man from another.

"Some things in life can't be bought or sold."

"You keep slaves here." He met her gaze defiantly. Let the Hundred folk preen and spout about their temples; that didn't make them better than the people of Kartu Town.

"Sure we do. There are folk who like that a person hasn't any choice. I think it's disgusting." She pressed his shoulder back until he was caught against the rock, then leaned against him. "What do you think?"

Ragged corners of rock poked painfully into his back. "Slaves have no will of their own," he said hoarsely. He could feel the pressure of her all along the length of his body.

"What does that mean?"

"They are disgraced. They have no honor."

"Maybe so, or maybe they were just unlucky." She licked her lips in a manner meant to make him crazy, and it did. "I wasn't asking about slaves anyway." She traced the line of his body from chest down his torso to a hip, and slid her hand around to cup one buttock. "Aui! You have a good, firm shape. We could do it in the crevice over there, and no one the wiser."

"Stop," he whispered.

She ground her hips against his until he thought he would burst. "You're not going to find any trace of your brother after four days looking over this cursed field. I'm bored waiting around, and when I get bored I get in a devouring mood, even if I am one of Hasibal's pilgrims. So I'm going to devour you, right now, because you want it, you're just too shy to say so. You need a little spice to heat you up, get that . . . tongue . . . of yours slick."

She steered him to the crevice, a slit mostly covered by a fall of vegetation sprinkled with orange flowers. He caught a whiff of their sweet scent as she dragged him through the vines. She pressed him down on the dry dirt floor and peeled back his clothing. At first she sat astride him fully clothed, teasing him with her hands and lips as he groaned and writhed, rocking herself against him until she gasped to a climax. Then she loosed her own trousers and straddled him.

He gasped and moaned, delirious, mounting, gone.

"I knew that would be fast," she said, hands on his shoulders, her pink tongue peeping out between slightly parted lips. "You'll last longer next time." She stroked his torso. "Whew! You have a body a woman could just devour again and again. Do you want to try it a second time?"

"Eridit," he said, but her name exhausted him; he could think of nothing to say to her except that all he could think of was wanting her to devour him over and over and over. No wonder they called their goddess merciless.

A fluttering bird's whistle rose on the air.

"The hells!" muttered Eridit. "That's the signal."

She scrambled to slip on her trousers as Shai rolled into a tangle of his own clothing. She ducked out from under the crevice as he tried to get everything straightened out so he could dress. By the time he crawled out and stood, an eagle flew so low overhead that he yelped and dropped to the dirt.

"Hurry!" Eridit dashed back to grab his wrist. "A reeve is here. They weren't supposed to contact us! Edard will be furious! They could break our cover."

They cut down over uneven ground between ridges of naked rock and bumpy grass-grown slopes. The eagle had come to earth beyond the eroded remnants of a once great spine of rock, a bit downslope toward the depths of the hollow, a landing spot that might conceal the eagle from any folk walking on nearby West Track or more distant Horn. The reeve had already unhooked, and he left his harness dangling free behind him as he strode up the slope.

Edard trotted down to meet him. "Be quick about it so we're not spotted, you rank fool!"

"Strange, I was here before," said the reeve, unaffected by Edard's snarling demeanor. "Be sure I wouldn't have cut my flight short if I'd not been commanded to deliver a personal message to one of your party. I'm called Volias, by the way. The man I'm looking for goes by the name of Shayi. An outlander." He bent his sour gaze on Shai, but was distracted by the sight of Eridit sauntering up. "Whew! What's *your* name?"

"No luck today," she said with a flirting smile.

"Didn't I see you in Olossi, at the arena? Aren't you the Incomparable Eridit?"

She did not take the bait. "Beautiful eagle. Is she friendly?"

"That might depend," he said.

She shook her head with a mocking frown. "You need work, ver. This is Shai. What's your message?"

"Yes," added Edard, "and then get gone. Cursed idiot. Where are you headed?"

"None of your cursed business, is it?" With a sneer, he turned to Shai. "Captain Anji's wife said to tell you—and I'm just repeating her words, they mean nothing to me, mind you—'Beware of Cornflower.' "

"What is a cornflower?" asked Eridit.

"She's haunting you, on your trail, out for revenge."

"If Mai meant the slave girl," said Shai, "then she's dead. She vanished in a sandstorm. No one could survive that."

"He's not too swift, is he?" said the reeve to Eridit.

"Umm. But tasty."

"Oof! That hurt! All right, *Shayi.*" The reeve mangled the name, and seemed to enjoy doing it. "I think what the captain's wife is trying to tell you is that you've got a demon stalking your tail."

Hu! His body recalled how it had responded to the sight of Cornflower's slight, pale form, her demon-blue eyes, her passive air. Every one of his brothers had tasted her, repeatedly; he had refrained, but not from disgust. Not from not wanting her. Not at all. He wiped sweat from his brow, shut his eyes, trying to wring from his memory the image of her lying on a pallet dressed in scanty bedroom silks, trying to freeze his body's fresh stirring of arousal.

"A lilu, eh?" said Eridit, who missed nothing.

Edard said, "if you've delivered your message, get moving."

"Where's the rest of your party?"

"The rest of the party is smarter than these two nimwits," said Edard. "They stayed hidden. You find what you were looking for, Shai, or are you ready to give up on it?"

As Shai opened his eyes, his gaze wandered to the reeve with his harness clipped tight around his torso and his tight leathers beneath, the trousers ornamented by a polished belt buckle engraved with a wolf's head.

He took in a sharp breath. "Where'd you get that?" he demanded.

"Get what?" asked the reeve indignantly.

"The belt buckle." Shai raised his right hand to display the wolf ring, sigil of the Mei clan into which he had been born. "That belonged to my brother. I recognize it." The shock of seeing it made him come alive, as if he were already moving, an axe in its downward swing.

The reeve leaped back, raising his baton. "The hells! Don't come any closer."

Shaking, Shai lowered his hand, now curled into a fist. He was about the same height as the reeve, but bulkier, and he felt his strength in the way his entire body was poised; but he also recognized the reeve's ready stance.

"Heya, Shai," said Eridit in a cool, amused tone. "We're playing for the same side, neh?"

"Want to get out of here now?" asked Edard. "If you would be so kind, reeve."

The reeve furrowed his brow, and slanted a glance at Shai. "Yet it's true, I found it. Here, on this field."

Shai's tongue rooted; he couldn't speak.

"Down this way," said the reeve.

"Stay here, Eridit," said Edard sternly. "Go gather your gear."

Shai stumbled over every bump and root that hooked his path, while the reeve glanced back several times, no doubt the better to eye Eridit from the rear. The reeve fetched up near where the stream cut through tussocks of flowering grass and white-barked saplings growing among low-lying rocks. Farther upslope, scrub trees and brush covered the hillside.

The reeve searched along the bank of the stream until he reached a spot dense with human remains left to the weather.

"It was . . . right . . . here." He probed with a boot, and lifted his foot a hand's width with a curved bone caught over the arch. "I found it under this fellow."

If a tree had hit him square in the back, Shai could not have dropped harder to his knees. A jumble of shapes and colors pulsed before him: green grass blowing; the white cradle of bare ribs; red-clay-colored cloth pressed into the loam, becoming part of the weave of earth. Nearby, a skull was lodged upside down between rocks in the stream, water flowing through the eye sockets. White flowers bobbed on a nearby bush. From deep in the branches, a bird peeped at him, black eyes gleaming.

"I need to get on." An object thudded to the ground by Shai's knees. The man walked away as Shai stared at the buckle; the wolf's head stared back at him, black on silver. He sucked in an inhalation as he grasped it.

Hari!

Dead. Dead. Dead.

With a trembling hand Shai touched the shattered rib cage. Closing his eyes, he tried to snare the lingering whispers of a spirit from the sun-warmed bones.

These were not Hari's bones.

A man shouted.

Shai started back, his hands cold and his chest heavy. He scrambled on hands and knees through the scatter of bones, touching leg bones, arms, fingers, a mandible. So many dead men, carved by death out of life and sent fleeing through the Spirit Gate. But none of them were Hari.

Yet Hari had been dead when he had last been wearing the belt buckle. Hari's wolf sigil ring had come to the family through convoluted channels, more by accident and chance than purpose, so Shai believed. Hari's ring, too, had whispered of its owner's death. But Hari's bones were nowhere to be found, or at least, not here where he had left his ring and his buckle. Weeping, Shai sank onto his heels, head cupped in his hands. The obvious answer sang in his ears: Hari had died elsewhere, and another man had robbed his corpse and worn his fine ring and buckle until he himself was caught by the death that attends those who march to war.

Enough.

An eagle rose out of the outcropping, whose bare stone shouldered above dirt in rough surfaces and ragged spills of rock like massive frozen waterfalls. Men flowed out of the rock, spurting from between ridges, cascading down the slope.

They had seen him.

They were armed.

He tied Hari's belt buckle into his sleeve and leaped the stream, landing up to his knees in the rushing cold water. He splashed through and scrambled up the far side as shouts were loosed at his back. He sprinted up the slope to the shelter of the low-lying scrub. Thin straggler vines whipped his face; branches caught in his clothes as he tore through. His cap came off. The racket he made as he thrashed through the brush was trail enough for his pursuers.

He dropped to hands and knees and scrambled among narrow trunks, squiggled into a thicket and lay, panting, on his belly. He eased around, to watch the way he had come. Branches snapped and slithered as four men pressed past not two body's lengths from him. He could not see their faces, only their legs. White and pale pink flowers danced in the taller scrub trees as the wind rose, melding with the stamp and disturbance made by the searching men. Maybe rain would blow through, discourage the hunters, and leave him free to—

A thorn pricked him. He shifted to get out from under it. The point pinched harder.

"Get up," said a man.

The point of a spear jabbed hard enough to break the skin.

Cautiously, he eased up to hands and knees.

A kick planted into his rear sent him sprawling into vines and thorns. A second kick caught a hip, and as he struggled to get out of the thorns, the kicks kept pushing him back in until he simply went limp and lay like he was dead. Blood tickled along his spine; his skin stung where the spear had poked him.

The spear jabbed a new spot.

"Get up," said the same voice, in the same flat tone, no pleasure in it, no giggling sneering gloat.

He had learned a few tricks from the Qin soldiers. With a spinning roll, he knocked the point off his back and got his hands on the shaft with a wide grip. He wrenched the spear out of the man's grip, twirled it, and smacked him upside the chin with the shaft.

The man dropped right into Shai, his weight smashing him backward into a bush. Shai shoved him off, then levered the spear under him to push himself up.

Too late.

Others pushed into view. Two had swords, three had spears, and one had a bow nocked with a ready arrow.

"Not bad," said the bowman, standing in back of the rest, partially screened by brush. "Kill him now, Sergeant?"

"Give us the spear, lad."

They looked like ordinary folk on the surface, bedraggled from tearing through the scrub, but their eyes were hard and their clothes mismatched, and they carried their weapons like they wanted an excuse to use them. Three had lips stained red, the sigil left by sweet-smoke, whose mark he'd seen on Girish. The addicts looked ready to kill if given the order. The fallen man groaned as he staggered to his feet.

"Cursed outlander!" he growled. "Can I rip his balls off?"

"Neh. The master will want to know what he's doing here pawing through the battlefield right where Lord Twilight was raised. Looks like he was traveling with that ordinand."

Had they captured Edard, too?

Was it better to fight and die, or give up your freedom now in the hopes of winning it back later?

He released the spear.

A man grabbed it and smacked him alongside the face. He blacked out.

And came to retching, with them dragging him through grass. They had been joined by more soldiers.

"Walk!"

They pulled him past a pile of clothing discarded on the ground, only there was a man still in that clothing, a face staring up at the sky and mist rising out of the nostrils in a roil of confusion.

"Why will folk never listen to me when I try to warn them? Heya! Shai!" Edard's ghost writhed toward him, mouth widening in an exaggerated grimace. "Did I tell you my clan's password to make contact in Toskala? Someone needs to know. 'Splendid silk slippers,' like in the tale. Same as our badge."

Shai had never been so afraid in his life, to see a ghost calling his name as its cloudy essence chased after him.

But of course, no one else could see. They just thought he was struggling to get free.

"No fighting, or I'll let Twist cook and eat your balls after he's cut them off."

"Don't want to eat them," said Twist, to the laughter of the others. "Want to make him eat them raw."

They chortled. Dizzied, Shai blinked as Edard's ghost hazed his vision.

"One moment I was walking down to find where Eridit had gone, and the next . . . Eiya! Am I dead?"

The ghost seemed less angry than puzzled as the gang of men marched through him. He drifted toward a ridge of rock adorned with curtains of orange-flowering vegetation. The way the vegetation fell down the crag made it seem there was rock all the way down, the crevice itself easily missed, unless you knew it was there because a young woman had recently dragged you in there and done what she wanted, not that he hadn't wanted it just as much.

"Aui!" said the ghost. "There Eridit is! Safe, at least."

Shai saw her eyes, a patchwork face behind orange flowers. As she saw him see her, fear made her face ghastly. Fear for him? Or for herself?

He stumbled purposefully, drawing their attention, and surged up so they crowded in to pressure him forward, weapons bristling like so many iron thorns ready to impale. They didn't examine the nearby rocks.

Edard's ghost had vanished.

And Shai was their living prisoner.

37

DEATH RODE AT twilight into High Haldia. Or so, Marit imagined, the tales might sing.

The broad avenue that bisected the city lay empty except for a scrap of cloth rippling along the paving stones, blown by a wind out of the north. Normally, she supposed this thoroughfare would be lit with lanterns, folk grabbing noodles or the savory buns common to Haldia for a quick bite while rushing about their last errands of the day. Apprentices released from their duties might be found traveling in packs for a night of carousing, or a shopkeeper seen sweeping her entry porch as she closed up for the night. Now, many buildings gaped as half-burned shells, roofs fallen in and broken tiles scattered. The intact shopfronts were shuttered, as closed up as a rich clan rejecting the marriage suit of a poor but ambitious neighbor.

Was High Haldia slain, or only licking its wounds?

Movement flashed to her right. Marit urged Warning into a trot down a side street. A figure dashed across the street, ducking into an alley. Marit slipped off Warning, ran in pursuit. In the depths of shadow between windowless walls, she grabbed a slight young person by his tunic.

He went limp, so she let go, and he sprawled at her feet. The side street lay behind them. Ahead, the alley met an intersection of murky lanes, the routes beyond too dim to trace.

"Jus' ran to fetch medicine." Despite short hair clipped close to the head, it was a girl. "I didna mean to break curfew, only my nephew needs the tisane for a fever." She opened a hand to reveal a stoppered vial with an orange ribbon wrapped around it to mark its medicinal virtue.

"I saw folk walking in from fields earlier," Marit said, hoping a friendly voice would stop the girl's convulsive shivering on a hot night. "All with stooped backs and bowed heads. The guards at the toll gate outside town let me pass without a word. Why's there a curfew?"

The back of her neck had a rash, and her feet were bare, newly blistered, as though she had formerly been accustomed to walking everywhere in slippers. "We've given our hostage to the garrison and kept the rules," she said into the dirt. "It was jus' that my nephew needed the medicine. He's jus' three. Cudna you let me go this one time?" Her hand closed around the vial.

Marit heard footfalls. She turned halfway, keeping an eye both on the girl and on the six soldiers who crowded into the alley's entrance

"Lord? Any trouble here? Got a curfew-breaker?"

Averting their eyes, they approached in file, blocking the alley.

The sergeant flung out an arm to halt the others. "Who are you?" His suspicion gave flavor to the air and made the others draw their short swords. The girl whimpered.

"I've not seen you before, lord," the sergeant added, words as tentative as a baby's first steps.

Now it's true that anyone might affect a long cloak, especially in the rainy season, although few would choose white as their ornament. As soon as she thought it, Marit wondered if a bold rebel might attempt a disguise and thereby walk through a city such as this one, imprisoned by a curfew that made an innocent girl cower when she was caught out at dusk with a vial of medicine.

"I've just come from Walshow," Marit said, looking them over as they glanced every way but at her.

"She's the one they warned us to look out for—" blurted the leftmost fellow, and his sergeant kicked him so hard on the shin that he yelped.

"Don't even try it," she said wearily. "Look at me."

Of course they didn't want to look. Joss's determination and misery had been laid bare to her sight: his nostalgic, regretful desire for the Marit he had once loved, a desire he knew he ought to have strangled long since but could not quite kill; his hunger for a young woman so vivid and sensual that Marit raged with envy while knowing perfectly well that she was dead and he had to get on with his own life.

With no one moving and she trapped in this pointless cycle of thoughts, she prodded the girl. "Get home."

"We bring curfew-breakers to the captain on duty, to be cleansed, lord," said the sergeant, trembling with the effort of staring at his hand so he would not forget and look at her.

"Take me to the captain in place of the girl. Who, if she knows what is good for her, will run off. *Now.*"

The girl bolted, and vanished down one of the lanes. Marit held her staff at the ready until she could no longer hear the patter of feet.

"No need to mention the incident to the captain," she said. "I'll know if you do."

"That's not how things work around here," muttered the sergeant. She didn't need a third eye and second heart to hear how disgruntled he was, having his authority undermined in front of his patrol by some cursed woman he'd never seen before in his life. She'd had a lot of experience as a reeve in unraveling the weave of conflicted human emotion, because it was rare indeed that any one person felt any one single pure feeling unadulterated by a dozen niggling other sentiments.

The sergeant lunged.

She sidestepped, and whacked him across the shoulders with the staff. He hit the ground face first. She turned on the others before they charged. Taken by surprise, they looked at her.

Aui! Humans are a monstrous roil of sensibilities, and by far the worst part of what she had now become was in being forced to know how true that was.

If I don't go along, they'll kill me. I wish I never left home.

I want Sergeant's job, that snot-nosed ass doesn't know what he's doing, not like I do, I would like to see him strung up and kicking.

Glad they didn't catch me cheating at dice hope my sister wasn't one of the girls taken for the army the wine isn't enough to drown this ache in my head I woulda kept lighting the houses on fire it was the hells grand to watch them burn and folk begging us to stop and anyway the commanders ordered us to make an example of them.

My tooth hurts.

The lords order us to kill, they like to kill, they like it when we kill, so she's just one cursed female breaking curfew, we can take her down and kill her—

"Drop your weapons! Down on your knees! Hands up!"

She hated them as they turned craven, heads tucked, hands high with palms open. She was breathing hard with the rush, and she wanted to crack them over the heads for what they had done to the people of this town. What they had done to countless others. What they had done to themselves.

"You." She thrust one tip of her staff hard into the chest of the man whose tooth hurt. He fell hard, tried to hide a groan as he righted himself, and she laughed, and was shocked at herself for finding amusement in his pain. "Unbuckle the sergeant's sword belt and give me sword and sheath."

Cringing, he did so. She slung the short sword at her own hip before poking him again.

"You're in charge now. You three will escort me to the captain. The others can carry your sergeant back to camp."

Even if the local captain tried to kill her, pain would be a temporary agony. *I can kill, but not be killed.* Yet that being so, what had happened to the man who wore the cloak before her?

HIGH HALDIA HAD begun its life in ancient days as a posting town, a string of buildings along the Istri Walk that led from Nessumara to Seven. From this spine, the city had grown outward into unequal halves. They walked into the eastern part of the city along a handsome avenue lined with merchant houses and trading emporia mostly untouched by the destruction that had visited the main road. These buildings, too, were entirely closed up for the night. No spark of light betrayed life within.

The streets had room to sprawl, nothing like the crowded streets of Toskala, the steep lanes in Olossi, the nerve-racking roped paths of Haorrenda, or the narrow canals and elaborate foot bridges of Nessumara-on-the-delta. Three squares were strung like beads along the thoroughfare. The entrances to four temples anchored the corners of the first square. The second was faced with two temples, north and south. On the third square, the assizes court and archon's hall stood opposite a massive compound dedicated to Taru the Witherer, beloved of farmers.

The captain in charge of High Haldia's garrison had set up his headquarters in the arkhon's hall. She rode Warning up the steps and through the main entrance hall into the courtyard. Men shrank back from her billowing cloak. A graveled path bisected the courtyard, flanked by terraces of white and pink tea flowers and decorative herbs set out in blocks like neighborhoods. A fountain depicted the island at Indiyabu where the Guardians had risen from the lake, but the spouts had dried up. Much like justice, Marit supposed. Run dry.

A dozen men edged out of the shadows into a loose circle around her.

"I've not seen you before," said their captain, a trim, muscular man flanked by a pair of gargantuan spear carriers. He had the imposing presence of a man who can make decisions without second guessing himself, but he did not look her in the face.

"No, you haven't. I want an escort down Istri Walk, to the main army."

"I'm under no obligation to assist you."

She snorted. "I suppose you get folk every day riding into High Haldia on a Guardian's horse and wearing a scrap of cloak so as to pretend they are a Guardian?"

His gaze met hers just long enough that she tasted the merest tangle of his complicated mind: He admired a bold woman with a sarcastic sense of humor. He didn't like the commanders he worked for, but he was good at fighting and they rewarded him well. He liked the job more than he disliked them. "They don't call themselves that. Which you'd have known, if you were one of them."

"As an attempt to intimidate me, it's not bad, Captain, but I'm up here on a winged horse, and you're down there wondering how much of your heart I've seen."

A smile ghosted onto his face and faded. "As it happens, Lord Twilight rode into town earlier today. He said a cloak, a woman wearing the color of death, might arrive soon. I just sent a man to fetch him."

Warning stamped. A door slid open on a long covered porch. The man who stepped into the courtyard wore a cloak very like hers, only the color of his was indistinguishable from the purpling-dark shadows. His hair was black, his eyes and complexion dark, and his expression ironic.

"You and your men can go, Captain," he said.

They departed hastily through gates and doors.

As he crossed the garden, she dismounted and released Warning to nose among the tea flowers. He halted beside the fountain. Lanterns hanging from tripods spread light on his face. He studied her as a smile twisted his lips.

"I wasn't sure if I had dreamed you, or really spoken to you. A wish is no better than a dream." His voice was softly mocking, but not of her. The accent dazzled.

" 'Lord Twilight'?" she asked with a laugh.

"It is grand, isn't it?" He let the grin emerge fully.

"It's ridiculous. Nor do you look like a Northerner, to carry the title."

"Lord?"

"It's an ancient claim, found only in the north. You're not a Northerner. You're not even born of the Hundred."

"As I admitted when we talked the first time."

"As your face proclaims. A good-looking face, I admit, but an outlander's face nevertheless. How in the hells did an outlander become a Guardian? A 'cloak,' as the soldiers call us."

He raised a hand, wincing. "Let's not spoil a pleasant evening with a painful subject. What am I to call you?"

She hesitated.

"If you won't give me something, I'll make up a name. And you won't like it, Lady Death."

"Aui! I'm wounded. You can call me Ramit."

"I suppose it's the best I can get."

"Yes. You said you're called Hari. Water-born, like me." And therefore forbidden, but she didn't say that out loud.

"Water-born? They said that before to me, but it means nothing. My father named me Harishil, which means fifth of his sons. Nothing about water."

Not forbidden, after all! She smiled. "I'll not mention it again. Why are you in High Haldia? Why not follow the army down the Istri Walk as I'm doing?"

His eyes shuttered. "Are you sure that's what you want?"

"I'm sure it's what I must do."

It was a relief to look at a man and not be flooded with his thoughts and feelings, and the longer she held his gaze in a kind of defiant counterstare the more it seemed they were flirting. And since he was not truly Water-born, she could enjoy the sensation. He had broad shoulders and the graceful strength of a man in his prime, about the age she had been when she'd died.

"I thought you might pass this way," he said. "I thought maybe we could travel together."

As invitations went, it had charm mostly because of his lazy smile. He wasn't a happy man; trouble shadowed those thick-lashed eyes. But he wasn't the kind to let trouble stop him from making an effort to please. And surely the gods knew how bitterly lonely she had become. Maybe she had hoped for this meeting more than she dared admit.

"I can leave any time," she said.

THEY RODE OUT of High Haldia soon after. Once on the Istri Walk, the hooves of their horses lit the road, a glow emanating like a mist formed of dying sparks. The city was silent except for the occasional barking of a dog or the noise of beasts as they passed, and inhaled the smell of, stabling yards. Twice, night patrols aggressively hailed them but, seeing them close, hurriedly bowed and let them pass.

"It's quiet," she said.

"But orderly. The troublemakers are dead or fled or in hiding. The rest do what they're told."

"Which is?"

"Farm. Mill. Manufacture. Pay a heavy tithe to the army in exchange for not being killed. That's the bargain they were offered. Most took it."

"And the ones who did not?"

"As I said."

"High Haldia has a decent population. There's a lot of land between here and Walshow, not to mention Haldia in general and Seven and the uplands of Teriayne beyond. And Gold Hall above the Falls. How can an army keep that much land and that many people under a reign of fear?"

"You Hundred folk don't understand the way of the world, do you? It seems the mountains and sea—and your reeves and Guardians—have protected you for a long time in your tiny enclaves. I was a troublemaker once, but I learned that a well-disciplined army with strong leadership can control a great deal of territory."

"How?"

"I and some others got in trouble with the Qin overlords of the trading town where I grew up. Instead of executing us, they sent us off to be useful elsewhere, which in my case meant being sold into a mercenary company as a soldier. One day about a hundred of us marched north over the high mountains and into the Hundred on a contract. We were betrayed, and I was killed. After that, I found myself prisoner of the cloak."

"Mine's a simpler tale. A country girl, sent to the city to find work. I was chosen as a reeve instead. I believe I was killed in the line of duty. Thus you find me."

"Here's the first toll gate." As they approached a stockade placed to control traffic on the road, Hari raised his voice to alert the guard. "We're passing through. I'm of no mind to mince words with your sergeant."

Men opened the gate, careful not to look up. They rode through without slackening their pace. Beyond this stockade the city turned into a scattered collection of threshing yards, stinking tanneries, aromatic corrals, and silent timber lots. High Haldia's environs seemed as deserted as the city itself.

"Have they no patrols to control thievery?" she asked.

"You'll see."

The roadside leading to a second barrier was lined with poles driven into the ground.

She sucked in a shocked breath. "This again!"

"You've seen the approach to Walshow, then."

"I have. Is this how they keep the peace?"

"Those who resist, who speak out, who cause trouble or break curfew—are cleansed. Their corruption removed."

Corpses dangled from poles, tied by ropes around the wrists, hands swollen and so deep a purple they were almost black and lower limbs puffy and distended. The dead stank, while the guards had bound linen kerchiefs over their mouths and noses. Beyond the gate, more poles rose. Flies buzzed in black clouds.

"I'd call it slaughtered, not cleansed! The hells! Those two aren't dead!"

A lad, his arms streaked with the jagged red of infection spreading down from his choked hands, was unconscious, spirit drifting deep. A man whimpered as he struggled to get enough purchase on the pole with his heels to ease the strangling pressure of the rope. She dismounted. His feet hung to about the level of her waist, making it impossible for her to reach the stake hammered into the top of the pole around which the chains looped.

Hari said, "They're already condemned."

"By what court?"

Beside the gate, the night watch gathered.

"By the only court that matters. Those who command the army hold the power."

" 'The cloaks rule all, even death.' Well, they don't rule me after all, do they? Help me."

"It serves no purpose to try to save one here and one there when they're all condemned."

"You disappoint me." Warning flicked her ears. "And you disappoint my good horse, too."

She walked to the barrier, a bulky fence set in front of debris piled to impede movement and with a gate set in place to allow wagons through in single file. "I need a ladder."

The taste of their sergeant's sullen anger at being ordered about so arbitrarily flavored the air even as he kept his gaze averted. A ladder was brought. She carried it over her shoulders to the pole where the hanging man scraped with a will, as if thinking to escape her efforts. As she braced the ladder behind the pole, Hari dismounted. He came up very close behind her, almost embracing her.

"I'll help you," he said in a low voice.

"Change of heart?"

"I'm not doing this for him. You catch him when he falls."

Grasping the man around the thighs, she lifted. He grunted in pain. His trousers were fouled; she sucked in a fetid breath through her mouth and held on, hoping Hari would be quick. The chain released. The man's body collapsed over her, and she staggered back to avoid falling under him as he began screaming. Then Hari had him, and together they eased him to the ground.

"Eiya!" She cut the ropes, then probed his shoulders as he writhed. "Nothing popped out, but he'll have a cursed painful time getting the blood back into his hands. The muscles must be torn from the weight. He can't have been up there long."

"What do you mean to do with him?" Hari asked.

"Cursed if I know. Find him a place he can heal."

"And thereby condemn whoever aids him as an accomplice, to be cleansed?"

"I can't just stand aside and do nothing! Help me with the other one."

"A waste of time. The lad's near death."

"How can you tell?"

"You're young to this yet, aren't you? It's a sweetness they get, when they cross beyond where they can be brought back. If you want, I'll kill him quickly."

"Are you going to help me, or not?"

His gaze shifted past her. Anger had made her careless. She turned. The sergeant, marked by his shoulder braids, stood a prudent distance away, gaze still averted, shaking as though terrified by his own audacity.

"Lord, if you will hear me, I would tell you that the man you cut down was cleansed for being a spy. He was sent from Toskala to infiltrate our territories and scurry back to his masters with what news he could tell them."

Marit rose. "Take the lad down. Also, bring me a pair of saddled horses, rope, wine, and a sack of rice." His abject obedience gave a rush that made her ears burn, and then at once she knew the shame of letting his fear feed her. Demons ate fear; that was what made them demons.

Hari nodded toward the lad. "Listen with your second heart, and look with your third eye. His spirit is passing."

The death rattle exhaled as softly as mist rises. The young spirit lightened within the night, a shudder of trembling confusion caught between death and the Spirit Gate. The wind quickened. Chains scraped on wood as bodies shifted. The odor of death grew strong, then faded abruptly. She sucked in breath—breath is life—and that quickly, the youth's spirit crossed over and was gone, joyful in its final release.

A pair of frightened soldiers brought a pair of saddled horses—decent mounts, to her surprise—and scuttled away. The accused spy screamed in pain as she and Hari bundled him onto the horse, and tied him on the saddle. Mercifully, he passed out. She tied the lead lines to her own saddle and strung the spare at the end.

They rode for a long while without speaking, her heart steaming hot with a bitter rage. The fields beyond High Haldia had a tidy architecture. This was fertile land, well populated, sufficient to feed High Haldia and besides maintain a brisk trade upcountry and downriver. The footfalls of the horses rang in the night, as loud as hammers. The unconscious man breathed in unsteady gasps, his pain like a haze of muddy pressure around his torso. Rain washed them, pouring for a while, and then they rode out of it. In the southwest, three stars shone in a break in the clouds.

"I don't know what I'll do with him now," she said at last.

"Why do you bother?"

"Because I can't walk away."

"Didn't you see the dead ones? The empty poles waiting? How will you save them?"

"I can't walk away from the one who is in front of me."

His glance was shadowed by night, but she felt its brooding force. "They'll feed on you. That's what they do."

"These poor souls feed on you?"

"No. The ones who control us. They feed on us, who are their slaves."

"Are they demons?"

"Maybe. If you turn around now, you might be free of them a while longer."

"No." She wiped her brow, still wet from the rains. "To run is to be their slave. I'm going to fight. All I ask is that you stay out of my way, and don't betray me."

"Don't trust me," he said. "I'm not like you."

"You're the only ally I have."

Looking at each other, they both laughed.

At length, she wiped away a tear. Within the strange shimmering gleam off the road, she watched his face, his wry smile, his habitual shrug as of a man who has trained himself to let water run where it may, making no effort to shield himself from the downpour.

"Don't make me like you too much," he said, "because it will end in grief."

"Will it? That's up to you."

38

The soldiers who had captured Shai had set up camp north of West Track, in woodland cover. It was dusk by the time the patrol reached a clearing with canvas shelters and one campfire. Men came to stare as the others tramped in.

"Make more noise, and you'll bring one of Horn's patrols down on us, you great cursed ass."

"More important, did you find anything?"

"Field was picked over," said the sergeant. "Not a cursed thing worth carrying."

One man pointed with his elbow, indicating Shai. "Found somewhat, you did."

"Waste of time bringing this big dumb ox with us," said the one called Twist.

A man holding an axe sniggered. "Look at those arms and shoulders! Whew! Bet he can chop wood! Save me the trouble."

"There was others with him, including an ordinand we killt," said the sergeant, "but I don't know how many or where they come from or why they was there. That's why I captured him and brung him back, you sorry fools. For your lack of thinking of it, is why I am sergeant and you will always be walking in my dust."

A few men spat.

But the man the sergeant had scolded merely laughed. "Got him a ring, doesn't he? I like that belt buckle, too. Very fancy."

"They're mine," said the sergeant. "Finder's rights."

"What about me?" demanded Twist.

"You can have his good-quality sandals, eh?"

Shai weighed his chances, and did not struggle as they stripped off his ring and belt, his sandals and good tunic. A mewling cry whispered from the trees, maybe a trick of his ears, but it made him terribly uneasy. He kept his mouth shut and his eyes open as they prodded him away from the campfire and into the shelter of a brake of lush ferns. A man sat on a stool under the curving fronds, braiding the hair of a girl seated on the ground with her head bowed.

"Who is this?" the man asked without looking up.

The sergeant said, "We found him on the battlefield you sent us to search, lord. We killed an ordinand. There were others that eluded us. You know how spies plague us."

The girl did not look up. The man did.

His was an unremarkable face, middle-aged and stout, not a man you would look at twice. He wore a cloak whose color Shai could not distinguish against the leaves. His hair was bound into a single long braid that fell almost to his waist, tied off around what Shai was sure was a finger bone.

Shai repressed a shudder as he regarded the cloaked man, awaiting the ugly verdict on his fate. He was afraid to die, but after all, what could he do about it now? Maybe he would use a few of the tricks Tohon had taught him, and at least take a few down before they slit his throat and punctured his belly.

Looking startled, the man dropped the girl's unfinished braid. "You're veiled to my sight. Yet you wear no cloak."

"Eh?" Shai took a step back, into the prodding point of a spear. He eased forward off the pain.

The man cocked his head, as dogs did sometimes, trying to figure out a thing they could not comprehend. "He must be simpleminded, Sergeant. He's got nothing in his head."

"He's an outlander."

"That shouldn't matter." The clipped arrogance of the cloaked man's tone made you want to answer. "Who are you? What are you doing here?"

"Eh, eh," said Shai, grunting to give himself time to think, cutting up his timing to make each word awkward. If they throw you rope, you're damned if you don't grab it. "Eh, ver. The master calls me Shai. I can chop wood."

The men behind him chortled.

The cloaked man grasped the fraying end of the girl's braid, although he seemed not to notice that she flinched. His attention shifted to her hair as suddenly as it had fixed on Shai before. "Best we take him to the lord commander, to explain this mystery. He should be easy to keep in line. We'll move at dawn."

They walked him back to camp, shoved him to the darkest corner of the encampment where other soldiers stood guard over many captives.

"Try to escape, and we kill you," said Twist congenially as Shai maneuvered among bodies huddled on the ground, not wanting to trip. There were at least thirty, and they were small.

They were children.

Most curled around others, sleeping or pretending to sleep. One boy watched as Shai found a patch of ground and sank down. He wrapped his arms around bent knees and laid his head against his legs, hoping he could doze, but sleep did not come. For a while it drizzled, and even though it was a warm rain, he shuddered. The mewling nagged on and on until, at length, a soldier kicked through.

"Shut up! Shut up! Who's making that cursed sound?"

The man reached into a bundle of shivering children and yanked a girl up by her braids, a little thing, not more than twelve or thirteen. She was sniveling, her shoulders bowing like the ferns as she folded forward to beg for forgiveness.

"Eihi! I can't take that sound!" He plunged his sword into her belly.

She screamed. Shai leaped to his feet as the children who had been huddling with her scrambled away like so many insects scattering from a disturbed nest. The soldier stuck her a second time, and a third, all done so quickly that Shai barely had time to take a step as her shrieks turned the air cold. A hand grasped Shai's ankle. He looked down into the dark face of the watchful boy.

"They'll just kill you, too," the boy whispered. "Sit down."

It had been too late already when the first thrust cut into her abdomen. The stink of entrails filled the air, and Shai coughed, retching, as the boy's hand clutched more tightly.

"Sit down, ver. You can't help her."

Her screaming twisted into a rising and falling moan as the pain tore into her and her life leaked out. The soldier slit her throat and let her go, stepping back from the gush of blood. Shai fell to his knees.

Merciful One! Give me refuge!

He mouthed the words, but uttered no sound. Not one of the captives made a noise as the girl died. Rain hissed in the leaves and wind rattled through the branches, almost drowning out her last hoarse gasp.

In night, the spirit rises like luminescent pale smoke out of lifeless flesh, twisting in confusion as the girl reached first here and then there toward those who could not see her. Even in death, she mewled, as though she had had her tongue cut out and could form no speaking sound. Her ghost drifted in the damp night wind, and then she saw him seeing her. He ducked his head, but her ghost sailed over and began to pluck at his sleeve to get his attention, although obviously her fingers had no substance with which to grasp.

A hush stilled the camp. Soldiers coughed and shuffled as a tangible presence moved among them.

"The stink offends me."

"Yes, lord. We'll move the corpse away at once, lord."

"Here, now." A man moved up beside Shai as captives shrank away. The hem of a long cloak brushed his right arm. "Look up."

Shai swallowed, hard to do with that choking knot in his throat, and slowly raised his head as he remembered all those awful family evenings when arguments had raged around the dining chamber while he kept his face empty and his mouth closed. The ghost was patting his hair, tugging at the unraveling topknot.

"Do you see her?" His gaze bent on Shai as though to dig deep into his heart, but Father Mei's rages were twice as frightening, and this man didn't look strong enough to have any force if he backhanded Shai. If they meant to kill him with a sword or spear, there was nothing he could do but run and be ready for arrows to take him in the back, but even if they chose to beat him it wouldn't be worse than what his older brothers had done to toughen him up. Even Hari had slapped him around to try to stop him sitting in dull silence while the others teased him. *Be a man. Speak up for yourself.* He'd gotten used to their ridicule.

"Eh, Master?" he said as stupidly as he could. "I'm cold. I'm hungry."

The cloaked man studied him and the ghost a moment longer, then turned away. "Get that stink away from camp."

"Up, you! Get rid of the body."

A whip descended on Shai's shoulders, and he yelped just because he was so surprised. But he shuffled over to the corpse as the captives scooted away. The smell gagged him, harder by far than the slash of a whip to suffer easily. Her limbs fell every which way as he grabbed her under the armpits. His hands became smeary with the blood that coated her chest. His feet pressed into moist, warm nubs and rubbery leavings that squelched as his feet shifted to gain purchase. He dragged her backward. A trio of soldiers hustled up to guard him as a thorn-ornamented thicket scraped his neck and back, branches catching in his hair.

"That's far enough!" barked one of the guards.

Her ghost shimmered up to him, child's face working in a distorted grimace as insubstantial tears sparked on white cheeks. He staggered away to heave, afterward made the mistake of wiping his mouth with a bloodstained hand, and the metallic taste made him retch again. His throat burned. He tried to wipe his hands on leaves, on dirt, but her blood wouldn't come off.

"Come on now." The guard poked him with a spear.

He took a slow step sideways, thinking to bolt. Even if the ghost followed him, they could not see it.

The haft of a spear cracked across his back, pitching him to his knees, and thwacked again, catching him at the base of the neck. Ears ringing, he stumbled up, too dazed to run, and they herded him at spearpoint back into camp. His face and hands and arms were scratched up by thorns, his head was pounding, and blinking made him dizzy. Once he grasped at the ghost, thinking to steady himself, but his hand passed right through her and he reeled to his left, brought up short by a soldier shoving him back.

"Aui! You reek!"

It started to rain.

"Heya! Get the big oaf over here to hold up the canvas what's coming down. Sergeant don't want to get wet while he's doing his business."

He caught his foot on a root and went down, his weight jarring up through the knee. Another soldier prodded him up, and he staggered to where a length of canvas tied up to form a lean-to was indeed caving in as rainwater pooled in a sag in the cloth. The watchful boy was already yanking on the cloth but he wasn't strong enough to keep it taut, so Shai grasped the cloth and tugged hard, making water splash onto the ground.

The side was wide open. It was too dark to see clearly, but he heard panting, a release, and a sigh. Rain poured. Another man slid under the canvas.

"Heya. My turn. Get out."

"Eiya! It's wet out there! Just go ahead."

"Get out!"

And so on, one grumbling as he slid out into the rain and another ducking under to take his turn, and then another, and another, men too wet to sleep or perhaps he had truly fallen into one of the hells where the rains, like lust and fear, could never slacken. The watchful boy swayed with exhaustion, and Shai took on more and more of the weight, sure that if the boy dropped he would be murdered right there for slacking his duty. His thoughts turned numb, the night blurred, but at length the rain eased and no more men came. The sergeant returned to chase out a girl.

"Eh! I want a dry cover for my head. Here, you, filthy slave. Get out. I'm going to sleep."

She crawled out and lay curled in a ball off to one side with drizzle spitting over her. She'd been wearing a taloos—women's garb—but the cloth was bunched up. The soles of her feet showed pale in the darkness. Shai eased the ache in his back by shifting. Wasn't there a way to hook the canvas up so the water didn't pool? He stretched, stood tiptoe, found a way to loop the guide-rope once around the stub of a broken branch. Carefully, he loosened his hold. Nodded to the boy who, waking from a standing doze, cautiously released his hold on his corner.

The lean-to held. Within, the sergeant snored peacefully.

The air had a thick texture, heavy enough to spoon; he'd never tasted so much moisture on the wind in his life. Kartu was desert country, the town alive because of its miraculous spring, which was said to rise from the heel print of the Merciful One walking the path of enlightenment, whatever that meant.

The ghost drifted in front of him, gesturing with open palms, trying to get him to listen to her, although her voice was a thread so fine he could not distinguish words. Had the blows to his head and back damaged his hearing?

"Uh, uh." The girl who had been used under the shelter started crawling.

He wasn't sure where she meant to go, but he leaned down to grasp her shoulders. Feeling her go rigid when he touched her was worse than being kicked.

"Here, now," he whispered. "I'm just helping you."

He eased her to her feet. She would have fallen without his arm braced around her back. He moved her toward the other captives, hoping he didn't trip over anyone in the dark.

"Uh, uh, uh." Her grunts were soft, a palliative against the pain, and he heard them only because she was pressed against him. He glanced back. Where had the watchful boy gone?

But it was all dark. They were lost in night. He had fallen into one of the hells, among demons.

BEFORE DAWN, SOLDIERS whipped the captives into line. Shai helped the shuddering girl to her feet. She was young, fifteen or sixteen, although it was hard to tell with her body made slight by lack of food. She flinched at everything, even his efforts to help her. Her hair was matted, her fingernails caked with dirt as though she had been digging with her hands. She could barely walk.

Once the captives stood in marching order, the soldiers led packhorses and mounts into line. The lord appeared from out of the forest cover, the watchful boy following three paces behind him with head bowed.

"We must move quickly through the Aua Gap." The lord had to work to make his voice carry; he did not have natural authority, but it was evident by the averted gazes and cringing stances that everyone there was frightened of him. "The Horn militia will have an eye open for armed companies traveling out of Olo'osson. They'll fight any small groups they see, like ours. So we make haste. Show no mercy to those who could talk about us if they fell into the hands of our enemies. Kill anyone who falls behind."

He walked into the trees as the watchful boy sidled into the line of captives. Ignored by the other prisoners, he stood beside Shai.

"Where did you go?" Shai asked him. "You just vanished last night. Did he— uh—hurt you?"

"Neh. There's two of us, that he likes to braid our hair." Indeed, the boy's hair was neatly combed and braided, not a strand out of place; his braid fell to his lower back, glossy hair cleaner than the rest of him. "The rest don't like me and Dena because of the attention he gives us, not that we asked for it! Maybe you'll scorn me now, too." He squared his shoulders, ready to move away.

"Can you help me with her?" Shai asked. "What's your name? I'm Shai."

"Vali." With a pleased smile, the boy slipped an arm around the girl's back. The order was called down the line and the ranks moved along a path cut through woodland. It was slow going, them in a narrow file never more than two abreast, but the pace remained steady and any captive who, by faltering, made the person behind cut their steps, got a whip slash across the back to chivvy her on. As dawn brightened into day, the ghost, her face set in a determined grimace, appeared as a wisp walking alongside a young lad who did not see her.

Under the cover of trees the light had a hazy glamour, and the smells seemed as thick as the muggy heat. Pockets of mud slurped under Shai's bare feet. Water dripped from leaves, and if he tilted his head back, he caught drops to moisten his parched mouth. Now and again the canopy opened into a clearing. Clouds glowed overhead, as if the sun was about to break through. Once, he saw a noble mountain blocking half of the northern sky, but the path twisted and trees rose, and the mountain vanished from view.

He got a better look at his companions. The youngest seemed to be ten or eleven—small enough!—and Shai was the only one with the heft of full growth. Vali slogged along in front of Shai, but soon enough one of the younger ones began to lag, so Vali put his arm around the littler girl's waist and kept her moving. Captives helped each other as well as they could. Even the ghost tried to aid that boy, maybe her kin, whenever he stumbled. But of course, she had no substance.

Shai was still dizzy from the blow to the head, and he was beginning to get truly hungry. Soldiers walked in groups of four, several always in view. Hard to sneak off into the forest cover with them so watchful. Anyway, if he let the girl go in order to save himself, she'd be killed.

"What's your name?" he whispered.

After a long time, she said, "Yudit." Nothing more.

They walked.

Rain washed through. Yudit stumbled more frequently. The path crossed a stream at a ford. The captives fell to their knees to scoop water in cupped palms. The soldiers led the horses upstream, muddying the water where the captives drank. Was it thoughtlessness, or cruelty?

He helped the girl kneel. She leaned on one arm, spilling more than got down.

"Slow down." Shai sucked water, savoring its cold bite. Then he cupped his hands so she could lie down and drink what he tipped into her mouth.

Vali knelt beside them, gaze darting along the bank, up into the trees, always seeking, never still. The ghost fluttered her hands helplessly as the boy she followed splashed into the water and flung himself into the current.

Roaring with anger, guards waded after him. They paddled; he dropped beneath the surface where the current streamed close against a high bank on the opposite shore. His hair floated atop the water, marking his position, and then he and his pursuers vanished around a bend. The ghost chased along the bank in their wake. Shai kept drinking, not sure when they'd be allowed to drink again.

"Drink more," he said to the girl.

"I can't walk." She rubbed at her grimy thighs. A runnel of blood had dried at one knee.

The soldiers came splashing back through the shallows, dragging the boy, who sobbed and struggled. They threw him on the stones and began beating him methodically with the hafts of spears as he tried to protect his head with upraised arms.

"Leave off!" The sergeant sauntered forward. "Find me stout sticks and big rocks." He surveyed the huddled mass of captives, with their knees dripping and their chins damp. "You want to join us, be a soldier, you learn how to kill." As soldiers brought him sticks he thrust them into the hands of the reluctant captives. "Just like the lords command us to do. Go on, then. Hit him as hard as you can. Aui! Don't make me mad at you."

He grabbed a boy and shoved him up to the prone youth, who was trying to crawl away, his face bloody and his look dazed. In Shai's eyes, all movement slowed.

The lad holding the stick tapped the lad's leg. The sergeant cuffed him so hard he reeled. "Hit. Or I'll kill you for disobedience."

Down the sticks came, one by one, some breaking over the body and others holding firm. The captives looked as dazed as if they were the ones being beaten, but they kept hitting and hitting and those who hesitated were struck until they, too, took a turn. Until the lad's face was crushed in.

But he wasn't yet dead. His spirit still inhabited his body, although from the blood running from his nose and the hollow where his skull had been caved in, it was hard to imagine how his spirit could reside there.

"Here, now, what about the ox?" Twist trotted over to where Shai crouched silently by the stream, the girl lying on the ground beside him, her head turned to watch the beating. He shoved on Shai's shoulder, but Shai had braced himself, so he wasn't shifted.

He grinned, looking right up into the man's ugly face. "I chop wood. I chop wood."

"Give him an axe," laughed the soldier. "Let's see if he can lop off its head in one go."

The sergeant waded over. "The hells! Are you a cursed horse's ass? You don't go giving a fellow with arms that size an axe, you gods-cursed lack-brain. Get on now. Time to get moving."

The horses were brought, the captives prodded into lines.

Vali uncurled from the ball he'd made of himself. "Whsst! They overlooked me, thank the gods."

Shai sat rigid, not sure he could ever move again. If he closed his eyes, he saw sticks rising and falling in the hands of frightened children; if he opened them, he saw the body, and the ghost girl patting the beaten lad to try to rouse him.

"Heya!" murmured Vali. "Best get moving, you don't want to get killed."

"He's not dead," muttered Shai.

Vali looked at him sideways. "He looks dead."

The familiar prickle of warning raced along Shai's skin. In Kartu Town, they burned those who could see ghosts, for being tainted with the evil eye. Here, they killed those who weren't obedient. No use taking chances.

"Get up," he said to the girl.

"I don't want to be beat like that," Yudit whispered, struggling to her knees although she hadn't the strength to rise.

"Get moving!" shouted the sergeant.

Whips cracked. Horses clopped through the shallows and plunged across breast-deep at the ford. The captives slogged through, shivering, but the worst cold was surely in their hearts, knowing what they had done.

"You there, ox! Get moving!"

He scooped up the girl and slung her over his back like a sack of wool to be brought down Dezara Mountain to market. Not much to carry. Vali slogged along beside, his expression thoughtful, his eyes seeking.

As he waded the ford, the sergeant yelled after him. "Best leave her if she can't walk on her own. You fall behind, too, and we'll kill you, too. You're not that much use to us, ox."

"He's too stupid to understand your meaning," said the one called Twist.

Shai clambered with difficulty up the far bank, Vali balancing him with a grip on one elbow, and shifted Yudit to a marginally more comfortable position over his shoulders. He filled his belly with breath, finding strength. Then he fell into line with the others, abandoning the dying boy and the ghost who would not leave him.

39

In the Barrens, underground, lamplight flickered. Nallo ceased cutting on the face of the tunnel immediately and crawled with mattock in hand back past the second lamp and toward the bottom of the shaft. She crouched under the hole, a hand gripping the rope in case she needed to tug for a lift out. Down the tunnel, the flame dimmed, pulsed twice, and flared to a steady flame. Behind her, Mas was using the back of his spade to tamp down the debris in a bucket, seemingly unconcerned. He'd done similar work before. He had an instinct for danger.

"Doesn't it get to you?" If she thought too much about the space in which they crouched, she'd scream.

"Neh. We're getting four times the rate of buyout toward our debt contracts as the ones working aboveground. Even the lads taking the extra shift of militia training only get half rates of what we do. It's worth it. I might stay on after I've paid off my debt, work for coin."

"They'll be working on these irrigation channels for years."

"So they will. I can make a tidy sum, hope to start a house of my own." He moved up beside her with the bucket. "Let me get this hooked up. You want me to do cutting?"

She refused to show weakness, although her shoulders and legs and back ached. The supervisor had told her this was man's work, best fit for short men so the tunnel roof didn't have to be cut very high, but a strong woman could fit into narrower spaces than most men. She had proved her worth. Wiping sweat from her brow, she returned to the face of the tunnel. Behind, the winch creaked as the full bucket was hauled up. Mas began to fill another.

She cut with the mattock, checking her direction by lining up on the two lamps. He shoveled and filled. Later, they switched out. Increasingly they heard the faint hammering vibrations of the team working in their direction from the shaft ahead, but they remained yet a fair distance apart. The winch reeled up full buckets and lowered empty ones. The work would have been monotonous, if not for the memory of the fall that last week had buried two men, and the water that had drowned the boy from Old Fort before that, and the old man who had asphyxiated when they'd sunk their first attempt at a mother well.

The second shift was lowered on the rope. Nallo and Mas chose to walk out along the conduit toward the mouth about half a mey distant. The gentle pitch and clay floor made the journey an easy one; shafts offered light and air about every two hundred paces. Mas was a scrawny older man, toughened by years of hard labor.

"You going to try for the militia, Nallo?"

"Neh. I'm too tired after my shift to do any drilling. The Qin don't want women in the militia units anyway. What about you?"

"Neh, I'm too old for that." He halted in the darkest part midway between two shafts. "Eihi! We've got debris here."

She swore under her breath, thrilled by discomfiting fear. As she bent to shovel at the tiny hills of debris heaped along the floor, he probed the ceiling for a breach. A grain spat onto her neck, followed by a hissing spill that got under her tunic, crawling along her spine.

"Seems like nothing," he said, "just a bit of loose—"

The sound crackled like a body turning over on a bed of pebbles. Mas grabbed at her.

"Move!"

She bent for the buckets, but he yanked harder as, in a downpour, loose material rained down. She ran with head bent under the low ceiling. A soft rumble expanded behind her and a cloud of dust nipped at her heels.

And faded.

Mas jogged on a ways farther, then halted to spit debris out of his mouth.

"Shouldn't we keep moving?"

"Neh, this is well packed, we dug this section ourselves if you recall."

Her neck was clammy, and her hands were hot. "I'll like to get out."

"Cursed fools were supposed to reinforce that area. Don't know what they're thinking not to have done it yet."

"Can we get out?" She was starting to shake.

"Eh, sure." As they walked mouth-ward, he chatted on like nothing had happened. "Listen, what I said before? About starting up my own house? I'll need a wife. You interested?"

She licked grit from her lips and thought about slapping him upside the back of the head. She was strong enough that it would really hurt him. "Eh, that's a kindness, Mas. I'm not interested, thanks."

"Well, then, what with there being no Devouring temple to visit, if you had a thought about a bit of sharing?"

Maybe a month's hard labor had mellowed her. Maybe it was knowing he had likely saved her life back there. Maybe it was just that the stone-lined mouth loomed before them, sun bright beyond the dim confines of the underground conduit down which water would someday flow to irrigate fields. As they ducked out through the stone-framed mouth of the conduit and blinked in the hard sunlight, she managed a polite reply.

"I appreciate you asking, but I don't want to get in trouble with the Qin."

Mas scratched dust from his scant beard. He looked across the flat depression that would become a reservoir and toward the higher practice ground where four black-clad Qin soldiers were forming up the trainees—men just off shift—into ranks. "Neh, I suppose I don't neither. They're hard, that's for sure. If fair. They don't overcharge us for sleeping space and food, like some masters do. Water's steep, though."

She tried in vain to slap dust off her tunic and kilted-up trousers, but she was coated in the sandy grit that passed for soil in these parts. Mas led her over to the supervisor's pavilion, and they got a hearing from the overseer, O'eki. The big man—an outlander—listened to Mas's detailed recounting with the resignation of a man who hears this every day.

"Hu! You got off easy. Maybe you'd like to set the reinforcement yourself, Mas. You're the best at it."

"If I get the same hazard pay as for digging the face."

"Come back at twilight. I'll let you know then."

They got into line by the supervisor's pavilion, waiting to turn in their mattock and spade. The four men ahead of them, coming off their own shift change, took sword-length wooden batons in exchange and trotted out to the formation. She walked away toward the canvas barracks. Mas kept pace beside her until they reached the canvas screens that set off the entrance to the women's barracks.

"If you're sure . . ." He was an ordinary fellow, without any least distinguishing characteristics except that, like her, he'd had some pressing reason to sell his labor to the Qin. He'd never said what it was, but then again, neither had she. "I just meant to say—"

"Sorry!"

He winced, so she knew she'd snapped.

"I'm just shaking after that," she added.

"Eh, truly, the murderer does get to people that way."

"And I'm tired." *And I'll never be interested in you, or maybe in any man.*

He sighed.

"Truth is, Mas," she added, for once thinking to spare him a bit of misery, "I really don't care to test the Qin's patience. You know how they are, all prim and dainty."

"Surely I do. Strange notions, they've got. Men sleep in one barracks tent and women in another, and once curfew falls, no mixing. Those who disobey are sent home, or whipped. Eiya! No use ruining your hopes for buying out your debt and gathering a nest egg of coin, just for an afternoon's pleasure."

She managed a smile, however insincere. Once safe within the women's area, she measured out her ration of wash water, which was only enough to wash her face and hands and even then not get off the grime. Coated with grit, she lay down on the blanket assigned to her, and she thought not of her husband, that kind and patient man who had never treated her with anything except gentle forbearance, but of the hierodule they had briefly traveled with. So be it. She was here, slaving in the Barrens, and no doubt that cursed interfering reeve had captured Zubaidit and taken her back to Olossi to serve out her own sentence for theft and debt-breaking. They'd not meet again. That's just how it was. She could never expect anything in life but leavings and scraps.

She hoped that Avisha and the children were doing well, but even that was out of her hands. After leaving Argent Hall, she had eked out a living doing day labor. In the meantime she had asked around at the Qin compound until she'd found out that a girl matching Avisha's description had been taken in to the household of the captain's wife. So at least they were being cared for. She'd heard a rumor that the captain's wife had come to live here in the Barrens, in the settlement, but since debt slaves remained in their camp, she'd never seen her. Even if it were true, what was the point of seeing Avisha and the children? She could do nothing for them, and no doubt it would upset them, as it had that day when Avisha had seen her in the labour gang in Olossi.

The hells! She could not rest, although she was weary to the bone and still feeling in her skin the way the cloud of soil and debris had raced after her like a monstrous lilu with mouth gaped wide to devour her. Digging was hard, dangerous work. Men like Mas called the shaft and conduit "the murderer," because men did die to bring water to barren settlements.

But the hard, dangerous work meant she didn't have to think about what she did not have, what she could not do, and how those cursed reeves had tried to trick her into enslaving herself to their cursed halls. If she was going to walk into debt slavery, at least she had done it of her own choice, with her eyes open to the consequences.

But which would be worse? Suffocating under a mass of dirt as it forced its way down your throat and nostrils? Or having your head ripped off by a bad-tempered eagle?

She wiped yet more dust from her brow. Or maybe she was just smearing it together with sweat to make herself a mottled complexion. Through a gap in the canvas, she watched the sun settle westward toward hazy peaks. Stamps and shouts from the practice ground marked the pace of the training. Men who showed promise would be allowed to join the Qin militia, an elite group being trained in the strictest and most arduous standard imaginable, and despite or perhaps because of this, young men did put in second shifts for the chance to be as tough as the sauntering Qin soldiers.

Nearby, women worked with cheerful banter in the kitchens. A pair of mules came in with fresh laundry from the washing house a couple of mey inland, closer to a good water source, where other female debt slaves worked. The shaded ground beneath the canvas grew stuffy. She dozed off.

As she often did these days after working underground, she dreamed of flying. The land below her dangling feet is seen as hollows and rises, a patchwork of color and texture like a rumpled blanket but breathtaking in each distinct detail. A tiny deer springs across a clearing, followed by a fawn. A man in a red cap crouches alone by a campfire. A wagon drawn by droving beasts glides down a road, accompanied by a trio of walking men more like ants than human beings. Black thunderclouds pile up over mountains, building strength, and after lightning flashes, a blue burst of light bolts into existence, winks coquettishly, and vanishes.

Thunder boomed, waking her. Shouts woke the alarm bell, rung thrice. Running footsteps scraped on the ground outside. She scrambled to the entrance of the women's compound, where debt slaves gathered.

"What happened?"

"A shaft fell in," said one of the women. Her hands were coated with grease. They watched as the men training on the practice ground ran for the supervisor's pavilion, grabbing spades and mattocks and rushing upland. A pair of Qin soldiers rode their horses inland, with a second man astride each carrying digging implements.

"Think it's worth it?" asked the woman with greasy hands. "Men dying for water?"

"They'll get irrigation all along here," said her companion. "Lookya—"

Hillward, the ground sloped in rugged stair-steps cut with gullies and ridges, a light dry soil. Seaward, they looked over level ground whose soil was built up by the accumulation of rainwater coursing down from higher ground during the wet season, which came here only during the Flood Rains, and fanning out to form stretches of richer soil suitable for planting, if only there was a steady supply of water. The mountains hoarded water, if it could be exploited. The Qin meant to do so.

Eagles circled above the distant shoreline. Off to the right snaked the low berm that ringed the quickly growing settlement and fort owned by the Qin outlanders. A pair of rowed cogs were coming in, headed for the shallow bay where they would beach and unload.

"Neh, there. Lookya!"

Thunderclouds boiled over a high mountain ridge to the northwest. A speck swooped out of the storm and, faster than seemed possible, glided close and, then, right over them.

The hells!

She began shaking harder than in the aftermath of the collapse. Best run and hide, and yet her feet took her out pace after pace until she found herself in the deserted parade ground as an eagle plummeted as on its death plunge and, pulling up at the last, thumped hard onto the dirt.

"Tumna." Her heart raced as her voice choked.

The eagle glared at her from beneath ridged brows, as if to say, "Why did you abandon me?"

"They tried to force me, like when Uncle dragged me to Old Cross to sell my labor. What did you expect me to do?"

"Heya!" Mas signaled from the edge of the parade ground. "Get back, Nallo. That thing could rip your head off!"

She was so fixed on Tumna's accusing stare that she did not notice the other eagles coming in until one landed with a delicate braking flutter of wings a safe distance away. Its harness held a reeve and a second person, hitched in front in a tangle of lines quickly unhooked. The woman walked out from under the hooked beak of the other raptor. Tumna swiveled her head to stare at the intruder, but the woman sketched a broad gesture, a signal that kept the bird in her place.

"You're Nallo." She carried a mass of lines and hooks draped over her right arm. "I'm Arda, training master of Naya Hall. That's what they call the training hall here. I hear Joss ran you off with some nonsense about reeves being slaves and how you best be grateful for shelter over your head and so on. He's astoundingly sanctimonious."

"He was a self-satisfied ass, it's true," said Nallo, warming to her but remaining cautious.

Arda looked her up and down in a way that made Nallo alert, and surprised, because she was more used to men looking her over that way—and then dismissing her. But Arda smiled, as if she liked what she saw. "He's a good reeve, but he's vain, if you ask me. Always thinking women will come round to his way of thinking just because he's got a handsome smile and a handsome face. Cursed tiresome, if you ask me."

Nallo's amusement at this plain speaking quickly sputtered. "How did you track me down?"

"I didn't. Tumna did." Arda nodded toward the raptor, now preening her wing feathers and seeming to ignore them. "She turned up a week ago at Naya Hall and began sweeps of the area, which told me that she'd tracked you. But there are hundreds of laborers brought here with Qin coin to build and dig. So I tracked her, tracking you. I have a proposition for you."

"So did Marshal Joss. Only his was more like an ultimatum."

"It does make you wonder how he manages to sweet-talk women into his bed, doesn't it? I'm just glad I'm not fashioned that way, to be susceptible to his charm." She smiled, and Nallo blushed as Arda went on. "I don't care whether you become a reeve or not, Nallo. That's your business, not mine. But I need my eagles jessed. An unjessed eagle not retired to the wild lands is an unpredictable eagle. Anyway, I need all the reeves I can get. In case you didn't know, we're living in troubled times."

"My husband was murdered by that army."

"I'm sorry to hear of it. Plenty more will suffer if we can't act. Here's my proposition. I don't care what you choose. Just fly first, and then tell me what you've decided."

Nallo felt every grain of dirt stuck to her sweaty skin. She remembered the spill of dirt on her shoulders as the ceiling gave way. She thought of crouching at the base of a narrow shaft, hoping to be hauled up before the air choked her as it sometimes choked out lamp flames.

She thought of her dreams.

"I have a debt contract," she said.

"If you choose the reeve hall, the Qin will release you. If you don't, you can come right back to whatever exciting work you're doing here." She studied Nallo closely.

"And I must say, we have a better water allowance at the hall. You can get a decent bath. For that matter, on your day off you can fly to Olossi and get a real bath in a real bathhouse. Cold scrub, hot soak, and all."

Nallo shut her eyes, woozy at the memory of a cold scrub and hot hot water in which to soak away all the angry voices that gnawed.

"Just one flight," she said, knowing it was a trap. Yet Tumna did sit there waiting for her, the only creature in the world who had actually gone to the trouble to seek her out on purpose.

Despite Tumna's fearsome reputation, Arda showed no fear of the eagle as she beckoned Nallo closer. "Help me get the harness slung."

"I'm flying *her*?"

"Of course. I'll show you how to rig this."

"Didn't she rip off her last reeve's head?"

"Yes, and disemboweled him, too. He had turned against his reeve's oath and, besides that, didn't treat her properly when she was injured. I don't blame her one bit. Did us a favor, I should think."

"That's a coldhearted way of looking at it."

"I train reeves. Nothing burns me more than a reeve who doesn't care properly for her eagle. I'd sooner feast a reeve who had betrayed all her companions but placed her eagle's welfare above her own, than one who neglected her raptor. Treat Tumna as she deserves, and she'll repay your loyalty with her own. She's a short-tempered, irritable bird, it's true, but we all have our quirks. I suppose my lack of sentimentality is mine. So. Are you going to help me, or should I leave? If I go now, I'm not coming back."

Maybe Arda was just playing on her contrary nature, or maybe it was that Tumna looked healthy and strong, no trace of injury like the other times Nallo had encountered her. Maybe it was the dreams, or the raptor's undeniable beauty and edge of danger.

"All right."

Arda walked over and showed her how to get into the harness. "It won't be the best fit. Reeves are measured for their harness to make sure there's no chafing. But it'll do. You can tighten it—that's right. Your feet go there—that's the training bar—so you can adjust your weight in flight. You're ready. I'll show you how to hook in."

She walked in under the cruel beak, right up to where the talons could puncture her. If Arda showed no fear, Nallo certainly was not going to. She followed her in under Tumna's shadow. The raptor huffed, straightening. Her feathers were gorgeous, golden-brown, splashed with white highlights. She wore a jess on each ankle and her own harness fastened over the shoulders and across the breast so it did not impede the wings. Working slowly and with the greatest patience, Arda showed Nallo how to hook the various tethers that allowed the bird to fly and the reeve to tuck in beneath.

"You get the best view. Free hands for signaling or to hold a weapon. As you saw, you can hook another person in front of you without oversetting the balance, although not every raptor is strong enough to manage two. With training, you'll learn how to hook in and out quickly."

"I didn't promise to become a reeve!"

"No need to rip my head off!" Then she grinned, leaned in, and kissed Nallo on the cheek. Nallo flushed like she hadn't since—well—since ever. With a laugh, Arda backed away. "Just one flight. That's all I ask."

"Oh, gods," murmured Nallo, as she realized she was well and truly hooked in. The rush went to her head, and then the raptor pushed so hard that Nallo thought her feet and her head were in two different places. Her feet slipped off the training bar, and she flailed, sure she was about to plunge to her death. Gripping the straps with knuckles gone white, she couldn't breathe. The powerful beat of Tumna's wings drowned out everything in the world except the plunge of the earth away from under her and, when she could see again, the many upturned faces staring as she rose. Air thrummed against her body. Tumna stopped beating her wings, simply held them out in that vast wingspan, and Nallo choked out a gulped cry, only they did not fall. They were rising as though in the hand of the gods, the earth dropping away to reveal the patterns of human handiwork below: the alluvial fan where the conduit had its exit; the holes marking the shafts; the gullies and hills. A pale berm, like rope, ran all around a hill where a brick palisade was also going up, plus many canvas tents and awnings to shelter the hundreds of folk now living and working here. The reeve hall was little more than canvas barracks for the reeves and fawkners, with massive perches set like skeletal trees rising off into the wilderness over a distance too broad for her to measure.

An eagle plunged past, the reeve in its harness whipping a flag signal at her that she did not understand. Tumna kept going, heading for the mountains. Off to her right the sea spread flat with the sun's light gilding the waters. Eihi! So beautiful!

The winds rumbled at crosscurrents as they rose over the foothills, heading straight into the black clouds. Thunder muttered above the mighty peaks. Lighting spiked.

"I don't—! I don't—!"

She had no cursed idea what to do; she was at the raptor's mercy, likely to get her head ripped off or—

She screamed as Tumna folded her wings and plunged down, down, down, wind shrieking in her ears. The wings unfurled, and they jerked up hard and Nallo began to laugh and sob together as the raptor found another rising stream of air and they sailed up along the face of the massive peaks of the thunderheads until the hair on her neck rose.

A dazzling form of blue light—not lightning—sizzled into being an arrow's shot away. It winked, and vanished.

Winked back, and vanished.

Winked back, and vanished.

All in the space of her taking in a shocked and heaving breath and letting it out.

The hells! It had eyes, of a kind, and it was *looking at her.*

It winked into being, and it *boomed*—like a laugh!—and vanished.

Tumna cut right, and they beat away from the face of the storm and glided down on the winds running before it. They dipped toward a valley cut deep into the foothills. Threads of light spun where a waterfall spilled over a cliff to cut a pool. A stream gushed through luxuriant vegetation. That same prickling feeling crawled on her skin, as though they were about to plunge back into the storm, but instead Tumna swept a wide turn and headed back toward the east. The sea glimmered in the distance. Nallo could not spot the settlement, but a strange web of light sparked to their left where two rocky hills joined in a saddle. Tumna swooped, and thumped down on the bare ground of the saddleback ridge.

Nallo was still laughing and crying as she wiped her eyes and looked around. Wind roared over the span of earth. A pattern carved into the rock glittered, tracing a labyrinth. Aui! Her skin went cold and she thought she would faint.

The eagle had brought her to a Guardian's altar.

"We can't stay here, Tumna! It's forbidden!"

On one side, an overhang offered shelter. Coals and ash smoldered in a fire pit, wood stacked neatly against one wall. Someone was living here, where all were forbidden to walk. All except Guardians.

"The hells! Move! Move!" She tugged on the uppermost jesses.

Tumna thrust, and they were up again, battered in the swirling currents, turning toward the sea. The winds fronting the storm buffeted them as they glided east, and once over the water the eagle had to beat her wings. It was getting dark, the setting sun occluded by the storm rolling out of the Spires. She banked, and ahead Nallo saw the flickering lights of watch fires and of scattered lamps and torches being lit against the gloom.

They sailed in over the settlement, and with a dainty dip Tumna landed by the reeve quarters. Nallo pulled her feet up out of reflex and, slowly, lowered herself within the angle of the harness to stand, legs shaking, on earth.

She swayed there, dazed, as folk called and Arda came out with a pair of fawkners to tend to the bird. They unhooked her and led her, unresisting and unable to speak, to a big tent covered in canvas, just in time, because rain began to fall, drumming on the taut canvas roof. Nallo hoped that everyone working in the conduit was out for the night but she didn't say so because she could not talk.

Arda sat her down on a bench and handed her a cup. The sharply spiced cordial scalded her throat. She coughed, blinking away tears.

Reeves—mostly young men and a few women and older men—came running in under cover. Out beyond the roped-back entrance a stocky black-haired young man who looked remarkably like one of the Qin soldiers—only he was dressed in reeve's leathers—was speaking with evident intensity to a pair of black-clad Qin soldiers. They shrugged and turned away, leaving him alone in the rain while everyone else laughed and talked around plank tables set up as an eating hall.

"You don't have to fly again if you choose not to." Arda poured cordial from a pitcher into the empty cup and sipped.

"I—I—I saw—" She wiped rain from her brow and blinked as another pair of lamps flared. The gods! This place was lit like they had oil to spare, and surely they did. Thunder boomed. "I saw a fireling, just like in the tales. It boomed, like thunder only so much smaller. Like it was laughing at me."

Nallo hadn't thought she could say anything that would surprise that competent woman, but the trainer's face went blank as she blew out breath between pursed lips. "Eihi!"

"You don't believe me!"

"Don't snap at me! I'm shaking my head because I do believe you. Here, now." Her gaze slipped away and her eyes narrowed. "What's he doing here?"

Nallo turned.

Volias sauntered up. "Greetings of the day to you, too, my darling Arda." He made a gesture of rudely passing a kiss before turning to Nallo. "Listen, Nallo, I have a proposition."

"Volias," said Arda with a sour grimace, "why you think she'd be interested in your ugly—"

"Neh, neh, not that kind of proposition. I'm not Joss, am I? Listen, Nallo." With a bright grin, like Jerad when he'd caught a fish, he straddled the bench, grabbed the cup out of Arda's hand, and drained it in one go. "Whew!" He screwed up his mouth, squinting. "That's strong stuff!" He set down the cup. "Listen, Nallo, I know you're angry about Joss and how he handled things, so I had a talk with the commander in Clan Hall. Plus in addition this trouble with Pil has got to be solved, so—"

"What are you doing here?" demanded Nallo.

He shut his mouth, ceased talking, and flushed.

Arda smirked. "Heard we'd tracked Tumna, did you, Volias?" She looked at Nallo. "He's been flying in and out of Argent Hall for weeks now, riding messages down from Clan Hall. He has become a pest, always asking if there's been any news of you and is anyone looking, like he thinks we're cursed fools who can't do a thing right. You followed me here!"

"I can't help worrying," muttered Volias without looking up. "Just like Joss to use too tight a rein. He must be honest in the very wrong way when maybe it would be better to let a person work things through with a bit of—I don't know—"

"A bit of dishonesty?" asked Arda with a laugh.

Nallo didn't know who to warm to, and who to snap at. "You knew, didn't you?" she said to Arda. "That once I flew, I would want to fly again."

Volias let out a whistle of breath. "So that's how you did it."

Arda said, "It does happen that way, often enough. How do you suppose I feel, Nallo? I'd have given anything to be chosen by an eagle. It's all I ever wanted. But it never happened. So I've dedicated my life to training those lucky enough to be jessed."

"To be slaves?"

She raised her hands, palms out, in the exact gesture she'd used to signal Tumna to lift. "I'm not treading that path, girl. Don't even try me."

Volias poured the last of the cordial into the cup and shoved it in front of Nallo. "You refuse to become a reeve because you say it's like being forced to sell your labor as a slave. And yet you go ahead, so I hear, and sell your labor as a slave, working for the outlanders. So wouldn't it make more sense to have remained a reeve, with autonomy, a hall filled with comrades, responsibility and authority?"

Nallo did not take the cup. "I myself chose to sell my labor. You at the hall—the marshal, everyone—made the choice for me."

"We made no choice. The eagle made its choice."

She shook her head. "Do you know how I got married? My father came up to me when I brought in the goats one afternoon and said, 'Nallo, the clan has sealed a contract for you to marry a ropemaker in a village on the West Track. About ten days' walk from here. You'll leave tomorrow.'"

Arda shrugged. "A story heard a hundred times. How are you different from most other lads and lasses married out to benefit the clan?"

Volias picked up the cup, thought better of drinking, and set it back down, turning it halfway and leaving his hands cupped around its curve. "I can see you may have felt roped—heh—into a bad situation. But Arda is right, as much as I hate to admit it." Arda rolled her eyes. "That's how contracts are arranged between clans."

She was boiling now, remembering the way her father had turned away with relief at finally being rid of her. "I didn't even get to meet him beforehand. No one asked if it was what I wanted."

"Was he cruel?" asked Arda suddenly. "Did he mistreat you?"

Volias pushed the cup closer to Nallo and removed his hand.

"No. He was a good man." She picked up the cup and gulped down the cordial, glad of how the spicy aftertaste burned her mouth and made her eyes water. "The truth is, he got the worse part of the bargain, but he never said one word in complaint."

"Ah," murmured Volias.

"Ah! What's that mean?"

"The hells! Just a way of making noise come out my throat. No need to rip my head off." As soon as the words were out of his mouth, he winced.

"A smooth talker," said Arda, "which accounts for his success with women."

Nallo said, "Tumna killed her reeve."

"Yes," said Volias. "And from everything I hear, he'd earned death. I am not a good man, not like your dead husband, may he rest beyond the Spirit Gate. But I do not fear Trouble."

"These days everyone fears trouble," said Nallo tartly.

"No, I mean, my eagle. Her name is Trouble. Now I admit she is a particularly good-natured bird, besides being as everyone acknowledges the most beautiful eagle known to be alive in the entire Hundred."

Nallo laughed. "You're boasting."

Arda sighed.

"It is not boasting if it is true. Like that Qin captain. You have to admit his wife is a lovely creature."

"I never saw her," said Nallo, thinking of Avisha and the children, and finding another tear on her cheek.

"And by all accounts a canny merchant," added Arda, "capable of twisting the knife with a smile and a compliment that makes you not even feel the pain. I think what Volias is saying is that no one could believe Trouble chose *him* when she could have had her pick of any decent person."

Volias grinned, and Nallo saw that he cared nothing for what people said about him and Trouble, because he had her, and they didn't. "Listen, Nallo. As I said, I have a proposition. I'm taking Pil back to Clan Hall to get his training. You come, too. Then you're away from all this, and you can make up your own mind. I admit that Arda is the best trainer we've got, but Ofri's experienced and cursed mellow, and a good man, for that matter."

Arda propped her chin on a hand as she examined Volias with a frown. "What's your angle?"

He wasn't a handsome man, but when he wasn't sneering, he had a nice face. "Get her away from Joss. He's the one who put her back up."

"You two must give up your feud. It bores the rest of us."

He turned a shoulder to Arda and fixed so warm a gaze on Nallo that she tried another swallow just to get the cup between her and his face. Arda reached across the table and patted Nallo's other wrist, stroking it teasingly, and Nallo shifted, feeling in that touch a promise that pleased her.

Volias sighed and rose. "I guess I'm too late."

"No," said Nallo, without pulling away from Arda's pleasant touch. "Just to be clear, I don't want any other kind of proposition from you. But if I go to Clan Hall, then maybe it'll seem like I'm starting new, of my own choice."

Thunder boomed overhead, and the rain pounded harder. Laughing reeves and hirelings dashed in under the cover of the canvas hall. Even Pil slouched in, looking like a drowned Rat, and with arms folded across his chest sank down on a bench alone, brooding.

"To be up there like that—I can't imagine never going aloft again."

"Jessed," said Volias, with heat or mockery. He was just speaking the truth.

Tumna had chosen her, and now they were bound.

*   *   *

THE BOOM OF thunder and the downpour that followed came as a relief to Mai after weeks enduring the dusty heat and dreary isolation of the Barrens, all too similar to the days of her childhood in Kartu Town. How far away the markets of Olossi seemed now. She pressed a hand over her swollen abdomen. The baby lay quiet, undisturbed by the storm. But she sighed, clutching a message brought midday by a reeve from Argent Hall.

She sat on a humble bench on a raised porch in the shelter of one of only four proper buildings in the entire settlement. From this vantage, sited advantageously on the slope, she watched rain make a haze of air, listened to its drumming on tile roof, on canvas, on dirt. Water tracked runnels into every crack and low spot, headed for the flat plain beyond the lower berm where in years to come fields would flourish if the massive irrigation project proved successful. An eagle spiraled in, battered by turbulence as it made for the training ground on Eagle Hill to the north. The rain was so dense she could not even see the hill where ancient ruins surrounded a rich vein of naya sinks. Water rushed down the gully, a muted roar rather like the thoughts in her head.

Soon it would be too dark to see. But since she could not read, it scarcely mattered. Priya had twice read out Miravia's message.

" 'Strangely, the terrible situation in the Hundred in which so many suffer works to my benefit. Contracts can be delivered by paying a fee to reeves flying between the halls, but bodies must travel by land. The uncles will not risk bodily harm coming to me by sending me on unsafe roads, even if they think nothing of those other harms that may come to me when the marriage is finally sealed. It's true that it says in the law that a girl must not be forced into marriage against her will, but were I to refuse, that would ruin my hopes of marriage forever, since no one else will want me because I will have proven myself to have a rebellious temperament. It will furthermore put a stain on my family's trading contacts with other Ri Amarah houses, and in the hopes my cousins cherish of contracting respectable marriages. For me to refuse would be to betray my family. My despair must remain in my heart. Yet while a person may hope to hide their face from the presence of the Hidden One, we are not hidden from that gaze even if we believe that because we cannot see that which is hidden, that it therefore does not exist.' "

Priya pushed past the curtained entrance—there were no actual walls, only canvas strung from beams—and offered Mai a bowl of rice covered with bean curd, slip-fried vegetables, and a red sauce swimming with slices of fish.

"Here, Mistress. You must be hungry."

"I am." She tucked the folded rice paper into her belt and accepted the bowl. Although the smell made her mouth water, she did not eat.

"You are still upset about the message."

"I am."

"Yet you accepted a marriage not of your choosing."

Mai looked up. Sheyshi shivered behind Priya, holding a burning lamp whose light spilled around them. "Did you become a priestess at the temple by your choice, or of your clan's choosing?"

"A meaningless question, Mistress. I came to the temple because it was the will of the Merciful One that I offer prayers there. Who spoke what words means nothing."

Lightning flashed, and thunder cracked right over them. They all jumped, and Sheyshi yelped in surprise, bringing Avisha running from inside.

"What happened? Sheyshi, what did you *do*? Here, let me take the lamp. You're shaking so hard you're going to drop it."

"No!" Sheyshi jerked the lamp away, and oil spilled, hissing on the planks.

"You two go inside and see after the children," said Priya sternly, taking the lamp from Sheyshi. "The noise has woken them."

Mai ate, listening to the anxious questions of children as rain pounded on the roof and spat in under the porch's eaves. Canvas thrummed, tugging on ropes.

"Does the storm frighten you, Mistress?"

"No. I like it. The rain will cut the dust. I'm so tired of tasting grit."

"You wish the captain returns soon?"

"Of course. It was easier to wait in Olossi. Still, there is more than enough to do here. After all, I must build a thriving settlement so I can have a market to enjoy."

Priya bent to kiss her cheek, lips cool on her skin, her breath smelling faintly of cloves. "Will you eat a second portion?"

Mai handed her the empty bowl. "Yes, I will. Do you think it is too early to allow those of the men who have particular women in mind to settle their betrothals?"

"The chief is having a difficult time keeping them in line, because the women here do not hesitate to have sex whenever they desire."

"That's what I was thinking. Get them settled before they get restless, and into trouble." As she shifted, the rice paper crackled, echoed by thunder rolling away over the water. "Miravia hasn't such freedom."

"You must accept that you cannot change certain things, Mistress, and bend your energy to those you can affect."

MAI ROSE WITH dawn's bell, after sleeping with the canvas walls rolled halfway up to admit some breeze into the inner chambers which would otherwise become stifling. The breath of morning had a special beauty, the sun rising over the flat waters and the Spires glinting as light sparked on ice-clad peaks. The clouds had vanished, although there was a constant, streaming mist above the peaks and a smear of pink-tinged white along the eastern horizon. The air was for the moment moist and cool. Sheep and goats grazed beyond the berm under the watchful eye of young shepherds, the children of women brave—or desperate—enough to travel to this barren reach to attempt a new life under the suzerainty of outlanders.

With her usual escort, Mai walked down the track, dodging carts pushed up by workmen, into what was already being called the lower town, although it looked more like a camp with many square tents and larger barracks built of hempen canvas tied over scaffolding. In the Barrens, wood was precious, so most of the building was in brick, and those few structures whose walls reached full height had canvas slung taut for a roof.

This early, Qin soldiers strolled the market lane, many gathered by the noodle sellers to eat before they began their training or patrolling for the day.

"A little bland today," she said as she and Priya sampled a cup from one of the stalls. She smiled at the young woman who wielded the ladle. "Running out of spice again, Darda?"

"But there's plenty of fish!" replied the girl cheerfully. She was young, strong, with a wide smile that displayed a full set of teeth. Good health mattered. Mai had been careful to favor women who looked robust and energetic. "I'm hoping the next boat brings more spice. Wish I could get shoots, but it's not worth the coin to ship them in, can't turn a profit, and they rot. The edible kind don't grow out here. That girl Avisha in your household told me she means to plant a garden when the fields go in. I've already told her what I'd buy."

"Hear any news of your family?"

Her brows furrowed. "It's kind of you to ask, verea, but I don't suppose I ever will. Even if they got away safely and made it to my kin, it's not likely they could go all the way to Olossi to ask after me. It's kind of you to think of keeping a list at the compound for those who do come looking."

"I lost an uncle that way. It's hard not to know what happened to him."

The girl sighed. "It's my younger brother I worry about most. I suppose he is dead, that he might be better dead than suffering, but then I must hope he will walk up alive and tease me like he was used to do." Her frown transformed abruptly to a brighter smile, lamp-lit as the songs called it. A Qin soldier, an older and very steady man, came up with his bowl to buy his morning's meal.

Mai retreated. "I sense an interest there," she said to Chief Tuvi as they paused to look in on a tailor's shop, a weaver's shed, a rope and braid maker, and a pair of shops whose proprietors shaped household items out of clay.

"You have a talent for finding skillful women," said the chief as he eyed a young woman who had thrown down a square of cloth beside the thoroughfare and, shading herself under an umbrella propped up between stacked bricks, was doing a brisk business with needle and thread repairing torn taloos, tunics, trousers, and other items of clothing. She was so intent on her mending that she did not look up as they passed, only paused as their shadows altered her light, then started up again with neat, even stitches.

"It's true I've favored women with skills, and ones who are interested in establishing shops. That way they can maintain their families and grow their clans, while leaving their husbands free to fight and herd. All of which suits Anji's purpose."

Chief Tuvi nodded. "It's a good site. Isolated. Hard for an invading army to attack us here without ruining their own supply lines and running out of water. We are scouting the routes up into the mountains, looking for fallback positions, a defensible refuge, better water sources."

"Yet it will be prohibitively expensive to ship in all our foodstuffs, even with the trade in oil of naya. We can't flood the market with a commodity that is currently high-priced because it is so hard to obtain."

"There's plenty of fish," said Tuvi, and they both laughed. "We'll run sheep and goats in the uplands. Its decent grazing land. If O'eki and the engineers can construct the conduit, we will have a steady supply of water and be able to maintain fields for the locals to work. Then the settlement will be viable beyond the spring in the gully. We could stay here a good long time."

"Have you picked out a wife, Tuvi?"

He sighed. "I left a good wife at home. It's hard to think about taking a new one when I think of her wondering what's become of me. Still, that Avisha is a pretty girl."

Mai shook her head. "No, Tuvi. You'll get bored of her. And you intimidate her. Let her go to someone who will enjoy her chatter."

"Hu! That's telling me! Do you have someone in mind for me, then? Or must I bide a bachelor for the rest of my days?"

"I'll keep an eye out. For you, Tuvi-lo, someone special only."

He laughed.

The noodle-maker came out to greet Mai, her face whitened with flour dust. Mai nodded toward the laborers out in back, muscular men stripped to their kilts and wearing faded caps to protect their eyes from the sun. They were adding on a second room out of brick.

"Expanding already?"

"I've had to hire on four more workers to keep up with the demand. But I've had some trouble with men drinking and fighting."

"Bring your complaint to the next assizes."

"I will, verea. As it happens, I'm hoping to send for my auntie and cousins. With your permission, verea."

"I'll be pleased to see them here if they are as industrious as you."

"You've offered us a chance to change our circumstances, verea. We won't forget it."

Priya stayed behind to haggle over a delivery of noodles to the captain's house, while Mai and her escort walked on. At the lower gate, she stood in a patch of shade as she surveyed the alluvial fan that spread toward the bay, its darker earth cut by shallow streambeds from the seasonal flow. A brickyard spread mountainward, sun-drying bricks laid in ranks. On the coastal side, fish racks stretched as far as she could see. Children crouched where women filleted caught fish, stringing fish heads. Where stonework marked the end of the underground channel, the color of the soil had darkened in a wide skirt.

"Did the reservoir take water from the rains?" she asked. "Is the underground channel going to work?"

Tuvi squinted, but said nothing.

Priya said, "It will take many years for the entire conduit to be dug. There was such a channel in Kartu Town, bringing water down off Dezara Mountain."

"That's where O'eki earned coin, didn't he?" said Mai. "The channel had to be repaired and cleaned out."

"Dangerous work," said Priya. "But he supervises now. Others take the risk."

Down on the flat land, fields might bloom, although the landscape looked dusty and brown. Last night's storm had been the first substantial precipitation since she had arrived weeks ago. The season of Flower Rains was giving way to that of Flood Rains.

"Strange to think of this place as becoming green," Mai said. "I would love an orchard, with sunfruit and almonds. And white-stone fruit. If it will grow here. Maybe it is too hot."

She wiped sweat from her brow. A stream of laborers hauled materials up into town. They wore kilts or long jackets much worn and faded, their caps sewn of scraps of material in every color: peacock green, dingy brown, clay red, fig yellow. Some acknowledged her with a nod; others ignored her. She noted those with a morning spring in their step, and those with a slump in their shoulders despite the early hour. She felt compassion for the weary, but in another part of her mind she toted up the cost of maintaining laborers who were not as strong. Shelter, now that they had set up the barracks tents, demanded little coin to maintain, but food enough to fuel labor did not come cheaply, since much had to be brought in from Olossi. She wanted her outlay on foodstuffs to be used at maximum efficiency, with strong workers, not lagging ones. Rice was easy to transport, but quantities of fresh water to boil it in remained problematic. All in all, the difficulties of this holding seemed overwhelming despite Chief Tuvi's assessment of its superior defensive capabilities.

Yet that did not mean that strangers did not on occasion walk into the settlement, seeking employment or, perhaps, less tangible goals.

"Is that a priest? An envoy of Ilu, by his clothing."

A man was climbing the road. He was a man of mature years, not yet elderly, and dressed in a bright blue cloak, dark-red trousers, and a tunic dyed a brilliant saffron yellow. As he approached the gates he looked up, saw her, and smiled as though they were old friends. She smiled back. He did look familiar, but she could not place where she had seen him.

"Greetings of the dawn," she called, abruptly sure that her day would pass without undue troubles to disturb her.

The guards shifted to take up flanking stations, but the envoy of Ilu flashed no weapons and made no threatening gesture.

"Greetings of the dawn." As he halted in a neighboring patch of shade along the raised gateway, he mopped his brow and chuckled in an amiable manner. "Whew! Hot today, despite the storm last night, neh?"

"So it is," she agreed.

"Where did you come from?" asked the chief.

"I walked down from north of here. That way lies the Ireni Valley. Isolated country."

"Why are you here?"

"Why does any envoy of Ilu walk the land? I come to pass on what little news I have, and to take away news in turn, if any have news to share. I can bide at the temple of Ilu here. If there is one. Where do the locals make their offerings?"

"We have no temples," said Tuvi.

"None are built yet," added Mai hastily, not wanting to offend the man. "Some among us say prayers to the Merciful One. How the rest manage their prayers and offerings I do not know."

"Is it forbidden to build temples to the gods?" he asked, although his tone remained congenial.

"Not at all. But you see, holy one, that we must first build shelter and set up our markets and walls."

"Folk must eat," added Tuvi, "and they wish to sleep with some surety they will not be murdered at their rest. Surely the gods do not begrudge us that much."

"Not at all, ver. And with the Flood Rains entering, you'll certainly wish for shelter. You are outlanders."

"Given title to this land," said Mai. "It is all perfectly legal, holy one. Perhaps you could advise me on where temples might be most properly sited."

"A worthy endeavor. I would be willing to bide a few days before going on my way. There's a substantial ruin a few mey distant. Do you know it?"

"I do," said Mai. "There are substantial sinks of naya there, and a cave where a flame burns without cease. But the city fell into ruin long ago."

"You know the place, truly."

"A Qin soldier was murdered there by a demon several months ago," said the chief.

"A demon! Eiya! I'll avoid it henceforth, then. My thanks for the warning, ver."

Yet somehow, he did not seem surprised. "What is the other thing you wished to consult me on, verea?"

"I was just thinking—you're the first holy priest who has walked out this way— a long way, I admit! I don't know what the proper customs are for the marriage ceremony, beyond a contract."

"That's simple enough, verea. But you'll need established temples here, nothing elaborate. An altar with a single attendant will do. However, no marriage can be sanctified without the proper offerings being made to each of the gods. Surely any of the local women who live here could have told you that." He reached into the sleeve of his robe and produced a sunfruit, small but perfectly ripe. This offering he presented.

"Thank you!" Mai blushed as she accepted it. "Where did you get this, holy one?"

"North of here, about twenty mey distant, there lies a deep valley of particular fertility nestled in the high foothills. Hard to spot from the ground, and difficult to enter. Now if you will, verea, I'll take my leave and go into camp, see if any wish to arrange evening prayers."

"Take a meal with me tomorrow, holy one," Mai called after him. He acknowledged her invitation with a wave as he strode up the hill into the lower town.

The fruit was perfectly ripe, fresh, moist, and sweet without tartness.

The chief meanwhile took his hand off his sword hilt and called over one of the guards. After a consultation, the soldier hurried after the envoy.

"I recognize him, Mistress, said Tuvi. "He walked with the caravan most of the way over the Kandaran Pass, and at some juncture left us and walked on ahead. He might be a holy man. I hear some among them walk into the empire to buy silk for their temples. Or he might be somewhat else."

"He can't be a spy for the Red Hounds, surely. He's local, a Hundred man."

"Locals can be bought. I'm not saying he was. He might be what he seems. I'm saying it's best to observe caution."

She thought of the demon who had ridden into her house and murdered two Qin soldiers. Indeed, the demon's actions had sent Mai and her household into exile in the Barrens.

"I'll be cautious," she assured Tuvi. "Yet I have so many fine guards that I cannot help but feel well protected."

He smiled.

"When do you think Anji will return?"

"That I cannot say. Yet look who approaches. A reeve may bring a message from the captain."

"Chief Tuvi?" The reeve wore a cap against the glare. He looked Mai up and down in a way that made the chief place himself between them.

"I am. You are?"

"This is the captain's wife, I take it. For once I must say that Joss did not exaggerate."

The words had no charm, and she wondered whether he meant them to cut, or whether he could not manage to utter a pleasing compliment because he expected it to be thrown back in his face.

"I don't know your name," said Mai in as pleasant a voice she could muster, al-though his sneer set her on edge.

"I'm Volias."

"Greetings of the dawn, Volias." She was careful to seem warm without being ef-fusive. In the market, she would have to work doubly hard to overcome his readi-ness to take offense, his surety that he would be rejected or mocked. "Are you come from Argent Hall? I am anxious to hear news of the captain."

His shoulders relaxed slightly. "I came through Argent Hall, but I've no message from the captain for you, verea. I'm here from Clan Hall." He shifted his gaze to the chief. "I'm taking the lad, Pil, like you requested, Chief Tuvi. It's been agreed he can train at Clan Hall."

Tuvi nodded.

"Why?" Mai asked. "Is there a problem because he is Qin?"

"Pil is no longer appropriate for the Qin troop," said Tuvi.

"Because he is an eagle rider, not a horseman? I thought Anji agreed that if the eagle chose him, then he would be allowed to train as a reeve."

"That's not why."

In the Mei household, she had learned when a man's expression told you he had nothing more to say on a subject. So she smiled with her blandest face, and nodded politely at the waiting reeve to show he could leave.

He blinked, as though the sun had gotten in his eyes. "Listen, verea. I have got news for you, now that I think of it."

"From the captain?" The eagerness broke in her voice. She coughed to control it, smoothed a hand over her belly. In answer, the baby moved rather like a fish might slip around within grasping hands.

"Neh, I never saw the captain. These days I mostly fly messages between Clan Hall, Nessumara, and Argent Hall. Joss some weeks past told me to keep an eye open for a scouting party sent out by the temples and council. Naturally they've been keeping under cover, so I didn't expect—"

"Did you see Shai?"

The reeve's frown made her heart go chill.

"It happened that I spotted the scouts outside Horn, combing through the re-mains from a battle fought a few years back. It was a stupid thing to do, coming to earth. A band of men attacked them. I had to fly out immediately. I don't know what happened. Likely they hid. There was plenty of cover."

The chief caught Mai under the elbow. He whistled sharply, and said to a guard, "Priya's in the market. Also, a drink."

The reeve's words kept stinging. "Maybe I alerted the bandits, or maybe they were already stalking them. I'm sorry if my flying in to warn them brought about the attack."

"Best you find a place to sit down, Mistress," said Tuvi in a firm voice.

"I warned him about the demon, though," finished the reeve.

As the sun rises, shade retreats. Light lanced her eyes, and one moment she was standing, and the next seated awkwardly on the ground with Chief Tuvi kneeling beside her.

"There, now, Mistress. We'll get you a cup of rice wine. Then we'll take you back to the house."

Down here she had settled back into shadow, but her head still hurt as though she had been standing in the sun all day. "What did I do?" she whispered.

"You wisely sent warning," said the chief sternly, "given the serious nature of the demon's threat. As for the rest, the scouts knew the risks. Those you are not responsible for."

But his words, like the shade, offered no comfort.

40

A whimper woke Shai just before dawn. It took him a moment to remember where he was: starving, thirsty, and a prisoner of a remnant of the army that had been defeated at Olossi and now fled north toward their allies. He was curled around Eska, the youngest and weakest of the girls. She still slept, her thin face looking gray and unhealthy in the twilight. He uncurled to a crouch, surveying the captives. He'd quickly learnt that the children who were not yet fourteen—the ones who hadn't celebrated a ceremony called their Youth's Crown—were not abused even by these crude soldiers except of course that they were daily hit, whipped, and at risk of being killed. The older ones—the eldest besides him was sixteen—were not so fortunate.

Yudit's eyes were already open. Seeing him, she nodded but stayed curled on the damp ground, knees tucked up to her chest as if that could protect her from the nightly assaults. On hands and knees, anxious not to alert the soldiers, he negotiated the cluster of prisoners until he tracked down the one crying: Dena, the other twelve-year-old whose hair the cloaked lord braided.

He placed a hand on her back. "Hush now," he murmured. "I'm here."

He knew better than to warn her that crying could get her murdered. They all knew, and to say it aloud would only frighten them more. Nor did he bother to ask what was wrong. If they wanted to speak, they would; otherwise, he respected their silence.

She pressed her face against his chest until her shudders ceased. "Shai, you'll always stay with us, won't you?"

"I'm here." The dawn whistle blew twice. "Get up now, Dena. Roust your banner. Get them up and moving."

"Yes, Shai."

Judging it safe to rise as the soldiers were now beginning to move, he hurried over to Yudit. "How are you this morning?"

"I can manage," she said wearily. "Jasya and Wori are bleeding again."

"I'll keep an eye on them. Get your banner together."

She began moving children toward the stream to drink before they formed into marching ranks. Mercifully, it had not rained last night and their clothing mostly remained dry but for dew and the moisture seeping up from damp earth. Four days ago, a boy sick with a phlegm-ridden cough had been cut out and killed before Shai could get to him. Now Shai watched constantly for signs of increasing sickness.

He walked through the assembling banners and chose the six strongest children. When the call came for prisoners to take down the canvas under which the soldiers sheltered, he led this group through their routine: stakes pulled, rope coiled, canvas shaken out and rolled up and bound onto the packhorses. He slouched through the tasks, grinning at the soldiers.

"Cold today," he said to the sergeant. "Didn't rain last night."

"A wise observation," replied the sergeant. "Now get on with you. We're moving out."

"Need wood chopped?" he asked a cadre of soldiers, who laughed as they shouldered axes and staves.

He peered into the surrounding woodland, but the lord—who always slept well away from the camp—had already departed on his daytime scouting. The watchful boy walked into camp lugging folded canvas over his thin shoulders.

"Vali," said Shai, stepping closer. "You are well today?"

The lad shrugged, his gaze downcast instead of prying.

"Dena was crying this morning," added Shai.

"It's my fault. I asked the lord for more food last night. Like you asked me to do. He got angry. I guess he took it out on Dena."

"Neh. It's my fault for suggesting it. It was brave of you to ask. Never doubt that."

"Heya! Heya! Up now! Get in line!"

The sergeant strode along the line with whip in hand. He was the kind of man, Shai had decided, who liked to wield his power to make people cringe, and he had a habit of whipping at dawn whichever girl he had raped the night before. There he strutted, and Shai quickly cut back to the line, falling in beside Yudit just as the sergeant reached her with whip raised. Shai made a show of blundering forward, just in time to catch the slash across his own back.

"Cursed idiot!" The sergeant raised the whip again, but the line lurched forward as the vanguard got moving, distracting him.

Yudit tapped Shai's wrist. "Eska's stumbling."

Back stinging, he walked backward as the others walked forward, and hoisted Eska to his back before her faltering drew the attention of the soldiers. Fortunately the whip had only welted him this morning, not drawn blood, so the pain wasn't too bad as her weight—such as it was, her being little more than skin and bones—rubbed his bare skin. But he was thirsty, and of course the hollow in his stomach was a constant torture. Yet he must not show the weakness he felt. Up and down the line of prisoners, faces turned to mark his progress at the rear of the ground. He nodded at Wori, with his tear-streaked face, and at Jasya, who had bruised eyes. Yudit plodded along, her chin lifted with stubborn defiance, and when Dena began dropping back through the line, Shai handed Eska to Yudit and carried the heavier Dena instead.

The soldier called Twist walked up alongside. "Heh. You there, packhorse. You tasted the girls yet? Or are you fashioned for men, eh?"

"Greetings of the day to you, ver," said Shai with his biggest grin. "You got food, maybe? I'm sure hungry."

Twist snorted and called to his comrades. "Cursed fool says the same thing every day. You think we should set him on the girls tonight, like? We could see if he's hung like a horse, way he packs them all day, eh?"

So they laughed, and when they laughed they weren't likely to be beating on the children.

All morning they struggled to keep the pace set by the soldiers. For days and days and days they had pushed north along the ragged skirts of a range of hills, through sparsely inhabited countryside. At midday they paused to water the horses at a stream. After setting down Dena, Shai ranged the line, making sure none of the children drank too much, which would cause them to founder, or too little, which would weaken them further.

"Drink more," he said, coaxing Jasya.

"I'd be better dead."

"If you let yourself die, then they've won. We're going to win by surviving."

She sighed, but she drank.

Once the horses were watered, they marched on. And on. To his sight, the woodland never seemed to change, but just as they waded across another stream, Yudit whispered, "we're getting close to a village," seeing something in the way trees were spaced and bushes flourished in open spaces. The children pointed at berry-laden branches, but none dared leave the line of march to grab them while the soldiers watched.

A command rang down from the vanguard. Abruptly, the captives were herded into a tight group and left with six guards while the rest ran down the path. The children shivered as they heard screams and shouts in the distance. Vegetation rattled in the woods, sounding exactly like folk running for their lives. Eska began to snivel, shocked by fear, and Shai hugged her against him to stifle her sobs. Of the rest, some stared at Shai while others covered their faces with their hands.

To his horror, a pair of ghosts drifted into view, wisps with still enough self-identity that one could identify them as farmers by their misty garb. They were so busy talking to each other, as if intent on escape, that they did not notice Shai's attention.

"Eiya! I thought we'd escaped the calamity! Now they come down on us, when they missed us last time! Did you hide the feast bread and the nai cakes?"

"Eh, I did. Under the boards on the weaving house porch. Good thing the children are still hidden at the refuge. Think you we bought time for the women to get away?"

"I heard them running out here—"

A living cry roused their guards. "Heya! Heya! Bring in the prisoners! We'll have roofs over our heads tonight, lads!"

As they marched in, Shai walked beside Yudit. "Listen," he whispered, "I'll create some manner of diversion. There might be loose boards on the porch of the weaving house, and food hidden beneath it. Be quick, if you can find it. Don't let the soldiers see. Everyone gets a share."

She looked startled, but nodded. The woods opened up into a small settlement, a village of three longhouses and a number of outbuildings, including a weaving shed. One of the longhouses and half of the outbuildings had been burned recently and left in disrepair, but the soldiers ripped through the intact ones, looting anything they could carry and smashing cupboards and walls as they laughed and howled. A trio ripped the roof off a thatched altar, while others trampled on prayer banners. Three farmers lay dead on the dirt, and two had faces Shai recognized: They'd been the ghosts on the path. Soldiers hooted as the sergeant opened the gate to the byre and was bowled over by a pair of nervous ewes rushing to escape.

Shai had spent much of his youth herding sheep up on Dezara Mountain, a good way to stay out of family quarrels. He knew every kind of story about shepherds, single men too poor to avail themselves of brothel fare, lads working the upper pastures for months at a time. Sometimes they did for each other, no shame in that up in the highlands among lads. But one time—hu!—he'd come across a man working at a ewe. Never would he forget that sight.

"Heya! Twist!" he shouted in a louder voice than he'd known he possessed. "I fancy those ones!"

He galloped after the ewes, grabbed clumsily at them and missed, purposefully tripped over his own feet in a mud-slopped puddle, and generally made such a horse's ass of himself that the soldiers, roaring with laughter, all rushed to watch, cheering him on. He was soon winded and aching, but he kept on until Yudit made a show of getting in his way, and then he collapsed, heaving on hands and knees while the soldiers caught the ewes and, just like that, killed both to make a feast. The prisoners, rounded in to haul wood and set up camp, were all surreptitiously licking their fingers and wiping their mouths on their arms.

"Heya!" he said to the sergeant. "I know how to carve up a sheep."

"Heh! Heh! Seems you do. But we're eating these, not devouring them." He walked away without handing Shai a knife. Indeed, the soldiers did all the work skinning and butchering the sheep, keeping the prisoners away from anything sharp. The big open hearth soon blazed, and Shai's mouth watered as meat began to sizzle.

Yudit crept up beside him and slipped a pair of nai cakes, like flat bread, into his hand. "How did you know?" she whispered.

"Eh, ah, it's a trick we did at home, eh?" He gulped them down when no one was looking.

She pressed leaves into his palm. "Se leaves. Very nourishing."

They had an unpleasant, spicy flavor, but they went down easily and for all that they weren't much to taste, they were filling. For the first time in days, he didn't feel light-headed.

"Did you really?" she asked him.

"With sheep? I did not!"

She laughed, and he saw she'd been teasing, that she'd understood all along, and the sight of a smile briefly on her face made it all worth it.

"Heya, girl!" called the sergeant, beckoning to Yudit. She winced, let go of Shai's hand, and rose. "Heh. He may have broad shoulders and brawny arms, but he's not fashioned for the likes of you, eh?" The soldiers chortled. Head bowed, Yudit trudged over to the sergeant, and he led her into one of the longhouses. The men's blood was up after the fight, and they quarreled, there being too many soldiers who wanted a piece and too few captives old enough to be marked for the taking.

"What about one of the younger ones?" said one of the soldiers, eyeing Vali and Dena, who sat apart with their perfectly groomed hair now rather undone by a day's hard walking.

The others jeered and cursed. "What? That's disgusting."

"If the lord does it, it must be good for the rest of us—"

"Shut up! You gods-rotted imbecile. You want to get us all punished?"

"Hush! Lookya. Here he comes."

The lord, his leaf-green cloak swagged behind him, walked into the clearing leading his winged horse. All fell silent, heads bowed, and after a troubling silence in which no one spoke, the sergeant burst out of the longhouse, tying up his trousers.

"Eh, lord, sorry to keep you waiting. What's your wish?"

"Why have you stopped marching while there's still light for walking?"

"Ah, eh, had a bit of a fight with some locals, here, and afterward I thought we might cook up two sheep to strengthen our blood."

The man's gaze cowed all. Shai watched with bent head, kneeling in the dirt with the other prisoners. "This lack of discipline is what got you defeated in Olossi. We must keep moving." He glanced at the sky, and licked his lips. He had a prim face, bland and ordinary, that of a man who in other circumstances you might meet with equanimity in the market about unexceptional business. "Anyway, I'm tasting a flavor in the air. We're being followed, but I can't . . . quite . . . grasp it. Still, the meat will strengthen you. Dena and Vali, come along."

They rose with shoulders set in shame, carrying the canvas that served as the lord's shelter.

At the edge of the clearing, the cloak paused and looked back. "Share meat with the prisoners. I'll know if you don't. Be generous. Sergeant, I'll speak with you now."

He went, and after a bit Yudit slunk out of the shelter and came over to Shai. He left her with the younger children and strode boldly up to the fire.

"Eh! I'm hungry!"

"What?" they laughed. "Going to eat your girlfriends?" But they dared not disobey the lord's direct order. Each child got cut a strip, not so much to sicken them except for Jolas, who threw up afterward, but even Eska looked better for the day's bounty of food.

At dusk, the sergeant returned and walked among the soldiers, speaking in such a low voice that Shai could not hear anything. Their voices buzzed afterward, like bees disturbed by smoke. They've had news, Shai thought.

Last of all, the sergeant beckoned to Shai. "You're to come with me," he said, and called over a pair of soldiers to accompany them. The stream they'd crossed earlier passed through one end of the clearing. With head bowed, Shai followed the sergeant upstream along the bank. On the far shore, water rippled through rocks below a dense growth of pipe-brush. The lord's shelter had been set up near the water, canvas strung between two trees and staked down on either side. Dena sat on a log outside the shelter with hands folded in her lap and tears flowing down cheeks still rounded with baby fat. The sergeant flung out a hand, and they all stopped. The soldiers grimaced, turning away. The sergeant wiped his brow nervously. None could see what was going on under the shelter, but they could all hear it.

The sounds of a man in rut forced Shai's mind back to that day in the desert when he had sold Cornflower's services to the Qin soldiers. Ripe peaches, one man had said: That had been Chaji, and now that Shai thought of it, he realized he'd never liked Chaji, who was meanspirited and vain. What men had gone for the first chance at Cornflower? The ones he had liked least, truly. The others had had more self-control, or perhaps they'd feared her too much to touch her. Perhaps a few had found the transaction distasteful.

Knowing it was Vali who suffered, Shai found the sounds unbearable. Yet even when he shut his eyes he could not hide from the puffing and panting, a groan of release, the wheezing sigh in the aftermath of pleasure. But truly, a pleasure taken, not shared.

Maybe Mai had been right. Maybe selling Cornflower's sex to the Qin soldiers had not been an act of prudent economy but one of thoughtless cruelty. He wept silently.

"Open your eyes and look at me."

Startled, Shai opened his eyes to find himself looking directly at the lord. The man bit his lips, as if he were nervous, or recalling the taste of something sweet.

"You puzzle me, with your dull mind and witless foreign face. Vali says you are the one who told him to request more food for the prisoners." Perhaps he meant to be intimidating, with a belligerent stare and restless hands so like Shai's detestable brother Girish, but Shai had faced far more formidable opponents. He had his story and words down cold.

"I'm so hungry, ver. Never get enough to eat. Makes me tired. Mutton was good, though." He smacked his lips.

"I don't understand you. I fear there is something I am missing. Best we get you to her. She'll know what to make of you." He shuddered, as though by invoking the nameless *her*, he remembered what fear was, he who obviously need fear nothing. "Sergeant, see our friend the woodcutter does not escape. Meanwhile, I must now return to Olo'osson to scout the plain and the Rice Walk for other remnants of Lord Twilight's broken army. I knew the plan would come to nothing under that outlander's incompetent command. Heh. Our lackwit looks something like him, doesn't he?"

"Yes, lord," said the sergeant in the tone of a man who is grateful when he is overlooked.

"You and your company must press onward without my guidance."

"We could wait here for you," said the sergeant, careful not to look up.

"In some ways this seems a safe enough place, very isolated. But I taste an odd flavor on the air, just out of my reach." He shook his head, rubbed his fingers together. "I can't name it. Keep moving. Do not lose the two I favor. You will bring them intact to the army, with the lackwit. If you fail me, I will be sure to make you personally pay for the loss."

The sergeant kept his gaze lowered as his voice quavered. "Yes, lord. All will be as you command. What of the other prisoners? What is your will with them?"

The lord whistled before replying. "The army needs recruits. Those who are ashamed of what they have done will not wish to escape home. No mercy for those who fall behind."

His winged horse paced into view, and the guards drew back fearfully. The lord wiped his hands on his trousers as though wiping off sweat. He did not look back as he rode into the dusk.

"Now what, Sergeant?" asked a guard.

"Bring me that girl I like," said the sergeant curtly, looking irritated.

"Right where the lord sheltered, Sergeant?"

"I'm captain of this troop now, aren't I?" He sauntered over to the shelter as Vali crawled out. Grabbing the boy by the shoulder, he yanked him out so roughly that the lad sprawled face-first on leaves and muck. "Bring Yudit. She's my favorite, and I'll thank you boys not to touch her any longer."

"Cursed getting above himself, he is," muttered the first guard. "Just like that."

The second said, to Shai, "Come on then, you and them."

Dena held Shai's hand, still crying, but Vali walked with arms clenched tight against his chest. After a bit, Shai said quietly, "How are you faring, Vali?"

The lad looked in the direction the cloak had ridden away. They saw a light rising above the trees: The horse had flown. "He doesn't touch us. He just wanks off in his hand."

The words were a lie, and Shai knew it, and Dena knew it, and the lad knew it. Their silence was their pact. If they must say so to endure it, then let them say so.

"You'll survive this," Shai said softly.

The lad caught Shai's other arm and both children leaned on him as they headed back to camp, guards walking before and behind. They blundered along the stream's edge in the darkness. Foot slipping, Shai careered into the water, and yelped as cold bit his skin. In the moment of surprised pain, his gaze lifted to the thicket of pipe-brush on the far shore.

Merciful God!

Memory is a ghost that haunts you. He saw within the pipe-brush Cornflower's face, her pale skin and light hair. She was staring at him.

"Get moving, you clumsy ewe-tupping oaf!" The man slammed him across the back with the haft of his spear.

Shai went down to his knees on the hard stones. Vali gulped down a sob and Dena yelped out a protest, then stifled the cry as the guards cursed at her.

"Here, now," said Shai quietly. He rose, joints popping. His knees smarted and his back ached. "We're just moving on, like you said." To the children, he spoke in a lower voice. "We'll survive this. Don't despair."

When he looked back into the pipe-brush, now behind them, it was too dark to see anything. Anyway, it had only been a trick of his mind.

41

It rained half the night, and twice Avisha woke, sure she heard Mai crying in the adjacent chamber and, in response, Priya's soothing whisper. Every slightest noise carried within the captain's house: the raised plank floor, the stout wood pillars, and the strong roof were of highest quality, but until more of the settlement in the Barrens was serviceable, Mai had insisted they make do with canvas walls.

The children slept soundly, crowded close. After the rains died, the air grew close and stifling, so Avisha tied up the entrance to let in air. Standing in a light cotton shift, she sighed in a blissfully cooling breeze. A pair of figures paced the lower porch that wrapped the structure. A face looked up at her.

"Early yet, Avisha," said Chief Tuvi in a voice hoarsened, perhaps, by the early hour.

She hurriedly shrank back into the shadows of the sleeping chamber as the two men—she hadn't recognized the other one—chuckled, their footfalls soft on the porch as they continued their circuit. Did the man never sleep? He was the captain's most trusted officer, which explained why he had been sent to the Barrens with the captain's beloved wife.

Who had woken again.

"I just can't sleep," Mai was saying in a low voice. "My back hurts. Every time I close my eyes I think of Shai."

Avisha dressed as quietly as possible so as not to wake the other women and children. The house had been built on three levels, to accommodate both their living situation and the vagaries of the ground. A walkway wrapped the greater structure, with the main house one step up, and the inner house another two steps farther up, its raised floor constructed around a courtyard with a cistern, an area for a small garden, and foundations dug out where a tower would be built. The kitchen and work area lay on the western edge of the house, and she slipped on sandals and crossed the walkway down into the kitchen yard. A fire burned on the outdoor hearth: Sheyshi was already up, brewing tea.

Avisha fetched a tray and a pair of cups from the pantry. "I'll take that in."

"I will do it," said Sheyshi. "You will go marry and leave. I will stay here."

Stupid girl!

Aui! She could take in a basin of washing water. She filled a pot from the cistern and heated it on the hearth. By the time she had a pitcher, basin, and cloths ready, Sheyshi was gone and the kitchen women were bustling. Lads were sent to haul water from the spring; rice was washed and readied for cooking. Fish again! But there were fresh spices, shipped in three days ago, to flavor the stew. In town, hammering started up, men getting to work while it was still cool. Although the heavy tray made her arms ache, she paused on the walkway where the view opened over the east. The sun was rising, a blush spread along the watery horizon.

"Need help with that?"

She turned to face Jagi.

"I can carry that in for you."

"My thanks." She handed him the tray, which he handled smoothly, the weight nothing to him.

"We're riding formation today," he said as she held aside the entry curtain to allow him into the formal room where Mai, looking pale, sat on pillows while Sheyshi offered her tea. "I told Jerad he could help me saddle up and get my armor on. If you'll allow it."

"That's very kind of you. Of course he can go. You're like a brother to him, truly."

He flicked a considering glance at her as he set the tray on the table, barely stirring the water. Then he retreated. Face flushed, Avisha waited by the table, wondering if anyone in the room would remark on the comment, on Jagi's kindness, on anything, indeed, but Mai sipped listlessly. She hadn't even noticed Avisha come in. Priya swept out from the sleeping chamber.

"Avisha has brought wash water, Mistress," Priya said, a bit tartly.

Mai glanced up. "Thank you, Vish."

"Are you well, Mai?" Avisha asked.

"Bring a wet cloth!" snapped Sheyshi. "Why be so slow?"

"No use me sitting here feeling sorry for myself." Mai got up awkwardly. The fine silk robes she had brought with her from the south no longer fit her, and she had taken to wearing a taloos, which could be wrapped to accommodate any stage of pregnancy. Dark circles hollowed her fine eyes, and after she had finished wiping her face and hands, she stood with the wet cloth dangling unregarded from a hand and stared out the opened curtain toward the sea.

A faint jangle sounded. Puzzled, Mai straightened. Footsteps sounded on the walkway, and a moment later—quite amazingly—an elderly man dressed in the blue traveling cloak and gaudy colors of an envoy of Ilu trotted up into the chamber.

"Here you are, verea," he said in an amiable voice, as if he were accustomed to entering her chambers every morning, like a favorite uncle. "I heard you were feeling poorly. Not that I have much in the way of healing knowledge or any cunning herbcraft—you'd need a mendicant for that—but I wanted to come tell you that I've consulted with various temples and your architect and we've come up with a proper siting for seven altars. Simple structures could be erected within the week. Once the altars are in place, there's no further impediment if you wish to see marriages go forward."

Chief Tuvi stamped in, sword drawn. "Where did you come from?"

The envoy's smile was sweet and harmless. "I walked in, ver. Didn't you give me permission yourself?"

This statement caused the chief to look confused.

Mai stepped forward. "It's all right, Chief, let him stay. I asked him to come see me when he had news about establishing local temples."

The chief glanced at Avisha, and she flushed. He was a good-looking man in his own way, if very old, probably as old as her father. But he was formidable and important, and everyone listened to him.

"Will you share tea, Your Holiness?" Mai asked.

"With thanks at your gracious offer." The man settled easily on a pillow. He indicated the disordered coverlet. "Not sleeping well? A common complaint later in pregnancy, so I am told. Hard to get comfortable, I should think."

She sighed as she looked at him, as if ready to speak.

"Missing your husband?"

She blushed and looked away. "He is very busy."

"Yes, indeed." The envoy frowned. "Very busy."

"Is something wrong, Your Holiness?"

"Neh, nothing. It's true enough, with the troubles in Haldia, that Olo'osson must consider how to protect itself."

"I don't like the Barrens," said Mai. "But I must not complain."

"Why not?" The envoy glanced at Avisha, and she looked away, wondering why his benign gaze seemed so discomfiting.

"Anji would be disappointed in me."

"Would he?"

Really! thought Avisha. *That holy man ought to know better than to grind his finger into an open sore!*

"There is plenty for me to do," said Mai. "Anyway, if I mope, then the baby will have a sullen personality."

"Is that so?"

"That's what Grandmother always said to her sons' wives. Although how it would explain Uncle Girish's cruel ways, or Uncle Shai's silence—I don't suppose Grandmother thought of that when she was criticizing the others, did she?" Cheered by this thought, Mai accepted the teapot from Priya and with dainty gestures poured four cups.

"Uncle Girish, eh?"

"Let's not talk about him. He's dead now, anyway." She offered him the first cup, which he took. She then offered Chief Tuvi a cup, and she and Priya picked up the third and fourth. With a nod from Mai, they all drank. Avisha smelled the sharp tang, and her mouth watered.

"More?" Mai asked.

"With thanks." The envoy returned the cup to her hand. She smiled at him as she received it. "You mentioned another uncle, Uncle Shai, eh?"

He spoke pleasantly, but Chief Tuvi touched the hilt of his sword, and Avisha took a step toward Mai as if a change in the air impelled her motion.

"Aiyi!" Mai passed a hand over her eyes and seemed on the verge of tears. "Probably dead, too. It's my fault."

Priya tucked a hand under Mai's elbow and firmly settled her on a pillow.

"How so?" asked the envoy as gently as a feather brushes.

Tears began to fall, some captured in the cup held in her hands. "There came a demon. A ghost." She shook her head. "A ghost turned into a demon, maybe. She rode into our compound in Olossi and killed two of the soldiers. Then I didn't mean to tell her but I did, so now she's gone after Shai."

"North," muttered the envoy.

"North," she echoed, or maybe he had echoed her.

Avisha shivered.

"And then I heard some days ago—that very day I met you at the gate, Your Holiness—that Shai had been attacked by bandits."

"Where did that happen?"

"Near the town of Horn. That's where the ring belonging to my Uncle Hari was found." Her shoulders slumped. The cup rolled out of limp hands, and Sheyshi deftly caught it as Mai covered her eyes. "What if Shai is dead?"

The envoy had the kind of cheerful modest demeanor that makes the day more pleasant when he walks into your shop and asks to purchase braid and rope. Yet beneath all lay a disquieting expression, hard to fathom.

He looked at Avisha, eyebrow cocked as if in a question.

Unbidden, words rose. "I miss my father," she whispered, but no one was listening. No one but him. His gentle smile lingered as he looked toward the door.

"Chief!"

Tuvi hurried outside. Mai looked up. Feet clattered on the walkway as male voices rose in greeting. The captain strode in, followed by guards and the handsome reeve, who halted to stare at the envoy of Ilu.

"Anji!"

The captain crossed to Mai, took both her wrists in his hands, and frowned as he examined her wan face. "Tuvi sent word you were not feeling well."

For a moment he matched gaze to gaze with the envoy, and his brow furrowed as if the captain was trying to place the man. Then he nodded at Tuvi.

"Everyone out," said the chief.

The chamber cleared with a bit of confusion, people getting in the way, Sheyshi running out and then running back in for the tea things and impeding the exit of others as she fussed. Avisha retreated to the walkway, wondered if she should collect the basin and pitcher, and then saw the reeve—marshal of Argent Hall, a very important man!—beckon to her.

Biting her lower lip, she went to him.

"I can't recall your name. I'm Marshal Joss. We met in the Soha Hills."

"It's Avisha, ver. I remember you."

His smile warmed. Maybe he was old enough to be her father, not that he was anything like. Aui! He was a handsome man even as old as all that. "There was an envoy of Ilu in there. Did you see where he went?"

"No, ver, but he can't have gotten far."

"What do you know of him?"

"He came into the settlement about a week ago, at least twelve days. The mistress asked him to site altars for the gods, so marriages can go forward in the proper way."

Chief Tuvi ambled over, his gaze sharp and his smile forced. "Is there a problem, Marshal?"

The marshal raised a hand as if to beckon Tuvi in. An unspoken message passed between the men, but she wasn't sure what it was. "See if you can find that envoy, Chief."

"He's harmless. The mistress likes him, and she is a good judge of character."

"If I'm not mistaken, the last time I saw that man was in Dast Korumbos. He was dead."

Eihi! Maybe the marshal wasn't quite right in the head. Age took folk like that.

"You recognized him, too, eh?" said Tuvi, nodding. "He walked with us over the Kandaran Pass, but I lost track of him before we reached Dast Korumbos. You say he was killed in the bandit attack?"

"He was dying."

"But you didn't see him dead?"

The marshal ran a hand over his tightly cropped hair. "I did not, it's true. It's hard to imagine he could have survived those injuries, though."

Chief Tuvi shook his head. "He's talked a few times with the mistress, ver, and I can tell you, he's no ghost. Ghosts don't drink tea, for one thing."

"Hard to imagine how they could." The charming smile flashed as the marshal's gaze shifted back to Avisha. "If the altars are built, then I suppose marriages will go forward. You must have a line waiting for you, Avisha. Yet whose rice will you eat?"

She wrapped a hand in the fabric of her taloos, angry at him for embarrassing her in front of Chief Tuvi, who might not like to see her in the company of such a good-looking man. But the marshal was not truly interested in her, he was just fashioned that way, flirting with women the same way he breathed.

"I must go, ver. I've work to do."

And Zianna to check in on. Eiya! She'd neglected the children, so caught up was she in running after the mistress. She hurried off. Jerad was nowhere to be found, and Zi was in the kitchen yard with little ones her own age, picking pebbles out of a bin of rice, careful-handed despite their youth.

"Zi, I'm off to the garden. You want to come?"

Zi barely glanced at her. "No."

Zi had been angry at Avisha since the day Nallo had left, as if that was Avisha's fault. Anyway, Zianna didn't really understand that their father was dead, only that he wasn't around to dote on her and someone had to be blamed for a world cast into disorder.

With a sigh, Avisha caught the attention of one of the kitchen workers. "I'm going down to my garden."

"I'm hoping those melons you planted give fruit," said the woman with a smile, tucking a strand of loose hair back into her kerchief with a sweaty hand.

Avisha trudged down through the growing settlement. Men expanded a second reservoir at the base of the irrigation channel. The main reservoir had captured a fair bit of water in the recent rains, which was routed into cisterns. Mai had extended credit for seeds, and Avisha had received a plot in one of the irrigated parcels. The soil was a fine-grained pale silt nothing like the black river-fed soils of her home. She hadn't much to enrich it with beyond peelings and scraps she composted with night soil, but while celestial star simply would not grow, she had coaxed along decent plantings of ginger, onions, pepper-heart, and various chilis. She watered and weeded the garden, then walked past the parade ground. Down by the shelter where folk could rest under shade after drilling, Jerad cracked sticks with another lad. Although she halted and waved, he did not notice her.

She wiped away a tear with a dirty finger and walked to the dry fields, where she had set up pot irrigation for her melons. She had also planted sapling figs, dates, and three ranks of precious woolly-plum seedlings; all but two had sprouted. Out here, all alone, she felt truly isolated. She did so badly miss her father.

Horsemen pounded into view in tight formation. She watched admiringly as the Qin soldiers pulled up, wheeled, turned again, and galloped away with dust spitting in their wake. Another group of ten raced up to attempt the same maneuver, the local riders awkward on their mounts while their black-clad Qin supervisor slashed his whip at those who fell out of line. A second unit of trainees attempted the drill, half of them hopelessly lagging on the first turn as the Qin soldier yelled at them and chased them back to the starting point. A third group came, holding together better at the first turn, but several fell off the line at the second turn and then whipped their horses to catch up, only to get themselves in a tangle, pulling up short before the horses crashed into each other.

Jagi was in charge of this group. He rode through the ranks laughing, and pointed with his whip here, and then there, indicating where they had gone wrong. He had the riders work back through the drill in pairs before a shout from the starting point called his group back. They rode off in paired rows; some of the local men had their hair up in topknots, like the Qin, while others had bound their long hair in horsetails that swagged down their backs. She admired their squared shoulders. Jagi, at the back, had so easy a seat on his horse that he and it might as well have been one creature.

A formation consisting only of Qin riders swept past. Jagi peeled off from his own group and raced with his comrades through an about-face back toward the starting line with a precision and speed that made her heart pound. No wonder they had defeated a much larger army!

"Vish!" Jerad trotted up, his face smeared and his clothes dirty. He wore a big grin of pure happiness as he watched the troop ride off. "Did you see that, eh? I'm going to be a soldier in the captain's army. Jagi is teaching me to ride. I'm going to become a black wolf, just like them."

42

"Why should you get to keep that girl for yourself, not sharing her?" The soldier confronting the sergeant squinted, holding an axe in one hand. "Who set you over us as if you was lord?"

Shai watched sidelong as he scoured out the pot that had been used to cook rice. The conflict had been taking shape over several days of marching, and now, having stopped for the night in yet another isolated, abandoned, burned village, the malcontents within the cadre of thirty-six had decided to confront their leader.

"I was named captain when the cloak left us," snarled the sergeant. "You going to argue with the lord?"

The man with the axe sneered. "You think that pervert cares about us? You ever think maybe we were led into a trap? I've been thinking the lords sent us west to test Olossi's strength, not caring what became of us. Like scarpers sent into a hole to see if an adder will bite. What do we owe them? Why go back at all, eh? Plenty of fields here. We've got slaves to do the work."

Shai sat on a charred beam out in front of a shed where most of the younger children, chores complete, already rested on such pallets as they could scrape together from grass or straw. They were always scratching, bodies speckled with bites and discolored with sores and bruises and welts. His foot itched. He leaned down and felt along the arch until he identified the bump where he'd been bitten. Aiye! He hurt everywhere, but he must never let it show.

Twenty-six men had congregated around the sergeant, so there were nine men not present. He identified four in visible watch positions where two paths entered the wide clearing. Two more would be in the woods on a ranging watch. Where were the other three? Yet he could not possibly lead twenty-four frail children and adolescents into the woods; even with a head start, they would be caught.

"Farming is hard work," said the sergeant as his allies muttered agreement. "I didn't sign up to farm."

"You say that because you get a good lie-down every night, when there aren't enough to go around who are old enough, eh? Or are you like the cloak, eh? The younger, the better?"

"You gods-rotted, pus-filled shit!" The sergeant flicked up a hand, and Twist and another pair of soldiers threw the challenger to the ground. Their bodies blocked Shai's view of the beating, but two girls who were carrying buckets on a pole down the lane faltered and dropped the pole, so frightened were they at the sight. Solid thumps changed tone to a meatier, more liquid sound; they were bashing in the man's head.

There is a way men have of breathing hard when their blood is up that Shai had come to recognize in these soldiers, a spillover that the Qin soldiers had, evidently, learned to rein in. Twist lurched out of the gathering, glaring around, hands clenched. Men moved back from him as he spotted the cowering girls. Shai leaped up and trotted forward.

"Here, now!" he called out. "I'm thirsty! Where's my water?" He affected the lop-sided gait that made the men laugh at him, but no one was laughing.

"Take the body away," snarled the sergeant. "If any of you have further complaints, let me know."

Twist grabbed Shai. "You're not what you pretend to be, that's what I think, cursed outlander." He spat in Shai's face.

The spittle landed beneath an eye, and he flinched, sparking with hatred as he forced a stupid grin. "Heya! My dear mom said spitting wasn't nice."

"I'd wick your dear mom until she wept for mercy!" Twist slugged him up under the ribs.

The impact doubled him over, but the spectacle had drawn the attention of the others, those slinking away to lick their wounds and those needing a bit of fun to work out the bloody aftermath of the killing of one of their own.

"Heya, Twist! I'm betting his mother was a ewe. I hear that's more to your liking."

"You ass-wiping turd."

Gagging and hacking, Shai stumbled out of the way. A fight broke, fists flying, and more men waded in, laughing with a high-pitched giggling, but as Shai staggered toward the girls the roil settled out and the knot dispersed, men grumbling as they headed to fires or shelters.

"Pick up the buckets." It was hard to choke out the words with his chest throbbing. "Get back to the well and get more water. Keep moving like nothing happened."

Faces gray with fear, the girls grabbed pole and empty buckets and hurried off. They were so scrawny their shoulders came to a point instead of a nice rounded curve. What remained of their tunics hung in flaps.

Shai rested on hands and knees as he waited for the worst of the pain to fade. Merciful One protect them! Tohon would be making a plan, while he did nothing more than react as each new blow fell. Maybe he was dull-witted in truth. He'd done his best, organizing the children into banners so they could look out for each other, carrying the weakest when they lagged. But it wasn't enough.

And yet the girls did come back with the water without being hit. The men mumbled, and ate their supper, and called for their favorites or waited their turn. The beaten man had been dragged away by the other soldiers and thrown into the trees, but despite the pulpy mess of his head, some glimmer of life still animated him because no ghost rose.

Shai crept back to the shelter as twilight mellowed the scene. It was easy to believe they sheltered in a peaceful backwoods hamlet, trees soughing in the breeze, candlewick flowers giving off dusk's perfume. An owl hooted, and a nightjar clicked.

After night fell, Jasya and Wori and the others old enough to be taken hobbled back to the shelter, ducking past him on the threshold and finding their places in their banner groups as he had assigned them. He waited until all were back except Yudit, who was forced to remain with the sergeant all night. He had to wait, because three nights ago they had lost Jolas, done to death in a rough way that Shai sheared away from recalling, having seen the aftermath. He hadn't thought to go looking for the lad until morning, and by then of course it was far too late.

Yet what could he have done anyway?

How was it possible he could not keep them all safe?

Too restless to sleep, he braced himself across the opening so no one could grab one without him knowing. He considered paths of escape. Could they sneak out at night? By the two sentry fires, shadowed forms paced on watch. The pair of men set to watch the prisoners' shelter kept up a steady murmur, an idiotic conversation about a game called hooks-and-ropes.

Rain passed over, out of the southeast. He dozed, woke when a child whimpered, but it was only a dreaming cry, not repeated. The watch fires glowed red. At the forest's edge, mist untangled from the vegetation to drift into what had been some poor soul's tended garden.

He rubbed his eyes. The mist took on a flowing shape, a ghost winged with a gleaming trail as if its spirit were blown back in an unseen wind from the land beyond the Spirit Gate.

The soldier was dead, then, his ghost wandering in confusion. That left thirty-five, still too many for a single woodchopper to take on.

Yet for an instant, as the ghost crossed the compound toward the byre where the sergeant slept, he saw in the misty shape the form of a woman who looked exactly like Cornflower.

Merciful One! Would her haunt never let him rest? He shut his eyes, wishing desperately for sleep, anything to shut down the fevered workings of his exhausted mind. If he breathed slowly, if he cupped hands before his heart in the attitude of prayer and murmured the beseeching phrases, perhaps he could find peace.

"I go to the Merciful One for refuge. Accept my prayers out of compassion. Peace."

Footsteps pattered on the ground like a fall of rain. He opened his eyes as Yudit crouched beside him.

"The sergeant's dead," she whispered. "They'll think I did it, and they'll kill me. But I was just lying there. A ghost came in and stole his spirit." Shivering, she clutched his arm.

"Who's dead?"

"The sergeant." She pressed two objects into his hands: the wolf ring and the belt buckle.

"Get inside."

Shaking, she crawled past him. Whispered questions greeted her. He eased out from the threshold and crawled to the corner of the shed, from which he could see down the central village path. No ghost emerged from the building where the sergeant slept. Maybe the sergeant's ghost had already passed through Spirit Gate. Or maybe Yudit, in her fear, had been mistaken.

A bird chirped, the herald of dawn's coming. Men slumbered. The watch paced. One man by the north path, just becoming visible, swayed as though dozing on his feet. An aura of gray touched the treetops as more birds assayed their predawn song. There was something he ought to have understood and acted on, but had missed.

"Heya!"

He ran back to the threshold. The south path guard was waving his hands, running toward the camp; he tripped and fell hard, cursing. Within the shelter, the children were already awake and alert.

A woman wearing a lord's cloak rode into the clearing, white cloth unfurling like wings as she raised a staff to command their attention.

"You ass-kissing turds. Rise as I command!" The voice carried without being a shout. Its resonance hung in the air as men scrambled up.

An armed woman rode beside her. He blinked twice, before he recognized her: *Zubaidit!* Had she betrayed them?

As the two females rode forward, his mind sorted out what he thought he was seeing from what was right in front of his face. The cloak was Eridit, but her bearing so changed and her aspect so frightening that it was hard to see in this cloaked woman the recklessly self-absorbed young actress who had dandled the other three men and afterward thrown Shai down beneath the overhand and, well, wicked him.

"Lord Radas sent me! Why are you loitering here when you are needed in Haldia? We are angry at your disobedience! Get your gear! Move out quickly!"

Her gaze passed over Shai as if she did not recognize him. Zubaidit, measuring the movements of the men as they grabbed gear or slouched out of lean-tos and ruined houses, marked him. Both women were dressed more conservatively than he was used to seeing them, far less flesh exposed; Bai was accustomed to having a lot of freedom of movement, while Eridit had just liked flaunting it. But now Bai wore a shift under her laced leather vest, and leather trousers for riding, while Eridit wore richer garb, a silk tabard and flowing trousers whose bright blue color shone in the rising dawn light. Her glossy black hair was twisted up on her head and held in place by lacquered sticks.

Twist and his cronies formed a tight knot, blocking the path into the village. They looked skittish, but they held their ground. "I see no winged horse," Twist said, although his voice quavered.

Eridit raised a hand, as if giving an order.

A hiss sounded. An arrow buried itself in Twist's throat. He crumpled, as the men around him shouted in fear and bumped into each other in their haste to get away from the stricken man. His body spasmed, legs pumping as he gurgled.

"We do not tolerate disobedience," cried Eridit, and even Shai shuddered at her imperious fury.

A man came running from the byre. "Heya! Heya!" Sweating and gray, he stumbled to a halt as he stared at the two mounted women with suspicion and fear. "Sergeant's dead. Not a cut, or welts, or bruises on his throat. He's just dead."

Zubaidit's gaze flickered, and Eridit glanced at her sidelong, the moment passing quickly as the soldiers gabbled in alarm and confusion.

"Thus are those who disobey us, punished!" cried Eridit. "Gather your gear. Move east. Quickly, now. Quickly."

Cowed, they hastened to their shelters and pallets.

One brave man shuffled forward with head bent to touch fisted hands. "What of the prisoners, lord?"

Neither looked toward Shai.

"Leave the prisoners!"

"Er, eh, as you command, lord. But what of the two favored ones the lord cloak, Lord Bevard, commanded us to bring safely to camp. And what of the lackwit? The lord cloak promised he would tear our hearts out if we did not do as he ordered."

"Show me the prisoners," said Eridit in that same full-throated voice, deeper than her speaking tone.

"You there, woodchopper! Get them out."

Shai ducked inside the shelter. Every child was standing, ready for anything, as he'd trained them to be. "File out in your banners. Stand close beside the door. Be ready to duck back inside if I tap my shoulder. Run like crazy for the woods on the north if I tap my head."

They filed out. Bai looked them over, her grim expression unchanged.

Eridit's anger scorched. "These are no longer your responsibility. I know which are chosen by Lord Bevard. I am responsible now. You have your orders."

Incredibly, the soldiers formed up in a ragged line and jogged out of the clearing and away down the southeastern path, their hulking forms vanishing into the trees one by one by one until—Merciful God!—they were all gone.

The children stared numbly after them. The rising sun brought the trees into color. In the long silence, birds twittered. They stood there for what seemed forever, unable to move. Shai's skin was atwitch like a thousand bugs crawling.

The brush beyond the path rustled. Vali began to sob. Shai clamped a hand over his mouth.

"Hush, Vali, hold it together!"

Tohon trotted out of the trees, carrying his bow. He jogged up to the two women, nodding at Shai as he halted. "They're moving off at speed." He looked at Eridit. "That was done well, lass."

Her high color sank to a dull sheen. She dismounted hastily and took only three steps before she doubled over and retched, heaving until she had nothing left to bring up.

"Where did you get the horses?" Shai could think of nothing else to say.

"That horse has no wings," said Dena. "The lord has a winged horse."

Tohon surveyed the children, then caught Bai's attention. "I'm going to track the soldiers. These young ones are a complication. Best if they return to their homes."

"Don't you think they would have done so long ago if they could have?" cried Shai. "They can't possibly walk so far now, even if they could find their way, which I doubt. Most would starve along the way or be captured again. The lord went back toward Olo'osson looking to round up more of the soldiers routed at Olossi. Do you want to send them walking back into his hands?"

"Work it out," said Tohon. He loped back into the forest on the trail of the soldiers.

"Why ever did they leave you alive, Shai?" asked Zubaidit.

"The cloak took me for a lackwit."

Eridit rose. "Can you blame them?" She spat, grimacing at the taste. "Aui! You've talked more just now than I heard you talk the first month we were out."

Shai tapped his shoulder, and the children hustled back into the shelter, even Vali, who was forcefully sucking down sobs, trying not to break out weeping.

"Why did you come back?" he said. "I assumed you would just go on with the mission."

Bai shrugged. "The less you know, the less can be tortured out of you. We figured if you reached the camp, you'd be questioned. We couldn't take the chance they'd learn of our situation from you."

He considered the cold nasty feeling he'd had in the presence of the cloak. "It's true. He was sending me to be questioned by the commander of the army."

"Lord Radas?"

"A female. He never named her. I can't leave the children behind, they depend on me."

"What can you possibly do with them?" asked Eridit. All imperious command had vanished. She looked exhausted.

"I don't know. Get them to a safe haven."

"Nothing like that around here," said Bai. "This entire district is pretty sparsely settled, but even so, every village we've come across as we've tracked you has been burned out or abandoned. Even the temples are empty. You can't lead them all the way back to Olo'osson, Shai. Or hope to find their families, if their families even survived."

"If I leave them now, I don't know who will die because I wasn't here to help them."

Mounted, Bai reminded him of the Qin soldiers: deadly, but rational, unlike the soldiers who had taken them prisoner. "They went inside quickly enough, at a signal from you."

"They're formed into banners. They'll take my orders."

"Is there a well around here?" asked Eridit. "Eihi! I want to rinse out my mouth."

"That way." He pointed.

She moved.

Bai said, "Don't go, Eridit. We've got to clear out now."

Eridit halted.

"All it takes is three of those cursed soldiers to ask a pair of questions and call each other cowards, and they'll be come running back here to kill us. Eiya!" Bai bit her lip. Raised her gaze to the heavens. Drew down her brows.

"We can't take them all," said Eridit.

"I'm not leaving the children," said Shai. "You go on. I'll manage. Come out, banners! Grab anything there is." They filed out briskly, looking frightened. "Yudit, take your warblers and the heron banner and run to the byre. See if the soldiers forgot the supplies stored there."

Yudit and Dena ran off with their groups, but to watch them go made obvious the ridiculousness of any plan to save them: too thin, too weak, too young. Still, he must try.

"Owls, scour the houses. Don't dawdle. You hawks, go to the storehouse beside the well and see if there are any ladles, buckets, or pouches left, and fill them with—"

A scream arced from the forest cover.

"The hells!" Bai drew her sword.

"Shit!" Eridit fumbled the mount as two men sprinted out of the woods, packs flapping on their backs. If they had held swords or spears, they had lost them.

A pale-haired, demon-eyed ghost rode out of the forest, with a light burning in her left hand and a mirror held in her left. Mist coiled around her, only it was not mist. It was a cloak that concealed her legs and, in its winding, blended into the furled wings of the mare she rode. One of the men looked back over his shoulder at the demon.

The mirror, catching light, flashed. The man collapsed to the ground.

The other stumbled gibbering to the ground and raised hands in supplication, but when the mirror flashed again, he slumped forward, then toppled sideways.

Bai sheathed her sword and yanked a strung bow from her quiver, fitting an arrow as the ghost rode forward. The hawk banner huddled around Shai, fixed in the silence they'd learned to keep. Other children, farther away, cried out and ran, some toward the byre where Yudit had gone, but others back to Shai.

All the tales said that demons were beautiful, that they aroused men and women to lust; this one was no different.

She pulled up her mount and faced him.

"You're a demon," he said, his voice strong enough that it surprised him to hear it issue so forcefully from his mouth. He wasn't accustomed to speaking up. "You've taken on the appearance of someone who is dead."

"I am a demon," she agreed, in the smoky voice he'd dreamt of so many nights, wishing to hear her speak even though in all the time she had served the Mei clan she had seemed mute. Meeting his gaze, her brow furrowed. "Yet your heart is veiled to my sight."

She looked at the others. Eridit choked down a cry; the children wept; Bai doubled over, a hand clapped to her heart, bow and arrow falling out of her hand to the ground to leave her helpless. The ghost looked back at him, the only one who could meet that cold blue demon gaze. Yet what is a demon, after all, but your fears and hopes stalking you?

"Those who hurt others must be punished," she said.

Vali clung to him, and Eska and Dena had thrown their arms around his body. Gently, he pushed them behind him. "Maybe I harmed you once, but these others did not. Spare them, I beg you."

A ghost retains emotion, but demons have been bled dry. Her round, pale face did not alter expression as she raised the mirror.

And lowered it.

"You act as I did once. What does that make you?" She shook her pale head, as at an unanswerable question, then rode off across fields green with untended weeds. The horse unfurled its wings and leaped, rising above the treetops. All stared as the demon and her horse vanished from sight.

First to recover, Eridit raised both hands and sang. "'Heaven-born, elegant in line, it rises above the mountains to where the stars burn.'"

"I feel sick," said Bai, straightening as slowly if she were an old woman afflicted with joint fever. "The hells! That cursed demon looked straight into my heart!"

Hooves thumped on earth. At a gallop, Ladon and Veras burst into the clearing from the path.

"They're all dead!" cried Ladon.

Another rider appeared, reining to a halt beside the two militiamen. Tohon's expression was pulled with shock, eyes white and almost rolling, but when he saw Shai and identified the others, he pressed the back of a hand against his chest and with several controlled breaths calmed himself.

"They're dead," the Qin scout said. "I counted thirty-four soldiers, these two the last. A demon killed them."

"That was a Guardian," said Eridit. "As it says in the chant. A Guardian saved us!"

"It was a demon, like the other cloak," said Vali hoarsely. "I'm glad the soldiers are dead. I'm glad! I wish I could have cut their throats myself! And then cut the lord cloak's throat, too, and made him bleed!"

"Hush, Vali."

Zubaidit looked at Shai. "You recognized her."

"The demon took on the appearance of a woman who was once a slave in the Mei clan. We called her Cornflower, for her eyes. But she died in the desert last year."

"What did she mean, that your heart is veiled?"

"I don't know."

Tohon said, "These children are a burden to our mission. Also, in this large a group, they will attract attention. They should be scattered."

" 'Your heart is veiled,' " muttered Bai. She swung down from her horse to pick up her fallen weapon. With the arrow, she tapped Tohon on the arm. "I have a better idea. These children are our gate into Lord Radas's army, don't you see? If we walk into the army with prisoners in tow, we'll look like we belong."

"How can you even say so?" cried Shai.

"Not into slavery," she said briskly. "Not to be abused. Shai, do you believe I would chain any person to what these have already suffered? But you know what we're facing. The children can help us, if they can be brave."

Hand closed around the shaft of the arrow, she raised it as a talisman. She stamped three times, marking the entry, and sang in a voice not as silky and prettified as Eridit's but more powerful. This was no guise or mask, meant to entertain, but a call to arms.

" 'Oliara-the-Bold raised the silk banners, all their color made bright in the sun. She cried out, "Forward! Forward!" and so they marched.' "

A few mouthed the words or, like Eridit, sketched the gestures with their hands.

"Can you be brave?" Bai asked them, echoing the tale. "Do you want to defeat those who harmed you and killed your comrades and kinfolk?"

"I want to go home," said Eska in a small voice.

"And you will, every one of you, I swear it by the knives of the Merciless One." She met each pair of eyes, because all watched her. "Any who wish can head home now."

But of course it was impossible that these children could walk hundreds of mey across unknown countryside without food or guidance. Bai knew that and, knowing it, manipulated them. Shai hated her even as he felt the pull of her words and of her strength.

"We're the ones who will destroy that which lies beyond the Shadow Gate. We are the ones who will walk into their camp and spy them out. Be bold. Strike the blow that will cripple them. We must go forward."

" 'Forward, forward,' " they whispered, the familiar echo from thé tale.

She swept them up in the flood of her righteous anger, so you drowned never knowing you had succumbed.

Eridit glowed, staring at Bai as at a lover. The militiamen likewise nodded eagerly. Even Tohon—who surely knew better!—tugged on an ear as he considered her words, her stance, her reckless proposal.

"You're crazy," said Shai.

"Maybe a bit of madness is what is needed. Not the Thunderer's strict ordinances or the Lantern's tidy accountings. Now enters the mistress of love, death, and desire, the All-Consuming Devourer. Swallowed up, we become the vessels that carry out her will, for it is not her will that we transgress against others. She will walk with us, as long as we walk in her."

" 'Praise to the glorious one,' " sang Eridit. " 'She who is lightning. She who devours us.' "

Passionate words engulf the unwary; strength lures the vulnerable. After all they had suffered, after all they had done and pretended to do, the young ones wanted, perhaps, to feel their degradation meant something. They weren't shamed; they were soldiers.

"Don't worry, Shai," said Zubaidit as she surveyed her frail, ragged troops. "I have no intention of seeing the innocent suffer. I have a plan."

43

"Do you hear that voice?" whispered Eliar.

"No."

"It's mumbling on and on. 'Mist flees,' and 'a night spanned with stars cloaks all.' I can't sleep."

Keshad rolled over in his blankets. Even that effort made him pant in the thin air of the Kandaran Pass. "The only cursed voice mumbling on and on is yours. Any chance you're likely to leave me alone so I can sleep?"

In the crumbling sod shack they were, of necessity, pressed close together under what remained of the turf roof. The rest of the party had refused to sleep in a place rumored to be haunted and instead huddled beneath canvas in the freezing night outdoors among rocks and snow. Now Kesh wished he had joined them, even though he had observed that the whole cursed place looked likely to slide away. But night had caught them on the road, and the rocks and shack seemed stable enough.

Eliar coughed hoarsely, as they all did up on the heights. "Did you know you are one of the most unpleasant men I have ever been forced to associate with?"

"I wasn't aware anyone forced you to come on this expedition. Are you done?"

"People like me, you know. Everyone likes me."

"Of course they do. You're young and rich and handsome, even if you are a hells-cursed Silver. Now can I sleep?"

"I wish you would stop using that word. I am Ri Amarah."

"Aui!" The exclamation caught in his weary lungs, and he coughed, once started unable to suck in enough air to stop.

Eliar plucked at his sleeve. "Hsst! Do you hear that?"

This time he did hear something. He covered his mouth and listened. It sounded like the jangling of harness. As with one thought, he and Eliar crawled to the remains of the door. Dawn would come soon, and as he peered into the gloom he was able to distinguish the road as a stripe below. Mercifully, the rest of their party were well hidden at the edge of the rocks.

The sound echoed off the high mountain escarpments, amplified by the predawn quiet and the eerie lack of wind. Men trotted into view, carrying lamps extended on poles. After them marched a force of soldiers, the men walking on the steep upgrade but each one leading a string of four horses, one saddled, one packing, and the other two as remounts. They wore swords slung at their hips and javelins or bow quivers across their backs; spears and bundles of javelins and arrows laded the pack horses. At speed, they passed quickly, moving north and vanishing from sight before the first birds woke to sing awake the dawn.

"Is that a trading company?" Eliar whispered. "Trying to get across before the snows close the pass?"

"Are you as stupid as you sound? Those are soldiers. Several hundred, I'd estimate."

"Eiya! Whose soldiers?"

"Sirniakan, by the look of them."

"But what if—?"

"I'm not listening. It's none of my business. I don't care. Let's roust the men and make an early start. I want to get down off the heights before more snow falls. Aui! I hate the cold!"

Eliar shut his mouth, but as they raised the grumbling company and set off in marching order while dawn lightened the cloudy sky, he loosed dark, brooding glances toward Keshad that were, Kesh supposed, meant to disturb Kesh into troubling himself over the matter.

None of the drovers had noticed anything, so their company of ten hirelings and ten doughty guards—in truth nothing more than reckless young men hankering for an adventure and, perhaps, a chance to slip chains binding them in Olossi—set off downroad, traveling south.

Keshad scanned the slopes, not that there was a cursed thing they could do about it if they were attacked by a numerically superior force of bandits. But as the morning unfolded and their knees ached from the jarring descent, they met no one walking north.

"I thought we'd see more people on the roads," said Eliar, who had moved up alongside Keshad at the front.

"Not this time of year. The big snows could come any day and block the pass. We'll be trapped in the empire for months."

"What will we see in the empire? I've read accounts, and talked to merchants, but—"

"We'll see no women, that's one thing. I suppose you'll like that."

"Is there some hidden meaning in your rude words?"

"Do you think there is? You Silvers keep your women hidden away. You wouldn't like your sister out walking around, would you?"

"I've already told you I don't talk about my female relatives with people who aren't kin."

"I might like you better if you did."

"It was a shameful thing that happened to my sister."

"It wasn't her fault."

"You know nothing of the matter. You know nothing."

Kesh knew that Eliar could not forgive him because he had glimpsed his sister's face that night in Olossi. Bai would urge him to befriend the man as an act of kindness, or maybe simply because it was the smart thing to do, but that gate was already closed, and it wasn't Kesh who had closed it. He'd have loved nothing more than to hear the other man talk on and on and on all he wanted if only the subject was his glorious sister.

"Heya, ver," called one of the guards. "Here comes someone."

Kesh whistled, and they tightened up their formation, guards slipping wicker shields off their backs. Kesh had a sword, but he left it sheathed. Surely bandits would ambush them, not march up in the open.

A trio of peddlers walked into view, each man leading a string of laden horses. They wore red caps and the distinctive tiered robes common among Sirniakan merchants. The guards relaxed.

Keshad acknowledged them with the believer's salute, speaking in the believer's language. "Peace to you, in the Name of the Exalted One, King of Kings, Lord of Lords, the Shining One Who Rules Alone."

"Peace to you," they replied, and there was an awkward moment while both parties slowed so as not to ram into each other. Kesh pulled his mount aside, and his company followed suit, but instead of simply passing upward the men halted. They stared pointedly at Eliar and the turban that wrapped his head.

Kesh approached them. He didn't like the way their gazes sucked him in, like they were spooling for secrets.

"A cold day higher up," he said with a smile, switching back to the modified Hundred speech that could be understood in every trading town he'd ever walked. "You'll be wanting more of a wrap, if you've got one. More snow ahead of you, but the road's open yet all the way across. What news from the empire?"

Sour men offer sour smiles, and one refused to smile, still squinting at Eliar.

"All praise to Beltak, King of Kings and Lord of Lords," said the eldest, and he also changed to the trade speech. "Sarida's markets are open to foreign men. Believers such as you will be charged a lower toll. As for ourselves, we hope for good trade in the Hundred, despite the cold weather. How are the markets?"

"They are open!" he said, wondering what kind of an idiot they took him for. "Silk is always welcome in the Hundred. No silk rivals Sirniakan silk, heh?" His chuckle did not elicit agreement, even though his statement was not flattery but truth.

"Seen you much traffic on the road?" asked the eldest with a sly glance toward the guards and drovers.

Eliar looked away.

Keshad lifted his chin, the Sirniakan way of motioning no. "No one in the last three days. Should we fear bandits on the pass?"

"The priests make all roads in the empire safe," said the eldest, as if Kesh had insulted them. "But we hear stories in Sarida, maybe there is trouble in the Hundred, maybe some fighting with outlanders? You know anything of that?"

"There's trouble in the north, but not in Olossi, where we come from."

"Are there many outlanders in Olossi? Like us?"

"Not like you." He wondered now why they wore red caps and not some other color. "We hope for a rich market in Sarida, eh?"

Another glanced at Eliar. "If you worship at the temple."

"I will worship at the temple."

They nodded, made their parting gestures, and took their leave.

Keshad got the men moving. Eliar waited perhaps four breaths before he began poking.

"What was that all about? What temple? Why do you think they were asking about outlanders in Olossi? Do you think we should return to Olossi to warn the captain?"

"Now, there's a fruitful idea. Naturally we can easily outpace trained soldiers racing at night out of the empire armed with numerous weapons and a string of remounts. Who may perhaps be on their way into the Hundred to assassinate Captain Anji. So when they catch us hounding their trail, they won't just kill us outright, do you think? I don't either."

"Why do you dislike me? What have I ever done to you?"

"Nothing." And then, because he couldn't speak the truth, he ate his anger and went on in a tight voice. "I apologize for my bad temper. This expedition means everything to me."

Everything.

Eliar's gaze drifted to sharp peaks so majestic that one might believe gods dwelt there, if one believed in gods. What Eliar saw in the crags and white-cloaked spires, Kesh could not guess, but when the young Silver frowned and looked back, his shoulders were taut and his expression scarred with something akin to grudging respect and a kind of weary pain. "Aui! How Miravia would love this! It's noble of you to risk everything to aid your sister."

"Yes, it is."

Flakes of snow spun past, and the rest of the company plodded steadily behind as they pushed down into the empire, where fortunes might be lost or won.

A fortune he would win, to use for unselfish reasons, not selfish ones. Unlike Eliar, he would risk everything to save a sister. His own. And now Eliar's. He would save her even if she never thanked him for it, even if that brief look they had shared in the inner court had meant nothing to her. Let others ride into Olossi on the trail of Captain Anji, if that's what those men were: spies, Red Hounds, assassins. Let others argue for prominence in the city council, guide the temples, or stand in authority over the reeve halls. Kesh had his eyes set on a far more precious prize, the one Eliar had already selfishly traded away.

Miravia.

44

"What's your name?" Marit asked.

The spy stared morosely into the campfire, cradling his left forearm on his right. They'd been traveling downriver along Istri Walk for days, and the man had remained silent the entire time.

"Easy enough to find out his name," said Hari as he untied the pouch of food they had commandeered from a passing patrol.

"He need tell me nothing," replied Marit tartly. "What do we have to eat? I'm hungry."

"We're better served to drink at the altars. That's what keeps us strong, and young."

"A fountain offering youth? Think you so?"

"It's what they tell me. It might be true. Or it might be a ruse to keep me returning to the altars, where they can spy out my movements."

"Good man," said Marit to the spy, who had maintained an intense interest in the fire. "You're listening, and pretending not to. If you're truly a spy for Toskala, then I hope you go to Clan Hall and report all you've seen and heard to the Commander."

"I'm no spy," he muttered to the fire. "I was walking to visit my sister in High Haldia, after hearing there was troubles in the north and worrying about her and her young ones."

If death, the release of the spirit, tasted sweet on the air, then a lie burned, like too much red-cap scalding the tongue. Anger was sour, and hope bitter, and what joy or happiness tasted of she did not know since she'd met with little enough in the last months.

"Don't lie, ver," she said, not unkindly, "because you can't lie to me. Here. Can you eat?"

He could not grip the rice ball, so she broke it off in portions and fed him, and his gratitude and suspicion spiced the air as Hari paced at the edge of the fire's light. She walked into the darkness to him.

"Why do you run at Lord Radas's beck and call?"

"Because they're the only ones who can free me."

"Release you, you mean? How would they manage it, if it takes five to destroy me?"

His shadow was made substantial by the twilight glamour of his cloak. "I don't know. I only know it can be done, for there was a frightened woman wearing the green cloak when I first woke, and now that cloak wears a man. Not a bad sort, precisely, not vicious or cruel like the others, but there is something about him that creeps me."

The spy had looked up, maybe trying to listen.

"Careful," called Marit, "or I'll guess your secrets."

The spy looked away.

"When he falls into the hands of our masters, he'll betray you, and then they'll know your true intentions," said Hari in a low voice. "If this campaign against them is what you truly intend."

"He can't possibly hear us from over there. Anyway, I want no part of an army that strings folk up by their wrists, leaves them to rot and die, and calls it a cleansing. One that burns villages, abuses women, and locks down High Haldia like a jail. Fear is their master, not Lord Radas."

"Lord Radas's pleasure is fear. That's why he commands the army."

"Who commands Lord Radas?"

"She is very old, although she doesn't look it. What she is truly, I do not understand."

"But she wears a Guardian's cloak." She thought of the night she had watched a woman walk out of the forest and, without touching them, kill two reeves. "A cloak of night, spanned with stars. She—whoever *she* is—and Lord Radas discovered how to kill Guardians, and then took their cloaks for their own. Find out how to kill a Guardian, Hari, and tell me, and then I promise you, if it's still your choice, that I will release you if it is in my power. After I have destroyed them."

"You'll never manage it."

He walked farther into the night, until she could not see him. Trees sighed in a wind out of the south, running up the river from the distant ocean, carrying the promise of more rain. They had camped on a stretch of beach where a bend in the river had led the current to undermine the far shore and smooth this one. Thorns bristled in plenty to shelter them from patrols, and stands of smoke tree and northern pipe separated them from the Istri Walk, a screen against prying eyes.

She walked back to the fire.

Without looking up, the spy said, "Folk are saying the Guardians were murdered. That demons took their place for the power they could wield."

"It's an explanation," she agreed.

After a while, he spoke again. "My name's Miken. Toskala's council sent me and four others to spy out Walshow, but I was caught in High Haldia. I don't know what became of the others. It's true I have a sister in High Haldia. That's why I went there."

The truth stings.

She looked away, reaching for the bag of provisions. "You want more rice? Maybe some wine to wash it down?"

"Why did you save me?"

He had a cautious gaze, and she found that if she struggled to draw an imagined curtain between her and him, his thoughts did not overwhelm her. He had nice eyes, but his face was thinned with hunger and hollow with the pain he still endured from the aftermath of beatings and then the final hanging, for he'd told his captors everything and they had laughed at his weakness.

"I was a reeve, once. In my heart, I'm still a reeve."

He indicated Hari's presence beyond the light. "What about the outlander?"

"Listen, Miken. You can go free now, make your own way. You can travel with us, pretend to be my prisoner or my hireling. We're headed for the army. I'll try to get you back into Toskala, but there's no guarantee I can manage it."

"I'll never know if it's true or not, what you're saying."

"No, you won't. But I give my oath as an apprentice to the Lady, where I took my year's service, that I'm telling you the truth. It's her honor I hold in my hands when I tell you that if I can bring them down, I will."

"You alone? That one seems to me a bit of a coward and an outlander besides, which might account for it."

"I can't stand aside and do nothing."

He was seated on a log, hands laid loose in his lap and arms slack, everything still too sore and abused to work properly. But he was stronger than he'd been when they'd cut him down.

"I know the back routes. I'll make my own way to Toskala."

"We'll leave you provisions then, if you can carry them."

He closed and opened his right hand, face scrunched up in pain, but he managed the movement, and then closed and opened his left hand to show it could be done.

"Tie the bag to my back, and help me shove this log into the river. They can't see me at night, and we're past the cataracts. It's smooth water more or less downstream."

"A reasonable plan, if you can hang on."

"I've hung on this long. I endured worse." He rose. "No point waiting. The council needs my report."

She rigged the provision bag around his torso, then dragged the log into the river. "You're sure?"

He flexed his shoulders, tested his range of motion. "My thanks to you for rescuing me. What's your name?"

The streaming current rushed, louder than the wind.

She smiled sadly. "Ramit."

He hooked himself into the fork where a branch had grown out from the bole. "My thanks, Ramit. May the gods honor you."

His words brought tears. "May you find a safe haven, Miken."

She shoved the log onto the river and watched until she could no longer see it on the dark waters. Then she walked back and sat by the fire, contemplating the lick and simmer of flames and the occasional spat spark. Was there a pattern to its burning, a truth in the way flames ran merry along a charring log or glowed in a blue-white shimmer where coals burned dense and hot?

If Guardians can be made, then they can be unmade.

If Lord Radas and his ally can kill, then so could she.

A branch snapped. She grabbed her sword.

Hari strolled into the light. "So you didn't trust him either. Wise of you, my sweet."

"When did I become your sweet?" She sheathed the sword.

He braced a foot on another drift log and stared at the sky, but it was overcast and thus starless. Ripples of firelight seemed to work through the fabric of his twilight cloak. Her own had a stubborn bone-white gleam, as pure as death.

"Two times I took off my cloak," she said, "and I couldn't breathe, and then it wrapped around me, and took me back, like it refused to let me die. So you can't just remove a cloak and kill them that way. You'd have to bind the cloak as well."

"You can't kill what is already dead. Anyway, if a living person touches the clasp which binds a cloak, their skin burns and blisters just as if they were touching fire."

"How do you know that?"

"Yordenas does it, if a person angers him. Makes them hold the clasp until the skin burns off their hands."

Marit shuddered. "Where is he now?"

"He was sent south to take charge of Argent Hall, and I was sent south with the army."

"Then you both failed."

"And I'm pleased to hear it!" His grin made her laugh. "I did my best to do as little as possible with my command. I marched as a mercenary with the Qin for a while, and I saw how disciplined their troops were, and how certain men could not bear the discipline. I was given the dregs, the criminals and the insane, I swear to you, and I let them give in to the worst that drove them. That's why they were so easy to defeat at Olossi."

"Whose side are you really on? Had you ridden them harder, you'd have led them to victory."

He bent to grab a stick, and poked into the fire until, with an oath, he flung the now-burning stick into the river. "Let's ride. No use lingering here."

She raised her arms, stretching. He watched her in silence, but she did not need the sense granted by her Guardian's cloak to recognize a stirring of arousal in his body.

"Harishil, eh? Hari being your short name. You're not Water-born?"

"I don't know what that means. Although my brothers complained that I was always too full of hot air."

She smiled, not wanting to think of Fire-born Joss. "Air, then. Which suits me. I can think of a reason to linger here, where it's quiet and isolated."

He sucked in a breath, moving neither toward nor away.

"I don't like being alone, Hari. And whatever else you may be, you're an attractive man. Despite everything"—she leavened the phrase with a cocky grin—"I like you."

Her dear friend Kedi had often said, "There's a reason it fits firmly in the hand, convenient for women to lead us around, for it's true that's what leads and we must follow."

Hari spoke a phrase in a language she had never heard before. He ran a hand over his hair to his nape. She rose, because surely he was not budging, and tested him by stroking up from his nape. He kept his coarse black hair clipped so short it was like bristles. A reeve's cut.

"That tickles!" she said, laughing.

His breath grew harsh, but not from fear.

The first time she'd bedded Joss, she'd played coy, to encourage his reckless streak, but Hari was a different man, so guarded it seemed likely he'd lost the habit of trust. Forget subtlety.

One kiss was all it took. And if he was a little desperate, in the manner of a drowning man, she didn't mind: She too was a little desperate, having swum in cold and lonely waters for far too long.

MARIT AND HARI rode at a leisurely pace south toward Toskala on the Istri Walk, in no hurry to reach the army although Marit knew they ought to move quickly.

"Eagles!" Hari squinted at specks in the sky.

"You seem pleased to see them."

"I wonder if they see us." He grinned. "And what they make of us if they do."

Nothing like sex to cheer up a man, reflected Marit. The edge was still there, but he chattered a lot more about nothing of importance. Good thing she liked his voice.

A wagon with a broken axle had been dragged to one side, its bed stripped bare. Vultures flapped heavenward from a pair of decomposed corpses sprawled at the edge of woods an arrow's shot off the road. If Hari had seen the bodies, he made no comment, but for a while they rode in silence. The road was wide and smooth, the powerful River Istri a noisy neighbor to their right. Normally in the rich heartland of Haldia a traveler would expect to meet steady traffic, but they encountered no one except for soldiers wearing the eight-pointed star who manned the occasional barricade.

Yet the land was green, and the sky today as much blue as cloud. It was a fine morning for a ride through handsome countryside. What *were* the eagles doing? What hall did they come from?

"I have to admit," said Hari with a laugh, "I wasn't sure I could manage it. It's a relief to know I still can."

"Manage—? Aui! Is that all men think of? I ask you." But it was true that, being dead, one might start to wonder. "Surely you could have . . ."

He had a way of tightening one side of his face, pulled by shameful thoughts he wished to cut loose. "That would be more than I could endure. Either to know her thoughts, and surely to find in them some thing I wished never to have known. Or to know I was forcing her and share every moment of dread and pain. I am not that sort of man. If you'd seen what Lord Radas had it in him to do, you'd feel as I do."

The day seemed darker. "You're right, of course. I'm sorry I made a jest of it, if it seemed I did."

"It makes me wonder about these Guardians your tales sing of. What manner of folk were they?"

"They were the guardians of justice!" But she faltered. "Surely the gods cannot have meant otherwise."

Yet Atiratu, the Lady of Beasts, had foreseen that one among the Guardians would betray the others. Marit had always thought it part of the tale only because any tale must include trouble and strife, setbacks and struggles, to make a good story. She had never really thought about it as if the goddess had actually seen as with the sight of eagles into what lay far ahead, and done her best to give warning.

Patrolling out of Copper Hall, she had learned the gullies and ridgetops of Haya and the Haya Gap, the skirts of the Wild, the bays and promontories of the North

Shore and the deep reaches of Istria Bay as well as the warrens and canals of Nessumara and the broad delta region with its ancient ruins and fisherman's reed houses. She had flown patrols over Iliyat and into Herelia. But she did not know Haldia well.

"Look," said Hari as they pulled up where the land dropped away. From this vista at least a dozen villages surrounded by fields and woodland could be seen, three on the western shore of the river in Farhal and the others in Haldia to the east. What transpired in those villages she could not tell; they were too far away. A dark stain oozed along the road.

"Eiya!" Her heart contracted and her will ebbed.

The army swarmed south, boiling along the road. So huge a force would surely prove impossible to defeat.

"There's an altar near here." Rudely, he pointed with a finger across the river. "On a promontory that overlooks this view. Best we take a drink, for strength."

Warning chafed at the bit, smelling the presence of an altar.

"All right, then. I'll follow you."

They approached a rocky hill whose lower reaches were blanketed with flowering thorn and evergreen ghost pine. An abutment of boulders rimmed the crown, and as they dipped to the flat ground, Hari shouted a warning. The horses clattered down to greet another mare, who nipped, forcing them to back off.

"The hells!" Hari swung out of the saddle and ducked away as his horse nipped back.

Warning trotted away from the altercation, and Marit reined her up hard. She dismounted and ran to Hari.

A person was walking the labyrinth. A ghost flickered into view on the straight stretches, vanished where the path took its twists, and shimmered again into existence. A demon's body might seem substantial walking in the world, but within the labyrinth its true nature was revealed.

Hari grabbed her wrist to stop her. "I don't recognize her."

Marit tugged away and stepped into the entrance. She strode, pushing as through water, each angle compressing as the landscapes flashed past: the quiet sea, the ruined tower, the pillar, the dunes, the marsh, and more places she'd had no time to mark and learn. Winded, she staggered into the center.

As she'd thought, she did recognize her.

A girl drank from cupped hands at the spring. Rising, she turned with liquid dripping off her chin. A polished bronze mirror hung from her belt, and she first grasped the mirror but then released it and with practiced skill slid a strung bow from its quiver, nocked an arrow, and drew the string just as Hari bumped into Marit.

"You can't kill us," said Hari, with a lopsided smile, "although I admit you can inflict a lot of pain. And I must say, I am cursed sick of the pain."

She seemed comfortable looking down the arrow at Marit, gaze fixed on target. "He said you were a traitor. He was right about that, at least."

"No," said Marit. "You do not know what you are seeing. How can you? My heart is veiled to your sight, as yours is veiled to mine."

"I want to meet others like me." She dipped the point so it menaced the ground instead of Marit. "You two are like me. Did you lie to him, about what you mean to do?"

"I did not lie. He rejected my offer of alliance, so I am forced to work on my own. Did he reject you?"

Her body had a woman's shape, yet there remained something girlish in her speech and aspect, as if the body had grown apace while the mind was trapped and now hurried behind trying to catch up. "No. I left him. I seek to punish those who harm others, but he is afraid to pass judgment. How can he be? I encounter people so twisted in their hearts. They are locusts, eating everything in their path. And I saw a man cloaked as we are, only he was twisted, too, like Uncle Girish. There must be others, like me, who are not afraid to pass judgment on the ones whose hearts are diseased. We are the wolves. It is our obligation to cull the sick ones, so the tribe remains strong."

Hari laughed bitterly. "The ones you seek are the ones who released the locusts."

"Best you go home, lass," said Marit, trying to sound kind, although the girl's words disturbed her. "Find your companion and return to him. He is wiser than you know."

But after they watered their horses and drank their fill, the girl followed them.

45

To fly lifted Nallo's spirits. To skim through low-lying clouds and get soaked to the skin with unshed moisture made her laugh. To glide on the wind—currents and thermals, which Volias told her she would learn to identify and anticipate—while the earth rolled away on all sides gave her joy. No chanter or tale-spinner, she could think of no better way to describe the earth from her harness than that it was like a textured carpet of greens and browns and yellows, ribboned and splotched with the variegated blues of water. Glorious!

Volias took them in easy stages so she would not get too badly chafed by the harness. Even so, the mey fell away with breathtaking speed. They could cover a day's journey in half a morning, and Volias said that *they were going slow.*

They flew upriver along the River Olo with the Lend rising to the south, its mysterious grasslands wavering like a dream in the distance. Then westward upriver along the River Hayi, with the Soha Hills rumpling the land to the north, air currents tangled. Surely they flew over the village where she had lived with her husband, but she could not pick out earth-bound landmarks from the air. Mount Aua reared his gleaming pate, and they were buffeted through the Aua Gap with the city of Horn seen below to resemble an onion chopped in half, its nested circles climbing the slope of a ridge that marked the terminus of a prominent range of hills whose name she did not know.

There was so much she did not know!

She'd never thought about it before.

Pil flew a ways off to her left and Volias to the right and out in front. Tumna kekked as they glided down the long descent to the Istrian Plain, known to Nallo only in the tales. She twisted in the harness, trying to see what Tumna had spotted. She kept her feet fixed on the training bar, while Volias hung with feet dangling, perfectly at his ease, and after a moment she realized something was moving where her feet blocked her view. Now it was behind them.

It was hard to know what Tumna might spy out: a deer, a bandit, an honest traveler. She tucked her knees up to her chest and scanned the earth. There sparkled a pond lined with mulberry trees, and a neighboring settlement, not more than six houses, storehouses and sheds flanked by an orchard and rice fields. This time of year the fields should have shone with green shoots working up through muddy water, but the fields lay brown and untended. No one had planted. From the air, the place looked abandoned.

Tumna dropped, and she shrieked and planted her feet on the training bar even though the harness held her. Aui! So far to fall!

Color flashed where the trees thinned by a stream. She knew in the crudest sense how to rein the eagle; she tugged the right jess, and Tumna responded with a tight circle that attracted Volias's attention. Fumbling in the pouch strapped to the harness, she got a hand around the red flag. As she yanked it free, her grip slipped, and it fell, brought up short by a leash.

She cursed, grabbed and waved it clumsily, trying to show where she had seen a person moving in the forest. Volias and Trouble plunged past her like a dropped stone, and Tumna's circling movement cut off her view. As she turned in her harness trying to get a clear line of sight, something happened because as they came around she saw Volias and Trouble had set down in a narrow patch of cleared ground stream-side and he was gesticulating to a person—a woman with a baby—who was possibly hysterical or furious.

Pil had gotten Sweet to come around at an altitude rather higher than Nallo and Trouble; he had a far better grasp of reining and leashing. He had barely settled into a holding pattern when Volias launched, the eagle beating upward until she found a rising current that would lift her. Volias set a course eastward over countryside smoothing into a plain that stretched to a cloudy horizon.

It was going to rain soon. She shivered, wondering what had happened below.

Volias stayed aloft late into the afternoon, not stopping as he usually did for an early camp and a lesson in short-range maneuvers. They passed over extensive forest lands and, increasingly, villages set amid fields and ponds and orchards and attended by the occasional temple building or compound. Every one of these had thrown up around it an earthwork or palisade, flimsy-looking barriers from this height. Folk worked in the closer fields, or hauled dirt as others shoveled.

According to the tales, fertile Istria boasted ten and a thousand villages, and it looked to Nallo like every one of them was surrounded by fresh fortifications.

Late in the afternoon, they set down in a clearing well away from village or temple. She followed Volias in checking her eagle's harness and feathers and then, like

Pil, hooding the bird for the night, making sure the two raptors remained at opposite sides of the open space. Volias released Trouble to hunt. Nallo trudged farther into the woods.

Her arms were sore, her legs and hip aching, and when she slipped down her leather trousers to pee, she saw that the harness had rubbed her right hip raw where the strap was too tight over her hip bone.

Finishing her business, she walked back to camp, wincing as her leathers rubbed the same raw spot. Eiya! Next thing you knew it would start bleeding.

Pil already had a fire going. Crouched beside it, he fed sticks into the flames while Volias tied canvas into a lean-to and spread a ground cloth beneath it.

The senior reeve looked up as Nallo approached. "That was good eyesight, spotting her like that."

"Who was she?"

"Eh, the usual tale. A squad of bandits hit her village, but fortunately they had a watch out and a palisade to slow the outlaws, so everyone escaped. But the houses took damage, and tools and food and the local temple's silk banners and silver altar settings were stolen."

"Desecrating the temple . . ." She shook her head. "That's the work of savages."

Pil glanced at them, then turned back to the fire.

"I won't argue with you," said Volias. "Here, hold this end while I tighten it."

"Where was she going? She had a baby."

"Eihi! You do have good eyesight. Maybe that's why."

"Why that woman was alone in the forest?"

"Neh, neh. Why the eagle chose you. It's as good an explanation as any, and we've all wondered. Not every reeve is a decent person. Some were murderers or become murderers, some have a thievish bent, or complain all the time. Envy, jealousy, spite, anger, vanity. Reeves boast of all these fine traits. Yet what manner of heart we have makes no difference in the choosing. Sure it is, if you eat far too much, your eagle can't carry you, but otherwise our bad behaviors don't really limit our ability to be reeves, they only limit our ability to be good reeves. So why one person over another? Why choose a reluctant recruit—" He gestured to her and then to Pil. "—over some poor lad who's dreamed of being a reeve all his young life? Maybe it's just the cursed eyesight."

Pil grabbed the iron traveling pot and walked to the stream that snaked through the clearing. The two eagles had tucked their heads under their wings, readying for sleep. Trouble chirped nearby, but Nallo could not see her.

"She's got her dinner," said Volias with a smile. He fished in his travel pouch for their leather bottle of rice. When Pil returned with the pot half full of water, Volias dumped in a double handful of rice and over the top crumbled two wafers of traveler's cake, a pungent blend of spices and dried, mashed nai. Pil set the pot on a tripod over the fire and settled back on his heels to watch it heat.

"What about that woman?" asked Nallo, thinking of her own journey with Avisha and the children.

He tucked his chin like the eagles readying for sleep, and the gesture made him seem, for an instant, ashamed. "She was angry at me for giving away her position. In case any folk were nearby to spot me. She'd gone on the forest track to see if the village her sister married into had been hit."

"Had it?"

"She hadn't reached yet." He grinned. "I think, from certain words that slipped, that she left her own village's hiding place because she'd gotten into an argument with her kin, or her husband, or the elders. Hard to say. She reminded me a little of you."

She glared at him, and he laughed. Pil looked at them, and Nallo stalked to the fire and plopped down next to him, promptly soaking her rear as she sat in a hole hidden by a luxuriant growth of spring-beam.

Pil raised an eyebrow.

"You could have warned me!" she said, shifting away.

He shrugged, then dug into his sleeves and handed her a stick of dried meat.

"Thanks." She chewed. He chewed. There was something about his silence that always got to her. She said, finally, "You're awfully good with the eagle. Is it a lot like riding a horse?"

He tucked his chin in the gesture she'd come to learn meant no.

"I'll tell you, I'm no good. I feel so clumsy up there, and thinking all the time how I'm going to fall, and then forgetting all that and just staring because it is so cursed amazing to see the land from the air. I just never knew!"

He chewed, watching the pot. He had exceptionally lovely thick straight black hair, which she had seen once when he let down his topknot to comb it out. Otherwise, as now, it was all gathered up tightly atop his head. He had a pleasant face once you got used to him looking so different, his eyes pulled at the corners and his cheeks broad and his nose a little flattened like someone had punched it down, only it wasn't crooked as it would have been if it had been broken. Not a bad-looking man, really; just an outlander. Nallo had never met an outlander before; she could count on one hand the times she'd even seen Silver merchants on the road, them being outlanders still with their hidden god despite their people having lived here for almost a full cycle of years and colors according to the clerks at the temple of Sapanasu.

"What temples do your people have?" she asked. "I mean, did your gods come with you, or stay behind?"

At first she thought he would, as usual, say nothing, so she went back to chewing on the tough stick of meat. But after a while, he cleared his throat and forced out words.

"In the upper world," he gestured toward the sky, "there are tribes. In the lower world there are tribes. They herd, and fish, and fight with each other. We walk the lands of the middle world and try to stay out of the way."

"Eh, that sounds like where I grew up. We herded our goats and sheep, but there was a bigger village eastbound and a bigger village westbound, and we got caught in the middle when they had their disputes over tolls, pastures, and contracts."

Volias walked over. "Hush. Do you hear voices?"

Pil stood and walked to the edge of the clearing, head bent and eyes shut as he listened. A male voice rang faintly in the distance, but after that it was quiet. They held still until the rice was done, and then they ate and, with darkness falling, stretched out under the shelter to sleep, sharing out the watch.

No one disturbed them. Trouble roosted elsewhere, appearing at dawn. She thumped down hard, agitated, and Volias called from the clearing's edge to Nallo, who was folding up the canvas shelter.

"Nallo! Get to your eagle and hook in. Where's Pil?"

"Off to do his business, I think. Or pray. I don't know what the hells he does every morning."

"Leave everything. *Now!*"

She dropped the half-folded canvas, abandoned the bedrolls and cooking equipment, but grabbed her gear pouch—fortunately with her gear neatly packed away—and the baton and short sword they had issued her, not that she had the faintest idea of how to use either one effectively. Of how to fight at all, if it came to that.

She ran across the clearing to Tumna, the eagle acting restive, talons digging into the earth, wings half open, neck feathers raised. Shouts broke from the far end of the clearing. Nallo whistled, and Tumna bent her huge head down and raked at the hood with her talons. Got stuck. Nallo released her, tugged off the hood, and hooked in just as three men carrying spears ran into the clearing.

An arrow sprouted—like sorcery!—in the chest of one of the men. His companions faltered as he tipped to his knees with a hand clutched around the shaft.

Volias had his sword drawn, but it was Pil, at the edge of the forest, who had loosed. He drew again, released, and hit a second man in the shoulder.

"Move!" shouted Volias.

A third arrow buried its point in the earth, shaft quivering, as the men grabbed their comrade and scrambled back, calling to fellows hiding in the trees.

Pil sprinted across the clearing to Sweet, and cursed if the cunning old bird didn't catch her hood with a talon and yank it off so that as Pil hooked in she was already thrusting. Volias, in his harness, waited on the ground until Pil and Nallo were aloft.

A shower of arrows painted the air with ghostly stripes. Volias swore, and then he, too, was up, but Trouble had an arrow in her right leg that shook loose and fell away. Blood dribbled earthward. Volias was still cursing, a stream of words less heard as discrete syllables than experienced like a river's flow. A cadre of men gathered in the clearing. Sweet caught an updraft, and the others followed. Nallo's pulse thundered in her ears and, slowly, quieted.

They flew north over the plain. In village after village, folk labored to complete walls and earthworks instead of tending freshly planted fields and gardens. Now and again a cadre of men rode, or marched, along a path, but Volias took no notice. Trouble flew point, but she began to labor. The sun rose higher. The day grew hot and moist. To the southeast, clouds piled up, but there wasn't much wind to move them.

Just when Nallo feared they would have to land to save the eagle, she spotted the glittering line of a river. The roads and tracks swarmed with people walking, riding, carting, draft beasts pulling wagons, all creeping in the same direction. Soon she realized that the strange cast of ground ahead, the red clay and patchwork fields and textured ground, was not a bizarre land-form but actually streets and buildings grown into the land between two rivers. The city had a massive outer wall, reinforced by a berm and ditch, although a straggle of new settlement grew up outside its protection. The main road seemed almost as wide as the river, its tributary roads and paths lined with villages and hamlets like so many beads on a string, each bracketed by green fields and flowering orchards. At the southern tip of the city, where the muddy yellow-brown waters of the larger river were joined by the blue of the smaller, a bold escarpment jutted out, its flat top almost the breadth of Olossi's inner city.

Trouble was dropping fast.

"The hells!" She had never landed in a prescribed space which, if overshot, would dump her into water. She shut her eyes as Tumna swooped. "Thunderer, give me courage, let me die without pissing myself—Oof!"

Tumna chirped interrogatively, and a cheerful voice close beside her said, "heya! Unclip, make room, there's another coming in."

She slid her feet off the training bar and found hard ground to stand on. Unhooking, she sagged, and was helped away by a young man in reeve leathers. Fawkners ran up to hood Tumna. Off to one side, Volias shouted his wrath into the skies, and Trouble listed *wrong* while fawkners clustered around her with various implements and bindings.

"Heya! Here she comes!" With a grin, the reeve caught Nallo's arm.

Sweet pulled up neat as you please and easily gripped one of the huge perches built into the wide parade ground. That left Pil dangling about his own height off the ground, but he unhooked and let go, catching himself in a deep crouch when he hit dirt, then straightening.

"Eihi!" The reeve had cropped hair, and muscular shoulders and arms revealed by his sleeveless leather vest. Watching Pil, he grinned. "Interesting. What is that?"

"That's Pil," she said irritably.

"That may be," agreed the reeve, "but what is he? He doesn't look like any man I've seen before, and I've seen plenty."

"He's Qin."

"One of those outlanders that fought the battle of Olossi? We heard rumors, mostly from Volias—" He flicked a glance toward Volias and his stricken eagle, then away as if to stare would be rude. "—but now I see the truth. What's he like?"

"He doesn't talk much." *Unlike you,* she thought, but held her tongue. "He saved us today from an ambush. He's an amazing archer."

"We'll be needing his skills. I'm Peddonon, by the way. An old-fashioned name, I admit. Everyone calls me Peddo." He grinned.

She laughed, because usually only women had names like that, and she liked him the better for being amused about it. "Maybe you're a bit like me, eh? I'm called Nallo."

"You'll fit right in. Let me find someone to get you to the barracks—Likard! Get over here and take her in hand." He nodded at Nallo. "I was just about to head out on patrol when we saw you three, and Trouble injured. Wsst!" His brows drew down. "Volias can be a bit of a jerk, but we all love that bird, and so does he. Will you be all right? Don't let that fat-ass Likard try to give you the bunk by the door. Glad you're here, Nallo. Sure as hells we need you."

He walked off, head cocked to size up Pil as the Qin carried weapons and gear over to Nallo. The soldier set everything down and glanced around. If he was as nervous as she felt, she could not tell by his bland expression.

A short, thin man with his long hair tied back in a tail hurried up. "You have the look of novices, eh? I'm Likard. If you'll come with me, I'll show you bunks where you can dump your gear, and then Ofri'll want to meet you." They followed him, feet crunching on the gritty dirt. "You been in training long?"

"I haven't," said Nallo. "I came here to be trained."

Likard looked at Pil, who shrugged, his gaze flickering down, and all at once Nallo realized he was not a stolid, laconic, arrogant outlander but a youth not much older than she was who was simply very shy.

"I figure he's been training at Naya Hall two or three months, since it was established."

"Naya Hall?" Likard squinched up his face.

"It's what they call it, because of the oil of naya. It's where they sent the overflow of novices out of Argent Hall."

"That Joss is now marshal over, eh? Who'd've thought that cursed drunken womanizer had it in him? I'm impressed, heh!" He led them up onto a porch and had them unlace their flying boots before they went inside. The barracks hall had an open room for work, unswept at this hour and littered with wood shavings and scraps of leather. Behind half-open screens lay a raised sitting room strewn with pillows and low tables. Pairs of doors opened off either side of the work room. Likard slid one open, gesturing to a shuttered room beyond.

"Unless you got any preference otherwise, I'll put you both in here where most of the younger reeves bunk."

She stepped into the chamber, which was long and narrow and had a musty odor, nothing unpleasant, just redolent of bodies. There were about twenty beds, most decorated with homely remembrances like a flower-patterned quilt or an embroidered pillow.

"Here's one for you, Pil," said Likard, gesturing toward the sole bed set against the same wall as the door.

"Neh, not that one," said Nallo. "It's likely too noisy."

Footsteps sounded on the floor, and a young woman in a hurry barged through the door, jerking to a halt before she slammed into Likard.

"Heya! Why be stopped like that in the middle of—Here, now. Who are these?"

"Novices from Argent Hall, sent to train here," said Likard. "Greetings of the day to you, too, Kesta."

"Fuck off, you turd." Then she turned a bright smile on the others. "I'm Kesta. Sorry, not much of a greeting, is it? Welcome to Clan Hall. Always glad to see a new face."

The words seemed sincere enough, and she had the grace not to stare at Pil. And she was cursed attractive, with her sleeveless vest laced tight over a muscular frame.

Nallo averted her eyes, trying for something safer, like the reeve's chin. "I'm

Nallo. This is Pil. He's an outlander, as you may have noticed, and he doesn't say much."

"Eh, so you talk for him?" She grinned, and lifted her chin in a gesture almost flirtatious. "Fair enough. Anyway, I'm late for duty—"

"There's a surprise," muttered Likard.

"—so I can't chat, but I'll see you at hall this evening, if I get back. The hells! There it is." She grabbed a baton off the bunk decorated with the embroidered pillow, and ran out.

Pil said, with his careful diction and heavy accent, "where lies the men's hall?"

"Men's hall?" Likard looked him up and down in an intrusive way that truly annoyed Nallo. "Can't wait to get to the temple and be devoured, eh?"

Pil blushed.

"Leave him be! Among the Qin, men and women who aren't kin or married don't bunk down together. So he'd be uncomfortable bunking in these quarters."

Likard scratched an eyebrow, as if this answer confounded him. "Why in the hells would we be wasting our time here with a men's hall and a women's hall? He want a private chamber, like a legate? Or his own cote, like the cursed commander?"

"He's got no idea of our ways and customs, so don't mock him. You know, Likard, it seems to me there are in general more male reeves than female. Maybe one of the bunk rooms has all men in it, or fewer woman, anyway."

"I never thought to count," he said with an exaggerated and sarcastic smile. "Aui! Just throw your gear in the workroom. I'll let Ofri sort it out."

But Pil would not leave his weapons or his gear, so in a show of solidarity, Nallo lugged her gear as well. Likard led them through the compounds into a private garden court where a fountain spilled water into a series of stone basins carved to look like giant nai leaves, whose root feeds all people.

An old man sat on the porch, studying a half-finished game of kot. Seeing them, he rose. "What's this, Likard?"

"Novices brought from Argent Hall to train here. Volias brought them."

"Where is Volias, then?"

"Trouble's injured."

"Eiya!" His expression darkened. "How bad is it?"

"It's the leg. She had to fly while losing blood."

Nallo faltered. "Will Trouble die?"

"No use courting worries, lass," said the old man. "The fawkners will have all in hand." He considered Pil with a frown, then gestured. "I'll let Commander know you're here."

They heard voices engaged in discussion as they took off their boots. They waited on the porch until the old man came back out to beckon them into a spacious audience chamber where six older men and two women sat on pillows, with a ninth seated behind a low desk.

"Your names?" The woman behind the desk had years, and pain, etched in her face.

"I'm Nallo. This is Pil."

"Can the outlander not speak for himself?"

"I am Pil," he said, curtly enough that it might be taken for arrogance, but Nallo recognized the way he had of looking at people without quite having the nerve to look at them. She could not reconcile his shyness with his killing arrows.

The woman nodded, not one to take offense at trifles. "I'm the commander. These are my council." She ran off names, pointing to each reeve, and ended with a middle-aged man called Ofri. "Why did Marshal Joss send you from Argent Hall? Why not keep you there?"

"I didn't want to train at Argent Hall, verea. As for Pil, here—you'll need to ask Volias—but I think it was determined he'd train better away from the other Qin soldiers."

"Is that true?" asked the commander, tone like a whip. "Pil, you'll answer me."

"Captain Anji asked it be done, Commander," he said in his soft voice. His mouth twisted as if he was in pain. "He said it is better I go away to train. I am no longer a proper Qin soldier."

"Because you are chosen as a reeve?"

He parted his lips to reply, then closed them.

"We'll sort it out later. At the moment, we can use you to ferry messages so more experienced reeves can patrol. Wait outside. When we're finished, Ofri will take charge of you."

Outside, they sat cross-legged on the porch. Pil had the knack of sitting perfectly still, hands at rest on his thighs, while he stared at the fountain and seemed, if anything, to be praying. Nallo could not find a comfortable seat. The raw burn on her hip smarted. Everything else itched, poked, ached. She listened to the reeve council discussing the approach of a vast and terrible army, the flight of refugees from burned villages, a spy recovered from the river, the death of two reeves and an eagle. What had happened to the Green Sun clan? They'd abandoned their warehouses and all left town, very odd, and the council wanted the reeves to search for traces of them. Should we use oil of naya, as they did at Olossi? How do we transport a lot of oil quickly, if we do, when river transport down the lesser Istri might be blocked?

The words, by themselves, had no tangible meaning, like a tale sung at festival time, but their voices had an edge so sharp that Nallo found her own shoulders tightening in response. A great ravening beast was lumbering down on them, and they just sat there helplessly in its path.

46

The Istri Walk was the great thoroughfare of the Hundred, wide enough to accommodate two wagons rolling abreast on the raised central pavement with well-trodden dirt paths flanking the walk on either side. Marit found it eerie to pace its measures in such solitude. Every village was closed down tight, not one person out on road or path except for gangs of farmers working the fields without the usual songs to pass the time. Everything was too quiet, Marit thought, not with the lull before the storm but with the shock of destruction after.

The trailing edge of the army appeared roadside, the detritus of their passage: A naked toddler with a distended stomach sucked its dirty thumb; a lad herded a paltry herd of skinny goats along the verge; a man with a crutch limped away when he saw them, keeping his head down. People had been scavenging for wood and kindling, for there was not a scrap of forest litter on the ground besides rotting vegetation.

Wagons blocked the road, but the riders broke into a canter and flew over them. The guards bobbed their heads in obeisance, afraid to look her in the eye.

"Who built this road?" Hari asked. "I've never seen anything like it. Not even in the Sirniakan Empire."

"No one knows," said Marit. "Even the tales don't say."

"I see such a path one time," said the girl, who called herself Kirit.

"Where?" asked Marit when it became obvious she wasn't about to say more.

"In the grasslands. Just one place. A big tower. No one lives there, only demons. A road like this one, I see there."

"Who built it?"

Kirit shrugged. "Demons."

They passed a second barrier, set at the outskirts of a village overrun with soldiers sitting at their ease on porches, but chatter died as the three cloaks passed. In the fields beyond the village, the army had set up its main bivouac, rank upon rank of traveling tents amid hundreds of campfires. As the long quiet spilled down to dusk, they rode into the camp, their cloaks billowing as the wind caught the edge of coming night. Twilight, mist, and death, they approached the heart of the enemy, identified by a trio of huge tents. Evidently Lord Radas liked his comforts.

Aui! Her chest felt tight, and her throat constricted. Hari was breathing raggedly, maybe not aware he was doing so. As for the girl, she likely was a demon, because as small and helpless as she looked, she acted no differently than if she'd been riding into her home village, not that Marit could begin to imagine a village filled with people with such ghastly pale faces and hair.

And for that matter, she thought, mind skittering at random as she shied away from the confrontation looming before her, did demons live in villages? Did they have kinfolk and lovers, or only prey?

The walls of the tents rippled as the wind sighed, like a beast breathing as it waited to consume them. Soldiers gathered at a distance. Marit and Hari dismounted, but Kirit remained on her mare, strung bow resting over her legs and three arrows caught in her left hand.

The entrance to the tent was swept back. Marit inhaled sharply, but the people who scurried out wore the badges common to prosperous merchants and householders, the kind of folk you met in the council hall. They kept eyes averted, and yet a stench of fear and greed rose off them as they hurried away under escort, soon vanishing into the crowded camp beyond. A second group strode out in their wake, captains outfitted in soldiers' gear and with the posture and authority of men accustomed to getting their way through physical prowess. She knew their type: Kotaru's ordinands, local militia commanders, any man who has built a fence around a territory and considers it his own and the gods help you if you think to challenge him. Yet they, too, kept their gazes lowered like children showing submission to a bullying parent.

Hari went inside, the pale cloth swallowing him. One gulp, and he was gone.

In the rightmost tent, cloth twitched. If someone had been peeking out, she had missed them. She looked at Kirit as the young woman surveyed the assembly with her cold blue gaze. Gawking soldiers hurried away, leaving the guards and the captains. Their fear pricked her.

Inside the tent, a man shouted, voice breaking into a ragged sobbing keen stabbed by grunts of pain.

"The hells!" Her lips were dry, and her hands cold. She gripped her staff and used its tip to flip the heavy entrance flap aside, then followed it into the interior.

Lamps burned in open space. A man writhed on a fine wool carpet, blood leaking over the green and gold pattern.

"Hari!"

Two men stood beside Hari, one holding a sword laced with blood and the other holding an arrow loosely woven between the fingers of his right hand. The swordsman looked up, revealing the face of a young man, grin twisted with cruel pleasure.

"Clean it, and sheath it," said the other man, and the soldier obeyed mutely.

Lord Radas faced her, looking no older than the day he had ordered her killed. He blinked, not startled but considering. His was a pleasant face, but something dwelt deep there that she could not call human. "The cloak of death. I glimpsed it many years ago, and thought it lost, but now you are come. I welcome you."

Hari twitched, hands clutching his stomach. From the stench, the soldier had done a serviceable job of gutting him, because his guts were leaking out. His gaze fixed on her, his soft "uh uh uh" enough to make your skin crawl, but he did not beg her for aid. Aui! She cursed herself for not having drawn her sword beforehand. Could she take them?

By his grip on the sword, the soldier was ready to strike again.

"Why did you do it?" she asked.

Radas's voice was as soft as his shadowed eyes. "He has to learn not to displease me. In this way, he comes to understand that for his carelessness there are consequences. He brought it on himself."

"What carelessness?"

"It's shameful, how carelessly he commanded the army we sent to support our allies in Olossi. Our task is made more difficult by his failure. It brings more harm and trouble to those who desire order. All the many people who suffer from these disturbed times want order, and they shall have it. Only now it will take longer and be more messy."

Perhaps he was insane. Perhaps he was simply the land's most selfish liar. Hard to say, since he was veiled to her sight, and she was cursed sure he could see nothing in her likewise. He did not even seem to recognize her as the reeve he had ordered killed twenty years ago. Maybe because of that, he did not frighten her.

"What is your name?" he asked, his tone an imitation of kindly concern.

"I'm called Ramit."

"That's right. Yet you fled from me. That was over a year ago."

"I was unaccountably detained. Otherwise I would have come sooner."

Perhaps he believed this bland pap. She found herself oddly irritated that she could not know, when all other people lay open to her third eye. Great Lady! Was she becoming accustomed to holding that axe over their heads?

"I'm satisfied. You are here now."

She gestured toward Hari, whose grunts faded as blood leaked out between his fingers. "May I assist him?"

"No. I would prefer you did not. He'll recover."

"So you can punish him again in like manner?"

Wise uncles might smile so, sadly shaking their head at youth's foibles. "He must suffer the agonies he has earned. Those who do harm must be punished."

"Who are you to judge and execute him?"

"I am lord here, master of this army, which serves at my will." He indicated the silent soldier.

"You're neither lord nor master to me! If he displeases you, why not release him? Why make him suffer?"

"We can't know how long it will take for the cloak to find a new master."

"Does the cloak find a master, or make a slave?"

His smile twisted, flattening to a thinner line. "That depends on you, doesn't it?"

The words struck deep, as they were intended to do. Disgusted with her cowardice, she threw herself to her knees beside the dying man. "Hari," she murmured, "I'm here. I'll bind your wounds—"

"Leave me be," he whispered hoarsely. ". . . knew it was coming . . . just leave me, it will heal . . ."

The inner walls stirred, and a young man wearing a cloak as red as Hari's blood hurried into the tent from a side chamber. He wore his hair in the same fashion as Lord Radas, the rich man's three loops, but his were lopsided. Seeing Marit, he stopped.

"What is it, Yordenas?" asked Lord Radas, voice clipped with impatience.

"That's death's cloak! The one you were looking for last year."

"So we had determined long since."

"I sniffed her out, that one time. Remember I told you? I told you this cursed outlander was hiding something from you, but you wouldn't listen to me." His tone grated.

Marit despised him at once, the feeling so strong it left a taste.

Lord Radas sighed. "What is it, Yordenas?"

"Cursed if there isn't another one out there, lord."

"Another what?"

"The cloak of mist you spoke of, lord. The lost one."

Lord Radas's expression changed, a tic by his eye jerking twice before it stilled.

Hari moaned, eyes rolling back in his head as his body sagged and his hands opened in a gesture of acquiescence; he had stopped breathing. His cloak fluttered, rippling as in wind, and slithered over his body like a lilu embracing her chosen one.

From deeper within the tent a calm voice spoke. "Death is come, as expected. Mist returned, a puzzle to tease us."

The brawny soldier dropped to both knees, cowering.

There is a kind of fear that begins formless, deep in the pit of the belly, and wells up with such speed that it catches you and blinds you before you know you've been taken. Marit pushed to her feet, not even sure what monster clawed at her heart, only that she was ready to run.

She had heard that voice before.

A woman pushed aside cloth to enter. She had a round, dark face, ordinary in its lineaments, no one who would stand out in a crowd. She wore a cloak, black as night. Under that she wore humble laborer's clothing, a linen tunic and wide trousers. Lord Radas and Yordenas wore best-quality silk tabards, embroidered with gold-thread trim, under-tunics dyed in subtle colors rarely seen outside wealthy homes and temple precincts. They looked like peacocks, like the scions of Nessumara's richest houses who strutted about the streets and canals in their finest to make sure folk did know they had the coin to be extravagant. Even their cloaks dazzled, while hers had no color at all.

"Radas," she said in a pleasant, ordinary voice, "go forth. Ask the young woman to enter. Treat her gently. Smile."

She looked Marit up and down, while Marit reined in her breath and her composure. This was the woman who had murdered two reeves in the forest beside West Spur without touching them.

"Death ever challenges, but in the end even death can be defeated. You are not so different than the one who came before you, although he was grandson to an outlander."

"Who is the one who came before me?" Images spun in Marit's memory of a handsome man with long black hair, a brown face, and demon-blue eyes.

The woman turned to Radas. "Yet a warning, Radas, before you go out to greet the new one. She is small and young, and quite ugly, as pale as a worm. Easy to discount. But she carries her staff."

He lifted his chin, as a man might who has just been slapped. "She carries her staff? Aui!"

"It is leashed to her belt." She did not bother to glance at Yordenas, who had not, evidently, noticed this crucial item. Nor for that matter had Hari mentioned it to Marit.

"An annoying development," murmured Lord Radas.

Marit thought of the envoy of Ilu, the one Kirit had left, the one who had refused Marit shelter and friendship. He had asked Marit if she carried her staff, but she had not known what he meant.

"Not at all," said the woman. "We must welcome her all the more kindly, and teach her to be wise."

He frowned. "If you say so." He went outside.

"Yordenas, move Hari. Drag out the entire carpet." She clucked at the mess, then beckoned. "If you will, Ramit, retire with me."

Marit followed cautiously past the inner wall and into another chamber, this one with dirt for floor except for a single humble carpet spread in the middle of the dim chamber. A low writing desk and a traveling chest sat on the carpet, squared off to match the corners. Pillows rested on the other end, one in each corner.

"Sit." She stepped over a spear lying behind the desk and sat. She touched the objects lying on the desk, shifting those that had moved out of line with the table's edge. "Come closer, Ramit. You are disturbed by what you have seen."

Marit pulled a pillow closer, settled down cross-legged with her short sword laid across her thighs, and said nothing.

"Radas has a cruel streak. Hari is reckless and does not understand the responsibilities that have fallen to him. I remain surprised that the cloak fell to an outlander, but the gods make these decisions, not us."

Her indignation got the better of her. "Surely Lord Radas could be commanded not to punish a man by torturing him."

"Yes, I came too late to stop that piece of petty brutality, for which I am sorry. Matters have long since gotten out of hand. The criminals should have been culled from our ranks, not formed into their own army and sent to Olossi. So be it. I had other things on my mind and let it pass. Now I do what I can to mitigate the worst."

"What do you mean?"

She raised a hand, palm up, in the gesture of receiving and questioning. "What respect do we owe the gods? When respect is no longer shown, is it not true that people wander into the shadows? That they ignore those laws which displease them personally? That they scorn the helpless and needy? That offerings are scanted, and tithes not properly paid? That a few who believe they know what is right for others begin to call for change? Yet change is all too often only a word to signify chaos."

The words seemed reasonable enough. "Yes."

"The weak should not suffer injustice simply because they are weak."

"No."

"Nor should the powerful twist justice to serve their own ends."

"Of course not."

"If those in power will not shift, what then is to be done? Have you a question, Ramit?"

Marit rubbed her jaw with the back of a hand. This unstable ground might collapse beneath her feet. Best to change the subject entirely. "What am I?"

"Ah." A keen look took her in from top to toe, with her threadworn, mismatched clothing, and her short sword, which naturally the woman could not know Marit had stolen from a sergeant in High Haldia. "You hold your sword close."

"I trust it, that's true."

"You are a soldier? One of the Thunderer's ordinands?"

"That's right," Marit lied. "I've had training. But I meant, what am I now?"

"You are a Guardian." She touched, again, the odd assemblage of objects on the desk: a serviceable dagger; a sharpened green stick cut from hollow pipe brush; a narrow wooden box that likely contained writing brushes.

Remembering how this woman had written on paper, and two reeves had fallen dead, Marit found her resolve strengthened. "Then why am I not presiding over assizes? Why are Guardians traveling with an army that invaded Haldia and now means to attack Toskala?"

"Have you asked yourself, when and why did the assizes fall into disuse? Indeed, the abandonment of the assizes by the Guardians is a sad tale, one not recorded in the annals of the Lantern. The hierophants of Sapanasu and the reeves certainly deserve an equal share of blame."

"The reeves have always served justice! I mean, so I always heard."

"Even the halls can become corrupted when those in power come to love power more than justice."

"Maybe. But it seems to me that first the Guardians vanished, and after that the assizes fell into disorder. What am I to think now, when I find you and the others—if you count me, seven all told." Too late she caught herself, having slipped in her accounting. She had meant to name six, rather than betray the envoy.

The woman nodded. "Seven, now that you and the outlander girl have come to us."

"I never saw so many," said Marit cautiously. "Where is the seventh?"

"On patrol."

Perhaps not the envoy, then. Perhaps she meant the one Kirit had mentioned, "twisted like Uncle Girish," whatever that meant. And if so, that meant eight Guardians were accounted for.

The woman went on. "All could be restored to what the gods intended, if only we discover where the last two are. What a blessing that would be for the Hundred, neh?"

If Marit had not seen this woman kill two apparently innocent reeves, she might have found the argument more convincing. As it was, she smiled, not needing to fake her uncertainty. "What happened to the council of Guardians?"

"Who among us has not succumbed to small greeds and unintended mistakes? Yet when those who clutch power turn all decisions to their own benefit, choosing to be ruled by selfishness, striking down those who have done nothing more than what they have done themselves, then the shadows have triumphed. Is it not so?"

"Truly, I think it is."

She inclined her head in agreement. "I was forced to act as I did. Let me ask you, Ramit. I would like to offer you my companionship for a few days. I would like to take you to the altars that lie in this region, to show them to you, to instruct you in their secrets."

"Their secrets?"

"How to locate the altar which is closest to you, if you are lost. How to memorize the angles of the labyrinth. How to properly groom and care for the mare you ride."

"A generous offer."

"You have entered into a heavy obligation. It matters that you comprehend your duty."

"What about Hari?"

She smiled ruefully. "There you must trust me. He'll not recover for many days, perhaps weeks. But I promise you he will recover. Will you come? I'd like the company, I admit it."

To enjoy the companionship of a seemingly reasonable human being, one who could teach her about what she had become! The temptation gnawed. She smiled tentatively. "I'd welcome such a lesson."

"Tomorrow, we will leave. Here they are."

Lord Radas walked in looking stormy and irritated with Kirit following, bow gripped in white hands.

"I smell blood," said the girl. "Who are you? Are you all of them? Are there more?"

"I wonder where you are from," said the woman softly, "and how you came to possess the cloak of mist, and its bowl and staff and Sapanasu's light."

The girl looked her up and down in a way Marit would never have dared do, knowing it more prudent to play the part of a supplicant. Then Kirit looked at Lord Radas. "Here are four. Where is Hari?"

"He has other business to attend to and will not be available for some days." If the woman was pleased, or angry, or worried, Marit simply could not tell. Even her age remained a mystery. She might be middling young, or middling old, but her demeanor suggested she had the experience to take hiccoughs in stride.

The girl, on the other hand, had youth's lightning ways. "That is a good arrow," she said to Radas. "What wood makes it? I would see it." She extended an arm.

"Don't touch!" He stepped back, rigid with anger.

"You have a bow, and arrows," said the woman in her pleasant voice. "And what a fine mirror that is hanging from your belt. May I see it?"

Those demon eyes really had a creepy shine, although Marit had to admire the girl's lack of fear. "No. It is mine. He—gave—" She faltered, and for an instant looked as young as she likely was, an inexperienced child confronting the old and treacherous.

"*He?*" The woman leaned forward. "Who is he?"

The girl hesitated.

"Hari gave her trouble about it," said Marit. "Sheh! I never saw a person spit fire like she did! Him just asking to use it one morning. Hari is a bit vain, wanting to look into the mirror, eh?" She finished more loudly than needed. The girl's look of confusion faded.

"A mirror is a woman's strength. I do not give away my strength." Kirit glanced first at Marit and then at the other woman. "You two do not display your woman's mirrors."

Something mattered here, something that eluded Marit.

The woman brushed a hand over the writing box. "Not all need mirrors."

"In the mirror, I see truth. Why do so many bad people walk in the land? You march with an army. Cannot you stop the bad people from what they do to hurt people?"

"It is our goal to restore order." The woman's voice sharpened. "It is our intent to be sure that none need ever fear for the safety of her own existence."

"We are already dead," said the girl.

"No, we are not dead!" The woman rose, paced to a canvas wall, and back to the desk, crouching to pick up the writing box. "We are Guardians, bringing justice to the land."

"I kill them," said the girl. "The ones who are bad. You also? You kill the bad ones?"

A gaze flashed between Lord Radas and the woman. He pulled the arrow to his chest. She stood with the writing box tucked under a sleeve, and then, as an after-thought but very smoothly, she picked up the dagger and the stick and after that she took one step backward so she was standing in her soft leather slippers across the haft of the spear that lay on the carpet.

"Perhaps you would like to rest, young one. What is your name?"

"I am Kirit," she said proudly. "A Water-born Red Crane. I am orderly in nature. I am ruthless in the quest for justice because I cannot rest where injustice is done."

"What is your companion's name?" asked the woman, indicating Marit with an elbow.

The girl looked at Marit, pale eyes cold.

The hells, thought Marit. *I've been careless.* She'd told the envoy her real name, within the hearing of this demon child. She shifted the sword on her thighs. Maybe she couldn't kill them, but she could hurt them badly enough that she could run.

"Maybe she doesn't have a name," Kirit said to the woman. "Do you have a name?"

The woman said nothing, and Kirit went on. "For a long time, I had no name. But this white-cloaked one has a cloak, a bowl, a light, and a horse. Only she has no staff. Why not?"

Why the hells not?

It got so quiet that Marit noticed distant sounds: the neighing of a horse, the rumble of cart wheels, the rhythmic clash of sticks as men trained. A faint gasp as lungs caught air, and feebly sucked it in. Was that Hari, breath returning to his body?

"Most of the staffs were lost," said the woman.

Marit knew she was lying because as a reeve Marit had learned to suss out liars, the way their jaw twitched up in defiance or their eyes did not blink as the weight of the lie held them open.

"Where is *my* staff?" Marit asked.

Lord Radas exhaled.

The woman shook her head. "Lost, with the others. We would dearly wish to find it."

"I don't even know what it is, or why it matters," added Marit, hoping to sound disingenuous. " 'The staff of judgment.' So the tales say."

"The symbol of our authority," said the woman. "So it is doubly a cause for cele-bration that you, Kirit, possess yours."

The girl's stare was so flat that Marit did wonder if a demon had crept into that cloak. "We pass judgment, then? We kill the many bad people?"

"Yes, Kirit. We will kill the many bad people."

47

On Wakening Rat, the last day of the Month of the Ox, Avisha woke trembling and wiped her face with dry hands as she rose. Sheyshi was still snoring. Outside, the Barrens still lay in shadow. Avisha lit a lamp and washed herself with water from a basin. She dressed in a taloos she had never worn, winding the cloth tight. After combing out her hair, she pinned it up in coils as for a festival day. Slipping on sandals, she padded to the kitchen gardens with the basin clasped against a hip and poured the water over flourishing rows of immortal sun, whose petals were edible and whose roots could be ground up into a soothing medicinal good for pregnant women taken by nausea. The sun broached the horizon, painting the sea with light.

One of the kitchen women looked up, smiling. "That's cloth I've not seen before. Good quality, too! You going to sit on the bench today?"

Avisha blushed.

"You know, that girl from Dekos village, she is already pregnant! So they are saying."

"Is that the girl who got a belly full in Olossi?" Avisha asked. "That one who had to come out here before all us? The chief wanted the soldier whipped."

"Aui! That one! Neh, those two made the offerings in Olossi and came here already married, but without a feast. That Dekos girl, first day the altars were up, she and her lover they sat the bench. Don't you remember? It was only a week ago."

Twelve days ago Avisha had been in the middle of a roaring conflict with Jerad about his fights with other boys, which had ended with him storming off to sleep in the stables. Chief Tuvi had assured her he was being looked after by the Qin soldiers, and anyway he was always following Jagi around.

"I was too busy to go down into town. Let me get Zi."

The little girl was snuggled in with other small children belonging to the kitchen workers.

The kitchen woman touched her on the shoulder. "Let her sleep, Avisha. You don't want her fussing to distract you, eh?"

"Maybe it would be better to wait until the next auspicious day. I'm not a Rat, to find good fortune on Wakening Rat, but I am an Ox, and I don't want to sit on the bench next month, Snake Month. Snakes are good people, of course, serene and wise, but that doesn't mean I want to make such a big decision in a month dedicated to an animal known to be strict and secretive, liable to hide its hostility in a crack in the ground and then strike when least expected."

The other woman kissed her on the cheek as a cousin might. "If you aren't sure, don't go. The mistress would never turn us out."

"I'm eighteen." She patted her hair again to make sure nothing had slipped out of place. "What use is there to remain an unmarried girl? You're already a married woman, with two children of your own."

"A widow, without kinfolk. Still, now that I've work, I'm in no hurry to marry again. I'm not sure I fancy any of the outlanders. There's a laborer come out of the village that was neighbor to mine before they got burned down. But he'll have to buy himself out of his debt before I'm likely to look in that direction!" She laughed, pleased at her independence, a capable woman who knew where her next meal was coming from.

"I'm going down," said Avisha in a rush.

"Eihi! As pretty as you are, and beloved by the mistress, I am sure you won't be sitting there long, not like that one poor woman last week. Here." She scooped rice into a humble bowl and handed it to her.

The simple gesture brought tears. Avisha thanked her tremulously, and walked away before she could lose her courage. She knew what her father would want her to do, what her mother would counsel. Even Nallo would tell her that being married was better than living on the sufferance of others, no matter how well they treated you.

The settlement did not yet have a council house, but brick benches had been placed to form a large square and canvas raised on rope to offer shade. In her village, the council house benches had been carved from wood, enclosed by a courtyard ringed with trellises heavy with falling-water and murmuring heart and decorated with festival cords braided by her father. Her village hadn't the coin to build a roofed council hall, but the courtyard was a particularly pretty one, especially when the vines were in bloom. Travelers said so. Once a poet had come just to sit there for three days and contemplate its beauty while the villagers fed him, but he hadn't composed any chants so afterward her father said, in private, that perhaps the man had been a fraud. Although why in that case he hadn't just come around as a beggar, Avisha could not imagine. The temples gave alms without question. She felt herself a beggar, living off another's handouts for one too many days.

Every day, now, you were likely to see one or two women sitting on the benches. Today two young women had already each taken a place, seated far enough apart that, if a suitor did arrive, there could be no confusion about who he meant to offer for. Because the council benches were sited at the upward edge of the growing settlement, only a few people passed on their way to and from their labors at the captain's hall above. But folk did come just to stare.

She sat, clutching the bowl of rice. A pair of young Qin soldiers had walked up from the barracks. One nudged his comrade, and that man ventured forward hesitantly and sat down by the young tailor, who smiled shyly as she handed him a bowl of rice.

Avisha looked at her hands. After a while, she heard a new rustle of arrivals. Over by the other corner, an older Qin soldier strolled up to the noodle-seller, Darda. He was received with a pretty greeting and an offered bowl of rice.

Her mouth was so dry. Again, she looked away. She had to be brave and determined. She had to take care of the children. Her life in the village was lost; she must build a life here.

The settlement lay in four pieces: the reservoir, irrigated fields, and parade ground beyond the embankment; the settlement growing out from the gate; the altars and council square sited on the upper hill; the captain's house on the farthest spur of ground with cliff-side for its skirts. There was plenty of room for the settlement to grow, both expanding across the low hill and out into the surrounding land.

From this corner she could see three of the altars. A simple wooden gate with three lintels, facing east, marked the Herald domain of Ilu. Adjacent to the council square, stone walls delineated enclosure of Kotaru, the Thunderer. A flat boulder, brushed clean and sprinkled with water every morning, offered a resting place for Hasibal, the Formless One.

The Lantern's accounting house, so far just a one-room hut, had been raised beside the market square, the Witherer's roof thatched by the fields, and the Lady's shelter planted farther out yet where a footpath ran south along the shore toward distant villages. As for the Devourer—

"Avisha!" Mai came lumbering down the path, dust kicked up by her sandals. Priya and Sheyshi walked close on either side, and Chief Tuvi and a pair of guards paced behind her. "I was looking for you everywhere!"

Mai assessed the situation with a sweeping glance. As she turned to speak to Priya, Chief Tuvi strode forward into the shadow of the canvas awning and right across the dirt square to Avisha. Up from town a Qin soldier came running, riding whip in hand as though he had been interrupted at drill.

Chief Tuvi glanced that way, and stopped, dust settling around his boots. Seeing him, Jagi slowed, then halted, hand tight around the whip. The chief made a gesture with his right hand, visible to Avisha from this angle only because she saw the chief's arm move. For an instant, Jagi remained poised; then he took two steps back like a horse under tight rein. Obedient to his superiors.

Not even willing to fight for her!

The chief sat down on the bench beside her. He had a pleasing smile; all of the Qin did, able to find humor in most everything. He was old, but the second most important man among the Qin.

Hands shaking, she handed him the bowl of rice, cold by this time. He took it, as they had all been instructed to do, carefully ate half of the rice, then returned the bowl. Its curve rested in her cupped hands, the weight of her future not so very heavy when measured in rice.

The other women had eaten and gotten up to laugh and talk with friends. Here no clans showered them with flower petals or set out a betrothal feast for the village. The Qin had no such customs, and the women had no family nearby to carry out the proper rites.

She could be the wife of an important man. She could expect to live in a substantial house, exert considerable influence over the settlement as it grew, and raise her children to positions of prominence.

Beyond the council benches, Mai smiled sadly. A few more soldiers had come, curious to see their chief catch himself a wife, but Jagi turned to walk away. A boy dashed up from the settlement, carrying an eating bowl covered with a warming lid. He said something to Jagi, then looked beyond the young soldier to see Avisha and Chief Tuvi sitting together. It was Jerad, of course, staring at her with a look of such *accusation* as he tugged on Jagi's sleeve to move him to Avisha. Jagi refused to budge.

Chief Tuvi followed her gaze with his own. "He's a good lad, is Jagi. If he can work his way up through the ranks, then he has a hope of getting what he wants."

But not before. Not if a man wielding more influence wanted it instead.

She thought of her father, braiding cord and rope day after day, year after year, investing the humble labor with something akin to prayer because he cared that his work itself be an offering.

She set the bowl down on the bench without eating.

Voices murmured, startled and speculating. Has the pretty clan-less girl turned down the chief? Impossible!

She hadn't thought the Qin could look surprised at anything. The chief's eyes widened as he looked at the bowl, her empty hands, and her face, which she knew was flaming. What if he was angry?

But he shrugged in good part, rose with the faintest of smiles, and left, scratching his chin as if trying to figure out where he had gone wrong.

Tears bloomed. She choked down a sob, felt it lodge in her heart. Was she simply too afraid to go through with it?

She had to cling to the one thing she knew: Her father had been a good man, a gentle man, a kind man. He had treated her mother well. They had been fond of each other. He had treated Nallo with the same kindness, and even Nallo had found a bud of kindness in herself, not much of one, but her surly nature had tempered in the house, only to surface again in its full fury after his horrible death.

"Vish?" Jerad cantered up, all gangly legs and arms. Aui! He was growing! He shoved the covered bowl of rice into her hands, and snatched the half empty one off the bench. "I *knew* you weren't that stupid!"

He bolted back to Jagi. Without really stopping, Jerad grabbed the man's sleeve and yanked, and tugged, and pulled, while the soldier stood blinking like he'd been blinded by the sun and could not quite make out what was going on right in front of his eyes.

Someone laughed.

Abruptly, Jagi shook free of Jerad, took two steps, then thrust the riding whip into the boy's hand and strode the rest of the way. Not smiling, not today. He plopped heavily down on the bench next to Avisha. He seemed about to say something, but then he let out all his breath as he fixed his gaze on the distant mountains. He was blushing.

The bowl of rice Jerad had given her was still warm, because he had been thoughtful enough to bring it covered. Just as her father would have. She laid the cover aside and handed the bowl to Jagi, because if a man sat on the bench next to a woman, the woman had to offer.

Hands trembling, he carefully ate half, and gave the bowl back into her hands.

Any man might eat, but to seal the agreement, the woman must finish the rice.

Chief Tuvi had an important position. Jagi did not; he ranked among the youngest and least experienced of the Qin soldiers.

Chaji—before his awful death—had been the best-looking of the Qin, since he looked more like the Hundred folk than his comrades. The scars of a childhood disease pocked Jagi's round face; he could not be called a handsome man, but he had nice eyes and a sweet smile.

Keshad, of course, had a bold, bright, intense spirit. Having met him, she would never forget him. Did she regret that he was never meant for her?

Jagi shifted nervously on the bench, and looked at her. Not accusingly, but questioningly, as if to say: What will happen now?

After all, a kind man is best.

She raised the bowl, and ate the rest of the rice.

48

The Qin had set up their main militia training compound outside the city of Olossi, separate from the camps in the Barrens and at Storos-on-the-water. For Joss, the journey from Argent Hall to the substantial military camp was an easy one, up on a thermal and a long, long glide down. The local militiamen standing guard at the gates waved him through. The Qin guards allowed him entry past the inner palisade to the captain's office, a raised platform built of planks and covered by a canvas roof. Its inner and outer walls were tied up in a configuration that let through light and air while concealing the innermost chamber. Rather like the man himself, Joss reflected as he navigated the brief maze.

Anji was seated at a low writing desk with paper unrolled on the slanting desk, one hand holding the missive open while he mouthed words.

As Joss entered, Anji looked up and smiled. "Sit, my friend. Let me finish, if you will. I have received a letter from my wife."

"Are you reading?"

"Is that so surprising?"

"Not in one of the Lantern's hierophants. Mai can write?"

"She can tally an accounts books. As for writing, I believe she may be learning the temple script. However, it is Priya who has written this to her dictation."

"Priya? The slave?"

"She was a priest before she was taken captive. She is an educated woman." His gaze drifted back to the page, and he smiled absently as if he could hear Mai's voice through the words. "Heh. That pretty girl Mai took in. It seems Chief Tuvi attempted to marry her, but she turned him down and chose one of the tailmen instead."

"A good-looking one? The young are enamored of looks."

Anji glanced up. "Not only the young."

"I'm hit!" Joss staggered, a hand clapped over his heart.

Anji laughed. "Sit. Since you came yourself, your message must be important. Let me just . . ." His voice trailed off as his gaze tracked lines from top to bottom. The smile drifted back.

Joss settled himself on one of the pillows. With Mai in the distant Barrens, he thought it likely that Anji had himself chosen the elegant furnishings: masterfully painted silk wall scrolls depicting lush green stands of pipe-brush, embroidered gold silk pillows, five vases filled with yellow and white flowers. The stubby legs of the desk had been lathed by a master into smooth curves. Was Anji's weakness that he loved beauty too well, starting with his wife? Hard to say. Certainly any man might stumble in the face of beauty, and desire yet more comforts. It was possible, and yet Mai herself possessed other qualities that made her formidable. Anji slept, it seemed, on a simple pallet on the floor, and a single ebony chest sufficed to hold his possessions.

"As news comes in that men in the Barrens settlement are finding wives, the men stationed here and at other postings become anxious, although I have given permission for a few to—how do you say it—sit on the bench. Have you ever married?"

Joss shrugged uncomfortably. "It always seemed I was too occupied with reeve's work."

Anji rolled up the letter and set it aside. "What news?"

Joss mentally scrambled back through thoughts of his mother and aunties inquiring in their gently persistent way about his prospects, now that he was getting older, and older. And older. "Eiya! Yes. A cloaked man like to a Guardian has been sighted on the Rice Walk, accompanied by about three hundred soldiers, marching northeast. They've been marching at night, when reeves can't spy them out, and camping under cover of trees during the day. A local villager alerted a pair of reeves on patrol after his village was ransacked for supplies. They scouted the road at dawn and dusk and caught a look."

"About three hundred? The reeves didn't count exact numbers?"

"Being inexperienced and therefore cautious, they kept elevation. I've lost four reeves in the last four months, and there's no knowing whether they're dead, captured, or run off. Meanwhile, I've sent an older reeve to confirm the sighting."

"Could this be a scouting force come out of the north and now headed back?"

"Perhaps. But I think these are stragglers he's rounded up and is leading back north."

"Men who went to ground for five months instead of running? It's possible." He tapped fingers on the desk, thinking. "I'd like to get my hands on a Guardian. Can we ambush the company and take prisoners?"

"I should think it would be impossible to take a Guardian as a prisoner. If it is a Guardian. Maybe it's a demon."

"I'm willing to try. How far ahead are they?"

Joss brushed a hand over his tightly shorn head. "I have a difficult time with earth-bound distances. Fifty or sixty mey."

"A strike force with remounts can travel that in two days."

"Impossible. A message rider would take four days to cover that distance. Regular traffic, ten or more."

"For a fixed distance, along a good road? If we changeover to remounts at Storos?" He was well started now, a wolf already begun its race after a herd of scattering red deer. "We've got militiamen in training who need experience fighting. Such a strike would build cohesion, and give them a sense of triumph."

"If we win."

"Against three hundred of the same rabble who besieged Olossi? If we remain steady, and allow for the troubles that invariably beset orderly plans, it could prove a small but significant victory." He stood, grabbing his sword belt and riding whip. "Especially if we capture a Guardian."

"The ghost-girl killed three of your men."

"She caught them by surprise. What if we can trap this one where it can't see us?"

His determination caught in Joss, tumbling his thoughts through possibilities. "A barrier to delay them." He grinned.

"What are you thinking?" asked Anji.

Joss told him.

*   *   *

ZUBAIDIT WAS SHARPENING her knives.

Shai glanced toward the awning strung low between trees. Their little cadre had set up camp off the path in a narrow clearing, not much more than an arm's reach of open ground where a pair of massive old trees had fallen, taking down smaller trees. The children huddled beneath the canvas, settling down for the night after a scant meal of rice and nai paste. He saw their forms as darkness churning, but maybe that was only the fear in his heart. Weren't they all captives, in a way, of Zubaidit's insane plan to join up with the northern army posing as merchants with slaves to sell?

"You're crazy," he said.

"Every dawn I tell those who wish to stay behind that they are free to go," said Bai without looking up. Eihi! How the whetstone grated his nerves! "Every day, they stay with us."

"You can strand a man in an oasis in the middle of the desert. You can tell him he is free to walk in whatever direction he wishes. But he knows he will die of thirst before he reaches the next water hole. Anyone can choose to die instead of live as a slave. That's not the same as freedom."

Veras, oiling harness, looked up. "Shut up, Shai. Bai knows best."

She smiled, stroking a blade. "Neh, let him talk. You're grown voluble, little brother. I like that. But remember. If we succeed, then even if we die our lives are an insignificant sacrifice compared to those who will suffer if we don't fight. Maybe brave children are clear-sighted enough to know what crucial part they can play."

"Think of what a tale it will make!" said Eridit, from her seat on a log.

Shai turned away in disgust. He would have taken the children and walked away, but he had no idea how to get back to Olossi, and he had no idea how to feed them. He was just afraid to take charge. It was easier to let Zubaidit and Tohon make the decisions.

He covered his eyes with a hand. What was he, after all? Just the useless unlucky seventh son, accustomed to taking orders from his elders.

"Hsst!"

Bai leaped to her knife, a knife in either hand. Veras dropped the harness and drew his sword. Eridit took in a sharp breath.

Ladon rattled out of the trees. "Patrol coming."

Bai nodded coolly. "Take positions."

Eridit ducked under the awning, crouching at the front. Pulse galloping, Shai grabbed a spear and stood, as if guarding prisoners.

Veras and Ladon took cover along the fallen trunks, one on each side. Ladon had his bow ready; Veras propped his supply of javelins beside him. Bai tied a belt of knives around her middle, checking each sheath. Tohon remained hidden.

Bodies pushed through undergrowth. A pair of men appeared at the edge of the clearing.

"Who're you?" one demanded.

"The hells!" Bai answered. "Who are you?"

"Just passing through. Where you headed?"

"I've no pressing need to tell you where I'm headed." The cheap tin medallion worn around her neck caught the firelight and winked.

"Heya! You headed to Walshow, maybe?"

"Come out of the shadows and I might be willing to talk."

"Sheh! You cursed lackwit." This compliment, delivered by a second voice, was directed at his comrade. "I only see two."

"And an awning that might be concealing more, and logs for cover. When did you get to be such a fool?" The first man whistled. Branches snapped and vegetation rustled as an unknown number of confederates approached. "We can make it a fight, or we can join forces. Up to you."

"Depends on who you are," Bai said. "I might be going to Walshow, or I might not."

"We might just escort you there." A dozen soldiers filed out to take up positions around the clearing's edge. Veras, flushed out, rose slowly with a javelin in hand. Men stiffened. Hands gripped weapons. Shoulders grew taut. Every man wore a tin medallion around his neck, just like the ones they'd taken from the corpses of their former captors.

"I'm willing to travel with you," said Bai, "but I have a few conditions."

"Not sure you're in a position to give conditions, verea," said their leader mockingly. He was a burly man with a scarred forehead and hair cropped against the skull.

"That's because you're thinking you know all my resources, but you don't."

The men looked nervously around at the trees.

"Told you not to rush in like a cursed bull," muttered the second.

"Shut up."

"I got no quarrel with you lot," added Bai in a reasonable tone. "I'm taking cargo to Walshow. I don't want any trouble."

"What manner of cargo?"

"Slaves. Children mostly. From the Olo Plain."

"Olo? How were you down there?"

"How do you think I was down there? Marched with the cursed army, didn't I? Got our asses kicked, didn't we? Cursed bad fortune, wasn't it? Captain Mani is dead, gods rot him, and the rest with him. That left me in charge of these dregs.

Here, Ladon, you pissing dog. Stand up." The youth stood, startling one of the soldiers so badly that the man yelped and thrust with his spear, but the jab wobbled and went far wide as Ladon jumped back into a rattle of branches.

"Settle!" barked the leader. "I heard of Captain Mani."

"Sheh! Let me not speak ill of the dead, though I'd like to. What a tight ass he had, eh?" Some man among the company snorted, as in agreement, but Shai couldn't tell which one it was. "We fled with the clothes on our backs, these horses, and our weapons."

"And slaves." He nodded toward the awning.

"We were told we'd get the pick of loot in Olossi, so we took what we could."

"I'd like to see your catch."

"Sure you would. Wait 'til dawn."

"I surely would wait, if I didn't suppose you might have a cadre of soldiers hidden under that awning like to murder us in our sleep."

Aui! They were two wolves facing off.

Bai bared her teeth. "Listen, ver, I'm happy to give you a look, but a look is all. I'm not one of those gods-rotted temples where anyone can go in as long as they show a little respect. I'm aiming to collect coin for leasing the older ones and to sell the younger." She spat. "You give me trouble, you've got a fight. And believe me, you'll go down first. You and your brother, there."

The leader glanced at his second, but the other man looked unsure as the fire played light over his face. Some people, Shai realized, simply were in charge and, being so confident, cowed others. Captain Anji was that kind of person. So was Zubaidit.

"Give me a cut of the action?" ventured the leader.

Zubaidit heaved her shoulders in a big sigh. "And then won't every cursed lout be wanting a cut, eh? Still. Keep your end of the bargain, and I'll consider your offer."

Even knowing what to expect, having heard Bai explain how she intended to con her way into camp, Shai shook with an anger he could not express. Yet when the children were called out, they kept heads bent obediently and shuffled into a tight huddle, youngest in the center. Yudit was trembling, arms crossed in front of her scrawny body, but she said nothing, did not bolt, did not cry. Vali clutched her arm.

One of the men checked inside the awning. Others stared at Eridit.

"She going for sale, too?" asked the leader finally, indicating her with an elbow.

"Neh. She was Captain Mani's bed warmer, although I don't see what she saw in him. I promised to see her safely back to the army."

The man leered. "Looking for a real man to take you on, eh? I'll consider it, but you'd have to show me what you have to offer."

Eridit looked about to say something rude, but she scanned him in a measuring way. "I'm looking for a man who will treat me decent. One with a bit of coin to keep me clothed and fed. Say what you will about Captain Mani, but he treated me decent and so I treated him decent. That's worth plenty."

Simple words, and yet with her tone and posture she did get those men to looking at each other as though sizing up their competition. Set their backs up. Sow a scattering of dissension. Good tactics. Bai signaled, and Eridit herded the children back under the awning.

"We'll move out at dawn," Bai said.

They settled into an uneasy truce, one man from each company set to the watch. Shai was dismissed, but although he settled down against the awning, he was twisted too tight to sleep. He fretted all night, wondering where Tohon was concealed, but neither saw sight nor heard sound of the Qin scout, not even when night's shroud lifted to reveal an overcast dawn.

They walked the next day on forest tracks, pushing east through heavily over-grown countryside. At their approach, birds ceased singing. The children ate nai paste in the morning, and afterward trudged with faces set, little soldiers who had lost all hope of returning home and, in doing so, gained new strength. Shai moved up and down the line as they marched, keeping an eye out for exhaustion, quietly making sure none of the soldiers bothered them.

In the afternoon they stumbled across an abandoned farmstead, blowing through like locusts, stripping any least thing that might be edible. Dena and Eska proved adept at crawling along the narrow eaves of the storehouse to collect bun-dles of drying herbs. It was strange to see how sharing food altered the behavior of the soldiers, some joshing the children good-naturedly as they might younger sib-lings. The landscape began to open with harvested woodland, large clearings suit-able for pasturage, a pair of charcoal pits, and strips of old field gone fallow. Twice again they moved through emptied farmsteads, and gleaned what they could.

Where had the farmers gone? No one made any guesses.

But in both farmsteads Shai collected an arrow fletched in the Qin style dis-carded in the dust beneath one of the storehouses. Tohon had been here before them.

As they traveled on, the shadows grew long. A murmur nagged at Shai's ears.

"Best we look for a camping site," said Bai.

The leader shook his head. "Neh. We're near enough. Keep moving."

"Near enough to what?"

The ground gave way to an incline thick with flowering brush, humming with bees and flitting birds. Shai's gaze skipped over these wonders to the vista beyond as the children clustered around him, murmuring in amazement, shocked out of their daze. It took him a while to realize that the wide strip of blue-green land that split the earth was not land but a river twice as wide as the River Olo. The spilling mur-mur was its voice.

He looked down. A second river flowed past, neither as wide nor as deep, but much closer, cutting a swath through cultivated land.

"Look." Bai nudged him.

Where the rivers met, a city rose, ringed by walls. Within the inner wall, canals quartered the inner city. A huge outcropping thrust into the confluence of the two rivers, tiny buildings visible like children's toys set atop the broad rock.

But this astounding city was not what Bai was pointing at. The soldiers had al-ready started down the track, which zigged and zagged through the flowering growth.

Between the rivers the land, of course, narrowed in the manner of a funnel. Tidy ranks of orchards and cultivated fields covered this tongue of land as far north as he could see. Above, a pair of eagles circled. Below, a vast army marched, rank upon rank descending on the city to the beat of drums. The drums stuttered a new rhythm, and in stages the ranks staggered to a halt, their line stretched from bank to bank. Merciful God! There were so many!

"We can't take the children into that," he whispered.

"It's exactly what we must do." With her body lit by the westering sun, Bai looked *eager*.

Vali held Yudit's hand, his gaze cold, hers exhausted like a hurt dog who knows it must keep limping. The other children watched Shai. Ladon and Veras walked up behind with the leader and his second, and Ladon shaded his eyes and gave a grunt of surprise, while Veras flung his head back like a startled horse catching sight of unfamiliar movement in dangerous country.

"Heya!" The second cheered, then laughed. "The main army beat us to Toskala, eh? I'll be glad of a dram of cordial tomorrow."

"Eh," agreed the leader. "If we can get it, which I doubt. We haven't much coin between us for cordial." He looked at Bai, whose gaze had not left the army settling into its new camp. "I'm counting on our arrangement, verea."

"Eiya! Both whores and slaves need cleaning and fattening. As it is, they're too scrawny to be of interest to any but the worst sort, if you take my meaning, and that sort hasn't more than a vey or two to rub together. I can't earn my fortune that way, eh?"

His gaze slid to Eridit's behind, and back to Bai. "Neh. Neh. I don't have many connections, I admit, but there's opportunity for those following the camp. It's true a better class of offerings will attract more coin."

Bai's answering smile made Shai shudder and the other man grin as at a gift. "Listen to your greed, ver. I know the temples say otherwise, yet they enrich themselves with our offerings, eh? I've a brother still in debt slavery, and mean to free him. So let's go. Before the army moves on."

He laughed. "Moves on? Lord Radas's army has reached its target."

The siege of Toskala had commenced.

*   *   *

THE FLIGHT OF reeves swung wide around the road until it reached the upper reaches of the River Olossi, here not wide but swollen to a green churning roar with the flood rains. They glided southwest, strung in a line at varying elevations along a valley's edge. Each eagle bore a reeve and a soldier.

Anji, harnessed in front of Joss, said, "Look there. A ford."

A rockslide broken off from a treeless ridgeline had filled part of the river, boulders and debris sunk halfway across and thereby making the shallows hard to defend. This time of year, the remaining deep channel boiled with white water. A booming sound pounded at intervals like a smith hammering on an anvil.

"Where's the next crossing?" shouted Anji.

"The Westcott ferry."

They covered about eight mey, passing hamlets and farmsteads set back from the river although mostly the land here was forest cover sprinkled with clearings, moister than the Barrens but not as lush as the countryside in the east.

They sighted a substantial village and the Rice Walk, which on the Westcott side of the river became known as the Lesser Walk. Folk in the fields spotted them. A figure ran into the village, and in its wake the rest fled toward the palisade. By the time Scar touched down in the nearest fallow field, sixty or more people stood at the gate with adzes, hoes, rakes, axes, spears, and staffs balanced in their hands.

Anji unhooked, and then Joss, but the reeve approached alone along a raised walkway between fields.

"Greetings of the day," he called. He addressed the eldest person, a stoop-shouldered man with the weathered face of one who has spent years working under the sun. "I am Joss, marshal of Argent Hall, come on urgent business. I hope you'll give me your respectful attention."

The old man walked forward accompanied by a middle-aged woman in a good quality silk taloos and a younger man carrying a spear. Joss heard his flanking eagles land.

"If you've come for one of us, we'll not allow your depredations," said the old man. "Not unless you present proof beyond doubt of guilt."

Maybe shock showed on Joss's face, because folk pointed at him. "Have reeves come here and demanded you give up individuals into their custody?"

"Last year it did happen. Said they hailed from Horn Hall. They took five young people. Into custody, so they said."

"Horn Hall!"

"Know you of Horn Hall?"

"The hells! Last year I had reason to visit Horn Hall, and found it abandoned." He wanted to slap himself until he woke up. Another mystery, and one he had no time to solve.

"Folk can say anything they want," agreed the elder. "There are plenty of rogues abroad these days. I'm called Menard. What's your business with us, and why have you brought so many eagles?" He gestured skyward.

"Rogues are my business," said Joss, wishing he had a drink. "I don't know if you've had the news, but at the end of the Fox year an army out of the north attacked Olossi."

"Might have heard a rumor of it. Might have had some trouble ourselves recently. Might have. I'm not saying we did."

"A coalition of reeves, Olossi militia, and outlanders come to make their fortune in the Hundred banded together to defeat this army. Most of the defeated survivors fled north over months ago, but some hid out on the Olo Plain. This group have finally made their move to get home."

"What's that to do with us?"

"They're marching up the Rice Walk. They'll hit this ferry and want to cross. They're being led by a man who pretends to be a Guardian."

The elder whispered for a bit to his fellows, then turned back. "The Guardians are long vanished from the Hundred. Everyone knows that."

"Maybe so, but I'm not the only one who has seen abroad creatures who in all parts resemble Guardians except that they rule not in favor of justice but against it."

"Sounds like demons to me. What's it to us?"

"You don't dispute my tale. Or ask to hear more particulars?"

"I don't."

"Then you've heard rumors, or have seen what I speak of. As for Westcott, the companies that now march up Rice Walk will not show your town any mercy, once they cross the river."

"You wish us to hold the ferry and defend the shore. This we can do easily enough. We've pulled the ferry to our side. We control its movements from the winch. Anyway, the river is swift this time of year. They'll not cross without our permission. They'll have two day's rugged march north to Hammering Ford, which is no easy crossing. There's neither ford or ferry south of here until Storos-on-the-water. That's a long way."

"I'm glad to hear you have your territory so well scanned, Menard. So tell me. What defense have you against demons?"

"Why, the same as you reeves. Or are you here to tell me you have a plan in mind and wish our help?"

Joss grinned. "That's exactly what I'm here to tell you. We haven't long, for we're not that far ahead. We've plans to make and snares to set. As for your people, those who have heart and strength to fight are welcome to join us. All others should flee to refuge."

"How many march in this army?" asked Menard grimly.

"Three hundred or so."

They dropped back to confer with the villagers, but the conference was a short one. Soon the trio returned. "What do you want us to do?"

Joss beckoned, and Anji walked up, surveying the assembly as they stared and muttered. "This is Captain Anji, commander of the Olossi militia by request and consent of the Olossi council."

"He's an outlander."

"So he is. Olossi would be a ruin today if not for him."

By their expressions, they weren't convinced.

"If you'll hear me out," said Anji, facing their skepticism without any sign of discomfort, "I'll tell you that I consider myself a Hundred man now. I have an estate in the Barrens. I have a pregnant wife."

"A cursed beautiful one," said Joss in the tone of a jealous man, which got a laugh.

"Go on," said Menard, who with the others had relaxed a bit at the mention of a child. If a man had children, and land, then he had something to defend.

Anji indicated Joss. "The marshal here will be sending four reeves, in pairs, to fly north and south to patrol the river and give us warning should the enemy decide to attempt a river crossing elsewhere. I'll need you to detail twenty or thirty men, if you have them, who can march at speed to any point of contact, should it be necessary."

"What about the village?" asked the woman.

"We've brought a cadre of trained militiamen from Olossi to aid with the defense here. Ver, I'll need three of your largest and sturdiest fishing nets and your heaviest stone weights. We will require all of the arrows, javelins, slings and stones you have in case they try to force their way across the river. Move the livestock out of the village and conceal it. We'll need, in addition, brave souls to remain in the village, working as if nothing is amiss, to lure in the demon. They'll be armed, ready to fight if we're forced to engage."

They listened eagerly. They'd been expecting this, Joss saw. They'd had trouble, and scant hope of defeating new trouble should it come. Because in times like these, trouble would come. Scar spread his wings, to catch the sun, and the villagers took a nervous step back.

Grinning, Anji examined the crowd, nodding at folk to acknowledge them. Young men, especially, moved toward him, despite the big eagle. "Know your vulnerabilities and defend them. Think how, if you were your enemy, they might overcome you. Prepare for the unexpected. As for the demon, I intend to confront him myself."

"BOLD WORDS," SAID Joss after the villagers had hurried away to make ready and the militia men carried by eagles from Olossi had received their instructions. "Chief Tuvi could not face the one that entered your house."

"Mai faced the creature. How am I to do less? It must be done, to understand what we battle. These Guardians of yours, upholders of justice, are nothing but tales. This is not a Guardian."

"Maybe not. Maybe it is. Either way, I agree we must confront it."

"You mean to stay here?"

"I do. The rest of the flight will move out of sight to the northeast."

A pair of older woman walked out from the village and, politely but without smiling, offered them cordial. He knocked back two cups, feeling the buzz of a headache recede. Anji thanked them, and the women walked over to offer drink to the pair of reeves who, waiting on Joss's orders, had volunteered for the hardest task of the day.

"I note," said Joss once he was sure the women were out of earshot, "that you didn't tell them about the strike force that's riding up from behind."

"What none know, no traitor can reveal."

"You think there's a traitor in this village?"

"Three hundred men hid out on the Olo Plain for almost five months, and only now make their break north? I choose not to take the chance."

BY EARLY AFTERNOON the eagles were flown, the village emptied, militia concealed, and volunteers loitering in places visible on the far shore where the road ended at river's edge. Menard had stayed, but every other elder, all the children, and most of the women had left.

The sun swung over the arc of the sky. As the afternoon grew late, its rays glinted off the water as if to blind the town to the coming threat. Forested slopes covered much of the land on the far side, although trees had been cut back on either side of the road by folk gathering fuel or supplying logs to villages downstream. It was a peaceful enough scene. Yet Joss, standing beside Anji in the town's watchtower with a good view, felt uneasy, as at the approach of an ill wind.

"Did you tell Mai you meant to face a Guardian?"

Anji ignored the question and indicated the covered platform that housed the ferry winch and operators. The ferry itself, a sturdy raft with railings, bumped against the dock. "Do you see it?"

At first Joss thought it was a trick of light scattering off the river. The hells! A winged horse flapped over the river, circled Westcott once, and descended, landing in the open ground between ferry and gate beside the Ladytree and traveler's trough where any soul might water. Wings folded, the horse stepped to the trough and dipped its nose toward the water.

Aui! It was such a stunningly beautiful creature that at first he noticed nothing except the elegance of its head and neck and the glorious pale wing feathers.

Then he blinked again, startling as though doused with water, and realized Anji was gone. The folk in fields had dropped to their knees.

Menard walked out from the gate alone, below Joss. "Greetings of the dusk, ver." His voice carried clearly in the silence, although he kept his head bowed.

The man riding the winged horse looked like exactly the sort of man you would find selling fans or eels in the marketplace or dipping cordial for customers at an inn. He wore a dark green cloak appropriate for the rainy seasons. "Greetings, Uncle. Now hurry yourself. Have your ferry released. I've men to cross over from the other side. We'll need food and drink and shelter for the night."

"Of course, ver. We'll be happy to accommodate. Before I send my lads to the winch, best we discuss how many travel with you and how much coin we'll need to lay on a feast. If you'll come with me to our council hall, modest I admit but I think we may be justly proud of our cordial, we can discuss—"

"Look at me!"

Surprised, the old man looked up. He stumbled, a hand pressed to one cheek as though he'd been struck. "Neh, neh! It wasn't only me that started the fight. I was drunk and he was jealous. My clan paid the fine—more coin than that vermin was ever worth—and the assizes court approved the finding and the reckoning."

"You always hated him. Your clan was respected, and his despised. So easily you atone for stealing his life, which can never be repaid. And yet still you think about it, every day it eats at your heart . . ."

From the safety of the watchtower, Joss clutched the railing as the old man buckled, knees folding, and sank to the ground.

"How can coin absolve blood?" the cloaked man pressed on. "I know all who have transgressed, and what they hide. There is not one I have faced, not even children, who does not seek to conceal wrongdoing, greed, petty and grand cruelties, the way he pinches and prods others just for the sake of—"

The shadows had lengthened, hiding that which plummeted out of the sky. Joss gasped, although he had not forgotten. Two eagles pulled up sharply, wings opening. Talons released weighted nets, and one fell directly atop the cloaked man, while the second tangled across the head and forequarters of the winged horse. It dipped its head and shook it off, backing toward its rider.

Two arrows thumped into the man's torso. In their wake, with two more arrows flying wide, Anji ran out with sword drawn.

Joss shouted. "Don't approach him! Captain! Stay back!"

The man let the arrows be as blood leaked through the cloth of his long jacket. He swung to face Anji, who pulled up short, face a study in concentration as the two stared at each other.

"You are veiled," said the man. "Just as the other outlander was. Are you Guardians?"

Anji lunged, sword cutting toward him.

The winged horse had come within range. It kicked, and its hoof caught Anji in the hip and sent him sprawling. Four Qin soldiers ran forward, but the cloaked man met them with a gaze that staggered them. They dropped back. He flung off the netting, mounted, and flew.

Joss cursed. He whistled for Scar, dropped down the ladder, and ran out the gate. Anji got to his feet, wincing as he tested his weight.

He looked at Joss. "What sorcery does he wield, to fell that old man without touching him, and confound my good soldiers likewise, with merely a look?"

Sengel and Toughid came up, rubbing their heads and muttering.

"What did you see?" asked Joss. "He never looked my way."

"I saw a creature who can remain standing with two Qin arrows buried deep in his chest. That is not a man."

"He's a demon," said Menard hoarsely from the ground. "He tried to eat out my heart."

Anji shaded his eyes against the setting sun. "Likely he is a demon. Meanwhile, he's escaped. Toughid, call in the militia. Pull in the strongest village men as well. The enemy will reach here soon." He winced again, took limping steps.

"Anything broken?" Joss asked. "That looked hard."

"I've taken worse. I must have been at the limit of the mare's range. Bad enough, as you can see." He looked up as Scar swooped low and came to rest by the river's shore. "Do you mean to fly?"

"Neh. I'll see this through."

Anji nodded. "Good. They'll try to cross at night. Here's my plan."

THE SUN YIELDED to night. Campfires sprang up on the far shore as the enemy reached the limit of the road. In teams of three, villagers and militiamen dispersed along the bank. Every flopping fish earned a start. If a branch floated past, a village man threw a stone. Across the river, axes chopped and falling trees splintered.

But night passed, and no one attacked.

In the morning, the remaining eagles and reeves took flight, all but Scar and Joss. Staying above arrow range, they scouted up and downstream while meanwhile a reeve flew south along the road to seek out the strike force.

The chopping continued. A reeve landed to report that the enemy was constructing a dozen rafts, logs lashed together with rope. The building site lay upstream.

"What do you think?" the villagers asked Anji.

"They'll come at night."

"We'll be overwhelmed!" cried Menard.

The sergeant in command of the twenty Olossi militia men who had been dropped in by the eagles stepped forward. "Can't we delay them, Captain? Destroy their rafts? Hold the shore?"

"What good will that do?" demanded Menard. "They'll just float downstream and put to shore elsewhere."

"Patience," said Anji with an unexpected smile. After a night off his feet, he was still stiff, but his gait was steady. He surveyed his troops: the Olossi militiamen, four Qin guardsmen, and forty or so locals. "We have to keep them pinned on the other bank. How deep is the river?"

"Shallow to the height of a man for more than a stone's throw from shore on this side. The current cuts closer to the far shore, and has for years. That's why the ferry leads on this side. You can see there's a ramp of paving stones somewhat eroded on the other side. It gets steep fast."

"The current will pull them downstream."

"Downstream the bank on our side gets steep, as the current shifts. If I were them, I'd put the rafts into the water upstream and aim for the shoals here."

Anji stared across the water. A great deal of movement was going on, upstream. "They seem to have the same idea. Yet I wonder. I read a tale once in the archives of the palace library . . . a hidden barricade under water that slowed the advance of a fleet."

"May the Great Lady come to our aid, Captain. If you have any ideas at all, let us know them."

Eyes still narrowed, Anji glanced at Joss. "Marshal?"

"We've some oil of naya, but with forest cover, wet ground, and mobile troops, it's unlikely to meet with the same success as at Olossi."

But Anji, Joss saw, had already ridden on in his own mind. He'd concocted a new plan, and like the others, Joss found himself wondering, waiting, and hoping.

"The oil of naya will find its use. But we don't want to scatter them. We want to kill them. Here's what we'll do."

FOR THE REST of the day, eagles ran sweeps over the enemy but raised no alert. Again, the sun surrendered the sky to the brilliant stars. With night, the winch turned and the ferry moved out into the channel, piled high with wooden furniture and bales of old hay, drenched with a bit of oil and a lot of lard. From the bank, Joss listened for and thought he heard the faint plops of villagers rolling off the back, each trio hauling a bundle of spears and poles. As the raft neared the deep channel, it burst into flame so bright that Joss blinked back tears. The winch cranked a few more times. Shouts rose from the far shore as arrows whistled across the water, many consumed by the fire. The raft blazed, rocked by the streaming current, a bright distraction as the swimmers did their best to drive poles into the shallows. They finished their work as the flames began to die. One by one, they emerged on shore. When the count was made, one had gone missing, but no one knew if he'd drowned, lost heart and fled downstream, or swum across to warn the enemy.

For a while longer the raft glowed and the enemy did not react.

Then their rafts hit the water. The splash and slop of poles in the water and occasional words of encouragement or barked obscenities bounced off the surface to carry farther, perhaps, than intended. Beside Joss, a youth crouched on the shore, carefully piling stones and moistening the straps of his sling by sucking on the leather.

As the rafts entered the channel and picked up speed, arrows arced out from the rafts, most dropping harmlessly in the water while a few peppered the shore. Anji's troops, even the raw village recruits, held position behind their own crude shields of planks or sturdy wicker.

The rafts angled toward shore. A thunk sounded from the lead raft as its bottom caught on one of the submerged poles. The four Qin soldiers lit pitch-stained arrows and loosed them at the first raft, then at a second and third that, scraping on poles, swirled in the current. Fire spurted. Panicked men shouted. Rafts rocked, and bodies tumbled into the river.

"On your left," Joss shouted to mark a swimmer paddling desperately into the shallows. Arrows followed him until his stroke ceased and his corpse floated away, borne on the current.

One group of six men made the shallows and, banding together, used a pair of wicker shields and their spears to push onto shore. Ten Olossi militiamen closed in a disciplined group to confront them, trying to drive them back. Menard had crafted a long pole with a thickly knotted rope fastening a club to one end, and driven bits of jagged metal into the club. Coming up on the flank of the militia, he hefted the flail and, grunting, swung it. The club crashed down twice on enemy shields, which shuddered but did not splinter. Again the old man raised the flail, but this time as he stretched, an arrow caught him in the belly and a javelin's bite drove him back. He fell, tried to raise himself, and collapsed. With a scream of rage, one of the village lads hoisted the flail and waded forward, club swinging so wildly that the Olossi militia men cried out both in warning and in laughter as the lad broke apart the enemy.

"Heya!" the youth next to Joss leaped back, abandoning his neat pile of stones.

Joss spun to face a man splashing up out of the shallows. Joss stabbed with his short sword, wrenched it free, and waded in as a second man lunged at him. He knocked aside a spear thrust and cut him down, and leaped back to realize he had just killed two men.

This was butcher's work. Reeves were never meant to chop and hack like ordinands.

"Marshal! Your back!"

Spinning, he faced one of the enemy, who had axe raised; the man slumped, toppling forward and bringing Joss down with him. He squirmed out as the man twitched, to find Sengel grinning at him as he offered a hand up.

"Hu! That was close!"

Six rafts had been released into the waters, and the stragglers, their arrows spent and their comrades dead, dove into the water to swim back to the far shore. A single raft floated downstream, spinning away in the night as arrows vanished harmlessly into the river behind it.

Above the eastern woodland, the Basket Moon rose.

Anji trotted out to Joss, streaks and splashes of blood revealing he'd done his share of fighting. "Thirty of the enemy accounted for, and more lost in the river, I expect. We lost one man in the river, another three in the fighting on shore, and have five wounded. But we've delayed them."

Joss wiped his brow. "I need a drink," he said, looking at the bodies littering the shore. Villagers were already cutting their throats to make sure they were dead, stripping anything of value, and then dragging the bodies into the river.

"Now we wait for the strike force?" Joss asked.

Anji nodded. "Now we wait."

JOSS WHISTLED SCAR in at dawn. The enemy camp was in turmoil, men arming, rafts abandoned. It looked as if they were readying to march upstream to Hammering Ford. He got high enough to scan several mey down the road, and he did suck in air, then, as Scar chirped interrogatively, feeling the shocked tightening of Joss's shoulders.

"The hells!"

He hadn't thought the strike force could really ride that far, that fast, but cursed if they hadn't managed it: about three hundred riders, a mix of Qin and local men who'd been training with them. Joss signaled with his flags.

Eagles closed in, thirty strong. Below, the strike force approached at a ground-devouring pace, pounding up the road with their remounts left behind for the final dash. Before the enemy could break north into the forest, the eagles flew low and dropped oil of naya in their path, driving them back toward the road. In confusion, they fled. The unluckiest caught a scrap of the unquenchable fire on their bodies. Those who ran screaming into the water still burned.

In the direction of the road, the clash of arms rang with ugly vigor, the shouts and screams of a battle engaged. But Joss's attention was caught by a throng clamoring after the cloaked man, who was riding away into the forest. He was abandoning his own troops. Reaching open space, the horse opened its wings and flew.

"There, Scar!" But the eagle did not fix his keen eyes on the other beast. Even Joss found himself losing track of the horse's flight, as if it literally possessed less substance in the air than on the ground, fading like mist under sun.

He wasn't going to lose the cursed Guardian after all this!

He yanked ruthlessly on the jesses, and at first Scar swept a full circle and only reluctantly pulled in the direction Joss directed him. There! A wink of light stung the reeve's eye. He followed sparks until he flew over a narrow ridge overlooking the booming ford. He tugged on the jesses and, sluggishly, Scar obeyed, gliding down until they skimmed low over the rock and, with a final tug on the jesses, landed at one end.

He'd seen Guardian altars as a young man, when he had defied the holiest law and, after the first transgression on Ammadit's Tit, gone looking for other altars, trying to understand why the Guardians were lost. Why Marit had died.

Now he had followed a man who by any measure could be identified as a Guardian. Yet he saw neither horse nor man on the ridge, only a shimmering of light above a glimmering pattern etched into the rock. Was that a shadow of horse pacing to the center of the labyrinth? Did a ghostly figure walk the maze, no more substantial than fog rising off the ground at dawn?

He unhooked and ventured forward, then looked back over the shoulder. Scar had fallen into a stupor, head tucked under a wing. The reckless anger that had scarred his youth slammed back in all of its bitter fury. He'd killed two men today, stuck them like pigs. A battle had been fought, and many had died, and even if he wasn't sure the enemy soldiers didn't entirely deserve death after the misery they had no doubt inflicted on others far more innocent, he still could not wipe the taste from his tongue. He did not like the world as it had become. But that didn't mean he could ignore it.

To the hells with the laws! What did it matter, when his dreams in the form of Marit whispered that Guardians walked again in the world to seek justice, and meanwhile those who met Guardians in the living world called them demons?

The path shone faintly. He set one foot down, followed with the second, and walked into the maze on the trail of a thing he could not explain. At each turn he looked onto a new vista, a distant landscape: smooth ocean waves; a ruined tower sited above a tumble of rocks which, before it flashed out of view, he recognized as Everfall Beacon; a tangled forest that was surely the Wild; the flat gleam of the Olo'o Sea just turning out of the shadows into the dawn's light.

The visions made him dizzy. Voices whispered urgently.

". . . I escaped from Indiyabu . . . she has corrupted them, thus are we lost . . . surely not, for if we keep our strength and our heart within us, we can still fight back . . . it is not possible for me to struggle any longer, take the mirror and give it to the one who returns in my place."

Don't turn your back, Marshal Alard had been used to say, but Joss could not bring himself to see if ghosts crowded behind him, murmuring in his ear.

He stumbled into a depression in the center of the labyrinth. A woman waited, plump, dark, attractive, smiling but with sorrow awake in her eyes, her hands talking in the secret language of the Guardians. He walked through her before he realized she wasn't there. The rock sloped sharply into a bowl-like hollow. Light flashed, blinding him. An unknown force spun him halfway around.

Aui! He clawed at rock as the ground gave way beneath his feet.

He clung to one side of the ridge, a finger's clutch away from falling to his death into the trees below. He'd been tossed out. He'd broken the boundaries once again.

But cursed if he'd let it go this time. Grunting and straining, he climbed to the top. By the time he flopped down on level ground, his hands were bleeding and the knees of his leathers were badly scraped. He lay there for a while, the wind blowing over him, and panted until his head stopped whirling and his muscles ceased quivering.

At last, he regained the strength to raise his head. Not a stone's throw away, Scar slumbered. As for the rest, the altar lay exactly as he had left it, glittering but empty. Forbidden ground, it had cast him away.

The Guardian had vanished.

49

"Recite again the hundred and one altars."

Marit laughed. "My head hurts from everything you've taught me."

Her companion, the nameless woman wearing the cloak of night, smiled. "A rest then, before we walk. This is a particularly lovely view."

They sat at their ease at the edge of a rock altar ringed by a thorny tangle of flowering purple and white heart's ease. The rocky ledge overlooked the vale of Iliyat, Lord Radas's ancestral home. Under clearing skies, neatly tended fields surrounded tidy villages, everything in order and no one moving on the roads.

"It's very quiet," said Marit.

"No trouble disturbs those who labor and build. Isn't that as it should be?"

"Yes."

"Why do you frown, Ramit?"

She could not speak her thoughts aloud: A pleasant woman with an agreeable philosophy and a concerned demeanor ought not to be marching with an army that burned villages and "cleansed" folk by stringing them up from poles to strangle under the weight of sagging arms.

"It's hard to explain," she said, testing a dozen phrases and discarding them all. "I see that the vale of Iliyat lies at peace, which Haldia surely does not. Yet how do I know those who live below have peace in their hearts and justice in their villages? How do I know that the folk in High Haldia deserved to be overrun? How can an army bring justice? Isn't that the question the orphaned girl asks in the Tale of the Guardians? Didn't the gods agree with her?"

"So they did." The woman nodded. Her hair was pulled back and braided without ornament, suggesting a woman of simple tastes but a complex mind. "We must never forget that the gods came because of her cry for justice. But there are many forms of coercion. Brute force is only one of them. It's not always easy to know which form of coercion causes the deepest harm, today, or next year, or when a child who is a toddling child now is stooped with age. Is it better to live quietly in servitude or die seeking freedom?"

"Why should those be our only choices?"

She nodded. "We ask questions because we want to understand. Yet knowledge can be painful. Still, despite pain, we desire knowledge because, like a sown seed, it will flourish and bear fruit if properly tended."

It was hard to argue with such platitudes, so Marit said nothing. In truth, the woman had instructed with seemingly infinite patience and a soothing demeanor: how the horse must be groomed and the wing feathers properly cared for; that the altars were holy spaces where Guardians replenished their spirit. They could survive for long periods without entering an altar, but they would grow weak and even appear to age without water from the holy spring to strengthen them.

"Are you ready to try again?" her companion asked.

"Aui! Yes."

They rose and set foot at the entrance to the labyrinth, Marit in front and her companion behind her with fingers brushing Marit's left shoulder blade. Marit imagined a knife thrust up under her ribs, and shook the image away.

"What is it, Ramit?"

"Just shaking the cobwebs loose. I was never good at memorization. That's why the Lantern's hierophant wouldn't take me for my apprentice year!"

She laughed, the slight pressure of her hand shifting Marit forward. "I, also. Impossible to line up one after the next. But here you need only look, and remember. Soon you will have visited all these places, and you will know them in your heart as well as with your eyes."

Marit paced the labyrinth, speaking each turn out loud. "Needle Spire. Everfall Beacon. Stone Tor. Salt Tower. Mount Aua." The first were easy, but soon she faltered, recalling some from her own travels and others too unfamiliar to place.

Her companion reminded her in the voice of a patient teacher. "Thunder Spire . . . Far Tumble . . ."

They twisted, now seeing onto an overcast ridge with a faint booming like an echo.

"Aui!" cried Marit, for a presence waited there, green and flowering, as ordinary as a burgeoning rice field and yet with a hidden layer of rot deep in its roots.

"Who are you?" Raising an arm, he swung like a man grabbing for and missing a thrown rope. "Eihi! Mistress! I was hoping you would walk!"

"What is it, Bevard?" asked the woman. "You are making progress gathering the troops?"

"Eiya! I got some, but now I'm pursued, my companies trampled and killed. We were ambushed at the river! They dropped fire out of the skies!"

"Come back," she said. "The army has reached Toskala. Negotiations should now be complete. You did as you were told."

He caught in a sob like a child reassured. Marit sheared away from his presence, not knowing why he creeped her so; she hurried on, forgetting to name the angles. Finding the spring and the mares at the center, she knelt, trembling, and gulped down the cold liquid until her throat burned.

"Sheh!" Her companion arrived, filled her bowl, and drank with polite sips.

"I'm sorry. I was just startled by coming across him like that, so suddenly."

"I didn't mean you. You'll learn in time to feel the presence of another before you meet. I meant rather his difficult circumstances. Bevard is not a true leader; he's working beyond his capabilities, not a problem you will have, I feel sure. Just be patient."

Just be patient, Marit thought. *Be patient, and learn everything you can.* She looked up, and the woman smiled so reassuringly that Marit opened her mouth to confess her real name. Warning stamped. Marit shut her mouth, leashing her bowl to her belt.

"What now?" she asked as she rose.

"We must cut short our journey and return to Toskala. Or I must, to oversee our meeting with the Toskala council."

"With Toskala's council? May I attend?"

"You are free to attend, if you wish."

Was it a genuine offer, or a test? If ever there was a person Marit could not comprehend, this woman was that one, calm, thoughtful, and yet nameless. Only demons have no names.

"I'll come with you."

She nodded, as if she had expected that answer all along.

BUT WHEN THEY returned to the army's camp outside the walls of Toskala, Marit found herself observing a council of war. The flavor of the air and the tension in the stances of the soldiers assembled in the tent kept her alert.

Lord Radas paced beside a large table on which lay a map of the city and the surrounding environs. "At the sixth bell, tonight, the gates of Toskala will be opened, and we will march in."

The hells! She'd missed something major, for sure.

"At first, there will likely be resistance from certain elements of Toskala's militia. Afterward, due to confusion sown in their ranks by our allies, we will triumph. Let this command pass back through the ranks, cohort commanders to company captains, company captains to cadre sergeants, and sergeants to each member of their cadre. Kill those who fight. The others, *do not touch*. Each soldier among you will be judged, and those who have broken this command will meet justice, which is death."

Marit twitched the hanging aside to look into the smaller interior room behind, where Hari lay on a carpet. His cloak still smothered him, but his chest rose and fell. Otherwise he gave no sign of being alive. Kirit, sitting in silence beside Marit, looked in, too, and her grim little face creased in such a grim little frown that Marit wished heartily she could know what the outlander was thinking, or what the girl had seen or heard during the days Marit and the woman wearing the cloak of night had been away from camp.

"How much fighting can we expect, lord?" asked one of the commanders, addressing the map. "Maybe some have allied themselves with us, but the rest of the defenders will fight fiercely since they are fresh, lacking neither food nor water and with their courage still high. Might we not sit out the siege a while longer to sap their strength?"

"Is your courage not equal to the task? The sooner we have taken over an intact Toskala, the less likely reeves will be willing to drop oil of naya lest they burn down the entire city even with us in it. Or do you question our plans?"

They all kept their heads down, like cringing dogs. Marit supposed a man could get used to having folk walk around him in that posture. He might come to like it, expect it, resent those who did not truckle.

She could no longer delay. She did not want to desert Hari. Curse him. Yet she must.

Tens of thousands of people lived in Toskala, and many thousands more had crowded into the city's five quarters in flight from the army. Someone had to warn the defenders of Toskala that traitors within the city meant to betray them— *tonight*.

Lord Radas went on. "At dusk, assemble your companies and move in silence to the gates. Account for me the disposition of your cohorts."

"What about you?" Marit asked Kirit in a low voice. "Do you mean to attack the city with them?"

The girl turned that inscrutable blue gaze on Marit. "I will ride with them. My mirror will show me what is truth, and what demons have corrupted with their shadow."

As the commanders rattled off numbers and composition of various cadres, Marit eased behind the cloth wall separating her from Hari and crawled over the rug to kneel beside him. She dared not touch the cloak lest she interrupt whatever sorcery healed him. Finally, she left the chamber through another entrance, ignoring a guard's surprised exclamation. He wasn't the one she need worry about.

Saddle and harness and saddle bags rested beside a rolled up mattress. She gathered her things and, choosing boldness over caution, walked to the corral. She hadn't finished saddling Warning when a procession with Lord Radas at the lead and Yordenas and Kirit trailing paraded to the corral. Kirit lugged her own gear, but soldiers carried the harness belonging to the two men.

"You are here before us," said Lord Radas with a gloating smile that told her, if she had not already suspected, that he had never trusted her. Had Kirit betrayed her? Or was she just so cursed obvious that anyone could have guessed? "We'll be ready shortly."

"I was just going to water my mare at the nearest altar, the one upriver by Highwater." She meant to play her game to the bitter end, anything to stall.

He laughed. "You will be surprised to learn that the nearest altar lies in Toskala, long forgotten but very much still there. Below the council chambers on the promontory most call Justice Square. We're expected for a council meeting."

The hells! She'd been outmaneuvered. Too late she realized that over the last eight days the others had been engaged in an elaborate form of misdirection, keeping her out of the way. Yet they had made no direct move against her. How could they? It wasn't as if they could kill her.

"I thought," said Yordenas peevishly, "you said Bevard was on his way back." He fidgeted like a distempered lad too spoiled for his own good.

"Patience," said Lord Radas. "Shall we go? Ramit?"

She'd have slugged him for all the good it would do. She had to go to Toskala and the council meeting. She had to try.

With night they flew, Lord Radas taking the lead and Yordenas flying in the rear, while in the camp below them the soldiers, like so many night-crawling serpents, began creeping into attack formation.

*   *   *

AS BAI'S CHOSEN escort when she trolled the camp pretending to be a merchant, Shai had plenty of opportunity to observe because folk tended to ignore him, thinking he was an outlander slave. The army that had laid siege to Toskala had good discipline, a neat camp, and clear lines of authority. An off-duty sergeant could drink a bit, knowing others had his back. He could afford to be expansive.

"You see, it's like this," said the sergeant, leaning close to Bai in a confiding manner. "There was a woman who wore the green cloak, but now the green cloak is a man. The woman displeased them, and Lord Radas raised someone else up to the honor, eh? So who's to say that some of us, the best and most obedient ones, might not have a chance at being raised to a cloak? Why not?"

"Do you think that's how it works?" Bai asked him. "That Lord Radas chooses? I thought the cloaks—Guardians, that is—were made by the gods."

"The cloaks rule all, even death. I think the Guardians that was, in the tales, that they're all gone. Dead, maybe. Maybe they never even existed. Our commanders, now, they're something else."

"What do you think they are?"

His gaze flickered toward the high banner pole, deep within the camp, that marked the big tents where the cloaks sheltered. He had a broken nose, healed crookedly, and a scar under his left eye. His expression shifted uneasily, and Bai quickly changed the subject.

"I'm getting my slaves fattened up and healthy, although it's costing me a cursed lot of vey. What do you think, sergeant? Think I should sell all of them outright? Or just the younger ones, and keep the older for a business? There's plenty here who will pay coin for sex. I could set right up in camp, maybe even work out of a pair of wagons if the army keeps moving south to Nessumara. I'm new to merchanting, as you might have guessed, but you seem like an experienced man who'll give me fair advice."

He cleared his throat and handed her his cup. "That woman who watches your slaves, is she your lover?"

"Neh." Bai sipped at the wine. "I'm not fashioned that way. We made a deal. She works for me while she's looking for a protector."

"Think she'd consider me?"

"Since I like you, I'll be honest, my friend. I think she's aiming for a captain, at the least. A commander, if she can reach so high. Where's your company's captain, anyway? I don't see his fat ass around."

"Eh, there's a council going up at the big tent, neh? My captain's all right, though. Some of the other sergeants, they have to put up with real turds, if I may say so."

Bai laughed. "You won't hear me arguing. Whew! What I had to put up with at the temple, I tell you! Heya! Look there. Is that your captain?"

The man was coming back at a trot, looking tense. He hailed his sergeants, and the man talking to Bai made his excuses and hurried over. Bai beckoned to Shai, and they moved off into camp.

"Something's up," she said in a low voice. "A council of war this late in the afternoon. The way he came running back to rope in his sergeants. He's got orders."

She led Shai back to the perimeter of camp where the camp followers and merchants had set up. When they arrived at the ragged tent she'd purchased for shelter, the children pressed forward to touch both her and Shai, as if making sure they were still alive and not ghosts.

"Where's Ladon?" she asked Veras and Eridit.

"A fellow came by wearing a badge marked with silk slippers, Edard's clan, the ones with river transport."

"Why in the hells would river transporters badge their clan with silk slippers?" Shai asked.

Veras rolled his eyes. Bai smiled.

Eridit just shook her head. "You don't know the tale, do you? Anyway, Ladon went off with him."

Bai frowned. "Did he say where they were going?"

"In fact he did. The abandoned Green Suns tanning yard. Not far from here."

Bai nodded. "I know where it is. That's where I meet Tohon to exchange news. The hells! I'm going after him, make sure it's not a trap."

"Heya," said Shai, "I forgot. Edard told me that the password is 'splendid silk slippers.'"

"Edard told *you*?" Bai looked at him with a narrowed gaze, then shrugged. "It's worth trying. Veras, you'll come with me. You two stay here with the children. Be alert. Keep them ready to move at short notice."

Eridit's eyes widened, and her look of alarm was real, not feigned. "What is it, Bai?"

"May be nothing. A feeling that's prickling my skin." She grabbed a pair of slender assassin's knives, concealed them under her kilt, and strode off with Veras hurrying after.

"Now what?" Eridit asked.

Shai stuck his head into the tent, where the children sat and lay crammed together, watchful as they stared at him. "Form into banners. Pack up everything."

"What's happening, Shai?" Yudit asked.

"Maybe nothing. Stay quiet, but be ready to move if I give you the signal. And for that matter, eat up now. Finish off the rice and nai. We can buy more tomorrow."

The children began gathering up scraps of clothing, eating utensils, leather bottles, and sacks of rice. He came outside and sat on the bench he'd built from scraps of lumber. Eridit twitched her ass down beside him and leaned flirtatiously against his shoulder.

"I like it when you talk with so much confidence," she purred.

"Stop it!" He moved away. After weeks marching with the prisoners, he could not bear to even think about sex. "Or are you truly as cursed stupid as Tohon must think you are?"

"That was a mean thing to say."

"Just because Tohon didn't do the thing with you?"

"You jealous? Of his self-control, I mean."

"You're being an ass."

"A horse's ass, you mean, Shai. It's from the tale of the Swift Horse. It's a bedtime story. You know, before you get into . . . bed?"

"Leave me alone."

"Great Lady," said Yudit from within the tent. "Are you two arguing again?"

A soldier stumbled up toward the tent, obviously drunk. "Heya! You there! Outlander! I hear there's lasses and lads for sale, eh? Nice and young and tasty. Celebrated their Youth's Crowns and ready for a treat! Heh!"

Eridit ducked inside as Shai blocked the entrance. He wasn't as tall as the soldier, but he knew how to brace as he shouldered the man back. "Mistress hasn't opened yet for business, ver."

"Sheh! You lot have sat here a week, eh? You've not fattened up that veal yet? I'll bring a tey of rice every evening, you just let me in." He pushed.

Shai sank to get his weight lower, and shoved hard back. The man staggered, unable to keep steady.

"Outlander bastard!" He turned around and shouted. "Divass! Avard! Get over here. About time we took a taste of what these cursed shut-holes are withholding from us, eh?"

A pair looked up from haggling with a man seated on a blanket who was selling white plums and heaps of cawl petals.

Nudged from behind, Shai glanced over his shoulder. Eridit thrust the hilt of a short sword into his back. "Here."

"That won't help me," he muttered as the drunken man stumbled back to his friends and began gesticulating his complaints in a thready whine. Yah yah yah. Merciful God! How much longer Bai expected them to keep up this cursed pretense, Shai could not imagine. Men were coming around every cursed evening after drill, and so far Bai had managed to put them off with various plausible excuses delivered in her drawling, contemptuous style. "Hu! Take the children out the back if you have to. Here they come."

The three swaggered with outraged privilege as they approached. Merciful One, act now!

A sergeant jogged through the ragged market street, pausing to grab men by the shoulders. "Heya! Heya! Three Circles cadre, report at once."

A second sergeant followed, calling another group. Men turned from browsing the wares on offer: fried vegetables, hot noodles, goat's milk, carved bowls and spoons, an old man repairing knife hilts, women skinny from the abuse they took to fetch a few vey.

"Avard! Divass! Kili! Get your cursed horses' asses over here."

"Assembly?" muttered the big one. "At dusk? After we've already been released from drill? The hells!" But he lumbered away.

Shai sagged, all his readiness blown.

"Did that man go away?" asked Vali, venturing up behind Eridit. "He was following me before. He tried to touch me."

"Sheh!" said Eridit in disgust. "You're not even of an age, Vali. But I'm not surprised by any crude thing I hear or see in this place." She loosed an accusatory glance at Shai, pushed past him, and crossed over the open space to the man selling white plums and cawl petals. There she smiled prettily, and she and the man entered into a protracted haggle, which she no doubt drew out to annoy the poor merchant.

"Why do you argue with her all the time?" asked Vali.

"Shai's a prude," said Yudit, laying her head against Shai's shoulder.

"Neh, he isn't," said Eska. Dena and others in the interior echoed her, defending him.

"Oh, shut it, little plum," said Yudit affectionately. "I'm not ragging him. I'm just saying so, because it's true. Nothing wrong with it." She shuddered, and he put an arm around her. Vali leaned against him on the other side, and they watched as the market street cleared of soldiers and the merchants packed away their wares for safekeeping.

He felt a prickling on his skin, maybe the same one Bai had spoken of, like the way air changed before a storm.

Eridit returned triumphant, her long jacket cradling cawl petals weighted down with white plums. "Look at all this, and for only two vey!" She pushed rudely past Shai. "Here, Eska. Let's put this in the pot. Then we can make soup later."

"I'm scared, too," said Yudit softly. "But that's no cause for you two to keep fighting. It worries the younger ones."

"I don't fight with her because I'm scared!"

She smiled, a rare gift, and shame shut him up. Maybe she was even right. He missed Tohon bitterly, but the Qin scout had been left in the woodland to scout the environs, meeting with Bai long past midnight on specified nights.

"Whsst!" Bai came striding out of the gloom, waving at them to fall back. "Here, now, Shai," she said, catching him by the arm. "The password worked. Although why Edard told you instead of anyone else I can't figure."

They retreated into the interior, stuffy with so many bodies crammed inside. After so long without a bath, they all stank. Eridit lit a lamp and hung it from a pole.

Bai surveyed her troops. "You're leaving tonight. You'll travel to the ford where we crossed ten days ago. You'll meet Ladon and Veras there, with a wagonload of supplies. You'll cross to the far shore and travel about a mey downstream. There, you'll meet Tohon on the road, and he'll lead you to a hidden dock where you'll rendezvous with a barge owned by our dead comrade Edard's kin. They're going to take you to Nessumara, to his clan's compound. Do you understand?"

They nodded.

"I want you to know something," she went on. "Lone wolves are rightly viewed with suspicion and treated as spies. I'd do the same, in their place. But having you here has given me entrance to every cursed company in this camp, talking up my wares, how juicy they'll be as soon as I get a bit more fat on them, all untouched, never bitten. Folk who want something from you are a cursed reach stupider than those who want nothing." She sketched a gesture in the air, and the children smiled in response. "By having the courage to walk in here and just wait, not knowing what might happen and if you'd get abused again, you've done more service to Olossi than the entire cursed Olossi militia."

"Should we stay, holy one?" asked Yudit in a low voice.

"No. Edard's kinfolk were tipped off by some woman who married into the clan from the Green Sun clan. They're getting out, and they're willing to take you lot downriver with them. Eridit, there's a passing phrase you must speak to get across the river at the ferry. 'Flying fours lost,' the sentry will tell you, and you reply, 'Five cloaks won.'"

Eridit mouthed the words twice, then nodded. "Got it."

"Shai, you can see them to the ford, make sure they get across safely. Then you have to come back to me."

The children groaned, and murmured rebelliously.

"What's happening?" asked Eridit, all saucy anger fled.

"Lord Radas's army is attacking Toskala tonight. I don't know the details, but I'm cursed sure there's treachery on the wind."

"Why does Shai have to stay behind?" Yudit and Vali asked at the same moment.

"He's the only one of us who is protected against the demons. Veiled to their sight. That's what both cloaks said."

"And what in the hells do you mean to do?" asked Eridit. "The two of you can't fight the entire cursed army."

Bai grinned, and everyone paused to admire her because she made them all want to be able to grin like that. "The Merciless One will guide me." She rocked back, listening to the murmur of a camp rising instead of settling. "Now get out of here."

They walked in a tight line, four abreast with the younger ones in the center rows, Eridit and Wori in the lead and Shai and Yudit as tailmen, the ones likeliest to get attacked from behind. If you acted like you were about your business, then folk did not question.

The vendors following the army had set up farthest away from the siege line, and the usual busy twilight market had gone to ground, blankets rolled up, folk hiding inside their tents or huddled in whatever scrap of protection they could find in ragged hedgerows or the remains of a lot of firewood commandeered by the army. It felt like it was about to rain, but the skies remained dry. They descended through a series of orchards, and held their noses as they skirted the edge of tanning yards before coming to the main crossing of the Lesser Istri, two sets of paired cables strung across the wide river.

The guards had lamps out at the barricade, and they considered Eridit with suspicion as she sauntered forward, playing too much, Shai thought, to their lust.

"Here, now," said the first. "Shouldn't you be at home with your husband, eh, verea?"

"I don't see your red bracelet, sweetheart," said the second. "But I'll give you a taste of married life."

The third man shushed them. "Flying fours lost," he said.

"Five cloaks won," she answered, and her posture shifted so swiftly that Shai blinked. She was another person now, someone rigid and irritated. "Didn't think I'd have trouble here. You lot need to attend to your duty."

The two who had been rude grumbled.

The third man shook his head. "Where are you going with all these children?"

"We were ordered to get them out of the area."

"Who ordered you?" demanded the first man, anxious to show he could be a hard-ass.

"Shut up," said the third man to his comrade. "I remember you lot. You in particular." He looked Eridit up and down, and Shai found that he'd closed a hand into a fist. Yudit patted him on the elbow, like calming a tense dog. "You lot crossed eight or ten days ago, neh?"

"Can't get buyers for what we're trying to sell, can we?" she said with a smirk.

The first two men looked at each other, frowning as they considered the insinuation in her words, while the third man grimaced. "Sheh! Are you saying—? Most of those kids aren't old enough—Eiya! People like you ought to be hanged up on a post, eh? I've got little sisters and brothers, eh? Haven't you any shame?"

"Those with plenty of coin don't need to bow before shame, eh? And we've got coin for the fare, don't we? Now just shut up and let us cross."

"What if I won't let you pass, you cursed foul degenerate—"

Down at the platform, the winch-turners had stirred from their cots, rising to get a look at the commotion. Wagon wheels ground on paved stones, and a wagon appeared out of the gloom lit by a lamp swaying on a pole. Ladon and Veras had arrived just in time.

Curiously, a slender man of mature years, not yet elderly, strode alongside the wagon, chattering in the most inanely cheerful manner. He wore a long cloak against the expected rains, and the garb Shai had come to recognize as typical of the priests known as envoys of the god Ilu.

"—then I said to him, 'Ver, death's wolves aren't greedy. They only eat when they're hungry, not like the wolves among men.' I was speaking, of course, of the Sirniakan toll collectors, who I will tell you charged me double and triple only because I was a foreigner in their lands! Outrageous!" As the wagon rattled to a halt, the envoy smiled at the guardsmen. "Greetings of the dusk, my friends. What's this? A full raft for the twilight pull, eh? Good fortune for those who collect the toll."

The guards took a step back, and the children shrank against each other. Eridit expelled a hot gasp, as though she'd just been insulted, and Ladon and Veras—the idiots—sat like nimwits on the box of the wagon, struck to silence. The big raft bumped gently at the dock. From the shelter of the platform, the winch-turners stared. No one moved.

Shai trotted forward, pushing right up to the guards. "We're in a hurry, ver. And I'd sooner piss on you than listen to you tell me what you think of our business. You want to fight? Call out your fellows, and let's fight, eh?"

"Neh, neh, you go on. Vermin."

Shai shouldered past them, and the children hurried after with the wagon rumbling in their wake. The winch-turners peered out as Shai strode out onto the landing stage and pulled open the railings to allow the wagon to maneuver onto the raft. He stepped back as the children flooded on afterward.

That cursed envoy was nattering to Eridit. ". . . Water-born Goats like you do have an unfortunate tendency to be self-centered, wanting the attention of others always fixed on them. They might not mean to be petty and selfish, but too often they don't notice if they've violated the honor of other people, which is why it can be hard to trust them—"

"Who asked you?" she demanded furiously, half crying as she stormed past Shai and hopped over the widening gap onto the raft. She grabbed a rope and yanked the raft's railings shut, latched them, and shouted to the laborers. "We're ready!"

Gears ratcheted. Rope trembled.

Shai gripped the outer railing. "Behave!" he called to the children. "Don't be stupid."

"You're not going with them," said the envoy.

"Neither are you!"

The envoy met his gaze for a long careful while and then, abruptly, smiled with great sweetness. "I remember you."

"Eh?"

"You see ghosts."

The winch clanked, and footsteps trod the boards on the platform behind.

"Shai! Shai!" cried the children as the raft lurched a hand's span out from the landing stage. The rope tautened.

"Aui!" continued the envoy. "So you are Shai, the one I've been searching for, eh? There's a young woman looking for you. I fear she means to do you ill."

"How do you know me?"

"You were with the Qin soldiers riding out of the empire. I saw your eyes follow the Beltak priest. A terrible thing to imprison their spirits in the bowl, isn't it? You're rare, you folk who see ghosts. You're veiled to our sight. I don't know why."

Words croaked up, made hoarse by everything happening at once. "Who are you?"

"Beware," said the envoy. "But be honest. Honesty might save you."

"Shai!" As the raft slid away from the river, rocking in the current, Yudit pressed to the railing, the others crowding behind, their faces fading into the night. Then he heard their voices as they began to chant.

> *I sing to the mountain,*
> *Mount Aua, who is sentinel*
> *who guards the traveler*
> *who watches over us.*
> *He carries us on his shoulders*
> *because he is strong, kissed by the heavens.*
> *We survive in his shelter.*

The river's voice drowned theirs. His face was wet with river mist and tears.

He ran to the winch and found a place to slide in with the other laborers, pushing pushing pushing until his shoulders ached and his legs strained, until the mechanism caught and the rope, sighing, slackened. They were safely across. The men grunted and, straightening, rubbed their lower backs.

"Thanks for that," they said. "Eihi! You've got good shoulders on you. Want our job?"

"Good fortune to you," he said, and stepped out from under the platform, remembering suddenly the envoy of Ilu who had known he could see ghosts. He scanned the docks, the road, but all he saw were the slouching guards and, strangely, a pair of lights weaving up and down in the heavens like candles carried aloft by drunken soldiers.

The envoy was gone.

Far away, horns blatted, and drums beat an angry rhythm. He stared toward the far bank, but of course he could not see it, nor hear the creak of wheels and the patter of feet as they headed downriver along the road. Not out of danger, never that, but away from the worst if their gods chose to be merciful.

The envoy had told him, *You're veiled to our sight.*

You're the only one protected against the demons, Bai had said.

Veiled against demons, Shai thought. *They can't eat out my heart the way they eat out the hearts of others.* He brought the wolf ring to his lips as he thought of his clan, of Mai, of Tohon, of the children. Even of Eridit. He thought of Hari, whose spirit was still not at rest.

Even at a distance of several mey, he heard a steady rumbling rising from the city: treachery on the wind.

I can fight them.

He headed back toward the city.

50

"Brought your shadow along, eh, Nallo?" said the vendor, scooping fried eel into her bowl.

She had walked down from Clan Hall into Toskala to haggle over a bed net, since no such item had been issued by the hall. With her purchase draped over her shoulders, she had stopped at her favorite stall for her favorite snack. Pil hung at her back.

"Sure you don't want some?" she asked him.

His shrug meant no.

"You can't just eat mutton and yoghurt," she said, but he looked at her in that way he had that made her feel bad for teasing him. Then he scanned the street. It was dusk, when villagers settled after a hard day's labor. In Toskala, market stalls were still selling food, folk chattering and haggling, on their way with lamps lit. Olossi had seemed unimaginably complicated to a country girl. Toskala overwhelmed, so huge, so busy, so crowded, so packed with shops and squares and streets selling grains and pies and oil and kites and banners and cord and dried fish and cloth and fans until it made her dizzy. So much! And with a hostile army camped outside their gates and the population swollen with refugees, folk lived as on a knife's edge. She always felt someone was about to jump out of the crowd and slug her. She liked having Pil at her back.

She chewed eel, sighing with pleasure. "Good today," she said to the vendor. "Even if you raised your prices."

The vendor was middle-aged and comfortably portly, wearing a mended tunic and broad-brimmed hat in case it rained. A small umbrella covered the pan and fire. "My thanks. Spice and fuel sellers raised their price, eh? What am I to do?" She laughed too brightly. "I hear tell they've sent reeves to Olo'osson, asking for help. You know anything about that?"

"I don't, and I couldn't say if I did."

"That's fair enough."

The neighboring vendor, selling noodles, broke in. "Our defenses are strong enough to hold off that cursed army."

Under cover of this conversation, Pil tugged at her sleeve. "I think we should go back," he muttered.

"My thanks to you," said Nallo, "greetings of the dusk."

She slurped down the last bits and set off, Pil striding alongside. "What is it?" she asked.

Then she heard shouts rising over the twilight clamor.

Pil edged into a trot as folk looked up from their shopping and eating and chatting; foreheads wrinkled; a man harrumphed irritably; a child whined, "Come on, Ma, come on." The knife sharpener's whetstone creaked to a halt as he forgot to pump. A noodle vendor's ladle tipped sideways as she strained to hear, and the steaming noodles slithered out to plop on the ground.

"Move." Pil broke into a run, pulling out his reeve's baton.

She fumbled as she slipped hers out of its loop. A tumult of shouting lifted as in a wave to wash over them. Dogs began barking and howling, the cry taken up throughout the city. Something had gone horribly wrong.

As they reached the Silk Street gate, Pil used his baton to shove folk aside as they cut across to the brick-paved walkway reserved for official business and hopped over the dividing rail. At first, the lane ran clear of traffic as far as they could see alongside Canal Street, and Pil ran full out with Nallo pounding along behind.

She glanced back. A *surge* like a rains-swollen flood roiled in their wake, people rushing toward Guardian Bridge. Was that a person crumpling to the earth, trampled by the press of those stampeding behind? The hells! They'd be crushed.

The approach to the bridge lay in the open space where Bell Quarter and Flag Quarter ended at the locks. A crowd was always waiting for passage over the bridge. Pil ruthlessly drove through the people clogging the walkways, using the baton as leverage to prod people out of the way.

"Heya! Watch that—"

"Cursed reeves—"

One side of the bridge was roped off for official traffic, but the press of people trying to get over the bridge had spilled over. Pil tucked up beside the railing and smacked bodies to move them out of the way so he and Nallo could squeeze past. The bed net caught on something, or someone, and was dragged off her shoulders. She let it go.

It took forever to get over the span, and as they pushed down to the spur where the stairs that led up to Justice Square began, panic hit the square in front of the bridge. Screaming drowned all other sounds. Flailing bodies plunged into the spillway pool and the empty locks.

"Let in the water! Let in the water!" a voice cried.

"Release the locks!"

"They've breached the gates!"

Like a storm, riot crashed down: the clatter of weapons, the dogs gone wild, and most of all the terror of thousands wailing and roaring until she thought her heart would burst from fear. Within the bodies pushing toward the single gate guarding the stairs, she had lost Pil.

"Nallo!"

She spotted his topknot, and she brought her baton into play, slapping and whacking. "I'm a reeve! Let me through!"

They fought their way to the gate, where a dozen frightened militiamen held the entrance, wicker shields overlapping to make a tight wall over the gap.

"What's going on?" demanded one lad, his voice breaking.

"We need to get to our eagles! Let us through!"

A slim crack opened. She and Pil squeezed past, and the crowd surged forward as the poor guardsmen tried to close up. They kept moving up. With night coming down it was hard to see, but with the rail under one hand they could guide themselves. A thousand steps were carved into the rock, wide enough that some might descend as others ascended, although today everyone struggled upward. Those who were slow hugged the rock face, and those who were stronger climbed along the outer rail, shouting at anyone who didn't get out of their way. Winded and sucking air, she and Pil reached Justice Square at the crest of the promontory only to stumble over folk collapsed on the ground right in their way.

Guardsmen carrying lit brands came running. "Move out of the way! Let those behind keep climbing!"

Pil staggered to the wide balcony that overlooked the city. The din rising off the city was indescribable, floodwaters drowning everything in its path. Lamps and torches flickered in the streets below like will-o'-the-wisps, darting at random.

"The hells," Nallo muttered. "Best we get to Clan Hall."

Four complexes fenced Justice Square, all swarming with lamplight. The night fire burned at the tip of the promontory beside Law Rock. They cut left to the gate into Clan Hall, and were immediately stopped by the reeve standing watch.

"Any more with you?" he demanded. "Ah, the hells, thank the gods it's you, Nallo. Heya, Pil! What is going on down there?"

"Peddo?" she said. "I thought you'd know something."

"The gates have been breached," said Pil. "The army has attacked. There's panic."

"How can the gates be breached? They're reinforced, doubled ranks of walls, a second ditch and entrenchment . . ."

"Sometimes," said Pil in a calm voice that cut through Peddo's mounting hysteria, "the Qin commanders bribe a local man who is discontented to open the gates. Maybe here, also? It is the easy way."

"No, that's not possible. Why would anyone betray—"

"Heya! Is that you, Peddo?"

"It is. Volias?"

"The same. We need a count of reeves. How many were caught down in the city—Nallo! By the Witherer's mercy!" He caught her arm, hugged her, and let go to slap Pil on the shoulder. "The hells!" His voice broke, he sucked in air. "The hells! It's what I think, isn't it? They've breached the gates."

"We think so," said Nallo.

"Good time to attack," said Pil. "No moon."

"No moon means the eagles won't fly until dawn," agreed Volias. "Peddo, why are you on gate duty?"

"Likard sent me. Commander was called away, over to Assizes Tower. Some kind of council meeting, I don't know. Her, and Ofri, and the legates, and—"

"Every senior reeve not off duty, twelve all told. I've been looking for them. Listen, I sent those two new fawkner's assistants over here to hold the gate, although I don't see them here, curse them. You grab every reeve you can find, and have them kit out. Ready to go. We'll need to release all the eagles."

"They'll not fly at night," said Peddo.

"Maybe not, but it's better if they're not trapped."

"What do you think is happening, Volias?"

"I don't know. Pil, you have military experience. You and Nallo come with me."

"Where are you going?" asked Peddo.

"To Assizes Tower. To find out what in the hells the council is doing over there. And why in the hells they didn't ask for oil of naya sooner. Eiya!"

Peddo laughed, tight and tense. "Didn't know you had it in you to prance around giving orders, Volias. Thought all you did was snipe."

"You and your grandmother." Volias slapped him on the chest.

Peddo swung at him.

"Stop it!" Nallo cried, and they both looked at her, and she realized they weren't fighting, they were just tipping back the lid to let a trickle of steam escape.

"And while you're at it," added Volias, still shouting to be heard above the onslaught of noise, "send Kesta to find Captain Ressi. Someone's got to block those steps."

Usually at night Justice Square lay in peaceful slumber, deserted except for the rounds made by the fire watch. Tonight, the three reeves pushed through a churning crowd, every person arguing and complaining, no one in charge.

"We had to leave everything."

"My children are hungry."

"My children are in the city! I have to go back down."

"What's happening?"

"Those cursed reeves have done nothing. They let the refugees flood us. They let the army march without resistance. They padded their own nests while others work. The Commander says she's in charge, and yet see what has happened—"

"And what in the hells have you ever done?" snapped Nallo to the man, dressed in his expensive silks with his hair done up in a rich man's threefold loops. "Let me see the calluses on your clean hands, eh?"

Volias took her arm. "Nallo, come on."

"You pissing coward," she shouted for good measure as they trotted off. The man waved his hands as though berating her and was then lost in the milling crowd.

Volias said nothing, not to scold, not to praise. He was mumbling under his breath as he let go of her arm, but she was pretty sure it was nothing to do with her or that gods-rotted whining fool behind them. Toskala's Assizes Tower rose higher than any structure she had ever seen, with its thick stone base and wooden tiers floating above. They ascended the wide ramp, lit by lamps hanging from tripods. Militia guards huddled in groups, talking as they glanced nervously into the night.

"What's that?" said Pil, gaze lifting.

Lights dipped in the sky. Folk scattered, and with their shrieks ringing close beside and the steady rumbling clamor from below, Nallo could not hear the clap of horses' hooves when the animals dropped down out of the sky and trotted to the ramp. A light steadier than a burning oil lamp gleamed from the hand of each Guardian, two men and two women.

She couldn't move. She couldn't even breathe, but when the four riders hit the base of the ramp, she grabbed a stunned Volias and yanked him to one side as the winged horses paced up the stone walkway and the militiamen leaped out of their way.

Guardians!

Everyone knew the tales. She wept to see them, so bright and beautiful, come to save the city. Guardians of justice. The servants of the gods.

Men cowered, or dropped to their knees. Some wept, while others covered their faces.

A ghost rode in their midst.

"The demon," said Pil, quite clearly, if not very loud.

A pallid face turned in their direction, and its gaze caught Nallo. Sheh! For shame! The rice she had stolen from a neighbor's storehouse before she was married, and how she let her cousin take the blame and the whipping. That time she had slapped Jerad until he cried, and then bullied him into keeping quiet about it. How much she had resented her husband, although he'd only ever been kind, smiling gently sometimes as if he knew what a bad bargain he'd gotten but was determined to accept his fate gracefully. That was the worst of it, hating yourself and never being brave enough to change.

The demon released her, and she swayed, a sob convulsing her. The demon's gaze snapped to Pil, fierce with challenge.

Yet he faced her. "I will not fear demons!"

She considered him with her flat demon gaze held over a shoulder until, passing upward and riding actually into the tower in the wake of the others, she vanished from sight.

"The hells!" said Volias. "Are those Guardians?"

Away across the square, an eagle shrieked in fury. A man screamed, the pitch ripping high, then cut off.

Volias heaved, staggered, and retched, although nothing came up. "Trouble," he said hoarsely. "Aui!" He collapsed, sprawling limp on the ground.

In Justice Square, a stilling hand had turned the crowd as into stone while the city below sank further into chaos.

*   *   *

NOW THAT SHE was trapped, her purpose suspected, Marit felt a sense of peace. Let them do their worst!

She rode behind Lord Radas into a hall lined with benches. The Toskalan council sat in expectant assembly, everyone facing the woman cloaked in night who stood on the elevated speaker's platform holding the lacquered speaker's stick. They watched her as if she were holding their hearts in her hand and meant to decide whose she would crush.

The air in the room was sweat-drenched. The size and weight of the horses devoured space so the women and men seated on the benches shrank back to give room. Marit knew the trick of quick assessment: there, twelve reeves, experienced men and women; a pair of militia captains and another dozen prosperous-looking council members, some of whom shifted nervously while the rest sat very still. Guardsmen stood behind the benches on which the reeves sat. A cloaked man stood in the shadows behind the speaker's platform, his face unfamiliar. Six Guardians assembled here. Kirit and her mare blocked the door; she watched the council through the reflection of her mirror, studying their faces.

Something terrible was going to happen.

"An ill day," said she who wore the cloak of night. "Trouble has risen to plague the Hundred. We the Guardians have returned on this day to restore peace."

As in the old days with Flirt, when the raptor's excitement at a reckless maneuver had burned in her blood as well, Marit grinned as she took the plunge. She stood in her stirrups.

"Don't believe her! These are ones who command the army that assaults Toskala. As we are speaking, in the city below, the gates have been opened by traitors and your enemy marches in. Don't trust them!"

One of the reeves stood, an older man whose black hair was streaked with silver. "Who are you? You look like a reeve who died twenty years ago. A dear friend of mine. Her eagle was slaughtered on the Iliyat Pass and yet her own body never found. Who are you?"

Lamplight flashed off a mirrored surface, illuminating his face. Aui! She hadn't recognized him. The years had not been kind, not in the way they had been to Joss. *"Kedi?"*

"Marit? Eiya! You have the same voice! Yet you've not aged a day. Commander, this is a ghost or a demon. How can it wear Marit's face?"

"Marit!" said Lord Radas beside her. "I recall you now. You are the foreseen traitor. 'One among the Guardians will betray her companions.'"

"Kedi, I beg you, believe me for the sake of the friendship we shared. They mean to betray you, they have already a plan in place, you are in danger—"

Of course they ran a hundred mey ahead of her down this road, swords and knives drawn before the words left her mouth. A militia captain stabbed the man beside him. Three council members turned on their own. The guardsmen standing behind the reeves drove knives into unprotected backs. By the time she got her sword out, those not yet dead were being swarmed by the killers.

"Kedi!"

Lord Radas reined his horse into hers, forcing her back. She slid off one side as Warning flicked a wing half open, and crawled under the horse's belly. A tremor stirred beneath the planking, a whispering pulse she recognized as the tracery of a Guardian's altar hidden under the Assizes Tower. Her skin throbbed, gooseflesh rising.

Coming up, she found herself face-to-face with Miken, the spy. "They caught me on the river," he murmured, and his blood-soaked shame pressed like a blade at her throat.

I had to kill, in exchange for the lives of my sister and her children.

"They've lied to you," she said.

She pushed past him, but the senior staff of Clan Hall were dead, dispatched cleanly. Despite being inside the tower, and with the riot of sound aloft in the air outside drowning out much else, she felt more than actually heard the distinctive squalls of eagles sundered from the bond that jesses them to their reeves.

Three of the killers knelt, heads bowed. A fourth was doubled over, fluid leaking out where he'd been stabbed by someone who had, briefly, fought back. Five guardsmen and merchants remained standing, weapons poised, but there was no one left to kill except a single gasping woman dressed in a merchant's tabard badged with a green sun.

"This isn't what I thought you meant!" she said accusingly to the air, or the cloaks, or the living captain—it was hard to be sure. "This isn't what I intended, at all!"

"Someone must bear the blame." Lord Radas touched his arrow to Miken's chest. "You are all traitors. Murderers! Do you deny it?"

Miken sobbed.

"So are you judged," said Lord Radas.

Miken exhaled sharply, his hand raised to grasp at a flicker of light that sparked before his face, then fell. He was dead.

"But you commanded us to kill them!" cried the militia captain.

"Did you commit the act?" asked the cloak of night from the speaker's platform.

Crouched by Kedi's lifeless body, Marit watched the murderers fall one by one, all but the merchant woman, who collapsed in a babble of hysteria. She rose, sheathing her sword.

"This one, who lied about her name, is also a traitor." Lord Radas pointed his arrow at her.

"You can't kill me," said Marit, edging toward Warning. "I'm already dead."

"It is time, Radas," said the cloak of night, "to grant our companions their full power. We are forced to pass judgement on one of our own, because of her deeds."

"Folk who are accused are allowed a hearing at an assizes," said Marit.

"We stand in an assizes court. We do not act out of haste. We will pass considered judgment, not like it happened the other time, long years ago, when those who had the majority acted out of spite and jealousy to condemn one who had done nothing wrong."

"How long ago was that? Who did they judge, and what had that person done wrong?"

"I had done nothing to warrant obliteration! But the majority passed judgment out of fear and anger. So in their actions, I saw the truth of what they had become."

"I can't argue with you," said Marit, stepping over Miken's corpse. "Words mean nothing when acts tell the true tale."

"You know nothing," she said. "You only think you do. You think you are dead, but you are living. It is others who tell you you are dead, and you believe them, and by believing them you corrupt the strength the gods pour into their chosen vessels."

"Maybe so," agreed Marit, fingers tangling in Warning's mane. "But if I know nothing, it's only because no one ever told me what became of the Guardians. And what became of me."

"Because you refused to come to us in the beginning! You never trusted us, and therefore we can never trust you. There must be trust between Guardians. There must be unanimity. All must agree. And when one does not agree, when one cannot be trusted, then for the good of all, that one must be destroyed."

"Agree about what is truth? Or just agree with *you*? With whatever you want, and whatever you have already decided?"

"Yordenas." The cloak of night tossed a knife, blade flashing. He caught the dagger easily, as if the hilt had twisted into his hand by sorcery.

He yelped, as if its touch stung. "I could have cut them down! Murderers and traitors! I could have punished them, if you'd given me my staff before."

"Bevard." She gave the green-cloaked man a pointed green stick, like a poor farmer's implement for digging out offending weeds. All were objects that pass judgment, that can sever spirit from flesh and that which is healthy from that which is diseased: a writing brush, a dagger, an arrow, a weeding stick. Even a mirror.

"A majority pass judgment on a renegade," the woman said. "Five, to judge one, standing on an altar, which completes their judgment." She touched her brush to paper.

Yordenas advanced cautiously toward Marit with dagger raised. Lord Radas stretched out his arrow. The green-cloaked man hesitated, but when the women gestured, he, too, approached.

All this the ghost girl watched, her pale figure overlooked, ignored, forgotten.

"Kirit," said Lord Radas. "Remember what I told you. She's not one of us. She must be killed, so we can remain safe. We need your strength added to ours."

She turned the mirror to reveal her own white face and blue eyes.

"In their actions, we see the truth of what they have become," said the girl. "You are not Guardians, seeking justice. You are demons. I will not be one of you."

She reined her horse around.

Marit tugged on Warning's mane, ducked as the mare opened a wing, and jumped up belly-down over the saddle. Yordenas grabbed at her, and she kicked hard, connecting with flesh, hearing him grunt and stumble backward. Lord Radas's arrow jabbed her shoulder, but Warning, once she knew she was going to get her way, nipped and kicked to force a way to the entrance. Kirit crossed the threshold and clattered down the ramp. Marit cleared the door as the other horse took wing, bearing west-southwest over the Lesser Istri.

What if it had been Hari, instead of Kirit? Eiya! Would he have resisted, or joined the others and betrayed her? *Killed* her?

Spreading her wings, Warning leaped into the sky while below the hundreds gathered in Justice Square shouted and wept, their voices rising as if it was their cries that lifted her.

51

IN THE SETTLEMENT, men and women ringed the council square, weaving a song to accompany the bridal couples who walked a circuit of the seven altars to present offerings to the gods.

> *A garland of flowers.*
> *A handful of rice.*
> *Nai, wrapped in se leaves.*
> *Silk as your banner.*
> *Build a house! Build a house!*
> *Walk this path into the next day.*

Flowers were hard to come by in the Barrens, even during the rainy season, but the reeves on training sweeps had discovered the lush valley hidden deep in the foothills mentioned by the envoy. With so many marriages waiting on a proper feast day, and every person in the settlement dreaming of a festival to interrupt the steady grind of labor, Mai had asked the reeves to fetch the appropriate offerings and assigned a propitious day after consultation with holy priests from the temples in Olossi.

She stood on the porch of the house with Anji, fanning herself as they watched the procession wind away from the benches. Twenty-seven couples in turn offered spikes of purple twilight-stupor at the flat boulder sacred to Hasibal. Bright red blooms of blood-star and falling-shields woven into necklaces draped the stone walls of the Thunderer's enclosure. They strewed petals beneath the Herald's gate, a path from west to east. The procession, accompanied by the singers, continued down to the market square.

Mai folded up her fan and, taking Anji's arm for balance, indicated the steps. "Now they'll go to the Lantern, the Witherer, the Lady, and the Merciless One. Then we'll gather here in front of our house for rice wine and a feast."

The kitchen yard was bustling, but he scanned the settlement sprawling below, the brick wall, the embankment, the green fields and, beyond all, the pale countryside, dotted with herds of sheep and tendrils of smoke where shepherds had set camps. Above, eagles circled. "Should you walk so far?"

"Would I be healthier if I lay in bed? Is that how Qin women spend their days when they are pregnant?"

His grin, like the day, was bright. "No, it is not. But you are getting very big, close to your time. Naturally, I worry. I have spoken to the Ri Amarah women. Maybe, after all, I must return you by ship to Olossi, so you can give birth surrounded by their medicine and sorcery."

"I wish you had thought of that before you exiled me here."

"Maybe so, but I am impressed with what you have built."

More people—the entire settlement, really, except for the women cooking in the kitchens—had fallen in behind the procession as the singers switched rhythms and began to chant a complicated and somewhat lewd tale that everyone seemed to know, about a blind woodcarver and the blacksmith who courted her by forging fine tools for her use. Voices were raised in answer to the singers, punctuating the long descriptive verses with quick refrains: "Too sharp!" "Too dull!" "Just right!"

Mai surveyed the settlement. "I have not built it. They are the ones who built it."

"Yours is the overseeing hand that guides them." He looked at Tuvi, and the chief nodded. They began walking down, guards ahead and behind, Priya and Sheyshi following. "That girl who knew about herbs and plants—why did she refuse Tuvi?"

"They wouldn't have suited. I have someone else in mind for Chief Tuvi."

"Do you? Does he know?"

"Of course not! These matters must be dealt with more subtly."

"So it seems."

She braced her hand on his elbow as they negotiated a rough patch of ground. Taking a breath, she ventured onto new ground. "I hear a rumor that you fought a battle."

"Was that meant to be subtle?"

"No. But I worry, so if you tell me the details, then I'll worry less because I will not be weaving stories in my own mind to pass the days while I wait for you to return."

"You are right to wish to know details."

He sketched the scene: night on the river, the demon he had faced, the battle that came afterward, the old villager who had died. Anji had been very brave, and foolhardy, she supposed, but perhaps he would not measure it as foolishness but rather as prudence. Know your enemy if you want to defeat him. It had worked out this time. That was all you could really hope for.

The Lantern's one-room counting house was ringed by twenty-seven stone cups filled with oil, the last one taking fire as Avisha and Jagi touched the wick with a burning stick, an offering of Sapanasu's fire. A new song rose as the procession descended to the gate, everyone clapping.

" 'Empty your basket! Don't carry stones! Heya! Heya! Today we celebrate.' "

"Our children will know these songs well," said Mai, "even if we stumble through them."

Beyond the gate, laborers from the fields and reeves and soldiers from the barracks joined them, the sung responses turning deep with so many male voices. They marched to the Witherer's altar and draped the thatched roof with curtains of green leaves strung on fishing line while Mai and Anji observed from a distance. Priya offered Mai juice. Sheyshi held an umbrella over her head to keep off the sun. Anji tilted his head back to watch the eagles overhead, marking, Mai supposed, the pattern of their sweeps. Chief Tuvi watched the crowd.

"I thought we made it clear that we wanted no temple raised to their Merciless One, not in our settlement," said Anji as they walked behind the procession toward the irrigation ponds. The singers formed up on either side of a walled garden.

"It's only a garden, planted with useful medicinal herbs and other spices. And it's all the way out here by the irrigation ponds."

"Near the training grounds and the laborers' camp." He frowned. "It's trouble, if you ask me."

She snapped open her fan. "Would it be less trouble if a merchant opened up a brothel? There are plenty of men here, just like in Kartu."

"Has that old woman been to see you? She's dangerous."

She laughed. "Anji! No, the Hieros has not visited, although I am sure I would enjoy her conversation, since so few interesting people travel to the Barrens. I am bereft of company, which I was not in Olossi." She fluttered her fan.

"Hu! I am struck."

Her belly tightened. She sucked in a breath and let it out as the contraction released its grip.

"Mai? Are you well?"

"It's nothing. It comes and goes, not often. Priya says it is perfectly normal."

"She is a trained midwife?"

"She attended births in our household in Kartu. Before that, she read texts written about medical matters."

"I am sure she did, but I will breathe more easily when you are shipped off to the Ri Amarah. Tomorrow, at first light."

So suddenly he changed his mind! She might have spent the last months in company with Miravia, and yet as she watched the couples enter the garden and pour rice wine onto the soil, she could not regret seeing the settlement expand and ripen. In the months to come, more Qin soldiers would cycle through and, she hoped, find wives, while meantime Anji had told her that another dozen or so men at other forts and stations looked ready to marry. Now they could truly say they were building homes in the Hundred.

Everyone was laughing, clapping rhythms. "Aiyiyi! Aiyiyi! Bring me . . . to a good family, bring me . . . to a warm hearth."

There were almost a thousand folk living in the various nearby camps or within the walled town with its market and burgeoning crafts and artisan quarter. So many! Anji halted, and his guards stopped, and she watched as the procession paced farther away toward the sapling Ladytree about half a mey distant down the track that led south along the shore of the sea, to other places and other villages not under Qin control.

"Too many people," said Anji. "Too far from the gate. We'll go back now, Mai."

She sighed and, fanning herself, went without protest. Anyway, her feet were swollen, and she was really getting hot as the long afternoon baked the earth. As they trudged past the irrigation ponds, the cheerful shouts and singing faded into the shimmering heat-haze behind them. The barracks and training grounds lay empty. Everyone had followed the procession, except for the soldiers on watch.

"What about this valley the reeves found?" Anji asked. "Who has been there?"

"Only the reeves. They say you can only fly in and out. It's lush and beautiful, so they say."

"I'll ask Marshal Joss."

"I thought I would see him here today, since he brought you in yesterday."

"He's on patrol. For a man who charms women so readily, I'm surprised he never married."

"There's a tale fit for a song. A sad, sad song."

"Not one I'm likely to enjoy."

She tapped him on the arm with the folded fan. "I forgive you for finding the old songs ridiculous, Anji. But I love them."

To her surprise, he kissed her lightly on the cheek. Certainly his Qin escort looked as startled as she was herself at such a bold, public gesture.

"Captain?" inquired Chief Tuvi with a look of concern.

"The heat has overcome me, Tuvi-lo," said Anji with a laugh.

An eagle plummeted out of the sky. Mai shrieked, caught by surprise. Her belly contracted, and she bent over as the muscle clenched with an iron grip around her middle.

"Priya, help me!" Anji supported her as Priya held her other arm. "Tuvi, that eagle is Scar. Go see what Joss wants. I want a cart for Mai—"

"It's easing. I can walk. A cart would jolt me worse."

"Let's move," said Anji as she straightened.

They halted in the shadow of the gate to wait for the reeve sprinting down from the empty market square where his huge eagle had landed.

"What is it, Marshal?" Anji called.

He shook his head, handsome face creased with a deadly frown. "Trouble." Then he had to stop to catch his breath.

"Call the alert," said Anji.

The reeve heaved a pair of breaths, trying to get enough air to speak. "Wait, wait! Give me a moment."

Anji waited.

"A group of perhaps two hundred armed men. About three mey south of here. Riding hard up the main track. They must have worked their way at night northward through the wilderness and only now broken cover."

"Soldiers?"

"Outlanders. Wearing red sashes or some such garb."

"The Red Hounds? Riding in such numbers?" He swore, such an ugly word that Mai flinched away and he did not even notice.

Tuvi said, "We did not expect a show of force, captain."

"Where are the agents we suspect?"

"All under observation. But they would have heard the plans for the wedding festival and could easily have passed out a message."

"And I arrived only yesterday, with no prior warning." Anji shook his head. "We should have expected them to strike today. Tuvi."

"Anji-hosh."

"Now the soldiers you've trained will prove their worth. We'll call a general alert, and proceed as we discussed."

"They'll know you're on to them," said Joss.

"It is a game of hounds and wolves, Joss. We knew the agents of the Red Hounds would penetrate this settlement, despite all our precautions, so the Hieros lent us certain of *her* agents to keep track of their agents."

"Aui! You never told me!"

"The fewer who know, the less can be spoken. Now they strike, seeing an opening, hoping and perhaps believing we do not suspect. They're taking a risk with an open attack knowing we have eagles who can spot them—" Abruptly, he grasped Mai's arm, harder than she expected, pinching her skin. "It's a feint, Tuvi. To make us careless. Joss, can you take Mai out of here? If I know she is safe, then I do not fear them."

"Anji?"

"No fears, Mai. We are prepared for them."

"For poisoned knives? Why not poisoned arrows?"

"Even so, Mai. Therefore, you must go immediately."

"I'll take her myself," said Joss.

"Too bad about the marriages!" she said, really angry now. "How unfair to interrupt the festival! Now it will have to be done all over again."

"If they've placed all the offerings, verea," said Joss, "then the ceremony is complete. The feast can be celebrated later. Will you come with me?"

She burst into tears and, hating herself for the weakness, sucked them down. "Yes. Of course. I'll do whatever is necessary."

Anji had never told her! He and Tuvi had kept secret from her all along the troubles they foresaw!

"Take her to the Ri Amarah," said Anji.

"I would attend the mistress as well," said Priya.

Joss nodded. "I'll assign a second reeve to convey you, verea."

"Mai, be strong." Anji released her, turned away and, with the chief and his guardsmen around him, took off at a run.

Sheyshi began to weep noisily. "Do you leave me behind, Mistress? Do you leave me?"

"Hush," snapped Priya.

Mai was shaking, but she began walking up into town, Joss beside her.

"Easier to make a quick break," he said, "than drag out the parting. And if it makes it any easier, he didn't tell me either about this secondary arrangement he made with the Hieros. A secretive man, your husband."

She wanted to defend Anji, or agree with Joss, but she was already out of breath. A second reeve landed in the market square. A woman ran to them.

"Marshal! Did you hear the news? There's a party of about two hundred men spotted two mey south on the track."

"Saw it myself. Miyara, you'll be transporting Priya to Olossi. Hitch her in now, but make a detour to the camp and give Arda these directions."

Pain gripped her midsection so tightly that she did not hear as Joss continued. Then it faded.

"—just make sure she coordinates the hall's actions with Captain Anji. Are you well, verea?" He took Mai's arm.

"Yes," she said, shaking him off. She had lost all that hard-won equilibrium, her market face burning away in the face of trouble.

Sheyshi trailed behind, irritating everyone with her wails. "Mistress, let me help you."

"No! I'm fine."

They reached the market square. Mai panted and puffed as the marshal hooked into his harness. To walk under the shadow of the huge eagle took courage, but Anji had done it, so she could, too. Then the harness had to be adjusted to fit over her distended belly, but at least the sling under her hips supported her weight comfortably. Priya was being hooked in by the female reeve. Sheyshi slunk away, still bawling, a Qin soldier in awkward pursuit.

"Are you ready?" asked Joss.

"Yes."

He blew a tone on his whistle: Up!

Mai laughed first as fear squeezed her heart, and then she laughed because, as the ground dropped away and they picked up and up, the entire settlement fell into her view in the most astonishing manner. She could see everything! The mountains striped with late afternoon shadows. Sheep pouring over a slope as they moved to pasture. The skin of water gleaming in the irrigation ponds and the net of canals moving water into greening fields. The racks of drying fish. The sky, so blue above, and the mirror of the sea so wide below, fading in the east to dusk.

No wonder reeves left their families behind and never looked back.

She spotted the procession returning from the Ladytree, everyone chanting and dancing, but as she watched, twisting because the view was falling away behind them, a pair of figures reached the crowd and a trickle of tiny figures spun out of the celebratory mass as oil separates from water. Anji was already spreading the word, putting his plan in motion.

Then they were over the water, and she lost sight of the settlement. Why did Anji not trust her? Or was it those around her he did not trust? Agents of the Red Hounds might infiltrate in many guises. As for the Hieros, that knife could cut both ways: Her agents could spy on foreign agents, but they could also spy on him.

With mighty wings outstretched, the eagle glided. The land receded behind them. She had never ever imagined anyone could travel so fast. The wind rumbled in her ears, and carved scallops in the glittering surface of the water far below.

On and on they flew. The sea darkened in the east, promising night. Joss had his arms around her shoulders in a discreet lover's embrace and, abruptly, he relaxed his grip and withdrew his hands.

She gasped, gripping the harness because she felt suddenly how fragile were the straps holding her in.

"How are you doing?" He was very close, accustomed to embracing women, no doubt, while she had never been this intimately close to any man except Anji.

"Hu! I have to pee, but I should have known that would happen! No, don't worry." She giggled, so giddy she thought her spirit must be flying even higher than her body. "I'm joking."

Her abdomen clenched so hard her next words were choked off, a fist clenched to squeeze her breath right out of her lungs. Warm liquid gushed down her thighs.

"The hells!" cried Joss. "I thought you said you were joking."

Eldest daughter, she had attended at every birth in the Mei clan since she was old enough to run errands in and out of the birthing room. "That was my water breaking. I'm going to give birth."

"Now? Right now? The hells you are!"

A spark of panic surged to a flame. She shut her eyes and let it run, as a pure, wild fire might rage along her skin. Let it fall away, like clothes shed from the body. Her fear died. She would live, or she would die. She must accept what was, in order to think and to act.

He was still babbling. "How could it—? Aren't you—? What do you mean, that was your water?"

Liquid ran down her leg; there was plenty of it, since the womb is a vessel of water and blood in which the growing seed is nurtured. In the desert, as the saying goes, without water there is no life, without blood you have no kin.

"My womb's water. Now I will deliver the baby."

"Eiya! What if it slips out and falls into the water?"

"It won't come right away. My womb's passage has to open. How long until we reach Olossi?"

"I am not flying over the sea all night with a laboring woman whose baby might drop out at any time." He tugged on the harness and the eagle began a low slow curve. The other reeve signaled with flags, querying, and Mai saw Priya dangling, like her, and staring toward her, trying to read the situation. "The hells! The nearest village is south, but there might be agents of the Red Hounds in hiding there. The Ireni Valley lies too far north through barren, uninhabited, rough country, not a place I want to have to set down. May those cursed Sirniakans have their balls eaten off by demons! Could they not have waited to attack?"

She began to laugh again, because she had never imagined him the kind of man to start raving. Then another pain caught, and he swore, and she rode it out by measuring each breath in four counts and out four counts, trying to picture the peaceful altar of the Merciful One, who brings ease to women in the throes of birth.

"Mai? Mai!"

"Oof! No, it's just—it's fine. What about that valley? The Naya Hall reeves say it can only be reached by air."

"True enough, and it's not far as the eagle flies. Aui. I've only been there once, though, and not so late in the afternoon as this with the cursed sun going down. The hells. Gods rot it, what choice have we?"

They swung around, flying toward the setting sun and the dull red gleam of far distant mountains. The female reeve followed, and for a while they flew in silence with the marshal breathing raggedly while Mai counted off the intervals between her pains. Not too close together, enough that she began to get tired of counting. Yet Joss was right: They could not fly all night over the water, with a chance the baby might drop before they reached Olossi.

"What can I do?" he said after pain had ripped away her breath again. "I'm cursed useless."

"Eh! Ah! The hells." She pressed a hand to her head as the pain receded, relieved she had a respite, however brief. "Get us put down in a safe place. The pains will come more quickly, and be more severe. We'll need a fire, boiled water, scraps of cloth or grass for the bleeding afterward. Priya knows a tea to brew for the pain, but she hasn't any with her, never mind." On she talked, because it kept him quiet and her mind busy, sorting through her memories of births she had attended, only one of which had ended in a mother's death.

Do not think of that, nor of early babies and how difficult it was for them to survive.

The shore rose into view. To the right she saw the settlement's embankment.

"Too close," muttered Joss. "Eh, well, now I know my heading."

They passed above the turbulent break between sea and land. Mai glimpsed a party of unknown mounted men wheeling to face trouble: a mass of Qin and local riders approaching both from the direction of the settlement and, somehow, from the road behind the outlanders. The outlander troop broke toward the sea, the Qin in steady pursuit over rugged ground. Down the Qin drove them. A pair of arrows tipped with fire traced a spectacular arc out of the Qin company and up into the sky before plunging into the sinks and shallows along the shoreline.

Flame licked the surface, boomed in a sink with a startling burst, and then raced in a flare of light along the shore as the oily smear that stained the surface caught fire and spread.

The Qin pushed their enemy down into the burning sea.

Then she and Joss were past, too far away to watch the course of the battle, but for a long time after as they flew inland, Mai could see the shoreline limned in fire as night overtook the east.

52

TWO RIDERS ON winged horses emerged from Toskala's council hall and rose, flying, into the gathering night. In quick succession, four more emerged and galloped into the heavens in pursuit. The people crowded into Justice Square began to call and scream and argue in a clamor that made Nallo wish she could smack each one until they all shut up.

Pil was crouched beside Volias, his own face hovering just above the reeve's parted lips. Straightening, he shook his head. "He's dead."

"The hells!" She ran up the ramp, pushed past some idiot shrieking woman in blood-soaked merchant's robes, and stopped at the threshold, slammed by the reek of blood and the stench of death. Gagging, she backed away, and bumped into a person crowding up behind. She turned and slugged; Pil caught her arm.

"Cursed demons slaughtered them all," she said, voice breaking on the words. "Nothing we can do here. Let's get back to the hall."

Pil slung Volias's corpse over his shoulder. Nallo took point, shoving down the ramp and through the crowd with vicious pleasure in seeing people flinch away. Tears washed her face. She wanted to rip someone's cursed ugly face off just for all the gods-rotted useless nattering, no one taking charge, an assembly of weak-hearted fools.

No one guarded the gate to Clan Hall, but a swarm of reeves and fawkners were streaming in and out of the lofts and buzzing in the torch-lit parade ground like bees smoked out of their hive. Seeing her and Pil, Peddo ran over.

"Ah, the hells!" he cried, but he wasn't surprised to find Volias dead.

"There's been a massacre at the council hall, demons guised as Guardians from the tales," said Nallo. "Then Volias just dropped dead. What's going on?"

"Bring him to the lofts."

Inside, she smelled blood enough to make her choke. Likard ran up. He'd been weeping. Others were still crying as they wriggled aimlessly here and there like so many decapitated eels.

"Are you just always that sloppy about fixing the cursed bird's hood?" Likard shouted at her.

"What?"

Unlike the big, open barracks rooms, the lofts had separate sections and separate entrances, linked by corridors for the fawkners to move quickly from one cote to another. She ran ahead, but the side door to the loft where Tumna sheltered was already open. She staggered to a halt inside. Two young men sprawled on the floor, one headless. Tumna's feathers were stuck out in a rage, and she was still swiping at them with her talons, rolling them over as if they were toys. Her hood was crumpled in a corner, as if it had hit the wall.

"Slow down," wheezed Likard, behind her. "Cursed if those two hells-bitten bastards weren't hopeful fawkner's assistants at all, but agents for the cursed army, come up here to kill the eagles while everyone slept. They slaughtered Trouble and Surri in the first two lofts. When they snuck in here ready to stab Tumna and Sweet, I tell you that cursed ill-tempered raptor must have torn off her hood and skewered them. She ripped the head clean off that one. May he rot and roast and freeze in the hells."

Tumna was alive. Exasperated, the huge raptor chirped, glaring at Nallo in the muzzy lamplight as if in complaint: Thugs disturbed my night's rest! How like them!

Nallo began sobbing. Folk came up to touch her as if to make sure she wasn't a ghost, while others ran up and down the corridors to see if anyone else was sneaking around, anyone not accounted for. *Murderers!*

The shouting and anger and all manner of voices churned as if a storm blew through. Trouble dead. Volias dead. Surri dead, whichever eagle she was, and her reeve with her. Nallo hadn't even learned every reeve's name yet, much less figured how to tell the eagles apart.

Sweet, still hooded, shifted restlessly on her night perch, much disturbed. Pil appeared at Nallo's side.

"The hells," he muttered, sounding very like a Hundred man. "After that time Sweet pulled off her hood, I made sure to fasten it correctly. I'm glad you didn't!" He fixed his eagle with a possessive stare.

"Where's Volias?" she asked, surprised into speech by his volubility.

"At rest by the dead eagles. Him and the other reeve. What now?"

"No one's in charge! All the senior reeves are cursed dead, aren't they? After that first day, I don't think I exchanged more than twenty words with the commander, eh? 'How's the training going? Ofri treating you well?'"

"Who will the others listen to?"

"How can you be so cursed calm! They're all *dead*. Volias just dropped dead. And those in the hall—the reeves, the council members, the cursed militiamen—they were cut down like sheep, stinking with it, and you can stand there because you're a cursed rotting outlander who doesn't know . . ." He took in the abuse that poured out of her until she ran out of breath and heaved, thinking she was going to retch out the boil of anger and heartbreak, but nothing came but dry sobs.

"Who will the others listen to, Nallo?" he said in the exact same tone.

She wiped her eyes. "Peddo, maybe."

He left.

"I'm a cursed idiot," she said to Tumna, who looked over at the sound of her voice, probably to agree with her. "You're the best raptor who ever lived. You know that, don't you?"

The bird tipped her head sideways, considering this statement.

"So you stay here, with your prizes. Eat them, for all I care, although their flesh will likely poison you. Ah, the hells!"

She stepped into the corridor and grabbed Likard and the fawkner next to him. "Are there other murderers on the loose?"

"Those are the only two hired in within the last year," said Likard. "So likely they were sent in on purpose, don't you think? Cursed traitors. Wish I could strangle them myself."

He seemed likely to go on in this vein, so she went back into the loft, untangled the hood, and approached Tumna, tapping the signal that made the raptor flutter back to her night perch and lower her head. But she couldn't bear to hood her. She turned to face a crowd of fawkners.

"What are you gawking at? Can you haul this rubbish out of here? It stinks!"

She remained by Tumna while others dragged away the corpses. Eiya! She hadn't believed Volias, had she? Just a cursed stupid thing to say, she'd thought, a crude form of arm-twisting: *If your eagle dies, you die.*

Tears flowing, she circled the compound but didn't find Pil. The commander's cote was empty, the old reeve who attended her sobbing so hard on the porch that he didn't notice Nallo come or go. Folk were poking spears into every hidey-hole and dark corner, making sure no one was sneaking around to strike again. Someone had set a dozen furious, frightened fawkners and assistants to guard the gate. They pointed her toward the stairs that led down into the city.

A cataract of sound poured up from Toskala. Rubbing against it in a chatter that irritated her even more, the refugees mobbing Justice Square waved their hands in the air to no purpose, jabbering and complaining and then having the nerve to yell at her as she elbowed them aside to get to the overlook. A pair of lamps hanging from posts illuminated the balcony that jutted out over the cliff face. She identified Pil's topknot. The two other reeves had very short hair, and the fourth person wore a firefighter's brimmed leather helmet and fitted leather coat. They made room for her at the railing.

They stared over the city, delineated by torches flaring in lines that snaked along avenues as the army spread out to overtake the population piece by piece. In one quarter, a fire burned, so far confined to a single block. A pair of guardsman stood at the edge of lamplight, posted at the gate marking the head of the stairs. All traffic in either direction had ceased.

"How did they block the stairs?" Nallo asked finally.

Kesta set a hand over hers on the railing. "Some old trap from ancient days. It made a terrible noise. Eiya! A lot of people on the steps died when it was sprung."

"Captain Ressi did that?"

Her usually lively face looked drawn and aged in lamplight. "Neh. Captain Ressi was at council hall. A sergeant sprang it. Killed himself in the process. Knew he was going to, I think."

"What do we do now?" asked the fire captain. He was surprisingly young, with a short-clipped beard and an annoying habit of drumming his fingers on the railing as he started talking. "The senior militia captains are dead in the council hall, or trapped in the city and surely dead by now."

"You are a captain," said Pil.

"Eiya! Through my mother's Green Sun connections, if you want to know the truth. I was so cursed proud of myself, wasn't I? Riding my gelding through the streets, strutting about with my fire hook." He glanced at Peddo, then away. "My kinfolk sent me up here three days ago to square the accounts on the various hall storehouses. This much water in the cisterns. That much oil. So many tey of rice. I tell you, I think they knew. I fear they sent me up here to keep me out of harm's way, curse them!" He began sobbing. "Gods-rotted traitors!"

They stepped away from him, and he looked over indignantly.

"I wasn't in on it! As soon as the trouble erupted, I secured the storehouses and cisterns with what firefighters remain up here, in case any of this crowd decides to grab what they can."

"Why come over here to the stairs, then?" asked Peddo. "Since it's the only way up or down from this rock besides flying, or the baskets?"

The young man gestured helplessly, a sweep of his arm that took in the city. Overhead, stars glittered in silence; below, Toskala roared as its thousands ran or fought or hid, or simply wailed and grieved. The wind blustered, but like them it could do nothing but witness.

"What's the point of staying?" asked Kesta. "We've lost."

"What's ever the point of staying?" said Nallo, thinking of the day she had walked into a strange village to marry a man she'd never met, to fulfill a contract other hands had sealed in her name. "To say you can. To show you will."

"And what the hells does it matter, Nallo, when those demons can fly? The steps are blocked, but the demons can come back any time they want."

"Maybe so, but if they'd wanted to kill us all, then why didn't they?"

"The winged ones carried no weapons," added Pil, "but the ones who died, died in blood. So then who stabbed them? Not the demons."

"A good point," said Peddo, smiling wanly at Pil, who blushed and looked away.

"Traitors stabbed them!" said the fire captain hoarsely. "Any of us might be a traitor!"

"The hells you say!" snapped Nallo. "I'm no gods-rotted traitor. And I'm not cursed ready to give up, either."

"We need a captain," said Pil. "If we mean to resist. This rock is a good fort. If we can protect ourselves against demons, and ration water and food."

"And throw the cursed traitors to their death!" screamed the fire captain with a howl of outraged grief.

Distant voices on Justice Square echoed his cries, and the guards at the stairs stirred restlessly, looking scared.

Nallo slapped the fire captain right across the face. That shut him up. Probably with his soft skin and well-kept hands he'd never done a day's worth of real work in his silk-wearing, pampered life.

"Do you think you're the only cursed person who's suffered? We either give up now, or we take stock of our situation and then we cursed well decide what we mean to do! I don't want to give up!"

The image of her husband lying dead in the road with the flies buzzing in and out of his gaping mouth sprang so vividly into her mind that she began to cry. He had stayed behind with the other men to hold off the army while the women and children ran into the forest to hide. Dazed from a day of hiding in the brush, Jerad and little Zi had not truly understood what had happened to their father. Avisha had trembled so close to hysterics that Nallo recognized only now how much strength it had taken the girl to suck it up and keep going for the sake of the little ones. And they'd done it. They'd walked away from the ruins of a life they could never have back, and by sheer stubbornness they had found other shelter. Not a safe place, for maybe there weren't any safe places left. But a decent place, a good place. A place they could find pride in.

"I didn't give up before, and the gods know I'm cursed well not going to give up now. What if we can hold this rock? Won't that give hope to others?"

"Who will be captain?" repeated Pil.

"That's right," she said fiercely, looking at each in turn: the fire captain still stricken and likely to break out in a whine; Peddo exhausted but thoughtful; Kesta twisted between despair and hope. Pil as always so calm that you didn't know whether to love him or shake him to see if he would ever yelp. "We need a commander, someone who knows Toskala and the other halls. Someone who has allies. Someone who might actually know what he's doing, even if he is a vain-hearted and insufferably smug horse's ass. I say, we send word to Argent Hall. To Marshal Joss."

53

Joss paced to the edge of darkness beyond which Scar drowsed on a rocky perch, but he heard and sensed nothing out of the ordinary. Yet he could not shake off a tingle along his skin, like ants crawling up and down his neck. He returned to the fire. Water boiled in a pot set on a tripod over the flames. He placed a bowl on a rock and poured water over leaves, then covered it to steep. Darkness had trapped them in the steep-sided, hidden valley, and he was himself confined to the circle of firelight with a blanket on the ground, if he even dared attempt sleep. Hearing the scuff of footsteps, he rose.

Miyara set down their lamp beside the bowl. She wiped sweat from her forehead with a cloth and sank into a crouch, rubbing her neck.

"How are things?" he asked, not sure how much he was permitted to know but desperate for any scrap.

"I'll take the tea. Thanks for brewing it. Priya and I could use a sharp pinch to keep alert."

"How are you managing without the lamp, if you don't mind my asking? Or did you find another in the shelter?"

"I did not." She grinned. "Us reeves taking a break from training at Naya Hall to spend a night in the cave aren't doing so because we need light, eh?" She laughed.

Joss ran a hand over his head. "What do you mean?"

"Surely you of all people would—" Then she laughed again. "As nervous as you are, Marshal, you'd think you were the father, eh?"

"Or responsible for Captain Anji's wife. This is scarcely the time for jokes."

"Aui! No more jokes, then!" Miyara shook her head, lifted up the bowl's cover, and inhaled. "Eihi! That's ready, eh? It's out of your hands, Marshal. The gods will favor her, or curse her, but if you ask me, she's a tough one. Never a word of complaint. She's managing as well as any can who must suffer through her first birth. Here, now, let's take this back. I've something I'd like you to see."

"Is that allowed—? I wouldn't want to—"

"Not all the way into the cave. If you will, Marshal, come and see. It's a puzzle. I thought you might have an answer."

She carried the lamp and he the bowl, warm against his hands. The path led through a tangle of growth unexpected after the dry tableland of the Barrens: candleflowers, plum, falls of sweet-scented heaven-kiss, moist ripe sunfruit, lush stands of uncultivated jabi. This burgeoning orchard of wild fruit was tended solely by the gods' blessing. He bumped his head on a ripe sunfruit dangling over the path.

Miyara balanced in the lamp in one hand and plucked it with the other. "This way."

No insects chattered, nor did night-waking animals rustle within the growth. The lack of animal noises was unnerving, but at least a stream babbled in the distance and wind caught among the surrounding crags. They reached the pool, deep and round, rimmed by the remains of an ancient building. A waterfall thundered into the pool from the height. They walked alongside walls no more than knee height, worn down by time and wind and rain. Who had built here? Lived here in such isolation? How had they found their way in, when truly it must be impossible to reach the valley by climbing?

Halfway around, as they neared the curtain of water, Miyara halted. The pool rippled with a constant churning. The waterfall glinted with filaments of light, and at first he thought the lamplight was reflecting within the falls and then he realized she had snuffed the wick. A glow emanated from tendrils of writhing light spilling out of the falling water and drifting, as if pushed by the action of wind and water, into a cave carved out of the rock that extended behind the falls.

In that protected cave, the reeves from Naya Hall had kitted out a shelter with a chest, flown in, in which they stored a lamp, oil, bedding, bowls and utensils, and a pot for cooking.

In that cave, Mai labored, and he was cursed sure that if anything bad happened to her, he'd be called—quite rightly—to account for their coming here instead of crossing the Olo'o Sea to deposit her into the capable hands of the Ri Amarah women.

"Were those—things—there before?" he asked nervously, as the glittering strands swirled in an eddy of wind and mist.

"I'm not sure. They'd be easy to miss in daylight. They're like finest quality silk thread, neh?"

"Miya! Are you there?" Priya called from behind the curtain of water, and because of the noise he could not tell if she was frantic or just searching with her voice.

The reeve set down the lamp and took the bowl of tea out of Joss's hands. "Keep the water hot."

"There's nothing else I can do?"

She shrugged. "This isn't men's business, eh?"

Walking on a narrow rim that hugged the rock wall, she vanished behind the spray.

A splash disturbed the pool. A dark shape shouldered out of the roil and so quickly slipped beneath that it might have been only a trick of the light, or a reminder from the gods that he was intruding. He started back around the pool, but before he reached the path he heard his name called and turned back.

Miyara waved wildly at him, both hands aloft.

He ran back. Wisps slithered in the air around him, and when one brushed his cheek he got such a jolt, like a stinging burn, that he yelped.

She called, "Marshal, we don't know what to do. You have to come."

He followed her along the narrow path, steadying himself with a hand along the rock wall on his right while water poured past to his left. The mist pelted him, an oddly iron taste on his tongue. They passed out of the spray and into the cave. She halted. A step behind, he stared into the cave, which extended deep into the rock, a haven lit so brightly that he blinked before he saw Mai.

"What do we do?" cried Miyara.

With a plank wedged across and between rocks, they had set up a birthing stool halfway back in the cave, over a hollow smoothed into the cave's dirt floor. Mai leaned into a cushion made by her folded clothing, but she was herself limned by filaments clustering around and over her as if to smother her. And yet she breathed; she grunted, and Priya said,

"Hold your breath as I say the prayer of opening. Now." She spoke words in a steady voice, while Mai gripped the edge of the plank and strained.

Priya was her own self, unencumbered, but the filaments traced Mai's form as if a translucent second skin wrapped her, so that she blazed.

"Here it comes, plum blossom. Look down. Do you see it? This is the head of your child."

Panting, seemingly oblivious of the threads of light, Mai bent her head to stare down between her legs. Her sweaty face changed expression. "I can't look!" she cried. And then, "I have to push again!"

"Take in a breath. Hold it." Priya spilled words Joss did not understand, as Mai pressed her mouth shut and bore down.

Miyara grabbed his elbow. "Quickly! We must weave a blessing. She has no clan to surround her. The child will be cursed if no blessing greets it!"

The hells!

She stamped to begin, and though he had no particular skill, he was like anyone who had heard the chants and songs all his life. He could stumble along in her company.

May the Earth Mother greet you, little flower.
May the Air Mother greet you, little breeze.
May the Fire Mother greet you, little flame.
May the Water Mother greet you, little wave.

From this angle, he could not see beyond Mai's gleaming body, but as Priya extended her hands to catch the baby as it was born, the threads poured off Mai to fill the hollow until it seemed to burn, drowning the newborn child.

Mai sagged back, reclining against the cloth-draped rock with a gasped sigh.

"Marshal!" cried Priya. "What are these things? Are they living creatures? Or something else? What do we do?"

The baby wailed, and the tendrils spun as though on the strength of that tiny voice and whirled into the air and blinked out. The child ceased crying.

Miyara faltered, voice breaking, but within the darkness she stamped and kept singing.

Be woven into the land with this song.
Be strong. We cherish you.

Joss stumbled out along the path and groped along the ruined wall until he found the lamp. It took him three tries to light the wick with his flint, and by the time he got back into the cave the infant had been placed on Mai's chest, still attached by a cord pulsing with faint flashes of blue as though the last tendrils had actually slipped into its umbilical. Above, a weave of light bridged the cave's high ceiling, glimmering faintly.

"One more!" exclaimed Mai, and she sucked in a breath and pushed again.

Priya caught a red mass in a bowl.

Miyara hurried forward to offer tea to the new mother. "You have to name the child before you cut the cord," she said to Mai.

Mai's eyes were closed, and at length she opened them to stare at the baby, who opened its tiny eyes as if in answer. "The father names a child," she said, in a remarkably ordinary voice. "I must wait for Anji."

Miyara glanced at Joss as if for support. "That's not our way," she said. "It's—"

"Never mind it," said Joss hastily. "She'll name the child, or he will, as they please."

"I guess we're uncle and aunt now," said Miyara. Then, as an afterthought, she added, "That's how we do things here, Mai."

Mai smiled wearily, too exhausted to move as Priya washed her and bound a pad of linen torn from Miyara's shirt to absorb her bleeding. "And I am glad of it, for I thank you, both of you. What is it, Priya? A girl, or a boy?"

"A boy, mistress."

"Just as Grandmother said. Aiyi! I thought it would never come out!" Her skin gleamed from sweat, and all at once Joss saw how naked she was.

"Marshal," said Priya, "please fetch water so I can wash child and mother. It must be cooled enough so as not to burn, but still generously warm."

He flinched as though he had been slapped, although she had spoken in an entirely pleasant tone. He hurried out, carrying the lamp. Thunder rumbled among the crags, and the air felt charged, ready to snap and spark. High in the air, almost out of range of his vision, a fireling winked into existence and vanished, and then a second, and ten more, and after that more than he could count, like kinfolk come to weave a new child into the heart of their clan, chanting the greeting.

He stopped to stare, but they were already gone.

Eiya! Never for him a child called from beyond the Spirit Gate to join father and mother; he must be content as an uncle, and unaccountably he wept as he trudged the long dirt path to the fire pit, where flames blazed and the wind caught sparks and sent them tumbling. Away up in the mountains, lightning flared, and thunder boomed, and as he hooked the pot off the tripod, rain washed over the valley, cleansing everything in its path.

*   *   *

"WHY DO YOU follow me?" asked Kirit.

"I'm the hells unlikely to follow them." Downstream along the bank of the River Istri, Marit indicated distant lights sweeping northward through the sky out of the Toskala.

"They are looking for us," said Kirit. "It is safer if we do not travel together."

"You don't trust me."

The girl shrugged.

"I thank you anyway," continued Marit, "for not joining them. I'm not your enemy, Kirit. But I have a cursed good idea that they're headed back to their camp, to see if Hari has woken. To give him his staff. Then they'll be after both of us."

"He will betray us?"

"I like him. But that doesn't mean we can trust him."

"Or that I can trust you," said the girl. "Do not follow me. Maybe you are their spy."

"I'm not," said Marit more with weariness than heat. "But I'm not going to debate that now. At the turn of the next month—when Lion falls into Ibex—I will walk the shore of the Salt Sea where the spine of the Earth Mother cradles the birthing waters." The girl stared at her, devoid of emotion. "If you don't know of it, you being an outlander, the Salt Sea lies northwest beyond Heaven's Ridge, where the gods cleft the Hundred from the lands beyond. When a new reeve finishes her first year of training, her circuit of the land, that's the last place she visits: to lay an offering of flowers at the Earth Mother's womb. You'll know the place when you see it."

"You go back to them, now?"

"I am not one of them, Kirit. Surely you saw they meant to destroy me. If you won't trust me enough to ally with me, then what if they find you in the end? Five, to judge one. They're after you now, just like they're after me. And most likely they're after the envoy, wherever he's hiding. As for me, I'm going to find my staff."

REEVES PATROLLING OVER the Liya Pass had once commonly met at Candle Rock to exchange news and to replenish wood for the signal fire kept ready in case of emergency. But the fire-pits were half filled with dust and debris, the white stones that had once ringed the hollows tumbled out of line. Under the craggy overhang, spiders and rock mice had made comfortable homes in the depleted woodpile.

What a bright day that had been, Joss waiting for her, him so young and her so eager. Where had that young woman gone? *What we have lost we can never get back again.*

Marit stood where she and Joss had so long ago shared the embrace of the Devourer. With the setting sun behind her, she looked east toward the ridge of hill held by the hierarchs to be sacred to the Lady of Beasts, to whom she had served her year's apprenticeship as a girl of fifteen. Ammadit's Tit could be mistaken for no other landmark.

Out of habit, out of respect, she cleared the stones, raked out the fire pit, and shifted such wood as was still usable into a new stack, splitting kindling. You had to leave things as you would hope to find them.

Herelia had been closed to reeves for so many years that she doubted any reeves chanced the Liya Pass in these more dangerous days, for fear of being ambushed, as she had been twenty years ago. Nor, in the circuitous route she had taken over many days and nights flying up here, had she seen much traffic on any of the tracks or roads in these parts. The land appeared quiet and orderly. Subdued. Probably it was. But looks could be deceiving.

In the gray light before true dawn, she flew Warning along the high ridgeline to the black knob of the Tit. The Guardian's altar tucked on a shelf of rock below the summit glittered with the first sparks of sunlight. She'd had a hard time maneuvering Flirt onto the ledge, but Warning simply galloped as on a ramp down to earth. Marit dismounted, and the mare trotted across the labyrinth, seeking the spring.

Now, the gamble, the sticks tossed, the game set in motion.

She set her right foot on the entrance, and her left. She named each turn as the woman wearing the cloak of night had taught her: Needle Spire bright with the morning sun; Everfall Beacon; Stone Tor; Salt Tower beside the Salt Sea; Mount Aua; Highwater stream; the Pinnacle; the Walshow overlook; Swamp Bastion; Horn Vista; the Dragon's Tower; Thunder Spire; the Five Brothers; the Seven Secret Sisters; the Face on the Kandaran Pass, where night still shadowed the Spires. A hundred and one altars sacred to the Guardians wove through the land and, together with the Ten Tales of Founding, held the garment together.

The Rocky Saddle. The Eagle's Talon. Haldia Overlook.

She tasted blood, a faint lingering taint. One of the others had stood at Haldia Overlook recently, was maybe even walking the labyrinth ahead or behind her. She pushed on. Unlike the last time she had walked this labyrinth, no voices whispered at her ears; no man's figure greeted her as she stepped into the hollow. But instead of being blinded by a flare of light, spun halfway around and thrown by the altar's sorcery to the peak of the knob, she simply halted beside Warning, who watered unconcernedly at the pool.

Marit knelt, dipped her bowl, and drank deeply. Rising, she ran a hand over the soft stubble of her hair, still and always the same length as the days when she'd kept it cut short because that was the fashion reeves wore.

You think that you are dead, but you are living. It is others who tell you you are dead, and you believe them, and by believing them you corrupt the strength the gods pour into their chosen vessels.

Yet why then did her hair not grow?

Sometimes you had to go with the evidence.

She walked back to the rim of the ledge. Remarkably, the rope she'd left here twenty years ago swayed in the morning breeze, still fastened above. She gripped the rope in a hand and tugged as hard as she could, and cursed if it didn't hold. Amazing how indestructible good hempen rope proved to be.

She curled up the trailing end of the rope and knotted it in a cradle around her hips. Climbing up on the ledge, she leaned backward into the air and, hand over hand, worked her way up the knob, pausing at intervals to rest with the rope looped up tight around her body. Arms and legs aching, she scrambled the last rugged slope up to the summit where a metal post had been hammered deep into the rock. The frayed remains of banners streamed around her: blood-red, black of night, heaven-blue, mist-silver, fiery-gold-sun, earth-brown, seedling-green, twilight-sky, and death-white. The cloaks of the Guardians.

And she laughed, because there it was. The metal post was hollow, like pipewood, and cursed if someone—maybe the handsome man with demon-blue outlander eyes set in a brown face—hadn't simply slipped a sword in at the top, the hilt peeping up above the blustery rumble of sun-bleached banners.

∗   ∗   ∗

NEVER IN HER life before had Mai enjoyed isolation, but after the birth she was content simply to rest on a pallet in the cave, seeing no one, food and drink and cleaning arranged by Priya and, later, Sheyshi. The baby was very small, but he seemed healthy, nursing and sleeping and eliminating. He rarely cried, and sometimes she sat outside on a pillow by the pool and cradled him in her arms as spray off the falls cooled her back. Probably she should not expose him to the moist air, but she felt an inexplicable kinship with the falls, as if it had soothed and comforted her during the final stages of labor when those eerie strands of light had filled the cave. The valley, too, was very beautiful, and its high walls cradled her, the crags and mountain peaks looming like stalwart guards. In this place, she was safe.

"Mistress, do you want to go lie down?" asked Sheyshi.

"No, I'm content here in the sun."

"You should lie down for one month," said Sheyshi. "Otherwise the evil spirits might eat you."

"I'm fine, Sheyshi. Maybe you could brew me some more of that nice tea with spices." Anything to stop her hovering!

Given a task, the slave hurried off to the small encampment newly set up down the path to accommodate the daily coming and goings of reeves out of Naya Hall bringing provisions and news. The baby slept, his tiny round face entirely peaceful, although he slept so much she had scarcely seen his eyes open except for that first startling moment after his birth when he had stared at her as if recognizing her. He weighed nothing, really, light to hold but so vast that her heart had opened to encompass heavens and earth, fire and water, all of creation.

"Mai."

She smiled down at the sleeping baby, and then she rose with careful dignity and turned to greet her husband. "Anji, greetings of the day."

He looked a bit ragged, as if he hadn't slept, but his clothes were neat and clean and his hair was tied tightly up in the Qin topknot, not a strand out of place. He held a basket in his hands. Awkwardly, he offered it to her, looking very serious.

"These gifts I bring, mare's milk, goat's butter, sheep's yoghurt, to strengthen your blood." He set the basket on the low wall and opened a pouch slung at his hip. From this he drew length after length of gold chain and jewel-set necklaces, a fortune beyond price. "Among my mother's people, a woman of honor wears her clan's wealth, for she alone possesses the vitality to resist its corrupting influence. This is yours now, which once belonged to my mother's mother."

He draped them over her neck, a heavy weight indeed, and only then did he bend his gaze to the child.

She gently unwrapped the sleeping baby, who stirred and stretched as his limbs were exposed. "He is whole, and although small he is so far healthy. He sleeps a lot, though."

He examined the child's head and torso and genitals and limbs and fingers and toes, and only then did he smile, the sudden brilliance quite staggering.

"He needs a name!" she said indignantly.

He nodded. "That's why I waited seven days. He'll be Atani, after my father, who loved his younger brother too much to see him murdered, although it cost him much on his own behalf. I've also been told that by Hundred custom it is a Waterborn name, proper to a child born under the shelter of a waterfall, during a storm."

"Atani," she murmured, tracing the infant's perfect tiny lips and his flat baby chin. He burbled, mouth rooting as he woke up. His eyes opened, black pools absorbing the mystery of the world, and shut again.

"You have done well, Mai. Not that I am surprised."

"Will you hold him?"

"After the moon's cycle is complete. Otherwise my touch may alert demons to his presence. It's enough that I can look at him, and at you, until that day." He did look, but at her more than at the child, eyes narrowed with the very slight look of satisfaction that meant he was well pleased, perhaps even gloating, if Anji ever gloated.

"Captain!"

He turned. "You are an uncle, Tuvi-lo."

The chief walked up as Mai displayed the naked baby. "So I am! What a fine lad."

"Whole with no blemishes," said Anji.

"Atani-hosh, I pledge my loyal service," said the chief. Then with a big grin he nodded at Mai. "To the mother, strength and honor."

"I'm hungry. I think I'm always hungry!"

As if she had heard, Priya walked out from the cave. "Captain Anji! You must not touch Mai or your son until the turn of the moon."

"I have not. But I have brought Mai foods that will strengthen her blood."

Priya took the infant to wrap it, and Mai sat on the wall an arm's length from Anji and ate the food he had brought, rich butter, voluptuous yoghurt, stingingly strong fermented mare's milk, while he related the tale of the skirmish and the fate of the Red Hounds.

"We killed all of the riders, except for two we took as prisoners. However, they did not talk. As for the agents in place within the settlement, three for sure we killed."

"Who were they?" She shuddered. "I hate to think of walking past such men every day and never knowing."

"Posing as laborers. I am sure there are others. We remain vigilant. My brother the emperor will attempt to strike again. He sees me as a threat to his position, more so even than my cousins."

"Although they are the ones who have challenged him over the throne."

"At the moment, my brother is the one who stands in the way of their ambition. Although it's hard to imagine that they can defeat the rightful heir, the one the priests have sealed as legitimate. Now, of course, this boy likewise, a new grandson of the former emperor. So I'm not sure what to do with you and the baby, Mai."

"Build me a cottage in this valley. Then it would be hard for the Red Hounds to reach me, neh?"

He surveyed the whitecapped mountains and the spilling water, inhaling the scent of sweet flowers, of extravagant leaves, of moist air. The deep cleft might harbor an entire village, and no one ever know.

"But I don't really want to live here forever," she added hurriedly, brushing a hand over the links of gold that weighed on her chest. "You know how I love the market. And I miss Miravia, if I'm ever to be allowed to see her again."

He sat, saying nothing as he regarded the ripples in the pool with an expression so even that she began to grow nervous, thinking maybe he was very angry.

"Anji?"

"Marshal Joss told me a disturbing tale. Is it true?"

"That spirits attended the birth? I think so. I don't know what to call them, truly, for they were like strands of silk more than spirits, but I felt such calm and protection at their presence. Now they're gone. Sometimes I wonder if I dreamed it." But when she turned to regard the waterfall, white skirts of mist rising where the water met the pool, she knew she had not.

"That he entered the chamber of birth," said Anji.

Chief Tuvi whistled under his breath.

"The marshal brought me here safely. If we hadn't turned back, I'd have lost the baby over the sea, for it came that quickly. Miyara—the other reeve—told me it is traditional for an aunt and uncle to witness the birth." She watched him closely, not sure how to interpret his steady expression, but he glanced at the chief and shrugged as if to dislodge a weight, his shoulders relaxing.

"Uncle, eh? Then we must accept how things are done here in the Hundred. He's a good man. It can't hurt the child to be related by such bonds to the man who now stands as commander over all the reeves of the Hundred."

Of course his words rolled out like so much nonsense. At first breath, she wondered what any of this had to do with the quiet woodland surrounding them, with the sun's glamour setting the peaks in bright relief against a rich blue sky, with the brown earth under her slippered feet, and the whisper of a breeze in her ear bringing with it the faintest chiming lure of a distant melody sung by unseen voices.

She licked dry lips. "What do you mean, Anji? What has happened?"

"Hu!" He laughed for the first time, and she laughed, seeing his happiness in the quickness of his smile and the way he looked sidelong at her, almost flirting. "Grim news, truly, and a difficult path ahead. But it's true it's hard to feel the shadows in this place, as if the gods hold their hearts here."

Sheyshi brought bowls of spiced tea, and the men settled more comfortably on the stone wall while Mai adjusted the pillow under her to cushion the places down there where she was still rather sore.

"I can't sing," he added with another smile, "although I know how you love your songs. So for you, plum blossom, and only for you, flower of my heart and mother of my son, I will tell you the story of the events of the last many days as a tale."

*   *   *

AT THE HIGH salt sea, on the edge of the Hundred, a vast escarpment splits the land and the mountains plunge downward to a flat plain. If you stand on the sharp ridge that separates the waters from the cliff, you can gaze over the drylands, a desert that extends for an unknown distance, inimical to life.

But Kirit can smell the grass of home, even if maybe it is only memory.

She said, "Uncle, I killed the ones who hurt me."

"I know," he said sadly.

"I killed a lot of bad people. Their hearts were rotten."

"Some hearts do rot. Although that does not give us leave to behave as they would."

The day was very hot, and the air so dry her lips were already cracking. "I thought revenge would heal me. I found Shai. I looked into his heart, only his heart was veiled. But I do not need the third eye and second heart to know him, since I lived for two years in the same household. He was tempted, but he did not succumb. And if he could resist the worst in himself, then so must I. I won't become a demon."

The wind tore at their cloaks. Far away above the southern range, raptors circled so high that they were nothing more than specks in the fierce blaze of the heavens.

"What happened to her?" she asked. "Ashaya, who wore the cloak before me."

He followed the distant eagles with his gaze, but finally looked at her. "When she walked out of the Hundred, she hoped the gods would abandon her, that she would be able to die and be free, without loosing the cloak into the hands of the others."

"But I found the cloak."

"Yes. You did. So maybe you freed her, or maybe she was already gone. It's something to consider. What living person has ever attempted to uncloak a Guardian, eh? Who could manage it? I've been thinking about what happened to you, Kirit. It can't have been the poison that killed you."

"The poison that killed Girish?"

"Maybe the brew wasn't strong enough to kill. Maybe he just choked to death on his vomit."

She grinned. "As he deserved."

"Eiya! There's a conversation I'm not wise enough to assay. You told me the Qin captain forced you to walk into the sandstorm."

"I wanted to rejoin my tribe. Their voices called to me from the storm."

"Demons, most likely. Did he seek you out?"

"The captain? Neh. I went to find Mountain to tell him that the slave bearers needed water. A storm can last days. What use is shelter if you die of thirst beneath it?"

"A humble request, but a just one."

"The captain saw me. He thought I would bring ill luck down on them because that's what demons do. He gave me a fair choice. I could walk into the storm of my own will, or he would make sure I died some other way before the journey was over. That was the first time since I walked into demon land that I got to choose." She hid her face behind a hand, and then, finding that the voices of her lost tribesfolk did not call to her as they had in the storm, she lowered the hand and looked at him.

He smiled gently.

"I can't go home, Uncle. I am a different person, not that one who lived before."

He sighed and said nothing, by which he meant he agreed.

Yet Rats can't stay quiet for long.

"Do you know the tale of how the wide lake came to rest here, caught between the mountains and the cliff? It happened in the Tale of Change, when the delvings captured a merling and decided that in order to keep it from escaping back into the sea they must dig a prison far from the ocean and joined to no stream or rivulet down which it could slip and slide. So they cut a path deep through the earth and under the watershed—"

"I missed you," she said.

For a breath, two breaths, and then five, he could not speak.

A rippling movement flashed above the drowsy waters.

"Look there!" she cried.

A rocky islet lay surrounded by the lifeless waters. The islet, too, revealed no sign of life except for the desiccated remains of flowers draped over a series of crude stone pillars. A horse flew gracefully over the sea and circled the islet, and then the rider noticed them standing exposed on the ridge.

They waited.

At length her mare clattered to earth on the ridge, and Marit dismounted. She halted a prudent distance away and drew from a leather sheath a serviceable short sword, nothing fancy to look at: plain, good steel. "The sword, called death, cuts the strand of life."

"Where did you find it?" he asked.

"The place no one else thought to look," she said with a grin. "I'm Marit, as I said before. Kirit I already know. Will you tell me who you are, ver?"

"No one who ever did a cursed thing in his life to deserve good or ill, verea. But my mother, who has long since crossed the Spirit Gate, gave me the name Jothinin."

" 'Foolish Jothinin, light-minded Jothinin.' An old-fashioned name. Just like in the tale."

He smiled but said nothing.

"What is a Guardian?" she asked, but answered herself. "It's not a thing already made. It's what we become of our own shaping."

He rested his staff against a shoulder and opened his hands in the gesture of welcoming. "Will you join us, little sister?" Kirit looked sharply at him but did not object. "We have scant hope of victory, but we must make the effort."

She laughed, and the air wicked away her tears. "Allies, then?"

"Indeed we are," he agreed with a sweet, sober smile. "The last of our kind."

54

At dawn, as the clangor of the temple bells called men to prayer, Keshad confronted the guards at the gate, holding his blessing bowl in cupped hands.

"I need to pray."

They looked at each other. One went into the guardhouse and emerged with the sergeant while the other stared straight ahead, pretending not to see Kesh.

"No foreigners allowed in Sarida today," said the sergeant. He was a big man with hair shaved short and powerful hands that looked ready to crush the windpipe of any clamoring fool who annoyed him.

"I need to pray." Again he displayed the bowl. "I am a believing man. Not like the others."

He did not look into the courtyard where sour-faced men gathered yawning and stretching to mutter among themselves at the locked gate. The foreign merchants had heard trumpets in the night, and now it seemed they were to be imprisoned all day, not even let free to buy and sell in the market. Mutters turned to cheerful greetings as Eliar emerged from the cubicle he shared with Keshad, and at once the conversation flowered with laughter and spirited banter. Everyone liked Eliar! Kesh could not understand how the others could stomach the Silver's convivial ways and inanely amiable chatter.

"All peace be upon Beltak, King of Kings, Lord of Lords, the Shining One Who Rules Alone," said the sergeant at last, having taken his time to think things through. "The priests bid us to open the exalted gates to all men. To turn away a man who wishes to enter would be like killing him. Therefore, go. But return here after. This guard will accompany you. He speaks nothing of the trade talk, so no point in trying to converse."

"My thanks," said Kesh. "I'm just surprised. We heard trumpets last night, and now we're told we can't go into the market. It's impossible to do business."

"Those are my orders."

And that, Kesh judged, was far enough to push this one. He waited while the inner gate was unlocked, a laborious process involving chains, locks, and keys, and cursed if Eliar didn't trot up behind.

"Heya, Keshad. Where are you going? How did you get permission to leave? Are they opening the gates for the day, finally?"

"Move back," said the sergeant in a curt way that made Eliar startle and Kesh smile. "No one allowed out."

"*He's* being allowed out!"

"Go on," said the sergeant to Kesh before turning his back on Eliar and lounging against the wall of the guardhouse with every evident intention of flaunting his power.

Keshad hurried out, hearing voices raised behind him as other merchants saw the threshold gap and, then, slam shut in their faces.

He knew the route well and was careful to follow it exactly with the silent young guardsman at his back, a lad with an unpleasant face and look of pinching scorn to make it yet uglier. The truth was, the Sirniakans were not a handsome people, not the men Keshad had seen anyway, and of course except in the most distant and isolated villages on the route to the border with Mariha, he'd not seen women at all. Nothing but men, which was a tedious way to live, and as he walked he noted how this morning every gate was shut, the compounds whose walls lined the streets closed up as if night's curfew hadn't yet been lifted. Elderly men draped in robes approached the white gates at the edge of the caravan market where all foreigners must bide when in Sarida to trade. A few younger men walked in pairs and fours, murmuring quietly, some glancing curiously at him as he passed. No one spoke to him. It was very quiet, none of the waking market bustle that was normally fiercest at this early hour before the midday heat clobbered everyone.

Of course any city has only one temple, supervised by holy priests. Any believing man must, by the Exalted One's decree, be permitted entry. But that didn't mean that all men entered through the same holy gate or worshiped in the same holy court. Here at the wall of the caravan market, a gate opened into an alley confined by high whitewashed walls. It twisted and turned through the city in a circuitous route, bridged at intervals for the convenience of imperial citizens so they need never set foot where lesser men trod. Believers of a class not permitted free access within the city might approach the holy court, but they would certainly remain separate. Along this narrow way Keshad trudged, and though he listened, he heard no gossip, no news, nothing beyond a few halting discussions of rice crops, a horse race, and fishing.

The city was large, and the alley a long path often sloping uphill or angled with steps, so he was sweating when he reached the humble gate through which they entered single-file. Kesh crossed the threshold and crouched to touch the naked feet of a white-clad priest. The holy man frowned as if suspicious of his looks, but gave him the sign to pass into the earth-floored court packed with worshipers: foreigners, slaves, indentured servants, impoverished laborers, the deformed and disfigured, the beggars and the lame. He paid a coin to have a priest fill his bowl with holy water and then he knelt, palms turned upward to face the heavens, as a priest led the sonorous prayer.

"Rid us of all that is evil. Rid us of demons. Rid us of hate. . . ." He dipped a thumb in the water and traced the sign of Straight Order across his forehead. "Increase all that is good. . . ." How easy it was to produce the words, but it was like sowing seed in barren ground. Words are only words, because the gods do not listen, no matter what Zubaidit, or the priests of Beltak, or the Ri Amarah said. They, who believed, were blind, because they preferred blindness. It was easier than seeing the dispassionate cruelty of the world where those in power closed their hands around the throats of the ones they wished to control. They shut their victims behind locked gates and then prayed to their gods to persuade themselves they were doing right.

"Teach me to hate darkness and battle evil. Teach me the Truth." Bai would scold him for pretending to pray, but by doing so he had escaped the locked gates of the merchants' compound, hadn't he? "Peace. Peace. Peace."

Fine words and noble sentiments. How bright and clean they washed the world. He brushed tears from his cheeks, thinking of Miravia.

Some of the worshipers stood in line for the priest's cleansing, but Kesh sat down on a bench and rubbed his feet. In courts built farther in toward the center of the temple complex, voices still rose in the extended prayer granted to men of higher rank, and trees offered shade to men who preferred to pray out of the blazing sun. It was already hot, the sun's light so strong on the white-washed walls that he had to shade his eyes as he scanned the lingering assembly, wondering if he would see any merchants he recognized from the market, men he might conceivably chat with as they walked back down the alley out of the city. Men who might say too much, or be prone to gossip. Folk did like to gossip. It gave them a sense of power to know what others did not.

"You are a Hundred man."

Startled, he looked up. Dropped off the bench to his knees. "Holy one. You honor me."

The priest from the gate stood before him. He had a beard, and his hair was shorn short and shaved bald at the crown. "They are stubborn, the Hundred men, praying to demons who mask as gods. But you pray to the Exalted One."

"Yes, holy one."

The priest's look was as good as a question.

"I have walked into the empire many times. Thus am I come to the Exalted One, King of Kings, Lord of Lords, the Shining One Who Rules Alone."

"A merchant may speak words he does not believe in order to avoid the tax fixed on barbarians."

"Yes," agreed Kesh without flinching, his gaze steady. "So he may."

"You will be cleansed today?"

"I will. In truth, holy one, I was waiting for the line to shorten. My feet hurt."

The priest nodded, and turned to leave.

"Holy one," said Kesh, "if I may be permitted a question."

The man turned back as smoothly as if he had expected the words. "What do you wish, believer?"

"I am a Hundred man, a foreign merchant. Our compound has been locked down, and we are not permitted into the market to trade. All will be as the Exalted One ordains, and I am a patient man, but I admit that I am concerned about my business. Might I be permitted to know if trade will resume today, or another day soon, or if we will be permitted to leave Sarida and return to our homes if the market has been closed indefinitely?"

No wind stirred the air, but men's voices filtered everywhere. Tense murmurs. Choppy gestures. Glances sent close and far as if in fear that some other man, listening, might call them to account for reckless words. And indeed, the prayers still winding from the inner courts had also a tight coil to them, every man clinging to the familiar cycle as a man in a storm huddles under the shelter he knows, the only place he feels safe.

"It is hard to know what will happen next," said the priest thoughtfully, looking intently at Kesh, as if measuring the sincerity of his heart.

But he didn't scare Kesh. What man could, now that he had been emboldened by Miravia's face and enigmatic smile?

"We wait for word from Dalilasah as to how to proceed. Meanwhile, the regulations and restrictions will be observed fourfold, as is proper."

"What do you mean, holy one? I am ignorant, truly."

Men filtered out the gate to vanish down the alley, and in the inner courts, the singing faded and died. A bell rang thrice, and a trumpet blew twice, and then came silence, a vastly populated and crowded city caught in a hush like the world waiting to discover from which way the storm would thunder in upon them.

The priest smiled awkwardly, which was perhaps an attempt to show sympathy and perhaps the curling bite of lofty scorn and perhaps only the man's own anxiety peeping through his stern façade.

"You have not heard, of course. Emperor Farazadihosh is dead, killed in battle by his cousin."

ABOUT THE AUTHOR

KATE ELLIOTT is the author of more than a dozen novels, including the Novels of the Jaran and, most recently, *Spirit Gate*, the first novel of Crossroads. *King's Dragon*, the first novel in the Crown of Stars fantasy series, was a Nebula Award finalist; *The Golden Key* (cowritten with Melanie Rawn and Jennifer Roberson) was a World Fantasy Award finalist; *Jaran* was named *Voya*'s Best Science Fiction, Fantasy, and Horror of 1992, and was a *Locus* Recommended fantasy novel of 1992. Born in Oregon, she lives in Hawaii.

9/14 bm

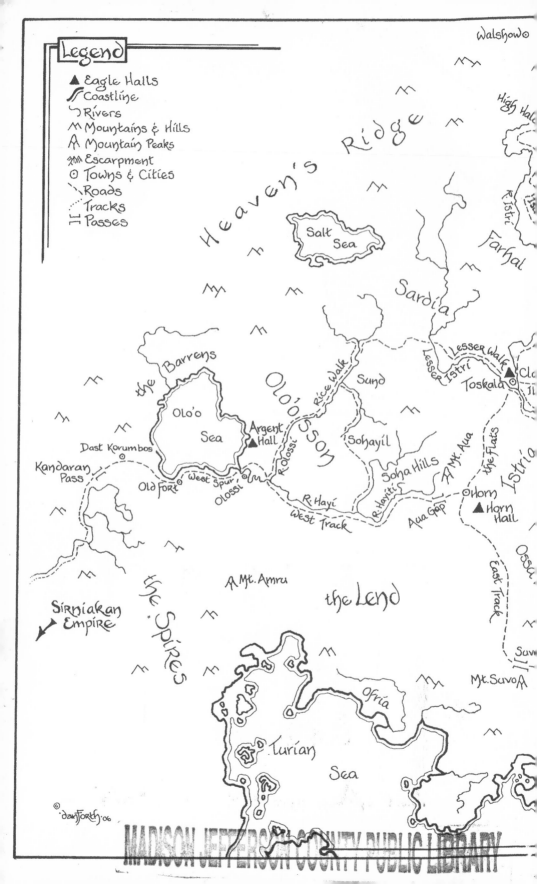